THE BONE CLOCKS

DAVID MITCHELL

THE BONE CLOCKS

A Novel

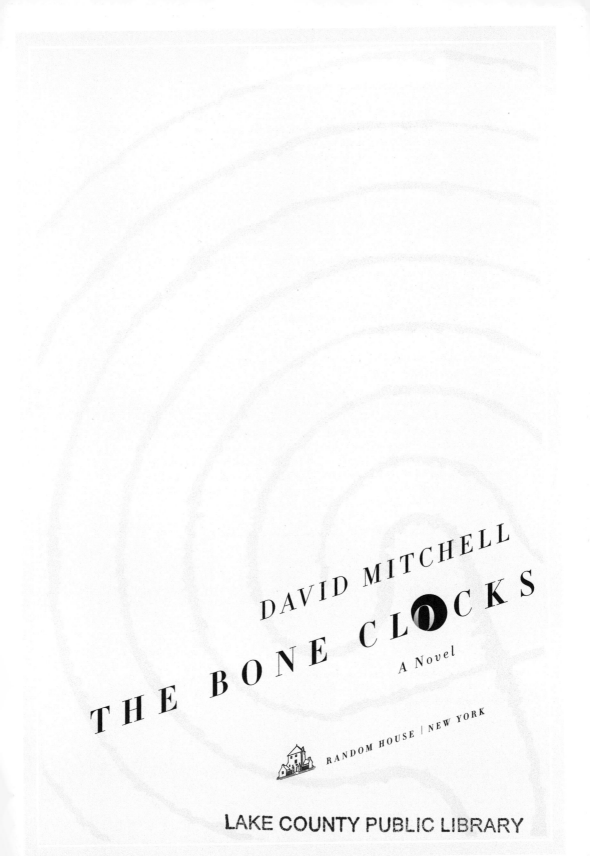

RANDOM HOUSE | NEW YORK

Published in the United States by Random House, an imprint and division of Random House LLC, a Penguin Random House Company, New York.

RANDOM HOUSE and the HOUSE colophon are registered trademarks of Random House LLC.

Published in the United Kingdom by Sceptre, an imprint of Hodder & Stoughton, London.

LIBRARY OF CONGRESS CATALOGING-IN-PUBLICATION DATA
Mitchell, David
The bone clocks : a novel / David Mitchell.
pages   cm
ISBN 978-1-4000-6567-7
eBook ISBN 978-0-8129-9473-5
1. Imaginary wars and battles—Fiction. I. Title.
PR6063.I785B66 2014
823'.914—dc23   2014008517

Printed in the United States of America on acid-free paper

www.atrandom.com

987654321

FIRST U.S. EDITION

Book design by Simon M. Sullivan

For Noah

A HOT SPELL

1984

I FLING OPEN MY BEDROOM CURTAINS, and there's the thirsty sky and the wide river full of ships and boats and stuff, but I'm already thinking of Vinny's chocolaty eyes, shampoo down Vinny's back, beads of sweat on Vinny's shoulders, and Vinny's sly laugh, and by now my heart's going mental and, God, I wish I was waking up at Vinny's place in Peacock Street and not in my own stupid bedroom. Last night, the words just said themselves, "Christ, I really love you, Vin," and Vinny puffed out a cloud of smoke and did this Prince Charles voice, "One must say, one's frightfully partial to spending time with you too, Holly Sykes," and I nearly weed myself laughing, though I was a bit narked he didn't say "I love you too" back. If I'm honest. Still, boyfriends act goofy to hide stuff, any magazine'll tell you. Wish I could phone him right now. Wish they'd invent phones you can speak to anyone anywhere anytime on. He'll be riding his Norton to work in Rochester right now, in his leather jacket with LED ZEP spelled out in silver studs. Come September, when I turn sixteen, he'll take me out on his Norton.

Someone slams a cupboard door, below.

Mam. No one else'd dare slam a door like that.

Suppose she's found out? says a twisted voice.

No. We've been too careful, me and Vinny.

She's menopausal, is Mam. That'll be it.

TALKING HEADS' *Fear of Music* is on my record player, so I lower the stylus. Vinny bought me this LP, the second Saturday we met at Magic Bus Records. It's an amazing record. I like "Heaven" and

"Memories Can't Wait" but there's not a weak track on it. Vinny's been to New York and actually saw Talking Heads, live. His mate Dan was on security and got Vinny backstage after the gig, and he hung out with David Byrne and the band. If he goes back next year, he's taking me. I get dressed, finding each love bite and wishing I could go to Vinny's tonight, but he's meeting a bunch of mates in Dover. Men hate it when women act jealous, so I pretend not to be. My best friend Stella's gone to London to hunt for secondhand clothes at Camden Market. Mam says I'm still too young to go to London without an adult so Stella took Ali Jessop instead. My biggest thrill today'll be hoovering the bar to earn my three pounds' pocket money. Whoopy-doo. Then I've got next week's exams to revise for. But for two pins I'd hand in blank papers and tell school where to shove Pythagoras triangles and *Lord of the Flies* and their life cycles of worms. I might, too.

Yeah. I might just do that.

Down in the kitchen, the atmosphere's like Antarctica. "Morning," I say, but only Jacko looks up from the window-seat where he's drawing. Sharon's through in the lounge part, watching a cartoon. Dad's downstairs in the hallway, talking with the delivery guy—the truck from the brewery's grumbling away in front of the pub. Mam's chopping cooking apples into cubes, giving me the silent treatment. I'm supposed to say, "What's wrong, Mam, what have I done?" but sod that for a game of soldiers. Obviously she noticed I was back late last night, but I'll let her raise the topic. I pour some milk over my Weetabix and take it to the table. Mam clangs the lid onto the pan and comes over. "Right. What have you got to say for yourself?"

"Good morning to you too, Mam. Another hot day."

"What have you got to *say* for yourself, young lady?"

If in doubt, act innocent. "'Bout what exactly?"

Her eyes go all snaky. "What time did you get home?"

"Okay, okay, so I was a bit late, *sorry*."

"Two hours isn't 'a bit late.' Where were you?"

I munch my Weetabix. "Stella's. Lost track of time."

"Well, that's peculiar, now, it really is. At ten o'clock *I* phoned Stella's mam to find out where the hell you were, and guess what? You'd left before eight. So who's the liar here, Holly? You or her?"

Shit. "After leaving Stella's, I went for a walk."

"And where did your walk take you to?"

I sharpen each word. "Along the river, all right?"

"Upstream or downstream, was it, this little walk?"

I let a silence go by. "What *diff'*rence does it make?"

There're some cartoon explosions on the telly. Mam tells my sister, "Turn that thing off and shut the door behind you, Sharon."

"That's not fair! Holly's the one getting told off."

"*Now,* Sharon. And you too, Jacko, I want—" But Jacko's already vanished. When Sharon's left, Mam takes up the attack again: "All alone, were you, on your 'walk'?"

Why this nasty feeling she's setting me up? "Yeah."

"How far d'you get on your 'walk,' then, all alone?"

"What—you want miles or kilometers?"

"Well, perhaps your little walk took you up Peacock Street, to a certain someone called Vincent Costello?" The kitchen sort of swirls, and through the window, on the Essex shore of the river, a tiny stick-man's lifting his bike off the ferry. "Lost for words all of a sudden? Let me jog your memory: ten o'clock last night, closing the blinds, front window, wearing a T-shirt and not a lot else."

Yes, I did go downstairs to get Vinny a lager. Yes, I did lower the blind in the front room. Yes, someone did walk by. *Relax,* I'd told myself. *What's the chances of one stranger recognizing me?* Mam's expecting me to crumple, but I don't. "You're wasted as a barmaid, Mam. You ought to be handling supergrasses for MI5."

Mam gives me the Kath Sykes Filthy Glare. "How old is he?"

Now I fold my arms. "None of your business."

Mam's eyes go slitty. "Twenty-four, apparently."

"If you already know, why're you asking?"

"Because a twenty-four-year-old man interfering with a fifteen-year-old schoolgirl is il*leg*al. He could go to prison."

"I'll be sixteen in September, and *I* reckon the Kent police have bigger fish to fry. I'm old enough to make up my own mind about my relationships."

Mam lights one of her Marlboro Reds. I'd kill for one. "When I tell your father, he'll flay this Costello fella alive."

Sure, Dad has to persuade piss-artists off the premises from time to time, all landlords do, but he's not the flaying-anyone-alive type. "Brendan was fifteen when he was going out with Mandy Fry, and if you think they were just holding hands on the swings, they weren't. Don't recall him getting the 'You could go to prison' treatment."

She spells it out like I'm a moron: "It's—different—for—*boys*."

I do an *I-do-not-believe-what-I'm-hearing* snort.

"I'm telling you now, Holly, you'll be seeing this . . . car salesman again over my dead body."

"*Actually*, Mam, I'll bloody see who I bloody well *want*!"

"New rules." Mam stubs out her fag. "I'm taking you to school and fetching you back *in the van*. You don't set foot outside unless it's with me, your father, Brendan, or Ruth. If I *glimpse* this cradle snatcher anywhere near here, I'll be on the blower to the police to press charges—yes, I *will*, so help me God. And—*and*—I'll call his employer and let them know that he's seducing underage schoolgirls."

Big fat seconds ooze by while all of this sinks in.

My tear ducts start twitching but there's no *way* I'm giving Mrs. Hitler the pleasure. "This isn't Saudi Arabia! You can't lock me up!"

"Live under our roof, you obey our rules. When *I* was your age—"

"Yeah yeah yeah, you had twenty brothers and thirty sisters and forty grandparents and fifty acres of spuds to dig 'cause that was how life was in Auld *feckin'* Oireland but this is England, Mam, *England*! And it's the 1980s and if life was so *feckin'* glorious in that West Cork *bog* why did you *feckin'* bother even coming to—"

Whack! Smack over the left side of my face.

We look at each other: me trembling with shock and Mam angrier than I've ever seen her, and—I reckon—knowing she's just broken something that'll never be mended. I leave the room without a word, as if I've just won an argument.

I ONLY CRY a bit, and it's shocked crying, not boo-hoo crying, and when I'm done I go to the mirror. My eyes're a bit puffy, but a bit of eyeliner soon sorts that out . . . Dab of lippy, bit of blusher . . . Sorted. The girl in the mirror's a woman, with her cropped black hair, her *Quadrophenia* T-shirt, her black jeans. "I've got news for you," she says. "You're moving in with Vinny today." I start listing the reasons why I can't, and stop. "Yes," I agree, giddy and calm at once. I'm leaving school, as well. As from now. The summer holidays'll be here before the truancy officer can fart, and I'm sixteen in September, and then it's stuff you, Windmill Hill Comprehensive. Do I dare?

I dare. Pack, then. Pack what? Whatever'll fit into my big duffel bag. Underwear, bras, T-shirts, my bomber jacket; makeup case and the Oxo tin with my bracelets and necklaces in. Toothbrush and a handful of tampons—my period's a bit late so it should start, like, any hour now. Money. I count up £13.85 saved in notes and coins. I've £80 more in my TSB bankbook. It's not like Vinny'll charge me rent, and I'll look for a job next week. Babysitting, working in the market, waitressing: There's loads of ways to earn a few quid. What about my LPs? I can't lug the whole collection over to Peacock Street now, and Mam's quite capable of dumping them at the Oxfam shop out of spite, so I just take *Fear of Music,* wrapping it carefully in my bomber jacket and putting it into my bag so it won't get bent. I hide the others under the loose floorboard, just for now, but as I'm putting the carpet back, I get the fright of my life: Jacko's watching me from the doorway. He's still in his *Thunderbirds* pajamas and slippers.

I tell him, "Mister, you just gave me a heart attack."

"You're going." Jacko's got this not-quite-here voice.

"Just between us, yes, I am. But not far, don't worry."

"I've made you a souvenir, to remember me by." Jacko hands me a circle of cardboard—a flattened Dairylea cheese box with a maze drawn on. He's mad about mazes, is Jacko; it's all these Dungeons & Dragonsy books him and Sharon read. The one Jacko's drawn's actually dead simple by his standards, made of eight or nine circles inside each other. "Take it," he tells me. "It's diabolical."

"It doesn't look all that bad to me."

" 'Diabolical' means 'satanic,' sis."

"Why's your maze so satanic, then?"

"The Dusk follows you as you go through it. If it touches you, you cease to exist, so one wrong turn down a dead end, that's the end of you. That's why you have to learn the labyrinth by heart."

Christ, I don't half have a freaky little brother. "Right. Well, thanks, Jacko. Look, I've got a few things to—"

Jacko holds my wrist. "Learn this labyrinth, Holly. Indulge your freaky little brother. Please."

That jolts me a bit. "Mister, you're acting all weird."

"Promise me you'll memorize the path through it, so if you ever needed to, you could navigate it in the darkness. *Please.*"

My friends' little brothers are all into Scalextric or BMX or Top Trumps—why do I get one who does this and says words like "navigate" and "diabolical"? Christ only knows how he'll survive in Gravesend if he's gay. I muss his hair. "Okay, I promise to learn your maze off by heart." Then Jacko hugs me, which is weird 'cause Jacko's not a huggy kid. "Hey, I'm not going far . . . You'll understand when you're older, and—"

"You're moving in with your boyfriend."

By now I shouldn't be surprised. "Yeah."

"Take care of yourself, Holly."

"Vinny's nice. Once Mam's got used to the idea, we'll see each other—I mean, we still saw Brendan after he married Ruth, yeah?"

But Jacko just puts the cardboard lid with his maze on deep into my duffel bag, gives me one last look, and disappears.

· · ·

MAM APPEARS WITH a basket of bar rugs on the first-floor landing, as if she wasn't lying in wait. "I'm not bluffing. You're *grounded.* Back upstairs. You've got exams next week. Time you knuckled down and got some proper revision done."

I grip the banister. " 'Our roof, our rules,' you said. Fine. I don't want your rules, *or* your roof, *or* you hitting me whenever you lose your rag. You'd not put up with that. Would you?"

Mam's face sort of twitches, and if she says the right thing now, we'll negotiate. But no, she just takes in my duffel bag and sneers like she can't believe how stupid I am. "You had a brain, once."

So I carry on down the stairs to the ground floor.

Above me, her voice tightens. "What about school?"

"*You* go, then, if school's so important!"

"*I* never had the bloody chance, Holly! I've always had the pub to run, and you and Brendan and Sharon and Jacko to feed, clothe, and send to school so *you* won't have to spend *your* life mopping out toilets and emptying ashtrays and knackering your back and never having an early night."

Water off a duck's back. I carry on downstairs.

"But go on, then. Go. Learn the hard way. I'll give you three days before Romeo turfs you out. It's not a girl's glittering personality that men're interested in, Holly. It never bloody is."

I ignore her. From the hallway I see Sharon behind the bar by the fruit juice shelves. She's helping Dad do the restocking, but I can see she heard. I give her a little wave and she gives me one back, nervous. Echoing up from the cellar trapdoor is Dad's voice, crooning "Ferry 'Cross the Mersey." Better leave him out of it. In front of Mam, he'll side with her. In front of the regulars, it'll be "It takes a bigger idiot than me to step between the pecking hens" and they'll all nod and mumble, "Right enough there, Dave." Plus I'd rather not be in the room when he finds out 'bout Vinny. Not that I'm ashamed, I'd just rather not be there. Newky's snoozing in his basket. "You're the smelliest dog in Kent," I tell him to stop myself crying, "you old fleabag." I pat his neck, unbolt the side door, and step into Marlow Alley. Behind me, the door goes *clunk*.

WEST STREET'S TOO bright and too dark, like a TV with the contrast on the blink, so I put on my sunglasses and they turn the world all dreamish and vivider and more real. My throat aches and I'm shaking a bit. Nobody's running after me from the pub. Good. A cement truck trundles by and its fumy gust makes the conker tree sway a bit and rustle. Breathe in warm tarmac, fried spuds, and week-old rubbish spilling out of the bins—the dustmen are on strike again.

Lots of little darting birds're twirly-whirlying like the tin-whistlers on strings kids get at birthdays, or used to, and a gang of boys're playing Kick the Can in the park round the church at Crooked Lane. *Get him! Behind the tree! Set* me *free!* Kids. Stella says older men make better lovers; with boys our age, she says, the ice cream melts once the cone's in your hand. Only Stella knows 'bout Vinny—she was there that first Saturday in the Magic Bus— but she can keep a secret. When she was teaching me to smoke and I kept puking, she didn't laugh or tell anyone, and she's told me everything I need to know 'bout boys. Stella's the coolest girl in our year at school, easy.

Crooked Lane veers up from the river, and from there I turn up Queen Street, where I'm nearly mown down by Julie Walcott pushing her pram. Her baby's bawling its head off and she looks knackered. She left school when she got pregnant. Me and Vinny are dead careful, and we only had sex once without a condom, our first time, and it's a scientific fact that virgins can't get pregnant. Stella told me.

BUNTING'S STRUNG ACROSS Queen Street, like it's for Holly Sykes's Independence Day. The Scottish lady in the wool shop's watering her hanging baskets, and Mr. Gilbert the jeweler's putting trays of rings into his front windows, and Mike and Todd the butchers're offloading a headless pig from the back of a van where a dozen carcasses are hanging from hooks. Outside the library a bunch of union men are collecting money in buckets for the striking miners with Socialist Workers holding signs saying COAL NOT DOLE and THATCHER DECLARES WAR ON THE WORKERS. Ed Brubeck's freewheeling this way on his bike. I step into the Indoor Market so he can't see me. He moved to Gravesend last year from Manchester, where his dad got sent down for burglary and assault. He doesn't have any friends and shows no sign of wanting any. Normally that'd get you crucified at our school, but when a sixth-former had a go at him Brubeck punched his nose out of shape, so he's been left alone since. He cycles by without seeing me, a fishing rod tied to his crossbar, and I carry on. By the games arcade a busker's playing funeral music on a clarinet. Someone lobs a coin into his case and he bursts into the theme from *Dallas*. When I get to Magic Bus Records I peer inside. I was looking at R for Ramones. Vinny says he was looking at H for Hot and Horny and Holly. There's a few secondhand guitars along the back of the shop, too. Vin can play the intro to "Stairway to Heaven," though he's never got past that. I'm going to teach myself to play Vin's guitar while he's at work. Vin and me could start a band. Why not? Tina Weymouth's a girl and she's the bassist in Talking Heads. Imagine Mam's face if she goes all, "She's not my daughter anymore," then sees me on *Top of the Pops*. Mam's problem's that she's never loved anyone as deeply as me and Vin love each other. She gets on okay with Dad, sure, though all her family in Cork were never crazy about him not being Irish and Catholic. My older Irish cousins enjoyed telling me that Dad got Mum pregnant with Brendan before they were married, but they've been married for twenty-five years now, which isn't bad going, I s'pose, but still, Mam's not got this amazing bond with Dad like me and Vin. Stella says me and Vin are soul mates. She says it's obvious, we're made for each other.

. . .

OUTSIDE NATWEST BANK on Milton Road, I run into Brendan. Moussed-back hair, paisley tie, and his blazer slung over his shoulder, you'd think he was off to Handsome School, not the offices of Stott and Conway. Bit of a heartthrob is my older brother, among my friends' older sisters—pass me the vomit bucket. He married Ruth, his boss Mr. Conway's daughter, at the town hall with a flashy reception at the Chaucer Country Club. I wasn't a bridesmaid 'cause I don't wear dresses, specially dresses that make you look like a *Gone with the Wind* collectible, so Sharon and Ruth's nieces did all that stuff, and loads of our Cork relatives came over. Brendan's Mam's golden boy and Mam's Brendan's golden mam. Later they'll be poring over every detail of what I say right now.

"Morning," I tell him. "How's it going?"

"Can't complain. All well at the Captain?"

"Fine. Mam's full of the joys of spring today."

"Yeah?" Brendan smiles, puzzled. "How come?"

I shrug. "Must've got out on the right side of bed."

"Cool." He notices my duffel bag. "Off on a trip, are we?"

"Not exactly. I'm revising French at Stella Yearwood's—then I'm staying overnight. It's exams next week."

My brother looks impressed. "Good for you, little sis."

"Is Ruth any better?"

"Not a lot. God only knows why it's called 'morning sickness' when it's worse in the middle of the night."

"Perhaps it's Mother Nature's way of toughening you up for when the baby arrives," I suggest. "All those sleepless nights, the arguing, the puke . . . Needs stamina."

My brother doesn't take the bait. "Guess so." It's hard to imagine Brendan being anyone's dad but, come Christmas, he will be.

Behind us the NatWest opens its doors and the bank clerks start filing in. "Not that Mr. Conway'll fire his son-in-law," I say to Brendan, "but don't you start at nine?"

"This is true. See you tomorrow, if you're back from your revision-a-thon. Mam's invited us over for lunch. Have a great day."

"It's the best day of my life already," I tell my brother and, in a secondhand way, Mam.

One flash of his award-winning smile and Brendan's off, joining the streams of people in suits and uniforms all going to work in offices and shops and factories.

ON MONDAY, I'LL get a key cut for Vinny's front door, but today I go the usual secret way. Up a street called the Grove, just before the tax office, there's this alley, half hidden by a skip overflowing with bin bags smelling of bubbling nappies. A brown rat watches me, like Lord Muck. I go down the alley, turn right, and now I'm between Peacock Street's back-garden fences and the tax-office wall. Down the far end, the last house before the railway cutting, that's Vinny's place. I squeeze through the loose slats and wade through his back garden. The grass and weeds come up to my waist and the plum trees are already fruiting up, though most of the fruit'll go to the wasps and the worms, Vinny says, 'cause he can't be arsed to pick it. It's like the forest in *Sleeping Beauty* that chokes the castle when everyone's asleep for a hundred years. Vinny's s'posed to keep the garden neat for his aunt but she lives up in King's Lynn and never visits and, anyway, Vinny's a motorbike guy, not a gardener. Once I'm settled in, I'll tame this jungle. It needs a woman's touch, that's all. Might make a start today, after a session teaching myself the guitar. There's a shed in the corner half hidden by brambles, with gardening gear and a lawnmower. Sunflowers, roses, pansies, carnations, lavender, and herbs in little terra-cotta pots, that's what I'll plant. I'll make scones and plum pies and coffee cakes and Vinny'll be all, "Jesus, Holly, how did I ever get by without you?" All the magazines say the way to a man's heart is through his stomach. By the rainwater barrel a fingery purple bush is swarming with white butterflies, all confetti and lace; it's like it's alive.

. . .

THE BACK DOOR'S never locked 'cause Vinny's lost the key. Our pizza boxes and wineglasses're still in the sink from last night, but no sign of breakfast—Vinny must've overslept and raced off to work, as per usual. The whole place needs a good tidying, dusting, hoovering. First a coffee and a fag's in order, though—I only ate half my Weetabix before Mam started her Muhammad Ali act on me. I forgot to get any ciggies on the way up—it flew out of my head after meeting Brendan—but Vinny keeps some in his bedside table, so I pad up the steep stairs and into his bedroom. Our bedroom, I should say. The curtains are still drawn and the air's like old socks so I let the light in, open the window, turn round, and jump out of my skin 'cause Vinny's in bed, looking like he's cacked himself. "It's me, it's only me," I sort of gupper. "Sorry, I—I—I—I thought you were at work."

He claps his hand over his heart and sort of laughs, like he'd just been shot. "*Jesus,* Hol. I thought you were a burglar!"

I sort of laugh too. "You're . . . at home."

"Cock-up with the rota—the new secretary's bloody hopeless—so Kev phoned to say I've got the day off, after all."

"Brill," I say. "That's great, 'cause . . . I've got a surprise."

"Great, I love them. But put the kettle on first, eh? I'll be right down. Shit, what am I saying? I'm out of coffee—be a sweetheart, pop out to Staffa's and get a jar of Gold Blend. I'll pay, uh, you when you get back."

I need to say this first: "Mam found out 'bout us, Vin."

"Oh? Oh." He looks thoughtful. "Right. How did she, uh . . ."

Suddenly I'm scared he won't want me. "Not great. Went a bit apeshit, actually. Told me I couldn't see you again and, like, threatened to lock me in the cellar. So I walked out. So . . ."

Vinny looks at me nervously, not taking the hint.

"So can I . . . like . . . stay with you? For a bit, at least."

Vinny swallows. "O-*kay* . . . Right. I see. Well. Okay."

It doesn't sound very okay. "Is that a yes, Vin?"

"Ye-es. Sure. Yes. But now I *really* need that coffee."

"Serious? Oh, Vin!" The relief's like a warm bath. I hug him. He's sweaty. "You're the best, Vinny. I was afraid you might not . . ."

"We can't have a furry-purry sex kitten like you sleeping under a bridge now, can we? But really, Hol, I need coffee like Dracula needs blood, so—" He doesn't finish the sentence 'cause I'm kissing him, my Vinny, my boyfriend who's been to New York and shaken David Byrne's hand, and my love for him sort of goes *whoosh,* like a boiler firing up, and I pull him back and we roll onto a lumpy hill of duvet, but the hill wriggles and my hand pulls the sheet away and here's my best friend Stella Yearwood. Stark naked. Like I'm in a bad sex dream, only it's not.

I just . . . gape at her crotch till she says, "It can't look so *very* different to yours, can it?"

Then I gape at Vinny, who looks like he's shat himself but then does this spazzo giggle: "It's not what it looks like."

Stella, cool as you please, covers herself with the sheet and tells Vinny, "Don't be dense. This is pre*cise*ly how it looks, Holly. We were going to let you know but, as you see, events have overtaken us all. Fact is, you've been dumped. Not pleasant, but it happens to the best of us, well, most of us, so c'est la vie. Don't worry, there are plenty more Vinnys in the sea. So why not cut your losses now and just go? With a little dignity intact?"

WHEN I STOP crying, finally, I find myself on a cold step in a little courtyard place, with five or six stories of old brick and narrow blind windows on each side. Weeds drilling up through paving slabs and dandelion seeds drifting around like snow in a snow globe. After I slammed Vinny's door my feet brought me here, round the back of the Gravesend General Hospital, where Dr. Marinus got rid of Miss Constantin for me when I was seven years old. Did I punch Vinny? It was like I was moving in treacle. I couldn't breathe. He caught my wrist and it hurt—still does—and Stella was barking, "Grow up and piss off, Holly. This is real life not an episode of *Dy-*

nasty!" and I ran out, slamming the front door and hurrying as fast I could, anywhere, nowhere, somewhere . . . I knew the moment I stopped I'd break down into a sobbing, snotting jelly, and then one of Mam's spies'd see me and report back and that'd be the cherry on her cake. 'Cause Mam was right. I loved Vinny like he was a part of me, and he loved me like a stick of gum. He'd spat me out when the flavor went, unwrapped another, and stuffed it in, and not just anyone, but Stella Yearwood. My best mate. How could he? How could she?

Stop *crying*! Think about something else . . .

HOLLY SYKES AND the Weird Shit, Part 1. I was seven years old in 1976. It didn't rain all summer and the gardens turned brown, and I remember queuing with buckets down the end of Queen Street with Brendan and Mam for water from standpipes, the drought got that bad. My daymares started that summer. I heard voices in my head. Not mad, or drooly, or specially scary, even, not at first . . . the Radio People, I called them, 'cause at first I thought there was a radio on in the next room. Only there never was a radio on in the next room. They were clearest at night, but I heard them at school, too, if everything was quiet enough, in a test, say. Three or four voices'd chunter away at once, and I never quite made out what they were saying. Brendan had talked 'bout mental hospitals and men in white coats, so I didn't dare tell anyone. Mam was pregnant with Jacko, Dad rushed off his feet at the pub, Sharon was only three, and Brendan was a plonker, even then. I knew hearing voices wasn't normal, but they weren't actually harming me, so maybe it was just one of those secrets people live with.

One night, I had a nightmare about killer bees loose in the Captain Marlow, and woke up in a sweat. A lady was sat at the end of my bed saying, "Don't worry, Holly, it's all right," and I said, "Thanks, Mam," 'cause who else could it be? Then I heard Mam laughing in the kitchen down the corridor—this was before my bedroom was up in the attic. That was how I knew I'd only dreamt the lady on my bed, and I switched on the light to prove it.

And sure enough nobody was there.

"Don't be afraid," said the lady, "but I'm as real as you are."

I didn't scream or freak out. Sure, I was shaking, but even in my fear, I felt it was like a puzzle or a test. There was nobody in my room, but someone was speaking to me. So, as calm as I could, I asked the lady if she was a ghost. "Not a ghost," said the lady who wasn't there, "but a visitor to your mind. That's why you can't see me." I asked what my visitor's name was. Miss Constantin, she said. She said she'd sent the Radio People away, because they were a distraction, and hoped I didn't mind. I said no. Miss Constantin said she had to go but that she'd love to drop by soon because I was "a singular young lady."

Then she was gone. It took me ages to fall asleep, but by the time I did, I sort of felt I'd made a friend.

WHAT NOW? Go home? I'd rather stick pins in my gums. Mam'll make me steaming shit pie, dripping in shit gravy, and sit there smug as hell watching me eat every shitty morsel, and from now until the end of time, if ever I'm anything less than yes-sir-no-sir-three-bags-full-sir, she'll bring up the Vinny Costello Incident. Okay, so I'm not living in Peacock Street but I can still leave home, at least for long enough to prove to Mam that I'm old enough to take care of myself so she can stop treating me like I'm seven years old. I've enough money to feed myself for a bit and the hot spell looks set to last, so I'll think of it as my summer holiday beginning early. Screw my exams, screw school. Stella'll twist things round so that I was this hysterical pathetic Clinging Ivy who just couldn't face the fact her boyfriend was tired of her. By nine A.M. on Monday morning, Holly Sykes'll be the Official Windmill Hill High School Laughing Stock. Guaranteed.

An ambulance siren gets closer, more urgent, echoes round the courtyard and stops, like, in mid-sentence . . . I rejiggle my duffel bag and get up. Right, where now? Every runaway teenager in England makes a beeline for London, imagining they'll get picked up by a talent scout or fairy godmother, but I'll strike out the opposite way, along the river, towards the Kent marshes; if you grow up in a pub you overhear exactly what sort of scouts and fairies pick up runaway teenagers in London. Maybe I could find a barn or an empty holiday chalet to stay in for a bit. That might work. So, off I set round the front of the hospital. The car park's full of windscreens flashing in the bright sunshine. In the cool shady hospital reception area, I see rows of people smoking and waiting for news.

Funny places, hospitals . . .

HOLLY SYKES AND the Weird Shit, Part 2. A few weeks went by, I must've turned eight, and I began to think I'd only dreamt Miss Constantin, 'cause she'd never come back. 'Cept for the fact I didn't know that word she'd called me, "singular" . . . I looked it up and wondered how it'd got into my head if Miss Constantin hadn't put it there. To this day I still don't know the answer to that. But then one night in September, after we'd gone back to school, I woke up and knew she was there, and I was more glad than I was scared. I liked being singular. I asked Miss Constantin if she was an angel, and she laughed a little, saying, no, she was human, like me, but she'd learned how to slip out of her own body, and go visiting her friends. I asked if I was one of her friends now, and she asked, "Would you like that?" and I said, Yes, please, more than anything, and she replied, "Then you shall be." And I asked Miss Constantin where she came from, and she said Switzerland. To show off, I asked if Switzerland was where chocolate was invented, and she said I was one of the brightest buttons she'd ever known. From then on she visited me every night, for a few minutes, and I'd tell her a bit about my day, and she'd listen, and sympathize or cheer me up. She was always on my side, like Mam or Brendan never seemed to be. I asked Miss Constantin questions, too. Sometimes she'd give me direct answers, like when I asked her her hair color and she told me "chromium blond," but as often as not she'd sidestep my questions with "Let's not spoil the mystery quite yet, Holly, shall we?"

Then one day our school's most gifted bully, Susan Hillage, got me as I walked home from school. Her dad was a squaddie in Belfast and, 'cause my mam's Irish, she knelt on my head and wouldn't let me go unless I admitted we kept our coal in the bathtub and that we loved the IRA. I wouldn't, so she threw my bag into a tree, and told me she was going to make me pay for her dad's mates who got killed in Belfast, and that if I told anyone, her dad's platoon'd set fire to my pub and my family'd all roast and it'd all be my fault. I was no pushover, but I was only little, and Susan Hillage had pulled all the right levers. I didn't tell Mam or Dad what'd happened, but I was worried sick about going to school the next day and what might happen. But that night, when I woke up in the warm pocket of my bed and Miss Constantin's voice came, it wasn't just her voice in my head—she was actually there, in person, sitting in the armchair at the end of my bed saying, "Wakey, wakey, sleepyhead." She was young, and had white-gold hair, and what must've been rose-red lips were purple-black in the moonlight, and she wore a gown thing. She was beautiful, like a painting. Finally I managed to ask if I was dreaming and she replied, "I'm here because my brilliant, singular child was so unhappy tonight, and I want to know why." So I told her about Susan Hillage. Miss Constantin said nothing until the end, when she told me that she despised bullies of all stripes, and did I want her to remedy the situation? I said, Yes, please, but before I could ask anything else Dad's footsteps were coming down the corridor and he'd opened the door, and the light from the landing shone in my eyes, dazzling me. How was I going to explain Miss Constantin sitting in my bedroom at, like, one o'clock in the morning? But Dad acted like she wasn't even there. He just asked me if I was okay, saying he'd heard a voice, and sure enough, Miss Constantin *wasn't* there. I told Dad I must've been dreaming and talking in my sleep.

Which was what I ended up believing. Voices are one thing, but women in gowns, sitting there? The next morning I went to school as usual, and didn't see Susan Hillage. Nobody else did, either. Our headmaster hurried late into school assembly and announced that Susan Hillage had been hit by a van while she cycled to school, that it was very serious and we had to pray for her recovery. Hearing all this, I felt numb and cold, and so much blood left my head that the school hall sort of folded up around me, and after, I had no memory even of hitting the floor.

THE THAMES IS riffled and muddy blue today, and I walk and walk and walk away from Gravesend towards the Kent marshes and before I know it, it's eleven-thirty and the town's a little model of itself, a long way behind me. The wind unravels clouds from the chimneys of the Blue Circle factory, like streams of hankies out of a conjurer's pocket. To my right, the A2 roars away over the marshes. Old Mr. Sharkey says it's built over a road made by the Romans in Roman times, and the A2's still how you get to Dover, to catch the boat to the Continent, just like the Romans did. Pylons march off in double file. Back at the pub, Dad'll be hoovering the bar, unless Sharon's doing it to get my three pounds. The morning's gone muggy and stretched, like it does in triple maths, and the sun's giving me eye-ache. I left my sunglasses in Vinny's kitchen, sat on the draining board. Fourteen ninety-nine they cost me. I bought them with Stella, who said she'd seen the same sunglasses on Carnaby Street for three times the price so I thought I was getting a bargain. Then I imagine myself strangling Stella and my arms and hands go all stiff, like I'm actually doing it.

I'm thirsty. By now Mam will've told Dad something 'bout why Holly went off in a teenage strop, but I bet a million quid she will've twisted it all. Da'll be joking 'bout "The Girls' Bust-up" and PJ and Nipper and Big Dex'll nod and grin like the shower of tossers they are. PJ'll pretend to read from the *Sun*. "It says here, 'Astronomers at the University of Bullshitshire have just found new evidence that, yes, teenagers really *are* the center of the universe.'" They'll all cackle, and Good Old Dave Sykes, everyone's favorite landlord, will join in with his you're-so-witty-I-could-wet-myself laugh. Let's see if they're still laughing by Wednesday when I haven't shown up.

Up ahead, in the distance, men are fishing.

WEIRD SHIT, LAST ACT. Even as I was half carried to the school nurse's room, I could hear the Radio People were back. Hundreds of them, all whispering at once. That freaked me out but not as much as the idea that I'd killed Susan Hillage. So I told the nurse about the Radio People and Miss Constantin. The old dear thought I was concussed at best and nuts at worst, so she called Mam, who called our GP, and later that day I was being seen by an ear doctor at Gravesend General Hospital. He couldn't find anything wrong, but suggested a child psychiatrist he knew from Great Ormond Street Hospital in London who specialized in cases like mine. Mam was all "My daughter's not mental!" but the doctor scared her with the word "tumor." After the worst night of my life—I prayed to God to keep Miss Constantin away, had the Bible under my pillow but, thanks to the Radio People, I could hardly sleep a wink—we got a call from the ear doctor saying that his friend the specialist was due in Gravesend in one hour, and could Mam bring me up right now?

Dr. Marinus was the first Chinese person I ever met, apart from the ones at the Thousand Autumns Restaurant, where me and Brendan were sometimes sent for takeaways if Mam was too tired to cook. Dr. Marinus spoke in posh, perfect English, quite softly, so you had to pay close attention to catch everything. He was short and skinny but sort of filled the room anyway. First he asked 'bout school and my family and stuff, then moved on to my voices. Mam was all, "My daughter's not crazy, if that's what you're implying— it's just concussion." Dr. Marinus told Mam that he agreed, I wasn't remotely crazy, but the brain could be an illogical place. To help him rule out a tumor, she had to let me answer his questions on my own. So I told him about the Radio People and Susan Hillage and Miss Constantin. Mam went all jittery again but Dr. Marinus assured her that auditory hallucinations—"daymares"—were not un-common in girls my age. He told me that Susan Hillage's accident was a big coincidence, and that coincidences even of this size were happening to people all over the world, right now; my turn had come, that was all. Mam asked if there was any medicine to stop these daymares, and I remember Dr. Marinus saying that, before we went down that route, he'd like to try a simpler technique from "the Old Country." It worked like acupuncture, he said, but it didn't use needles. He got Mam to squeeze a point on my middle finger—he marked it with a Biro—then touched a place on my forehead, in the middle, with his thumb. Like an artist putting on a dab of paint. My eyes shut . . .

. . . and the Radio People were gone. Not just quiet, but gone-gone. Mam knew from my face what'd happened, and she was as shocked and relieved as me. She was all, "Is that it? No wires, no pills?" Dr. Marinus said, Yes, that ought to do the job.

I asked if Miss Constantin'd gone forever, too.

The doctor said, Yes, for the foreseeable future.

The End. We left, I grew up, and neither the Radio People nor Miss Constantin ever came back. I saw a few documentaries and stuff about how the mind plays tricks on you, and now I know that Miss Constantin was just a sort of imaginary friend—like Sharon's Bunny Bunny Boing Boing—gone haywire. Susan Hillage's accident was just a massive coincidence, like Dr. Marinus'd told me. She didn't die, but moved to Ramsgate, though some people'd say it's the same difference. Dr. Marinus did some sort of hypnotism thing on me, like those cassettes you can buy to stop yourself smoking. Mam stopped saying "Chink" from that day on, and even today she's down like a ton of bricks on anyone who does. "It's 'Chinese' not 'Chink,'" she tells them, "and they're the best doctors in the National Health."

MY WATCH SAYS it's one o'clock. Far behind me, stick-men are fish-ing in the shallows off Shornemead Fort. Up ahead's a gravel pit, with a big cone of stone and a conveyor belt feeding a barge. I can see Cliffe Fort, too, with windows like empty eye sockets. Old Mr. Sharkey says it used to house antiaircraft batteries in the war, and when people in Gravesend heard the big guns, they knew they had sixty seconds—tops—to get into their air-raid shelters under the stairs or down the garden. Wish a bomb'd fall on a certain house in Peacock Street, right now. Bet they're scoffing pizza for lunch—Vinny lives on pizza 'cause he can't be arsed to cook. Bet they're laughing about me. I wonder if Stella stayed over last night. You just fall in love with each other, I thought, and that's all there is to it. Stupid. *Stupid!* I kick a stone but it's not a stone, it's a little outcrop of rock that mashes my toe. Pain draws a jagged line up to my brain. And now my eyes are hot and watering—where's all the water coming from, f'Chrissakes? The only water I've drunk today is when I cleaned my teeth and the milk on my Weetabix. My tongue's like that oasis stuff they use for flower arranging. My duffel bag's rubbing a sore patch on my shoulder. My heart's a clubbed baby seal. My stomach must be empty, but I'm too miserable to feel it yet. I'm not turning round and going home, though. No bloody way.

BY THREE O'CLOCK, my whole head's parched, not just my mouth. I've never walked so far in my life, I reckon. There's no sign of a shop or even a house where I can ask for a glass of water. Then I notice a small woman fishing off the end of a jetty thing, like she's sort of sketched into the corner where nobody'll spot her. She's a long stone-throw away, but I see her fill a cup from a flask. I'd never normally do this but I'm *so* thirsty that I walk down the embankment and along the jetty up to her, clomping my feet on the old wooden planks so as not to scare her. " 'Scuse me, but could you spare a drop of water? Please?"

She doesn't even look round. "Cold tea do you?" Her croaky voice sounds from somewhere hot.

"That'd be great, thanks. I'm not fussy."

"Help yourself, then, if you're not fussy."

So I fill the cup, not thinking about germs or anything. It's not normal tea but it's the most refreshing thing I've ever drunk, and I let the liquid swoosh all round my mouth. Now I look at her properly for the first time. Sort of elephanty eyes in a wrinkled old face, with short gray hair, a grubby safari shirt, and a leathery wide-brimmed hat that looks a hundred years old. "Good?" she asks.

"Yeah," I say. "It was. Tastes like grass."

"Green tea. Lucky you're not fussy."

I ask, "Since when's tea been green?"

"Since bushes made their leaves that color."

There's a splish of a fish. I see where it was, but not where it is. "Caught much today?"

A pause. "Five perch. One trout. A slow afternoon."

I don't see a bucket or anything. "Where are they?"

A bee lands on the brim of her hat. "I let them go."

"If you don't want the fish, why do you catch them?"

A few seconds pass. "For the quality of the conversation."

I look around: the footpath, a brambly field, a scrubby wood, and a choked-up track. She must be taking the piss. "There's nobody here."

The bee's happy where it is, even when the woman stirs herself to reel in the line. I stand off to one side as she checks the bait's still secure on the hook. Drips of water splash the thirsty planks of the jetty. The river slurps at the shore and sloshes round the wooden pillar things. Still seated, and with an expert flick of the wrist, the old woman sends the lead weight loopy-looping away, the reel makes its zithery noise, and the weight lands in the water where it was before. Circles float outwards. Dead calm . . .

Then she does something really weird. She takes out a stick of chalk from her pocket and writes on a plank by her foot, MY. On the next plank along she writes, LONG. Then on the next plank, it's the word NAME. Then the old woman puts the chalk away and goes back to her fishing.

I wait for her to explain, but she doesn't. "What's all that about?"

"What's what about?"

"What you just wrote."

"They're instructions."

"Instructions for who?"

"For someone many years from now."

"But it's chalk. It'll wash off."

"From the jetty, yes. Not from your memory."

Okay, so she's mad as a sack of ferrets. Only I don't tell her so 'cause I'd like more of that green tea.

"Finish the tea, if you want," she says. "You won't find a shop until you and the boy arrive at Allhallows-on-Sea . . ."

"Thanks a lot." I fill the cup. "Are you sure? This is the last of it."

"One good turn deserves another." She turns a crafty sniper's eye on me. "I may need asylum."

Asylum? She needs a mental asylum? "How d'you mean?"

"Refuge. A bolt-hole. If the First Mission fails, as I fear it must."

Crazy people are hard work. "I'm fifteen. I don't have an asylum, or a, uh, bolt-hole. Sorry."

"You're ideal. You're unexpected. My tea for your asylum. Do we have a deal?"

Dad says the best way to handle drunks is to humor them, then dump them, and maybe the doo-lally are like drunks who never sober up. "Deal." She nods and I drink until the sun's a pale glow through the thin bottom of the plastic.

The old bat's gazing away again. "Thank you, Holly."

So I thank her back, and return to dry land. Then I turn around and go back to her. "How do you know my name?"

She doesn't turn round. "By what name was I baptized?"

What a stupid game this is. "Esther Little."

"And how do you know *my* name?"

" 'Cause . . . you just told me." Did she? Must've.

"That's that settled, then." And that was Esther Little's final word.

. . .

AROUND FOUR O'CLOCK I get to a strip of shingly beach by a wooden groyne thing sloping into the river. I take my Docs off. There's a doozy of a blister on my big toe, like a trodden-on blackberry. Yum. I take my *Fear of Music* LP out of my duffel bag, roll my jeans right up, and wade in to my knees. The curving river's cool as tap water and the sun's got a punch to it, but not as hard as it was when I left the crazy old woman fishing. Then I frisbee the LP as hard and far as I can. It's not specially aerodynamic, and flies upwards till the inner sleeve with the record in drops out, plops into the water. The black album cover falls like a wounded bird and floats for a while. Tears, more tears, seep from my aching eyes and I imagine wading over to where the record's spiraling down now, down the slope of the riverbed, strolling through the trout and perch to the rusty bicycles and bones of drowned pirates and German airplanes and flung-away wedding rings and God knows what.

But I wade back to shore and lie down on a bed of warm shingle, next to my Docs. Dad'll be upstairs with his feet up on the sofa: "Reckon I'll go and pay this Costello feller a call, Kath," he'll be saying. Mam'll drown her cigarette in the cold coffee at the bottom of her mug. "No, Dave. That's what Her Ladyship wants. Ignore her Big Statement long enough, and she'll start appreciating just how much we do for her . . ."

But, come tomorrow evening, Mam'll start fretting 'bout school on Monday, 'cause once school asks where I am and why I'm not sitting the exams, she'll be a whole load less snotty about my Big Statement. She'll march round to Vinny's house, all guns blazing. Mam'll tear strips off of Vinny—good, ha!—but she still won't know where I am. Decided. I camp out for two nights, and then see how I'm feeling. So long as I don't buy any cigarettes, my £13.85 in coins is enough for two days' worth of chip butties, apples, and Rich Tea biscuits. If I get to Rochester I could even take some money from the TSB and extend my little vacation.

A massive freighter heading downstream blasts its horn. STAR OF

RIGA is written in white letters on the orange hull. Wonder if Riga's a place, or something else. Sharon and Jacko'd know. I do a huge yawn, lie back on the clacking pebbles, and watch the wash from the massive ship lap the shingle by the shore.

Christ, I'm dead sleepy all of a sudden . . .

"SYKES? YOU ALIVE? Oy . . . Sykes." The afternoon breaks in and it's *Where am I?* and *Why am I barefoot?* and *What the hell is Ed Brubeck doing touching my arm?* I jerk it back, get up, and scuttle a couple of yards while the soles of my feet go *ow ow ow* on the hot pebbles and then I bang my head on the wooden groyne thing.

Ed Brubeck hasn't moved. "That hurt."

"I know it bloody hurt. It's my bloody head."

"I only wanted to make sure you weren't dead."

I rub my head. "Do I *look* like I'm dead?"

"Well, yeah, a second ago, you did, a bit."

"Well, I'm bloody not." I see Brubeck's bike lying on its side with its wheel still spinning. His fishing rod's still strapped to its cross-bar. "I was just . . . snoozing."

"Don't tell me you *walked* here from town, Sykes?"

"No, I came by space hopper but the fecker bounced off."

"Huh. Never had you down as the great-outdoors type."

"I never had *you* down as the Good Samaritan type."

"We live and learn." A bird's singing, a loopy-loony-tweety one, a mile up. Ed Brubeck pushes his black hair back from his eyes. His skin's so tanned he could be Turkish or something. "So where are you going?"

"As far away from that shit hole as my feet can carry me."

"Oh dear. What's naughty Gravesend done to you now?"

I lace up my Docs. My blister hurts. "Where are *you* going?"

"My uncle lives thataway." Ed Brubeck waves an arm inland. "He's not too mobile these days and almost blind, so I go and keep him company a bit. I was cycling off to Allhallows for a bit of fishing when I saw you and . . ."

"Thought I'd died. Which I haven't. Don't let me keep you."

He makes a suit-yourself face, and climbs up the embankment.

I call after him, "How far is it to Allhallows, Brubeck?"

He picks up his bike. "About five miles. Want a backie?"

I think of Vinny and his Norton and shake my head. He mounts his bike, poser-style, and he's gone. I scoop up a fistful of stones and fling it over the water, hard and angry.

A SPECK-SIZED ED Brubeck vanishes behind a clump of pointy trees way up ahead. He didn't look back. Wish I'd said yes to his offer, now. My knees are stiff and my feet are two giant throbs and my ankles feel like they've been attacked with tiny drills. Five miles at this rate'll take me forever. But Ed Brubeck's a guy, like Vinny's a guy, and guys are all sperm-guns. My stomach growls with dry hunger. Green tea's great while you're drinking it, but it makes you pee like a racehorse, and now my mouth feels like a dying rat crapped in it. Ed Brubeck's a guy, yes, but he's not a total tosser. Last week he got into an argument with Mrs. Binkirk, our RE teacher, and got sent to Mr. Nixon for calling her "Bigot of the Year." A grown-up insult, that. People are icebergs, with just a bit you can see and loads you can't. I try not to think about Vinny, but I do, and remember how only this morning I dreamt of starting a band with him. Up ahead, from behind the clump of pointy trees, comes a speck-sized Ed Brubeck, cycling back my way. Probably he's decided it's too late to fish, and he's heading back to Gravesend. He grows bigger and bigger until he's life-sized, and does a show-offy skid-turn that reminds me he's still a boy as well as a guy. His eyes are white in his dark face. "Why don't you get on, Sykes?" He slaps his bike saddle. "Allhallow's *miles*. It'll be dark before you get there."

We wobble along the track at a decent clip. Whenever we go over a bump Brubeck says, "You okay?" and I tell him, "Yeah." The sea breeze and bike breeze slip up my sleeves and stroke my front like a pervy Mr. Tickle. Sweat's gluing Brubeck's T-shirt to his back. I refuse to think 'bout Vinny's sweat, and Stella's . . . My heart cracks again and goo dribbles out and stings, like Dettol on a graze. I grip the bike rack with both hands, but then the track gets rucklier so I steady myself by hooking one thumb through a belt loop on Brubeck's jeans. Probably Brubeck's getting a hard-on from this, but it's his problem, not mine.

Fluffy lambs are nibbling grass. Ewes watch us, like we're planning to serve up their babies with sprouts and mash.

We scare birds on stilts with spoony beaks; they skim off across the river. Their wing tips touch the water, sending out circles.

Here the Thames is turning into the sea and Essex is turning gold. That smudge is Canvey Island; farther on, Southend.

The English Channel's Biro-blue; the sky's the blue of snooker chalk. We judder across a footbridge over a rusty creek, half-marsh, half-dune, inland: WELCOME TO THE ISLE OF GRAIN.

It's not a real island, mind. Once upon a time, perhaps.

That loony, loopy, tweety bird's followed us. Must of.

ALLHALLOWS-ON-SEA'S BASICALLY A big holiday park spilling up to the shorefront from a nothingy village behind. It's all rows of caravans and those oblong cabins on little stilts they call trailer homes in American films. There's half-naked kids and totally naked toddlers all over the shop, firing water pistols and playing Swingball and running about. Half-sloshed mums're rolling their eyes at sun-pinked dads burning bangers on barbecues. I try to eat the smoke. "Dunno about you," says Brubeck, "but I'm starving."

Too enthusiastically I say, "Just a bit," so he parks his bike at the fish-and-chip place, next to Lazy Rolf's Krazy Golf. Brubeck orders cod and chips, which is two pounds, but I just order chips 'cause it's only fifty p. But then Brubeck tells the bloke at the counter, "*Two* cod and chips, please," and hands over a fiver, and the bloke glances at me and gives Brubeck that nice-one-son look that men give each other, which pisses me off 'cause me and Brubeck aren't boyfriend and girlfriend and we're not bloody going to be, however many battered cods he gives me. Brubeck gets us two cans of Coke too and notices my face. "It's only fish and chips—no strings attached."

"You're damn right there's no strings attached." It comes out spikier than I meant. "But thanks."

We walk past the last cabin and on a bit to a concrete shelter, just on the lip of the dunes. A whiff of wee leaks through the slitted window but Brubeck climbs onto its low, flat roof. "This is a pillbox," he says. "They were machine-gun posts during the war, in case the Germans invaded. There's still hundreds of them around, if you keep your eyes peeled. This is peace, if you think about it—machine-gun nests being used as picnic tables." I look at him: You'd never dare say something that clever at school. I scramble up on my own and take in the view. Southend's across the wider-than-a-mile mouth of the Thames and the other way I can see Sheerness docks on the Isle of Sheppey. Then we open our Cokes and I peel off the ring carefully to put in the can after. They slice open dogs' pawpads. Brubeck holds his can towards me so I clunk it, like it's a wineglass, but I don't meet his eyes in case he gets any ideas, and we drink. My first gulp's a *booom* of freezing fizz. The chips are warm and vinegary and the batter's hot in our fingers as we pull it back to get at the fat flakes of cod. "It tastes great," I say. "Cheers."

"Not as good as a Manchester chipper," says Brubeck.

A stunt kite writes on the blue with its pink tail.

I FILL MY lungs with one of Brubeck's Dunhills. That's better. Then I think of Stella Yearwood and Vinny smoking his Marlboros in bed, and suddenly I have to pretend I've got something in my eye. To distract myself, I ask Brubeck, "So who's this uncle of yours, then? The one you visited earlier."

"Uncle Norm. My mum's brother. Used to be a crane operator at Blue Circle Cement, but he's stopped working. He's going blind."

I take another deep drag. "That's awful. Poor guy."

"Uncle Norm says, 'Pity is a form of abuse.'"

"Is he completely blind, or just partly, or . . ."

"He's lost about three-quarters of his sight in both eyes, and the rest's going. What gets him down most is that he can't read the papers anymore. It's like searching for your keys in dirty snow, he says. So most Saturdays I cycle out to his bungalow and read him pieces from the *Guardian*. Then he talks about Thatcher versus the unions, why the Russians are in Afghanistan, why the CIA are taking down democratic governments in Latin America."

"Sounds like school," I say.

Brubeck shakes his head. "Most of our teachers just want to get home by four and retire by sixty. But my uncle Norm loves talking and thinking and he wants you to love it too. He's sharp as a razor. Then my aunt makes a big late lunch, and my uncle nods off, and I go fishing, if the weather's nice. Unless I see someone from my class at school lying dead on the beach." He stubs out his cigarette on the concrete. "So. What's your story, Sykes?"

"What do you mean, what's my story?"

"At eight forty-five I see you walking up Queen Street, ducking—"

"You *saw* me?"

"Yep—ducking into the Indoor Market, but seven hours later the target is sighted ten miles east of Gravesend, along the river."

"What is this? Ed Brubeck, Private Investigator?"

A little tailless dog that's all waggling bum comes up. Brubeck chucks it a chip. "If I *was* a detective, I'd suspect boyfriend trouble."

My voice goes sharp. "None of your business."

"This is true. But the tosser's not worth it, whoever he is."

Scowling, I drop the dog a chip. He scoffs it so hungrily I wonder if he's a stray. Like me.

Brubeck makes a funnel out of his chip paper to pour the crispy bits into his mouth. "You planning on going back to town tonight?"

I abort a groan. Gravesend's a black cloud. Vinny and Stella and Mam are in it. *Are* it. My watch says 18:19 and the Captain Marlow'll be cheerful and chattery as the evening regulars drift in. Upstairs Jacko and Sharon'll be sat on the sofa watching *The A-Team* with cheese thingies and a slab of chocolate cake. I'd like to be there, but what about Mam's slap? "No," I tell Brubeck, "I'm not."

"It'll be dark in three hours. Not a lot of time to find a circus to run away with."

The dune grass sways. Clouds're unrolling across the sky from France. I put my jacket on. "Maybe I'll find a nice cozy pillbox. One that's not used to pee in. Or a barn."

Here come seagulls on boingy elastic, scrawking for chips too. Brubeck stands up and flaps his arms at the gulls like the Mad Prince of Allhallows-on-Sea to make them scatter, just for the hell of it. "Maybe I know somewhere better."

WE'RE CYCLING ALONG a proper road again. Big fields in the pancake-flat arse-end of nowhere, with long black shadows. Brubeck's being all mysterious 'bout where we're going—"Either you trust me, Sykes, or you don't"—but he says it's warm, dry, and safe and he's stayed there himself five or six times when he's been out night-fishing, so I'll go along with it, for now. He says he'll head off home after Gravesend. That's the problem with boys: They tend to help you only 'cause they fancy you, but there's no unembarrassing way to find out their real motives till it's too late. Ed Brubeck seems okay, and he spends his Saturday afternoons reading for a blind uncle, but thanks to bloody Vinny and Stella, I'm not so sure if I'm a good judge of character. With night coming on, though, I don't have much choice. We pass a massive factory. I'm 'bout to ask Brubeck what they make there when he tells me it's Grain Power Station and it provides electricity for Gravesend and half of southeast London.

"Yeah, I know," I lie.

THE CHURCH IS stumpy with a tower that's got arrow-slits and it's gold in the last light. The wood sounds like never-ending waves, with rooks tumbling about like black socks in a dryer. ST MARY HOO PARISH CHURCH says a sign, with the vicar's phone number underneath. The village of Saint Mary Hoo is up ahead, but it's really just a few old houses and a pub where two lanes meet. "The bedding's basic," says Brubeck, as we get off the bike, "but the Father, the Son, and the Holy Spirit handle security, and at zero quid a night, it's priced competitively."

Does he mean the church? "You're joking, right?"

"Check-out's seven sharp or the management get shirty."

Yes, he means the church. I make a dubious face.

Brubeck makes a face that says, *Take it or leave it.*

I'll have to take it. The Kent marshes are not dotted with cozy barns full of warm straw, like in *Little House on the Prairie.* The only one I've seen was a corrugated-iron job a few miles back, guarded by two Dobermans with rabies. "Don't they lock churches?"

Brubeck says, "Yeah," in the same way I'd say, "So?" After checking no one's around, he wheels his bike into the graveyard. He hides it between dark brushy trees and the wall, then leads me to the porch. Confetti's piled up in dirty drifts. "Keep an eye on the gate," he tells me. From his pocket he digs out a leather purse-thing and inside's a dangly row of spindly keys and an L-shaped piece of thin metal. One last look at the lane, then he pokes a key into the lock, and jiggles it a bit.

I feel a lurch of fear we'll get caught. "Where did you learn to break into buildings?"

"It wasn't footy or repairing punctures that Dad taught me."

"We could get done for this! It's called, it's called—"

"Breaking and entering. That's why you keep your eyes peeled."

"But what am I s'posed to do exactly if somebody comes?"

"Act embarrassed, like we've been caught snogging."

"Uh—I don't *think* so, Ed Brubeck."

He does a half-hiss half-laugh. "*Act* it, I said. Relax, you only get nicked if the cops can prove *you* picked the lock. If you don't confess, and if you're careful not to bugger the mechanism . . ." he feeds a skeleton key into the keyhole, ". . . then who's to say you didn't just happen along, find the door left ajar, and go in to satisfy your interest in Saxon church architecture? That's our story, by the way, just in case." Brubeck's got his ear against the lock as he's twizzling. "Though I've stayed here three Saturday nights since Easter and not heard a dickie-bird. Plus it's not like we're taking anything. Plus you're a girl, so just sob your eyes out and do the 'Please, Mr. Vicar, I'm running away from my violent stepfather' bit and, chances are, you'll walk away with a cup of tea and a Penguin biscuit." Brubeck holds up a hand for hush: a click. "Got it." The church door swings open with the perfect Transylvanian hinge-creak.

Inside, Saint Mary Hoo's Church smells of charity shops, and the stained-glass gloom's all fruit-salady. The walls're thick as a nuclear bunker and the *thunk* when Brubeck shuts us in echoes all around, like a dungeon. The roof's all beams and timbers. We walk down the short aisle, past the ten or twelve pews. The pulpit's wooden, the font's stone, the organ's like a fancy piano with exhaust pipes. The lectern-thingy must be fake gold, or a burglar—Brubeck's dad, for example—would've swiped it long ago. We reach the altar table and look up at the window showing the crucifixion. A dove in the stained-glass sky has spokes coming off it. The Marys, two disciples, and a Roman at the foot of the cross look like they're discussing whether it's starting to rain or not. Brubeck asks, "You're Catholic, right?"

I'm surprised he's ever thought 'bout this. "My mum's Irish."

"So do you believe in heaven and God and that?"

I stopped going to church last year; that was me and Mam's biggest row till this morning. "I sort of developed an allergy."

"My uncle Norm says religion's 'spiritual paracetamol,' and in a way I hope he's right. Unless God issues personality transplants when you arrive, heaven'd mean a never-ending family reunion with the likes of my uncle Trev. I can't think of anything more hellish."

"So Uncle Trev's no Uncle Norm, then?"

"Chalk and cheese. Uncle Trev's my dad's older brother. 'The Brains of the Operation,' he says, which is true enough: He's got brains enough to get losers like Dad to do the dirty work. Uncle

Trev fences the merchandise if the job's a success, does his Mr. Non-stick Frying Pan when it goes belly-up. He even tried it on with my mum after Dad got sent down, which is partly why we moved south."

"Sounds a total scuzzball."

"Yep, that's Uncle Trev." The psychedelic light on Brubeck's face dims as the sun fades. "Mind you, if I was dying in a hospice, maybe I'd want all the spiritual paracetamol I could get my hands on."

I put my hand on the altar rail. "What if . . . what if heaven *is* real, but only in moments? Like a glass of water on a hot day when you're *dying* of thirst, or when someone's nice to you for no reason, or . . ." Mam's pancakes with Mars Bar sauce; Dad dashing up from the bar just to tell me, "Sleep tight don't let the bedbugs bite"; or Jacko and Sharon singing "For She's a Squishy Marshmallow" instead of "For She's a Jolly Good Fellow" every single birthday and wetting themselves even though it's not at all funny; and Brendan giving his old record player to me instead of one of his mates. "S'pose heaven's not like a painting that's just hanging there forever, but more like . . . like the best song anyone ever wrote, but a song you only catch in snatches, while you're alive, from passing cars, or . . . upstairs windows when you're lost . . ."

Brubeck's looking at me like he's *really* listening.

And, *feck it,* I'm blushing. "What're you looking at?"

Before he can answer, a key rattles in the door.

Slow-motion seconds lurch by me, like a conga of pissheads, and Brubeck and me are Laurel and Hardy and Starsky and Hutch and two halves of a pantomime horse, and he bundles me through a wooden door I'd not noticed behind the organ, into this odd-shaped room with a high ceiling and a ladder going up to a trapdoor. I think it's called a vestry, this room, and the ladder must lead to the bell tower. Brubeck listens through the door crack; there's no other way out, only a cupboard thing in the corner. Coming our way are at least two men's voices; I think I hear a third, a woman. *Shit.* Brubeck and me look at each other. Our choices are: Stay here and try to talk our way out; hide in the cupboard; or squirrel it up the ladder and hope the trapdoor opens for us, and whoever's coming doesn't follow. We probably wouldn't make it up the ladder now. Suddenly Brubeck's bundling me into the cupboard, then he gets in too and pulls the door shut the best he can. It's smaller than it looked from the outside; it's like hiding yourself in half a vertical coffin—with a boy you have no interest in being crushed up against. Brubeck pulls the door shut . . .

"But the man believes he's the Second Comin' of Fidel soddin' Castro!" The voices enter the vestry. "Love Maggie Thatcher or loathe her, and there's plenty who do both, she *did* win an election, which Arthur Scargill hasn't. He didn't even ballot his own union."

"None of that's the point," says a Londoner. "This strike's about the future. That's why the government's using every dirty trick in the book—MI5 spies, lies in the media, no benefits for miners' families . . . Mark my words, if the miners lose, your children'll be working Victorian hours for Victorian wages."

Brubeck's kneecap in my thigh's giving me a slow dead leg.

I swivel a bit; his *ow ow ow* is quieter than a whisper.

"We can't keep dying industries alive forever," the yokel's arguing back, "that's the point. Otherwise we'd still be forkin' out for castle builders or canal diggers or druids. Scargill's arguing for the economics of Fantasy Island and the politics of Bullshit Mountain."

I feel Brubeck's chest, rising and falling against my back.

"Ever been to a mining town?" asks the Londoner. "You can't go now 'cause the fuzz won't let you near, but when the mine goes, the town dies. Wales and the north ain't the south, Yorkshire ain't Kent, and energy ain't just another industry. Energy's security. The North Sea oil fields won't last forever, and then what?"

"A quality debate, gents," says the woman, "but the bells?"

Feet clop up a wooden ladder; lucky we didn't choose the bell tower. A minute goes by. Still no sound from the vestry. I think all three've gone up. I shift a fraction and Brubeck gasps in pain. I risk whispering, "Are you okay?"

"No. You're crushing my nuts, since you asked."

"You can adopt." I try to give him more room, but there isn't any. "Think we should make a run for it?"

"Perhaps a silent creep, once the—"

The stuffy darkness booms with bells. Brubeck opens the door— fresher air floods in—half hobbles out, then helps me climb out. High above, two chubby calves are dangling down through the hatch. We tiptoe to the door, like a pair of total wallies from *Scooby-Doo* . . .

ME AND BRUBECK leg it down the lane, like we've escaped from Colditz. The bells sound sloshy and shiny in the blue dark. I get a stitch so we stop at a bench by the village sign. "Typical," says Brubeck. "I want to show off my 'How to Survive in the Wild' skills, and it's the Invasion of the Wurzels instead. I need a fag. You?"

"Okay. Will they be ding-donging for a while?"

"Guess so." Brubeck hands me a cigarette and holds out a lighter; I dip the tip in the flame. "I'll let you back in when they've gone. Yale locks are a cinch, even in the dark."

"But shouldn't you be getting home?"

"I'll call my mum from the phone box by the pub and say I'm staying out night-fishing after all. Little white lie."

I need his help, but I'm nervous 'bout a price tag.

"Don't worry, Sykes. My intentions are honorable."

I think of Vinny Costello and flinch. "Good."

"Guys don't *just* think 'bout getting off with girls, y'know."

I fire a beam of smoke straight at Brubeck's face, so he has to squint and look away. "I've got an older brother," I tell him. We're by an overgrown orchard, so when we've finished our cigarettes we climb in and scrump a few unripe apples. There's a brick wall to clamber up. The apples are tart as limes, but good after an oily dinner. Lights blink on the power station we passed earlier. "Out that-away," Brubeck chucks an apple core in the general direction, "past them hazy lights on the Isle of Sheppey, there's a fruit farm, Gabriel Harty's. I worked the strawberry season there last year and made twenty-five quid a day. There's dorms for the pickers, and once the exams are over, I'm going back. I'm saving for an InterRail in August."

"What's an InterRail?"

"Seriously?"

"Seriously."

"A train pass. You pay a hundred and thirty quid and then you can travel all over Europe, for a month, for free. Second-class, but still. From the tip of Portugal to the top of Norway. Eastern-bloc countries too, Yugoslavia and places. The Berlin Wall. Istanbul. In Istanbul, there's this bridge, right. One side's in Europe and the other's in Asia. I'm going to walk across it."

Far away, a lonely dog barks, or perhaps a fox.

I ask, "What do you do in all these countries?"

"Look around. Walk. Find a cheap bed. Eat what the locals eat. Find a cheap beer. Try not to get fleeced. Talk. Pick up a few words in the local lingo. Just *be* there, y'know? Sometimes," Brubeck bites into an apple, "sometimes I want to be *every*where, all at once, so badly I could just . . ." Brubeck mimes a bomb going off in his ribcage. "Do you never get that feeling?"

A bat flaps by, like it's on a string in a naff vampire film.

"Not really, if I'm honest. The furthest I've ever been's Ireland, to see my mum's relatives in Cork."

"What's it like?"

"Different. It's not all checkpoints and bombs like up north, though the Troubles are still in the air a bit, and it's best to shut up about politics. They *hate* Thatcher 'cause of Bobby Sands and the hunger strikers. I've got this one great-aunt, my mam's aunt Eilísh— she's brilliant. She keeps hens and has a gun in her coal hole, and when she was younger she cycled all the way to Kathmandu. Really, she did. She felt that wanna-be-everywhere *boom* thing, for sure. I've seen photos and newspaper cuttings and stuff. She lives on this long headland near Bantry—the Sheep's Head peninsula. It's like the edge of the world. There's nothing there, no shops or anything, but"—there's not many people I'd admit this to—"I really loved it."

There's a moon sharp enough to cut your finger on.

We say nothing for a bit, but it's not an awkward nothing. Then Brubeck says, "D'you know 'bout the second umbilical cord, Sykes?"

I can't make out his face anymore. "You what?"

"When you're a baby in the womb, there's this cord—"

"I know what an umbilical cord is, thanks. But a second one?"

"Well, psychologists say there's a second umbilical cord, an invisible one, an emotional one, which ties you to your parents for the whole time you're a kid. Then, one day, you have a row with your mum if you're a girl, or your dad if you're a boy, and that argument cuts your second cord. Then, and only then, are you ready to go off into the big wide world and be an adult on your own terms. It's like a rite-of-passage thing."

"I argue with my mam, like, *daily*. She treats me like I'm ten."

Brubeck lights another fag, takes a drag, and passes it to me. "I'm talking a bigger, nastier fight. Afterwards you know it happened. You're not the kid you were."

"And you're sharing these pearls of wisdom with me why?"

He lines up his answer carefully. "If you're running off because your dad's a petty crim who beats your mum up and throws you downstairs when you try to stop him, then running away's the clever thing to do. Go. I'll give you my InterRail money. But if you're sat on this wall tonight just because your umbilical cord got snipped, then, yeah, it hurts, but it had to happen. Cut your mum a bit of slack. It's just a part of growing up. You shouldn't be punishing her for it."

"She *slapped* me."

"Bet she feels like shit about it now."

"You don't even know her!"

"Are you sure you do, Sykes?"

"What's *that* s'posed to bloody mean?"

Brubeck lets it drop. So I let it drop too.

. . .

THE CHURCH IS quiet as the grave. Brubeck's asleep in a nest of dusty cushions. We're up on this gallery thing along the back wall, so we won't be spotted if any Satan worshipers drop by for a black mass. My calves are sore, my blister's throbbing, and my mind keeps rewinding to the scene with Vinny and Stella. Wasn't I good enough at sex? Didn't I dress right, talk right, like the right music?

22:58, glows my Timex. The maddest minutes of the week at the Captain Marlow are right now: last orders on a Saturday night. Mam, Dad, and Glenda, who just works weekends, will be going full pelt; a roaring wall of drinkers flapping fivers and tenners through the fog of smoke and the racket of chatter, shouts, laughs, curses, flirting . . . Nobody'll care where Holly's ended up tonight. On the jukebox "Daydream Believer" or "Rockin' All Over the World" or "American Pie" will be booming through the building. Sharon's fallen asleep with her flashlight on under the blanket. Jacko's asleep with people murmuring foreign languages on his radio. Up in my room, my bed's unmade, my schoolbag's slung over my chair. A basket of washed laundry's just inside the door, where Mam puts it when she's pissed off with me. Which is most days now. The big glow of Essex at night'll be shining orangy light across the river, through my undrawn curtains, over the *Zenyattà Mondatta* and *The Queen Is Dead* posters I scavved from the Magic Bus. But I'm not going to start missing my room now.

No fecking way.

TIN WHISTLES, SCRATTY NOISES, birdsong, and a stained-glass angel. The little church on the Isle of Grain, I remember now, lit by sun through the first crack of the day. Mam. The row. Stella and Vinny, waking up in each other's arms. My throat goes tight. I s'pose if some man's been inside you often enough, it'll take a while to get rid of him. Love's pure free joy when it works, but when it goes bad you pay for the good hours at loan-shark prices. 06:03, says my Timex. Sunday. Ed Brubeck: There he is, asleep on his cushiony things, mouth squashed open, hair floppy. His baseball cap sits on his neatly folded lumberjack shirt. I rub the sleep from my eyes. I was dreaming about Jacko and Miss Constantin holding open a curtain of air, and stone steps going up like in an *Indiana Jones* film . . .

Who cares? I lost Vinny. Stella stole Vinny.

Ed Brubeck snores like a bear. Brubeck wouldn't two-time his girlfriend. If he has one. Most boys in my year drop hints 'bout losing their virginity at a mate's party, specially boys who haven't, stroking their bum-fluff moustaches . . . Ed Brubeck doesn't do any of that, which means probably he has done it. If it was with someone at our school, I'd've heard. Dunno, though. He keeps his mouth shut.

Mind you, he told me quite a bit yesterday.

His dad, his family, everything. Why me?

Watch his sleeping, pointy, half-man-half-boy's face.

And the answer's obvious: 'Cause *he fancies you, you prawn!*

If he fancies me, why didn't he make a pass at me?

He's clever, I realize. *First he makes you grateful.*

Right. Of course. I do believe it's time I was off.

DANDELIONS AND THISTLES grow along the cracked track and the hedges are taller than me. The early sun's like laser beams. Dunno why I nicked Brubeck's cap as I crept away, but I'm glad I did. He won't mind, much. Should be able to cut across the fields to the main road to Rochester—six, seven miles away, I reckon. My blisters'll take it. They'll have to; I don't have a first-aid box in my duffel bag. I feel a jab of hunger, but my stomach'll just have to put up and shut up—I'll find something to eat at Rochester. Perhaps I should've said bye and thanks to Brubeck but if he'd have answered, "No worries, Sykes, but are you sure I can't give you a backie back to Gravesend?" all cheerful-like, I'd've found it too hard to say no.

Up ahead, I see the track ending at a farmyard.

I climb a gate and skirt round a field of cabbages.

Another gate. A hawk thing's a speck in the sky.

Six days should do it. The police only get interested in missing teenagers once a week's up. Six days'll show Mam I *can* look after myself in the big bad world. I'll be in a stronger, whatchercallit?, a stronger negotiating position. And I'll do it on my own, without a Brubeck to get all boyfriendish on me. I'll have to be careful to make my money last. Remember that time I tried my hand at shoplifting?

One Saturday last year a bunch of us went to Chatham Roller Disco for Ali Jessop's birthday, but it was so lame that me and Stella and Amanda Kidd sneaked off to the high street. Amanda Kidd said, "Who wants to go fishing, then?" I didn't want to but Stella said okay, so I acted all cool too and we went into Debenhams. I'd never nicked anything in my life and really I almost peed myself, but I watched Stella. She asked the shop assistant something pointless and a bit later, accidentally on purpose, dropped two lipsticks from the cosmetics stand. When she bent down to pick them up she put one of them in her boot. I did the same with some earrings I liked, and on my way out of the shop, I even asked the assistant what time they were open till. Once we were safe outside, the world felt different, like the rules had been changed. If you keep your nerve, you get what you want. Amanda Kidd had got a pair of sunglasses worth a tenner, Stella had some Estée Lauder lippy, and my fake diamond earrings sparkled like real ones. Next we went to the Sweet Factory, where me and Amanda Kidd stuffed sweets into our clothes while Stella told the Saturday boy she'd seen him here every week for ages, and even dreamt about him, and would he like to go for a walk with her somewhere private after work? Last we went to Woolworths. Stella and me drifted away to look at the Top 40 singles, innocent enough, but the next minute the manager and an assistant were walling us in, and this store-detective guy had Amanda Kidd— shaking and white as a sheet—by the arm and saying, "These are the two she came into the shop with." The manager ordered us upstairs to his office. All my willpower and attitude withered away, but Stella snapped back, "By *whom* am I being addressed?" Her voice came out posh and sharp.

The manager said, "Just come quietly, sweetheart," and tried to put his hand on her shoulder.

Stella slapped it away and snapped at full volume, "Keep your grubby paws *off me,* you horrid little man! I neither know why you've linked my sister and me with this . . . *shoplifter,*" she sneered at Amanda Kidd, who now shook and sobbed, "but you'll tell us *exactly* why we'd steal any of the crap you sell in your ghastly little shop"—here she emptied her handbag onto the record counter— "and you'd *better be right,* Mr. Manager, or my father will serve you a writ first thing Monday. Make no mistake: I know my rights." Lots of customers were rubbernecking our way and, miracle of miracles, the manager backed down, and muttered that perhaps the store detective was mistaken and we were free to go. Stella snapped, "I *know* I'm free to go!," put her things back in her handbag, and out we huffed.

We sneaked back to the roller disco and didn't tell anyone what'd happened. Amanda Kidd's mum had to go and get her in the end. I was panicking she'd grass us off, but she didn't dare. Amanda Kidd ate lunch with a different bunch of girls that week, and we've never really spoken since. She's in the second-from-top class in our year now, so perhaps getting caught was good for her, sort of. The point is, unlike Stella, I'm not a natural thief, or a natural liar. That day in Woolworths, she even convinced *me* we were innocent. And look what a fool she made of me, when my turn came to be Amanda Kidd–ed. Doesn't Stella need friends? Or for Stella, are friends just a way to get what you want?

ON MY LEFT'S a steep embankment, with a dual carriageway running along the top, and on my right a field's been cleared for a massive housing estate by the look of it. There's diggers and bulldozers and Portakabins and tall wire fences and notices saying HARD HATS MUST BE WORN, and over a sign saying UNAUTHORISED ENTRY IS FORBIDDEN someone's sprayed AINT NO BLACK IN THE UNION JACK, plus a couple of swastikas for good measure. It's still early: 07:40. Brubeck'll be cycling home, but back at the pub Mam and Dad'll still be in bed. Up ahead's the entrance to an underpass going under the fast road above. When I'm about a hundred meters away, I see a boy there, and I stop, and this is really odd, but I could swear . . .

It's Jacko. He just stands there, watching me. The real Jacko's twenty-odd miles away, I know, drawing a maze or reading a chess book or doing something Jacko-ish, but the kid I'm looking at's got the same floppy brown hair, shape, way of standing, even a red Liverpool FC top. I know Jacko and this is him or an identical twin nobody knows about. I keep walking, not daring to blink in case he vanishes. When I'm fifty meters away I wave, and the kid who can't be my little brother waves. So I shout his name. He doesn't shout back, but turns and walks down into the underpass. I don't know what to make of it, but I jog along now, nervous that Jacko's done a runner to come and find me, even though the sensible part of me is sure it can't be him 'cause how'd Jacko know where to look?

I run as fast I can, now, knowing something strange is going on, but not knowing what. The underpass is for walkers and cyclists only so it's quite narrow, and as long as the width of the four traffic lanes and the grass in the middle it goes under. Ahead, down and then up a bit, the far exit's a square of fields, sky, and roofs. I've taken a few steps in before I notice it: Instead of getting darker towards the middle of the underpass, it's actually getting lighter; instead of getting echoier, it's getting more muffled. I tell myself, *It's just an illusion, don't worry,* but after a few more steps, I'm sure of it: The underpass is changing its shape. It's wider and higher, with four corners, a big diamond-shaped room . . . It's becoming somewhere else. It's incredible and it's terrifying. I know I'm awake but I know this can't be real. I stop walking altogether; I'm scared of hitting the wall. Where is this? I've been nowhere like it. Is it a daymare? Is all that stuff waking up again? There are narrow windows to my left and right, about ten paces away. I'm not going to look through them—they'd be well past the underpass walls—but through the left window I see dunes, gray dunes, climbing up towards a high ridge, but through the right-hand window it's darker: The dunes roll down towards a sea, but it's a black sea, utterly black-black, like darkness in a box in a cave a mile underground. A long table's appeared in the middle of the chamber, wherever we are, and I'm walking down on the left side of it, and look, there's a woman, keeping pace with me, on the right. She's young and beautiful in a cold way, like an actress who can't be touched; she's got white-blond hair and bone-pale skin, rich rose-red lips and a midnight-blue ball gown like a woman from a story . . .

Miss Constantin, from my armchair when I was seven years old. Why's my mind doing this to me now? We head towards a picture hanging in a sharp corner, of a man like a saint from Bible times, but his face has no eyes. I'm inches away now. There's a black spot on the saint's forehead, a bit above where the eyebrows meet. It's growing. The spot's a dot. The dot's an eye. Then I feel one on my own forehead, in the same place, but I'm not quite sure I'm still Holly Sykes, not exactly, though if I'm not me, who else could I be?

From the spot between my eyes something comes out and hovers there. If I look straight at it, it goes, but if I look away a bit, it's like a small, shimmery planet thing. Then another comes out, and another, and another. Four shimmerings. I taste green tea. Then it's like bombs going off and Miss Constantin's howling and her hands are talons, but she's flung away, bowled down the table by whip-cracking blue light. The old saint's mouth's opened, full of animal teeth, and metal screams and stone groans. Figures and shadows appear like a shadow-puppet show in the mind of someone going mad. One older man springs onto the table. He has piranha-fish eyes, curly black locks, a busted nose, a black suit, and there's a strange indigo light coming off him, like he's radioactive. He helps Miss Constantin up, and she points a silver-tipped finger straight towards me. Black flames and a roaring loud as jet engines fill the place, and I can't run and I can't fight, and I can't even see anymore so all I can do is stand there and listen to voices, like voices shouting as a building collapses on their owners, but I catch one clear voice saying, *I'll be here*. Then there's a new shaking, and a light brighter than suns is powering up and up and up until my eyeballs melt in their sockets . . .

. . . and gray comes in through the cracks, birdsong too, and the sound of a lorry passing overhead, and a sharp pain from a knocked ankle, and I'm crouching on the concrete ground of an underpass, just a few yards from the exit. A breeze that smells of car fumes washes over my face, and it's over, my daymare, my vision, my whatever-it-was, is over. There's no one to ask, *Did you see that too?* There's just those three words, *I'll be here*. I wobble out into the light, into the dry blue morning, still shaking with the gutted weirdness of it all, and sit on the grass bank. Perhaps daymares are like cancer, which goes away and comes back when you think you're all clear. Perhaps whatever Dr. Marinus did to fix me is wearing off. Perhaps the stress of yesterday, of Mam and Vinny and everything, triggered some sort of relapse. I just dunno. There was no sign of

Jacko, so I must've imagined seeing him, too. Good. I'm glad he's safe at the Captain Marlow, twenty miles away, even though I'd love to see him, to know he's okay, even though I know he's fine and there's nothing to worry about.

THE FIRST TIME I saw Jacko, he was in an incubator 'cause he was born too soon. That was in Gravesend General Hospital, too, though the maternity wing's in a different building. Mam, who'd just had a C-section, looked tireder than I'd ever seen her, but happier, too, and told us to say hi to our new brother, Jack. Dad had been at the hospital all the previous day; he looked and smelt like he'd been sleeping in a car park for a week. Sharon, I remember, was most dischuffed at losing her cutest-thing-at-the-Captain-Marlow crown, specially to this monkey-shrimp in a nappy with tubes coming off of him. Brendan was fifteen and spooked by all the bawling, breast-feeding, sick and poo in the ward. I tapped on the glass and said, "Hi, Jacko, I'm your big sister," and his fingers waggled, just a tiny, tiny bit, like he was waving. The God's honest truth, that; nobody else saw but I felt a tickle in my heart and I felt willing and able to kill to protect him, if I had to. I still feel it, when some twat talks 'bout the "weirdo" or the "freak" or the "premature one." People can be so crap. Why's it okay to draw spaceships if you're seven, but not okay to draw diabolical mazes? Who decides that spending money on Space Invaders is fine, but if you buy a calculator with loads of symbols you're asking to be picked on? Why's it okay to listen to the Top 40 on Radio 1 but not okay to listen to stations in other languages? Mam and Dad sometimes decide Jacko needs to read less and play footy more, and for a bit he'll act more like a normal seven-year-old kid, but it's only acting, and we all know it. Just now and then who he really is smiles out at me through the blacks of Jacko's eyes, like someone watching you from a train zipping past. At those times, I almost want to wave, even though he's just across the table, or we're passing on the stairs.

. . .

HALLUCINATIONS OR NOT, I can't just sit on my arse all day. I need food and a plan. So off I walk, and after a roundabout, the fields stop and I'm back in the world of garden fences, billboards, and zebra crossings. The sky's hazing over a bit and I'm thirsty again. I haven't had a proper drink since me and Brubeck got some water from a tap in the church, and the rules say that you can't knock on a door and ask for a glass of water in a town the way you can in the middle of nowhere. A park with a water fountain'd be perfect, or even a public toilet, but there's no sign of either. I'd like to brush my teeth, too; they're all scaly like the inside of kettles. I smell bacon from a window and stomach pangs wake up, and here comes a bus with GRAVESEND written on it. Hop aboard, I could be home in forty-five minutes . . .

Sure, but picture Mam's face when she opens the side door. The bus wafts by, and on I trog under a railway bridge. Up ahead there's a row of shops and a newsagent where I can buy a can of drink and a pack of biscuits. There's a Christian bookshop, a knitting shop, a betting shop, a shop that just sells Airfix models and stuff, and a pet shop, with scabby hamsters in cages. Everything's mostly closed and a bit sad. Okay, so I'm arriving in Rochester. Now what?

Here's a phone box, strawberry red.

Strawberries. That's an idea.

THE DIRECTORY ENQUIRIES woman finds Gabriel Harty and Black Elm Farm on the Isle of Sheppey, no bother, and asks if I want to be put straight through. I say yes, and a moment later the ringing tone rings. My watch says 08:57. Surely not too early for a farm, even on a Sunday. Nobody's answering. I don't know why I'm so nervous but I am. If it rings ten times and no one answers, I'll hang up and assume this wasn't meant to be.

On the ninth ring the phone's picked up. "Ye-es?"

I ram in my ten pence. "Hi. Is that Black Elm Farm?"

"It was when last I looked, ye-es." A rusty drawl.

"Are you Mr. Harty?"

"When I last looked I was, ye-es."

"I'm phoning to ask if you're hiring pickers."

"Are we hiring pickers?" In the background a dog's going mental and a woman yells, *Boris, shut your cake-hole!* "Ye-es."

"A friend worked on your farm a couple of summers back, and if you're hiring, I'd like to come and pick fruit for a bit. Please."

"Done picking before, have you?"

"Not on an actual farm, but I'm used to hard work, and"— I think of my great-aunt Eilísh in Ireland—"I've helped my aunt with her vegetable garden, which is massive, so I'm used to getting my hands dirty."

"So all us farmers have dirty hands, have we?"

"I just meant I'm not afraid of hard work, and I can start today, even." There's a pause. A very long pause. Very, very long. I'm worried I'll have to put more money in. "Mr. Harty? Hello?"

"Ye-es. No picking on a Sunday. Not at Black Elm Farm. We let the fruit grow on a Sunday. We'll start tomorrow at six sharp. There's dorms for pickers, but we're not the Ritz. No room service."

Brilliant. "That's fine. So . . . have I got a job?"

"Thirty-five pence a tray. Full punnets, no rotten fruit, or you'll be picking the whole tray again. No stones, or you're out."

"That's fine. Can I turn up this afternoon?"

"Ye-es. Do you have a name?"

I'm so relieved I blurt out, "Holly," even as I realize giving a false name might be cleverer. There's a poster by the railway bridge advertising Rothmans cigarettes so I say, "Holly Rothmans," and regret it straightaway. Should have chosen something forgettable like Tracy Smith, but I'm stuck with it now.

"Holly Bossman, is it?"

"Holly *Rothmans*. Like the cigarettes."

"Cigarettes, is it? I smoke a pipe, me."

"How do I get to your farm?"

"Our pickers make their own way here. We're no taxi service."

"I know. That's why I'm asking you directions."

"It's very simple."

I bloody hope so, 'cause at this rate I'll run out of coins. "Okay."

"First you cross the bridge onto the Isle of Sheppey. Then you ask for Black Elm Farm." With that, Gabriel Harty hangs up.

ROCHESTER CASTLE SITS by the Medway River like a giant model, and a big black lion guards the iron bridge. I pat its paw for good luck as I pass. The girders groan as trucks go over and my feet are aching, but I'm pretty pleased with myself; only twenty-four hours ago I was a weeping bruise, but I just passed my first-ever job interview and next week's sorted, at least. Black Elm Farm'll be a place to lie low and get some money together. I think of small bombs going off in Gravesend, one by one. Dad'll go round to Vinny's later, I reckon: "Oh, morning, I believe you've been sleeping with my underage daughter; I'm not leaving till I've spoken with her." *Kabooom!* Vinny's ferrety face. *Ka-boom!* Dad'll rush back to tell Mam I'm not there either. *Ka-boom!* Mam'll start replaying that slap, over and over. Then she'll march round to Vinny's. Shit, meet Fan. Fan, this is Shit. Mam'll leave Vinny splattered down the hallway and hurry to Brendan and Ruth's to see if I'm there. Brendan'll report I was on my way to Stella Yearwood's yesterday morning, so he and Mam'll stomp off there. Stella'll be all, "No, Mrs. Sykes, she was never here, actually I was out, I've got no idea," but she knows a heat-seeker missile's heading her way. Monday comes and goes, and Tuesday, then on Wednesday school'll phone 'cause I'm missing exams. Mr. Nixon'll say to her, "So let me get this straight, Mrs. Sykes. Your daughter's been missing since Saturday morning?" Mam'll mumble 'bout a small disagreement. Dad'll start wanting details, like what she said to me, and what she means by "a little slap." How little? *Ka-boom, ka-boom, ka-boom.* She'll lose it and

and snap, "I already feckin' told you, Dave!" and go upstairs to the kitchen, and as she's looking out over the river, she'll be thinking, *She's only fifteen, anything could've happened* . . . Serve her bloody right.

Gulls kick up a racket on the river, below.

A police boat buzzes under the bridge. I walk on.

Up ahead, there's a Texaco garage—it's open.

"WHERE'S THE BEST place to hitch a ride to Sheppey from?" I ask the bloke at the till, after he's handed me change and my two cans of Tizer, my Double Decker, and pack of Ritz biscuits. My £13.85 is down to £12.17.

"I never hitch," he says, "but if I did, I'd try the A2 roundabout, the top of Chatham Hill."

"How do I get to the top of Chatham Hill?"

But before he answers, a woman with raspberry-red hair comes in and the Texaco bloke just drinks her in.

I have to remind him I'm there. " 'Scuse me? How do I get to the top of Chatham Hill?"

"Head left out of the forecourt, over the first set of traffic lights, past the Star Inn, and up the hill to the clock tower. Take the left turn to Chatham and follow your nose a bit further, past Saint Bart's Hospital. Keep going till you get to an Austin Rover dealer and you're at the Chatham roundabout. Stick your thumb out there, wait for a knight in a shining Jag to stop." He deliberately said it all too quick for me to take in. "You might get lucky, or you might be waiting hours. You never know with hitching. Make sure you're dropped at the turnoff to Sheerness—if you find yourself in Faversham, you've gone too far." He readjusts his crotch and turns to the woman. "Now, what can I do for you, sweetheart?"

"Not calling me 'sweetheart' would be a good start."

I don't hide my laugh. The guy stares daggers at me.

. . .

LESS THAN A hundred yards later this knackered Ford Escort van pulls over. It might've been orange once, or perhaps that's just rust. The passenger winds down the window. "Hi." I've got a gobful of Ritz biscuit and must look like a total spaz, but I recognize who it is straight off. "It's not quite a shiny Jaguar," the woman with the raspberry-red hair slaps the door cheerfully, "and Ian here definitely isn't a knight," the guy driving does a little lean-over and a wave, "but if you're after a lift to Sheppey, we're going nearly to the bridge. Guide's honor, we're not axe murderers or chainsaw killers, and it's got to beat standing on a slip road for six hours waiting for someone like *that*"—she cocks her head towards the Texaco garage—"to stop and 'What can I do for you, sweetheart?' all over you."

My feet are killing me, and a lift off a couple's safer than a single man, she's right. "That'd be brill, thanks."

She opens the back of the van and shunts some boxes to make space. I wedge myself in, but there's windows on all sides so I've got a nice enough view. Ian, who's midtwenties, baldish, and has a nose as big as a Concorde, asks, "Not too crushed back there, I hope?"

"Not at all," I say. "It's dead cozy."

"It'll only be twenty-five minutes," Ian says, and we move off.

"I was saying to Ian," the woman tells me, "if we didn't give you a lift, I'd spend all day worrying. I'm Heidi, anyway. Who are you?"

"Tracy," I answer. "Tracy Corcoran."

"You know, I never met a Tracy I didn't like."

"I could find you one or two," I say, and Ian and Heidi laugh, like that was pretty witty, and I s'pose it was, yeah. "Heidi's a nice name, too."

Ian does a dubious *mmm,* and Heidi gives him a poke in the ribs. "Stop interfering with the driver," he says.

We pass a school ordered from the same catalogue as Windmill Hill Comprehensive—same big windows, same flat roofs, same muddy football pitch. I'm actually starting to believe I've left school: It's like old Mr. Sharkey says, "Life's a matter of Who Dares Wins."

Heidi asks, "Do you live on Sheppey, Tracy?"

"No. I'm going there to work on a fruit farm."

Ian asks, "Gabriel Harty's place, would that be?"

"That's right. D'you know him?"

"Not personally, but he's known for having a subjective grasp of arithmetic when it comes to totting up your pay, so keep your wits about you. Errors are likely to be in his favor."

"Thanks, I will. But it should be okay. A friend at school was there last summer." I find myself gabbling to make myself more believable. "I've just done my O levels 'cause I'm sixteen, and I'm saving for an InterRail in August."

That all sounded like I read it off a card.

"InterRails look great fun," says Heidi. "Europe's your oyster. So where's home, Tracy?"

Where would I *like* home to be? "London."

The lights are red. A blind man and his guide dog step out.

"Big city, London," says Ian. "Whereabouts, exactly?"

Now I panic a bit. "In Hyde Park."

"What—*in* Hyde Park? Up a tree, with the squirrels?"

"No. Our actual house is closer to, uh, Camden Town."

Heidi and Ian don't answer at first—have I said something stupid?—but then Ian says, "I'm with you," so it's okay. The blind man reaches the other side of the road, and Ian struggles with the gearbox before we move off. "I stayed in Camden Town when I first went to London," he says, "sleeping on a mate's sofa. In Rowntree Square, by the cricket ground next to the Tube station. Know it?"

"Sure," I lie. "I go past there, like, all the time."

Heidi asks, "Have you hitched from Camden this morning?"

"Yes. I got a lift off a truck driver to Gravesend, then a German tourist brought me to Rochester Bridge, and then you pulled up. Jammy or what?" I look for a way to change the subject. "What's in all these boxes, then? Are you moving house?"

"No, it's this week's *Socialist Worker*," says Heidi.

"They sell that in Queen Street," I say. "In Camden."

"We're with the Central London branch," says Ian. "Me and

Heidi are postgrads at the LSE, but we spend our weekends near Faversham so we're a sort of distribution hub. Hence all the boxes."

I pick up a copy of the *Socialist Worker*. "Good read, is it?"

"Every other British newspaper is a propaganda sheet," replies Ian. "Even *The Guardian*. Take one."

It seems rude to refuse, so I say "Thanks" and study the front page: the headline is WORKERS UNITE NOW! over a photo of striking miners. "So do you, like . . . agree with Russia?"

"Not at all," says Ian. "Stalin butchered Russian communism in its cradle, Khrushchev was a shameless revisionist, and Brezhnev built luxury stores for Party sycophants while the workers queued for stale bread. Soviet imperialism's as bad as American capitalism."

Houses loop past, like the background on cheap cartoons.

Heidi asks, "What do your parents do for a living, Tracy?"

"They own a pub. The King's Head. Near Camden."

"Pub landlords," says Ian, "get bled white by the big breweries. Same old story, I'm afraid. The worker makes the profit and the bosses cream it off. Hello-hello, what's all this about?"

The traffic ahead's come to a standstill, halfway up a hill.

"An invisible war's going on," says Heidi, which confuses me till I realize she doesn't mean the slow traffic, "all through history—the class war. Owners versus slaves, nobles versus serfs, the bloated bosses versus workers, the haves versus the have-nots. The working classes are kept in a state of repression by a mixture of force and lies."

So I ask, "What sort of lies?"

"The lie that happiness is about borrowing money you haven't got to buy crap you don't need," says Ian. "The lie that we live in a democratic state. And the most weasely lie of all, that there *is* no class war. That's why the Establishment keeps such an iron grip on what's taught in schools, specially in history. Once the workers wise up, the revolution will kick off. And, as Gil Scott-Heron tells us, it will not be televised."

I don't know who the heron is, but it's hard to think of our history teacher Mr. Simms as a cog in a vast plot to keep the workers down. I wonder if Dad's a bloated boss for employing Glenda. I ask, "Don't revolutions often end up making things even worse?"

"Fair point," says Heidi. "Revolutions *do* attract the Napoleons, the Maos, the Pol Pots. But that's where the Party comes in. When the British revolution kicks off, we'll be here with our structure in place, to protect it from Fascists and hijackers."

The traffic inches forward; Ian's van rumbles on.

I ask, "D'you think the revolution'll be soon, then?"

"The miners' strike could be the match in the gas tank," says Ian. "When workers see the unions being gunned down—first with laws, then bullets—it'll be clear that a class-based revolution isn't some pie-in-the-sky lefty dream, but a matter of survival."

"Karl Marx," says Heidi, "proved how capitalism eats itself. When it can't feed the millions it spits out, no amount of lies or brutality will save it. Sure, the Americans will go for our jugular—they'll want to keep their fifty-first state—and Moscow will try to grab the reins, but when the soldiers join in, as they did in 1917 in Russia, then we'll be unstoppable." She and Ian are so sure of everything, like Jehovah's Witnesses. Heidi leans out to look ahead: "Police."

Ian mutters about Thatcher's pigs and attack dogs, and we reach a roundabout where a lorry's lying on its side. Bits of windscreen are scattered across the tarmac, and a policewoman's merging three lanes of traffic into one. She looks calm and in control—not piggish or wolfish or on the lookout for a runaway teenager at all, so far as I can see.

"Even if Thatcher doesn't trigger the revolution this year," Heidi turns to say, strands of her raspberry-red hair blowing in the wind, "it's coming. In our lifetimes. You don't need a weatherman to know which way the wind blows. By the time we're old, society'll be run like this: 'From each according to his or her abilities, to each according to his or her needs.' Sure, the bosses, the liberals, the Fascists, they'll all squeal, but you can't make an omelet without breaking eggs. And speaking of eggs," she looks at Ian, who nods, "fancy breakfast at our place? Ian cooks a five-star full English."

. . .

HEIDI'S BUNGALOW'S SURROUNDED by fields and isn't what I'd imagine as Kent's HQ for a socialist revolution, with its net curtains, cushion covers, porcelain figurines, and Flower Fairies. There's even carpet on the bathroom floor. Heidi told me it was her gran's house before she died, but her mum and stepfather live in France somewhere so Ian and she come here most weekends to make sure squatters haven't moved in and to distribute the magazine. Heidi shows me how to lock the bathroom from the inside and makes a joke about the Norman Bates Motel, which I pretend to get. I've never used a shower before—we only have a bath at the Captain Marlow—so I freeze myself and boil myself before I get the water right. Heidi has a whole shelf of shampoos, conditioners, and soaps with labels written all in foreign, but I try a bit of everything till I smell like the ground floor of a department store. When I get out, I see the ghost of letters written in last time's steam: WHO'S A PRETTY BOY THEN? Did Heidi write it for Ian? Wish I hadn't lied 'bout my name, now; I'd really like to be friends with Heidi. I smear a bit of Woods of Windsor moisturizer on my suntanned skin, thinking how easily Heidi might have been born in a grotty Gravesend pub, and me the one who's clever and confident and studying politics in London, and who has French shampoo, and a kind, funny, caring, and loyal boyfriend who leaves messages on the mirror and cooks a five-star English breakfast. Being born's a hell of a lottery.

"THEY'VE GOT THIS bridge in Turkey," I harpoon a sausage and juice dribbles from the prong holes, "with Europe on one side and Asia on the other. I'm going there. The Leaning Tower of Pisa. And I love Switzerland. Well, I love the idea of Switzerland, though the closest I've ever been is eating a bar of Toblerone . . ."

"You'll adore it." Heidi swallows her toast and dabs her lips with a tissue. "La Fontaine Saint-Agnès is one of my favorite places on Earth, nestled up near Mont Blanc. My mother's second husband had a lodge there so we'd go skiing most Christmases. Switzerland's pricey, that's the only thing."

"Then I'll drink snow and eat Ritz biscuits. And thanks again for breakfast, Ian. These sausages are incredible."

He shrugs modestly. "I'm from three generations of Lincolnshire butchers, so I ought to know my stuff. Will your Grand Tour be a solo expedition, Tracy, or will you take a traveling companion?"

"The poor lass's love life is none of your business," Heidi tells him, "Captain Snoop. Ignore him, Tracy."

"It's okay," I say, swallowing. "Actually I don't have a boyfriend right now. I—I—I did up till recently, but . . ." My throat sort of closes.

"Any brothers and sisters?" As Heidi changes the subject I can tell she's kicked Ian under the table.

"One sister, Sharon, and my brother Jacko." I slurp some tea and leave Brendan out of it. "But they're both a few years younger so, yeah, it'll be a solo expedition. How 'bout you two? Any holidays planned?"

"Well, between the Party conference and helping the miners," says Heidi, "we'll try to get to Bordeaux in August. Visit my mother."

"Can't wait," Ian mimes being hanged, "I *don't* think. I've used my wicked wiles to seduce Heidi into an evil cult of lefty loonies, you see."

"The joke is that Ian's parents are sure I've done the same to him," says Heidi. "We should have an anti-wedding and split up." She dabs her lips. "Is Corcoran an Irish name, Tracy?"

I nod and fork a tomato. "Mum's from West Cork."

"Whatever the rights and wrongs of the Troubles," Ian reaches for the ketchup, "every post-1920 revolution owes a debt to the Irish. The English reckon they handed Ireland over out of magnanimity, but no; the Irish *won* it back, by inventing modern guerrilla warfare."

"My aunt Roisín," I reply, "says the English never remember and the Irish never forget."

Ian's still slapping the bottom of the ketchup bottle, but nothing's coming out. "I despair of humanity. We can put a man on the moon but can't invent a way of getting tomato sauce out of a bottle without—" A huge dollop glollops out, smothering his bacon.

I'M DOING THE washing-up. Ian and Heidi were all "No no no, you're our guest," but I insisted. Secretly I'm hoping they'll offer to give me a lift over to Black Elm Farm later, or maybe invite me again next Sunday, if I don't go back to Gravesend. Heidi might share her hair dye with me. I rinse the glasses first and wipe them with a dry cloth, like we do at the pub so you don't get streaks. Suds drip off the marble chopping board, and I let it drain next to a lethal carving knife. A song called "As I Went Out One Morning" by Bob Dylan's on the cassette player; Ian told me to choose anything so I chose this *John Wesley Harding* tape. The mouth organ would normally put me off, but this song's great; his voice is like the wind swerving through a weird day. "Cool choice," says Heidi, passing through the kitchen barefoot. "I haven't heard this for eons." Inside I glow. She goes outside with a book called *Inside the Whale* by George Orwell; we did his *Animal Farm* in English, so maybe I can impress her later. Heidi leaves the patio door open so the smell of grass drifts in. Then Ian comes in and puts a Pyrex jug of milk into the microwave. I've never seen one close up. Turn the dial, push a button, and forty seconds later, *ping,* the milk's steaming. I tell Ian, "That's like *Star Trek.*"

"The Future," says Ian, in a film-trailer voice. "Coming soon, to a Present near you." He puts the jug on a tray with three mugs and posh coffee made in a plunger-thing. "When you're done, join us outside for café au lait."

"Okay," I say, wondering what one of them is.

Ian takes the tray out to the patio. I check the time: ten-thirty. Mam'll be going to church now, maybe with Jacko, who sort of goes to keep her company. Dad'll take Newky along the river for a run in the Ebbsfleet direction, towards London. Or are they walking up to

Peacock Street now? Here am I, doing fine, carrying on with the washing-up, and Dylan moves on to a song called "I Dreamed I Saw Saint Augustine." It's a ploddier, howl-at-the-moon sort of song, but finally I get why everyone raves 'bout Dylan. Through the window, down the long garden, foxgloves and red-hot pokers sway a bit. The lawns and flower beds are pretty as a picture on a tin of shortbread, and earlier I asked Ian and Heidi if they're gardeners as well as postgrads. Heidi says a man from Faversham comes a few hours a fortnight "To breathe order into chaos." That didn't sound very socialist to me either, but I kept my mouth shut 'cause I don't want to come over smart-arsy.

THE WASHING-UP WATER glurps down the plug-hole, a teaspoon clatters in the sink, and Bob Dylan has a cardiac arrest halfway through "All Along the Watchtower." Oh, no! The tape's being eaten: When I press eject, a tangle of brown spaghetti spills out. I'm a dab hand at fixing tapes with a little rectangle of Sellotape, though, so I go onto the patio to ask Ian and Heidi where they keep it. They're both lying on these wooden lounger things, behind a wall of Ali Baba pots with herbs. Heidi's book's dropped to the ground, with her thumb still sandwiched in it; she's out for the count. Ian's snoozing, too, his head tilted to one side and his sunglasses skewed. The tray of coffee things is on a low wall. They must've been exhausted. Cautiously I call Heidi's name but she doesn't stir. Bees graze the herby hedge, sheep *baaa*, a tractor drones away. That low bump half a mile away is the Isle of Sheppey, and that sticky-up thing's the bridge. Then I notice three, four, more busy black dots zigzagging up Heidi's arm.

I take a proper look 'cause they can't be ants . . .

They are. "Heidi! You've got ants crawling up you!"

But she doesn't react. I sort of brush the ants off her, but I smear a couple by mistake. What's wrong with them? "Heidi!" I shake her arm harder, and she slides over onto the side arm of the lounger, like a comedy drunk, but this isn't funny. Her head slumps over and her sunglasses slide off and then I see her eyes—they're all iris and no black bit in the middle. I sort of leap back with a scared *gaaa!* noise and almost fall over. Ian hasn't stirred so, frantic now, I call his name—and see a furry fly crawling along his plump lips. My hand's unsteady as I lift the baseball cap off his face. The fly buzzes off. His eyes are the same as Heidi's—like he's just died of some new plague— and I drop the hat and that same shaky gasp judders out of me. A bird in the pink roses threads sharp and shiny notes together, and my mind's throbbing and woozy and only half here, but it serves up one explanation regardless: Heidi and Ian have food poisoning from breakfast. *Food poisoning from breakfast.* But after only twenty minutes? Possibly, but I don't have the same symptoms. We all ate the same stuff. Next I think, *Heart attack,* but that's not much of a theory. *Drug overdose?* Then I think, *Stop thinking, Sykes—call for an ambulance* now . . .

. . . the phone's on a stand thing in the lounge, through the kitchen. Dash through, dial 999, and wait for the operator. *Answer, hurry hurry hurry, now now now!* The line's silent. Then I notice a man in the mirror, watching from the armchair in the corner. The gears of what's real slip. I turn round and there he is, in the archway be- tween the kitchen and lounge. I know him. The piranha eyes, the curly black locks, the busted nose—the man from my daymare in the underpass, in the kite-shaped room. His chest's heaving like he's run uphill. He barks at me, "Which one are you?"

"I—I—I—I'm—I'm a friend of Ian and Heidi, I—I—"

"Esther Little or Yu Leon Marinus?" His voice is all hate and ice.

There's a small sort of flickering on his brow, like, well, nothing like I've ever seen. Did he say, "Marinus"? Who cares? He's a man from a nightmare, 'cept when you're this afraid you usually wake up. I step back and fall onto the sofa. "My friends need an ambu- lance."

"Tell me your name, and I'll give you a clean death."

This isn't an empty threat. Whoever he is, he killed Heidi and Ian and he'll kill you too, like snapping a matchstick. "I—I—I—don't understand, sir," I curl up into a terrified ball, "I—"

He takes another step my way. "Name yourself!"

"I'm Holly Sykes, and I just want to go—please, can I just—"

"Holly Sykes . . ." He re-angles his head. "Yes, I know the name. One of those who got away. Using the brother as bait was clever, but look what you're reduced to now, Horologist. Trying to hide in this slut-gashed bone clock. Xi Lo would shudder! Holokai would puke! *If,* of course, they were alive, which," he sneers, "they are not, after your midnight raid went horribly, horribly awry. Did you think the Shaded Way has never heard of burglar alarms? Did you not know the Chapel is the Cathar and the Cathar is the Chapel? Holokai's soul is ash. Xi Lo's soul is nothing. And *you,* whichever you are, you *fled.* As per your sacred Script, no doubt. We *love* your Script. Thanks to your Script, Horology is *finished.* This is a great day for Carnivores everywhere. Without Xi Lo and Holokai, what are you? A troupe of conjurers, mind readers, and spoon benders. So tell me before you die: Are you Marinus or Esther Little?"

I'm shaking: "Swear to God, I—I'm not who you think I am."

He reads me, suspiciously. "Tell you what. Those two sunbathers outside, they're not quite dead yet. Use your Deep Stream voodoo now, you might save one. Go on. It's what Horologists do."

Far, far away, a dog's barking, a tractor's grundling . . .

. . . the man's so close now I can smell him. Burnt ovens. My voice has gone all anorexic. "So can I call a doctor, then?"

"You can't heal them yourself?"

I manage to shake my head.

"Then they'll need a coffin, not an ambulance. But I need proof you're not Horology. Marinus is a coward, but he's a devious coward. Run away. Go on. Run. Let's see how far you can get."

I don't trust him or my ears. "What?"

"There's the door—go. Run, little mouse." He steps aside to open up an escape route. I'm expecting a trick, or a knife, I don't know what, but he leans in so close, I see grazes and tiny cuts on his face, and his big black eyes, with a halo of gray, and he shouts at the top of his lungs: "RUN BEFORE I CHANGE MY MIND!"

THROUGH THE THORNY roses, between swaying bushes, down the dusty lawn, I run. I run like I've never run. The sun's in my face and the wall's not far. Halfway there, when I get to the trellis thing, I look back; he's not running after me, like I dreaded, just standing there, a few steps from Ian and Heidi, who're still lying dead so he's letting me go—why who cares why he's a mental psycho so *run* run *run* run *run* run, but, run, but, but, *run,* but . . . But I'm slowing, slowing, how, why, what, my heart's straining like crazy, but it's like the brake and accelerator are being pressed at the same time but whatever's slowing down isn't inside me, it's not poison, it's outside me, it's time slowing up or gravity pulling harder, or air changing to water, or sand, or treacle . . . I have dreams like this—but I'm awake, it's daytime, I *know* I'm awake . . . But, impossibly, I've stopped, like a statue of a runner, one foot raised for the next stride that'll never come. This is mad. In*fecking*sane. It occurs to me I ought to try to scream for help, it's what people do, but all that comes out is this grunty spasm noise . . .

. . . and the world starts shrinking back towards the bungalow, hauling me along with it, helplessly. There's ivy on the arch thing, I grab it, and my feet lift off the ground, like I'm a cartoon character in a hurricane hanging on for dear life, but the pain in my wrists makes me let go, and I fall to earth with a bruising whack and I'm dragged along the ground, scraping my elbows and bumping my tailbone, and I swivel onto my back and try to dig my heels in but the lawn's too hard, I can't get a grip, I sort of trip myself upright, onto my feet, and a pair of butterflies flutter by, up-current, like this unfightable force only works on me. Now I'm back at the rose beds, and the pale man's still framed in the patio doorway, his hands and fingers threading away, like sign language for aliens, with a sort of hooked smile on his lips, and he's doing this, he's fishing me in, over the patio, past Heidi and Ian, who're still as corpses, corpses this man killed somehow, this man stepping back into the kitchen to make room, and once I'm in this bungalow I'll never ever leave it, so I desperately clutch at the door frame and the handle, but then it's like twenty thousand volts shoot through me and I'm tossed like a doll across the living room and bounce off the sofa, onto the carpet, and flashbulbs go *kapow kapow kapow* in my eye sockets . . .

. . . the daymare ends with the scratchy carpet digging into my cheek. It's over. It was like epilepsy or something. A photo of Heidi as a schoolgirl and a white-haired gran draws into focus, an inch away, must've fallen—maybe I knocked it off the dresser when I fell. I should go home and go to hospital. I need a brain scan. Heidi'll give me a lift to Gravesend. I'll call Mam from the hospital. Everything'll be forgotten, all the Vinny stuff. It felt so *real*. One moment I was about to repair Bob Dylan with scissors and sticky-tape, the next . . . ants up Heidi's arm, that daymare man with the busted nose, and the elasticky shoving air. What nutso part of my mind dreams up shit as weird as that, f'Chrissakes? I heave myself up, 'cause if Heidi or Ian finds me lying here they'll think I've died in their living room.

"I believe you, dear heart." He's sitting on the leather armchair, one foot resting on one knee. "You're an artless, vapid nothing in our War. But why would two dying, fleeing incorporeals blunder their way to *you*, Holly Sykes? That's the question. What are you for?"

I've frozen. What's he talking about? "Nothing, I swear, I just want to—to—to go away and—"

"Shut *up*. I'm thinking." He takes a Granny Smith apple from a bowl on the sideboard, bites and chews. In the dull quiet, the sound of his munching is the loudest thing. "When did you last see Marinus?"

"My old doctor? At—at—at Gravesend General Hospital. Years ago, I—"

He holds up his hand for silence, like my voice hurts his ears. "And Xi Lo never told you that Jacko wasn't Jacko?"

Till now the horror's been high-pitched; with Jacko's name, there's a bass of dread. "What's Jacko got to do with anything?"

He peers at his Granny Smith with disgust. "The sourest, blandest apples. People buy them for ornamental value." He tosses it away. "There's no Deep Stream field here, so we aren't in a safe house. Where are we?"

I daren't repeat my Jacko question, in case it brings this evil, 'cause evil's the right word, to my brother. "Heidi's gran's bungalow. She's in France, but she lets Heidi and . . ." *They're dead*, I remember.

"The *location*, girl! County, town, village. *Act* like you have a brain. If you're the same Holly Sykes whom Marinus fouled, we must be in England, presumably."

I don't think he's joking. "Kent. Near the Isle of Sheppey. I—I don't think where we are actually has a . . . has a name."

He drums the leather armchair. His fingernails are too long. "Esther Little. You know her?"

"Yes. Not really. Sort of."

The drumming stops. "Do you want me to tell you what I'll do to you if I think you're lying, Holly Sykes?"

"Esther Little was by the river yesterday, but I never met her before. She gave me some tea. Green tea. Then she asked . . ."

The pale man's stare drills into my forehead, like the answer's written there. "*What* did she ask?"

"For asylum. If her . . ." I hunt for her exact words, ". . . plans went up in flames."

The pale man lights up. "*So* . . . Esther Little wanted you for an oubliette. A mobile safe house. I see. You! A used pawn so insignificant, she thought we'd forget you. Well." He stands up and blocks the way out. "If you're in there, Esther, we found you!"

"Look," I manage to say, huddling, "if this is like MI5 stuff, about Ian and Heidi's communism, I'm nothing to do with it. They just gave me a lift, and I . . . I . . ."

He steps towards me, suddenly, to scare me. It does. "Yes?"

"Don't come near me." My voice sort of shrivels up. "I'll—I'll—I'll fight. The police—"

"Will be baffled by Heidi's gran's bungalow. Two lovers on the loungers, the body of teenager Holly Sykes. Forensics will have a proper farrago to disentangle by the time you're found—especially if the triple murderer leaves the patio door ajar for the foxes, crows, stray cats . . . The *mess*! You'll go national. The great, gory, unsolved British crime of the eighties. Fame at last."

"Let me go! I—I—I'll go abroad, I'll . . . go. *Please*."

"You'll look adorable dead." The pale man smiles at his fingers as he flexes them. "An unprincipled man would have some fun with you first, but I'm against cruelty to dumb animals."

I hear a hoarse gasp. "Don't don't don't please *please*—"

"Sssh . . ." His fingers make a twisting gesture and my lips, my tongue, and my throat shut down. All the strength drains from my legs and arms, like I'm a puppet with its strings cut, pushed into the corner. The pale man sits on the same rug I'm on, cross-legged, like a storyteller but sort of savoring the moment, like Vinny when he knows he's going to have me. "What's it like, knowing you'll be dead as a fucking stone in sixty seconds, Holly Sykes? What pictures does your insectoid mind flick through just before the end?"

His eyes aren't quite human. My vision's going, like night's falling, my lungs're drowning, not in water but in nothing and I realize it's been ages since I last breathed, so I try to but I can't and the drumming in my ears has stopped 'cause my heart's shut down. Out of the swarmy dusk the pale man reaches out his hand and brushes my breast with the backs of his fingers, tells me, "Sweet dreams, dear heart," and my last thought is, Who is that doddering figure in the background, a mile away, at the far end of the lounge . . . ?

The pale man notices, looks over his shoulder, and jumps up. My heart restarts and my lungs fill with oxygen, so quick I choke and cough as I recognize Heidi. "Heidi! Get the police! He's a killer! Run!" But Heidi's ill, or drugged, or injured, or drunk, her head's lolling about like she's got that disease, multiple sclerosis. Her voice isn't the same, either—it's like my granddad's since his stroke. She pushes out the words all ragged: "Don't worry, Holly."

"On the contrary, Holly," snorts the pale man, "if *this* specimen is your knight in shining armor, it's time to despair. Marinus, I presume. I smell your unctuousness, even in that perfumed zombie."

"Temporary accommodation," says Heidi, whose head flops forward, back, then forward: "Why kill the two sunbathing youths? *Why?* That was gratuitous, Rhîmes."

"Why not? You people, you're so why why *why?* Because my blood was up. Because Xi Lo started a firefight in the Chapel. Because I *could.* Because you and Esther Little led me here. She died, didn't she, before she could claim asylum in this female specimen of the great unwashed? A hell of a pounding she took, fleeing down the Way of Stones. I know, I gave it to her. Speaking of poundings, my sincere condolences over Xi Lo and poor Holokai—your little club of good fairies is de*cap*itated. What about you, Marinus? You're more a healer than a fighter, I know, but offer me some token resistance, I implore you." Rhîmes does his finger-weaving thing and— unless I'm seeing things—the marble chopping board rises up from the counter in the kitchen and hovers towards us, like the invisible man's bringing it over. "Cat got your tongue, Marinus?" asks the pale man called Rhîmes.

"Let the girl go," says head-flopping Heidi.

The chopping board hurtles across the living room into the back of Heidi's head. I hear a noise like a spoon going into an eggshell. It should've knocked Heidi's body forward, like a skittle, but instead she's picked up by—by—by—nobody, while Rhîmes spins his hands and makes sort of snapping motions, and Heidi's body spins too, herkily-jerkily. Snap, crackle, pop, goes her spine, and her lower jawbone's half off and blood's trickling from a hole in her forehead, like a bullet went in. Rhîmes does a backhand slap in the air, and Heidi's mangled body's flung against a picture of a robin sat on a spade, then lands on its head and tumbles in a heap.

Now it's like I've got headphones superglued over my ears and through one speaker I've got "None of This Is Happening" blaring and through the other "All of This Is Happening" going over and over at full blast. But when Rhîmes speaks, he speaks quietly and I hear every wrinkle in every word. "Don't you ever have days when you're just so glad to be alive you want to"—he turns to me—"howl at the sun? Now, I believe I was squeezing the life out of you . . ." He pushes the air towards me, palm-first, then lifts his hand; I'm slammed against the wall and shoved upwards by some invisible force till my head bumps the ceiling. Rhîmes leaps onto the arm of the sofa, like he's going to kiss me. I try to hit him but both my hands are pinned back and once again my lungs've closed off. One of the whites of Rhîmes's eyes is darkening to red, like a tiny vein's burst: "Xi Lo inherited Jacko's fraternal love for you, which pleases me. Killing you won't bring my lost Anchorites back, but Horology owes us a blood debt now, and every penny counts. Just so you know." My vision's fading and the pain in my brain's blotting everything out, and—

The tip of a sharp tongue slides from his mouth.

Reddened, metallic, an inch from my nose. A knife?

Rhîmes's eyeballs roll back, and as his eyelids shut, I slip down to the floor, and he falls off the arm of the sofa. When the back of his head hits the floor, the knife blade is rammed out a couple more inches, flecky with white goo. It's easily the most disgusting thing I've seen in my life and I can't even scream.

"Lucky shot." Ian drags himself in, gripping the counters.

It can only be me he's talking to. There's nobody left. Ian frowns at Heidi's twisted body. "See you next time, Marinus. It's time you got a newer vehicle, anyhow."

What? Not "Oh, Holy Christ!" or "Heidi, no, Heidi, no, no!"? Ian looks at Rhîmes's body. "On bad days you wonder, 'Why not just back off from the war and lead a quiet metalife?' Then you see a scene like this and remember why." Last, Ian twists his busted head my way. "Sorry you had to witness all this."

I slow my breathing, slower, and—"Who . . ." I can't do more.

"You weren't fussy about the tea. Remember?"

The old woman by the Thames. Esther Little? How could Ian know that? I've fallen through a floor and landed in a wrong place.

In the bungalow hallway a cuckoo clock goes off.

"Holly Sykes," says Ian, or Esther Little, if it is Esther Little, but how's that possible? "I claim asylum."

Two dead people are lying here. Rhîmes's blood's soaking into the carpet.

"Holly, this body's dying. I'll redact what you've seen from your present perfect, for your own peace of mind, then I'll hide deep, deep, deep in—" Now Ian-or-Esther-Little topples over like a pile of books. Only one eye's open now, with half his face shoved up on the squashed sofa cushion. His eyes look like Davenport's, the collie we had before Newky, when we had him put down at the vet's. "Please."

The word lifts a spell, suddenly, and I kneel by this Esther-Little-inside-Ian, if that's what it is. "What can I do?"

The eyeball twitches behind its closing lid. "Asylum."

I just wanted more green tea, but a promise is a promise. Plus, whatever just happened, I'm only alive 'cause Rhîmes is dead, and Rhîmes is only dead 'cause of Ian or Esther Little or whoever this is. I'm in debt. "Sure . . . Esther. What do I *do*?"

"Middle finger." A thirsty ghost in a dead mouth. "Forehead."

So I press my middle finger against Ian's forehead. "Like this?"

Ian's leg twitches a bit, and stops. "Lower."

So I move my middle finger down an inch. "Here?"

The working half of Ian's mouth twists. *"There . . ."*

THE SUN'S WARM on my neck and a salty breeze has picked up. Down in the narrow channel between Kent and the Isle of Sheppey a trawler's blasting its honker: I can see the captain's picking his nose, and looking for somewhere to put the bogie. The bridge is a *Thomas the Tank Engine* job—the whole middle section rises up between two stumpy towers. When it reaches the top a klaxon sounds and the trawler chugs underneath. Jacko'd love this. I hunt in my duffel bag for my can of Tango and find a newspaper—the *Socialist Worker*. What's this doing here? Did Ed Brubeck put it in for a joke? I'd chuck it over the barrier, but this cyclist bloke's just arriving, so I open my Tango and watch the bridge. The cyclist's 'bout Dad's age, but he's slim as a snake and nearly bald, where Dad's a bit chubby, and it's not for nothing his nickname's Wolfman. "All right," says the man, wiping his face on a folded cloth.

He doesn't look like a pervert, so I answer him: "All right."

The guy looks up at the bridge, a bit like he built it. "They don't make bridges like that anymore."

"Guess not."

"The Kingsferry Bridge is one of only three vertical-lift bridges in the British Isles. The oldest is a dinky little Victorian affair over a canal in Huddersfield, just for foot traffic. This one here opened in 1960. There's only two like it, for road and rail, in the world." He drinks from his water bottle.

"Are you an engineer, then?"

"No, no, just an amateur rare-bridge spotter. My son used to be as mad about them, though. In fact"—he takes out a camera from his saddlebag—"would you mind taking a snap of me and the bridge?"

I say sure, and end up crouching to fit in both the man's bald head and the bridge's lifted-up section. "Three, two, one . . ." The camera whirrs, and he asks me to take another, so I do, and hand him back the camera. He thanks me and fiddles with his gear. I slurp my Tango and wonder why I'm not hungry, even though it's almost noon and all I've eaten since I left Ed Brubeck asleep is a packet of Ritz crackers. I keep doing sausagey burps, too, which makes no sense. A white VW camper drives up and stops at the barrier. Two girls and their boyfriends are smoking and looking at me, all *What does she think* she's *doing here?* even though they've got an REO Speedwagon song on. To prove I'm not a no-friends sad-sack I turn back to the cyclist. "Come a long way, then?"

"Not far, today," he says. "Over from Brighton."

"Brighton? That's like a hundred miles away."

He checks a gizmo on his handlebars. "Seventy-one."

"Is taking photos of bridges, like, a hobby of yours, then?"

The man thinks about this. "More a ritual than a hobby." He sees I don't understand. "Hobbies are for pleasure, but rituals keep you going. My son died, you see. I take the photos for him."

"Oh, I . . ." I try not to look shocked. "Sorry."

He shrugs and looks away. "It was five years ago."

"Was it"—why don't I just shut up?—"an accident?"

"Leukemia. He would have been about your age."

The klaxon blasts again, and the road section's lowering. "That must've been awful," I say, hearing how lame it sounds. A long, skinny cloud sits over the humpbacked Isle of Sheppey, like a half-greyhound half-mermaid, and I'm not sure what else to say. The VW revs up and moves off the moment the barrier's up, leaving a trail of soft rock in the air behind it. The cyclist gets on his bike. "Take care of yourself, young lady," he tells me, "and don't waste your life."

He circles around and heads back to the A22.

All that way, and he never crossed the bridge.

CARS AND TRUCKS wallop by, gusting seeds off dandelion clocks, but there's no one to ask the way to Black Elm Farm. Lacy flowers sway on long stalks as trucks shudder by, and blue butterflies are shaken loose. The tigery orange ones cling tighter. Ed Brubeck'll be working at the garden center now, dreaming of Italian girls as he lugs bales of peat into customers' cars. Must think I'm a right moody cow. Or perhaps not. The fact Vinny dumped me is fast becoming exactly that, a fact. Yesterday it was a sawn-off shotgun wound but today it's more like a monster bruise from an air-rifle pellet. Yes, I trusted Vinny and I loved him, but that doesn't make me stupid. For the Vinny Costellos of the world, love is bullshit they murmur into your ear to get sex. For girls—me, anyway—sex is what you do on page one to get to the love that's later on in the book. "I'm well rid of that lechy bastard," I tell a cow watching me over a gate, and though I don't feel it yet, I reckon one day I will. Maybe Stella's done me a favor, in a way, by tearing off Vinny's nice-guy mask after only five weeks. Vinny'll get bored of her, sure as eggs is eggs, and when she finds him in bed with another girl it'll be *her* dreams of motorbike rides with Vinny that'll get minced, just like mine were. Then she'll come crawling back, eyes as red and sore as mine were yesterday, and ask me to forgive her. And I might. Or I might not. Up ahead there's a roundabout and a café.

And the café's open. Things are looking up.

THE CAFÉ'S CALLED Smoky Joe's Café and it's trying hard to be an American diner off *Happy Days* with tall booths you can't see into, but it's a bit of a shit-hole, really. There's not many customers, most of them glued to the footy on the knackered telly up on the wall. A woman sits by the door, reading the *News of the World* in a cloud of cigarette smoke coming from her pinched nostrils. Buttony eyes, stitched lips, frizzy hair, a face full of old regrets. Over her head is a faded poster of a brown goldfish bowl with two eyes peering out and a caption saying: JEFF'S GOLDFISH HAD DIARRHEA AGAIN. She sizes me up and waves her hand towards the booths, meaning, *Sit where you want.* "Actually," I say, "I just wanted to ask if you know how to get to Black Elm Farm."

She looks up, shrugs, looks back, and breathes smoke.

"It's here, on Sheppey. I've got a job there."

She returns to her paper and taps her fag.

I decide to phone Mr. Harty: "Is there a pay phone?"

The old moo shakes her head, without looking up.

"Would it be possible just to make a local call using your—"

She glares at me, like I've asked her if she sells drugs.

"Well . . . might anyone else here know Black Elm Farm?" I hold her gaze for long enough to tell her the quickest way to get back to her paper is to help me.

"Peggy!" she bawls, into the kitchen. "Black Elm Farm?"

A clattery voice answers: "Gabriel Harty's place. Why?"

Her button eyes swivel my way. "Someone's askin' . . ."

Peggy appears: she has a red nose, gerbil cheeks, and a smile like a Nazi interrogator's. "Off fruit-picking for a few days, is it, pet? It was hops in my day, but hops is all done by machines nowadays. You take the Leysdown road—thataway"—she points left out of the door—"past Eastchurch, then take Old Ferry Lane on the right. On foot, are you, pet?" I nod. "Five or six mile, it is, but that's a stroll in the park for—"

There's a godalmighty clatter of tin trays from the kitchen and Peggy hurries back. I deserve a packet of Rothmans now I've got what I came in for, so I go to the machine in the main part of the café: £1.40 for a packet of twenty. Total rip-off, but there'll be a bunch of new people at the farm so I'll need a confidence booster. In go the coins before I can argue myself out of it, round goes the knob, plop go the ciggies. Only when I straighten, box of twenty Rothmans in hand, do I see who's sat behind the machine, bang across the aisle: Stella Yearwood and Vinny Costello.

I duck down, out of sight, wanting to puke. Did they see me just now? No. Stella would've said something breezy and poisonous. There's a gap between the machine and the screen. Stella's feeding Vinny ice cream across the table. Vinny looks back like a lovesick puppy. She runs the spoon over his lips, leaving dribbly vanilla lipstick. He licks it off. "Give me the strawberry."

"I didn't hear the magic word," says Stella.

Vinny smiles. "Give me the strawberry, *please*."

Stella spikes the strawberry from the ice-cream dish and pushes it up Vinny's nostril. He grabs her wrist with his hand, his beautiful hand, and guides the fruit into his mouth, and they look at each other, and jealousy burns my gut like a glass of neat Domestos. What sicko anti-guardian angel brought them to Smoky Joe's right here, right now? Look at the helmets. Vinny's brought Stella here on his precious untouchable Norton. She hooks her little finger through his, and pulls, so his arm and body follow, until he's leaning all the way over the table and kissing her. His eyes are shut and hers aren't. Vinny only mouths the next three words, but he never said them to me. He says it again, eyes wide open, and she looks like a girl un-wrapping an expensive present she knew she was getting.

I could erupt and hurl plates, call them every name under the sun, and get a ride back to Gravesend in gales of tears and a police car, but I blunder back to the heavy door, which I pull instead of push and push instead of pull 'cause my vision's melting away, watched by the old moo, oh, Christ, yeah, 'cause I'm bags more interesting than the *News of the World* now, and those button eyes of her don't miss one single detail . . .

OUT IN THE open air my face dissolves into tears and snot, and a Morris Maxi slows down for the old fart at the wheel to get a good eyeful and I shout, "What are *you* bloody looking at?" and, God, it hurts it hurts it *hurts,* and I clamber over this gate into a wheatfield, where I'm hidden from the roundabout, and now I sob and sob and sob and sob and sob and sob and punch the ground and punch the ground and sob and sob and sob . . . And *That's it,* I think, *I've no more tears left now,* and then Vinny murmurs, "I love you," and reflected in his beautiful brown eyes is Stella Yearwood and here we go again. It's like puking up an iffy Scotch egg—every time I think I'm done, there's more. When I calm down enough for a cigarette, I realize I dropped them by the machine in Smoky Joe's. Bloody great. I'd rather eat cat shit on toast than *ever* set foot inside that place. Then, of course, I recognize the growl of Vinny's Norton. I creep to the gate. There they are, sat on the back, smoking—I just fucking *bet*—my fags, the fags I just paid £1.40 for. Stella would've spotted the box at the foot of the machine, still in its cellophane, and picked it up. First she steals my boyfriend, now it's my fags. Then she climbs onto the Norton, puts her arms round Vinny's waist, and buries her face in his leather jacket. Away they go, down the road to the Kings-ferry Bridge, into the streaky blue yonder, leaving me grimy and hidden like a tramp with crows in a tree going *What a laaarf . . . What a laaarf . . .*

The wind strokes and stirs the wheat.

The wheat ears go *pitter patter pitter.*
I'll never get over Vinny. Never. I know it.

TWO HOURS AFTER the roundabout I get to an end-of-the-world village called Eastchurch. There's a sign saying ROCHESTER 23. Twenty-three miles? Little wonder I've got blisters like Ayers Rock on my feet. Strange thing is, after the Texaco garage in Rochester it's all a bit of a blur till the Kingsferry Bridge onto Sheppey. Actually, it's a total blur. Like a section of a song that's been taped over. Was I walking along in a trance? Eastchurch is in a trance. There's one small Spar supermarket, but it's shut 'cause it's Sunday and the newsagent next to it's shut, too, but the owner's moving about inside so I knock till he opens up and get a packet of Digestive biscuits and a jar of peanut butter, plus another pack of Rothmans and a box of matches. He asks if I'm sixteen so I look him straight in the eye and say I turned seventeen in March, *actually,* which does the trick. Outside I light up as a mod and his modette drive by on a scooter, staring at me, but my mind's on the shrinking pounds and pence I've got left. I'll get more money tomorrow, as long as Mr. Harty doesn't play funny buggers, but I don't know how long this working holiday of mine's likely to last. If Vinny and Stella were out when Mam or Dad went to find me at Vinny's house, they won't know I'm not with him, so they won't know I've left Gravesend.

There's a phone box by the bus stop. Mam'd go all sarky and Mammish if I phone her, but if I phone Brendan's hopefully Ruth'll answer, and I'll say to get the message to Dad—not Mam, Dad—that I'm okay but I've left school and I'll be away for a bit. Then Mam won't be able to send me on a you-could've-been-abducted guilt trip the next time we meet. But when I open up the phone box I find the receiver's been ripped off its cord, so that's that.

Perhaps I'll ask to phone from the farm. Perhaps.

. . .

IT'S NEARLY FOUR P.M. by the time I turn down Old Ferry Lane onto the chalky track that leads to Black Elm Farm. On-and-off sprinklers in the fields spray cool clouds, and I sort of drink the vapor in like super-fine water-floss, and look at the little rainbows. The farmhouse itself is an old, hunkered-down brick building with a modern bit stuck on the side, and there's a big steel barn, a couple of buildings made from concrete blocks, and a windbreak of those tall thin trees. Here comes this black dog, like a fat seal on stumpy legs, barking its head off and wagging its whole body, and in five seconds flat we're best mates. Suddenly I miss Newky, and I pet the dog's head.

"I see you've met Sheba." A girl in dungarees steps out of the older part of the house; she must be about eighteen. "You've just arrived for picking?" Her accent's funny—Welsh, I think.

"Yeah. Yes. Where do I . . . check in?"

She finds my "check in" amusing, which pisses me off 'cause how am I s'posed to know the right word? She jerks her thumb at the door—she's wearing wristbands over both wrists like some tennis star but they just look spaz to me—and walks over to the brick barn to tell all the other pickers 'bout the new girl who reckons she's staying at a hotel.

"THERE'LL BE TWENTY pallets' worth by three o'clock tomorrow, see," comes a man's voice from the office down the hall, "and if your truck isn't here at one minute past three, then the lot'll be going to the Fine Fare depot in Aylesford." He hangs up and adds, "Lying twat." By now I've recognized Mr. Harty from my phone call this morning. The door behind me flies open and an older woman in stained overalls, green wellies, and a spotted neckerchief thing sort of shoos me on. "Chop suey, young lady, the doctor will see you now. Mush-mush. New picker, yes? Of course you are." She bustles me forwards into a poky office smelling of potatoes in a sack. There's a desk, a typewriter, a phone, filing cabinets, a poster with GLORIOUS RHODESIA on it and photos of wildlife, and a view of a farmyard and a decomposing tractor. Gabriel Harty's in his sixties, has a low-tide sort of face and hair tufting out of his nose and ears. Ignoring me, he tells the woman, "Bill Dean was just on the blower. Wanted to discuss 'a distribution niggle.'"

"Let me guess," says the woman. "His drivers have all got bubonic plague, so could we run tomorrow's strawberries over to Canterbury."

"Ye-es. Know what else he said? 'I wish you landowners would try to help the rest of us.' Landowner. The bank owns the land and the land owns you. That's what being a landowner means. He's the one taking his family to the Seychelles, or wherever it is." Mr. Harty relights his pipe and stares out of the window. "Who are you?"

I follow his gaze to the dead tractor until I realize he means me. "I'm the new picker."

"New picker, is it? Not sure if we need any more."

"We spoke on the phone this morning, Mr. Harty."

"A long time ago, this morning. Ancient history."

"But . . ." If I don't have a job here, what'll I do?

The woman looks over from the filing cabinet: "Gabriel."

"But we've already got this—this Holly Benson-Hedges girl on her way. She rang up this morning."

"That's me," I tell him, "but it's Holly Rothmans and . . ." Hang on, is he being funny? He's got one of those faces where you can't tell. "That's me."

"That was you, was it?" Mr. Harty's pipe makes a death-rattle noise. "That's lucky, that is. Then we'll see you tomorrow at six, sharp. Not two minutes past six. No. Nobody sleeps in, we're not a holiday camp. Now. I have more telephone calls to make."

"THE PLACE IS rather deserted on Sundays," says Mrs. Harty, as we walk back across the farmyard. She's posher than her husband and I wonder what their story is. "Most of our Kentish pickers go home on Sundays for a few creature comforts, and the student mob have decamped to the beach at Leysdown. They'll be back by evening, unless they get waylaid at the Shurland Arms. So: The shower's over there, the loo's down there, and there's the laundry room. Where did you say you've come from today?"

"Oh, just . . ." Sheba dashes up and runs happy rings round us, which gives me longer to get my story straight ". . . Southend. I just took my O levels last month. My parents are busy working and I want to save a bit of money, and a friend of a friend worked here a couple of summers ago, so my dad said okay, now I'm sixteen, so . . ."

"So here you are. Is it sayonara to school?"

Sheba follows a scent trail behind a pile of tires.

"Will you be going back to do A levels, Holly?"

"Oh, right. Depends on my results, I s'pose."

Satisfied, and not that interested, Mrs. Harty leads me into the brick barn through the wide-open wooden door. "Here's where most of the lads sleep." Twenty or so metal beds are arranged in two rows, like in a hospital but with barn walls, a stone floor, and no windows. What I think of sleeping among a bunch of snoring, farting, wanking guys must show on my face, 'cause Mrs. Harty says, "Don't worry—we knocked some partitions up this spring," she points to the end, "to give the ladies some privacy." The last third of the barn's walled off to a height of two men or so with a plywood partition thing. It's got a doorway with an old sheet across it. Someone's chalked THE HAREM above the doorway, which someone's drawn an arrow from to the words SIZE *DOES* MATTER GARY SO DREAM ON. Through the sheet, it's a bit darker, and like a changing room in a clothes shop, with three partitions on either side, each with its own doorway, two beds, plus a bare electric bulb dangling from the rafters. If Dad was here he'd wince and mutter about health and safety regs, but it's warm and dry and safe enough. Plus there's another door in the barn wall with an inside bolt, so if there was a fire you could get out in time. Only thing is, all the beds look taken with a sleeping bag, a backpack, and stuff, until we get to the last cubicle, the only one with the light on. Mrs. Harty knocks on the door frame and says, "Knock-knock, Gwyn."

A voice inside answers, "Mrs. Harty?"

"I've brought you a roommate."

Inside, the Welsh dungaree-wearing smirker is sitting cross-legged on her bed, writing in a diary or something. Steam's rising from a flask on the floor, and smoke from a cigarette balanced on a bottle. Gwyn looks at me and gestures at the bed, like, *It's all yours.* "Welcome to my humble abode. Which is now our humble abode."

"Well, I'll leave you two girls to it," says Mrs. Harty, and goes, and Gwyn gets back to her diary. Well, that's bloody nice, that is. F'Chrissakes, she could *try* to make a bit of small talk. *Scratty scrat-scrat* goes her Biro. Probably writing 'bout me right now, and probably in Welsh, so I can't read it. Well, if she's not talking to me, I'm not talking to her. I dump my duffel bag on the bed, ignoring a Stella Yearwood–sounding voice saying that Holly Sykes's great bid for freedom has ended in a total shit-hole. I lie next to my duffel bag 'cause I've got nowhere else to go and no energy. My feet feel well and truly Black & Deckered. I don't have a sleeping bag, either.

MY GOALIE WHACKS the ball clean down the table and, *slam!,* straight into Gary the student's goal and the impressed onlookers cheer. Brendan calls that shot my Peter Shilton Special, and used to whinge 'bout my left-handed goalie's unfair advantage. Five-nil to me, my fifth victory in a row, and we're playing winner stays on. "She bloody demolished me, what can I say?" says Gary, his face fiery and speech slurred after a few Heinekens. "Holly, you're a progeny, no, a progidy, thassit, a prodigy, a bona fide bar-football prodigy—and there's no dishonor in losing to . . . one of them." Gary does a pantomime bow and reaches over the table with his can of Heineken so that I have to clink mine against his. "How d'you get to be so good?" asks this girl who's easy to remember 'cause she's Debby from Derby. I just shrug and say I always used to play at my cousin's. But I remember Brendan saying, "I cannot believe

I've been beaten by a girl," which I've only just realized he said to make my victory sweeter.

I've had enough bar football for now, so I go out for a smoke. The common room's the old stables and it still whiffs a bit of horse poo, but it's livelier than the Captain Marlow on a Sunday night. Must be twenty-five pickers sat round the tables yacking, snacking, smoking, drinking, flirting, and playing cards, and although there's no telly someone's got a paint-spattered ghetto blaster and a Siouxsie and the Banshees tape. Outside, the fields of Black Elm Farm slope down to the sea, and lights dot-to-dot the coast past Faversham, past Whitstable, and further. You'd never believe it's a world where people get murdered or mugged or kicked out by their mothers.

It's nine P.M.; Mam'll be saying "Lights out and God bless" to Jacko and Sharon, then pouring herself a glass of wine and watching *Bergerac* on the telly. Or maybe tonight she'll go downstairs to bitch about me to one of her supergrasses: "I don't know where I went wrong with that one, so help me, God, I don't." Dad'll be telling Nipper the plumber and TJ the sparky and old Mr. Sharkey, "It'll all come out in the wash," or something else that sounds wise but means nothing.

I get my box of Rothmans out of my shirt pocket—eight gone, twelve left—but before I can light up Gary appears in his REALITY IS AN ILLUSION CAUSED BY A LACK OF ALCOHOL T-shirt and offers me one of his Silk Cut, saying, "This one's on me, Holly." I thank him and he says, "You won it fair and square," and his eyes flicker up and down my chest, like Vinny's do. Did. Gary's 'bout to say something else but one of his mates calls him over, and Gary says, "I'll see you later," and goes. *Not if I see you first,* I think. I've had it with boys.

Three-quarters of the pickers are students at college or uni or waiting to go this September, and I'm the youngest by a couple of years, even counting my age as sixteen, not fifteen. I'm trying not to act all shy, 'cause that might give my age away, but they aren't going to be plumbers or hairdressers or bin collectors: They'll be computer programmers or teachers or solicitors, and it shows. It's in how they speak. They use precise words, like they own them, like Jacko does, in fact, but not like any kid in my year at school'd dare to. Ed Brubeck'll be one of them in two years. I look over at Gary and just at that moment he sort of senses me and gives me a fancy-meeting-you-here look, and I glance away before he gets the wrong idea.

The pickers who aren't students sort of stand out. Gwyn's one. She's playing draughts with Marion and Linda and, apart from a "Hi" and a fake smile when I came in, she's ignored me. Cheers very much, Gwyn. Marion's a bit simple and her sister Linda fusses all mummishly and finishes her sentences for her. Picking fruit at Black Elm Farm's their annual holiday, sort of. There's a couple, Stuart and Gina, who have their own tent, tucked away in a dip. They're late twenties, look like folk singers, with earrings, and hair in pony-tails, and actually they *are* amateur folk singers, and busk in market towns. Gina's taking me and Debby food shopping to the Spar at Eastchurch after I've been paid. They act as go-betweens to the other pickers and Mr. Harty, Debby told me. Last, there's a kid called Alan Wall, who sleeps in a tiny caravan parked round the side of the farmhouse. I saw him hanging out washing to dry when I was having a look around. He can't be more than a year or two older than me, but his scrawny body's tough as cables and he's tanned like tea. Debby told me he's a gypsy, or a traveler, as you're s'posed to say these days, and that Mr. Harty hires someone from his family every year, but Debby didn't know if it's a tradition or debt or superstition, or what.

COMING BACK FROM the toilet, I see a narrow canyon between the farmhouse and a shed. Someone's waiting. A match strikes. "Fancy meeting you here," says Gary. "Care for another smoke?"

Yes, Gary's good-looking, but he's at least a bit drunk, and I've known him all of two hours. "I'll get back to the common room, thanks."

"Nah, you'll share a smoke with me. Go on, Hol, everyone's got to die of something." He's already stuck his box of Silk Cuts in my face with one stuck out for me to take with my lips. I can't refuse without making it into a big issue so I use my fingers and say, "Thanks."

"Here's a light . . . So tell me. Your boyfriend in Southend must be missing you something rotten."

I think of Vinny and heave out a "Christ, no," think, *You idiot, Sykes,* and add, "Kind of, yeah, he is, actually."

"Glad that's sorted." In the glow of his fag, Gary grins dead slinkily. "Let's go for a stroll and see the stars. Tell me about Mr. Christ-no-sort-of-yeah."

I really don't want Gary's fingers inside my bra or anywhere else, but how do I tell him to piss off without bruising his pride?

"Shyness is cute," says Gary, "but it stops you living. C'mon, I've got alcohol, nicotine . . . anything else you might need."

Christ, if guys could be girls being hit on by guys, just for one night, lines as cheesy as that'd go extinct. "Look, Gary, now's not a good time." I try to walk around him to get back to the farmyard.

"You've been eyeing me up." His arm comes down like a car-park barrier, pressing against my stomach. I smell his aftershave, his beer, and his horniness, sort of. "All night. Now's your chance."

If I tell him to feck right off, he'll probably turn all the pickers against me. If I go nuclear and call for help it'll be his version against the Hysterical New Girl's, and how old is she again, and do her parents really know she's here anyway?

"Polish your mating rituals, Octopus Boy," says a Welsh voice. Me and Gary both jump a mile. It's Gwyn. "Your seductions look very like muggings to me."

"We were—we were—we were just talking." Gary's already scuttling away to the common room. "That's all."

"Annoying but harmless." Gwyn watches him go. "Like mouth ulcers. He's propositioned every female on the farm except Sheba."

Being rescued's humiliating and what comes out is a grumpy "I can look after myself."

Gwyn says, a bit too sincerely, "Oh, I don't doubt that."

Is she taking the piss? "I could've handled him."

"You don't half remind me of me, Holly."

How do you answer that? "Up the Junction" by Squeeze booms from the ghetto-blaster. Gwyn stoops. "Look, Octopus Boy dropped his ciggies." She lobs them my way and I catch the box. "Hand them back or keep them as compensation for harassment. Your call."

I imagine Gary's version of this. "He'll hate me now."

"He'll be scared shitless you'll tell everyone what a horse's arse he made of himself. Rejection makes lads like our Gaz feel four feet tall and two inches long, full size. Anyhow, I came to say I borrowed a sleeping bag off Mrs. Harty for you. God only knows how many previous owners it's had, but it's been washed so the stains aren't sticky at least, and the barn can get chilly at night. I'm turning in, so if I'm asleep before you, sweet dreams. The hooter goes at five-thirty."

M Y PERIOD'S ONLY A FEW DAYS LATE, so I don't see how I can be pregnant, so what's this belly doing, or this blue-veined third boob pushing out below my normal two, which Vinny named Dolly and Parton? Mam is not taking the news well and doesn't believe that I don't know who the father is: "Well, *someone* put the baby inside you! We both know you're not the Virgin Mary, don't we?" But I really don't know. Vinny's the chief suspect, but am I quite sure nothing happened with Ed Brubeck in the church? Or Gary at Black Elm Farm, or even Alan Wall the gypsy? When you know your memory's been monkeyed around with once, how can you ever be sure of any memory again? Smoky Joe's old moo glares over her copy of the *Financial Times:* "Ask the baby. *It* ought to know."

Everyone starts chanting, *"Ask the baby! Ask the baby!"* and I try to say I can't, it hasn't been born yet, but it's like my mouth's stitched up, and when I look at my belly it's grown. Now it's a sort of massive skin tent that I'm attached to. The baby's lit red inside, like when you shine a torch through your hand, and it's as big as a naked grown-up. I'm afraid of it.

"Ask it, then," hisses Mam.

So I ask it, "Who's your dad?"

We wait. It swivels its head my way and speaks in a badly synched-up voice from a hot place: *When Sibelius is smashed into little pieces, at three on the Day of the Star of Riga, you'll know I'm near . . .*

. . .

. . . and the dream caves in. Relief, a sleeping bag, brothy darkness, I'm not pregnant, and a Welsh voice is whispering, "It's okay, Holly, you were dreaming, girl."

Our plywood partition, in a barn, on a farm; what was her name? Gwyn. I whisper back, "Sorry if I woke you."

"I'm a light sleeper. Sounded nasty. Your dream."

"Yeah . . . Nah, just stupid. What time is it?"

The light on her watch is mucky gold. "Five-and-twenty to five."

Most of the night's gone. Is it worth trying to go back to sleep?

A big fat zoo of snorers is snoring in all different rhythms.

I feel a stab of homesickness for my room at home, but I stab my homesickness back. *Remember the slap.*

"You know, Holly," Gwyn's whisper rustles the sheets of the dark, "it's tougher than you think out there."

That's a weird thing to say and a weird time to say it. "If that lot can do it," I mean the students, "I bloody know I can."

"Not fruit picking. The running-away-from-home deal."

Quick, deny it. "What makes you think I've run away?"

Gwyn ignores this, like a goalie ignoring a shot going a mile wide. "Unless you know for a fact, a *fact,* that going back'll get you . . ." she sort of sighs, ". . . damaged, I'd say go back. When the summer's gone, and your money's gone too, and Mr. Richard Gere hasn't pulled up on his Harley-Davidson and said, 'Hop on,' and you're fighting for a place by the bins behind McDonald's at closing time, then, whatever Gabriel Harty says to the contrary, you *will* think of Black Elm Farm as a five-star hotel. You make a list, see. It's called 'All the Things I'll Never, Ever Do to Get By.' The list stays exactly the same, but its name changes to 'All the Things I've Had to Do to Get By.'"

I keep my voice calm. "I'm not running away."

"Then why the false name?"

"My name *is* Holly Rothmans."

"And mine's Gwyn Aquafresh. Fancy a squirt of toothpaste?"

"Aquafresh isn't a surname. Rothmans is."

"That's true enough, but I bet you a pack of Benson & Hedges it's not yours. Don't get me wrong, a false name's clever. I changed mine often, in my first few months away. But all I'm saying is, if you're weighing possible trouble ahead against the trouble you've left behind, times the 'ahead' trouble by twenty."

It's appalling she's seen through me so easily. "Too early for Thoughts for the Day," I growl. "Good *night*."

The first bird of the morning starts twittering.

AFTER I'VE WASHED down three peanut-butter-and-Digestive-biscuit sandwiches with a glass of water we head out to the big south field, where Mrs. Harty and her husband're putting up a big tent thing. It's cool and dewy but another sticky day's ahead, I reckon. I don't hate Gwyn or anything, but it's like she saw me naked and I'm not sure how to meet her eyes, so I stick with Marion and Linda. Gwyn seems to understand and she's picked a row next to Stuart and Gina, and Alan Wall, ten rows or so away, so we couldn't talk now even if we wanted to. Gary acts like I'm totally invisible and is working on the far side of the students. Suits me.

Strawberry picking's boring work, sure, but it's calming, too, compared to bar work. It's nice being out in the open air. There's birds, and sheep, and the sound of a tractor somewhere, and the students' chattering, though that dies away after a bit. We've each got a cardboard tray with twenty-five punnets in, and our job's to fill each punnet with ripe strawberries, or nearly ripe. You snip through the stalk with your thumbnail, put the berry in the punnet, and on you go like that. I start off squatting on my haunches but it murders my calves so I kneel on the straw as I go along. Wish I'd brought a looser pair of jeans, or shorts. If a strawberry's a bit over-ripe and mushes in my fingers, I lick the fruity smear, but it'd be stupid to scoff the perfect ones 'cause that's like eating your own wages. When all the punnets are full, you carry the tray to the tent, where Mrs. Harty weighs it. If it's on or over the right weight she pays you a plastic token, otherwise you have to go back to your row for a few more strawbs to bring it up to weight. Linda says at three o'clock we all troop back to the office to swap the tokens for money, so you keep your tokens safe: no token, no money.

Once we get going, it's pretty obvious who's used to field-working: Stuart and Gina move up their rows twice as fast as the rest of us, and Alan Wall's even faster. Some of the students are a bit crap, which means I'm not the slowest at least. The sun gets higher and stronger and now I'm glad I've got Ed Brubeck's cap to shield the back of my neck. An hour goes by and I've sort of slipped into autopilot. The punnets fill, strawberry by strawberry by strawberry, and my earnings go up, 2 p by 5 p by 10 p. I keep thinking 'bout what Gwyn said this morning. Sounds like she's learned a lot of bad stuff the hard way. I think about Jacko and Sharon eating breakfast with my empty chair there, like I've died or something. Bet Mum's all, "I refuse to even discuss that young mademoiselle, I do." She sounds really Irish when she's angry or wound up. I think about pinball, and how being a kid's like being shot up the firing lane and there's no veering left or right; you're just sort of propelled. But once you clear the top, like when you're sixteen, seventeen, or eighteen, suddenly there's a thousand different paths you can take, some amazing, others not. Tiny little differences in angles and speed'll totally alter what happens to you later, so a fraction of an inch to the right, and the ball'll just hit a pinger and a dinger and fly down between your flippers, no messing, a waste of 10 p. But a fraction to the left and it's action in the play zone, bumpers and kickers, ramps and slingshots and fame on the high-score table. My problem is, I don't know what I want, apart from a bit of money to buy food later on today. Until the day before yesterday all I wanted was Vinny, but I won't make that mistake again. Like a shiny silver pinball whizzing out of the firing lane, I've not got the faintest bloody clue where I'm going or what'll happen next.

. . .

AT EIGHT-THIRTY WE break for sweet, milky tea, served in the tent by a woman with a Kent accent thicker than the Earth's crust. You're s'posed to have your own mug but I'm using an old marmalade jar fished out of the kitchen bin, which raises a few eyebrows but it gives my tea an orangy tang. Gary the student's Benson & Hedges are stashed in my Rothmans box, and I smoke a couple; they're that bit toastier than Rothmans. Linda shares her packet of Custard Creams with me, and Marion says, "Picking's hungry work," in her flat, bunged-up voice, and I say, "Yeah, it is, Marion," and Marion's really happy, and I wish her life could be easier than it's going to be. Then I go over to where Gwyn's sitting with Stuart and Gina and offer her a fag, and she says, "Don't mind if I do, thanks," and we're friends again; it's that simple. Blue sky, fresh air, aching back but three pounds richer than I was when I picked my first strawberry. At eight-fifty, we start picking again. At school right now, Miss Swann our form teacher'll be taking the register, and when she reads out my name, there'll be no reply. "She's not here, miss," someone'll say, and Stella Yearwood should start to sweat, if she's got half a brain, which she has. If she's bragged about nicking my boyfriend, people'll guess why I'm not at school, and sooner or later the teachers'll hear and Stella's going to get summoned to Mr. Nixon's office. Maybe a copper'll be there too. If she's kept schtum about nicking Vinny, she'll be acting all cool like she knows nothing but she'll be panicking inside. So'll Vinny. Sex with a bit of young fluff's all well and good, I s'pose, as long as nothing goes wrong, but things'll look pretty different pretty quickly if I stay at Black Elm Farm for a couple more days. Suddenly I'm an under-age schoolgirl whom Vincent Costello seduced with presents and alcohol for four weeks before she vanished without a trace; and Vincent Costello, twenty-five-year-old car salesman of Peacock Street, Gravesend, becomes a chief suspect. I'm not an evil person or anything, and I don't want Jacko or Dad or Sharon to lose sleep over me, specially Jacko, but putting Vinny and Stella through the mangle at least a bit is very, very tempting . . .

WHEN I CARRY my next full tray over to Mrs. Harty's tent, everyone's crowding round the radio looking dead serious—Mrs. Harty and the tea lady both look horrified—and for a horrible moment I think that I've been announced missing already. So I'm almost relieved when Derby Debby tells me that three bodies have been found. I mean, murder's awful, of course, but bodies are always being found on the news and it never actually affects you. "Where?" I ask.

"Iwade," says Stuart, of Stuart and Gina.

I've never heard of it, so I ask, "Where's that?"

" 'Bout ten miles away," says Linda. "You'd've passed by it yesterday. It's just off the main road to the Kingsferry Bridge."

"Shush," someone says, and the radio's cranked up: *"A police spokesman has confirmed that Kent police are treating the deaths as suspicious, and urge anyone who may possess information relating to the deaths to contact Faversham Police Station, where an inquiry room is being set up to coordinate the investigation. Members of the public are urged not to—"*

"My God," blurts out Derby Debby, "there's a *murderer* about!"

"Let's not jump to conclusions," says Mrs. Harty, turning down the volume. "Just because something's on the radio doesn't mean it's true."

"Three dead bodies is three dead bodies," says Alan Wall the gypsy. "Nobody's made them up." I haven't heard him speak till now.

"But it doesn't follow that Jack the Ripper Mark Two's roaming the Isle of Sheppey with a meat cleaver, does it? I'll make some inquiries from the office. Maggs here," Mrs. Harty nods at the tea lady, "will be in charge." Off she strides.

"That's all right, then," says Debby. "Sherlock Harty's on the case. But I'll tell you this: Unless there's a lock as thick as my arm on the barn door tonight, I'm off, and *she* can drive me to the station."

Someone asks if the radio said how the people'd been killed, and Stuart answers that the exact words were "a violent and brutal attack," which sounded more like sharp objects than guns, but nobody could be sure at this point. So we may as well get back to work for the time being, 'cause we're safest in the open air with lots of people about.

"Sounds to me like a love-triangle thing," says Gary the student. "Two men, one girl. Classic crime of passion."

"Sounds to me like a drug deal gone wrong," says Gary's mate.

"Sounds to me like you're both talking out your arses," says Debby.

ONCE THE THOUGHT gets into your head that a psycho *might* be hiding in that huddle of trees at the end of the field, or over there in that hedgerow, figures start appearing in the corners of your eyes. Like the Radio People you quarter-see instead of half-hear. I think about the timing of the murders; who's to say it didn't happen just as I was walking only a field or two away to the Kingsferry Bridge? S'pose it was that cyclist I met, driven mad by grief for his son? He didn't look like a psycho, but who does, in real life? Or how about those boyfriends and girlfriends in the VW camper van? As we're having lunch—Gwyn's made me cheese and Branston sandwiches and gives me a banana 'cause she's worked out my food situation—we spot a helicopter over where the bridge is, and on the one o'clock news Radio Kent's saying that a forensic team's arrived at the bungalow, and they've tracker dogs and everything there. The police still haven't issued the names of the victims, but Mrs. Harty knows the local farmer's wife and apparently the bungalow's lived in at the weekends by a young woman called Heidi Cross. She studies in London during the week, and it looks like the dead woman's her. There's a rumor that Heidi Cross and her boyfriend were into "radical politics" so now Gary the student's saying it was a political hit, possibly sponsored by the IRA or the CIA, if they were anti-American, or maybe MI5 if the couple were pro–coal miner.

I thought universities only let you in if you're dead brainy, but I sort of want to believe Gary, too, 'cause it'd mean there wasn't a random psycho hiding behind the haystacks, an idea I can't quite shake.

We put in another couple of hours after lunch, and when we've finished we traipse back to the office, where Mrs. Harty changes our tokens into cash. I earned over fifteen pounds today. Back at the barn where we sleep, Gabriel Harty's fitting a lock onto the inside of the barn door, just like Derby Debby wanted. Obviously our employer can't have all his pickers deserting while the strawberries ripen and rot on the plants. Gwyn tells me that normally a bunch of pickers all walk into Leysdown for food shopping and a bevvy or two, but today it's only the students with cars who've gone. I'll save my money, and dinner can be a bowl of muesli, from the leftovers cupboard, and the last of the Ritz biscuits, plus Gwyn's promised to give me a hot dog. Her and me then sit smoking in the warm shade of the crumbling wall on a grassy bank by the farm entrance. From where we're sitting we can see Alan Wall hanging up washing on a line. His top's bare and he's all muscled and coppery and blond, and Gwyn fancies him, I reckon. He's unflappable, only speaks when there's something worth saying, and he's not worried by a murderer in the undergrowth. Gwyn's pretty laid-back about the murders, too: "If you'd just bludgeoned three people to death yesterday, would you go to an island that's as flat as a pancake less than a mile away, where strangers stick out like a three-headed Adolf Hitler? I *mean . . .*"

Must admit, it's a good argument. Drag by drag we share the last Benson & Hedges. I sort of apologize for being grumpy this morning.

"What," Gwyn sort of teases, "my little sermon? Nah, you should've seen me when I left home." She does a piss-take dozy-cow voice: "I don't need *your* help so you can just *get lost,* can't you?" She stretches and lies back. "Godalmighty. I had not a clue. Not a clue."

The supermarket van trundles off with the day's strawberries.

I think Gwyn's wondering whether to say nothing, a bit, or a lot . . .

"I was born in a valley above this village, Rhiwlas, near Bangor, in the top left-hand corner of Wales, like Ivor the Engine. I'm an only child, and my father owned a chicken farm. Still does, for all I know. Over a thousand birds, all in these little cages not much bigger than a shoebox that the animal-rights campaigners talk about. Egg to supermarket shelves in sixty-six days. Home was a cottage hidden behind the big chicken-house. My father inherited the house and land from his uncle, and built up the business over time. When God was ladling out charm, my father got a triple helping. He sponsored the Rhiwlas rugby team, and once a week he'd go to Bangor to sing in an all-male choir. Firm but fair employer. Donations to Plaid Cymru. You'd be hard put to find a man in all Gwynedd with a bad word to say about him."

Gwyn's eyes are shut. There's a faint scar across her eyelid.

"Thing is about my father, there were two of him. The public one, the pillar of the community. And the indoors one, who was a cruel, twisted, lying control freak, to put it nicely. Rules, he loved rules. Rules about dirt in the house. How the table had to be laid. Which way the toothbrushes faced. What books were allowed in the house. Which radio stations—we had no television. Rules that kept changing because, see, he *wanted* my mother and me to break them, so he could punish us. Punishment was a length of lead piping, padded with cotton wool so the skin wouldn't show it. After the punishment, we had to thank him. My mother, too. If we weren't thankful enough, it'd be round two."

"Bloody hell, Gwyn. Even when you were little?"

"It was always his way. His da'd done the same."

"And your mum just . . . stayed put and let him?"

"If you've not been through it, you can't understand, not really. Lucky you, I say. Control is about fear, see. If you're afraid enough of the reprisals, you don't say no, you don't fight back, you don't run away. Saying yes is how you survive. It becomes normal. Horrible, but normal. Horrible, because it's normal. Now, lucky you can say, 'Not standing up to him is giving him permission,' but if you've been fed this diet since the year dot, there *is* no standing up. Victims aren't cowards. Outsiders, like, they never have a clue how brave you have to be just to carry on. My mum had nowhere to go, see. No brothers, no sisters, both her parents dead by the time she married. Da's rules kept us cut off. Making friends down in the village was being neglectful of home, and that meant the pipe. I was too scared to make friends at school. Asking anyone home was out of the question, and asking to go and play at other houses meant you were ungrateful, being ungrateful meant the pipe. A lot of method in that man's madness."

Alan Wall's gone in. His shirt and jeans hang, dripping.

"Couldn't you or your mum report your dad?"

"Who to? Da sang in Bangor choir with a judge and a magistrate. He charmed my teachers. A social worker? It was our word against his, and Da was a war hero, with a commendation for bravery from the Korean War, if you please. Mum was a husk of a woman, on Valium, and I was a messed-up teenager, who could hardly string a sentence together. And his final threat," Gwyn adds a note of false jollity, "on my last night at home, was to describe how he'd kill Mum and me, if I tried to blacken his name. Like he was describing a DIY job. And how he'd get away with it. I won't spell out what he'd just done to me to bring things to that pass, but what you're probably suspecting, it's that. I was fifteen." Gwyn steadies her voice and I wish I'd not started this. "Your age now, right?" I've nodded before I know it. "Five years ago, this. Mum knew what he did to me—it's a small cottage—but she didn't dare try to stop him. The day after it happened I left for school with some clothes in my gym bag, and I've not set foot in Wales since. Any more smokes, by the way?"

"Gary's are gone, so we're back to mine."

"I much prefer Rothmans, if I'm honest."

I pass her the box. "It's Sykes. My name."

She nods. "Holly Sykes. I'm Gwyn Bishop."

"I thought you were Gwyn Lewis."

"They've both got an *i* and an *s* in them."

"What happened after you left Wales?"

"Manchester, Birmingham, semi-homeless, homeless. Begging in the Bull Ring shopping center. Sleeping in squats, in flats of friends who weren't so friendly after all. Surviving. Barely. It's one miracle I'm here to tell the tale, and another that I dodged getting sent back—until you're eighteen, see, all Social Services'll do is pass you back to the local authority you came from. I still have nightmares about my father welcoming home the prodigal daughter while the liaison officer looks on, thinking, *All's well that ends well,* and then my father after he's locked the door. Now, why I'm telling you this tale of joy and light is to show you how bad it has to be before running away is a smart move. Once you've fallen through the cracks, you don't get out. It's taken me five years until I can dare to think the worst is behind me. Thing is, I look at you, and—" She breaks off 'cause a boy on a bike's skidded to a halt smack bang in front of us. "Sykes," he says.

Ed Brubeck? Ed Brubeck. "What're *you* doing here?"

His hair's spiky with sweat. "Looking for you."

"Don't tell me you *cycled*? What 'bout school?"

"Maths exam this morning, but I'm free now. Put my bike on the train and just rode over from Sheerness. Look—"

"You must *really* want your baseball cap back."

"The cap doesn't matter, Sykes, but we need—"

"Hang on—how did you know where to find me?"

"I didn't, but I remembered talking about Gabriel Harty's farm, so I phoned him earlier. No Holly Sykes, he said, only a Holly Rothmans. I thought it might be you, and I was right, wasn't I?"

Gwyn mutters, "I'm saying nothing."

I say, "Brubeck, Gwyn, Gwyn, Brubeck," and they nod at each other before Brubeck turns back to me.

"Something's happened."

Gwyn gets up. "See you in the penthouse suite." She gives me a go-for-it-girl look and waltzes off.

I turn back to Brubeck, a bit annoyed. "I heard."

He looks uncertain. "Then why are you here?"

"It's on Radio Kent. The three murders. At that Iwade place."

"Not that." Brubeck bites his lip. "Is Jacko here? Your brother?"

"Jacko? Course not. Why would he be here?"

Sheba comes running up, barking at Brubeck, who's hesitating, like someone who's got abysmal news. "Jacko's gone missing."

My head spins as it sinks in. Brubeck tells Sheba, "Shut *up*!" and Sheba obeys.

I ask feebly, "When?"

"Between Saturday night and Sunday morning."

"Jacko?" I must've heard it wrong, over the noise. "Missing? But . . . I mean, he can't be. The pub's locked at night."

"The police were at school earlier, and Mr. Nixon came into the exam hall to ask if anyone had information about where you were. I almost spoke up but I'm here instead. Sykes? Can you hear me?"

I've got that nasty floaty feeling you get in a lift when you can't trust the floor. "But I haven't seen Jacko since Saturday morning . . ."

"*I* know, but the cops don't. They probably think that you and Jacko cooked something up between you."

"But that's rubbish, Brubeck—you know it is."

"Yes, I *do* know it is, but you have to tell them that, otherwise they won't start searching for Jacko as hard as they should."

My mind zigzags from trains to London, to police frogmen dredging the Thames, to a murderer in the hedgerows. "But Jacko doesn't even know where I am!" I'm shaking and the sky's slipped and my head's splitting. "He's not a normal kid and—and—and—"

"Listen, listen." Brubeck's caught me and is holding my head like a boy about to kiss me, but he's not. "*Listen.* Grab your bag. We're going back to Gravesend. On my bike, then on the train. I'll get you through this, Holly. I promise. Let's go. Now."

MYRRH IS MINE,
ITS BITTER PERFUME

1991

"**B**OOMIER FROM THE TENORS**," commands the choirmaster. "Get our firm diaphragms wobbling, boys! Wibble-wobble, wibble-wobble. Trebles, le*sss sssybilanccce* on the e*sss*—we aren't a troupe of Gollums, now, are we?—and *t*ap ou*t* those *t*s. Adrian B—if you can nail the top C in 'Weep You No More Sad Fountains,' you can nail it here. Once more with more welly! A-*one*, a-*two,* and a—" King's College Choir's sixteen bat-eared choristers, bereft of hairstyles, and fourteen choral scholars exhale in unison . . .

> *Of one that is so fair and bright,*
> *Velut maris stella . . .*

Benjamin Britten's "Hymn to the Virgin" launches, chasing its echoey tail around the sumptuous ceiling before dive-bombing the scattering of winter tourists and students sitting there in the chancel in our damp coats. For me, Britten's a hit-and-miss composer; prolix on occasion but, when pumped and primed, the old queen binds your quivering soul to the mast and lashes it with fiery sublimity . . .

> *Brighter than the day is light,*
> *Parens et puella . . .*

In my idler moments, I do wonder what music I'll hear as I lie dying, surrounded by a bevy of hot nurses. Nothing more exultant than "Hymn to the Virgin" occurs to me, but I worry that when the big moment arrives DJ Unconscious will launch me off on the back of that "Gimme Gimme Gimme (A Man After Midnight)" and for once in my life I'll have no redress. World, shut yer mouth, for one of the canon's most glorious musical orgasms, on the "Cry":

> *I cry to thee, thou see to me,*
> *Lady pray thy Son for me . . .*

The hairs on my neck prickle, as if blown on. By her, for example, sitting across the aisle. She wasn't there when I last looked. Her eyes are closed to drink in the music so I drink her in. Late thirties . . . vanilla hair, creamy-skinned, beaujolais lips, cheekbones you'd slice your thumb on. Slim beneath a midnight-blue winter coat. A defected Russian opera singer, waiting to meet her handler. You never know, this is Cambridge. A true, rare ten . . .

> *Tam pia,*
> *That I might come to thee . . .*
> *Maria.*

Let her stay put after the choir troop out. Let her turn to the young man across the aisle and murmur, "Wasn't that the very breath of heaven?" Let us discuss the *Peter Grimes* Interludes, and Bruckner's Ninth. Let us avoid talk of her domestic arrangements as we drink coffee at the County Hotel. Let coffee turn into trout and red wine, and to hell with my last pint of the Michaelmas term with the boys at the Buried Bishop. Let us climb the carpeted stairs to that snug suite where Fitzsimmons's mother and I frolicked during fresher's week. Ouch. The Kraken in my boxer shorts wakes. I'm male, twenty-one, it's been ten days since I last got laid, what do you expect? But I can hardly adjust myself with a lady watching. Oh? Well well well, if she isn't discreetly studying me. I watch Rubens's *Adoration of the Magi* above the altar, and wait for her to make a move.

. . .

THE CHOIR TROOPS out but the woman stays put. A tourist aims his fat camera at the Rubens before Security Goblin snarls, "No flash!" The chancel empties, the goblin returns to his booth by the organ, and minutes trickle by. My Rolex says three-thirty. I've an essay to polish on Ronald Reagan's foreign policy, but an eerie goddess is sitting six feet away, waiting for me to make a move. "I always think," I tell her, "that seeing the choir's blood, sweat, and tears as they work on a piece deepens the mystery of music, not lessens it. Does that make sense?"

She tells me, "In an undergraduate way, yes."

Oh, you sultry minx. "Post-grad? Staff?"

Ghost of a smile. "Do I dress like an academic?"

"Definitely not." There are Francophone curves in her soft voice. "Though I'm guessing you can sting like one."

No acknowledgment. "I just feel at home here."

"Almost true for me—my rooms are at Humber College, only a few minutes away. Most third-years live off campus, but I can drop in to hear the choir most days, supervisions allowing."

A droll look, saying, *Someone's a quick worker, isn't he?*

I shrug cutely. *I might get hit by a bus tomorrow.*

She says, "Cambridge has met your expectations?"

"If you don't use Cambridge well, you don't deserve to be here. Erasmus, Peter the Great, and Lord Byron all lodged in my rooms. It's a fact." Bullshit, but I love to act. "I think of them, lying on my bed, staring up at the very same ceiling, in our respective centuries. That, for me, is Cambridge." And that's one tried-and-tested pick-up line. "My name's Hugo, by the way. Hugo Lamb."

Instinct warns me off attempting a handshake.

Her lips say, "Immaculée Constantin."

My, oh, my. A seven-syllable hand grenade. "French?"

"I was born in Zürich, as a matter of fact."

"I'm fond of Switzerland. I go skiing in La Fontaine Sainte-Agnès most years; one of my friends has a chalet there. Do you know it?"

"Once upon a time." She places a suede-gloved hand on her knee. "You major in politics, Hugo Lamb."

That's impressive. "How could you tell?"

"Speak to me about power. What is it?"

I do believe I'm being out-Cambridged. "You want me to discuss power? Right here and now?"

Her shapely head tilts. "No time except the present."

"Okay." *Only for a ten.* "Power is the ability to make someone do what they otherwise wouldn't, or deter them from doing what they otherwise would."

Immaculée Constantin is unreadable. "How?"

"By coercion and reward. Carrots and sticks, though in bad light one looks much like the other. Coercion is predicated upon the fear of violence or suffering. 'Obey, or you'll regret it.' Tenth-century Danes exacted tribute by it; the cohesion of the Warsaw Pact rested upon it; and playground bullies rule by it. Law and order relies upon it. That's why we bang up criminals and why even democracies seek to monopolize force." Immaculée Constantin watches my face as I talk; it's thrilling and distracting. "Reward works by promising 'Obey and feel the benefit.' This dynamic is at work in, let's say, the positioning of NATO bases in nonmember states, dog training, and putting up with a shitty job for your working life. How am I doing?"

Security Goblin's sneeze booms through the chapel.

"You scratch the surface," says Immaculée Constantin.

I feel lust and annoyance. "Scratch deeper, then."

She brushes a tuft of fluff off her glove and appears to address her hand: "Power is lost or won, never created or destroyed. Power is a visitor to, not a possession of, those it empowers. The mad tend to crave it, many of the sane crave it, but the wise worry about its long-term side effects. Power is crack cocaine for your ego and battery acid for your soul. Power's comings and goings, from host to host, via war, marriage, ballot box, diktat, and accident of birth, *are* the plot of history. The empowered may serve justice, remodel the

Earth, transform lush nations into smoking battlefields, and bring down skyscrapers, but power itself is amoral." Immaculée Constantin now looks up at me. "Power will notice you. Power is watching you now. Carry on as you are, and power will favor you. But power will also laugh at you, mercilessly, as you lie dying in a private clinic, a few fleeting decades from now. Power mocks all its illustrious favorites as they lie dying. 'Imperious Caesar, dead and turn'd to clay, might stop a hole to keep the wind away.' That thought sickens me, Hugo Lamb, like nothing else. Doesn't it sicken you?"

Immaculée Constantin's voice lulls like rain at night.

The silence in King's College Chapel has a mind all its own.

"What do you expect?" I say eventually. "We all have to die one day. End of. But in the meantime, doing unto others is a damn sight more attractive than being done to by others."

"What is born must one day die. So says the contract of life, yes? I am here to tell you, however, that in rare instances this iron clause may be . . . rewritten."

I look at her calm and serious face. "What level of nuts are we talking here? Fitness regimes? Vegan diets? Organ transplants?"

"A form of power that allows one to defer death in perpetuity."

Yes, she's a ten, but if she's Scientologically slash cryogenically oriented, Ms. Constantin needs to understand that I don't eat bullshit. "Did you just cross the border into the Land of the Crazy People?"

"The lie of the land has no notion of borders."

"But you're talking about immortality as if it's real."

"No. I'm talking about the perpetual deferral of death."

"Hang on, did Fitzsimmons send you? Or Richard Cheeseman? Is this a setup?"

"No. This is a seed."

This is too creative to be a Fitzsimmons prank. "A seed that grows into what, exactly?"

"Into your cure."

Her sobriety is unsettling. "But I'm not ill."

"Mortality is inscribed in your cellular structure, and you say you're not ill? Look at the painting. Look at it." She nods towards *The Adoration of the Magi.* I obey. I always will. "Thirteen subjects, if you count them, like the Last Supper. Shepherds, the Magi, the relatives. Study their faces, one by one. Who believes this newborn manikin can one day conquer death? Who wants proof? Who suspects the Messiah is a false prophet? Who knows that he is in a painting, being watched? Who is watching you back?"

THE SECURITY GOBLIN is waving his palm in front of my face. "Wakey-wakey! So sorry if I'm dis*turb*in' you, but would you an' the Almighty resume your business tomorrer?"

My first thought is, *How dare he?* There isn't a second thought because his Gorgonzola-and-paint-thinner breath makes me gag.

"It's closin' time," he says.

"The chapel's open until *six*," I tell him tersely.

"Uh—*yeah.* Exactly. And what's the time now?"

Then I notice the windows; they're shiny dark.

17:58, insists my watch. It can't be. It's only just gone four. I peer around my tormentor's belly to find Immaculée Constantin, but she's gone. Long gone, I feel. But no no no no no; she told me to look at the Rubens, just a few seconds ago. I did, and . . .

. . . I frown up at Security Goblin for an answer.

"Out at six," he says. "Closing time's closing time."

He taps his watch in front of my face and, even upside-down, its cheap and nasty digital face is quite clear: 17:59. I mutter, "But . . ." But what? Two whole hours do not vanish in the space of two minutes. "Was there . . ." my voice is thin, ". . . was there a woman here? Sitting there?"

He looks where I point. "Earlier? This year? Ever?"

"About . . . half three, I think. Dark blue coat. A real looker."

Security Goblin folds his stumpy arms. "If you'd kindly get your herbally enhanced arse into gear, I've got a home to go to."

. . .

ME, RICHARD CHEESEMAN, Dominic Fitzsimmons, Olly Quinn, and Jonny Penhaligon clunk our glasses and bottles in the roar and slosh of the Buried Bishop, across the cobbled lane behind Humber College's west gate. The place is heaving: Tomorrow the Christmas exodus begins, and we're lucky to have found a table in the furthest nook. I hole-in-one my Kilmagoon Special Reserve, and the fat Scotch slug scorches a trail from tonsils to stomach. Here, it gets to work on the knot of gut-worry I've been suffering from since my zone-out in the chapel earlier. I've been rationalizing. It's been a tiring month with essays and deadlines; Mariângela keeps leaving those nagging messages; and I've endured two all-nighters at Toad's in the last week to tenderize Jonny Penhaligon. Losing track of time isn't proof of a brain tumor; it's hardly as if I keeled over, or found myself wandering among the chimneys of the college, naked. I lost track of time while sitting in the finest Late Gothic church in the country, meditating upon a Rubens masterpiece—surroundings de-signed to transport you. Olly Quinn puts down his half-drunk pint and suppresses a belch. "So, did you solve the mystery of How Ron-ald Reagan Accidentally Won the Cold War, Lamb?"

I can barely hear him: The Humber College Young Conservatives in the next room are howling along to Cliff Richard's probably im-mortal Christmas hit "Mistletoe and Wine." "Done, dusted, and slipped under Professor Dewey's door."

"Don't know how you've stuck at politics for three years." Rich-ard Cheeseman wipes Guinness foam from his Young Hemingway beard. "I'd rather circumcize myself with a cheese grater."

"Too bad you missed dinner," Fitzsimmons tells me. "Pudding was the last of Jonny's Narnian weed. We couldn't very well let Mrs. Mop find it during her end-of-term clean-up, assume it was a turd nugget, and chuck it out with Jonny's gluey copies of *Scouting Ahoy!*" Jonny Penhaligon, still draining his bitter, gives Fitzsim-mons the finger; his knobbly Adam's apple bobs up and down. Idly, I imagine slicing it with a razor. Fitzsimmons sniffs and asks Cheeseman, "Where's your leather-trousered friend from the Mysterious Orient?"

Cheeseman glances at his watch. "Thirty thousand feet over Siberia, turning back into an upstanding Confucian eldest son. Why would I risk my reputation on being seen with a gang of notorious heterosexuals if Sek was still in town? I'm a fully converted rice queen. Crash us a cancer-stick, Fitz; I could bloody murder a fag, as I delight in telling Americans."

"You don't need to light up in here." Olly Quinn is our pet non-smoker. "Just breathe in."

"Weren't you giving up?" Fitzsimmons passes Cheeseman his box of Dunhills; Penhaligon and I take one too.

"Tomorrow, tomorrow," says Cheeseman. "Your Hermann Göring lighter, Jonny, if you'd be so kind? I adore its frisson of evil."

Penhaligon produces his Third Reich lighter. It's genuine, obtained by his uncle in Dresden, and these fat boys fetch three thousand pounds at auction. "Where's RCP tonight?"

"The future Lord Rufus Chetwynd-Pitt," answers Fitzsimmons, "is scoring drugs. Pity for him it's not an academic discipline."

"It's a recession-proof sector of the economy," I note.

"This time next year," Olly Quinn picks at the label of his non-alcoholic lager, "we'll all be out in the real world, earning a living."

"Can't bloody wait," says Fitzsimmons, stroking his chin cleft. "I despise being poor."

"My heart bleeds." Richard Cheeseman holds his ciggie in the corner of his mouth à la Serge Gainsbourg. "People see your parents' twenty-roomed mansion in the Cotswolds, your Porsche, your Versace gear and jump to *all* the wrong conclusions."

"It's my parents' loot," says Fitzsimmons. "It's only fair that I have my *own* obscene bonus to squander."

"Daddy's still sorting you a job in the City?" asks Cheeseman, then frowns as Fitzsimmons brushes the shoulders of Cheeseman's tweed jacket. "What are you doing?"

"Flicking the chips off your shoulders, our Richard."

"They're superglued on," I tell Fitzsimmons. "And don't knock nepotism, Cheeseman; my well-connected uncles all agree, nepotism made this country what it is today."

Cheeseman blows smoke my way. "When you're a burned-out *ex*-Citibank analyst having your Lamborghini repossessed and your third wife's lawyer's got your nuts under a judge's gavel, you'll be sorry."

"Right," I say, "and the Ghost of Christmas Future sees Richard Cheeseman working on a charity project for Bogotá street-children."

Cheeseman ponders Bogotá street-children, purrs, and desists. "Charity breeds fecklessness. No, it's the way of the hack for me. A column here, a novel there, bit of broadcasting now and then. Speaking of which . . ." He fishes in his jacket pocket and retrieves a book: *Desiccated Embryos* by Crispin Hershey. REVIEW COPY ONLY is emblazoned in red across the cover. "My first paid review for Felix Finch at *The Piccadilly Review*. Twenty-five pence a word, twelve hundred words, three hundred quid for two hours' work. Result."

"Fleet Street beware," says Penhaligon. "Who's Crispin Hershey?"

Cheeseman sighs. "The son of Anthony Hershey?"

Penhaligon blinks at him, none the wiser.

"Oh, *c'mon*, Jonny! Anthony Hershey! Filmmaker! Oscar for *Box Hill* in 1964, made *Ganymede 5* in the seventies, *the* best British SF film ever made."

"That film robbed me of the will to live," remarks Fitzsimmons.

"Well, *I'm* impressed by your commission, our Richard," I say. "Crispin Hershey's last novel was superb. I picked it up in a hostel in Ladakh on my gap year. Is this one as good?"

"Almost." Monsieur Le Critic places his fingertips together. "Hershey Junior *is* a gifted stylist, and Felix—Felix Finch, to you plebs—Felix puts him up there with McEwan, Rushdie, Ishiguro, et al. Felix's praise is premature, but in a few books' time, he'll ripen nicely."

Penhaligon asks, "How's your own novel going, Richard?" Fitzsimmons and I do hanged-men faces at each other.

"Evolving." Cheeseman gazes into his glorious literary future and likes what he sees. "My hero is a Cambridge student called Richard Cheeseman, working on a novel about a Cambridge student called Richard Cheeseman, working on a novel about a Cambridge student called Richard Cheeseman. No one's ever tried anything like it."

"Cool," says Jonny Penhaligon. "That's sounds like—"

"A frothy pint of piss," I announce, and Cheeseman looks at me with death in his eyes until I add, "is what's in my bladder right now. The book sounds incredible, Richard. Excuse me."

THE GENTS SMELLS well fermented and the only free urinal is blocked and ready to brim over with the amber liquid so I have to queue, like a girl. Finally a grizzly bear of a man ambles away and I fill the vacancy. Just as I'm coaxing my urethra open, a voice at the next urinal says, "Hugo Lamb, as I live and breathe."

It's a stocky, swarthy man in a fisherman's sweater with wiry dark hair, whose "Lamb" sounds like "Limb"—a New Zealander's vowels. He's older than me, around thirty, and I can't place him. "We met back in your first year. The Cambridge Sharpshooters. Sorry, it's appalling men's-room etiquette to put a guy off his stride like this." He's pissing no-handedly into the gurgling urinal. "Elijah D'Arnoq, postgrad in biochemistry, Corpus Christi."

A memory flickers: that unique surname. "The rifle club, yes. You're from those islands, east of New Zealand?"

"The Chathams, that's right. Now, I remember *you* because you're a natural bloody marksman. Still room at the inn, you know."

Now I know there's no cottagey thing going on, I start pissing. "You're overestimating my potential, I'm afraid."

"Mate, you could be a contender. I'm serious."

"I was spreading myself a bit thin, extracurricular-wise."

He nods. "Life's too short to do everything, right?"

"Something like that. So . . . you've enjoyed Cambridge?"

"Bloody love it. The lab's good, got a great prof. You're economics and politics, right? Must be your final year."

"It is. It's flown by. Do you still shoot?"

"Religiously. I'm an Anchorite now."

I wonder if "Anchorite" means "anchorman," or if it's a Kiwi-ism or a rifle club–ism. Cambridge is full of insiders' words to keep outsiders out. "Cool," I tell him. "I enjoyed my few visits to the range."

"Never too late. Shooting is prayer. And when civilization shuts up shop, a gun'll be worth any number of university degrees. Happy Christmas." He zips his fly. "See you around."

PENHALIGON ASKS, "So where's this mystery woman of yours, Olly?"

Olly Quinn frowns. "She said she'd be here by half seven."

"Only ninety minutes late," offers Cheeseman. "Doesn't *prove* she's dumped you for a gym rat with the face of Keanu Reeves, the anatomy of King Dong, and the charisma of moi. Not necessarily."

"I'm driving her home to London tonight," says Olly. "She lives in Greenwich—so she's bound to be along by and by . . ."

"Confide in us, Olly," says Cheeseman. "We're your friends. Is she a real girlfriend, or have you . . . y'know . . . made her up?"

"*I* can vouch for her existence," says Fitzsimmons, enigmatically.

"Oh?" I glower at Olly. "Since when did *this* cuckolding crim take precedence over your stairs neighbor?"

"Chance encounter." Fitzsimmons tips his roasted-nut crumbs into his mouth. "I espied Olly-plus-companion at the drama section in Heffer's."

"And speaking as a reformed postfeminist new man," I ask Fitzsimmons, "where would you position Queen Ness on the Scale?"

"She's hot. I presume an escort agency is involved, Olly?"

"Screw *you*." Olly smiles like the cat who got the cream. "Ness!" He jumps up as a girl squeezes through the crush of student bodies. "Talk of the devil! Glad you got here."

"*So* sorry I'm late, Olly," she says, and they kiss on the lips. "The bus took about eight hundred years to arrive."

I know her, or knew her, but only in the biblical sense. Her surname escapes me, but other parts I remember very well. An afterparty in my first year, though she was "Vanessa" back then; potty-mouthed Cheltenham Ladies College, if memory serves; a big shared house down the arse-end of Trumpington Road. We necked a bottle of Château Latour '76, which she'd nicked from the cellar in the pre-party house. We've sighted each other around town since and nodded to avoid the crassness of ignoring each other. She's a craftier operator than Olly, but even as I wonder what's in him for her, I recall a drunk-driving offense and a suspended license—and Olly's warm, dry Astra. All's fair in love and war, and although I'm many things, I'm not a hypocrite. Ness has seen me and a fifth of a second is enough to agree upon a policy of cordial amnesia.

"Have my seat," Olly's saying, removing her coat like a gentletwat, "and I'll . . . er, kneel. Fitz, you've met. And this is Richard."

"Charmed." Cheeseman offers her a four-fingered handshake. "I'm the malicious queer. Are you Nessie the Monster or Ness the Loch?"

"And I'm as charmed as you are." I remember her voice, too: slumming-it posh. "My friends have no trouble with just 'Ness' but you can call me Vanessa."

"I'm Jonny, Jonny Penhaligon." Jonny jumps up to shake her hand. "A pleasure. Olly's told us shedloads about you."

"All of it good." I hold up my palm to say hi. "Hugo."

Ness misses no beat: "Hugo, Jonny, the malicious queer, and Fitz. Got it." She turns to Olly. "And sorry—who are you again?"

Olly's laugh is a notch too loud. His pupils have morphed into love-hearts and, for the nth time squared, I wonder what love feels like on the inside because externally it turns you into the King of Tit Mountain.

"Richard was about to buy a round," says Fitzsimmons. "Right, Richard? Aerate your wallet?"

Cheeseman feigns confusion. "Isn't it your turn, Penhaligon?"

"Nope. I bought the round before this one. Nice try."

"But you own half of Cornwall!" says Cheeseman. "You should see Jonny's manor, Ness—gardens, peacocks, deer, stables, portraits of three centuries' worth of Captain Penhaligons up the main staircase."

Penhaligon snorts. "Tredavoe House is *why* we've got no bloody money. The upkeep's crippling. And the peacocks are utter bastards."

"Oh, don't be a Scrooge, Jonny, the poll tax must be saving you a king's ransom. I'm going to have to pimp myself later just to get a National Express ticket home to my Leeds pigeon-loft."

Cheeseman is a fine misdirector—he still has ten thousand pounds from the money his grandfather left him—but I want no ruffled feathers tonight. "I'll get the next round in," I volunteer. "Olly, you'll need to stay sober if you're driving, so how about a tomato juice with Tabasco to warm the heart of your cockles? Cheeseman's on the Guinness; Fitz, fizzy Australian wee; and Ness, your poison is . . . what?"

"The house red isn't bad." Olly wants a drunk girlfriend.

"Then a glass of red would hit the spot, Hugo," she tells me.

I recall that quirky lilt. "Wouldn't risk it, unless you carry a spare trachea in your handbag. It's hardly a Château Latour."

"An Archers with ice, then," says Ness. "Better safe than sorry."

"Wise choice. Mr. Penhaligon, would you help me bring these six drinks back alive? The bar will not be pretty, I fear."

THE BURIED BISHOP'S a gridlocked scrum, an all-you-can-eat of youth: "Stephen Hawking and the Dalai Lama, right; they posit a unified truth"; short denim skirts, Gap and Next shirts, Kurt Cobain cardigans, black Levi's; "Did you see that oversexed pig by the loos, undressing me with his eyes?"; that song by the Pogues and Kirsty MacColl booms in my diaphragm and knees; "Like, *my* only charity shop bargains were headlice, scabies, and fleas"; a fug of hairspray, sweat and Lynx, Chanel No. 5, and smoke; well-tended teeth with zero fillings, revealed by the so-so joke—"Have you heard the news about Schrödinger's Cat? It died today; wait—it didn't, did, didn't, did . . ."; high-volume discourse on who's the best Bond; on Gilmour and Waters and Syd; on hyperreality; dollar-pound parity; Sartre, Bart Simpson, Barthes's myths; "Make mine a double"; George Michael's stubble; "Like, music expired with the Smiths"; urbane and entitled, for the most part, my peers; their eyes, hopes, and futures all starry; fetal think-tankers, judges, and bankers *in statu pupillari;* they're sprung from the loins of the global elite (or they damn well soon will be); power and money, like Pooh Bear and honey, stick fast—I don't knock it, it's me; and speaking of loins, "Has anyone told you you look like Demi Moore from *Ghost*?"; roses are red and violets are blue, I've a surplus of butter and Ness is warm toast.

"Hugo? You okay?" Penhaligon's smile is uncertain.

We're still logjammed two bodies back from the bar.

"Yeah," I have to half shout. "Sorry, I was light-years away. While I have you to myself, Jonny, Toad asked me to invite you to his last all-nighter tomorrow, before we all jet off home. You, me, Eusebio, Bryce Clegg, Rinty, and one or two others. All cool."

Penhaligon makes a not-sure face. "My mother's half-expecting me back at Tredavoe tomorrow night . . ."

"No pressure. I'm just passing the invitation on. Toad says the ambience is classier when you're there."

Penhaligon sniffs the cheese. "Toad said that?"

"Yes, he said you've got gravitas. Rinty's even christened you 'the Pirate of Penzance' because you always leave with the loot."

Jonny Penhaligon grins. "You'll be there too?"

"Me? God, yeah. Wouldn't miss it for the world."

"You took quite a clobbering last week."

"I never lose more than I can afford. 'Scared money is lost money.' You said that. Wise words for card players *and* economists."

My partner in recreational gambling does not deny authorship of my freshly minted epigram. "I *could* drive home on Sunday . . ."

"Look, I won't try to sway you one way or the other."

He hums. "I could tell my parents I've a supervision . . ."

"Which would not be untrue—a supervision on probability theory, psychology, applied mathematics. All valid business skills, as your family will appreciate when you get the green light for the golf course at Tredavoe House. Toad's proposing we raise the pot limit to a hundred pounds per game: a nice round figure, and quite a dollop of holiday nectar for *you,* sir, if your luck holds. Not that the Pirate of Penzance seems to need luck."

Jonny Penhaligon admits: "I *do* seem to have a certain knack."

I mirror his chuckle. *Who's a pretty turkey, then?*

FIFTEEN MINUTES LATER we're bringing our drinks back to our nook to find that trouble has beaten us to it. Richard Cheeseman, *The Piccadilly Review*'s rising star, has been cornered by Come Up to the Lab, Cambridge's premier Goth-metal trio, whose concert at the Cornmarket was acidly ridiculed in *Varsity* last month—by Richard Cheeseman. The bassist guy's a Frankenstein, lipless and lumbering; but She-Goth One has mad-dog eyes, a sharky chin, and knuckles of spiky rings; She-Goth Two has a *Clockwork Orange* bowler hat, exploding fuchsia-pink hair, a fake diamond hatpin, and the same eyes as She-Goth One. Amphetamines, I do believe. "Never done anything yourself, have yer?" Number Two is prodding Cheeseman's chest with jet-black fingernails to italicize key words. "Never performed live to a real audience, have yer?"

"Nor have I fucked a donkey, destabilized a Central American state, or played Dungeons & Dragons," retorts Cheeseman, "but I reserve the right to hold opinions on those who do. Your show was a bobbing turd and I don't take a word back."

She-Goth One takes over: "*Scribble scribble scribble* with your faggoty pen in your faggoty notebook and *snipe* and *bitch* and *slag off* real artists, you hairy lump of dick cheese."

"'Dick Cheese,'" says Cheeseman, "from 'Richard Cheeseman,' yeah, that's *really* clever. Original, too. Never once heard it."

"What d'you expect," She-Goth One snatches up *Desiccated Embryos,* "from a Crispin Hershey fan? He's a prick, too."

"Don't pretend you read books." Cheeseman gropes for his review copy in vain and I catch a distant glimpse of a tortured gay child having his satchel emptied off a sooty bridge over the Leeds–Bradford railway line. She-Goth Two rips the book down its spine and tosses the halves away. The male Goth goes *gur-hur-hur.*

Olly retrieves one half, Cheeseman the other. He's riled now. "Crispin Hershey's last crap has more artistic merit than your lifetime's output. Your music's derivative wank. It's parasitic. It's a hatpin through the eardrum, darling, and not in a good way."

He was doing quite well until the last sentence, but if you bare your arse to a vengeful unicorn, the number of possible outcomes dwindles to one. By the time I've put the drinks on a handy shelf, She-Goth Two has indeed extracted her hatpin and flown at Monsieur Le Critic, who topples operatically; the table upends and glasses slide off; female spectators gasp and shriek and go, "Oh, my God!"; She-Goth Two pounces on the fallen one and stabs downwards; I grab the hatpin (glistening?) and Penhaligon pulls her off Cheeseman by her hair; the bassist's fist misses Penhaligon's nose by a whisker; Penhaligon staggers onto Olly and Ness; and She-Goth One's screeching becomes audible to the human ear—"Get your hands *off her*!" Fitzsimmons is kneeling down, with Cheeseman's head on his lap. Cheeseman looks like a guy in a comedy seeing stars and birdies, but the ear dribbling blood is more worrying; I examine it closely. Good: Only the lobe's torn, but the attackers don't need to know that. I arise and shout at Come Up to the Lab in a fisticuff-quelling roar: "A *monsoon* of piss and shit is headed straight at you for this."

"The wanker was asking for it," states She-Goth Two.

"He started it," insists her friend. "He provoked us!"

"Multiple witnesses," I indicate the scandal-hungry onlookers, "know *exactly* who was attacked by *whom.* If you think 'verbal provocation' is an admissible defense for grievous bodily harm, then you're even stupider than you look. See that hatpin there?" She-Goth Two sees the blood on the tip and drops it; two seconds later it's in my pocket. "Lethal weapon used with intent. Got your DNA all over it. Custodial term, *four years*. Yes, girls: four years. If you've punctured the ear canal, make it seven, and by the time *I've* finished in court, seven years *will mean seven*. So. Reckon I'm bluffing?"

"Who," the bassist's aggression is shaky, "the fuck are you?"

I perform my craziest L. Ron Hubbard laugh. "Postgrad in law, genius. What's more interesting is who *you* are—an *accomplice*. Do you know what that means, in nice plain English? It means you get sentenced too."

She-Goth Two's braggadocio is wilting. "But I . . ."

The bassist's pulling her by the arm. "C'mon, Andrea."

"Run, Andrea!" I jeer. "Melt into the crowd—oh, but wait! You've glued posters of your mugshots all over Cambridge, haven't you? Well, you *are* fucked. Well and truly." Come Up to the Lab decide it's time to vacate the building. I yell after them, "See you at the hearing! Bring phone cards for the detention wing—you'll need them!"

Penhaligon rights the table and Olly gathers the glasses. Fitzsimmons hauls Cheeseman onto the bench, and I ask him how many fingers I'm holding up. He winces a bit, and wipes his mouth. "It was my ear she went for, not my sodding eye."

A very pissed-off landlord appears. "What's going on?"

I turn on him. "Our friend was just assaulted by three drunken sixth-formers and needs medical attention. As regulars, we'd hate to see your license revoked, so at A and E Richard and Olly here will imply the assault happened *off* your premises. Unless I've read the situation wrongly, and you'd prefer to involve the authorities?"

The landlord susses the state of play. "Nah. 'Preciated."

"You're welcome. Olly: Is the Magic Astra parked nearby?"

"In the car park at the college, yes, but Ness here—"

"Um, my car's available too," says helpful Penhaligon.

"Jonny, you're over the limit and your father's a magistrate."

"The breathalyzers'll be out tonight," warns the landlord.

"You're the only sober party, Olly. And if we phone for an ambulance from Addenbrookes, the cops will come along too, and—"

"Questions, statements, and all *sorts* of how's-yer-father," says the landlord, "and then your college'd get involved, too."

Olly looks at Ness, like a boy who's lost his finger of fudge.

"Go on," Ness tells him. "I'd join you, but the sight of blood . . ." She makes a *yuck* face. "Help your friend."

"I'm supposed to be driving you to Greenwich tonight."

"Don't worry. I'll get home by train—I'm a big girl, remember? Call me on Sunday and we'll talk Christmas plans, okay? Go."

MY RADIO ALARM is glowing 01:08 when I hear footsteps on the stairs, the pause, the timid *tap-tap-tap* on my outer door. I put on my dressing gown, close my bedroom door, cross my parlor, and open up, leaving the chain on. I squint out: "Olly? Wassa time?"

Olly looks Caravaggian in the dim light. "Half twelve-ish."

"Shit. Poor you. How's the bearded one?"

"If he survives the self-pity, he'll be fine. Antitetanus booster and a glorified Elastoplast. A and E was the Night of the Living Dead. I only just dropped Cheeseman off at his flat. Did Ness get to the station?"

"For sure. Penhaligon and I escorted her to the taxi rank at Drummer Street, Friday night being Friday night. Fitz met Chetwynd-Pitt and Yasmina after you left and went off clubbing. Then, once Ness was safely off, Penhaligon followed on. I wussed out, spent a sexy hour here with I.F.R. Coates's *Bushonomics and the New Monetarism,* then called it a night. Look, I'd"—I do a whale-sized yawn—"invite you in, but I'm bushed."

"She didn't . . ." Olly thinks, and Connect 4 counters drop, ". . . stick around for a drink or—or anything? At the Buried Bishop?"

"I.F.R. Coates is a *bloke,* Olly. He teaches at Blithewood College in upstate New York."

"I meant," how Olly aches to believe me, "Ness, actually."

"*Ness?* Ness just wanted to get to Greenwich." I'm mildly hurt; Olly ought to trust me not to hit on his girlfriend. "She'd have made the nine fifty-seven to King's Cross, thence to Greenwich, where she's no doubt tucked up and dreaming of Olly Quinn, Esquire. Lovely girl, by the way, from the little I saw of her. Obviously besotted with you, too."

"You reckon? This week she's been a bit, I don't know, ratty. I've been half afraid she might be . . ."

I continue to act dumb. Olly lets his sentence fizzle out.

"What?" I say. "Thinking of dumping you? Hardly the impression I got. When these huntin', shootin', fishin' types *really* fall for a guy they go all headmistressy to hide it. But don't discount the more obvious cause of female crankiness, either; Lucille used to turn into a scorn-flobbing psychopath every twenty-eight days."

Olly looks cheerful. "Well. Yeah. Maybe."

"You'll be meeting up over Christmas, right?"

"The idea was to sort out our plans tonight."

"Too bad our Richard needed a Good Samaritan. Mind you, the way you took charge of things back at the pub impressed her to pieces. She said it showed how self-possessed you are when a crisis strikes."

"She said that? Actually said it?"

"Pretty much verbatim, yes. At the taxi rank."

Olly's glowing; if he was six inches tall and fluffy, Toys R Us would ship him by the thousands.

"Olly, mate, I'll bid thee a fair repose."

"Sorry, Hugo, sure. Thanks. G'night."

BACK IN MY bed of woman-smelling warmth, Ness hooks a leg across my thighs: " 'Headmistressy'? I should kick you out of bed now."

"Try it." I run my hands over her pleasing contours. "You'd better leave at the crack of dawn. I sent you to Greenwich just now."

"That's hours away, yet. Anything could happen."

I draw twirls around her navel with my finger, but I find myself thinking about Immaculée Constantin. I didn't mention her to the boys earlier; turning her into an anecdote felt unwise. Not unwise: prohibited. When I zoned out on her, she must have thought . . . What? That I'd entered a sort of seated coma, and left me to it. Pity.

Ness folds back the coverlet for air. "The problem with the Ollies of the world is—"

"Glad you're so focused on me," I tell her.

"—is their *niceness*. Niceness drives me mental."

"Isn't a nice boy what every girl is looking for?"

"To marry, sure. But Olly makes me feel trapped inside a Radio 4 play about . . . *fright*fully earnest young men in the nineteen fifties."

"He did mention you'd been out of sorts lately. Ratty."

"If I'm ratty, he's an overgrown wobbly puppy."

"Well, the course of true love never did—"

"Shut up. He's so em*bar*rassing socially. I'd already decided to dump him on Sunday. Tonight just seals the deal."

"If poor doomed Olly's a Radio 4 play, what am I?"

"You, Hugo," she kisses my earlobe, "are a sordid, low-budget French film. The sort you'd stumble across on TV at night. You know you'll regret it in the morning, but you keep watching anyway."

A lost tune is whistled in the quad below.

"A ROBIN." Mum points through the patio windows at the garden, clogged with frozen slush. "There, on the handle of the spade."

"He looks freshly arrived off a Christmas card," says Nigel.

Dad munches broccoli. "What's my spade doing out of the shed?"

"My fault," I say. "I was filling the coal scuttle. I'll put it back after. Though, first, I'll put Alex's plate to keep warm: Hot gossip and true love shouldn't mean cold lunches." I take my older brother's plate to the new wood-burning oven and put it inside with a pan lid over it. "Hell's bells, Mum. You could fit a witch in here."

"If it had wheels," says Nigel, "it'd be an Austin Metro."

"Now *that*," crap cars are one of Dad's loves, "was a pile of."

"What a pity you'll miss Aunt Helena at New Year," Mum tells me.

"It is." I sit back down and resume my lunch. "Give her my love."

"*Right,*" says Nigel. "Like you'd rather be stuck in Richmond over New Year than skiing in Switzerland. You're *mega*-jammy, Hugo."

"How many times have I told you?" says Dad. "It's not—"

"What you know but who you know," says Nigel. "Nine thousand, six hundred, and eight, including just now."

"That's why getting to a brand-name university matters," says Dad. "To network with future big fish and not future small-fry."

"I forgot to mention," remembers Mum. "Julia's covered herself in glory—again. She's won a scholarship to study human-rights law, in Montreal."

I've always had a thing for my cousin Julia, and the thought of covering her in anything is Byronically diverting.

"Lucky she takes after your side of the family, Alice," says Dad, a dour reference to my ex-uncle Michael's divorce ten years ago, complete with secretary and love child. "What's Jason studying again?"

"Something psycho-linguisticky," says Mum, "at Lancaster."

Dad frowns. "Why do I associate him with forestry?"

"He wanted to be a forester when he was a kid," I say.

"But now he's settled on being a speech therapist," says Mum.

"A st-st-stuttering sp-sp-speech therapist," says Nigel.

I grind peppercorns over my mashed pumpkin. "Not grown-up and not clever, Nige. A stammer has to be the best possible qualification for a speech therapist. Don't you think?"

Nigel does a guess-so face in lieu of admitting I'm right.

Mum sips her wine. "This wine is divine, Hugo."

"Divine's the word for Montrachet seventy-eight," says Dad. "You shouldn't be spending your money on us, Hugo. Really."

"I budget carefully, Dad. The office-drone work I do at the solicitor's adds up. And after everything you've done for me down the years, I ought to be able to stand you a bottle of decent plonk."

"But we'd hate to think of you going short," says Mum.

"*Or* your studies suffering," adds Dad, "because of your job."

"So just let us know," says Mum, "if money's tight. Promise?"

"I'll come cap in hand, if that ever looks likely. Promise."

"*My* money's tight," says Nigel, hopefully.

"You're not living out in the big bad world." Dad frowns at the clock. "Speaking of which, I only hope Alex's fräulein's parents know she's calling England. It's the middle of the day."

"They're Germans, Dad," says Nigel. "Big fat Deutschmarks."

"You say that, but reunification is going to cost the earth. My clients in Frankfurt are *very* jumpy about the fallout."

Mum slices a roasted potato. "What's Alex told you about Suzanne, Hugo?"

"Not a word." With my knife and fork I slide trout flesh off its bones. "Sibling rivalry, remember."

"But you and Alex are the firmest of friends, these days."

"As long as," says Nigel, "no one utters those six deadly words, 'Anyone fancy a game of Monopoly?'"

I look hurt. "Is it *my* fault if I can't seem to lose?"

Nigel snorts. "Just 'cause no one knows *how* you cheat—"

"Mum, Dad, you heard that hurtful, baseless aspersion."

"—isn't proof you *don't* cheat." Nigel wags his knife. My baby brother lost his virginity this autumn: chess magazines and Atari console out, the KLF and grooming products in. "Anyway, *I* know three things about Suzanne, using my powers of deduction. If she finds Alex attractive, then (*a*) she's blind as a bat, (*b*) she's used to dealing with toddlers, and (*c*) she has no sense of smell."

Enter the Alex: "Who's got no sense of smell?"

"Fetch Firstborn's dinner from the oven," I order Nigel, "or I'll rat you out and you'll deserve it." Nigel obeys, sheepishly enough.

"So how's Suzanne?" asks Mum. "All well in Hamburg?"

"Yeah, fine." Alex sits down. He's a brother of few words.

"She's a pharmacology student, you said?" states Mum.

Alex spears a brain of cauliflower from the dish. "Uh-huh."

"And will we be meeting her at some point, do you think?"

"Hard to say," says Alex, and I think of my own poor dear Mariângela's vain hopes.

Nigel puts Alex's lunch in front of our elder brother.

"What I can't get over," says Dad, "is how distances have shrunk. Girlfriends in Germany, ski trips to the Alps, courses in Montreal: This is all normal nowadays. The first time I left England was to go to Rome, when I was about your age, Hugo. None of my mates had *ever* gone so far. A pal and I got the Dover-Calais ferry, hitched a ride down to Marseille, then across to Turin, then Rome. Took us six days. It felt like the edge of the known world."

Nigel asks, "Did the wheels come off the mail coach, Dad?"

"Funny. I didn't go back to Rome until two years ago, when New

York decided to hold the European AGM there. Off we all jetted in time for a late lunch, a few supervisions, schmoozing until midnight, then the next day we were back in London in time for—"

We hear the phone ring, back in the living room. "It's for one of you boys," Mum declares. "Bound to be."

Nigel skids down the hall and into the living room; my trout gazes up with a disappointed eye. A few moments later, Nigel's back. "Hugo, that was a Diana on the phone for you—Diana Spinster, Spankser, Spencer, didn't quite catch it. She said you could pop over to the palace while her husband's touring the Commonwealth . . . Something about Tantric plumbing? She said you'd understand."

"There's this operation, little brother. It would help that one-track mind of yours. Vets do it cheaply."

"Who *was* on the phone, Nigel?" asks Mum. "Before you forget."

"Mrs. Purvis at the Riverside Villas. She said to tell Hugo that the brigadier's feeling better today, and if he'd still like to visit this afternoon, he'd be welcome to call between three and five o'clock."

"Great. If you're sure you can spare me, Dad . . ."

"Go go go. Your mother and I are very proud of how you still go to read to the brigadier, aren't we, Alice?"

Mum says, "Very."

"Thanks," I shrug awkwardly, "but Brigadier Philby was so brilliant when I went to see him for my civics class at Dulwich, and so full of stories. It's the least I can do."

"Oh, God." Nigel groans. "Someone's locked me up inside an episode of *Little House on the Prairie*."

"Then let me offer you a way out," says Dad. "If Hugo's visiting the brigadier, you can help me collect the tree."

Nigel looks aghast. "But Jasper Farley and I are going to Tottenham Court Road this afternoon!"

"What for?" Alex loads his fork. "All you do is slobber over hi-fi gear and synthesizers you can't afford."

We hear a small crash out on the patio. From the corner of my eye

I see a flash of black. A toppled flower pot skitters across the patio, the spade tips over, and the black flash turns into a cat with a robin in its mouth. The bird's wings are flapping. "Oh." Mum recoils. "That's *horrible*. Can't we do something? The cat looks so pleased with itself."

"It's called survival of the fittest," says Alex.

"Why don't I lower the blinds?" asks Nigel.

"Better let nature take its course, darling," says Dad.

I get up and go out through the back door. The cold air shocks my skin as I go, "Shoo, shoo!" to the cat. The feline hunter leaps onto the garden shed. It watches me. Its tail sashays. The mangled bird is twitching in the black cat's mouth.

I hear the boomy scrape of an airplane.

A twig snaps. I am intensely alive.

"ACCORDING TO MY husband," Nurse Purvis steams along moppable carpet to the library of Riverside Villas, "the youth of today are either scroungers-on-benefits, queers, or I'm-all-right-Jacks." The smell of pine-scented disinfectant stings my nostrils. "But as long as Great Britain breeds fine young men of your cut, Hugo, *I* for one say we shan't be collapsing into barbarism any time soon, *mmm?*"

"Please, Nurse Purvis, my head won't fit through the library door." We turn the corner and find a resident clinging to the hand-rail. She's frowning at the wintry garden, as if she's left something out there. A string of drool connects her lower lip to her spearmint-green cardigan.

"Standards, Mrs. Bolitho," says the nurse, hipping out a tissue from her sleeve. "What do we watch? Our standards, *mmm?*" She scoops up the saliva stalactite and deposits the tissue in the bin. "You'll remember Hugo, Mrs. Bolitho—the brigadier's young friend."

Mrs. Bolitho turns her head; I think of my trout at lunch.

"Great to see you again, Mrs. Bolitho," I say cheerfully.

"Say hello to Hugo, Mrs. Bolitho. Hugo's a guest."

She looks from me to Nurse Purvis and whimpers.

"What's that? *Chitty Chitty Bang Bang* is on the television, in the lounge. The flying car. Why don't we go and join them, *mmm*?"

A fox's head watches us from the wall with a faint smile.

"Stay here," Nurse Purvis tells Mrs. Bolitho, "while I take Hugo to the library. Then we'll go to the residents' room together."

I wish Mrs. Bolitho a Merry Christmas but the chances are low.

"She has four sons," Nurse Purvis leads me on, "all with a London post code, but they never visit. You'd think old age was a criminal offense, not a destination we're all heading to."

I consider airing my theory that our culture's coping strategy towards death is to bury it under consumerism and *Sansara*, that the Riverside Villas of the world are screens that enable this self-deception, and that the elderly *are* guilty: guilty of proving to us that our willful myopia about death is exactly that.

But, no, let's not complicate Nurse Purvis's opinion of me. We reach the library where my guide continues sotto voce: "I know you won't be put out, Hugo, if the brigadier doesn't recognize you."

"Not at all. Does he still suffer from the postage stamp . . . delusion?"

"It rears its head from time to time, yes. Oh, here's Mariângela—Mariângela!"

Mariângela approaches with a stack of neatly folded bed linen. "Yugo! Nurse Purvis, she told me you visit today. How is Norwitch?"

"Hugo is at Cambridge University, Mariângela." Nurse Purvis shivers. "*Cambridge*. Not Norwich. Quite different."

"Pardon, Yugo." Mariângela's puckish Brazilian eyes arouse not only my hopes. "My geography of England, still a bit rubbish."

"Mariângela, perhaps you'd bring some coffee to the library for Hugo and the brigadier. I ought to be getting back to Mrs. Bolitho."

"Of course. It's been wonderful catching up, Nurse Purvis."

"Be sure to say goodbye before you leave." Off she marches.

I ask Mariângela, "What's she actually like to work for?"

"We are accustomed to dictators in my continent."

"Does she sleep at night or plug herself into the mains?"

"Is not a bad boss, if you agree with her always. At the least, she is dependable. At the least, she says what she is thinking, honestly."

I'd describe Mariângela as pouty but not vitriolic. "Look, Angel, we both needed some space."

"*Eight weeks,* Yugo. Two letters, two calls, two messages on my answer machine. *I* need contact, not space." Okay, so she's between pouty and wronged woman. "You not an expert on what I need."

Tell her it's over, Hugo the Wise advises, but Hugo the Horny loves a uniform. "I'm not an expert on you, Mariângela. Or any other woman. Or myself, even. I had two or three girlfriends before you—but . . . you're *different*. By the end of last summer, the inside of my eyelids was a TV station showing Mariângela Pinto-Pereira, all day, all night. It freaked me out. The only way I could handle it was space. So often, I *nearly* phoned . . . but . . . but . . . I was an inexperienced boy, Angel, not a malicious one." I open the library door. "Thanks for some great memories, I'm sorry my insensitivity hurt you. Really."

Her foot's in the door. Pouty and sultry. "Nurse Purvis ask I bring you and the brigadier coffee. Is still dark, with one sugar?"

"Yes, please. But no Amazonian voodoo stuff that shrivels up testicles, if that's okay."

"Sharp knife is better than voodoo." She scowls. "Milk or Coffee-mate in your coffee, like you drink it at Came-bridge University?"

"White coffee brings me out in a nasty rash."

"So if—*if*—I find you real Brazilian coffee, you drink?"

"Mariângela. Once you've tasted the real thing, everything else is a cheap imitation."

"NEAR THE END now, Brigadier," I tell the old man, and turn the page. " 'But for me all the East is contained in that vision of my youth. It is all on that moment when I opened my young eyes on it.

I came upon it from a tussle with the sea—and I was young—and I saw it looking at me. And this is all that is left of it! Only a moment; a moment of strength, of romance, of glamour—of youth! . . . A flick of sunshine upon a strange shore, the time to remember, the time for a sigh, and—goodbye!—Night—Goodbye . . .' " I slurp lukewarm coffee: Brigadier Philby's cup remains untouched. The vital, witty man I knew five years ago is one and the same as the wheelchair-bound husk. Back in 1986 he was seventy going on fifty, living in a big old place in Kew with his devoted widowed sister, Mrs. Hatter. The brigadier was an old friend of my headmaster, and although I was supposed to be mowing his lawn while his broken leg recovered, he recognized a kindred spirit and we ended up spending my civics-class hours on poker, cribbage, and blackjack. Even after his leg had healed I'd go round most Thursday evenings. Mrs. Hatter would "fatten me up" and we'd retire to the card table, where he taught me ways to "Entice Lady Luck to drop her bloomers" that not even Toad guesses at. A dapper dresser and quite the ladies' man in his day, an obsessive philatelist, linguist, and raconteur. After a glass of port he would talk about days in the Special Boat Section in wartime Norway, and later in the Korean War. He insisted I read Conrad and Chekhov, and taught me how to get a fake passport by finding a name in a graveyard and writing off to Somerset House for a birth certificate. I knew this but pretended I didn't.

Brigadier Philby hardly stirs nowadays. His head sways now and then, like Stevie Wonder's at the piano, and dandruff gathers in the furrows of his jacket. His shave was done by a male nurse with a mind on other matters and the old man wears an incontinence nappy. A few malformed words escape the brigadier's mouth from time to time, but he's otherwise nonverbal. I've no idea whether Conrad's *Youth* is bringing him the pleasure it used to, or whether it's a torment to be reminded of happier days. Or perhaps he has no idea what I'm saying, or even who I am.

Still. Mariângela says that the best way to work with dementia is to act as if the person you knew is still inside the wreckage. If you're wrong, and the person you knew is gone, then no damage is done but the standards of care stay high; if you're right, and the person you knew is still bricked up inside, then you are the lifeline. "On to the final page, now, Brigadier. 'By all that's wonderful it is the sea, I believe, the sea itself—or is it youth alone? Who can tell? But you here—you all had something out of life: money, love—whatever one gets on shore—and, tell me, wasn't that the best time, that time we were young at sea; young and had nothing, on the sea that gives nothing, except hard knocks—and sometimes a chance to feel your strength—that only—what you all regret?'"

Something flutters in the brigadier's throat.

A sigh? Or just air, strumming vocal cords?

Through a gap in the trees at the end of the garden I see the Thames, silver and gunmetal.

A five-man boat flits from left to right. Blink and you miss it.

The flat-capped gardener gathers leaves with a rake.

Last paragraph in the dying light: "'And we all nodded at him: the man of finance, the man of accounts, the man of law, we all nodded at him over the polished table that like a still sheet of brown water reflected our faces, lined, wrinkled; our faces marked by toil, by deceptions, by success, by love. Our weary eyes looking still, looking always, looking anxiously for something out of life, that while it is expected is already gone—has passed unseen, in a sigh, in a flash—together with the youth, with the strength, with the romance of illusions.'"

I shut the book, and put on the lamp. My watch says 4:15. I rise, and draw the curtains. "Well, sir." It feels like I'm addressing an empty room. "I shouldn't tire you out too much, I guess."

Unexpectedly, the brigadier's face tautens with alertness and his mouth opens, and although his voice is ghostly and stroke-slurred, I can discern his words: "My . . . bloody . . . stamps . . ."

"Brigadier Philby—it's Hugo, sir. Hugo Lamb."

His shaky hand tries to clutch my sleeve. "Police . . ."

"Which stamps, Brigadier? Which do you mean?"

"Small . . . fortune . . ." Intelligence enters his eyes and, for a moment, I think he's ready to fire off an accusation, but the moment goes. In the corridor outside, a trolley squeaks by. The brigadier I knew has left his bombed-out face, leaving me alone with the clock, shelves of handsome books nobody ever reads, and one certainty: that whatever I do with my life, however much power, wealth, experience, knowledge, or beauty I'll accrue, I, too, will end up like this vulnerable old man. When I look at Brigadier Reginald Philby, I'm looking down time's telescope at myself.

MARIÂNGELA'S DREAM-CATCHER SWINGS when I biff it, and I find my lover's crucifix among her boingy curls. I hold the Son of God in my mouth, and imagine him dissolving on my tongue. Sex may be the antidote to death but it offers life everlasting only to the species, not the individual. On the CD player, Ella Fitzgerald forgets the words to "Mac the Knife" one broiling night in Berlin over forty summers ago. A District Line train rumbles down below. Mariângela kisses the fleshy underside of my forearm, then bites, hard. "Ow," I complain, enjoying the pain. "Is that Portuguese for 'the Earth moved for me, my lord and master, how was it for you?' "

"Is Portuguese for 'I hate you, you liar, you cheat, you monster, psycho, pervert, go to rot in the hell, you son of the bitch.' "

My erect bishop is unburying itself; the anticipation makes us both laugh, which squishes me out prematurely. I rescue the condom before its gluey viscera stains her purple sheets, and wrap it in a tissue shroud. Coupling is frenzy; decoupling is farce. Mariângela squirms around to face me and I wonder why women are uglier once they're unpeeled, encrusted, and had. She sits up and sips some water from the glass guarded by Jesus of Rio. "You want?" She brings the glass to my lips. Mariângela guides my hand over her heart: *Love love love love love love love,* it beats.

Ah, I should have listened to Hugo the Wise . . .

. . .

"Yugo, when can I meet your family?"

I'm putting on my boxers. I'd like a shower, but the Aston Martin dealership is closing soon so I need to hurry. "Why do you want to meet my family?"

"Is normal I want. We see each other six months now. June twenty-first, when you come here first. Tomorrow is December twenty-first."

God, an anniversary counter. "Let's go for a meal to celebrate, Angel, but let's leave my family out of it, hey?"

"I *want* meet your parents, your brothers . . ."

Right: *Mum, Dad, Nigel, Alex; may I present Mariângela. She hails from a nondescript suburb of Rio, works at Riverside House as a geriatric nurse, and after visiting Brigadier Philby, I shag her scarlet. So: What's for dinner?* I find my T-shirt down the side of her bed. "I don't really take girlfriends home, to be honest."

"So, I will be number one. Is very nice."

"Separate areas of my life"—jeans, zip, belt—"I keep separate."

"I am your girlfriend, not an 'area.' You shamed of me?"

What a sweet stab at emotional blackmail. "You know I'm not."

Mariângela's brain knows she should let this drop, but her heart has seized the wheel. "So, you shamed of your family?"

"No more than an average middle son of three."

"Then . . . you shamed I am too older than you?"

"You're twenty-six, Angel. That's hardly old."

"So . . . I am not white enough for your parents?"

I button up my Paul Smith shirt. "Not a factor."

"So for why I cannot meet my boyfriend's family?"

Sock one, sock two. "We're just . . . not at that stage."

"Is *bool*-shit, Yugo. In relationships, you share more than just bodies, yes? When you in Cambridge, drinking shit coffee with all the PhD white girls, I don't sit here, praying you call, waiting for letters. No. One guy is consultant at private clinic, he ask for date at

Japanese restaurant in Mayfair. My friends say, 'You crazy to say no!' But I say no—for you."

I try not to smile at her amateurishness.

"So what am I for? Just for sex when you on vacation?"

Okay, my coat's over by the door, ditto cowboy boots; she's still naked as a snowman and no weapons within easy reach. "You're a friend, Mariângela. Today you're an intimate friend. But do I want to introduce you to my parents? No. Move in with you? No. Plan a future, fold laundry with you, get a cat? No."

Another train passes below the window and cue crying scene: a scene as old as hominids and tear glands. It's happening all over Planet Earth, right now, in all the languages there are. Mariângela wipes her face and looks away, and the Olly Quinns of the world sink to their knees, promising to make things right. I put on my coat and boots. She notices and the tears stop. "You are leaving? *Now?*"

"If this is our big goodbye, Angel, why prolong the agony?"

Hurt to hatred in five seconds. "Sai da minha frente! Vai pra puta que pariu!"

Good. It's a cleaner ending if she hates me. With one foot over her threshold, I tell her, "If that consultant of yours wants lessons on Mariângela Pinto-Pereira, tell him I'll give him a few pointers."

One murderous scowl, one flash of muscular arm, and one glimpse of prime Brazilian breast later, Jesus of Rio is hurtling my way at meteor velocity; I react with a tenth of a second to spare, and Jesus hits the door and turns into a thousand plaster hailstones.

THE SIX O'CLOCK gloom promises snow. I put on my possum-hair hat. All's well in Richmond's prosperous backstreets. House owners draw curtains on middle-class rooms lined with books, hung with art, lit by Christmas trees. I make my short detour via Red Lion Street. The girl at reception in the Aston Martin dealership has curves as pert as the cars' but facially she's an out-and-out ET. She's gossiping on the phone as I stroll by—I give her a curt your-boss-is-expecting-me nod and cross the showroom floor to the open door of VINCENT COSTELLO, SALES TEAM. The occupant looks to be in his early thirties, has a gelled mullet, an off-the-peg suit from a mid-range high-street outfitter, and is making a dog's dinner of wrapping a big box of Scalextric. "Hi," he says to me. "Can I help you?" Jack-the-lad accent, east London; a photo of him and a little boy on his desk, but no mummy and no wedding ring.

"Vincent Costello, I presume?"

"Yes. Like it says on the door."

"I'd like to inquire about the resale value of an Aston Martin Coda. But first," I peer at the half-wrapped box, "you need an extra thumb."

"No, no, really, you're fine."

"I am, yes, but you are not. Let me help."

"Okay, cheers. It's for my five-year-old."

"Formula One fan, then, is he?"

"Crazy about cars, motorbikes, anything with engines. His mother does the wrapping normally but . . ." A tongue of Sellotape tears off a strip of paper, and Costello refines an "Oh, shit" into "Oh, sugar."

"Wrap boxes diagonally." Before he can argue, I nudge him away. "Get the little squares of Sellotape ready beforehand, persuade the paper to fold, and . . ." A few seconds later, a perfectly gift-wrapped box sits on his desk. "Good to go."

Vincent Costello's duly impressed. "Where d'you learn that?"

"My aunt runs a small chain of upmarket gift shops. It has been known for her wayward nephew to lend a hand."

"Lucky her. So. Aston Martin Coda, you say?"

"1969, hundred and ten on the clock, one careful owner."

"*Very* low mileage for such a mature specimen." He takes out an A4 sheet of numbers from a drawer in his desk. "May I ask who this careful owner is? 'Cause *you* haven't been driving since 1969."

"No, a friend inherited from his father. I'm Hugo, by the way, Hugo Lamb, and my friend's one of the Penzance Penhaligons." We shake hands. "When my friend's father passed away, he left his family one ungodly financial mess and a humongous bill for inheritance tax."

Vincent Costello makes a sympathetic grimace. "Right."

"My friend's mother's a lovely woman, but hasn't got a financial bone in her body. And, to cap it all, their family solicitor cum financial adviser's just been banged up for fraud."

"Blimey, it's one thing after another, isn't it?"

"Just so. Now, when I last spoke with Jonny, I offered to mention his Aston Martin to our local dealer—you. My parents live on Chislehurst Road. Cowboys outnumber sheriffs in the vintage motor business and I'm guessing a London dealer like yourself could offer a degree of discretion that my friend wouldn't enjoy if he went to someone in Devon or Cornwall."

"Your instinct is bang-on, Hugo. Let me consult an up-to-date price list . . ." Costello opens a file. "Is your own father a client here?"

"Dad's a BMW man at present, but he may be in the market for something niftier. Beamers are such a yuppie cliché. I'll mention how helpful you've been."

"I'd appreciate that. Rightio, Hugo. Tell your friend that the ballpark figure for a 1969 Aston Martin Coda with around a hundred K on the clock, all things being equal, is . . ." Vincent Costello runs his finger down a column, ". . . in the *region* of twenty-two thousand. However, London weighting'd work in his favor—I'm thinking of an Arab collector on my client list, a gentleman who'll pay a bit extra, knowing we sell a sound vehicle, so I *could* stretch to twenty-five K. We'd need to have our in-house mechanic inspect the vehicle, and Mr. Penhaligon'd need to bring in the paperwork himself."

"Naturally, we want everything to be aboveboard."

"Here's my card, then—I'll be ready if he calls."

"Excellent." I put it in my snakeskin wallet and we shake hands as I leave. "Merry Christmas, Mr. Costello."

BERNARD KRIEBEL PHILATELY of Cecil Court, off Charing Cross Road, envelops me with pipe-tobacco fug as the bell jingles. It's a long, narrow shop with a central stand where sets of midprice stamps are displayed, like LPs. Pricier items live in locked cabinets along the walls. I unwind my scarf, but my old satchel stays around my neck. The radio is warbling *Don Giovanni,* Act 2. Bernard Kriebel, clad in green tweed and a navy cravat, glances around the customer at the desk to ensure I come in peace; I send him a take-your-time face and stay at a tactful distance, perusing the mint condition Penny Blacks in their humidity-controlled display cabinets. It soon becomes clear, however, that the customer ahead of me is not a happy bunny: "What do you mean, *fake*?"

"This specimen is closer to a hundred days old," the proprietor removes his delicate glasses to rub a watery eye, "than a hundred years."

The customer pinches the air like a comedy Italian: "What about the faded dye? The browned paper? That paper's not contemporary!"

"Period paper isn't hard to obtain—although the crosshatch fibers suggest the 1920s more than the 1890s." Bernard Kriebel's unhurried English has a Slavonic burr: He's Yugoslav, I happen to know. "Dunking the paper in weak tea is an old gambit. The blocks must have taken many a night to craft, I'll admit—though with a list price of twenty-five thousand pounds, the prize justifies the labor. The ink itself is modern—Windsor and Newton Burnt Sienna?— diluted, slightly. Not an inept forgery."

Appalled falsetto huff: "You accuse me of *forgery*?"

"I accused someone, not you. Interestingly."

"You're trying to beat the price down. Admit it."

Kriebel grimaces with distaste. "A part-timer at Portobello may bite, or one of the traveling stamp and coin fairs. Now, if you'd excuse me, Mr. Budd, a genuine customer is waiting."

Mr. Budd snarls a *gaaagh* and storms out. He tries to slam the door—but it's not slammable—and he's gone. Kriebel shakes his head at the ways of the world.

I ask, "Do many forgers bring you their handiwork?"

Kriebel sucks in his cheeks to show he'll ignore the question. "I know your face . . ." he searches for me in his mental Rolodex, ". . . Mr. Anyder. You sold me a Pitcairn Island set of eight in August. A good clean set."

"I hope you're well, Mr. Kriebel."

"Passably. How are your studies? Law at UCL, wasn't it?"

I think he's trying to catch me out. "Astrophysics at Imperial."

"So it was. And have you found any sentient life up there?"

"At least as much as there is down here, Mr. Kriebel."

He smiles at the old joke and looks at my satchel. "Are you buying or selling this afternoon?"

I bring out the black folder and remove a strip of four stamps.

A Biro in Kriebel's hand goes *tap-tap-tap* on the benchtop.

The philatelist and his Anglepoise lamp peer closer.

The Biro falls silent. Bernard Kriebel's old eyes look my way inquisitorially, so I recite: "Four Indian Half-Anna Deep Blues; 1854 or 1855; from the right of sheet, with part marginal inscription; fresh condition; unused. How am I doing so far?"

"Well enough." He renews his inspection under a Sherlock-sized magnifying glass. "I won't pretend that a plethora of these pass through my hands. Did you have any . . . price in mind?"

"A single franked specimen sold at Sotheby's last June for two thousand one hundred pounds. Times four, gives us eight thousand four hundred. Add fifty percent for the pristine set, and we're in the neighborhood of thirteen grand. However. You have Central London overheads, you pay on the nail, and I have high hopes for a long-term relationship, Mr. Kriebel."

"Oh, I think we are on 'Bernard' terms from now on."

"Then call me Marcus, and my price is ten thousand."

Kriebel's already decided to accept, but pretends to agonize out of courtesy: "Commonwealth stamps are underperforming at present." He lights his pipe and the aria ends. "The highest I can go is eight and a half, alas."

"It's an icy day for chasing me to Trafalgar Square, Bernard."

He sighs through hairy nostrils. "My wife will pull me limb from limb for my softness, but young philatelists should be encouraged. We can agree to split the difference: nine thousand two hundred and fifty?"

"Ten is a simpler, rounder number." I put on my scarf.

A final sigh. "Ten it is." We shake. "You'll take a check?"

"Yes, but, Bernard . . ." he turns in the doorway to his cubbyhole, ". . . would *you* let your sweet Half-Annas out of sight prior to getting your hands on the payment?"

Bernard Kriebel tilts his head at my professionalism. He returns my stamps and goes to prepare my check. A terminally ill bus hauls itself up Charing Cross Road. Demons drag Don Giovanni down into the underworld: The fate of all amateurs who neglect their homework.

I WEAVE THROUGH Christmassy Soho, blaring, steamy, and hazardous with icy slush, cross the glacial stampede of traffic on Regent Street, and arrive at Suisse Integrité Banc's discreet London office, tucked away behind Berkeley Square. Security Ape holds the bulletproof door open with a nod of recognition; I have an appointment. Once within its airy, mahogany and cream interior, I deposit my check with the petite female teller across the polished desk, who asks no questions beyond, "How are you today, Mr. Anyder?" There's a little Swiss flag by her computer terminal, and as she fills out my deposit slip, I wonder if Madam Constantin, as a Swiss expatriate of understated means, ever graces this same plush chair. That odd encounter in King's College Chapel keeps returning to me, even if I've experienced no more time-slips. "Until next time, Mr. Anyder," the teller says, and I agree, Yes, until next time. The money is only the side product of my art, but I still leave feeling armed and flak-jacketed; when Kriebel's check clears, my account will cross the fifty K mark. This is, of course, a tadpole-sized account for Integrité's sheets, but it's a tidy enough stash for an undergraduate paying his own way in the world. And it will multiply. Half of my fellow Humberites—unless their parents are good and willing milkers—are so up to their nostrils in debt and denial that for their first five working years they'll have to take whatever shit gets flung their way and act like it's caviar. Not I. I'll throw it back. Harder.

IN A SHELTERED walkway off Piccadilly Circus, two men in suits and raincoats are blocking off a doorway and haranguing someone, hidden from view. The bright windows of Tower Records shine out through the feeble sleet, and early commuters are pouring into Piccadilly Circus Tube, but my curiosity is piqued. Between the men's backs I glimpse a shrunken Yeti huddled in an entrance. "Nice business strategy you've got worked out," says one. "You watch people buy flowers *there* and collar them for money *here* so they can't walk off without feeling like callous bastards." The tormentor sounds drunk. "We're in marketing, too, see. So what's your hit rate?"

"I"—the Yeti's blinking and scared—"I don't hit no one."

The tormentors laugh in each other's face: not a nice sound.

"All—all I'm askin' for's a bit of change. The hostel's thirteen quid a night."

"Then get yourself a shave and get a job stacking shelves!"

"Nobody'll give me a job without I've got a perm'nent address."

"Get a permanent address, then. *Duh.*"

"Nobody'll rent me a room without I've got a job."

"This one's got excuses for everything, hasn't he, Gaz?"

"Hey. Hey. Want a job? I'll give you a job. Want it?"

The burliest one leans down: "My colleague's asking you *very nicely* if you want a job."

The Yeti swallows and nods. "What's the job?"

"Hear that, Gaz? Beggars can be choosers, after all."

"Money collector," says Gaz. "Ten quid a minute, guaranteed."

The Yeti has a facial tic. "What do I have to do?"

"The clue's in the job title." The guy turns and lobs a pocketful of coins into a gap in the traffic roaring into Piccadilly Circus. "Collect the fucking money, Einstein!" Coins roll between tires and under cars, scattering in ruts of dirty ice. "Look at that, the streets of London *are* paved with gold." The two tormentors shuffle off, delighted with themselves, leaving the shrunken Yeti calculating the odds of picking up coins without getting whacked by a bus. "Don't," I tell the homeless guy.

He glares at me. "*You* try sleepin' in a skip."

I take out my wallet and offer him two twenties.

He looks at the money and looks at me.

I say, "Three nights in the hostel, right?"

He takes the notes and slips them inside his dirty coat. "Obliged."

My sacrifice to the gods duly performed, I let Piccadilly Circus Tube Station suck me down into its vortex of body odor and bad breath.

THE LINES ARE simple enough: "Men have imagined republics and principalities that never really existed at all. Yet the way men live is so far removed from the way they ought to live that anyone who abandons what 'is' for what 'should be' pursues his downfall rather than his preservation; for a man who strives after goodness in all his acts is sure to come to ruin, since there are so many men who are not good." For this plainspoken pragmatism, Cardinal Pole denounced Niccolò Machiavelli as the devil's apostle. After Earl's Court my carriage lurches into the dying light. Gasworks and Ed-

wardian roofs, chimneys and aerials, a supermarket car park, Premises for Rental. Commuters sway like sides of beef and slump like
corpses: red-eyed office slaves plugged into Discmans; their podgier
selves in their forties buried in the *Evening Standard;* and nearly
retired versions gazing over West London wondering where their
lives went. *I am the System you have to beat,* clacks the carriage. *I
am the System you have to beat.* But what does "beating the system" mean? Becoming rich enough to buy one's manumission from
the daily humiliation of employment? Another train on a parallel
track overtakes us slowly enough for me to glimpse the young City
worker I'll have turned into this time next year, squashed against
the window, only a meter away. Good skin, good clothes, drained
eyes. *How to Get Seriously Rich by Thirty* reads the cover of his
magazine. The guy looks up and sees me. He squints at my Penguin
Classic to make out the title, but his train swings away down a different track.

If I have doubts that you beat the system by moving up, I damn
well know you don't beat it by dropping out. Remember Rivendell?
The summer before I went up to Cambridge a few of us went clubbing at the Floating World in Camden Town. I took Ecstasy and got
off with a waifish girl wearing dried-blood lipstick and clothes
made of black cobwebs. Spidergirl and I got a taxi back to her place:
a commune called Rivendell, which turned out to be a condemned
end-of-terrace squat next to a paper recycling plant. Spidergirl and
I frolicked to an early Joni Mitchell LP about seagulls and drowsed
until noon, when I was shown downstairs to the Elrond Room,
where I ate lentil curry and the squat's "pioneers" told me how their
commune was an outpost of the postcapitalist, postoil, postmoney
future. For them everything was "inside the system"—bad—or
"outside the system"—good. When one asked me how I wanted to
spend my sojourn on Earth, I said something about the media and
was bombarded with a collective diatribe about how the system's
media divides people, not connects them. Spidergirl told me that
"here in Rivendell, we actually talk to each other, and share tales

from wiser cultures, like the Inuit. Wisdom's the ultimate currency." As I left, she asked for a "loan" of twenty pounds to buy a few things from Sainsbury's. I suggested she recite an Inuit folktale at the checkout, because wisdom is the ultimate currency. Some of her response was radical feminist, most was just Anglo-Saxon. What I took from Rivendell, apart from pubic lice and an allergy to Joni Mitchell that continues to the present day, was the insight that "outside the system" means poverty.

Ask the Yeti how free he feels.

As I TAKE off my hat and boots on the porch, I hear Mum in the front room: "Hold on a moment. That may be him now." She appears, holding the phone with its cord stretched to the max. "Oh, it *is*! Superb timing. I'll put him on. Wonderful to put a voice to the name, as it were, Jonny—season's greetings and all that."

I go in after her and mouth, "Jonny Penhaligon?" and Mum nods and leaves, closing the door behind her. The dark front room is lit by the fairy lights on the Christmas tree, pulsing on and off. The receiver lies on the wicker chair; I hold it against my ear, taking in the sound of Penhaligon's nervous breathing, and the trancey *Twin Peaks* theme wafting from another room in Tredavoe House. I count from ten to zero, slowly . . . "Jonny! What a surprise! So sorry to keep you."

"Hugo, hi, yeah, it's Jonny. Hi. How are things?"

"Great. All revved up for Christmas. Yourself?"

"Not so great, to be brutally honest, Hugo."

"Sorry to hear that. Anything I can help with?"

"Um . . . I don't know. It's a bit . . . awkward."

"O-*kay*. Speak."

"You know the other night, at Toad's? You remember I was four thousand up when you called it a night?"

"Do I remember? Cleaned out in the first hour, I was. Not so the Pirate of Penzance, eh?"

"Yeah, it was . . . one of those charmed runs."

" 'Charmed'? Four thousand quid is more than the basic student grant."

"Well, yeah. It went to my head a bit, a lot, that and the mulled wine, and I thought how fantastic it'd be not to go groveling to Mum for funds every time the account goes low . . . So, anyway, you'd left, Eusebio was dealing, and I got a flush, spades, jack high. I played it flawlessly—acted like I was bluffing over a pot of crap— till over two thousand quid was on the table."

"Shitting hell, Jonny. That's quite a bucketful."

"I know. We'd agreed to scrap the pot limit, and there were three of us bidding up and up, and nobody was backing down. Rinty only had two pairs, and Bryce Clegg looked at my flush and said, 'Shafted by the Pirate again,' but as I scooped up the pot he added, 'Unless I've got—oh, what is this? A full house.' And he had. Three queens, two aces. I should have gone then, wish to *Christ* I had. I was still two grand up. But I'd lost two grand and I thought it was just a blip, that if I kept my nerve I'd win it all back. *Fortune favors the brave,* I thought. *One more hand, it'll turn around . . .* Toad asked me if I wanted to drop out a couple of times, but . . . by then I was . . . I was . . ." Penhaligon's voice wobbles, ". . . ten thousand down."

"Wow, Jonny. Them's grown-up numbers."

"So, yeah, we carried on, and my losses piled up, and I didn't know why the King's College bells were ringing in the middle of the night, but Toad opened up the curtains and it was daylight. Toad said his casino was closing for the holidays. He offered to scramble eggs for us, but I wasn't hungry . . ."

"You win a few," I console him, "you lose a few. That's poker."

"No, Hugo, you don't get it. Eusebio took a hammering, but I took a . . . a pulverizing, and when Toad wrote down what I owe, it's"—a strangled whisper—"*fifteen thousand, two hundred.* Toad said he'll round it down to fifteen in the interest of nice round numbers, but . . ."

"Your sense of honor brings out the best in Toad," I assure him, peering through the blue velvet curtain. It's a cold, dark indigo, streetlight-amber night out. "He knows he's not dealing with an underclass scuzzball with a can't-pay-won't-pay attitude."

Penhaligon sighs. "That's the awkward thing, you see."

I act puzzled. "To be honest, I don't quite see, no."

"Fifteen thousand pounds is . . . is quite a lot. A shit of a lot."

"For a financial mortal like myself, sure—but not for old Cornish aristocracy, surely?"

"I don't actually have that much in . . . my main account."

"Oh. *Right.* Right! Look, I've known Toad since I got to Cambridge and, I promise you, there's nothing to worry about."

Penhaligon croaks a hope-tortured "Really?"

"Toad's cool. Tell him that, with the banks closed over Christmas, you can't transfer what you owe until the New Year. He knows that a Penhaligon's word is his bond."

Here it comes: "But I don't have fifteen thousand pounds."

Take a dramatic pause, add a dollop of confusion and a pinch of disbelief. "You mean . . . you don't have the money . . . *anywhere*?"

"Well . . . no. Not at present. If I could, I would, but—"

"Jonny. Stop. Jonny, these are your debts. *I* vouched for you. To Toad. I said, 'He's a Penhaligon,' and that was that. Enough said."

"Just because your ancestors were admirals and you live in a listed building, that doesn't make you a billionaire! Courtard's Bank owns Trevadoe House, not us!"

"Okay, *okay.* Just ask your mother to write you out a check."

"For a poker debt? Are you mad? She'd refuse point-blank. Look, what could Toad actually *do* if, y'know . . . that fifteen thousand . . ."

"No no no no no. Toad's a friendly chap but he's a businessman, and business trumps friendly chap–ness. Please. Pay."

"But it's only a poker game. It's not like . . . a legal contract."

"Debt's debt, Jonny. Toad believes you owe him this money, and I'm afraid I do too, and if you refuse to honor your debt, I'm afraid the gloves would come off. He wouldn't put a horse's head in your bed, but he'd involve your family and Humber College, which, by the by, would take a dim view of its good name being dragged through the gutter press."

Penhaligon hears his future, and it sounds like a bottle-bank heaved off the roof of a multistory car park. "Oh, shit. Shit. *Shit*."

"One possibility *does* occur to me—but, no, forget it."

"Right now, I'd consider anything. Anything."

"No, forget it. I already know what the answer would be."

"Spit it out, Hugo."

Persuasion is not about force; it's about showing a person a door, and making him or her desperate to open it. "That old sports car of yours, Jonny. An Alfa Romeo, is it?"

"It's a 1969 vintage Aston Martin Coda, but—sell it?"

"Unthinkable, I know. Better just to grovel at your mother's feet."

"But . . . the car was Dad's. He left it to me. *I* love it. How could I explain away a missing Aston Martin?"

"You're an inventive man, Jonny. Tell your family you'd prefer to liquidate your assets and put them in a steady offshore bond issue than tear up and down Devon and Cornwall in a sports car, even if it was your father's. Look—this just occurs to me now—there's a dealer in vintage cars here in Richmond. *Very* discreet. I *could* pop round before he closes for Christmas, and ask what sort of numbers we're talking."

A shuddered sigh from the chilblained toe of England.

"I guess that's a no," I say. "Sorry, Jonny, I wish I could—"

"No, okay. Okay. Go and see him. Please."

"And do you want to tell Toad what's happening or—"

"Could you call him? I—I don't think I . . . I don't . . ."

"Leave everything to me. A friend in need."

I DIAL TOAD's number from memory. His answering machine clicks on after a single ring. "Pirate's selling. I'm off to the Alps after Boxing Day, but see you in Cambridge in January. Merry Christmas." I hang up and let my eye travel over the bespoke bookshelves, the TV, Dad's drinks cabinet, Mum's blown-glass light fittings, the old map of Richmond-upon-Thames, the photographs of Brian, Alice, Alex, Hugo, and Nigel Lamb at a range of ages and stages. Their chatter reaches me like voices echoing down speaking tubes from another world.

"All fine and dandy, Hugo?" Dad appears in the doorway. "Welcome back, by the way."

"Hi, Dad. That was Jonny, a friend from Humber. Wanted to check next term's reading list for economics."

"Commendably organized. Well, I left a bottle of cognac in the boot of the car, so I'm just popping out to—"

"Don't, Dad—it's *freezing* out and you've still got a bit of a cold. My coat's there on the peg, let me fetch it."

"HERE WE ARE again," says a man, who appears as I shut the rear door of Dad's BMW, "in the bleak midwinter." I damn nearly drop the cognac. He's bundled in an anorak, and shadow from his hood, thrown by the streetlight, is covering his face. He's only a few paces from the pavement, but definitely on our drive.

"Can I help you?" I'd meant to sound firmer.

"We wonder." He lowers his hood and when I recognize the begging Yeti from Piccadilly Circus, the bottle of cognac slips from my grip and thumps onto my foot.

All I say is, "*You?* I . . ." My breath hangs white.

All he says is, "So it seems."

My voice is a croak. "Why—why did you follow me?"

He looks up at my parents' house, like a potential buyer. The Yeti's hands are in his pockets. There's room for a knife.

"I've got no more money to give you, if that's what—"

"I didn't come all this way for banknotes, Hugo."

I think back; I'm sure I didn't tell him my name. Why would I have done? "How do you know my name?"

"We've known it for a couple of years, now." His underclass accent's vanished without trace, I notice, and his diction's clear.

I peer at his face. An ex-classmate? "Who are you?"

The Yeti scratches his greasy head; he's got gloves with the finger-ends snipped off. "If you mean 'Who is the owner of this body?'

then, frankly, who cares? He grew up near Gloucester, has head lice, a heroin addiction, and a topical autoimmune virus. If you mean, 'With whom am I speaking?' then the answer is Immaculée Constantin, with whom you discussed the nature of power not very long ago. I know you remember me."

I take a step back; Dad's BMW's exhaust pipe pokes my calf. The Yeti of Piccadilly couldn't have even pronounced "Immaculée Constantin." "A setup. She prepped you, what to say, but how . . ."

"How could she have known which homeless beggar you would pay your alms to today? Impossible. And how could she know about Marcus Anyder? Think larger. Redraw what is possible."

In the next street along a car alarm goes off. "The security services. You're both—both part of . . . of . . ."

"Of a government conspiracy? Well, I suppose it's larger, but where does paranoia stop? Perhaps Brian and Alice Lamb are agents. Might Mariângela and Nurse Purvis be in on it? Maybe Brigadier Philby isn't as gaga as he appears. Paranoia is so all-consuming."

This is real. Look at the Yeti's footprints in the crusty snow. Smell his mulchy odor of sick and alcohol. Feel the cold biting my lips. You can't hallucinate these things. "What do you want?"

"To germinate the seed."

We stare at each other. He smells of greasy biscuit. "Look," I say, "I don't know what's happening here, or why she sent you, or why you'd pretend to be her . . . But Ms. Constantin needs to know she's made a mistake."

"What species of mistake have I made, exactly?" asks the Yeti.

"I don't want this. I'm not what you think I am. I just want a quiet Christmas and a quiet life with—"

"We know you better than that, Hugo Lamb. We know you better than you do." The Yeti makes a final amused grunt, turns, and walks down the drive. He tosses a "Merry Christmas" over his shoulder, and then he's gone.

ERE AN ALP, THERE AN ALP, everywhere an Alp-Alp. Torn, castellated, blue-white, lilac-white, white-white, scarred by rock faces, fuzzed by snowy woods … I've visited Chetwynd-Pitt's chalet often enough now to know the peaks' names: the fanglike Grande Dent de Veisivi; across the valley, Sasseneire, La Pointe du Tsaté, and Pointe de Bricola; and behind me, Palanche de la Cretta, taking up most of the sky. I drink in two lungfuls of iced atmosphere and airbrush modernity from all I survey. That airplane in the evening sunlight: gone. The lights of La Fontaine Sainte-Agnès, six hundred meters below: off. The chalets, bell tower, steep-roofed houses, not unlike a little wooden village I had as a kid: erased. The hulking Chemeville station—a seventies concrete turd—with its rip-off coffee shop and its discus-shaped platform where we four Humberites stand: demolished. The *télé-cabines* bringing up us skiers and the chair lifts going on up to the summit of Palanche de la Cretta: gone in a *pfff*! The forty or fifty or sixty skiers skiing downhill on the meandering blue run or the far steeper black route: *What skiers? I see no skiers.* Rufus Chetwynd-Pitt, Olly Quinn, and Dominic Fitzsimmons, nice knowing you. Up to a point. There. Now that's what I call medieval. Did La Fontaine Sainte-Agnès exist back then? That skinny girl in the mint-green ski suit leaning on the railing, smoking like all French girls smoke—is it on the school curriculum?—let her stay. Every Adam needs an Eve.

. . .

"WHAT SAY WE add a dash of glory to this run?" Rufus Chetwynd-Pitt lifts his £180 Sno-Fox ski goggles. "The three losers can pick up the winner's bar tab, from dawn till dusk. Takers?"

"Count me out," says Olly Quinn. "I'm taking the blue run down. I don't want to end my first day in the clinic."

"Hardly a fair contest," says Dominic Fitzsimmons. "You've skied here more often than you've siphoned your python."

"Grannies Quinn and Fitz have made their excuses." Chetwynd-Pitt turns to me. "What about the Lamb of Doom?"

Chetwynd-Pitt is a better skier than the rest of us, here or any-where else, and at Sainte-Agnès nightlife prices the "dash of glory" will cost me dearly, but I mime spitting on my palms. "May the best man win, Rufus." My logic is sound. If he wins the race, he'll bet more rashly at pool later, but if he takes a tumble and loses, he'll bet even more rashly later to restore his alpha-male credentials.

Chetwynd-Pitt grins and pulls down his Sno-Foxes. "Glad *some-one* has his balls stitched on. Fitz, you're our starter." We go to the top of the run, where Chetwynd-Pitt draws a notional starting line in the dirty snow with his pole. "First to the giant fluffy snowman at the end of the black run is the winner. No griping, no ifs, a direct race to the bottom, as one Etonian said to the other. We'll see *you* pair of delicate woollens"—he looks at Fitzsimmons and Quinn—"back at chez moi."

"Under starter's orders, then . . ." declares Fitzsimmons.

Me and Chetwynd-Pitt crouch like Winter Olympians.

"Ready, steady—*bang*!"

BY THE TIME I've settled into my crouch Chetwynd-Pitt is a snow-ball lob ahead. We barrel it down the first stretch, passing a wedge of Spanish kids who have chosen the middle of the run for a group photo. The run divides into two—blue to the right, black over a sharp lip to the left. Chetwynd-Pitt takes the latter and I follow, grunting at my poor landing a few meters later, but at least I stay upright. The old snow here is glassy but fast and my skis sound like knives being sharpened. I'm accelerating, but so is my opponent's black-and-orange-Lycra-clad arse as it passes the *télécabine* pylon. The run curves into the upper wood and the gradient steepens. At thirty, thirty-five, forty klicks an hour, the air scours my cheeks. The four of us zigzagged down this section this morning, but now Chetwynd-Pitt's taking it straight as a javelin—up to forty-five, fifty kph—as fast as I've ever gone on skis, my calves and thighs are aching, and the rushing air's howling in my ear canals. An unseen but vicious bump launches me for three, five, eight meters . . . I nearly lose it on landing, but just maintain my balance. Fall at this speed and your only protection against multiple breakages is blind luck. Chetwynd-Pitt disappears around a deep bend up ahead, fifteen seconds before I hit it, misjudging its sharpness and whipping through the overhanging claws of fir trees before wrenching myself back onto the piste. Here come the slalomlike snake-curves: I watch Chetwynd-Pitt weaving in and out of eyeshot; try to follow his angles of incidence; duck on reflex as crows bowl up the tunnel of branches. Suddenly out of the woods, I shoot onto the slower strip between a sheer flank of rock and a neck-breaking drop. Yellow diamond signs with skulls and crossbones warn you away from the edge. My rival slows down a little and glances back . . . He's stick-man-distant now, passing the Lonesome Pine on its finger of rock—the halfway point. Four or five minutes in now, surely. I straighten up to rest my stomach muscles and glimpse the town in its hollow below—see the Christmas-tree lights, in the plaza? My bastard goggles are starting to fog up, even though the salesgirl swore they wouldn't. Chetwynd-Pitt is already entering the lower woods, so I thrust with my poles as far as the Lonesome Pine, then settle back into my racing crouch. Soon I'm up to forty-five, fifty kph again, and I should ease off but the wind in my ears will speak if I dare to go faster, and the lower woods smother me and the tunnel's a blur and it's fifty-five, sixty, and I'm flying over a ridge with a savage dip beyond, and the ground's fallen away . . . And I soar like a stoner archangel . . . This freedom is eternal for as long as it lasts . . . Why are my feet level with my chin?

MY RIGHT FOOT hits the ground first, but my left one's gone AWOL, and I'm cartwheeling, my body mapped by local explosions of pain—ankle, knee, elbow—*shit,* my left ski's gone, whipped off, vamoosed—ground-woods-sky, ground-woods-sky, ground-woods-sky, a faceful of gravelly snow; dice in a tumbler; apples in a tumble dryer; a grunt, a groan, a plea, a *shiiiiiiiit* . . . Gravity, velocity, and the ground; stopping is going to cost a fortune and the only acceptable currency is *pain*—

OUCH. WRIST, SHIN, rib, butt, ankle, earlobe . . . Sore, walloped, sure . . . but unless I'm too doped on natural painkillers to notice, nothing's broken. Flat on my back in a crash-mat of snow, pine needles, and mossy, stalky mulch. I sit up. My spine still works. That's always useful. My watch is still working, and it's 16:10, just as it should be. Tiny silver needles of birdsong. Can I stand? I have an ache instead of a right buttock; and my coccyx feels staved in by a geologist's hammer . . . But, yes, I can stand, which makes this one of my luckiest escapes. I lift my goggles, brush the snow off my jacket, unclip the ski I still have and use it as a staff to hobble uphill, searching for its partner. One minute, two minutes, still no joy. Chetwynd-Pitt will be giving the fluffy snowman a victory punch down in the village just about now. I backtrack, searching through the undergrowth along the side of the piste. There's no dishonor in taking a fall on a black run—it's not as if I'm a professional or a ski instructor—but returning to chez Chetwynd-Pitt forty minutes after Fitzsimmons and Quinn with one ski missing would be, frankly, crap.

Here comes a whooshing sound—another skier—and I stand well back. It's the French girl from the viewing platform—who else wears mint green this season? She takes the rise as gracefully as I was ele-phantine, lands like a pro, sees me, takes in what's happened, straightens up, and stops a few meters away on the far side of the piste. She bends down to retrieve what turns out to be my ski and brings it over to me. I muster my mediocre French: "Merci . . . Je ne cherchais pas du bon côté."

"Rien de cassé?"

I think she's asking if I've broken anything. "Non. À part ma fi-erté, mais bon, ça ne se soigne pas."

She hasn't removed her goggles so, apart from a few loose strings of wavy black hair and an unsmiling mouth, my Good Samari-taness's face stays unseen. "Tu en as eu, de la veine."

I'm a jammy bugger? "Tu peux . . ." "Bloody well say that again," I'd like to say. "C'est vrai."

"Ça ne rate jamais: chaque année, il y a toujours un couillon qu'on vient ramasser à la petite cuillère sur cette piste. Il restera toute sa vie en fauteuil roulant, tout ça parce qu'il s'est pris pour un champion olympique. La prochaine fois, reste sur la piste bleu."

Jesus, my French is rustier than I thought: "Every year someone breaks their spine and I ought to stick to the blue piste"? Something like that? Whatever it was, she launches herself without a goodbye and she's gone, swooping through the curves.

BACK AT CHETWYND-PITT's chalet, floating in the tub, Nirvana's *Nevermind* thumping through the walls, I smoke a joint among the steam serpents and peruse the Case of the Body-Hopping Mind for the thousandth time. The facts are deceptively simple: Six nights ago, outside my parents' home, I encountered one mind in posses-sion of someone else's body. Weird shit needs theories and I have three.

Theory 1: I hallucinated both the second coming of the Yeti and his secondary proofs, like his footprints and those statements that only Miss Constantin—or I—could have known about.

Theory 2: I am the victim of a stunningly complex hoax, involving Miss Constantin and an accomplice who poses as a homeless man.

Theory 3: Things are exactly as they appear to be, and "mind-walking"—what else to call it?—is a real phenomenon.

The Hallucination Theory: "I don't feel insane" is a feeble retort, but I really don't. If I was hallucinating a character so vividly, surely I'd be hallucinating other things too? Like hearing, I don't know, Sting singing "An Englishman in New York" from inside light-bulbs.

The Complex Hoax Theory: "Why me?" Some people may hold a grudge against Marcus Anyder, if certain fictions were known. But why seek revenge via some wacky plot to loosen my grip on sanity? Why not just kick the living shit out of me?

The Mind-walking Theory: Plausible, *if* you live in a fantasy novel. Here, in the real world, souls stay inside the body. The paranormal is always, *always* a hoax.

Water drops go *plink, plink, plink* from the tap. My palms and fingers are pink and wrinkly. Someone's thumping upstairs.

So what do I do about Immaculée Constantin, the Yeti, and the weird shit? The only possible answer is "Nothing, for now." Perhaps I'll be served another slice tonight, or perhaps it's waiting for me back in London or Cambridge, or perhaps this will just be one of life's dangly plot lines that one never revisits. "Hugo?" It's Olly Quinn, bless him, knocking on the door. "You still alive in there?"

"Yes, the last time I checked," I shout, over Kurt Cobain.

"Rufus says we should get going before Le Croc fills up."

"You three go on ahead and get a table. I'll be along soon."

LE CROC—A.K.A. LE Croc of Shit to its regulars—is a badger's set of a drinking hole down an alley off the three-sided plaza in Sainte-Agnès. Günter, the owner, gives me a mock salute and points to the Eagle's Nest—a tiny mezzanine cubbyhole occupied by my three fellow Richmondians. It's gone ten, the place is chocka, and Günter's two *saisonniers*—one skinny girl in Hamlet black, the other plumper, frillier, and blonder—are busy with orders. Back in the 1970s Günter was ranked the 298th best tennis player in the world (for a week) and has a framed clipping to prove it. Now he supplies cocaine to wealthy Eurotrash, including Lord Chetwynd-Pitt's eldest scion. His Andy Warhol flop of bleached hair is stylistic self-immolation, but a Swiss-German drug dealer in his fifties does not welcome fashion advice from an Englishman. I order a hot red wine and climb to the Nest, past a copse of seven-foot Dutchmen. Chetwynd-Pitt, Quinn, and Fitzsimmons have eaten—Günter's daube, a beef stew, and a wedge of apple pie with cinnamon sauce—and have started on the cocktails which, thanks to my lost bet, I have the honor of buying for Chetwynd-Pitt. Olly Quinn's tanked and glassy-eyed. "Can't get my head round it," he's saying morosely. The boy's a crap drunk.

"Can't get your head round what?" I take off my scarf.

Fitzsimmons mouths, "Ness."

I mime hanging myself with my scarf, but Quinn doesn't notice: "We'd *planned* it. I'd drive her to Greenwich, she'd introduce me to Mater and Pater. I'd see her over Christmas, we'd go to Harrods for the sales, skate on the rink at Hyde Park Corner . . . It was all planned. Then that Saturday, after I took Cheeseman to hospital for his stitches, she calls me up and it's 'We've come to the end of the road, Olly.'" Quinn swallows. "I'm like . . . huh? *She* was all, 'Oh, it's not your fault, it's mine.' She said she's feeling conflicted, tied-down, and—"

"I know a Portuguese tart who enjoys that tying-down stuff, if that oils your rooster," says Chetwynd-Pitt.

"Misogynist *and* unfunny," says Fitzsimmons, inhaling vapors from his *vin chaud*. "Splitting up's an utter bitch."

Chetwynd-Pitt sucks a cherry. "Specially if you buy an opal necklace Christmas prezzie and get dumped before you can turn the gift into sex. Was it from Ratners Jewellers, Olly? They issue gift tokens for returned items, but not cash. Our groundsman had a wedding called off, that's how I know."

"No, it wasn't from bloody Ratners," growls Quinn.

Chetwynd-Pitt lets the cherry stone drop into the ashtray. "Oh cheer up, for shitsake. Sainte-Agnès plus New Year equals more Europussy than the Schleswig-Holstein Feline Rescue Society would know what to do with. And I'll bet you a thousand quid that the feeling-conflicted line means she's got another boyfriend."

"Not Ness, no way," I reassure poor Quinn. "She respects you— and herself—way too much. Trust me. And when Lou dumped *you*," this is for Chetwynd-Pitt, "you were a train wreck for months."

"Lou and I were serious. Olly 'n' Ness lasted what, all of five weeks? And Lou didn't dump me. It was mutual."

"Six weeks, four days." Quinn looks tortured. "But it's not time that matters. It felt . . . like a secret place just us two knew about." He drinks his obscure Maltese beer. "She *fitted* me. I don't know what love is, whether it's mystical or chemical or what. But when you have it, and it goes, it's like a . . . it's like . . . it's . . ."

"Cold turkey," says Rufus Chetwynd-Pitt. "Roxy Music were right about love being *the* drug, and when your supply's used up, no dealer on earth can help you. Well: There *is* one—the girl. But she's gone and won't see you. See? I *do* know what poor Olly's suffering. What I'd prescribe is"—he waggles his empty cocktail glass—"an Angel's Tit. Crème de cacao," he tells me, "and maraschino. Pile au bon moment, Mo*nique,* tu as des pouvoirs télépathiques." The plumper waitress arrives with my hot wine, and Chetwynd-Pitt deploys his smart-arse French: "Je prendrai une Alien Urine, et ce sera mon ami ici présent"—he nods at me—"qui réglera l'ardoise."

"Bien," says Monique, acting bubbly. "J'aimerais bien moi aussi avoir des amis comme lui. Et pour ces messieurs? Ils m'ont l'air d'avoir encore soif." Fitzsimmons orders a cassis, and Olly says, "Just another beer." Monique gathers the used dishes and glasses and off she's gone.

"Well, *I'd* fire my unsawn-off shotgun up *that,*" says Chetwynd-Pitt. "A cuddly six and a half. Yummier than that Wednesday Adams lookalike Günter's also taken on. Frightmare or what?" I follow his gaze down to the skinnier bargirl. She's filling a schooner of cognac. I ask if she's French, but Chetwynd-Pitt's asking Fitzsimmons, "You're the answer man tonight, Fitz. What's this love malarkey all about?"

Fitzsimmons lights a cigarette and passes us the box. "Love is the anesthetic applied by Nature to extract babies."

I've heard that line elsewhere. Chetwynd-Pitt flicks ash into the tray. "Can you do better than that, Lamb?"

I'm watching the skinny barmaid making what must be Chetwynd-Pitt's Alien Urine. "Don't ask me. I've never been in love."

"Oh, listen to the poor lamb," mocks Chetwynd-Pitt.

"That's crap," says Quinn. "You've had lots of girls."

Memory hands me a photo of Fitzsimmons's yummy mummy. "Anatomically, I have some knowledge, sure—but emotionally they're the Bermuda Triangle. Love, that drug Rufus referred to, that state of grace Olly pines for, that great theme . . . I'm immune to it. I have not once felt love for any girl. Or boy, for that matter."

"That's a pile of steaming bollocks," says Chetwynd-Pitt.

"It's the truth. I've never been in love. And that's okay. The color-blind get by just fine not knowing blue from purple."

"You can't have met the right girl," decides Quinn the idiot.

"Or met too many right girls," suggests Fitzsimmons.

"Human beings," I inhale my wine's nutmeggy steam, "are walking bundles of cravings. Cravings for food, water, shelter, warmth; sex and companionship; status, a tribe to belong to; kicks, control, purpose; and so on, all the way down to chocolate-brown bathroom suites. Love is one way to satisfy some of these cravings. But love's not just the drug; it's also the dealer. Love wants love in return, am I right, Olly? Like drugs, the highs look divine, and I envy the users. But when the side effects kick in—jealousy, the rages, grief, I think,

Count me out. Elizabethans equated romantic love with insanity. Buddhists view it as a brat throwing a tantrum at the picnic of the calm mind. I—"

"I spy an Alien Urine." Chetwynd-Pitt smirks at the skinny barmaid and the tall glass of melon-green gloop on her tray. "J'espère que ce sera aussi bon que vos Angel's Tits."

"Les boissons de ces messieurs." Lips thin and unlipsticked, with a "messieurs" that came sheathed in irony. She's gone already.

Chetwynd-Pitt sniffs. "There goes Miss Charisma 1991."

The others clink their glasses while I hide one of my gloves behind a pot-plant. "Maybe she just doesn't think you're as witty as you think you are," I tell Chetwynd-Pitt. "How does your Alien Urine taste?"

He sips the pale green gloop. "Exactly like its name."

THE TOURIST SHOPS in Sainte-Agnès's town square—ski gear, art galleries, jewelers, chocolatiers—are still open at eleven, the giant Christmas tree's still bright, and a *crêpier,* dressed as a gorilla, is doing a brisk trade. Despite the bag of coke Chetwynd-Pitt just scored off Günter, we decide to put off Club Walpurgis until tomorrow night. It's beginning to snow. "Damn," I say, turning back. "I left a glove at Le Croc. You guys get Quinn home, I'll catch you up . . ."

I hurry back down the alley and get to the bar as a large party of He-Norses and She-Norses leaves. Le Croc has a round window; through it I can see the skinny barmaid preparing a jug of Sangria without being seen. She's very watchable, like the motionless bass player in a hyperactive rock band. She combines a fuck-you punkishness with a precision about even her smallest actions. Her will would be absolutely unswayable, I sense. As Günter takes the jug away into Le Croc's interior she turns to look at me so I enter the smoky clamor and make my way between clusters of drinkers to the bar. After she's wiped the frothy head off a glass of beer with the flat of a knife and handed it to a customer, I'm there with my forgotten glove gambit. "Désolé de vous embêter, mais j'étais installé là-haut"—I point to the Eagle's Nest, but she doesn't yet give away whether or not she remembers me—"il y a dix minutes et j'ai oublié mon gant. Est-ce que vous l'auriez trouvé?"

Cool as Ivan Lendl slotting in a lob above an irate hobbit, she reaches down and produces it. "Bizarre, cette manie que les gens comme vous ont d'oublier leurs gants dans les bars."

Fine, so she's seen through me. "C'est surtout ce gant; ça lui arrive souvent." I hold up my glove like a naughty puppet and ask it scoldingly, "Qu'est-ce qu'on dit à la dame?" Her stare kills my joke. "En tout cas, merci. Je m'appelle Hugo. Hugo Lamb. Et si pour vous, ça fait"—shit, what's "posh" in French?—"chic, eh bien le type qui ne prend que des cocktails s'appelle Rufus Chetwynd-Pitt. Je ne plaisante pas." Nope, not a flicker. Günter reappears with a tray of empty glasses. "Why do you speak French with Holly, Hugo?"

I look puzzled. "Why wouldn't I?"

"He seemed keen to practice his French," says the girl, in London English. "And the customer *is* always right, Günter."

"Hey, Günter!" An Australian calls over from the bar football. "This bastard machine's playing funny buggers! I fed it my francs but it's not giving me the goods." Günter heads over, Holly loads up the dishwasher, and I work out what's happened. When she returned my ski on the black run earlier, she used French, but she said nothing when my accent gave me away because if you're female and working in a ski resort you must get hit on five times a day, and speaking French with Anglophones strengthens the force field. "I just wanted to say thanks for returning my ski earlier."

"You already did." Working-class background; unintimidated by rich kids; very good French.

"This is true, but I'd be dying of hypothermia in a lonely Swiss forest if you hadn't rescued me. Could I buy you dinner?"

"I'm working in a bar while tourists are eating their dinner."

"Then could I buy you breakfast?"

"By the time *you're* having breakfast, I'll have been mucking out this place for two hours, with two more hours to go." Holly slams shut the glass-washer. "Then *I* go skiing. Every minute spoken for. Sorry."

Patience is the hunter's ally. "Understood. Anyway, I wouldn't want your boyfriend to misinterpret my motives."

She pretends to fiddle with something under the counter. "Won't your friends be waiting for you?"

Odds of four to one there's no boyfriend. "I'll be in town for ten days or so. See you around. Good night, Holly."

"G'night," *and piss off,* add her spooky blue eyes.

THE BAYING OF THE PARISIAN MOB drains into the drone of a snowplow, and my search through French orphanages for the Cyclops-eyed child ends with Immaculée Constantin in my tiny room at the family Chetwynd-Pitt's Swiss chalet telling me gravely, *You haven't lived until you've sipped Black Wine, Hugo.* Then I'm waking up in the very same garret groinally attached to a mystifying dawn horn as big as a cruise missile. A bookshelf, a globe, a Turkish gown hanging from the door, a thick curtain. "This is where we put the scholarship boys," Chetwynd-Pitt only half joked when I first stayed here. The old pipe lunks and clanks. Dope + Altitude = Screwy Dreams. I lie in my warm womb, thinking about Holly the barmaid. I find I've forgotten Mariângela's face, if not other areas of her anatomy, but Holly's face I remember in photographic detail. I should have asked Günter for her surname. A little later, the bells of Sainte-Agnès's church chime eight times. There were bells in my dream. My mouth is as dry as lunar dust and I drink the glass of water on the bedside table, pleased by the sight of the wedge of francs by the lamp—my winnings from last night's pool session with Chetwynd-Pitt. *Ha.* He'll be eager to win the money back, and an eager player is a sloppy player.

I pee in my garret's minuscule en suite; hold my face in a sinkful of icy water for the count of ten; open the curtains and slatted shutters to let in the retina-drilling white light; hide last night's winnings under a floorboard I loosened two visits ago; perform a hundred push-ups; put on the Turkish gown and venture down the steep wooden stairs to the first landing, holding the rope banister. Chetwynd-Pitt's snoring in his room. The lower stairs take me to the sunken lounge, where I find Fitzsimmons and Quinn buried under tumuli of blankets on leather sofas. The VHS player has spat out *The Wizard of Oz,* but Pink Floyd's *Dark Side of the Moon* is still playing on repeat. Hashish perfumes the air and last night's embers glow in the fireplace. I tiptoe between two teams of Subbuteo soccer players, crunching crisps into the rug, and feed the fire a big log and crumbs of fire lighter. Tongues of flame lick and lap. A Dutch rifle from the Boer War hangs over the mantelpiece, whereon sits a silver-framed photograph of Chetwynd-Pitt's father shaking hands with Henry Kissinger in Washington, circa 1984. I'm pouring myself a grapefruit juice in the kitchen when the phone there discreetly trills: "Good morning," I say cutely. "Lord Chetwynd-Pitt the Younger's residence."

A male voice states, "Hugo Lamb. Got to be."

I know this voice. "And you are?"

"Richard Cheeseman, from Humber, you dolt."

"Bugger me. Not literally. How's your earlobe?"

"Fine fine fine, but listen, I've got serious news. I met—"

"Hang on, where are you? Not Switzerland?"

"Sheffield, at my sister's, but shut up and listen, this call's costing me a bollock a minute. I was speaking with Dale Gow last night, and he told me that Jonny Penhaligon's dead."

I didn't mishear. "*Our* Jonny Penhaligon? No fucking way."

"Dale Gow heard from Cottia Benboe, who saw it on the local news, *News South-West.* Suicide. He drove off a cliff, near Truro. Fifty yards from the road, through a fence, three-hundred-foot drop onto rocks. I mean . . . he wouldn't have suffered. Apart from whatever it was that drove him to do it, of course, and the . . . final drop."

I could weep. *All that money.* Through the kitchen window I watch the snowplow crawl by. A well-timed young priest follows, his cheeks pink and breath white. "That's . . . I don't know what to say, Cheeseman. Tragic. Unbelievable. Jonny! Of all people . . ."

"Same here. Really. The *last* person you'd expect . . ."

"Did he . . . Was he driving his Aston Martin?"

A pause. "Yeah, he was. How did you know?"

Be more careful. "I didn't, but that last night in Cambridge, at the Buried Bishop, he was saying how much he loved that car. When's the funeral?"

"This afternoon. I can't go—Felix Finch has got me tickets for an opera and I could never get to Cornwall in time—but maybe it's for the best. Jonny's family could do without an influx of strangers arriving at . . . at . . . wherever it is."

"Tredavoe. Did Penhaligon leave a note?"

"Dale Gow didn't mention one. Why?"

"Just thought it might shed a little light."

"More details will emerge at the inquest, I suppose."

Inquest? Details? Sweet shit. "Let's hope so."

"Tell Fitz and the others, will you?"

"God, yes. And thanks for phoning, Cheeseman."

"Sorry for putting a downer on your holiday, but I thought you'd prefer to know. Happy New Year in advance."

TWO P.M. THE passengers from the cable car pass through the waiting room of the Chemeville station, chattering in most of the major European languages, but she's not among them, so I direct my mind back to *The Art of War*. My mind has ideas of its own, however, and directs itself towards a Cornish graveyard where the skin-sack of toxic waste recently known as Jonny Penhaligon is joining its ancestors in the muddy ground. Like as not it's howling with rain, with an east wind clawing at the mourners' umbrellas and dissolving the words of "For Those in Peril on the Sea" Xeroxed yesterday onto sheets of A4. Nothing throws the chasm between me and normals into starker relief than grief and bereavement. Even at the tender age of seven, I was embarrassed by—and for—my own family when our dog Twix died. Nigel wept himself sore, Alex was more upset than he had been the time his Sinclair ZX Spectrum arrived minus its transformer, and my parents were morose for days. Why? Twix was out of pain. We no longer had to endure the farts of a dog with colon cancer. Same story when my grandfather died: a tearing-out of hair, gnashing of teeth, revisionism about what a Messiah the tight-arsed old sod had been. Everyone said I'd handled myself manfully at his funeral, but if they could have read my mind, they would have called me a sociopath.

Here's the truth: Who is spared love is spared grief.

GONE THREE P.M. Holly the barmaid sees me, frowns, and slows: a promising start. I close *The Art of War*. "Fancy meeting you here."

Skiers stream by, behind her and between us. She looks around. "Where are your highly amusing friends?"

"Chetwynd-Pitt, which rhymes with Angel's Tit, I notice—"

"As well as 'piece of shit' and 'sexist git,' *I* notice."

"I'll file that away. Chetwynd-Pitt's hungover, and the other two passed through about an hour ago, but I slipped on my ring of invisibility, knowing that my chances of sharing your ski lift up to the top"—I twirl my index finger towards Palanche de la Cretta's summit—"would be a big fat zero if they were here too. I was embarrassed by Chetwynd-Pitt last night. He was crass. But I'm not."

Holly considers this and shrugs. "None of it matters."

"It does to me. I was hoping to go skiing with you."

"And that's why you've been sitting here since . . ."

"Since eleven-thirty. Three and a half hours. But don't feel obligated."

"I don't. I just think you're a bit of a plonker, Hugo Lamb."

So my name has sunk in. "We're all of us different things at different times. A plonker now, something nobler at other times. Don't you agree?"

"Right now I'd describe you as a borderline stalker."

"Tell me to sod off and off I will duly sod."

"What girl could resist? Sod off."

I do an urbane as-you-wish bow, stand, and slip *The Art of War* into my ski jacket. "Sorry for embarrassing you." I head out.

"Oy." It's a lightening more than a softening. "Who says *you're* capable of embarrassing *me*?"

I knock-knock my forehead. "Would 'Sorry for finding you interesting' go down any better?"

"A certain type of girl after a holiday romance would lap it up. Those of us who work here get a bit jaded."

Machinery clanks and a big engine whines as the down-bound cable-car begins its journey. "I understand that you need armor, working in a bar where Europe's Chetwynd-Pitts come to play. But jadedness runs through you, Holly, like a second nervous system."

An incredulous little laugh. "You don't know me."

"*That's* the weird part: I know I don't know you. So how come I feel like I do?"

She does an exasperated grunt. "There's *rules* . . . You don't talk to someone you've known five minutes like you've known them for years. Bloody stop it."

I hold up my palms. "Holly, if I am an arrogant twat, I'm a harmless arrogant twat." I think of Penhaligon. "Virtually harmless. Look, would you let me share your ski lift up to the next station? It's, what, seven, eight minutes? If I turn into a date from hell, it'll soon be over—no no no, I know, *not* a date, it's a shared ski chair. Then we'll arrive and, with one expert thrust of your ski poles, I'm history. Please. Please?"

THE SKI LIFT guy clicks our rail into place, and I resist a joke about being swept off my feet as Holly and I are swept off our feet. December 30 has lost its earlier clarity and the summit of the Palanche de la Cretta is hidden in cloud. I follow the ski lift cable from pylon to pylon up the mountainside. The ravine opens up below us and, as I'm mugged by vertigo and grip the bar, my testicles run and hide next to my liver. Forcing myself to look down at the distant ground,

I wonder about Penhaligon's final seconds. Regret? Relief? Blank terror? Or did his head suddenly fill with "Babooshka" by Kate Bush? Two crows fly beneath our feet. They mate for life, my cousin Jason once told me. I ask Holly, "Do you ever have flying dreams?"

Holly looks dead ahead. Her goggles hide her eyes. "No."

We've cleared the ravine again and pass sedately over a wide swath of the piste we'll be skiing down later. Skiers curve, speed, and amble downhill to Chemeville station.

"Conditions look better after last night's snow," I say.

"Yeah. This mist's getting thicker by the minute, though."

That is true; the mountain peak is blurry and gray now. "Do you work at Sainte-Agnès every winter?"

"What is this? A job interview?"

"No, but my telepathy's a bit rusty."

Holly explains: "I used to work at Méribel over in the French Alps for a guy who knew Günter from his tennis days. When Günter needed a discreet employee, I got offered a transfer, a pay hike, and a ski pass."

"Why ever would Günter need a discreet employee?"

"Not a clue—and, no, I don't touch drugs. The world's unstable enough without scrambling your brain for kicks."

I think of Madam Constantin. "You're not wrong."

Empty ski chairs migrate from the mist ahead. Behind us, Chemeville is fading from view, and nobody's following us up. "Wouldn't it be freaky," I think aloud, "if we saw the dead in the chairs opposite?"

Holly gives me a weird look. "Not dead as in undead, with bits dropping off," I hear myself trying to explain. "Dead as in your own dead. People you knew, who mattered to you. Dogs, even." Or Cornishmen.

The steel-tube-and-plastic chair squeaks. Holly's chosen to ignore my frankly bizarre question, and to my surprise asks this: "Are you from one of those army-officer families?"

"God, no. My dad's an accountant and Mum works at Richmond Theatre. Why do you ask?"

" 'Cause you're reading a book called *The Art of War.*"

"Oh, that. I'm reading Sun Tzu because it's three thousand years old, and every CIA agent since Vietnam has studied it. Do you read?"

"My sister's the big reader, really, and sends me books."

"How often do you go back to England?"

"Not so often." She fiddles with a Velcro glove strap. "I'm not one of those people who'll spill their guts in the first ten minutes. Okay?"

"Okay. Don't worry, that just means you're sane."

"I *know* I'm sane, and I wasn't worried."

Awkward silence. Something makes me look over my shoulder; five ski chairs behind sits a solo passenger in a silver parka with a black hood. He sits with his arms folded, his skis making a casual X. I look ahead again, and try to think of something intelligent to say, but I seem to have left all my witty insights at the ski-lift station below.

AT THE PALANCHE de la Cretta station, Holly slides off the chairlift like a gymnast, and I slide off like a sack of hammers. The ski-lift guy greets Holly in French, and I slope off out of earshot. I find I'm waiting for the skier in the silver parka to appear from the fast-flowing mist; I count a twenty-second gap between each ski chair, so he'll be here in a couple of minutes, at most. Odd thing is, he never arrives. With mild but rising alarm, I watch the fifth, sixth, seventh chairs after us arrive without a passenger . . . By the tenth, I'm worried—not so much that he's fallen off the ski chair, but that he wasn't there in the first place. The Yeti and Madam Constantin have shaken my faith in my own senses, and I don't like it. Finally a pair of jolly bear-sized Americans appear, thumping to earth with gusts of laughter and needing the ski-lift guy's help. I tell myself the skier behind us was a false memory. Or I dreamt him. Holly joins me at the lip of the run, marked by flags disappearing into cloud. In a perfect world, she'll say, *Look, why don't we ski down together?*

"Okay," she says, "this is where I say goodbye. Take care, stay between the poles, and no heroics."

"Will do. Thanks for letting me hitch a ride up."

She shrugs. "You must be disappointed."

I lift my goggles so she can see my eyes, even if she won't show me hers. "No. Not in the least. Thank you." I'm wondering if she'd tell me her surname if I asked. I don't even know that.

She looks downhill. "I must seem unfriendly."

"Only guarded. Which is fair enough."

"Sykes," she says.

"I'm sorry?"

"Holly Sykes, if you were wondering."

"It . . . suits you."

Her goggles hide her face but I'm guessing she's puzzled.

"I don't quite know what I meant by that," I admit.

She pushes off and is swallowed by the whiteness.

THE PALANCHE DE la Cretta's middle flank isn't a notorious descent, but stray more than a hundred meters off-piste to the right and you'll need near-vertical skiing skills or a parachute, and the fog's so dense that I take my own sweet time and stop every couple of minutes to wipe my goggles. About fifteen minutes down, a boulder shaped like a melting gnome rears from the freezing fog by the edge of the piste. I huddle in its leeward side to smoke a cigarette. It's quiet. Very quiet. I consider how you don't get to choose whom you're attracted to, you only get to wonder about it, retrospectively. Racial differences I've always found to have an aphrodisiac effect on me, but class difference is sexuality's Berlin Wall. Certainly, I can't read Holly Sykes as well as I can girls from my own income-tax tribe, but you never know. God made the whole Earth in six days, and I'm in Switzerland for nine or ten.

A group of skiers weave past the granite gnome, like a school of fluorescent fish. None notices me. I drop my cigarette butt and follow in their wake. The jolly Texans either decided they'd bitten off more than they could chew and went back down on the ski lift, or they're following at an even more cautious pace than mine. No skier in a silver parka, either. Soon the fog thins, crags, ridges, and contours sketch and shade themselves in, and by the time I reach Chemeville station I'm under the cloud rafters again. I line my innards with a hot chocolate, then take the gentler blue piste down to La Fontaine Sainte-Agnès.

"WELL WELL WELL, the talented Mr. Lamb." Chetwynd-Pitt's making garlic bread in the kitchen, or trying to. It's gone five o'clock but he's still in his dressing gown. A cigar is balanced across a wine glass and George Michael's *Listen Without Prejudice* is on the CD player. "Olly and Fitz went off in search of you two or three hours ago."

"It's a big old massif. Needles, haystacks, and all that."

"And where did your Alpine foray take you aujourd'hui?"

"Up to Palanche de la Cretta, then cross-country. No more nasty black pistes for me. How's your hangover?"

"How was Stalingrad in 1943? The hair of the dog: ouzo on ice." He jiggles a small glass of milky liquid and knocks back half.

"Ouzo always reminds me of sperm." I wish I had a camera as Chetwynd-Pitt swallows the stuff. "Tactless. Sorry."

He glares at me, puffs on his cigar, and returns to chopping garlic. I fish in a drawer. "Try this revolutionary device: the 'garlic-crusher.'"

Now Chetwynd-Pitt glares at the implement. "The housekeeper must have bought it before we arrived."

I used it here last year, but never mind. I wash my hands and turn on the oven, which Chetwynd-Pitt had not. "C'mon, make way." I squeeze the garlicky pulp into the butter.

Grumpy but glad, Chetwynd-Pitt parks his arse on the counter. "I suppose it's compensation for fleecing me at pool."

"You'll get your revenge." Pepper, parsley, stir with a fork.

"I've been thinking about why he did it."

"I gather we're talking about Jonny Penhaligon?"

"There's more to this than meets the eye, Lamb."

My fork stops: His gaze is . . . accusing? A code of *omertà* operates at Toad's, but no code can be 100 percent secure. "Go on." Absurdly, I find myself scanning the kitchen for a murder weapon. "I'm all ears."

"Jonny Penhaligon was a victim of privilege."

"Okay." My fork's stirring again. "Elaborate."

"A pleb is someone who thinks privilege is about living off the fat of the land and getting chambermaids to nosh you. Truth is, blue blood's a serious curse in this day and age. First off, the great unwashed laugh at you for having too many syllables in your name *and* blame you, personally, for class inequality, the deforestation of the Amazon, and the price of beer going up. The second curse is marriage: How can I know if it's me my future wife loves—as opposed to my eleven hundred acres of Buckinghamshire and the title Lady Chetwynd-Pitt? Third, my future is shackled to estate management. Now, if *you* want to be a broker earning gazillions or an Antarctic archaeologist or a zero-gravity vibraphonist, it's 'If you're happy we're happy, Hugo.' Me, I've tenants to keep afloat, charities to sponsor, and a seat in the House of Lords to fill one day."

I fork garlic butter into grooves in the bread. "My heart bleeds. You're, what, sixty-third in line to the throne?"

"Sixty-fourth, now whatsisname's born. But I'm serious, Hugo, and I haven't finished: The fourth curse is the county hunt. I bloody *hate* beagles, and horses are moody quad-bikes that piss on your boot and cost thousands in vets' fees. And the fifth curse is the kicker: the dread that *you*'ll be the one who loses it all. Start out in life as a social nobody, like you and Olly—no offense—and the only direction you can go is up. Start off with your name in the Domesday Book, like me and Jonny, and the only direction is down the sodding crapper. It's like an intergenerational pass-the-parcel with bankruptcy instead of a tube of Rolos, and whoever's alive when the money dries up gets to be the Chetwynd-Pitt who has to learn how to assemble flat-pack furniture from Argos."

I wrap the garlic bread in foil. "And you reckon this posy of curses was what made Jonny drive off a cliff?"

"That," says Rufus Chetwynd-Pitt, "and the fact he had nobody to call in his darkest hour. Nobody to trust."

I put the tray into the oven and crank up the heat.

ICICLES ARE DRIPPING all down the alley, catching the slanted sun. There's a barstool propping open the door of Le Croc, and inside Holly is hoovering, attired in baggy army trousers, a white T-shirt, and a khaki baseball cap, which doubles as a ponytail scrunchie. A droplet from an icicle above finds the gap between my coat and my neck and sizzles between my shoulder blades. Holly senses me and turns. As the Hoover's groan dies, I say, "Knock-knock."

She recognizes me. "We're not open. Come back in nine hours."

"You say, 'Who's there?' It's a knock-knock joke."

"I refuse even to open the door, Hugo Lamb."

"But it's already a *bit* open. And look," I hold up the paper bags from the patisserie, "breakfast. Surely Günter has to let you eat?"

"Some of us had breakfast two hours ago, Poshboy."

"If you go to Richmond Boys College you get ridiculed for the crime of not being posh *enough*. How about a midmorning snackette, then?"

"Le Croc doesn't clean itself."

"Don't Günter and your colleague ever help?"

"Günter's the owner, Monique's hired just as bar staff. They'll be wrapped up in each other until after lunch. Literally, as it happens: Günter left his third wife a few weeks ago. So the privilege of sloshing out the sty falls to the manager."

I look around. "Where's the manager?"

"You're looking at her, y'eejit. Me."

"Oh. Then if Poshboy does the men's lavvy, will you take a twenty-minute break?"

Holly hesitates. A part of her wants to say yes. "See that long thing? It's called a mop. You hold the pointy end."

"TOLD YOU IT was a sty." Like a time traveler operating her machine, Holly pulls the handles and swivels the valves of the chrome coffeemaker. It hisses, belches, and gurgles.

I wash my hands and take a couple of barstools off a table. "That was one of the most disgusting things I've ever done. Men are pigs. They wipe their arses, then *miss* the toilet bowl, and just leave the scrunched-up shitty tissue where it fell. And the splattered puke in the last cubicle—*nice*. Vomit sets if it's just left there. Like Polyfilla."

"Switch your nose off. Breathe with your mouth." She brings over a cappuccino. "And someone had to clean every toilet you've ever used. If your dad had run a pub instead of a bank, like mine did, it might've been you. Thought for the Day."

I take out an almond croissant and slide the other bags to Holly. "Why don't you do the cleaning the night before?"

Holly unravels the edge of an apricot pastry. "Günter's regulars don't piss off till three in the morning, if I'm lucky. *You* try facing the cleaning at that time after nine hours' worth of serving drinks."

I concede the point. "Well, the bar's looking battle-ready now."

"Sort of. I'll clean the taps later, then restock."

"There was I, thinking bars just ran themselves."

She lights a cigarette. "I'd be out of a job if they did."

"Do you see yourself in, uh, hospitality long-term?"

Holly's frown is a warning. "What's it to you?"

"I just . . . Dunno. You seem capable of doing *anything*."

Her frown is both wary and weary. She taps ash from her cigarette. "The schools the lower orders go to don't exactly encourage you to think that way. Hairdressing courses or garage apprenticeships were more the thing."

"You can't blame a crap school forever, though."

She taps her cigarette. "You're clever, obviously. But there are some areas where you really don't know shit, Mr. Lamb."

I nod and sip my coffee. "Your French teacher was brilliant."

"My French teacher was nonexistent. I picked it up on the job. Survival. Fending off Frenchmen."

I dig a bit of almond from my teeth. "So where's the pub?"

"What pub?"

"The one your dad works in."

"Owns. Co-owns, in fact, with my mam. It's the Captain Marlow, by the Thames at Gravesend."

"Sounds picturesque. Is that where you grew up?"

"'Gravesend' and 'picturesque' don't exactly waltz around arm in arm. It's a lot of closed-down factories, paper mills, Blue Circle cement works, council estates, pawn shops, and bookies."

"It can't all be misery and postindustrial decay."

She searches the bottom of her cup. "The older streets are nice, I s'pose. The Thames is always the Thames, and the Captain Marlow's three centuries old—apparently there's a letter by Charles Dickens that proves he used to drink there. How 'bout that, Poshboy? A literary reference."

My blood's zinging with coffee. "Is your mum Irish?"

"What leads you to that deduction, Sherlock?"

"You said 'with my mam,' not 'with my mum.'"

Holly exhales a fat loop of smoke. "Yeah, she's from Cork. Don't your friends get annoyed when you do that?"

"Do what?"

"Sifting what they say for clues instead of listening."

"I'm a detail nerd, that's all. Have you started the clock on my twenty minutes, by the way?"

"You're down to"—she checks—"sixteen."

"Then I'd like to spend the remainder playing bar football."

Holly scrunches her face. "Bad idea."

I never know if she's serious. "How come?"

"'Cause I'll scalp your arse, Poshboy."

. . .

THE TOWN SQUARE is patchy with melting snow and busy with shoppers, and a red-cheeked brass band's playing carols. I buy a fund-raising calendar from some school kids and their teacher at a stall by the statue of St. Agnès, and get a chorus of "Merci, Monsieur!" and "Happy New Year," because my accent tells them I'm English. Holly Sykes did indeed scalp my arse at bar football; she scored rebound goals off the sides, she can lob, and her left-handed goalie's a lethal weapon. She didn't smile but I think she enjoyed her victory. We made no plans, but I said I'd drop by the bar tonight, and instead of answering Eeyore-ishly or sarcastically, she just said I'd know where to find her. Stunning progress, and I almost fail to recognize Olly Quinn in the phone box by the bank. He's looking agitated. If he's using a phone box instead of Chetwynd-Pitt's phone, he doesn't want to be overheard. Would I be fully human if curiosity didn't get the better of me occasionally? I hide behind the solid wall of the booth where Olly can't see me. Thanks to a bad line and his angst, Olly's voice is loud and every punched-out sentence is pretty clear. "You *did,* Ness. You *did*! You said you loved me too! You said—"

Oh dear. Despair is as attractive as cold sores.

"Seven times. The first was in bed. I remember . . . Maybe it was six, maybe eight, who cares, Ness, I . . . So what's that about, Ness? Was it one big lie? . . . Then was it some—some mind-fucking experiment?"

Too late to slam on the brakes now; we're over the edge.

"No no no, I'm *not* getting hysterical, I just . . . No, I'm *not,* I don't get what happened, so . . . What? What was that last bit? This line's shit . . . No, not what *you* said—I said the *phone* line's shit . . . What's that? You *thought* you meant it?"

Olly punches the glass of the phone box, hard. "How can you *think* you love someone? . . . No, Ness, no, no—don't hang up. Look. Just . . . I want things back to how we were, Ness! . . . But if you'd explain, if you'd talk, if you'd . . . I *am* calm. I'm calm. No, Ness! No no no—"

A phony peace, then an explosive *"Fuck* it!"

Quinn hammers his fist on the glass a few times. This attracts attention, so I slip back into the stream of shoppers and loop back around the way I came, sideways as I pass, for long enough to see my lovesick classmate folded over, hiding his face in his hands. Crying—in public! The unedifying sight sobers me a tad with regard to Holly. Remember: What Cupid gives, Cupid takes away.

THE AUSTRIAN-ETHIOPIAN DJ is silent and hooded, won't take requests, and, in the last hour alone, has loped through remixes of the KLF's "3 A.M. Eternal," Phuture's "Your Only Friend," and the Norfolklorists' "Ping Pong Apocalypse." Club Walpurgis is housed in the basement annex of the vast and elderly Hôtel Le Sud, a six-floor, hundred-room angular labyrinth converted in the 1950s from a sanatorium for the tubercular and very wealthy. A recent refit has stripped Club Walpurgis down to a bare-brick Bowie-in-Berlin look, and expanded the dance floor to the size of a tennis court. Submarine lights are strobing and a decent percentage of the two to three hundred dancing skeletons clad in young flesh and high-end apparel is young and female. A snort or two of devil's dandruff has reerected the Mighty Quinn from his emotional crash earlier, so all four of us have come clubbing. Unusually, I'm the only one who isn't in the act of pulling; my three fellow Humberites are sitting on a horseshoe-shaped sofa, each nursing a young, attractive black girl. No doubt Chetwynd-Pitt is playing his nineteenth-in-line-to-the-throne card—the drunker he gets, the bluer his blood—Fitzsimmons is flashing his francs, and presumably Quinn's squeeze just finds him cute and fluffy. Fair play to them all. Any other night I'd go fishing too, and I won't pretend my Alpine glow, Rupert Everett sultriness, charcoal Harry Enna shirt, and Makoto Grelsch jeans wrapping my rower's torso aren't drawing long-lashed attention, but this New Year's Eve I'd rather get blown by a dance track. Could

I be on to a Temptation of Christ deal whereby an act of continence at Club Walpurgis tonight earns me credit in the Bank of Karma to be redeemed by a certain girl from Gravesend? Only Dr. Coke has the answer, and after this archangelic remix of "Walking on Thin Ice" by somebody or other, I'll go and consult with the good medicine man . . .

THE CUBICLES IN the Gents are as commodious as Le Bog du Croc is not, and seemingly designed for the insufflation of cocaine: frequently cleaned, spacious, and sans that incriminating gap between the top of the door and the ceiling so common in British clubs. I seat myself upon the throne and produce my compact mirror—borrowed from an elfin Filipina who was angling for a spouse's visa—and Foo Foo Dust, won from Chetwynd-Pitt at blackjack this very night and stored in a little plastic wrapper inside a bag of menthol Fisherman's Friends to confuse any canine investigators in the unlikely event . . . My tooter is a straw made from coarse paper and Sellotape. With superb precision I deposit the last of my coke in a swirl on the mirror and—kids, don't try this at home, don't try it anywhere, Drugs Are Bad—toke it up my left nostril in a powerful snort. For five seconds it stings like a nettle being threaded down my throat via my nose, until . . .

We have liftoff.

The bass is reverberating in my bones and godalmightythat'sgood. I flush the paper straw away, dampen a sheet of loo paper in the cascade, and wipe my mirror clean. Tiny lights I can't quite see pin-prick the hedges of my field of vision. I emerge from the cubicle like the Son of God rolling away the stone, and inspect myself in the mirror—all good, even if my pupils are more *Varanus komodoensis* than *Homo sapiens*. Exiting the bogs, I encounter an Armani-clad stoner known as Dominic Fitzsimmons. He smoked a joint earlier, and his habitual sharp-wittedness has bungee-jumped from the bridge and is yet to return. "Hugo, what's a shit like you doing in a nice place like this?"

"Powdering my nose, dear Fitz."

He peers up my nostril. "Looks like a blizzard blew in." He does a melted grin and I can't help but think of his mother wearing the same smile and nothing else. "We met *girls,* Hugo. One for CP, one for Olly, one for moi. Come and say hello."

"You know how shy I am around women."

He finds this too funny to laugh at. "Pants—on—*fire.*"

"Really, Fitz, no one loves a gooseberry. Who are they?"

"This is the best part. Okay. Remember that African pop song "Yé Ké Yé Ké"? Summer of . . . 1988, I think. Massive hit."

"Uh . . . Not well, but yeah. What's his name—Mory Kanté?"

"*We* are a-wooing Mory Kanté's backing singers."

"*Riiiiight.* And doesn't Mory Kanté need them tonight?"

"They did a big gig last night in Geneva, but tonight they're free and they've never learned to ski—lack of snow in Algeria, I pre-sume—so they've all come to Sainte-Agnès for two or three days to learn."

I find this story semi-plausible, more semi than plausible, but be-fore I can voice my skepticism Chetwynd-Pitt rocks up. "It's the season of *lurrrve* back at chez CP. There's a still a slab of Gruyère in the fridge for you to impregnate, Lamb, so you won't feel left out."

Southern Comfort, cocaine, and horniness turns my old friend Chetwynd-Pitt into an A1 shithead and compels me to retaliate: "I don't want to shit in your baguette, Rufus, but hasn't it occurred to you you're pulling a trio of tarts? They have that air of paid sex about them. I'm only asking."

"You *may* be better at cheating at cards than us but tonight you've failed to pull." Chetwynd-Pitt pokes my chest and I imagine ripping off the offending index finger. "*We've* got three dusky maid-ens zero-to-gagging for it in less than sixty minutes, so Lamb de-cides we're paying them. Well, actually, *no,* they're discerning women, so you'd better put your earplugs in: Shandy's a screamer, I can tell."

I can't let that pass: "I *don't* fucking cheat at cards."

"Oh, I believe you *do* fucking cheat at cards, Scholarship Boy."

"Take your finger off my chest, Gaylord Chetwynd-Pitt, and prove it."

"Oh, you're too fucking clever to leave proof, but year in, year out, you've fleeced your friends for thousands. Intestinal parasite."

"If you're so sure I cheat, *Rufus,* why do you play me?"

"I won't again, and in-fucking-fact, Lamb, why don't—"

"Guys, guys," says Fitz the stoned peacemaker, "this isn't you; it's Colombian snort or whatevertheshit it was that Günter sold you. C'mon, c'mon, *c'mon*! Switzerland! New Year's Eve! Shandy's into lovers, not fighters. Kiss and make up."

"Cheat-boy can kiss my fat one," mutters Chetwynd-Pitt, pushing past me. "Get our coats, Fitz. Tell the girls it's afterparty time."

The door to the Gents swings behind us. "He didn't mean it," said Fitzsimmons, apologetically.

I hope not. For several reasons, I hope not.

I STAY ON the dance floor for DJ Aslanski's remix of Damon MacNish's mid-eighties anthem "Exocets for Breakfast," but Chetwynd-Pitt's parting shot has disfigured my night by shaking my faith in the whole Marcus Anyder project. I created Anyder not only as fake account holder to own and obscure my ill-gotten gains, but to be a better, sharper, truer version of Hugo Lamb. But if a privileged clot like Chetwynd-Pitt can see through me so easily, I'm not as clever and Anyder isn't as hidden as I've believed up until now. And even if I am a master dissembler, so what? So what if I join a City firm in eight months, and stab and bluff my way to a phone-number income within two years? So what if I own a Maserati convertible, a villa in the Cyclades, and a yacht in Poole harbor by the turn of the century? So what if Marcus Anyder builds his own empire of stocks, properties, portfolios? Empires die, like all of us dancers in the strobe-lit dark. *See how the light needs shadows.* Look: Wrinkles spread like mildew over our peachy sheen; beat-by-beat-by-beat-by-beat-by-beat-by-beat, varicose veins worm through plucked calves; torsos and breasts fatten and sag; behold Brigadier

Philby, French kissing with Mrs. Bolitho; as last year's song hurtles into next year's song and the year after that, and the dancers' hairstyles frost, wither, and fall in irradiated tufts; cancer spatters inside this tarry lung, in that aging pancreas, in this aching bollock; DNA frays like wool, and down we tumble; a fall on the stairs, a heart attack, a stroke; not dancing but twitching. This is Club Walpurgis. They knew it in the Middle Ages. Life is a terminal illness.

PAST THE QUEUE for the gorilla-man's *crêperie* on the plaza, under lights strung between the spiky pines, through air shimmering with bells and cold as mountain streams, my feet know the way, and it's not back to family Chetwynd-Pitt's Swiss chalet. I take off my gloves to light a cigarette. My watch says 23:58. All Praise the God of Perfect Timing. After giving way to a police 4x4—its snow chains clink, sleigh-bell-like—I walk down the narrow alley to Le Croc and peer in through the round window at the scrum of natives, visitors, and shady in-betweeners; Monique's fixing drinks but Holly's not in eyeshot. I go in anyway, and ease myself through flesh, jackets, smoke, chatter, clatter, and phrases of Herbie Hancock's *Maiden Voyage*. No sooner do I reach the bar than Günter turns down the volume and clambers onto a stool, whirling a soccer rattle for attention. Our host points at the large clock with the handle of a tennis racket: Less than twenty seconds remain of the old year. "Mesdames et messieurs, Herr und Herren, ladies and gentlemen, signore e signori—le countdown, s'il vous-plaît . . ." I'm allergic to choruses so I abstain, but as the unified clientele reaches five I feel her eyes pulling mine down from the clock and we watch each other like kids playing a game where the first one to smile loses. A lunatic cheering breaks out, and I lose the game. Holly pours a measure of Kilmagoon over a single cube of ice and slides it my way. "What mystery object did you forget this time?"

I tell her, "Happy New Year."

THIS MORNING I WAKE in my garret at Chetwynd-Pitt's, knowing that the phone in the lounge, two floors down, will ring in sixty seconds and that the caller will be my father, with bad news. Obviously it won't; obviously it's the dregs of a dream—otherwise I'd have powers of precognition, which I don't. Obviously. What if Dad's calling about Penhaligon? What if Penhaligon blabbed in his suicide note, and an officer from Truro has spoken to Dad? Obviously this is postcocaine paranoia, but just in case, *just* in case, I get up, slip into the Turkish dressing gown, and go down to the sunken lounge where the phone sits silent, and will stay silent, obviously. Miles Davis's *In a Silent Way* dribbles out of Chetwynd-Pitt's room, no doubt to beef up his wigga credentials. The lounge is empty of bodies but full of debris: wineglasses, ashtrays, food wrappers, and a pair of silk boxer shorts over the Boer War rifle. When I got home last night, the Three Musketeers and their backing singers were frolicky and high, so I went straight to bed.

Perching on the back of the sofa, I watch the phone.

09:36, says the clock. 08:36 in the U.K.

Dad's peering over his glasses at the number I left.

+36 for Switzerland; the area code; the chalet's number . . .

Yes, I'll say, *Jonny did play cards from time to time.*

Just a bunch of friends. Relaxation, after a long week.

Absolute tops was fifty pounds a sitting, though. Beer money.

How much? Thousands? I'll laugh, once, in disbelief.

That's not relaxation, Dad. That's lunacy. I mean . . .

He must have fallen in with another bunch altogether.

09:37. The molded plastic phone sits innocuously.

If it doesn't ring by 09:40, I've been scaring myself . . .

09:45 AND ALL'S well. Thank Christ. I'll lay off the cocaine for a while—maybe longer. Didn't the Yeti warn me about paranoia? An orange-juice breakfast and a vigorous ski from Pointe les Hlistes will flush last night's toxins away, so—

The phone rings. I grab it. "Dad?"

"Morning . . . Hugo? Is that you?"

Damn it, it *is* Dad. "Dad! How are you?"

"A bit startled. How the Dickens did you know it was me?"

Good question. "There's a display on Rufus's phone," I lie. "So, uh, Happy New Year. Is everything okay?"

"Happy New Year to you too, Hugo. Can we talk?"

I notice Dad's subdued tone. Something's up. "Fire away."

"Well. The damnedest thing happened yesterday. I was watching the business news at lunch when I had a phone call from a police detective—a lady detective, no less—at Scotland Yard."

"Good God." *Think think think,* but nothing joins up.

"One Superintendent Sheila Young from the Art and Antiques Recovery Division. I had no idea such a thing existed, but apparently if Monet's *Water Lilies* gets stolen, say, it's their job to get it back."

Either Bernard Kriebel's shopped me or someone's shopped Kriebel. "A fascinating job, I guess. But why phone you?"

"Well, actually, Hugo, she wanted a word with you."

"What about? *I* certainly haven't nicked a Monet."

A worried little laugh. "She wouldn't actually say. I explained you're in Switzerland, and she said she'd appreciate your calling her when you get back. 'To assist in an ongoing inquiry.'"

"And you're sure this wasn't some idiot's idea of a practical joke?"

"She sounded real. There was a busy office in the background."

"Then I'll call Detective Sheila Young the moment I'm home. Some manuscript got nicked from Humber Library, I wonder? They have a few. Or . . . nope, I'm *clue*less, but I'm *itch*ing with curiosity."

"Super. I—I must admit, I didn't tell your mother."

"Tactful, but feel free to tell her. Hey, if I end up in Wormwood Scrubs, she can do the 'Free Hugo' campaign."

Dad's laugh is brighter. "I'll be there, with my placard."

"Splendiferous. So, apart from Interpol hounding you about your criminal-mastermind son, is everything else okay?"

"Pretty much. I'm back to work on the third, and Mum's rushed off her feet at the theater, but that's panto season for you. You're quite sure you don't need a lift from the airport when you get home?"

"Thanks, Dad, but the Fitzsimmonses' driver is dropping me off. See you in eight days or so, when our mystery will be resolved."

I GO UPSTAIRS with scenarios flashing by at twenty-four frames a second: The brigadier's died and a legal executor is asking, "*What valuable stamps?*"; Nurse Purvis is asked about the brigadier's visitors; Kriebel points the finger at Marcus Anyder; CCTV footage gets reviewed; I'm identified; I conduct a taped interview with Sheila Young; I deny her accusations, but Kriebel appears from behind a one-way mirror—"It's him." Formal charges; bail denied, expulsion from Cambridge, four years for theft and fraud, two suspended; if it's a quiet news day I'll make the national papers—OLD RICHMONDIAN STEALS STROKE VICTIM'S FORTUNE; out in eighteen months for good behavior, with a criminal record. The only profession open to me will be wheel clamping.

In my garret, I wipe a clear bit on the misted-up window. Snowy roofs, Hôtel Le Sud, sheer peaks. No snow's falling yet, but the granite sky is full of oaths. January 1.

A compass needle is turning. I feel it.

Pointing to prison? Or somewhere else?

Madam Constantin doesn't choose people at random.

I hope. Hard rabbitty thumps from below: Quinn.

He comes soon, like a disappointed brontosaurus.
Detective Sheila Young isn't a trap; she's a catalyst.
Pack a bag, my instinct says. *Be ready. Wait.*
I obey, then find my place in *The Magic Mountain.*

THE CHALET OF Sin is astir. I hear Fitzsimmons on the first landing below: "I'll have a quick shower . . ." The boiler wakes, the pipes growl, and the shower spatters; women are speaking an African language; earthy laughter; Chetwynd-Pitt booms, "Good morning, Oliver Quinn! Tell me that wasn't what the doctor ordered!" One of the women—Shandy?—asks, "Rufus, honey, I call our agent, so he know we are okay?" Footsteps go down to the sunken lounge; in the kitchen, the radio leaks that song "One Night in Bangkok"; Fitzsimmons comes out of the shower; male muttering on the landing: "The scholarship boy's still up in his holding pen . . . On the phone earlier . . . If he wants to sulk, let him sulk . . ." I'm half tempted to yell down, "I'm not bloody sulking, I'm *really* happy that you all got your rocks off!" but why should I spend my energy on rectifying their assumption? Someone whistles; the kettle's boiling; then I hear a half-falsetto half-croak half-shout: "You are *shitting* me!"

I give my full attention. A quiet few seconds . . . For the second time on this oddest of mornings I experience an inexplicable certitude that something's about to happen. As if it's scripted. For the second time, I obey my instinct, close *The Magic Mountain,* and stow it in my backpack. One of the singers is talking fast and low so I can't make out what she's saying, but it prompts a *thud-thud-thud* up the stairs to the landing, where Chetwynd-Pitt blurts out, "A thousand dollars! They want a thousand fucking dollars! *Each!*"

Drop, drop, drop, go the pennies. Or dollars. Like the best songs, you can't see the next line coming, but once it's sung, how else could it have gone? Fitzsimmons: "They've got to be fucking joking."

Chetwynd-Pitt: "They're very very not fucking joking."

Quinn: "But they . . . they didn't *say* they were hookers!"

Chetwynd-Pitt: "They don't even look like hookers."

Fitzsimmons: "I don't *have* a thousand dollars. Not here!"

Quinn: "Me neither, and if I did, why should I just hand it over?"

Tempting as it is to emerge from my room, stroll on down with a cheery "Would you Romeos like your eggs scrambled or fried?," Shandy's call to her "agent" is a klaxon with flashing lights blaring out the word *pimp, pimp, pimp.* Some would say it's merely a fluke that I have a new pair of Timberland boots in my room, still in their box, but "fluke" is a lazy word.

Chetwynd-Pitt: "This is extortion. I say, fuck 'em."

Fitzsimmons: "I agree. They've seen we have money, and they're thinking, *How do we get a slice of this?*"

Quinn: "But, I mean, if we say no, I mean, won't they—"

Chetwynd-Pitt: "Club us to death with tampons and lipsticks? No, we establish that piss off means piss off, that this is Europe, not Mombasa or whereverthefuck, and they'll get the idea. Who'll the Swiss cops side with? Us, or a trio of sub-Saharan rent-a-gashes?"

I wince. From the Bank of Floorboards I withdraw my assets and redeposit the wedge of banknotes in my passport bag. This I secure inside my ski jacket, contemplating that, while the wealthy are no more likely to be born stupid than the poor, a wealthy upbringing compounds stupidity while a hardscrabble childhood dilutes it, if only for Darwinian reasons. This is why the elite *need* a prophylactic barrier of shitty state schools, to prevent clever kids from working-class post codes ousting them from the Enclave of Privilege. Angry voices, British and African, are jostling down below. From the street outside I hear a *beep.* I look through my window and see a gray Hyundai with a skullcap of snow, crawling thisaway with ill intent. It stops, of course, at the mouth of Château Chetwynd-Pitt, blocking the drive. Out step two burly guys in sheepskin jackets. Then Candy, Shandy, or Mandy appears, beckoning them in . . .

THE FRACAS IN the lounge falls silent. "*You,* whoever you are," shouts Rufus Chetwynd-Pitt, "get off my property *now* or I call the police!"

Camp-Psycho-German with a nasal voice: "You ate in a fancy restaurant, boys. Now it is the time to pay the bill."

Chetwynd-Pitt: "They never *said* they were hookers!"

Camp-Psycho-German: "*You* did not say you are crafted of penis yogurt, yet you are. You are Rufus, I believe."

"None of your *fucking* business *what* my—"

"Disrespectful language is unbusinesslike, Rufus."

"Get—out—now!"

"Unfortunately, you owe three thousand dollars."

Chetwynd-Pitt: "Really? Let's see what the police—"

That must be the TV expiring in a tinkly boom. The bookcase slams on the stone wall? Smash, clang, wallop: glassware, crockery, pictures, mirrors; surely Henry Kissinger won't escape unscathed. And there's Chetwynd-Pitt shrieking, "My hand, my f'ck'n' *hand!*"

An inaudible answer to an inaudible question.

Camp-Psycho-German: "I CANNOT HEAR YOU, RUFUS!"

"We'll pay," whinnies Chetwynd-Pitt, "we'll pay . . ."

"Certainly. However, you obliged Shandy to call us, so the price is higher. This is a 'call-out fee' in English, I think. In business, we must cover costs. You. Yes, you. What is your name?"

"O-O-Olly," says Olly Quinn.

"My second wife owned a Chihuahua named Olly. It bit me. I threw it down a . . . *Scheiss,* what is it, for an elevator to go up, to go down? The big hole. Olly—I am asking you the English word."

"A . . . an elevator shaft?"

"Precisely. I threw Olly into the elevator shaft. So, Olly, you will not bite me. Correct? So. You will now gather your monies."

Quinn says, "My—my—my what?"

"Monies. Funds. Assets. Yours, Rufus's, your friend's. If there is enough to pay our call-out fee, we leave you to your Happy New Year. If not, we do some lateral thinking about how you pay your debts."

One of the women speaks, and more mumbling. A few seconds later Camp-Psycho-German calls up the stairway. "Beatle Number Four! Join us. You will not be hurt, if you do no heroic actions."

Soundlessly, I open the window—it's cold!—and swing my legs over the window ledge. A Hitchcock *Vertigo* moment: Alpine roofs you're planning to slide down look suddenly much steeper than Alpine roofs admired from below. Although the angle of Chetwynd-Pitt's chalet becomes shallower over the kitchen, there's a real risk that in fifteen seconds I'll be the screaming owner of two broken legs.

"Lamb?" It's Fitzsimmons, up on the stairway. "That money you won off Rufus . . . He needs it. They have knives, Hugo. Hugo?"

I lower myself onto the tiles, gripping the windowsill.

Five, four, three, two, one . . .

LE CROC IS locked, dark, and there's no sign of Holly Sykes. Perhaps the bar's closed tonight, so Holly won't be in to clean it until tomorrow morning. Why didn't I ask for her number? I hobble to the town square but even the hub of La Fontaine Sainte-Agnès is in an end-of-the-world mood: few tourists, fewer vehicles, the gorilla-*crêpier*'s nowhere to be seen, most shops have *Fermé* signs up. How come? Last year January 1 had quite a buzz. The sky presses lower, the gray of sodden mattresses. I go into La Pâtisserie Palanche de la Cretta, order a coffee and a *carac,* and slump in the corner by the window, ignoring my throbbing ankle. Detective Sheila Young won't be thinking about me today, at least. What now? What next? Activate Marcus Anyder? I have his passport in a safety-deposit box at Euston station. A bus to Geneva, a train to Amsterdam or Paris; across on the hovercraft; flight to Panama; the Caribbean . . . Job on a yacht.

Really? Do I pack in my old life, just like that?

Never see my family again? It's so abrupt.

Somehow this isn't what the script says.

Olly Quinn passes the window, just three feet and a pane of glass away, accompanied by a cheerful-looking man in a sheepskin jacket. Camp-Psycho-German's right hand, I presume. Quinn looks pale and sick. The duo march past the phone box where our Olly had his

Ness-based meltdown only yesterday and into Swissbank's auto-mated lobby where the cashpoints live. Here Quinn makes three withdrawals with three different cards, before being frog-marched back. I hide behind a conveniently to-hand newspaper. A Normal would feel guilt or vindication; I feel as if I just watched a middle-of-the-road episode of *Inspector Morse*.

"Morning, Poshboy," says Holly, holding a hot chocolate. She's beautiful. She's utterly herself. She's got a red beret. She's percep-tive. "So, what sort of trouble are you in?"

I don't know why I deny it. "Everything's fine."

"Can I sit down, or are you expecting company?"

"Yes. No. Please. Sit down. No company."

She removes her ski jacket, the mint-green one, sits opposite me, places her red beret on the table, unwinds her cream scarf from her neck, rolls it up into a ball, and places it on her beret.

"I just went to the bar," I admit, "but figured you were skiing."

"The slopes are shut. Because of the blizzard."

I glance outside again. "What blizzard?"

"You really should listen to the local radio."

"There's only so much 'One Night in Bangkok' a man can take."

She stirs her hot chocolate. "You ought to be getting back—the forecast's for whiteout conditions, within the hour. You can't see three yards in a whiteout. It's like being blinded." She eats a spoon-ful of froth and waits for me to confess what sort of trouble I'm in.

"I just checked out of the Hotel Chetwynd-Pitt."

"I'd check in again, if I were you. Really."

I do a downed-plane hum. "Problematic."

"Unhappy families in the House of Rufus Sexist-Git?"

I lean forward. "Their hot totties from Club Walpurgis turned out to be prostitutes. Their pimps are extracting every last centime they can scare out of them as we speak. I exited via an escape hatch."

Holly shows no surprise at this common ski-resort tale. "So what's your plan?"

I look into her serious eyes. A dum-dum bullet of happiness tears through my innards. "I don't know."

She sips her hot chocolate and I wish I was it. "You don't look as worried as I would be, if I was in your shoes."

I sip my own coffee. A pan hisses in the bakery kitchen. "I can't explain it. It's . . . impending metamorphosis." I can see she doesn't understand, and I don't blame her. "Do you ever . . . know stuff, Holly? Stuff that you cannot possibly know, yet . . . Or—or lose hours. Not as in, 'Wow, time flies,' but as in," I click my fingers, "there, an hour's gone. Literally, between one heartbeat and the next. Well, maybe the time thing's a red herring, but I *know* my life's changing. Metamorphosis. That's the best word I've got. You're doing a good job of not looking freaked, but I must sound utterly, utterly, utterly bonkers."

"Three too many utterlies. I work in a bar, remember."

I fight a strong urge to lean over and kiss her. She'd slap me away. I feed my coffee a sugar lump. Then she asks, "Where do you plan to stay during your 'metamorphosis'?"

I shrug. "*It's* happening to *me*. Not me to it."

"Which sounds cool, but it hardly answers my question. The buses out aren't running and the hotels are full."

"Like I said, it's a very poorly timed blizzard."

"There's other stuff you're not telling me, isn't there?"

"Oh, tons of stuff. Stuff I'll never tell anyone, probably."

Holly looks away, making a decision . . .

WHEN WE LEFT the town square there were just a few scratchy snowflakes prowling at roof height, but a hundred yards and a couple of corners later it's as if the vast nozzle of an Alp-sized pump is blasting godalmighty massive coils of snow up the valley. Snow's up my nose, snow's in my eyes, snow's in my armpits, snow howls after us through a stone archway into a grotty yard with dustbins already half buried under snow, snow, snow. Holly fumbles with the key and then we're in, snow gusting through the gap and the wind *whoo-whoo*ing after us until she slams the door shut, and it's suddenly very peaceful. A short hallway, a mountain bike, stairs going

up. Holly's cheeks are hazed dark pink. Too skinny; if I were her
mum I'd get a few fattening desserts down her. We take off our
coats and boots and she gestures me up the carpeted stairs first.
Above, there's a light, airy flat with paper lampshades and varnished floorboards that squeak. Holly's flat's plainer than my rooms
at Humber, and obviously 1970s, not 1570s, but I envy her it. It's
tidy and very sparsely furnished: The big room has an ancient TV
and VHS player, a hand-me-down sofa, a beanbag, a low table, a
neat pile of books in a corner, and that's a near-complete inventory.
The kitchenette, too, is minimalist: a single plate, dish, cup, knife,
fork, and spoon wait on the drainer. Rosemary and sage grow in
pots on a shelf. The top three smells are toast, cigarettes, and coffee.
The only nod to ornament is a small oil painting of a pale blue cottage on a green slope over a silver ocean. Holly's large window must
offer an amazing view, but today it's obscured by a blizzard, like
white-noise static on an untuned telly. "It's unbelievable," I say. "All
that snow."

"It's a whiteout." She fills the kettle. "They happen. What did
you do to your ankle? You're limping."

"I left my old accommodation à la Spiderman."

"And landed à la sack-of-Spudsman."

"My Scout pack did the Leaping from Buildings to Escape Violent Pimps badge the week I was away."

"I've got some stretchy bandages you can borrow. But first . . ."
She opens the door of a box room with one window as big as a
shoebox lid. "My sister slept here okay, with the sofa cushions and
blankets."

"It's warm, it's dry." I dump my bag inside. "It's great."

"Good. I sleep in my room, you sleep here. Yep?"

"Understood." When a woman is interested in you, she'll let you
know; if not, there's no aftershave, gift, or line you can spin to make
her change her mind. "I'm grateful, Holly. God only knows what I
would have done if you hadn't taken pity on me."

"You'd have survived. Your sort always does."

I look at her. "My sort?"

She huffs through her nose.

"F'CHRISSAKES, LAMB, *bandage* it, it's not a tourniquet." Holly is less than impressed by my first aid skills. "Obviously you missed the Junior Doctor badge too. What badges *did* you get? No, forget I asked. All *right*," she puts down her cigarette, "I'll do it—but if you make any idiotic nurse jokes, your other ankle gets cracked with a breadboard."

"Definitely no nurse jokes."

"Foot on the stool. I'm not kneeling at your feet."

She unravels my cack-handed attempt, tutting at my ineptitude. My sockless swollen foot looks alien, naked, and unattractive against Holly's fingers. "Here, rub in some arnica cream first—it's pretty miraculous for swellings and bruises." She hands me a tube. I obey, and when my ankle's shiny she wraps the bandage around my foot with just the right degree of pressure and support. I watch her fingers, her loopable black hair, how her face hides and shows her inner weather. This isn't lust. Lust wants, does the obvious, and pads back into the forest. Love is greedier. Love wants round-the-clock care; protection; rings, vows, joint accounts; scented candles on birthdays; life insurance. Babies. Love's a dictator. I *know* this, yet the blast furnace in my ribcage roars *You You You You You You* just the same, and there's bugger-all I can do about it. The wind attacks the window. "It's not too tight?" asks Holly.

"It feels perfect," I tell her.

"LIKE SNOW IN a snow globe," Holly says, watching the blizzard. She tells me about UFO hunters who come to Sainte-Agnès, which somehow leads on to working as a strawberry picker in Kent and a grape-picker in Bordeaux; why the Troubles in Northern Ireland won't end without desegregated schools; how she once skied through a valley three minutes before an avalanche swept through. I light a cigarette and talk about how a bus I missed in Kashmir skidded off the Ladakh road and fell five hundred feet; why townies in Cambridge hate students; why roulette wheels have a zero; how great it is to row on the Thames at six A.M. in the summer. We discuss the first singles we bought, *The Exorcist* versus *The Shining,* planetariums and Madame Tussaud's. We spout a lot of rubbish, but watching Holly Sykes talk is a fine thing. I empty the ashtray again. She quizzes me about my three months' study program at Blithewood College in upstate New York. I give her the edited highlights, including getting shot at by a hunter who thought I was a deer. She tells me about her friend Gwyn, who worked last year at a summer camp in Colorado. I tell her about how Bart Simpson phones Marge from his summer camp and declares, "I'm no longer afraid of death," but Holly asks who Bart Simpson is, so I have to explain. Holly talks about the band Talking Heads, like a Catholic discussing her favorite saints. The morning's gone, we realize. Using a half bag of flour and bits and pieces from her fridge I make us a pizza, which I can tell impresses her more than she lets on. Aubergine, tomatoes, cheese, pesto, and Dijon mustard. There's a bottle of wine in the fridge, too, but I serve us water in case she thinks I want to get her drunk. I ask if she's a vegetarian, having noticed that even the stock cubes are veggie. She is, and she tells me how when she was sixteen she was at her great-aunt Eilísh's house in Ireland, "and this ewe walked by, bleating, and I realized, 'Sweet fecking hell, I'm eating its children!'" I remark how people are superb at not thinking about awkward truths. After I've done the dishes—"to pay my rent"—I discover she's never played backgammon, so I make us a board using the inside of a Weetabix box and a marker. She finds a pair of dice in a jar in a drawer, and we use silver and copper coins for pieces. By the third game she's good enough for me to plausibly let her win.

"Congratulations," I tell her. "You're a fast learner."

"Ought I to thank you for letting me beat you?"

"Oh no I didn't! Seriously, you beat me fair and—"
"And you're a virtuoso liar, Poshboy."

LATER, WE TRY the TV but the reception's affected by the storm and the screen's as blizzardy as the window. Holly finds a black-and-white film on a videotape inherited from the flat's last tenant. She stretches out on the sofa, I'm sunk into the beanbag, and the ashtray's balanced on the arm between us. I try to focus on the film and not her body. The film's British and made, I guess, in the late 1940s. Its opening minutes are missing so we don't know the title, but it's quite compelling, despite the Noël Cowardy diction. The characters are on a cruise liner crossing some foggy expanse, and it takes a while for the passengers, Holly, and me to twig that they're all dead. Each character gets deepened by a backstory—a good Chaucerian mix—before a magisterial Examiner arrives to decide each passenger's fate in the afterlife. Ann, the saintly heroine, gets a pass into heaven, but her husband, Henry, the Austrian-pianist-resistance-fighter hero, killed himself—head in a gas cooker—and has to work as a steward aboard a similar ocean liner between the worlds. The wife tells the Examiner she'll exchange heaven to be with her husband. Holly snorts. "Oh, *please*!" Ann and Henry then hear the sound of breaking glass and wake up in their flat, saved from the gas by the fresh air flooding in through the broken windows. String crescendo, man and wife embrace each other and a new life. The End.

"What a pile of pants," says Holly.

"It kept us watching."

The window's dim mauve except for snowflakes tumbling near the glass. Holly gets up to draw the curtains but stands there, under the spell of the snow. "What's the stupidest thing you've ever done, Poshboy?"

I fidget in my beanbag. It rustles. "Why?"

"You're so megaconfident." She draws the curtains and turns

around, almost accusingly. "Rich people are, I s'pose, but you're up on a different level. Do you never do stupid things that make you cringe with embarrassment—or shame—when you look back?"

"If I worked through the hundreds of stupid things I've done, we'd still be here next New Year's Day."

"I'm only asking for one."

"Okay, then . . ." I guess she wants a flash of vulnerable underbelly— it's like that witless interview question, "What's your worst fault?" What have I done that's stupid enough to qualify as a proper answer, but not so morally repugnant (à la Penhaligon's Last Plunge) that a Normal would recoil in horror? "Okay. I've got this cousin, Jason, who grew up in this village in Worcestershire called Black Swan Green. One time, I'd have been about fifteen, my family was visiting, and Jason's mum sent Jason and me to the village shop. He was younger than me and, as they say, 'easily led.' As his sophisticated London cousin, how did I amuse myself? By stealing a box of cigarettes from his village shop, luring poor Jason into the woods, and telling him that to fix his picked-on, shitty life, he had to learn to smoke. Seriously. Like the villain in some antismoking campaign. My meek cousin said, 'Okay,' and fifteen minutes later he was kneeling on the grass at my feet, vomiting up everything he'd eaten in the previous six months. There. One stupid, cruel act. My conscience goes 'You bastard' whenever I think of it," I wince to hide my fib, "and I think, *Sorry, Jason.*"

Holly asks, "Does he smoke now?"

"I don't believe he's ever smoked."

"Perhaps you inoculated him that day."

"Perhaps I did. Who got you smoking?"

"OFF I WENT, across the Kent marshes. No plan. Just . . ." Holly's hand gestures at the rolling distance. "The first night, I slept in a church in the middle of nowhere and . . . that was when it happened. That was the night Jacko disappeared. Back at the Captain Marlow he had his bath, Sharon read to him, Mam said good night.

Nothing seemed wrong—apart from the fact that I'd gone off. After shutting up the pub, Dad went into Jacko's room as usual to switch his radio off—that's how he used to fall asleep, listening to foreign voices chuntering away. But, come Sunday morning, Jacko wasn't there. He wasn't in the pub. Like some crappy whodunnit puzzle, the doors were locked from the inside. At first the cops—Mam and Dad, even—thought *I'd* hatched a plot with Jacko, so it was only when . . ." Holly pauses to stabilize herself, ". . . I was tracked down, on the Monday afternoon, on this fruit farm on the Isle of Sheppey where I'd blagged a job as a picker, only then did the police start a proper search. Thirty-six hours later. First it was dogs and a radio appeal . . ." Holly rubs her palm around her face, ". . . then chains of locals combing wasteland around Gravesend, and police divers checking the . . . y'know, the obvious places. They found nothing. No body, no witnesses. Days went by, all the leads fizzled out. My parents shut the pub for weeks, I didn't go to school, Sharon was crying the whole time . . ." Holly chokes. "You'd pray for the phone to go, then when it did, you'd be too scared it'd be bad news to pick it up. Mam shriveled up, Dad . . . He was always joking, before it happened. Afterwards, he was . . . like . . . hollow. I didn't go out for weeks and weeks. Basically I left school. If Ruth, my sister-in-law, hadn't weighed in, taken over, got Mam to go over to Ireland in the autumn, I honestly don't think Mam'd still be alive. Even now, six years later, it's still . . . Terrible to say, but now when I hear on the news about some murdered kid, I think, That's hell, that's your worst nightmare, but at least the parents *know*. At least they can grieve. We can't. I mean, I *know* Jacko would've come back if he could've done, but unless there's *proof*, unless there's a"—Holly's voice catches—"a body, your imagination never shuts up. It says, *What if this happened? If that happened? What if he's still alive somewhere in some psycho's basement praying that today's the day you find him?* But even *that's* not the worst part . . ." She looks away so I can't see her face. There's no need to tell her to take her time, even though, unbelievably, her travel clock on the shelf says it's nine forty-five P.M. I light her a cigarette and put it in her fingers. She fills her lungs and slowly empties them. "If I hadn't run off that weekend—over some stupid fucking boyfriend—would Jacko've let himself out of the Captain Marlow that night?" Still turned away, Holly rubs her face. "No. The answer's no. Which means it's my fault. Now my family tell me that's not true, this counselor I went to told me the same, everybody says it. But they don't have that question—*Was it my fault?*—drilling into their heads every hour, every day. Or the answer."

The wind hammers out mad organist's chords.

"I don't know what to say, Holly . . ."

She finishes her glass of white wine.

". . . except 'Stop it.' It's *rude*."

She turns to me, her eyes red, her face shocked.

"Yes," I say. "Rude. It's rude to Jacko."

Obviously nobody's ever said this to her.

"Switch places. Suppose Jacko had stormed off somewhere; suppose you'd gone looking for him, but some . . . evil overtook you and stopped you ever returning. Would you want Jacko to spend his life as self-blame junkie because once, one day, he committed a thoughtless action and made you worry about him?"

Holly looks as if she can't quite believe I'm daring to say this. Actually, I can't either. She's *this* far from kicking me out.

"You'd want him to live fully," I go on. "Wouldn't you? To live *more* fully, not less. You'd need him to live your life for you."

The VCR chooses now to trundle out its videotape. Holly's voice comes out serrated: "So I'm s'posed to act like it never happened?"

"*No.* But stop beating yourself up because you failed to see how a seven-year-old kid might respond to your ordinary act of teenage rebellion in 1984. Stop burying yourself alive at Le Croc of Shit. Your penance isn't helping Jacko. Of course his disappearance has changed your life—how could it not?—but why does that make it right to squander your talents and the bloom of your youth serving cocktails to the likes of Chetwynd-Pitt and for the enrichment of the likes of Günter the employee-shagging drug dealer?"

Holly snaps back, "What am I s'posed to do, then?"

"*I* don't know, do I? I haven't had to survive what you've had to survive. Though, since you ask, there are countless other Jackos in London you *could* help. Runaways, homeless teenagers, victims of God only knows what. You've told me a lot today, Holly, and I'm honored, even if you think I'm betraying your trust by talking to you like this. But I haven't heard *one thing* that forfeits your right to a useful and, yeah, even a content life."

Holly stands up, looking angry and hurt and puffy-eyed. "Half of me wants to hit you with something metal." She sounds serious. "So does the other half. So I'll go to sleep. You'd better leave in the morning. Switch off the light when you go to bed."

WHEN I'M WOKEN by the wedge of dim light, my head's in a fog and my body's gripped in a tangled sleeping bag. Tiny room, more of a walk-in cupboard; silhouetted girl in a man's rugby shirt, long, loopy hair . . . Holly: good. Holly, whom I ordered out of a six-year period of mourning for a missing little brother—presumably dead and skillfully buried—come now to turf me out without breakfast into a very uncertain future . . . pretty bad. But the little window's black as night still. My eyes are still gouged with tiredness. My dry, cigarette-and-pinot-blanc-caked mouth croaks, "Is it morning already?"

"No," says Holly.

THE GIRL'S BREATHING deepens as she drifts off. Her futon's our raft and sleep is the river. I sift through all the scents. "I'm out of practice," she told me, in a blur of hair, clothing, and skin. I told her I was out of practice too, and she said, "Bull*shit,* Poshboy." A long-dead violinist plays a Bach partita on the clock radio. The crappy speaker buzzes on the upper notes, but I wouldn't trade this hour for a private concert with Sir Yehudi Menuhin playing his Stradivarius. Neither would I want to travel back to my and the Humberites' very undergrad discourse on the nature of love at Le Croc the other night, but if I did I'd tell Fitzsimmons et al. that love is fusion in the sun's core. Love is a blurring of pronouns. Love is subject and object. The difference between its presence and its absence is the difference between life and death. Experimentally, silently, I mouth *I love you* to Holly, who breathes like the sea. This time I whisper it, at about the violin's volume: "I love you." No one hears, no one sees, but the tree falls in the forest just the same.

STILL DARK. THE Alpine hush is miles deep. The skylight over Holly's bed is covered with snow, but now that the blizzard's stopped I'm guessing the stars are out. I'd like to buy her a telescope. Could I send her one? From where? My body's aching and floaty but my mind's flicking through the last night and day, like a record collector flicking through files of LPs. On the clock radio, a ghostly presenter named Antoine Tanguay is working through *Nocturne Hour* from three till four A.M. Like all the best DJs, Antoine Tanguay says almost nothing. I kiss Holly's hair, but to my surprise she's awake: "When did the wind die down?"

"An hour ago. Like someone unplugged it."

"You've been awake a whole hour?"

"My arm's dead, but I didn't want to disturb you."

"Idiot." She lifts her body to tell me to slide it out.

I loop a long strand of her hair around my thumb and rub it on my lip. "I spoke out of turn last night. About your brother. Sorry."

"You're forgiven." She twangs my boxer shorts' elastic. "Obviously. Maybe I needed to hear it."

I kiss her wound-up hair bundle, then uncoil it. "You wouldn't have any ciggies left, perchance?"

In the velvet dark, I see her smile: A blade of happiness slips between my ribs. "What?"

"Use a word like 'perchance' in Gravesend, you'd get crucified on the Ebbsfleet roundabout for being a suspected Conservative voter. No cigarettes left, I'm 'fraid. I went out to buy some yesterday, but found a semiattractive stalker, who'd cleverly made himself homeless forty minutes before a whiteout, so I had to come back without any."

I trace her cheekbones. "Semiattractive? Cheeky moo."

She yawns an octave. "Hope we can dig a way out tomorrow."

"I hope we can't. I like being snowed in with you."

"Yeah well, some of us have these job things. Günter's expecting a full house. Flirty-flirty tourists want to party-party-party."

I bury my head in the crook of her bare shoulder. "No."

Her hand explores my shoulder blade. "No what?"

"No, you can't go to Le Croc tomorrow. Sorry. First, because now I'm your man, I forbid it."

Her *sss-sss* is a sort of laugh. "Second?"

"Second, if you went, I'd have to gun down every male between twelve and ninety who dared speak to you, plus any lesbians too. That's seventy-five percent of Le Croc's clientele. Tomorrow's headlines would all be BLOODBATH IN THE ALPS and LAMB THE SLAUGHTERER, and as a vegetarian-pacifist type, I know you wouldn't want any role in a massacre so you'd better shack up"—I kiss her nose, forehead, and temple—"with me all day."

She presses her ear to my ribs. "Have you *heard* your heart? It's like Keith Moon in there. Seriously. Have I got off with a mutant?"

The blanket's slipped off her shoulder: I pull it back. We say nothing for a while. Antoine whispers in his radio studio, wherever it is, and plays John Cage's *In a Landscape*. It unscrolls, meanderingly. "If time had a pause button," I tell Holly Sykes, "I'd press it. Right"—I press a spot between her eyebrows and up a bit—"there. Now."

"But if you did that, the whole universe'd be frozen, even you, so you couldn't press play to start time again. We'd be stuck forever."

I kiss her on the mouth and blood's rushing everywhere.

She murmurs, "You only value something if you know it'll end."

NEXT TIME I wake, Holly's room is gray, like underneath a hole in pack ice. Whispering Antoine is long gone; the radio's buzzing with

French-Algerian rap and the clock says 08:15. She's showering. To-day's the day I either change my life or I don't. I locate my clothes, straighten the twisted duvet, and deposit the tissues in a small wicker bin. Then I notice a big round silver pendant, looped over a postcard Blu-Tacked to the wall above the box that serves as a bedside table. The pendant is a labyrinth of grooves and ridges. It's hand-made, with great care, though it'd be too heavy to wear for long and it's too big not to attract constant attention. I try to solve it by eye, but get lost once, twice, a third time. Only by hold-ing it in my palm and using my little fingernail to trace a path do I get to the middle. If the maze was real and you were stuck in it, you'd need time and luck. When the moment's right, I'll ask Holly about it.

And the postcard? It could be one of a hundred suspension bridges anywhere in the world. Holly's still in her shower, so I pull the postcard off the wall and turn it over . . .

ISTANBUL ve GÜZELLİKLERİ - TÜRKİYE
Boğaziçi Köprüsünün Beylerbeyinden görünüşü
The view of Bosphorus Bridge from Beylerbeyi village
Une vue du Pont du Bosphore par Beylerbeyi

Keskin Color
KARTPOSTALCILIK LİMİTED ŞİRKETİ
Ankara Caddesi. No. 98 — İSTANBUL Tel: 22 24 06

HER HAKKI MAHFUZDUR

TÜRKİYE CUMHURİYETİ POSTA 70 LİRA
TÜRKİYE CUMHURİYETİ POSTA 70 LİRA
I.MİLLETLERARASI TÜRK HALI KONGRESİ
AJANS-TÜRK/ANKARA

Today I crossed the Bosphorus Bridge! You're not allowed to walk across it so I hopped be-tween continents on a bus with schoolkids and grannies. Now I can say I've been to Asia. Istanbul is amazing! Mosques and spinarets, Kami-kaze traffic, Hot as hell at noon, street-kids flogging knock-off cigarettes (Rothmans 25p a pack), markets with fruit I've never seen only shady squares with pigeons, glasses of lemon tea, a zoo with depressed animals (including terriers!) a funfair with happy-hmm-mmm, (in a hostel with thin walls and squeaky beds and sheets that always lead to the sea, hundreds of small boats (like the Thames in the old days, I guess) and freighters - wonder if any of them will go Past the Captain Marlow to Tilbury Dats? Next stop Athens. Cheers + take care, Ed x

Holly Sykes,
The
Captain Marlow,
West Street,
Gravesend,
UK
Ingiltere

19th Aug '85

UÇAK İLE PAR AVION AIR MAIL

GÜZEL SANATLAR - KESKİNCOLOR LTD. ŞTİ. MATBAASI

Hugo Lamb, meet Sexual Jealousy. Wow. "Ed." How *dare* he send Holly a postcard? Or—worse—was it a string of postcards? Was there a follow-up from Athens? Is he a boyfriend? So this is why Normals commit crimes of passion. I want to get Ed's head fastened into stocks and hurl two-kilo plaster statues of Jesus of Rio at his face until he doesn't have one. This is what Olly Quinn would want to do to me if he ever found out that I'd poked Ness. Then I notice the 1985 date—deliverance! Hallejulah. But hang on: Why has Holly been carting his postcard around for six years? The cretin doesn't even know "spinarets" are "minarets." Unless it's a private joke. That'd be worse. How *dare* he share private jokes with Holly? Did Ed give her the maze pendant, too? Makes sense. When she had me inside her, was she imagining I was him? Yes yes yes, I know these snarly thoughts are ridiculous and hypocritical, but they still sting. I want to feed Ed's postcard to my lighter and watch the Bosphorus Bridge and its sunny day and its sub-sixth-form reportage burn, baby, burn. Then I'd flush its ashes down the sewers, like the Russians did to what was left of Adolf Hitler. No. Deep breath, calm down, keep Hitler out of it, and consider the breezy "Cheers, Ed." A real boyfriend would write "Love, Ed." There is the "x," though. Consider also that if Holly in 1985 was in Gravesend receiving postcards, she wasn't being gobbled by an Ed on a squeaky European mattress. Ed must've been a not-quite-lover-not-quite-friend.

Probably.

"HELP YOURSELF TO the shower," she says round the door, and I call back, "Thanks," in a neutral tone to match. Normally I admire uncommitted matter-of-factness the morning after, but with this wooden stake called "Love" whacked through my heart, I want proof of intimacy and have to ignore a strong urge to go and kiss Holly. What if it's a no? Don't force it. I have a skin-scalding shower, change into fresh clothes—what do fugitives do for clean laundry?—and go to the kitchenette, where I find a note:

Hugo—I'm a coward about goodbyes, so I've gone to Le
Croc to start the cleaning. If you want to stay over tonight,
bring me breakfast and I'll find you a feather duster and a
frilly apron. If you don't show up, then such is life, and good
luck with your metamorphisis (is that how you spell it?). H.

Not a love letter, but this note of Holly's is more precious than
any piece of correspondence I've ever owned, bar none. That Zorro-
like three-stroke *H* is both intimate and runic. Her handwriting's
not girly, it's a bit of train wreck, really, calligraphically speaking,
but it's legible if you squint and it's hers. Discoveries. I fold the note
into my wallet, grab my coat, clatter down the stairs, and I'm out,
treading in Holly's ten-minutes-old footsteps through knee-deep
snow in the courtyard, where the morning cold is a plunging cold;
but the blue sky's blue as Earth from space, and the warmth from
the sun's a lover's breath; and icicles drip drops of bright in steep-
sloped streets from storybooks whose passersby have mountain
souls; the kids are glad to be alive and snowballs fly from curb to
curb; I raise my hands and say, "Je me rends!" but a snowball scores
a direct hit; I turn to find the little shit and clutch my heart—pretend
to die—"Il est mort! Il est mort!" the snipers cry, but when I resur-
rect myself they fly away like fallen leaves; around the corner here's
the square, my favorite square in Switzerland, if not the world;
Hôtel Le Sud, the gabled eaves, with Legolandish civic pride, the
church clock chimes nine golden times; an Alp rears up on every
side; the crêpeman's setting up his stall across from the patisserie
where yesterday this all began; "I'm Not in Love," claim 10cc but,
au contraire, I know *I* am; the crêpeman looks as if he knows that
Holly's face is all I see on every surface, there transposed; plus nape,
lips, jaw, hair, and clothes; I hear her "Sort of," "Bull*shit*," "This is
true"; recall her slightly elfish ears; her softnesses; her flattish nose;
her guarded eyes of strato-blue; Body Shop tea tree oil shampoo;
she's nearer now with every step; I wonder what she's thinking . . .
Wondering if I'll really show? The traffic's moving pretty slowly, but
I'll wait until the man turns green . . .

A slush-spattered cream-colored Land Cruiser draws level with where I stand. Before I can feel miffed at having to walk around it, the mirrored window of the driver's door slides down, and I assume it'll be a tourist after directions. But, no, I'm wrong. I know this stocky, swarthy driver in a fisherman's sweater. "G'day, Hugo. You look like a man with a song in his heart."

His New Zealand accent gives it away. "Elijah D'Arnoq, king of the Cambridge Sharpshooters." There's somebody else in the back of the car, but I'm not introduced.

"Your lack of surprise," I tell D'Arnoq, "suggests this isn't a chance encounter."

"Bang on. Miss Constantin sends you her regards."

I understand. I get to choose between two metamorphoses. One is labeled "Holly Sykes" while the other is . . . What, exactly?

Elijah D'Arnoq slaps the side of the Land Cruiser. "Hop aboard. Find out what this is all about, or die wondering. Now or never."

Past the patisserie, down the alley, I can see the crocodile pub sign hanging over Günter's bar. Fifty paces away? "Get the girl!" counsels the love-drunk, reformed-Scrooge Me. "Imagine her face as you walk in!" The soberer Me folds his arms and looks at D'Arnoq and wonders, "What then?" Well, we'll eat breakfast; I'll help Holly clean up the bar; lie low in her place until my fellow Humberites have flown home; we'll hump like rabbits until we can hardly walk; and while our breaths are coming hard and fast, I'll blurt out "I love you" and mean it and she'll blurt out "I love you too, Hugo" and mean it just as much, right then, right there. Then what? I'll phone the registrar at Humber College to say I've suffered a minor breakdown and would like to put my final year on hold. I'll tell my family—something, no idea what, but I'll think of something—and buy Holly a telescope. Then what? I find I'm no longer thinking about her every waking moment. Her way of saying "Sort of" or "This is true" begins to grate, and the day comes when we understand that "All You Need Is Love" is rather less than the whole truth. Then what? By now Detective Sheila Young has tracked me down, and her colleagues in Switzerland interview me at the station and only allow me back to Holly's flat if I surrender my passport. "What's this about, Poshboy?" Then I'll have to confess either to stealing an Alzheimer victim's valuable stamp collection, or luring a fellow student at Humber so deeply into debt that he drove himself off a cliff. Or possibly both, it hardly matters, because Holly will give me back the telescope and get the locks changed. Then what? Agree to go back to London to be interviewed but pick up Marcus Anyder's passport and book a cheap flight to the Far East or Central America? Such narrative arcs make good movies but shitty existences. Then what? Eke out Anyder's money until I succumb to the inevitable, open a bar for gap-year kids and turn into Günter. I notice a silver parka on the passenger seat next to D'Arnoq. "Can I just ask for an outline—"

"Doesn't work like that. You need a leap of faith to leave your old life behind. True metamorphosis doesn't come with flowcharts."

All around us life goes on, oblivious to my quandary.

"But I'll tell you this," says the New Zealander. "We've all been headhunted, except for our founder." D'Arnoq jerks with his head to the unseen man in the compartment behind. "So I know what you're feeling right now, Hugo. That space there, between the curb and this car, it's a chasm. But you've been vetted and profiled, and if you cross that chasm, you'll thrive here. You'll matter. Whatever you want, now and always, you'll get."

I ask him, "Would you make the same choice again?"

"Knowing what I now know, I'd *kill* to get into this car, if I had to. I'd kill. What you've seen Miss Constantin do—that pause button of time at King's College, or the puppeteering of the homeless guy—that's just the prelude to lesson one. There's so much more, Hugo."

I remember holding Holly in my arms, earlier.

But it's the *feeling* of love that we love, not the person.

It's that giddy exhilaration I just experienced, just now.

The feeling of being chosen and desired and cared about.

It's pretty pathetic when you examine it clearheadedly.

So. This is a real, live Faustian pact I'm being offered.

I almost smile. *Faust* tends not to have happy endings.
But a happy ending like whose? Like Brigadier Philby's?
He passed away peacefully, surrounded by family.
If that's a happy ending, they're fucking welcome to it.
When push comes to shove, what's Faust without his pact?
Nothing. No one. We'd never have heard of him. Quinn.
Dominic Fitzsimmons. Yet another clever postgrad.
Another gray commuter, swaying on the District Line.
The Land Cruiser's rear door clunks open an inch.

THE MAN—THE FOUNDER—IN the rear of the car acts as if I'm not there, and D'Arnoq says nothing as he drives us away from the town square, so I sit quietly examining my fellow passenger via his reflection in the glass: midforties, frameless glasses, thick if frosted hair; chin cleft, clean-shaven, and a scar over his jawbone, which surely has a story to tell. He has a lean, tough physique. Mittel Europe ex-military? His clothes offer no clues: sturdy ankle-length boots, black moleskin trousers, a leather jacket, once black but battered grayish. If you noticed him in a crowd you might think "architect" or "philosophy lecturer"; but you probably wouldn't notice him.

There are only two roads out of La Fontaine Sainte-Agnès. One climbs up to the hamlet of La Gouille, but D'Arnoq takes the other, heading down the valley towards Euseigne. We pass a turning for Chetwynd-Pitt's chalet, and I wonder if the boys are worried about my safety or just pissed off that I abandoned them to their hookers' pimp. I wonder, but I don't care. A minute later we've passed the town boundary. The road is banked by rising, falling walls of snow, and D'Arnoq drives with caution—the car has snow tires and the road's been salted, but this is still Switzerland in January. I unzip my coat and think of Holly looking at the clock above the bar, but regret is for the Normals.

"We lost you last night," states my fellow passenger, in a cultured European accent. "The blizzard hid you from us."

Now I study him directly. "Yes, I had a disagreement with my host. I'm sorry if it caused you any trouble . . . sir."

"Call me Mr. Pfenninger, Mr. Anyder. 'Anyder.' A well-chosen name. The principal river on the island of Utopia." The man watches the monochrome world of valley walls, snow-buried fields, and farm buildings. A river rushes alongside the road, black and very fast.

The interview begins. "May I ask how you know about Anyder?"

"We've investigated you. We need to know about everything."

"Do you work for the security services?"

Pfenninger shakes his head. "Only rarely do our circles overlap."

"So you have no political agenda?"

"As long as we are left alone, none."

D'Arnoq slows and drops a gear to take a perilous bend.

Time to be direct: "Who are you, Mr. Pfenninger?"

"We are the Anchorites of the Dusk Chapel of the Blind Cathar of the Thomasite Monastery of Sidelhorn Pass. It's quite a mouthful, you'll agree, so we refer to ourselves as the Anchorites."

"I'd agree it sounds freemasonic. Are you?"

His eyes show a gleam of amusement. "No."

"Then, Mr. Pfenninger, why does your group exist?"

"To ensure the indefinite survival of the group by inducting its members into the Psychosoterica of the Shaded Way."

"And you're the . . . the founder of this . . . group?"

Pfenninger looks ahead. Power lines dip and rise from pole to pole. "I am the First Anchorite, yes. Mr. D'Arnoq is now the Fifth Anchorite. Ms. Constantin, whom you met, is the Second."

Cautiously, D'Arnoq overtakes a salt-spitting truck.

" 'Psychosoterica,' " I say. "I don't know the word."

Pfenninger quotes: "A slumber did my spirit seal, I had no human fears." He looks like he's just delivered a subtle punch line, and I realize he just spoke without speaking. His lips were pressed together. Which is not possible. So I must be mistaken. "She seemed a thing that could not feel the touch of earthly years." Again. His voice sounded in my head, a lush and crisp sound, as if through top-of-the-range earphones. His face defies me to suggest it's a trick. "No motion has she now, no force; she neither hears nor sees." No muffled voice, no wobbling throat, no tell-tale gap at the corner of his mouth. A recording? Experimentally, I put my hands over my ears but Pfenninger's voice is just as clear: "Rolled round in Earth's diurnal course, with rocks, and stones, and trees."

I'm gaping. I close my mouth. I ask, "How?"

"There is a word," Pfenninger says aloud. "Utter it."

So I manage to mumble, "Telepathy."

Pfenninger addresses our driver: "Did you hear, Mr. D'Arnoq?"

Elijah D'Arnoq's peering at us in the rearview mirror. "*Yes, Mr. Pfenninger, I heard.*"

"Mr. D'Arnoq accused me of ventriloquism, when I inducted him. As if I were a performer on the music-hall circuit."

D'Arnoq protests: "*I didn't have Mr. Anyder's education, and if the word 'telepathy' was coined back then, it hadn't reached the Chatham Islands. And I was fried by shell shock. It was 1922.*"

"We forgave you decades ago, Mr. D'Arnoq, I and my little wooden puppet with the movable jaw." Pfenninger glances my way, humor in his eyes, but their banter just makes everything weirder. 1922? Why did D'Arnoq say "1922"? Or did he mean to say 1982? But that doesn't matter: Telepathy's real. Telepathy exists. Unless I hallucinated the last sixty seconds. We pass a garage where a mechanic shovels snow. We pass a field where a pale fox stands on a stump, sniffing the air.

"So," my mouth's dry, "psychosoterica is telepathy?"

"Telepathy is one of its lesser disciplines," replies Pfenninger.

"Its *lesser* disciplines? What else can psychosoterica do?"

A cloud shifts and the fast river's strafed with light.

Pfenninger asks, "What is today's date, Mr. Anyder?"

"Uh . . ." I have to grope for the answer. "January the second."

"Correct. January the second. Remember." Mr. Pfenninger looks at me; his pupils shrink and I feel a pinprick in my forehead. I—

. . .

—BLINK, AND THE Land Cruiser is gone, and I find myself on a
wide, long rocky shelf on a steep mountainside in high-altitude sunshine. The only reason I don't fall over is that I'm already sitting on
a cold stone block. I huff a few times in panicky shock; my huffs
hang there, like vague, blank speech bubbles. How did I get here?
Where is here? Around me are the roofless ruins of what might once
have been a chapel. Perhaps a monastery—there are more walls farther away. Knee-deep snow covers the ground; the shelf ends at a
low wall, a few feet ahead. Behind the ruins a sheer rock face rears
up. I'm in my ski jacket, and my face and ears are throbbing and
warm, as if I've just undergone hard exertion. All these details are
nothing alongside this central, gigantic fact: Just now I was in the
back of a car with Mr. Pfenninger. D'Arnoq was driving. And
now . . . now . . .

"Welcome back," says Elijah D'Arnoq, to my right.

I gasp, *"Christ!"* and jump up, slip over, jump up, and crouch in
fight-or-flight mode.

"Cool it, Lamb! It's freaky, I know"—he's seated and unscrewing
a Thermos flask—"but you're safe." His silver parka gleams in the
light. "As long as you don't run over the edge, like a headless
chicken."

"D'Arnoq, where . . . What happened and where are we?"

"Where it all began," says Pfenninger, and I whirl the other way,
fending off a second heart attack. He's wearing a Russian fur hat
and snow boots. "The Thomasite Monastery of the Sidelhorn Pass.
What's left of it." He kicks through the snow to the low wall and
gazes out. "You'd believe in the divine if you lived out your life up
here . . ."

They drugged me and lugged me here. But why?

And how? I drank nothing and ate nothing in the Toyota.

Hypnotism? Pfenninger was staring at me as I went under.

No. Hypnotism's a cheap twist in crap films. Too stupid.

Then I remember Miss Constantin and King's College Chapel. What if she caused my zone-out—like Pfenninger just did?

"We hiatused you, Mr. Anyder," says Pfenninger, "to search you for stowaways. It's intrusive, but we can't be too careful."

If that makes sense to him or to D'Arnoq, it makes none to me. "I don't have a clue what you're talking about."

"I'd be worried if you did, at this stage."

I touch my head for signs of damage. "How long was I under?"

Pfenninger produces a copy of *Die Zeit* and hands it to me. On the front page Helmut Kohl is shaking hands with the Sheikh of Saudi Arabia. So what? Don't tell me the German chancellor is mixed up in this. "The *date*, Mr. Anyder. Examine the date."

There, under the masthead: *4. Januar 1992.*

Which cannot be right: today is 2 January 1992.

Pfenninger told me to remember it, in the car. Just now.

Just now. Yet still *Die Zeit* insists today is 4 January 1992.

I feel like I'm falling. Unconscious for two days? No, it's more likely the newspaper's a fake. I rustle through its pages, desperate to find evidence that things aren't what they appear to be.

"It *could* be a fake," Pfenninger concedes, "but why construct a falsehood that could be readily demolished?"

I'm head-smashed and, I realize, ravenously hungry. I check my stubble. I shaved this morning, at Holly's. It's grown. I stagger back, afraid of Elijah D'Arnoq and this Mr. Pfenninger, these . . . paranormal . . . Whateverthefuck they are, I have to get away to— to . . .

. . . to where? Our tracks in the snow disappear around a bend. Maybe there's a car park with a visitor's center and telephones just out of sight, or maybe it's thirty kilometers of glacier and crevasses. Back the other way, the narrow mountain shelf on which we stand narrows to a stubborn clump of firs, then it's near-vertical ice and rock. Pfenninger is studying me, while D'Arnoq is pouring a lumpy liquid into the Thermos cup. I want to scream, *"A picnic?"* I squeeze the sides of my skull. Get a grip and calm down. It's late in the afternoon. Clouds are smeared across the sky, beginning to turn metallic. My watch—I left it in Holly's bathroom. I walk to the low wall, a few paces from Pfenninger, and the ground swoops down fifty meters to a road. There's an ugly modern bridge over a deep crevasse, and a road sign that I can't read at this range. The road climbs to the bridge from half a kilometer away, twisting up from slopes dunked in shadow. Beyond the bridge, the road disappears behind a shoulder of the mountain we stand on, near a glassy waterfall that textures the profound silence. Us, the sign, the bridge, and the road surface: there are no other signs of the twentieth century. I ask, "Why did you bring me here?"

"It seems apt," says Pfenninger, "since we're in Switzerland, anyway. But first line your stomach: You've eaten nothing since Tuesday." D'Arnoq's next to me with a steaming cup. I smell chicken and sage and my stomach groans. "Don't burn your tongue."

I blow on it and sip it cautiously. It's good. "Thanks."

"I'll let you have the recipe."

"Being moved under hiatus is a double hand grenade in the brain, but"—Pfenninger clears the snow off the low wall and motions for me to sit down next to him—"a quarantine period was necessary before we let you into our realm. You've been in a chalet near Oberwald since noon of the second, not far from here, and we brought you here this morning. This peak is Galmihorn; that one is Leckihorn; over there, we have Sidelhorn."

I ask him, "Are you from here, Mr. Pfenninger?"

Pfenninger watches me. "The same canton. I was born in Martigny, in 1758. Yes, 1758. I trained as an engineer, and in spring 1799, in the employ of the Helvetica Republic, I came here to oversee repairs to an ancestor of that bridge, spanning the chasm below."

Now, if Pfenninger believes that, he's insane. I turn to D'Arnoq, hoping for supportive sanity.

"Born in 1897, me," says D'Arnoq, drolly, "as a *very* far-flung subject of Queen Victoria, in a stone-and-turf house out on Pitt Island—three hundred klicks east of New Zealand. Aged eighteen, I went on the sheep boat to Christchurch with my cousin. First time on the mainland, first time in a brothel, and first time in a recruiting office. Signed up for the Anzacs—it was either foreign adventures for king and empire or sixty years of sheep, rain, and incest on Pitt Island. I arrived in Gallipoli, and you know your history, so you'll know what was waiting for me there. Mr. Pfenninger found me in a hospital outside Lyme Regis, after the war. I became an Anchorite at twenty-eight, hence my eternal boyish good looks. But I'm ninety-four years old next week. So, hey. The lunatics have you surrounded, Lamb."

I look at Pfenninger. At D'Arnoq. At Pfenninger. The telepathy, the hiatuses, and the Yeti merely ask me to redefine what the mind can do, but this claim violates a more fundamental law. "Are you saying—"

"Yes," says Pfenninger.

"That Anchorites—"

"Yes," says D'Arnoq.

"Don't die?"

"*No,*" frowns Pfenninger. "Of course we die—if we're attacked, or in accidents. But what we don't do is age. Anatomically, anyway."

I look away at the waterfall. They're mad, or liars, or—most disturbing of all—neither. My head's too hot so I remove my hat. Something's cutting into my wrist—Holly's thin black hair-band. I take it off. "Gentlemen," I address the view, "I have no idea what to think or say."

"Far wiser," says Pfenninger, "to defer judgement than rush to the wrong one. "Let us show you the Dusk Chapel."

I look around for another building. "Where is it?"

"Not far," says Pfenninger. "See that broken archway? Watch."

Elijah D'Arnoq notices my anxiety. "We won't put you to sleep again. Scout's honor."

The broken archway frames a view of a pine tree, virgin snowy ground, and a steep rock face. Moments hop by, birdlike. The sky's blue as a high note and the mountains nearly transparent. Hear the waterfall's skiff, spatter, and rumble. I glance at D'Arnoq, whose eyes are fixed where mine should be. "Watch." So I obey, and notice an optical illusion. The view through the archway begins to sway, as if it were only printed on a drape, caught by a breeze, and now pulled aside by an elegant white hand in a trim Prussian-blue sleeve. Miss Constantin, bone-white and golden, looks out, flinching at the sudden bright cold. "The Aperture," murmurs Elijah D'Arnoq. "Ours."

I surrender. Portals appear in thin air. People have pause buttons. Telepathy is as real as telephones.

The impossible is negotiable.

What is possible *is* malleable.

Miss Constantin asks me, "Are you joining us, Mr. Anyder?"

THE WEDDING BASH

2004

"IF YOU'RE ASKING whether I'm a war junkie," I tell Brendan, "then the answer's no, I am not." I sound pissed off. I am, I suppose.

"Not *you*, Ed!" My virtual brother-in-law disguises his backpedaling behind a Tony Blairish suavity. Brendan looks like, and is, a workaholic property developer in his midforties having a rare weekend off. "We know *you* aren't a war junkie. Obviously. I mean, you flew all the way back to England for Sharon's wedding. No, I was only asking if it ever happens that a war reporter gets sort of hooked on the adrenaline of life in war zones. That's all."

"Some do, yes," I concede, rubbing my eye and thinking of Big Mac. "But I'm not in any danger of that. The symptoms are pretty obvious." I ask a passing teenage waitress for one more Glenfiddich. She says she'll bring it right over.

"What are the symptoms?" Sharon's four years younger than Holly and rounder in the face. "Just out of curiosity."

I'm feeling cornered, but Holly's hand finds mine on the bench and squeezes it. "The symptoms of war-zone addiction. Well. The same as the clichés of the foreign correspondent, I guess. Rocky marriages; estrangement from family life; a dissatisfaction with civilian life. Alcohol abuse."

"Not Glenfiddich, I trust?" Dave Sykes, Holly's mild-mannered dad, lightens the mood a little.

"Let's hope not, Dave." Let's hope the subject goes away.

"You must see some pretty hard-core, full-on stuff, Ed," says Pete Webber, accountant, keen cyclist, and tomorrow's groom. Pete's bat-eared and his hairline's beating a hasty retreat, but Sharon's marrying him for love, not hair follicles. "Sharon was saying you've covered Bosnia, Rwanda, Sierra Leone, Baghdad. Places most people try to get away from."

"Some journos carve a career in the business pages, others out of the plastic surgery of the stars. I've made mine out of war."

Pete hesitates. "And you've never wondered, 'Why war?' "

"Guess I'm immune to the charms of silicone."

The waitress brings me my Glenfiddich. I look at Pete, Sharon, Brendan and his wife Ruth, Dave, and Kath, Holly's ever-vigorous Irish mum. They're still waiting for me to say something profound about my journalistic motives. The Sykeses aren't without their scars—Holly's youngest brother, Jacko, went missing in 1984 and his body was never found—but the loss I see, work with, has been on an industrial scale. This makes me different. I doubt this difference is explicable. I doubt even I understand it.

"Do you write to bring the world's attention to the vulnerable?" asks Pete.

"God no." I think of Paul White, on my first assignment in Sarajevo, lying dead in a puddle because he wanted to Make a Difference. "The world's default mode is basic indifference. It'd like to care, but it's just got too much on at the moment."

"Then to play the devil's avocado," says Brendan, "why risk your neck to write articles that won't change anything?"

I fabricate a smile for Brendan. "First, I don't really risk my neck; I'm rigorous about taking precautions. Second, I—"

"What precautions can you take," Brendan interrupts, "to stop a massive car bomb going off outside your hotel?"

I look at Brendan and blink three times to make him vanish. Damn. Maybe next time. "I'll be moving into the Green Zone when I go back to Baghdad. Second, if an atrocity isn't written about, it stops existing when the last witnesses die. That's what I can't stand. If a mass shooting, a bomb, a whatever, *is* written about, then at least it's made a tiny dent in the world's memory. Someone, somewhere, some time, has a chance of learning what happened. And, just maybe, acting on it. Or not. But at least it's there."

"So you're a sort of archivist for the future," says Ruth.

"Sounds pretty good, Ruth. I'll take that." I rub my eye.

"Are you going to miss it all," asks Brendan, "after July?"

"After June," says Holly, cheerfully.

No one sees me squirm. I hope. "When it happens," I tell Brendan, "I'll let you know how I feel."

"So have you got anything lined up, workwise?" asks Dave.

"Ed's got a lot of strings to his bow, Dad," says Holly. "Maybe with the print media, or the BBC, and the Internet's really shaking up the news world. One of Ed's ex-editors at the *FT* is lecturing at UCL, now."

"Well, I think it's *great* you'll be settling in London for good, Ed," says Kath. "We do worry, when you're away. I've seen pictures of this Fallujah place—those bodies they strung up on the bridge! *Shock*ing. And baffling. I thought the Americans won, months ago. I thought the Iraqis hated Saddam. I thought he was a monster."

"Iraq's a lot more complicated than the Masters of War realized, Kath. Or wanted to realize."

Dave claps his hands. "Now we've got the chitchat out of the way, let's get down to the serious stuff: Ed, are you joining us on Pete's stag do tonight? Kath'll babysit for Aoife, so you've got no excuse."

Pete tells me, "A few mates from work are meeting me at the Cricketers—a lovely pub, just round the corner. Then—"

"I'd rather stay blissfully ignorant about 'then,' " says Sharon.

"Oh, right," says Brendan, "as if the hens are going to play Scrabble all evening." In a stage whisper he tells me, "Male strippers at the Brighton Pavilion followed by a crack den at the end of the pier."

Ruth play-cuffs him: "You slanderer, Brendan Sykes!"

"Too right," says Holly. "You wouldn't catch respectable ladies like us going anywhere near a Scrabble board."

"Remind me what you're really up to again," says Dave.

"A sedate wine tasting," replies Sharon, "with tapas, at a bar owned by one of Pete's oldest friends."

"Wine-tasting session," scoffs Brendan. "Back in Gravesend they call a piss-up a piss-up. So how about it, Ed?"

Holly's giving me a go-ahead face, but I'd better start proving what a great father I am while Holly's still talking to me. "No offense, Pete, but I'm going to wuss out. The jet lag's catching up with me, and it'll be nice to spend time with Aoife. Even if she will be fast asleep. That way Kath can join the wine-tasting session, too."

"Oh, I don't mind babysitting, pet," says Kath. "I've got to watch my blood pressure, anyway."

"No, really, Kath." I finish my Scotch, enjoying the blast-off. "You spend as much time as you can with your relatives from Cork—and I'll grab an early night, otherwise I'll be one giant yawn-in-a-suit at the church today. I mean tomorrow. God, see what I mean?"

"All right, then," says Kath. "If you're really sure . . ."

"Absolutely sure," I tell her, rubbing my itchy eye.

"Don't rub it, Ed," Holly tells me. "You'll make it worse."

ELEVEN O'CLOCK AT night, and all's well, kind of, for now. Olive Sun wants me flying out again by Thursday at the latest, so I'll have to tell Holly soon. Tonight, really, so she doesn't make plans for the three of us next week. Fallujah is the biggest deployment of marines since the battle for Hue City in Vietnam, and I'm stuck here on the Sussex coast. Holly'll hit the frigging roof, but I'd better get it over and done with, and she'll have to calm down for Sharon's wedding tomorrow. Aoife's asleep in the single bed in the corner of our hotel room. I only got here after her bedtime, so I still haven't said hi to my daughter, but the First Rule of Parenting states that you never wake a peacefully sleeping child. I wonder how Nasser's girls are sleeping tonight, with dogs barking and gunfire crackling and marines kicking down doors. CNN's on the flat-screen TV with the sound down, showing footage of marines under fire on rooftops in Fallujah. I've seen it five times or more and even the pundits can't think of anything fresh to say until the news cycle starts up again in a few hours, when Iraq begins a new day. Holly texted a quarter of an hour ago to say she and the other hens'll be heading back to the hotel soon. "Soon" could mean anything in the context of a wine bar, though. I switch off the TV, to prove I'm no war junkie, and go to the window. Brighton Pier's all lit up like Fairyland on Friday night, and pop music booms from the fairground at the far end. By English standards it's a warm spring evening, and the restaurants and bars on the promenade are at the end of a busy evening. Couples walk hand in hand. Night buses trundle. Traffic obeys the traffic laws, by and large. I don't knock a peaceful and well-functioning society. I enjoy it, for a few days, weeks, even. But I know that, after a couple of months, a well-ordered life tastes like a flat, non-alcoholic lager. Which isn't the same as saying I'm addicted to war zones, as Brendan helpfully implied earlier. That's as ridiculous as accusing David Beckham of being addicted to playing soccer. Just as soccer is Beckham's art and his craft, reporting from hot spots is my art and my craft. I wish I'd said that to the clan earlier.

Aoife giggles in her sleep, then groans sharply.

I go over. "You okay, Aoife? It's only a dream."

Unconscious Aoife complains, "No, silly! The *lemon* one." Then her eyes flip open like a doll's in a horror movie: "We're going to a hotel in Brighton later, 'cause Aunty Sharon's marrying Uncle Pete, and we'll meet you there, Daddy. I'm a bridesmaid."

I try not to laugh, and stroke Aoife's hair back from her face. "I know, love. We're all here now, so you go back to sleep. I'll be here in the morning and we'll all have a brilliant day."

"Good," Aoife pronounces, teetering on the brink of sleep . . .

. . . she's gone. I pull the duvet over her My Little Pony pajama top and kiss her forehead, remembering the week in 1997 when Holly and I made this precious no-longer-quite-so-little life-form. The Hale-Bopp Comet was adorning the night sky, and thirty-nine members of the Heaven's Gate cult committed mass suicide in San Diego so their souls could be picked up by a UFO in the comet's tail and be transported to a higher state of consciousness beyond human. I rented a cottage in Northumbria and we had plans to go hiking along Hadrian's Wall, but hiking didn't turn out to be the principal activity of the week. Now look at her. I wonder how she sees me. A bristly giant who teleports into her life and teleports out again for mystifying reasons, perhaps—not so different from how I saw my own father, I guess, except while I'm away on various assignments, Dad went away to various prisons. I'd love to know how Dad saw me when I was a kid. I'd love to know a hundred things. When a parent dies, a filing cabinet full of all the fascinating stuff also ceases to exist. I never imagined how hungry I'd be one day to look inside it.

When I was back in February she was having her period.

I hear Holly's key in the door. I feel vaguely guilty.

Not half as guilty as she'll make me feel, though.

Holly's having trouble with the lock so I go over, put the chain on, and open it up a crack. "Sorry, sweetheart," I tell her, in my Michael Caine voice. "I never ordered no kinky massage. Try next door."

"Let me in," says Holly, sweetly, "or I'll kick you in the nuts."

"Nope, I didn't order no kick in the nuts, neither. Try—"

Not so sweetly: "Brubeck, I need to use the loo!"

"Oh, all right, then." I unchain the door and stand aside. "Even if you have come home too plastered to use a key, you dirty stop out."

"The locks in this hotel are all fancy and burglar-proofed. You need a PhD to open the damn things." Holly bustles past to the bathroom, peering down at Aoife in passing. "Plus I only had a *few* glasses of wine. Mam was there as well, remember."

"Right, as if Kath Sykes was ever a girl to put the dampeners on a 'wine-tasting session.'"

Holly closes the bathroom door. "Was Aoife okay?"

"She woke up for a second, otherwise not a squeak."

"Good. She was *so* excited on the train down, I was afraid she was going to be up all night dancing on the ceiling." Holly flushes the toilet to provide a bit of noise cover. I go over to the window again. The funfair at the end of the pier is winding down, by the look of it. Such a lovely night. My proposed six-month extension for *Spyglass* in Iraq is going to wreck it, I know. Holly opens the bathroom door, smiling at me and drying her hands. "How did you spend your quiet night in? Snoozing, writing?"

Her hair's up, she's wearing a low-cut figure-hugging black dress and a necklace of black and blue stones. She hardly ever looks like that anymore. "Thinking impure thoughts about my favorite yummy mummy. Can I help you out of that dress, Miss Sykes?"

"Down, boy." She fusses over Aoife. "We're sharing a room with our daughter, you might have noticed."

I walk over. "I can operate on silent mode."

"Not tonight, Romeo. I'm having my period."

Thing is, I haven't been back often enough in the last six months to know when Holly's period is. "Guess I'll have to make do with a long, slow snog, then."

" 'Fraid so matey." We kiss, but it's not as long and slow as advertised, and Holly isn't as drunk as I was half hoping. When was it that Holly stopped opening her mouth when we kiss? It's like kissing a zipped-up zip. I think of Big Mac's aphorism: In order to have sex, women need to feel loved; but in order for men to feel loved, we need to have sex. I'm keeping my half of the deal—so far as I know—but sexually, Holly acts like she's forty-five or fifty-five, not thirty-five. Of course I'm not allowed to complain, because that's pressurizing her. Once Holly and I could talk about anything, anything, but all these no-go areas keep springing up. It all makes me . . . I'm not allowed to be sad either, because then I'm a sulky boy who isn't getting the bag of sweets he thinks he deserves. I haven't cheated on her—ever—not that Baghdad is a hotbed of sexual opportunity, but it's depressing still being a fully functioning thirty-five-year-old male and having to take matters into my own hands so often. The Danish photojournalist in Tajikistan last year would've been up for it if I'd been less anxious about how I'd feel when the taxi dropped me off at Stoke Newington and I heard Aoife yelling, "It's Daaaaddyyy!"

Holly turns back to the bathroom. She leaves the door open, and starts to remove her makeup. "So, are you going to tell me or not?"

I sit on the edge of the double bed, alert. "Tell you what?"

She dabs cotton wool under her eyes. "I don't know yet."

"What makes you think I . . . have anything to tell you?"

"Dunno, Brubeck. Must be my feminine intuition."

I don't believe in psychics but Holly can do a good impression of one. "Olive asked me to stay on in Baghdad until December."

Holly freezes for a few seconds, drops the cotton wool, and turns to me. "But you've already told her you're quitting in June."

"Yeah. I did. But she's asking me to reconsider."

"But you told *me* you're quitting in June. Me and Aoife."

"I told her I'd call back on Monday. After discussing it with you."

Holly's looking betrayed. Or as if she's caught me downloading porn. "We a*greed,* Brubeck. This would be your final final extension."

"I'm only talking about another six months."

"Oh, f'Chrissakes. You said that the *last* time."

"Sure, but since I won the Sheehan-Dower Prize I've been—"

"*And* the time before that. 'Half a year, then I'm out.' "

"This'll cover a year of Aoife's college expenses, Hol."

"She'd rather have a living father than a smaller loan."

"That's just"—you can't call angry women "hysterical" these days; it's sexist—"hyperbole. Don't stoop to that."

"Is that what Daniel Pearl said to his partner before he jetted off to Pakistan? 'That's just hyperbole'?"

"That's tasteless. And wrongheaded. And Pakistan's not Iraq."

She lowers the toilet lid and sits on it so we're roughly at eye level. "I'm *sick* of wanting to puke with fear every time I hear the word 'Iraq' or 'Baghdad' on the radio. I'm *sick* of hardly sleeping. I'm *sick* of having to hide from Aoife how worried I am. Fantastic, you're an in-demand award-winning journalist, but you have a six-year-old who wants help riding a bike with no stabilizers. Being a crackly voice for a minute every two or three days, *if* the satphone's working, isn't enough. You *are* a war junkie. Brendan was right."

"No, I am *not.* I am a journalist doing what I do. Just as he does what he does and you do what you do."

Holly rubs her head like I'm giving her a headache. "Go, then!

Back to Baghdad, to the bombs taking the front off your hotel. Pack. Go. Back to 'what you do.' If it's more precious than us. Only you'd better get the tenants out of your King's Cross flat 'cause the next time you're back in London, you'll be needing somewhere to live."

I keep my voice low: "Will you *please* fucking *listen* to yourself?"

"No, *you* fucking listen to *yourfuckingself!* Last month you agree to quit in June and come home. Your high-powered American editor says, 'Make it December.' You say, 'Uh, okay.' Then you tell me. Who are you with, Brubeck? Me and Aoife, or Olive Sun and *Spyglass*?"

"I'm being offered another six months' work. That's all."

"No, it's *not* 'all' 'cause after Fallujah dies down or gets bombed to shit it'll be Baghdad or Afghanistan Part Two or someplace else, there's *always* someplace else, and on and on until the day your luck runs out and then I'm a widow and Aoife has no dad. *Yes,* I put up with Sierra Leone, *yes,* I survived your assignment in Somalia, but Aoife's older now. She needs a dad."

"Suppose I told you, 'No, Holly, you can't help homeless people anymore. Some have AIDS, some have knives, some are psychotic. Quit that job and work for . . . for Greenland supermarkets instead. Put all those people skills of yours to use on dried goods. In fact, I'm *ordering* you to, or I'll kick you out.' How would *you* respond?"

"F'Chrissakes, *the risks are different.*" Holly lets out an angry sigh. "Why bring this up in the middle of the bloody night? I'm Sharon's matron of honor tomorrow. I'll look like a hungover panda. You're at a crossroads, Brubeck. Choose."

I make an ill-advised quip: "More of a T-junction, technically."

"Right. I'd forgotten. It's all a joke to you, isn't it?"

"Oh, Holly, for God's sake, that's not what I—"

"Well, *I'm not* joking. Quit *Spyglass* or move out. My house isn't just a storage dump for your dead laptops."

THREE O'CLOCK IN the morning, and things are fairly shit. "Never let the sun set on an argument," my uncle Norm used to say, but my uncle Norm didn't have a kid with a woman like Holly. I said "Good night" to her peaceably enough after switching off the lights, but her "Good *night*" back sounded very like "Screw you," and she turned away. Her back's as inviting as the North Korean border. It's six o'clock in the morning in Baghdad now. The stars will be fading in the freeze-dried dawn, as skin-and-bone dogs pick through rubble for something to eat, the mosques' Tannoys summon the devout, and bundles by the side of the road solidify into last night's crop of dead bodies. The luckier corpses have a single bullet through the head. At the Safir Hotel, repairs will be under way. Daylight will be reclaiming my room at the back, 555. My bed will be occupied by Andy Rodriguez from *The Economist*—I owe him a favor from the fall of Kabul two years ago—but everything else should be the same. Above the desk is a map of Baghdad. No-go areas are marked in pink highlighter. After the invasion last March, the map was marked by only a few pink slashes here and there: Highway 8 south to Hillah, and Highway 10 west to Fallujah—other than that, you could drive pretty much wherever you wanted. But as the insurgency heated up the pink ink crept up the roads north to Tikrit and Mosul, where an American TV crew got shot to shit. Ditto the road to the airport. When Sadr City, the eastern third of Baghdad, got blocked off, the map became about three-quarters pink. Big Mac says I'm re-creating an old map of the British Empire. This makes the pursuit of journalism difficult in the extreme. I can no longer venture out to the suburbs to get stories, approach eyewitnesses, speak English on the streets, or even, really, leave the hotel. Since the new year my work for *Spyglass* has been journalism by proxy, really. Without Nasser and Aziz I'd have been reduced to parroting the Panglossian platitudes tossed to the press pack in the Green Zone. All of which begs the question, if journalism is so difficult in Iraq, why am I so anxious to hurry back to Baghdad and get to work?

Because it is difficult, but I'm one of the best.

Because only the best *can* work in Iraq right now.

Because if I don't, two good men died for nothing.

WINDSURFERS, SEAGULLS, AND SUN, a salt-'n'-vinegar breeze, a glossy sea, and an early walk along the pier with Aoife. Aoife's never been on a pier before and she loves it. She does a row of froggy jumps, enjoying the flicker of the LED bulbs in the heels of her trainers. We'd have killed for shoes like that when I was a kid, but Holly says it's hard to find shoes that *don't* light up these days. Aoife has a Dora the Explorer helium balloon tied to her wrist. I just paid a fiver for it to a charming Pole. I look behind us, trying to work out which window of the Grand Maritime Hotel is our room. I invited Holly out on the walk but she said she had to help Sharon get ready for a hairdresser who isn't due until nine-thirty. It's not yet eight-thirty. It's her way of letting me know she hasn't shifted her position from last night.

"Daddy? Daddy? Did you hear me?"

"Sorry, poppet," I tell Aoife. "I was miles away."

"No, you weren't. You're right here."

"I was miles away metaphorically."

"What's meta . . . frickilly?"

"The opposite of literally."

"What's litter-lily?"

"The opposite of metaphorically."

Aoife pouts. "Be *serious*, Daddy."

"I'm always serious. What were you asking, poppet?"

"If you were any animal, what would you be? I'd be a white Pegasus with a black star on its forehead, and my name'd be Diamond Swiftwing. Then Mummy and me could fly to Bad Dad and see you. And Pegasuses don't hurt the planet like airplanes—they only poo.

Grandpa Dave says when he was small *his* daddy used to hang apples on very tall poles over his allotment, so all the Pegasuses'd hover there, eat, and poo. Pegasus poo is so magic the pumpkins'd grow really really big, bigger than me, even, so just one would feed a family for a week."

"Sounds like Grandpa Dave. Who's the Bad Dad?"

Aoife frowns at me. "The place where *you* live, silly."

"Baghdad. '*Bagh*-dad.' But I don't live there." God, it's lucky Holly didn't hear that. "It's just where I work." I imagine a Pegasus over the Green Zone, and see a bullet-riddled corpse plummeting to earth and getting barbecued by Young Republicans. "But I won't be there forever."

"Mummy wants to be a dolphin," says Aoife, "because they swim, talk a lot, smile, and they're loyal. Uncle Brendan wants to be a Komodo dragon, 'cause there're people on Gravesend Council he'd like to bite and shake to pieces, which is how Komodo dragons make their food smaller. Aunty Sharon wants to be an owl because owls are wise, and Aunt Ruth wants to be a sea otter so she can spend all day floating on her back in California and meet David Attenborough." We reach a section of the pier where it widens out around an amusement arcade. Big letters spelling BRIGHTON PIER stand erect between two limp Union flags. The arcade's not open yet, so we follow the walkway around the outside of the arcade. "What animal would you be, Daddy?"

Mum used to call me a gannet; and as a journalist I've been called a vulture, a dung beetle, a shit snake; a girl I once knew called me her dog, but not in a social context. "A mole."

"Why?"

"They're good at burrowing into dark places."

"Why d'you want to burrow into dark places?"

"To discover things. But moles are good at something else, too." My hand rises like a possessed claw. *"Tickling."*

But Aoife tilts her head to one side like a scale model of Holly. "If you tickle me I'll wet myself and then you'll have to wash my pants."

"Okay." I act contrite. "Moles don't tickle."

"I should think so too." How she says that makes me afraid Aoife's childhood's a book I'm flicking through instead of reading properly.

Behind the arcade, seagulls are squabbling over chips spilling from a ripped-open bag. Big bastards, these birds. A row of stalls, booths, and shops runs down the middle of the pier. I can't help but notice the woman walking towards us, because everything around her shifts out of focus. She's around my age, give or take, and tall for a woman though not stand-outishly so. Her hair is white-gold in the sun, her velvet suit is the dark green of moss on graves, and her bottle-blue sunglasses will be fashionable some decades from now. I put on my own sunglasses. She compels attention. She compels. She's way out of my class, she's way out of anybody's class, and I feel grubby and disloyal to Holly, but look at her, Jesus Christ, *look* at her—graceful, lithe, knowing, and light bends around her. "Edmund Brubeck," say her wine-red lips. "As I live and breathe, it's you, isn't it?"

I've stopped in my tracks. You don't forget beauty like this. How on earth does she know me, and why don't I remember? I take off my sunglasses now and say, "Hi!," hoping that I sound confident, hoping to buy time for clues to emerge. Not a native English accent. European. French? Bendier than German, but not Italian. No journalist looks this semidivine. An actress or model I interviewed, years ago? Someone's trophy wife from a more recent party? A friend of Sharon's in Brighton for the wedding? God, this is embarrassing.

She's still smiling. "I have you at a disadvantage, don't I?"

Am I blushing? "You have to forgive me, I—I'm . . ."

"I'm Immaculée Constantin, a friend of Holly's."

"Oh," I bluster, "Immaculée—yes, of course!" Do I half-know that name from somewhere? I shake her hand and perform an awkward cheek-to-cheek kiss. Her skin's as smooth as marble but cooler than sun-warmed skin. "Forgive me, I . . . I just got back from Iraq yesterday and my brain's frazzled."

"There's nothing to forgive," says Immaculée Constantin, whoever the hell she is. "So many faces, so many faces. One must lose a few old ones to make space for the new. I knew Holly as a girl in Gravesend, although I left town when she was eight years old. It's curious how the two of us keep bumping into each other, every now and then. As if the universe long ago decided we're connected. And *this* young lady," she gets down on one knee to look eye-to-eye at my daughter, "must be Aoife. Am I correct?"

Wide-eyed Aoife nods. Dora the Explorer sways and turns.

"And how old are you now, Aoife Brubeck? Seven? Eight?"

"I'm six," says Aoife. "My birthday's on December the first."

"How grown up you look! December the first? My, my." Immaculée Constantin recites in a secretive, musical voice: " 'A cold coming we had of it, just the worst time of the year for a journey, and such a journey: the ways deep and the weather sharp, the very dead of winter.' "

Holidaymakers pass us by like they're ghosts, or we are.

Aoife says, "There's not a cloud in the sky today."

Immaculée Constantin stares at her. "How right you are, Aoife Brubeck. Tell me. Do you take after your mummy most, do you think, or your daddy?"

Aoife sucks in her lip and looks up at me.

Waves slap and echo below us and a Dire Straits song snakes over from the arcade. "Tunnel of Love" it's called; I loved it when I was a kid. "Well, I like purple best," says Aoife, "and Mummy likes purple. But Daddy reads magazines all the time, whenever he's home, and I read a lot too. Specially *I Love Animals*. If you could be any animal, what would you be?"

"A phoenix," murmurs Immaculée Constantin. "Or *the* phoenix, in truth. How about an invisible eye, Aoife Brubeck? Do you have one of those? Would you let me check?"

"Mummy has blue eyes," says Aoife, "but Daddy's are chestnut brown and mine are chestnut brown, too."

"Oh, not *those* eyes"—now the woman removes her strange blue sunglasses. "I mean your special, invisible eye, just . . . here." She rests her fingers on Aoife's right temple and strokes her forehead with her thumb, and deep in my liver or somewhere I know something's weird, something's wrong, but it's drowned out when Immaculée Constantin smiles up at me with her heart-walloping beauty. She studies a space above my eyes, then turns back to Aoife's, and frowns. "No," she says, and purses her painterly lips. "A pity. Your uncle's invisible eye was magnificent, and your mother's was enchanting, too, before it was sealed shut by a wicked magician."

"What's an invisible eye?" asks Aoife.

"Oh, that hardly matters." She stands up.

I ask, "Are you here for Sharon's wedding?"

She replaces her sunglasses. "I'm finished here."

"But . . . You're a friend of Holly's, right? Aren't you even going to . . ." But as I look at her, I forget whatever it was I meant to ask.

"Have a heavenly day." She walks towards the arcade.

Aoife and I watch her shrink as she moves further away.

My daughter asks, "Who was that lady, Daddy?"

So I ask my daughter, "Who was what lady, darling?"

Aoife blinks up at me. "What lady, Daddy?"

We look at each other, and I've forgotten something.

Wallet, phone; Aoife; Sharon's wedding; Brighton Pier.

Nope. I haven't forgotten anything. We walk on.

A boy and girl are snogging, like the rest of the world doesn't exist. "That's *gross!*" declares Aoife, and they hear, and glance down, before resuming their tonsil-tickling. *Yeah,* I tell the boy telepathically, *enjoy the cherries and cream because twenty years on from now nothing tastes as good.* He ignores me. Up ahead, a picture spray-painted on a rolled-down metal shutter captures Aoife's attention: a Merlinesque face with a white beard and spiral eyes in a halo of Tarot cards, crystals, and stardust. Aoife reads the name: "D-wiggert?"

"Dwight."

" 'Dwight . . . Silverwind. For-tune . . . Teller.' What's that?"

"Someone who claims to be able to read the future."

"*Class!* Let's go inside and see him, Daddy."

"Why would you want to see a fortune-teller?"

"To know if I'll open my animal-rescue center."

"What happened to being a dancer like Angelina Ballerina?"

"That was *ages* ago, Daddy, when I was little."

"Oh. Well, no. We won't be visiting Mr. Silverwind."

One, two, three—and here's the Sykes scowl: "Why not?"

"First, he's closed. Second, I'm sorry to say that fortune-tellers can't really tell the future. They just fib about it. They—"

The shutter is rattled up by a less flattering version of the Merlin on the shutter. This Merlin looks shat out by a hippo, and is dressed up in prog-rock chic: a lilac shirt, red jeans, and a waistcoat en-crusted with gems as fake as its wearer.

Aoife, however, is awestruck. "Mr. Silverwind?"

He frowns and looks around before looking down. "I am he. And you are who, young lady?"

A Yank. Of bloody course. "Aoife Brubeck," says Aoife.

"Aoife Brubeck. You're up and about very early."

"It's my aunty Sharon's wedding today. I'm a bridesmaid."

"May you have an altogether sublime day. And this gentleman would be your father, I presume?"

"Yes," says Aoife. "He's a reporter in Bad Dad."

"I'm sure Daddy tries to be good, Aoife Brubeck."

"She means Baghdad," I tell the joker.

"Then Daddy must be very . . . brave." He looks at me. I stare back. I don't like his way of talking and I don't like him.

Aoife asks, "Can you *really* see the future, Mr. Silverwind?"

"I wouldn't be much of a fortune-teller if I couldn't."

"Can you tell *my* future? Please?"

Enough of this. "Mr. Silverwind is busy, Aoife."

"No, he isn't, Daddy. He hasn't got one customer even!"

"I usually ask for a donation of ten pounds for a reading," says the old fraud, "but, off-peak, to *special* young ladies, five would suffice. Or"—Dwight Silverwind reaches to a shelf behind him and produces a pair of books—"Daddy could purchase one of my books, either *The Infinite Tether* or *Today Will Happen Only Once* for the special rate of fifteen pounds each, or twenty pounds for both, and receive a complimentary reading."

Daddy would like to kick Mr. Silverwind in his crystal balls. "We'll pass on your generosity," I tell him. "Thanks."

"I'm open until sunset, if you change your mind."

I tug at my daughter's hand to tell her we're moving on, but she flares up: "It's not *fair*, Daddy! I want to know my *future*!"

Just bloody great. If I take back a tearful Aoife, Holly'll be insufferable. "Come on—Aunty Sharon's hairdresser will be waiting."

"Oh dear." Silverwind retreats into his booth. "I foresee trouble." He shuts a door marked THE SANCTUM behind him.

"*Nobody* knows the future, Aoife. These"—I aim this at the Sanctum—"*liars* tell you whatever they think you want to hear."

Aoife turns darker, redder, and shakier. "No!"

My own temper now wakes up. "No what?"

"No no no no no no no no no no."

"Aoife! Nobody knows the future. That's why it's the future!"

My daughter turns red, shaky, and screeches: *"Kurde!"*

I'm about to flame her for bad language—but did my daughter just call me a Kurd? *"What?"*

"Aggie says it when she's cross but Aggie's a *million* times nicer than *you* and at least she's there! You're never even home!" She storms off back down the pier on her own. Okay, a mild Polish swearword, a mature dollop of emotional blackmail, picked up perhaps from Holly. I follow. "Aoife! Come back!"

Aoife turns, tugs the balloon string off and threatens to let it go.

"Go ahead." I know how to handle Aoife. "But be warned, if you let go, I'll *never* buy you a balloon again."

Aoife twists her face up into a goblin's and—to my surprise, and hurt—lets the balloon go. Off it flies, silver against blue, while Aoife dissolves into cascading sobs. "I *hate* you—I *hate* Dora the Explorer—I wish you were back—back in Bad Dad—forever and *ever*! I *hate* you I *hate* you I *hate* you I *hate your guts*!"

Then Aoife's eyes shut tight and her six-year-old lungs fill up.

Half of Sussex hears her shaken, sobbing scream.
Get me out of here. Anywhere.
Anywhere's fine.

NASSER DROPPED ME near the Assassin's Gate, but not too near;
you never know who's watching who's giving lifts to foreigners, and
the guards at the gate have the jumpiest trigger fingers, the poor
bastards. "I'll call you after the press conference," I told Nasser, "or
if the network's down, just meet me here at eleven-thirty."

"Perfect, Ed," replied my fixer. "I get Aziz. Tell Klimt, all Iraqis
love him. Seriously. We build big statue with big fat cock pointing
to Washington." I slapped the roof and Nasser drove off. Then I
walked the fifty meters to the gate, past the lumps of concrete placed
in a slalom arrangement, past the crater from January's bomb, still
visible; half a ton of plastic explosives, topped with a smattering of
artillery shells, killing twenty and maiming sixty. Olive used five of
Aziz's photos, and the *Washington Post* paid him a reprint fee.

The queue for the Assassin's Gate wasn't too bad last Saturday;
about fifty Iraqi staffers, ancillary workers, and preinvasion residents of the Green Zone were ahead of me, lining up to one side of
the garish arch, topped by a large sandstone breast with an aroused
nipple. An East Asian guy was ahead of me, so I struck up a conversation. Mr. Li, thirty-eight, was running one of the Chinese restaurants inside the zone—no Iraqi is allowed near the kitchens for fear
of a mass poisoning. Li was returning from a meeting with a rice
wholesaler, but when he found out my trade his English mysteriously worsened and my hopes for a "From Kowloon to Baghdad"
story evaporated. So I turned my thoughts to the logistics of the day
ahead until it was my turn to be ushered into the tunnel of dusty
canvas and razor wire. "Blast Zone" security has been neo-
liberalized, and the affable ex-Gurkhas who used to man Checkpoint One have been undercut by an agency recruiting Peruvian
ex-cops, who are willing to risk their lives for four hundred dollars
a month. I showed my press ID and British passport, got patted

down, and had my two Dictaphones inspected by a captain with an epidermal complaint who left flakes of his skin on them.

Repeat the above three times at Checkpoints Two through Four and you find yourself inside the Emerald City—as the Green Zone has inevitably come to be known, a ten-square-kilometer fortress maintained by the U.S. Army and its contractors to keep out the reality of postinvasion Iraq and preserve the illusion of a kind of Tampa, Florida, in the Middle East. Barring the odd mortar round, the illusion is maintained, albeit it at a galactic cost to the U.S. taxpayer. Black GM Suburbans cruise at the thirty-five miles per hour speed limit on the smooth roads; electricity and gasoline flow 24/7; ice-cold Bud is served by bartenders from Mumbai who rename themselves Sam, Scooter, and Moe for the benefit of their clientele; the Filipino-run supermarket sells Mountain Dew, Skittles, and Cheetos.

The spotless hop-on, hop-off circuit bus was waiting at the Assassin's Gate stop. I hopped on, relishing the air-conned air, and the bus pulled off at the very second the timetable promised. The smooth ride down Haifa Street passes much of the best real estate in the nation and the Ziggurat celebrating Iraq's bloody stalemate against Iran—one of the ugliest memorials on Earth—and several large areas of white Halliburton trailers. Most of the CPA's staff live in these trailer parks, eat in the chow halls, shit in portable cubicles, never set foot outside the Green Zone, and count the days until they can go home and put down a deposit on a real house in a nice neighborhood.

When I got off the bus at the Republican Palace, about twenty joggers came pounding down the sidewalk, all wearing wraparound sunglasses, holsters, and sweat-blotted T-shirts. Some of the T-shirts were emblazoned with the quip WHO'S YOUR BAGHDADDY NOW?; the remainder declared, BUSH-CHENEY 2004. To avoid a collision I had to jump out of their way. They sure as hell weren't going to get out of mine.

. . .

I STEP ASIDE for a stream of flouncy-frocked girls who run giggling down the aisle of All Saints' Church in Hove, Brighton's genteel twin. "Half the florists in Brighton'll be jetting off to the Seychelles on the back of this," remarks Brendan. "Kew bloody Gardens, or what?"

"A lot of work's gone into it, for sure." I gaze at the barricade of lilies, orchids, and sprays of purples and pinks.

"A lot of *dosh* has gone into it, our Ed. I asked Dad how much all this set him back, but he says it's all . . ." he nods across the aisle to the Webbers' side of the church and mouths *taken care of*. Brendan checks his phone. "He can wait. Speaking of dosh, I meant to ask before you fly back to your war zone about your intentions regarding the elder of my sisters."

Did I hear that right? "You what?"

Brendan grins. "Don't worry, it's a bit late to make an honorable woman out of our Hol now. Property, I'm talking. Her pad up in Stoke Newington's cozy, like a cupboard under the stairs is cozy. You'll have your sights set a bit higher up the property ladder, I trust?"

As of right now, Holly's sights are set on kicking me out on my arse. "Eventually, yes."

"Then see me first. London property's dog-eat-dog right now, and two nasty words of the near future are 'negative' and 'equity.'"

"Will do, Brendan," I tell him. "I appreciate it."

"It's an order, not a favor." Brendan winks, annoyingly. We shuffle along to a table where Pete-the-groom's mother, Pauline Webber, gold and coiffured like Margaret Thatcher, is handing out carnations for the men's buttonholes. "Brendan! Bright-eyed and bushy-tailed after last night's 'entertainments,' are we?"

"Nothing a pint of espresso and a blood transfusion couldn't fix," says Brendan. "Pete's not the worse for wear, I hope?"

Pauline Webber's smile is a nose-wrinkle. "I gather there was an afterparty party in a 'club.'"

"I heard rumors of that, yes. Some of Sharon's and my Corko-nian cousins were introducing Pete to the subtleties of Irish whisky. That's a work of art you're wearing, Mrs. Webber."

To me Pauline Webber's hat looks like a crash-landed crow with turquoise blood, but she accepts the tribute. "I swear by a hatter in Bath. He's won awards. And call me Pauline, Brendan—you sound like a tax inspector with bad news. Now, a buttonhole—white for the bride's side, red for the groom's."

"Very War of the Roses," I offer.

"No, no," she frowns at me, "these are carnations. Roses would be too thorny. And you'd be?"

"This is Ed," says Ruth. "Ed Brubeck. Holly's partner."

"Oh, the intrepid reporter! De*light*ed. Pauline Webber." Her handshake is gloved and crushing. "I've heard *so* much about you from Sharon and Peter. Let me introduce you to Austin, who—" She turns to her missing husband. "Well, Austin's dying to meet you too. We're glad you got here in time. Delayed flights and bovva?"

"Yes. Iraq's not the easiest of places to depart from."

"No doubt. Sharon was saying you've been in that place, Fa—Faloofah? Falafel? Where they strung up the people on the bridge."

"Fallujah."

"Knew it began with 'Fa.' Appalling. Why *are* we meddling in these places?" She makes a face like she's smelling possibly gone-off ham. "Beyond the ken of us mere mortals. Anyway." She hands me a white carnation. "I met Holly and your daughter, yesterday—Aoife, isn't it? I could eat her with a spoon! What—a—*sweet*ie."

I think of the sulky goblin on the pier. "She has her moments."

"Pippa! Felix! There's a *live baby* in that pushchair!" Mrs. Webber dashes off and we proceed up the aisle. Brendan has a lot of hello-ing, handshaking, and cheek-kissing to do—there's a big contingent of Holly's Irish relatives in attendance, including the legendary Great-aunt Eilísh, who cycled from Cork to Kathmandu in the late 1960s. I drift up to the front. By the vestry door, I spot Holly in a white dress, laughing at a red-carnation young male's joke. Once upon a time I could make her laugh like that. The guy's admiring her, and I want to snap his neck, but how can I blame him? She looks stunning. I stroll up. My new shirt is rubbing my neck, and my old suit is pinching the temporary bulge around my middle, which I'll dispose of soon with a rigid regime of diet and exercise. "Hi," I say. Holly basically ignores me.

"Hi," says the guy. "I'm Duncan. Duncan Priest. My aunt's buttonholed you onto Sharon's side, I see."

I shake his hand. "So you're, um, Pauline's nephew?"

"Yep. Peter's cousin. Have you met Holly, here?"

"We bump into each other at weddings and funerals," Holly says, deadpan. "These irksome family events that get in the way of one's meteoric career."

"I'm Aoife's father," I tell Duncan Priest, who's looking baffled.

"*The* Ed? Ed Brubeck? Your"—he points to Holly—"other half? Such a pity you missed Pete's stag do last night, though."

"I'll learn to cope with the disappointment."

Duncan Priest senses my pissed-offness and makes an o-*kay* face. "Rightio. Well, I'll go and check up on, um, stuff."

"You have to forgive Ed, Duncan," says Holly. "His life is so full of adventure and purpose that he's allowed to be rude to the rest of us lemmings, wage slaves, and sad office clones. By rights we ought to be grateful when he even notices we exist."

Duncan Priest smiles at her, like a fellow adult in the presence of a misbehaving child. "Well, nice meeting you, Holly. Enjoy the wedding, maybe see you at the banquet." Off he walks. Tosser.

I refuse to listen to the onboard traitor who says I'm the one being the tosser. "Well, that was nice," I tell Holly. "Loyal too."

"I can't hear you, Brubeck," she says witheringly. "You're not here. You're in Baghdad."

FLANKED BY THE Stars and Stripes and the widely reviled new Iraqi flag, Brigadier General Mike Klimt gripped his lectern and addressed a press room as full and wired as I'd seen it since Envoy L. Paul Bremer III announced Saddam Hussein's capture to loud cheers last December. We had hoped that Envoy Bremer would make an appearance today, too, but the de facto Grand Vizier of Iraq has cultivated an imperial distance between himself and a media that daily grows ever more critical and ever less "post–9/11." Klimt referred to his notes: "The barbarity we saw in Fallujah on March 31 runs counter to any civilized norms in peacetime or wartime. Our forces will not rest until the perpetrators have been brought to justice. Our enemies will come to learn that the Coalition's resolve is *strengthened*, not weakened, by their depravity. And why? Because it proves the evildoers are desperate. They now know that Iraq has turned a corner. That the future belongs not to the Kalashnikov but to the ballot box. And this is why President Bush has pledged his ongoing full support to Envoy Bremer and our military commanders for Operation Valiant Resolve. Operation Valiant Resolve will prevent the dead-enders of history from terrorizing the vast majority of peace-loving Iraqis, and move this nation closer to the day when Iraqi mothers can let their children play outside with the same peace of mind as American mothers. Thank you."

"Clearly," Big Mac muttered in my ear, "General Klimt's never been a mother in Detroit."

Shouts broke out as Klimt agreed to take a few questions. Larry Dole, an Associated Press guy, won the verbal brawl for attention: "General Klimt, are you able to confirm or deny the figures from Fallujah Hospital, claiming that six hundred civilians have been killed in the last week, with over one thousand seriously wounded?"

The question generated a buzz; the U.S. doesn't, and probably couldn't, keep a record of Iraqis killed in crossfire, so even to ask the question is an act of criticism. "The Coalition Provisional Authority," Klimt lowered his head bullishly at Dole, "is not an office of statistics. We have a counterinsurgency to prosecute. But I say this: Whatever innocent blood has been spilled in Fallujah is on the insurgents' hands. Not ours. When a mistake is made, compensation is paid. Thank you."

I did a piece about compensation for *Spyglass:* Blood money payments had fallen from $2,500 to $500 per life—less than a visit to an ATM for many Westerners—and the untranslated English legal-ese of the forms was as comprehensible as Martian to most Iraqis.

"General Klimt," said a German reporter, "do you have sufficient troops to maintain the occupation or will you ask Defense Secretary Rumsfeld to supply more battalions for these widespread revolts we are seeing all over Iraq?"

The general swatted away a fly. "First, I dislike this 'occupation' word; we're engaged in a 'reconstruction.' And these 'widespread revolts'—have you actually seen them with your own eyes? Have you been to these places yourself?"

"The highways are too dangerous, General," answered the German. "When did *you* last tour the provinces by car?"

"If *I* was a journalist," Klimt smiled on one side of his face, "I'd be careful about confusing hearsay with reality. Security *is* returning to Iraq. One last question, before—"

"I wanted to ask, General," veteran *Washington Post* man Don Gross got in first, "whether the CPA now concedes that Saddam Hussein's weapons of mass destruction were imaginary?"

"Ah, this old chestnut." Klimt drummed on the side of the lectern. "Listen, Saddam Hussein butchered tens of thousands of men, women, and children. If we hadn't toppled this Arab Hitler, he would've slaughtered tens of thousands more. To my mind, it's the pacifists who would have done nothing about this architect of geno-cide who have the case to answer. What stage had his program of building weapons of mass destruction reached? We may never know. But for the ordinary peace-loving Iraqis who want a better future for their families, it's an irrelevance. Okay, we'll wrap it up here . . ." More questions were called out, but Brigadier General Mike Klimt exited in a snowstorm of flashlights.

"And the moral of the tale *is*," I smelt hash browns and whisky on Big Mac's breath, "if you're after news, avoid the Green Zone."

I switched off my recorder and shut my notebook. "It'll do."

Big Mac sniffed. "For an 'Official Bullcrap Versus the Facts on the Ground' piece? You still planning a little drive out west?"

"Nasser's got the hamper packed, ginger beer, the lot."

"Likely there'll be fireworks to go with your picnic."

"Nasser knows a few back roads. And what else can I do? Recycle these pasteurized tidbits from the Good Soldier Klimt and hope they get mistaken for journalism? Try to get *Spyglass* back on the approved list so I can trundle around in a Humvee for six hours and wire Olive another identical marine's-eye-view piece? ' "Incoming!" yelled a gunner as the RPG ricocheted off the armor cladding and all hell broke loose.' "

"Hey, that's *my* line. And, yes, I am joining our gallant warriors this afternoon. If you're six foot four, a hundred and eighty pounds, and blue-eyed as Our Lord Jesus Christ, a Humvee's the only way into Fallujah."

"First one back to the hotel buys the beers."

Big Mac clamped a shovel-sized hand on my shoulder. "Watch yourself, Brubeck. Tougher men than you get burned out there."

"Tasteless pun referring to Blackwater contractors intended?"

Big Mac looked away, chewing gum. "Kinda."

"BEFORE SHARON AND Peter tie the knot, I'd like us all to consider for a moment what they're getting themselves into . . ." The Reverend Audrey Withers has a puckish smile. "What *is* marriage, exactly, and how could we explain it to an alien anthropologist? It's more than just a living arrangement. Is it an endeavor, a pledge, a symbol, or an affirmation? Is it a span of shared years and shared experiences? A vessel for intimacy? Or does the old joke nail it best? 'If love is an enchanted dream, then marriage is an alarm clock.' " Mostly male laughter in the congregation is shushed. "Maybe marriage is difficult to define because of its array of shapes and sizes. Marriage differs between cultures, tribes, centuries, decades even, generations, and—our alien researcher might add—planets. Marriages can be dynastic, common-law, secret, shotgun, arranged, or, as is the case with Sharon and Peter"—she beams at the bride in her dress and the groom in his morning suit—"brought into being by love and respect. Any given marriage can—and will—go through rocky patches and calmer periods. Even within a single day, a marriage can be stormy in the morning, yet by evening turn calm and blue . . ."

Aoife, in her pink bridesmaid's finery, is sitting next to Holly by the font. She's holding the velvet tray with the bride's and groom's wedding rings on. Look at them both. About two months after our Northumbrian sojourn, I called Holly from a phone kiosk in Charles de Gaulle airport, with actual francs. I was on my way back from the Congo, where I'd done a lengthy piece on the Lord's Resistance Army's child soldiers and sex slaves. Holly picked up the phone, I said, "Hi, it's me," and Holly said, "Why, hello, Daddy."

I said, "It's not your dad, it's me, Ed."

Holly said: "I know, you idiot. I'm pregnant."

I thought, *I'm not ready for this,* and said, "That's fantastic."

"On marriage," continues the Reverend Audrey Withers, "Jesus made only one direct remark: 'What God has joined, let no man strike asunder.' Theologians have debated what this means down the ages, but it profits us to consider Jesus's actions as well as his words. Many of us know the story of the wedding at Cana, as it's trotted out at most Christian wedding sermons you'll ever hear, this one included. The banquet at Cana was down to its last drop of wine, so Mary asked Jesus to save the day and not even the Son of God could refuse a determined mother, so he told the servants to fill the wine jars with water. When the servants poured the jars, out came wine—and not your mediocre plonk, either. This was vintage. The master of the banquet told the bridegroom, "Everyone brings out the choice wine first, and then the cheaper stuff after the guests are legless, but you have saved the best until last." How human of the Son of God—to make his debut as a miracle worker, not as raiser of the dead, a healer of leprosy, or a walker on the water, but as a good son and loyal friend." The Reverend Audrey gazes over our heads, as if watching a home video of Cana. "I believe that *if* God cared what size and shape and form human marriage should take, He would have given us clear instructions, via the Gospels. I believe, therefore, that God is willing to trust us with the small print."

Brendan's next to me. His phone, set to silent, buzzes. His hand goes to his jacket, but a glare from Kath in front aborts the mission.

"Sharon and Peter," the vicar carries on, "have written their own wedding vows. I am a big fan of self-penned vows. To get the job done, they had to sit down, talk, and listen, both to what *was* said aloud and to what *wasn't,* which is where the real truth so often hides. They had to compromise—a holy word, that, as well as a practical art. Now, a vicar isn't a fortune-teller," I see Aoife prick up her ears, "so I can't tell Sharon and Peter what awaits them in the years ahead, but marriage can, should, and must evolve. Don't be alarmed, and don't resent it. Be patient and kind, unflaggingly. In the long run, it's the unasked-for hot-water bottles on winter nights that matter more than the extravagant gestures. Express gratitude, especially for work that tends to get taken for granted. Identify problems as they arise, remembering that anger is flammable. When you've behaved like a donkey, Peter," the groom smiles at his toes, "remember that a sincere apology never diminishes the apologizer. Wrong turns teach us the right way."

What grade, I wonder, would me and Holly get, on the relationship scorecard of the Reverend Audrey Withers? C+? D–?

"When's the bit where Uncle Peter *kiss*es her?" asks a kid.

The congregation laughs. "Great idea." The Reverend Audrey Withers looks like a woman who enjoys her job. "Why not just skip to the good bit?"

NASSER DROVE THE half-Corolla half–Fiat 5. Aziz occupied the passenger seat with his camera under a blanket at his feet, and I sat in the back behind a screen of dry cleaning, ready to burrow into the footwell under sheets and boxes of infant formula. Baghdad's low-rise western suburbs stretched out along the four-lane highway to Fallujah. After a mile or two the apartment blocks gave way to middle-class streets from the money-slick 1970s: whitewashed, flat-roofed houses surrounded by high walls and steel gates. Then we passed a few miles of two-story cinder-block buildings, with shops or workshops below and meager living quarters above. These acquired the visual repetition of a cheap cartoon. We passed several petrol stations, whose queues went on for many hundreds of vehicles. The drivers would be waiting there all day. Even in April, the sun was more of a glaring sky zone than the bright disk of northern latitudes. Unemployed men of all ages stood around in dishdashas, smoking and talking. Women in hijabs or full-length burkas walked in small groups, carrying plastic bags of vegetables: It struck me that Iraq was looking more Iranian by the week. Kids Aoife's age played at Insurgents Versus Americans. Nasser fed a cassette into the player, and Arabic music blammed out through the tinny speakers. A woman sang scales I'm not hardwired for, and the song must have been a classic because both Nasser and Aziz got to work on the backing vocals. During an instrumental break, I asked Nasser—half shouting above the din of the car and the music—what the song was about. "A girl," my fixer half-shouted back. "Man she love go to Iran to fight the war, but he never come back. She *very* beautiful, so other men say, 'Hey, honey, I got money, I got big house, I got *wasta,* you marry me?' But the girl she say, 'No, I wait one thousand years for my soldier.' Sure, this song is very . . . How you say?—like sugar too much? I forget word—santi-mantle?"

"Sentimental."

"*Veeery* sentimental, and my wife say, the girl of this song, she is crazy! If she don't marry, what happen to her? Dead soldiers can't send money! She gonna starve! Only a man write so stupid song, my wife say. But I say, 'Ah . . .' " Nasser made a dismissive motion with his hand. "This song touch me." He thumped his chest. "Love is more strong than the death." He turned around. "You know?"

IVANO DEL PIO at the *Sydney Morning Herald* had recommended Nasser as a fixer when he left Baghdad, and he was one of the best

I've ever employed. Preinvasion, Nasser had worked in broadcasting and had reached management level, which meant he'd had to join the Ba'ath Party. He had a decent house and could support his wife and three children, even in a society starved by U.S. and UN sanctions. Postinvasion, Nasser scraped a living from working for foreign press. Under Saddam's regime the official fixers were a shifty crew, paid to feed you Saddam's line and inform the Mukhabarat about any ordinary Iraqis foolish enough to try to tell you anything true about life under the dictator. Nasser, however, had a journalist's nose and eye, and on some of my best stories for *Spyglass* I insisted he received credit and pay as co-writer. He never used his real name, however, in case an enemy denounced him to any of a dozen insurgency groups as a collaborator. Aziz the photographer was an ex-colleague of Nasser's, but his English was as limited as my Arabic so I didn't know him as closely as I did my fixer. He knew his trade, though, and was cautious, crafty, and brave in pursuit of a good shôt. Photography is a dangerous hobby in Iraq; the police assume that you're recceing for a suicide mission.

We passed crumbling walls and decrepit shops.

"You break it," Colin Powell had warned Bush, in what's become known as the Pottery Barn Anecdote, "you'll own it . . ."

Bedraggled families sifted giant tumuli of rubbish.

"You'll be the proud owner of twenty-five million people . . ."

Lines of streetlamps, most leaning over, some fallen.

"All their hopes, aspirations, problems. You'll own it all."

We passed a buckled crash barrier by a small crater: the site of an IED attack. We hit an official checkpoint manned by the Iraqi police that cost us forty minutes. Official police shouldn't hassle a foreign journalist but we were all relieved that they didn't seem to notice my foreignness. Nasser's car is in a bad way even by Iraqi standards, but its shiteness acts as professional camouflage. What self-respecting journo, agent, or jihadist would travel in such a pile of crap?

The further west we drove, the riskier our venture became. Nasser's local knowledge grew scantier, and both the Abu Ghraib Highway and the N10 would be littered with dozens of roadside IEDs. The obvious targets for these were the U.S. military convoys, but knowing that any dead dog or cardboard box or bin-bag of crap might conceal enough explosives to roast a Humvee put you on permanent edge. Then there was the danger of kidnapping. My darkish complexion, beard, brown eyes, and local attire let me pass as a pale Iraqi at first glance, but my basic Arabic betrays me as a foreigner within a few words. I had my fake Bosnian passport to explain my poor language skills while claiming a Muslim affinity, but subterfuge is a high-risk game, and if a mob could be calmly reasoned with, it wouldn't be a mob. Bosnians aren't obvious kidnappees for ransom bounty, but neither were Japanese NGO workers until a fortnight ago. If my press pass was found, my value would go up; I'd be sold as a spy to an Al Qaeda affiliate, and they're less interested in money than in a recorded "confession" and a beheading for the webcam. Midway between Baghdad and Fallujah we reached the town of Abu Ghraib, famous for decaying factories, palm dates, and a vast prison complex where Saddam's enemies, or potential enemies, used to be tortured in submedieval conditions. Big Mac hears rumors that not a lot has changed under the CPA. We passed its high, kilometer-long fortified wall on the left and Nasser translated a slogan daubed on a bombed-out building facing it: *We will knock on the gates of Heaven with American skulls.* That was a killer opening or closing line for an article. I jotted it down in my notebook.

In front of a mosque, Nasser pulled over to give plenty of space to a U.S. convoy joining the highway. Aziz took a few pictures from inside the car, but didn't dare get out; to a jumpy gunner, a telephoto lens looks like an RPG launcher. I counted twenty-five vehicles in the Fallujah-bound convoy, and wondered if Big Mac was sweating his butt off in any of the Humvees. Then Aziz said something in Arabic and Nasser told me, "Ed, trouble!" Half a dozen men were walking towards us from a row of low buildings alongside the mosque.

"Let's go," I said.

Nasser turned the ignition.

Nothing.

Nasser turned the ignition.

Nothing.

Three seconds to decide whether to bluff it, or hide . . .

I slid down under the milk cartons, a few seconds before a man exchanged greetings with Nasser through the driver's window. The man asked us where we were going. Nasser said he and his cousin were taking supplies to Fallujah. Then the man asked Nasser, "Are you a Sunni or a Shi'a?"

A dangerous question; preinvasion, I seldom heard it.

Nasser replied, "While Fallujah burns, we are all Iraqis."

Like I said, Nasser's good. The voice asked for a cigarette.

After another pause, the man asked what supplies we had.

"Baby milk," said Aziz. "For the hospitals." Nasser said how his imam told them the American pigs were throwing baby milk into the sewers, to stop Iraqi babies growing up to become jihadists.

"We have hungry babies here, too," said the man.

Neither Aziz nor Nasser had an answer to hand.

"I said," repeated the man, "we have hungry babies too."

If the car was unloaded, I'd be found, a foreigner, within spitting distance of Iraq's Ground Zero of Incarceration. By hiding, I'd already put my Bosnian Muslim journalist story beyond use. Nasser sounded cheerful. They'd be happy to donate a box of baby powder to the babies of Abu Ghraib. Then, innocently, he asked for a favor in return. His damn car wouldn't start, and he needed a push.

I couldn't catch the man's reply. When the Corolla's door opened, I had no way of knowing if Nasser was being ordered out at gunpoint, or if every box of baby formula was about to be removed. The seat was flipped forward and the box covering my face was lifted away . . .

. . . I saw a hairy wrist with a Chinese Rolex and the underside of the box covering my face. I waited for a shout. Then the driver's seat flopped back, and no more boxes were taken. I heard laughter, then the car sagged under Nasser's weight and goodbyes called out. Soon after, I felt the car being pushed along, heard the tires crunch gravel, and felt the car jolt before the engine started.

Aziz half gasped: "I thinked we dead men."

I was lying under the boxes twisted and breathless.

Thinking, *When I get back home, I'll never leave again.*

Thinking, *When I get back home, I'll never feel this alive.*

"HOKEY-DOKEY, WE'LL START with the two families," says the beagle-faced photographer in his Hawaiian shirt. It's sunny on the church steps, and all the leaves are fresh and lime-green. They'd be microwaved brown by a single afternoon in Mesopotamia, where flora has to equip itself with armor and thorns to survive. "Webbers on the left," says the photographer, "and Sykeses on the right, if you will." Pauline Webber gets her family into position with martial efficiency, while the Sykeses drift into place unhurriedly. Holly looks around for Aoife, who's scooping up drifts of confetti for a confetti fight. "Picture time, Aoife." Aoife snuggles against Holly and neither think to look for me. So I stay where I am, out of shot. Like all belongers, the Sykeses and Webbers don't notice how easily they slip into groups, lines, ranks, gangs. But we nonbelongers know what we are, all right. "*Squeeze* in both ends, if you will," says the photographer.

"Wakey-wakey, Ed." Kath Sykes beckons me. "You're in on this."

The devil suggests I answer, "Holly seems to disagree," but I step between Kath and Ruth. Holly, below, doesn't turn around, but Aoife, with flowers in her hair, looks back and up. "Daddy, did you see me take up the ring tray?"

"I've never seen a ring tray held so skillfully, Aoife."

"*Daddy,* flattery will get you anywhere," and everyone who hears laughs, so much to Aoife's delight that she repeats the phrase.

Once I hoped that, by not getting married, me and Holly might avoid the scenes that Mum and Dad played out before Dad got sent down for his twelve years. True, me and Holly don't shout and throw stuff, but we sort of do, invisibly.

"Hokey-dokey," says the photographer. "All aboard?"

"Where's Great-aunt Eilísh?" asks Amanda, Brendan's eldest.

"Great-*great*-aunt Eilísh to you, technically," notes Brendan.

"Right, Dad, whatever." Amanda's sixteen.

"We're on *rather* a tight schedule," declares Pauline Webber.

"She was talking to Audrey the vicar . . ." Amanda scoots off.

The photographer straightens up, his smile drooping. I tell my sort-of sister-in-law, "Beautiful ceremony, Sharon."

"Cheers, Ed." Sharon smiles. "Lucky with the weather, too."

"Blue skies and sunshine all the way from here on in."

I shake Peter's hand. "So, Pete, how does it feel to be Mr. Sykes?"

Peter Webber smiles at what he imagines is my mistake. "Er, you mean Mr. Webber, Ed. Sharon's now Mrs. Webber."

My expression should tell him, *You just married a Sykes, matey,* but he's too in love to read it. He'll learn. Just like I did.

Holly's acting like I'm not there. Getting some practice in.

"Ancient lady coming through, make way, make way," says Great-aunt Eilísh, in her freewheeling Cork accent, escorted by Amanda. "Audrey—the vicar—is off to Tanzania next week and she was asking for a few pointers. Kath, might I just slip in here . . ." So I step forward and find myself next to Holly after all, wishing I could just slip my hand into hers without it being such a big bloody deal. But it is. I don't.

"All present and correct," Pauline Webber tells the photographer. "At last."

A lithe roller-blader glides past the church. He looks so free.

"Hokey-dokey," says the photographer, "on the count of three I'd like a big cheesey 'Cheeeeeeeeese!' Yes? A-one, a-two, and . . ."

THROUGH A HOLE blasted in a dry block wall, Aziz snapped a family hurrying across the wasteland north of the doctors' compound. An Arabic *Grapes of Wrath,* on foot. I told him it could be a cover shot, if it came out well. "I bring to your hotel tomorrow, after I develop. If on cover," Aziz rubbed his thumb against his first two fingers in the universal symbol, "Miss Olive, she pay more?"

"*If* it's used, yeah," I said. "But you ought to—"

A helicopter hammered by very low, blasting up sand and grit, and Aziz and I both ducked. A Cobra gunship? Kids appeared in the road from the next-door compound, shouting and pointing in the ballooning clouds, and watched it disappear. One boy threw a symbolic stone after it. A woman in hijab anxiously called the children in, shot us a hostile glance, and shut the gate. We were about as close as it was possible to get to Fallujah, a golf shot shy of the "Cloverleaf" intersection, where the Abu Ghraib highway knots into Highway 10. South, through the baked and wavery air, was the bad-tempered holding pen of vehicles, pooling at the verges of the outer checkpoint. Large numbers of marines and a couple of Bradleys—mini-tanks, basically—blocked the road. The second checkpoint was just beyond the Cloverleaf, flanked by a bulldozed-up berm, a ridge of dirt and rubble topped with razor wire. Nobody was allowed into Fallujah today, and only women and children were allowed out.

The rumors about this makeshift clinic for refugees set up by a couple of Iraqi doctors turned out to be true. Nasser was inside recording interviews, thanks to his Al Jazeera press accreditation, which was every bit as authentic as my Bosnian passport. Aziz and I had joined him for a while; at least a hundred patients were being attended to by two doctors and two nurses with little more in the way of equipment than donated first aid boxes. "Beds" were blankets on the floor of what had been a spacious living room, and the main operating table had until recently been a pool table. There was no anesthetic. Most patients were in various degrees of pain, a few in agony, and some dying. The mortuary was an inner room, where six unclaimed bodies lay. The flies and the smell were intolerable; some guys were digging graves in the garden. The nurses promised to distribute the infant formula, but the doctors asked us for painkillers and bandages.

Aziz took a few photographs while Nasser conducted interviews. I'd been introduced as Nasser's Bosnian cousin, also working for Al Jazeera, but anti-foreign sentiment was acute so Aziz and I soon left to wait by the car and let Nasser work unimpeded. We sat on a broken curb and each drank a bottle of water. Even in spring Mesopotamia is so hot you can drink all day and never need to piss. From Fallujah, just a kilometer to the west, we heard gunfire and, every few minutes, big explosions. The air tasted of burning tires.

Aziz stowed his camera in the car. He returned with cigarettes and offered me one, but I was still on the wagon. "Bush, I understand," said Aziz, as he lit his. "Bush father, he hate Saddam, then Twin Towers, so Bush want revenge. America need many oil, Iraq has oil, so Bush get oil. Friends of Bush get money also, Halliburton, supply, guns, much money. Bad reason, but I understand. But why your country, Ed? What Britain want here? Britain spend many many dollars here, Britain lose hundreds men here—for why, Ed? I not understand. Long ago people say, 'Britain good, Britain gentleman.' Now people say, 'Britain is whore of America.' Why? I want understand."

I sifted through possible answers for Aziz. Did Tony Blair really believe that Saddam Hussein possessed missiles capable of destroying London in forty-five minutes? Did he really believe in the Neocon fantasia about planting a liberal democracy in the Middle East and watching it spread? I could only shrug. "Who knows?"

"Allah know," said Aziz. "Blair know. Blair wife know."

I'd give a year of my life to see inside the prime minister's head. Three, maybe. He's an intelligent man. You can tell by his gymnastic evasions in interviews. Does he not think, when he's looking at himself in the mirror, *Oh, fuck, Tony, Iraq has gone well and truly tits-up—why oh why oh* why *did you ever listen to George?*

A drone circled above us. It would be armed. I thought of its operator, picturing a crewcut nineteen-year-old called Ryan at a base in Dallas, sucking an ice-cold Frappuccino through a straw. He could open fire on the clinic, kill everyone in and near it, and never smell the cooked meat. To Ryan, we'd be pixellated thermal images on a screen, writhing about a bit, turning from yellow to red to blue.

The drone flew off, and a white pickup truck hurtled up the dirt-track from the checkpoint area. It skidded to a halt by the clinic gate and the driver—head wrapped in a bloodstained kaffiyeh—jumped out and ran around to the passenger door. Aziz and I walked over to help. The driver, a guy about my age, pulled out a bundle wrapped in a sheet. He tried to carry it but he tripped over a cinder block, cushioning the bundle against his body as he fell. As we helped him up I saw he was holding a boy. The kid was unconscious, a sickly color, only five or six, and had blood oozing from his mouth. The man fired out a frantic volley of Arabic—I only knew the word for "doctor"—and Aziz led him into the clinic compound. I followed. Inside what had been a reception room a woman felt for a pulse on the boy's arm, said nothing, and called to one of the doctors, who shouted something back from the far corner. As my eyes adjusted to the shade inside the house I saw Nasser speaking with a hollow-faced old guy in a wife-beater's vest, fanning himself. Then a soft-spoken man, who, even here, smelt of aftershave, was in my face, asking a complex question in dialect—or a question that turned into a threat—containing the words "Bosnia," "America," and "kill." He finished by slashing his throat with his finger. I half nodded, half shook my head, hoping to imply that I'd understood but things were too complicated for me to give him a straightforward answer. Then I walked off. Foolishly, I looked back; the guy was still watching. Aziz followed me out, and around to the Corolla. He told me, "He militia. He test you."

"Did I pass the test?"

Aziz didn't answer. "I bring Nasser. If man come, hide. If men with guns come . . . Goodbye, Ed." Aziz hurried back to the compound. The open landscape was wasteland, pretty much devoid of cover. Unlike my previous brush with capture outside the mosque, I had time to think. I thought of Aoife in Mrs. Vaz's classroom at her Stoke Newington primary school, singing "Over the Rainbow." I thought of Holly at the homeless shelter off Trafalgar Square, helping some runaway kid make sense of a social-security form.

But the figure who stepped out of the compound, maybe twenty paces away, was neither Aziz nor Nasser nor an AK47-wielding Islamist. It was the driver of the pickup truck, the father of the boy. He stared past his car, towards Fallujah, where helicopters *thucker-thucker-thucker*ed over a quarter of a million humans.

Then he collapsed and sobbed in the dirt.

"Cop a load o' this!" Dave Sykes comes into the Gents at the Maritime Hotel as I'm washing my hands, thinking how precious water is in Iraq. The lounge band in the banquet hall are doing a jazzy rendition of Chris de Burgh's "Lady in Red." Dave gazes around the echoey space. "You could fit a crazy-golf course in here."

"Classy, as well," I say. "Those tiles are real marble."

"A classy khazi for the perfect Mafia hit. You could have five machine-gunners leaping out of the cubicles."

"Though maybe not on your daughter's wedding day."

"Nah, maybe not." Dave walks over to the urinal and unzips his fly. "Remember the bogs in the Captain Marlow?"

"Fondly. That sounds weird. I remember the graffiti. Not that I ever contributed, of course."

"The smuttiest graffiti in Gravesend, we had at the Captain Marlow. Kath used to make me paint over it, but a fortnight later it'd be back."

The journo within asks, "Do you miss life as a landlord?"

"Bits and pieces, sure. The *craic*. Some of the regulars. Can't say I miss the hours, or the fights. Or the taxes and the paperwork. But the old place was home for forty years, so it'd be strange if I didn't, y'know, have memories wrapped up in it. The kids grew up there. I can't go back. I couldn't bear to see it. 'The Purple Turtle,' f'Chrissakes! Yuppies on their poserphones. Upstairs all converted into 'executive apartments.' Do you go back to Gravesend ever?"

"Not since Mum died, no. Not once."

Dave zips up his trousers and walks over, placing one foot in front of the other, like an old man who could do with losing a few pounds. At the sink, he tentatively reaches out for the soap dispenser; a frothy blob blooms and drops onto his hand. "Look at that! Life's more science-fictiony by the day. It's not just that you get old and your kids leave; it's that the world zooms away and leaves you hankering for whatever decade you felt most comfy in." Dave holds his soapy hands under the warm tap and out spurts the water. "Enjoy Aoife while you can, Ed. One moment you're carrying this lovable little tyke on your shoulders, the next she's off, and you realize what you suspected all along: However much you love them, your own children are only ever on loan."

"What I'm dreading is Aoife's first boyfriend," I say.

Dave shakes the water from his hands. "Oh, you'll be fine."

Me and my big mouth might've just reminded Dave of Vinny Costello and the prelude to Jacko's disappearance, so I grope for a topic changer: "Pete seems like a decent enough bloke, anyway."

"Reckon so. Mind you, Sharon always was choosy."

I find myself searching Dave's reflection in the mirror for any signs of an unspoken "unlike Holly," but he's on to me: "Don't worry Ed, you'll do. You're one of the very few other blokes I've ever met who can really carry off a beard as well as I can."

"Thanks." I hold my hands under the dryer and wonder, *Would I actually do it? Leave Holly and Aoife for the sake of my job?*

I'm angry that Holly's forcing me to choose.

All I want is for Holly to share me with my job.

Like I share Holly with her job. It seems fair.

"It'll come as a bit of a jolt, I guess," says Dave, the intuitive ex-pub landlord, "being back in England full-time, like. Will it?"

"Um . . . yeah, it will, all things being equal."

"Ah. So all things might not be equal?"

"*Spyglass* offered me an extension to December."

Dave exhales through his teeth in sympathy.

"Age-old dilemma. Duty versus family. Can't advise you, Ed, but for what it's worth, I've met a fair few fellers down the years just after they've been told by a doctor that they're going to die. Stands to reason—if a quack ever tells me I've only got X weeks to live, I'll need a bar, a sympathetic ear, and a stiff drink, too. You won't be surprised when I tell you that not a one of them fellers ever said, 'Dave, if only I'd spent more time at work.'"

"Maybe they were doing the wrong jobs," I say, and regret straight away how flippant it sounds. Worse, I don't get the chance to clarify what I meant because the door flies open and a trio of Holly's Irish cousins burst in, laughing at a lost punch line: "Ed, Uncle Dave, here you are," says Oisín, whose blood relationship to Holly I can never get my head around. "Aunt Kath dispatched us to hunt you both down and bring you back alive."

"Blimey O'Riley, what've I done now?"

"Chil*lax,* Uncle Dave. Time to cut the cake, is all."

AZIZ DROVE US back towards Baghdad so Nasser could tell me about the patients he'd interviewed at the clinic. With Aziz's photos, we had the bones of a good *Spyglass* story. Before we reached Abu Ghraib, however, we hit a long tailback. Nasser hopped out at a roadside stall and returned with kebabs and two items of news: A fuel convoy had been attacked earlier and the main road back to Baghdad was part blocked by a thirty-foot crater, hence the holdup; and that an American helicopter had been brought down on farmland southeast of the prison complex. We decided to make a detour in search of the crash site. We chewed the chunks of stringy lamb—or possibly goat—and Aziz turned south at the mosque where we'd run into trouble earlier. Once the prison complex was behind us, we saw a reedy column of black smoke rising from behind a windbreak of tamarisk trees. A boy on a bicycle confirmed that, yes, the American helicopter, a Kiowa, had been brought down over there, Allah be praised. Boys growing up in occupied Iraq know about weaponry and military hardware just as I knew about fishing gear, motorbikes, and the Top 40 in the 1980s. The boy mimed a *boom!* and laughed. Some marines had removed the two dead Americans thirty minutes ago, he told Nasser, so now it was safe to go and see.

A track led over an irrigation canal, through the tamarisks and into a field of weeds. The smoldering carcass of the crushed and blackened Kiowa lay on its side, with its tail section lying half the field away. "Ground-to-air missile," speculated Nasser, "cut in middle. Like sword." Maybe twenty men and boys were standing around. Farm buildings stood on the far side, and machinery lay neglected. Aziz parked in the corner and we got out and walked over. The late afternoon was filled with insect noises. Aziz took pictures as we approached. I thought of the pilots, and wondered what had spun through their heads as they careered to Earth. An old man in a red kaffiyeh asked Nasser if we were with a newspaper, and Nasser said, Yes, we worked for a Jordanian one. We were here to counter the lies of the Americans and their allies, Nasser said, and asked the man if he had seen the helicopter crash. The old man said, No, he knew nothing, he only heard an explosion. Some other men, maybe the Mahdi Army, drove off, but he had been too far away, and look—he pointed to his eyes—his cataracts were clouding over.

Seeing too much in Iraq can get you killed.

Suddenly we heard the rumble of army vehicles, and the crowd scattered, or tried to; we clustered into a group again as we realized both exits from the field were blocked by two convoys of four Humvees. Marines emerged from the vehicles in full body armor, pointing their M16s at us. A disembodied roar filled the field: "Hands above your heads! Hands where I can see them! *All* of you on the fucking ground now or I swear, you gloating fucking Ali Baba pigfuckers, I'll put you *in* the ground!" No translation was provided, but we all got the idea.

"HANDS HIGHER!" another marine yelled at a man in a mechanic's oil-stained overalls, who said, "Mafee mushkila, mafee mushkila," No problem, no problem, but the marine shouted, "Don't contradict me! Don't contradict me!" and booted the man in the stomach—all our guts jerked tight in sympathy—and he folded over, gasping and coughing. "Find out who owns this farm," the marine ordered an interpreter, whose face was hidden in a sort of head-wrapping, like a ninja. The marine spoke into his headset, saying the area was secured while the interpreter asked the old man in the red kaffiyeh who owned the farm.

I didn't hear the answer because a black marine was standing over Aziz, saying, "Souvenirs, huh? This your handiwork, huh?" Fate sent a Chinook thundering out of the sun; it drowned my voice as the marine yanked Aziz's camera off his neck with such force that the strap broke, and Aziz fell forward headfirst. Next thing I knew the marine was kneeling by Aziz with his handgun pressed against my photographer's head.

I shouted, "No—stop! He's working for me," but the din of the Chinook drowned me out, and suddenly I was flipped to the ground and an armored kneecap was pressing my windpipe into the dirt, too, and I thought, *They won't discover their mistake till I'm dead.* Then, *No, they won't discover their mistake at all; I'll be deposited in a shallow pit on the edge of Baghdad.*

"WHY *AREN'T THEY* grateful, Ed?"

A cube of wedding cake is halfway to my mouth, but Pauline Webber has a penetrating voice, and now I'm being watched by four Webbers, six Sykeses, Aoife, and a vase of orange lilies. My problem is, I have no idea who or what she's talking about, as I've spent the last few minutes mentally composing an email to the accounts department at the corporation that owns *Spyglass*. I look at Holly for a hint, but she blanks me from behind her wronged-woman mask. Though I wouldn't be too sure it is a mask.

Luckily, Peter's younger brother and best man, Lee, comes to my aid; his "core competence" may be "tax evoision" but that doesn't stop him being an authority on international affairs too. "Iraq under Saddam used to be a concentration camp aboveground and a mass grave below. So us and the Yanks, we come along and take their dictator down for them, gratis and for free—and how do they pay us back? By turning on their liberators. Ingratitude is deeply, *deeply,* ingrained into the Arab races. And it's not just our lads in uniform they hate; it's *any* Westerner, right, Ed? Like that poor reporter who got offed last year, just for being American? Gro*tesque.*"

"You've got spinach stuck in your teeth, Lee," says Peter.

Of course Aoife asks, "What does 'offed' mean, Daddy?"

"Why don't you and I," Holly says to Aoife, "go and see Lola and Amanda at the big kids' table? I think they've got Coca-Cola."

"You always say Coca-Cola stops you sleeping, Mummy."

"Yes, but you worked so hard being Aunty Sharon's bridesmaid, we can make an exception this once." Holly and Aoife slip away.

Lee still hasn't caught on. "Has the spinach gone?"

"It has," says Peter, "but the tactlessness is still there."

"Huh? *Oh.*" Lee does a contrite smirk. "Oops. No offense, Ed. Imbibed too freely of the old vino, methinks."

I should say, "No offense taken," but I just shrug.

"Thing is," says Lee in a let's-face-it tone, "the invasion of Iraq was about one thing and one thing only: oil."

If I had a tenner for every time I heard that I could buy the Outer Hebrides. I put down my fork. "If you want a country's oil, you just buy it. Like we did from Iraq up until Gulf One."

"Cheaper just to install a puppet government, surely." Lee pokes out the very tip of his tongue to show how provocative he is. "Think of all those lucrative oil contracts. Favorable terms. Yum-yum."

"Maybe that's what the Iraqis object to," says Austin Webber, father of Peter and Lee, a retired bank manager with drooping eyes and a fascinating forehead like a Klingon's. "Being governed by puppets. Can't say I'd relish the prospect much, either."

"Could we *please* let Ed answer my questions?" Pauline says. "Why has the Iraqi intervention gone so horribly off script?"

My head's humming. After Holly's ultimatum last night, I didn't sleep so well, and I've drunk too much champagne. "Because the script was written referring not to Iraq as it was, but to a fantasy Iraq as Rumsfeld, Rice, and Bush et al. wanted it to be, or dreamt it to be, or were promised by their pet Iraqis-in-exile it would be.

They expected to find a unified state like Japan in 1945. Instead, they found a perpetual civil war among majority Shi'a Arabs, minority Sunni Arabs, and Kurds. Saddam Hussein—a Sunni—had imposed a brutal peace on the country, but with him gone, the civil war reheated, and now it's . . . erupted, and the CPA is embroiled. When you're in control, neutrality isn't possible."

The band at the far end of the hall strikes up "The Birdy Song."

Ruth asks, "So the Sunni are fighting in Fallujah because they want a Sunni leader back in charge?"

"That's one reason, but the Shi'a elsewhere are fighting because they want the foreigners out."

"Being occupied's unpleasant," says Austin. "I get that. But surely Iraqis can see that life's better now than it used to be."

"Two years ago your average Iraqi—male—had a job, of some type. Now he hasn't. There was water in the taps and power in the grid. Now there isn't. Petrol was available. Now it isn't. Toilets worked. Now they don't. You could send your kids to school without being afraid they'll be kidnapped. Now you can't. Iraq was a creaking, broken, sanction-ravaged place, but it sort of, kind of, worked. Now it doesn't."

An Arab-looking waiter fills my cup from a silver pot. I thank him and wonder if he's thinking, *This guy's talking out of his hole.* Sharon, meanwhile, a girl happy to discuss Middle Eastern politics over her wedding cake, asks, "Who's to blame?"

"It entirely depends who you ask," I reply.

"We're asking you," says Peter the groom.

I sip my coffee. It's good. "The de facto king of Iraq is a Kissinger acolyte named L. Paul Bremer III. On taking office, he passed two edicts that have shaped the occupation. Edict number one ruled that any member of the Ba'ath Party above a certain rank was to be sacked. With one stroke of the pen Bremer consigned to the scrapheap the very civil servants, scientists, teachers, police officers, engineers, and doctors that the coalition needed to rebuild the country. Fifty thousand white-collar Iraqis lost their salaries, pensions, and futures and wanted the occupation to fail from that day on. Edict number two disbanded the Iraqi Army. No back pay, no pension, no nothing. Bremer created 375,000 potential insurgents—unemployed, armed, and trained to kill. Hindsight is easy, sure, but if you're the viceroy of an occupied country, it's your job to possess foresight—or at least to listen to advisers who do."

Brendan's phone goes off; he answers it and turns away, saying, "Jerry, what news from the Isle of Dogs?"

"If this Bremer's doing such an appalling job," asks Peter, loosening his white silk tie, "why isn't he recalled?"

"His days are numbered." I plop a lump of sugar into my coffee. "But *everyone,* from the president to the lowliest staffer in the Green Zone, has a vested interest in peddling the bullshit that the insurgents are just a few fanatics and that the corner is always being turned. The Green Zone's like the Emperor's New Clothes, where speaking the truth is an act of treason. Bad things happen to realists."

"Surely," asks Sharon, "the truth must be obvious when they set foot outside the Green Zone."

"Most staffers never do. Ever. Except to go to the airport."

If Austin Webber wore a monocle, it would drop. "How do you run a country from inside a bunker, for God's sake?"

I shrug. "Nominally. Sketchily. In a state of ignorance."

"But the military must know what's going on, at least. They're the ones getting blown up and shot at."

"They do, Austin, yes. And the infighting between Bremer's faction and the generals is ruthless, but the military, too, often acts as if it *wants* to radicalize the population. My photographer, Aziz, has an uncle in Karbala who farms a few acres of olive orchards. Well, he *did* farm a few acres of olive orchards. Last October, a convoy was attacked on a stretch of road running through his land, so the coalition forces asked the locals for information on the 'bandits.' When none was forthcoming, a platoon of marines chopped down every last tree: 'To encourage the locals to be more cooperative in future.' Imagine the cooperation that act of vandalism earned."

"It's like the British in Ireland in 1916," says Oisín O'Dowd.

"They repeated the ageless macho mantra 'Force is the only thing these natives understand' so often that they ended up believing it. From that point on they were doomed."

"But I've been visiting the States for thirty years, on and off," says Austin. "The Americans I know are as wise, compassionate, and decent a bunch as you could ever hope to meet. I don't understand it."

"I suspect, Austin, that the Americans you've met in the banking world aren't high school dropouts from Nebraska whose best friend got shot by a smiley Iraqi teenager holding a bag of apples. A teenager whose dad got shredded by a gunner on a passing Humvee last week while he fixed the TV aerial. A gunner whose best friend took a dum-dum bullet through the neck from a sniper on a roof only yesterday. A sniper whose sister was in a car that stalled at an intersection as a military attaché's convoy drove up, prompting the bodyguards to pepper the vehicle with automatic fire, knowing they'd save the convoy from a suicide bomber if they were right, but that Iraqi law wouldn't apply to them if they were wrong. Ultimately, wars escalate by eating their own shit, shitting bigger and eating bigger."

I can see that my metaphor has overstepped the mark.

Lee Webber's chatting with a friend at the neighboring table.

His mum asks, "Can I tempt anyone with the last slice of cake?"

MY FREE EYE, the one not pressed into the dust and grit, located the black marine and I found myself endowed with lip-reading powers as he told Aziz, "Here's a shot for you, motherfucker!"

"He's working for me!" I spat out grit.

The soldier glared my way. "*What* did you say?"

The Chinook was moving away, thank God, and he could hear me. "I'm a journalist," I mumbled, trying to twist my mouth upwards, "a British journalist." My voice was dry and mangled.

A midwestern drawl above my ear said, "The *fuck* you are."

"I'm a British journalist, my name's Ed Brubeck, and"—I did my best to sound like Christopher Hitchens—"I'm working for *Spy-glass* magazine. Good photographers are hard to find so, please, ask your man not to point that thing at his head."

"Major! Fuckface here says he's a British journalist."

"Says he's a *what*?" A crunch of boots approached. The boots' owner barked into my ear: "You speak English?"

"Yes, I'm a British journalist, and if—"

"You're able to sub*stant*iate this claim?"

"My accreditation's in the white car."

There's a sniff. "What white car?"

"The one in the corner of the field. If your private would take his knee off my neck, I'd point."

"Media representatives are s'posed to carry credentials *on* their persons."

"If a militiaman found a press pass on me, they'd kill me. Major, my neck, if you wouldn't mind?"

The knee was removed. "Up. Real slow." My legs were stiff. I wanted to massage my neck but daren't in case they thought I was reaching for a weapon. The officer removed his aviator glasses. His age was hard to gauge: late twenties, but his face was encrusted with grime. HACKENSACK was stitched under his officer's insignia. "So whythefuck's a British journalist dressed like a raghead partying in a field with genu*ine* ragheads round a shot-down OH-58D?"

"I'm in this field because there's news here, and I'm dressed like this because looking too Western gets you shot."

"Looking too fuckin' Arabic almost got you shot."

"Major, would you please let that man go?" I nodded towards Aziz. "He's my photographer. And"—I found Nasser—"the guy in the blue shirt, over there. My fixer."

Major Hackensack let us dangle for a few seconds. "Okay." Aziz and Nasser were allowed to stand and we lowered our arms. "British—that's England, right?"

"England plus Scotland plus Wales, with Northern Ire—"

"Nottingham. 'S that England or Britain?"

"Both, like Boston's in Massachusetts and the U.S."

The major thought I was a smartass. "My brother married a nurse in Nottingham and I never saw such a rancid shit-hole. Ordered a ham sandwich and they gave me a slice of pink slime between two pieces of dried shit. Guy who made it was an Arab. Every last cabdriver was an Arab. Your country's an occupied fuckin' territory, my friend."

I shrugged. "There has been a lot of immigration."

The major leaned to one side, hoicked up a bomb of spit, and let it drop. "You live in the Green Zone, British journalist?"

"No. I'm staying in a hotel across the river. The Safir."

"Up close and personal with the real Iraqis, huh?"

"The Green Zone's one city, Baghdad's another."

"Lemme tell you the deal with real Iraqis. Real Iraqis say, 'There's no security since the invasion!' I say, 'Then try not killing, stabbing, and robbing each other.' Real Iraqis say, 'Americans raid our houses at night, they don't respect our culture.' I say, 'Then stop shooting at us *from* your houses, you fuckfaces.' Real Iraqis say, 'Where's our sewers, our schools, our bridges?' I say, 'Where's the shrinkwrapped billions of dollars we gave you to *build* your sewers, schools, and bridges?' Real Iraqis say, 'Why don't we have power or water?' I say, 'Who blew up the substations and tapped the fuckin' pipes we built?' Oh, and their clerics say, 'Hey, our mosques need painting.' I say, 'Then get your holy asses up a ladder and paint them your-fuckin'-selves!' Put that in your newspaper. What *is* your newspaper, anyhow?"

"It's *Spyglass* magazine. It's American."

"What's it like—like *Time* magazine?"

"It's a liberal jizz rag, sir," said a nearby marine.

"Liberal?" Major Hackensack said it like the word "pedophile." "You a liberal, British journalist?"

I swallowed. The Iraqis were watching us too, wondering if their fates were being decided by this incomprehensible but clearly ill-tempered exchange. "You've been sent here because of *the* most conservative White House in living memory. Truly, Major, I'd value your opinion: Do you consider your leaders to be smart, courageous people?"

Immediately I saw I'd misplayed my shitty hand. You don't suggest to a sleepless, angry officer that his commander in chief is a clueless jerk-off and that his comrades-in-arms have died for nothing. "Here's a question for you," Hackensack growled. "Which of those gentlemen know who shot down our helicopter?"

My feet no longer touched the floor of the pool of shit Aziz, Nasser, and I found ourselves in: "We only got here minutes before you did." Insects buzzed, distant vehicles clattered. "These people told us nothing. They aren't living in times when you trust strangers, specially a foreign one." The officer was reading me as I said this; a subject change would be a good idea. "Major Hackensack, please could I quote your views about the real Iraqis by name?"

He leaned back and squinted forward: "You *are* shittin' me?"

"Our readers would value your perspective."

"No, you cannot quote me, and if—" Hackensack's radio headset crackled into life and he turned away. "One-eight-zero? This is Two-sixteen; over. Negative, negative, One-eight-zero, nobody here but Caspar the fuckin' Ghost and a bunch of gawpers. I'll make inquiries for form's sake but the fuckers'll be laughing at us from under their fuckin' head-towels. Over . . . Uh-huh . . . Roger that, One-eight-zero. Last thing: Did you hear already if Balinski made it? Over." The major's nostrils flared and his jaw clicked. "Shit, One-eight-zero. Shit shit shit. Shit. Over." He booted a stone; it richocheted off the Kiowa's fuselage. "No, no, don't bother. Base admin couldn't dig shit out of their asses. Inform his unit liaison directly. Okay, Two-sixteen, over and out." Major Hackensack looked at the black marine and shook his head, then turned a malevolent gaze my way. "You just see a sewer-mouthed military man, don't you? You just see a cartoon character and a platoon of grunts. You think we deserve this"—he nods at the wreckage—"just for being here. But the dead, they had children, they had family, same as you. They wanted to make something of their lives, same as you.

Hell, they were lied to about this war, same as you. But unlike you, British journalist, they paid for other peoples' bullshit with their lives. They were braver than you. They were better than you. They deserve more than you. So you and Batman and Robin there, get the fuck out of my sight. Now."

"A salaam aleikum." The elderly Irishwoman has a foamy cloud of white hair and a zigzag cashmere poncho. You wouldn't cross her.

I place her Drambuie on the table. *"Waleikum a salaam."*

"How did it go now? *Shlon hadartak?*"

"Al hamdulillah. You've earned your whistle-wetter, Eilísh."

"Most kind. Now, I hope I didn't send ye astray?"

"Not at all." It's just me and Eilísh in the corner of the banquet room. I can see Aoife, playing a clapping-chanting game with a niece of Peter the groom's, and Holly's chatting to yet more Irish cousins. "They had a bottle in the lounge upstairs."

"Did ye bump into any extraterrestrials on the way?"

"Lots. The lounge looks like the bar scene from *Star Wars*." I guess an Irishwoman in her eighties won't know what I'm talking about. "*Star Wars* is an old science fiction film, and it's got this bit—"

"I saw it in Bantry picture house when it came out, thank ye. My sister and I went to see it on our penny-farthings."

"Beg your pardon, I didn't mean to imply . . . Uh . . ."

"Sláinte." She clinks her schooner of Drambuie against my G-and-T. "Bless us, that's the stuff. Tell me a thing now, Ed. Did ye ever get up to Amara and the marshes, in Iraq?"

"No, more's the pity. When I was in Basra I was due to interview the British governor in Amara but that morning the UN headquarters got bombed in Baghdad, so I drove back for that. Now Amara's too dangerous to visit, so I missed my chance. Did you visit?"

"A few months before Thesiger, yes, but I only stayed a fortnight. The village headman's wife took a shine to me. D'ye know, I still dream of the marshes? Not much left of them now, I hear."

"Saddam had them drained, to deny his enemies cover. And what's left is riddled with land mines from the war with Iran."

Eilísh bites her lip and shakes her head. "That one wretched man gets to eradicate an entire landscape and a way of life . . ."

"Did you never feel threatened on your epic ride?"

"I had a Browning pistol under my saddle."

"Did you ever use it?"

"Oh, only the once now."

I wait for the story, but Great-aunt Eilísh smiles like a sweet old dear. " 'Tis grand meeting you in the flesh, Ed, at long, *long* last."

"Sorry I've never come over with Holly and Aoife. It's just . . ."

"Work, I know. Work. Ye've wars to cover. I read your reportage when I can, though. Holly sends me clippings from *Spyglass*. Tell me, was your father a journalist as well? Is it in the blood?"

"Not really. Dad was a . . . sort of businessman."

"Is that a fact now? What was his line, I wonder?"

I may as well tell her. "Burglary. Though he diversified into forgery and assault. He died of a heart attack in a prison gym."

"Well, aren't *I* the nosy old crone? Forgive me, Ed."

"Nothing to forgive." Some little kids rush by our table. "Mum kept me on the straight and narrow, down in Gravesend. Money was tight, but my uncle Norm helped out when he could, and . . . yeah, Mum was great. She's not with us anymore either." I feel a bit sheepish. "God, this is sounding like *Oliver Twist*. Mum got to hold Aoife in her arms, at least. I'm happy about that. I've even got a photo of them." From the band's end of the room comes cheering and clapping. "Wow, look at Dave and Kath go." Holly's parents are dancing to "La Bamba" with more style than I could muster.

"Sharon was telling me they're after taking lessons."

I'm ashamed to admit I didn't know. "Holly mentioned it."

"I know ye're busy, Ed, but even if it's just a few days, come over to Sheep's Head this summer. My hens'll find room for ye in their coop, I dare say. Aoife had a gas time last year. Ye can take her pony trekking in Durrus, and go for a picnic out to the lighthouse at the far tip of the headland."

I'd love to say yes to Eilísh, but if I say yes to Olive, I'll be in Iraq all summer. "If I possibly can, I will. Holly has a painting she did of your cottage. It's what she'd rescue if her house was on fire. Our house."

Eilísh puckers her pruneish old lips. "D'ye know, I remember the day she painted it? Kath came over to see Donal's gang in Cork, and parked Holly with me for a few days. 1985, this was. They'd had a terrible time of it, of course, what with . . . y'know. Jacko."

I nod and drink, letting the icy gin numb my gums.

"It's hard for them all at family occasions. A fine ball of a man Jacko'd be by now, too. Did ye know him at all, in Gravesend?"

"No. Only by reputation. People said he was a freak, or a genius, or a . . . Well, y'know. Kids. I was in Holly's class at school, but by the time I got to know Holly well, he was . . . It'd already happened." All those days, mountains, wars, deadlines, beers, air miles, books, films, Pot Noodle, and deaths between now and then . . . but I still remember *so* vividly cycling across the Isle of Sheppey to Gabriel Harty's farm. I remember asking Holly, "Is Jacko here?" and knowing from her face that he wasn't. "How well did you know Jacko, Eilísh?"

The old woman's sigh trails off. "Kath brought him over when he'd've been five or so. A pleasant small boy, but not one who struck you as so remarkable. Then I met him again, eighteen months later, after the meningitis." She drinks her Drambuie and sucks in her lips. "In the old days, they'd've called him a 'changeling,' but modern psychiatry knows better. Jacko at six was . . . a different child."

"Different in what way?"

"He *knew* things—about the world, about people, all sorts . . . Things small boys just don't—can't—shouldn't know. Not that he was a show-off. Jacko knew enough to hide being a dandy, but," Eilísh looks away, "if he grew to trust ye, ye'd be given a glimpse. I was working as a librarian in Bantry at the time, and I'd borrowed *The Magic Faraway Tree* by Enid Blyton for him the day before he arrived because Kath'd told me he was a fierce reader, like Sharon. Jacko read it in a single sitting, but didn't say if he'd enjoyed it or not. So I asked him, and Jacko said, 'My honest opinion, Auntie?' I said, 'I'd not want a *dis*honest one, would I?' Jacko said, 'Okay, then I found it just a little *puerile, Aunt.*' Six years old, and he'd use a word like 'puerile'! The following day, I took Jacko to work with me and—not a word of a lie—he pulled *Waiting for Godot* off the shelves. By Beckett. Truth be told, I assumed Jacko was just attention-seeking, wanting to amaze the grown-ups. But then at lunchtime we ate our sandwiches by the boats, and I asked him what he'd made of Samuel Beckett, and"—Eilísh sips her Drambuie—"suddenly Spinoza and Kant were joining our picnic. I tried to pin him down and asked him straight, 'Jacko, how can you know all this?' and he replied, 'I must have heard it on a bus somewhere, Auntie—I'm only six years old.'" Eilísh sloshes her glass. "Kath and Dave saw consultants, but as Jacko wasn't ill, as such, why would they care?"

"Holly's always said that the meningitis somehow rewired his brain in a way that . . . massively increased its capacity."

"Aye, well, they do say that neurology's the final frontier."

"You don't buy the meningitis theory, though, do you?"

Eilísh hesitates: "It wasn't Jacko's brain that changed, Ed, it was his soul."

I keep a sober face. "But if his soul was different, was he still—"

"No. He wasn't Jacko anymore. Not the one who'd come to visit me when he was five. Jacko aged seven was someone else altogether." Octogenarian faces are hard to read; the skin's so crinkled and the eyes so birdlike that facial clues are obscured. The band have been nobbled by the Corkonian contingent; they strike up "The Irish Rover."

"I presume you've kept this view to yourself, Eilísh?"

"Aye. They'd be hurtful words as well as mad-sounding ones. I only ever put it to one person. That was himself. A few nights after the Beckett day there was a storm, and the morning after Jacko and I were gathering seaweed from the cove below my garden, and I came right out with it: 'Jacko, who are ye?' And he answered, 'I'm a well-intentioned visitor, Eilísh.' I couldn't quite bring myself to ask, 'Where's Jacko?' but he must've heard the thought, somehow.

He told me that Jacko couldn't stay, but that he was keeping Jacko's memories safe. That was the strangest moment of my life, and I've known a few."

I flex my leg; it's gone to sleep. "What did you do next?"

Eilísh face-shrugs. "We spread the seaweed over the carrot patch. As if we'd agreed a pact, if you will. Kath, Sharon, and Holly left the next day. Only," she frowns, "when I heard the news that he'd gone . . ." she looks at me, ". . . I've always wondered if the way he left us wasn't related to the way he first came . . ."

An uncorked bottle goes *pop!* and a table cheers.

"I'm honored you're telling me all this, Eilísh, honestly—but why are you telling me all this?"

"I'm being told to."

"Who . . . who by?"

"By the Script."

"What script?"

"I've a gift, Ed." The old Irishwoman has speckled woodpecker-green eyes. "Like Holly's. Ye know what it is I'm talking of, so ye do."

Chatter swells and falls like the sea on shingle. "I'm guessing you mean the voices Holly heard when she was a girl, and the, well, what in some circles would be called her moments of 'precognition.'"

"Aye, there's different names for it, right enough."

"There are also sound medical explanations, Eilísh."

"I'm quite sure there are, if ye set store in them. The *cluas faoi rún*, we'd call it in Irish. The secret ear."

Great-aunt Eilísh has a bracelet of tiger's-eye stones. Her fingers fret at it while she's talking and watching me.

"Eilísh, I have to say—I mean, I respect Holly very much, and y'know . . . she's definitely highly intuitive—bizarrely, sometimes. And I'm not rubbishing any traditions here, but . . ."

"But ye'd as soon eat your arm off as buy into this mumbo-jumbo about second sight and secret ears and whatever else this mad old West Cork witch is banging on about."

That's exactly what I think. I smile an apology.

"And that's all well and good, Ed. For ye . . ."

I notice a headache knocking at my temples.

". . . but not for Holly. She has to live with it. It's hard—I know. Harder for Holly in shiny modern London, I'd say, than for me in misty old Ireland. She'll need your help. Soon, I think."

This is probably the weirdest conversation I've ever had at a wedding. But at least it's not about Iraq. "What do I do?"

"Believe *her,* even if you don't believe in *it.*"

Kath and Ruth walk up, glowing from their Latin dance action. "You two have been sat here thick as thieves for *ages.*"

"Eilísh has been telling me about her Arabian adventures," I say, still wondering about the old woman's last line.

Ruth asks, "*Did* you see Kath and Dave dancing?"

"We did and fair play to ye both," says Great-aunt Eilísh. "That's a mighty set of tail feathers Dave's sprouted—at his time of life, too."

"We'd go dancing when we first met," says Kath, who sounds more Irish in the midst of the tribe, "but it stopped when we took on the Captain Marlow. No nights off together for thirty-odd years."

"It's almost three o'clock, Eilísh," says Ruth. "Your taxi'll be here soon. You might want to start your goodbyes."

No! She can't go all paranormal on me and just leave. "I thought you'd be around for tonight, at least, Eilísh."

"Oh, I know my limits." She stands up with the aid of her stick. "Oisín's chaperoning me to the airport, and my neighbor Mr. O'Daly'll meet me at Cork airport. Ye have your invitation to Sheep's Head, Ed. Use it before it expires. Or before I do."

I tell her, "You look pretty indestructible to me."

"We all of us have less time than we think, Ed."

CLOUDS CURDLED PINK in the narrow sky above the blast barriers lining the highway into Baghdad from the southwest. Traffic was chocka and slow, even on the side lanes, and for the last mile to the Safir Hotel the Corolla was moving at the speed of an obese jogger. Overladen motorbikes lurched past. Nasser was driving, Aziz was snoozing, and I slumped low behind my screen of hanging shirts. Baghdad's a dark city now in all senses—there's no power for the streetlights—and dusk brings a Transylvanian urgency to get home and bar the door behind you. We'd seen some ugly things and Nasser was in a bleaker-than-usual mood. "My wife, okay, Ed, she had good childhood. Her father worked at oil company, she go to good school, money enough, she smart, she study, Baghdad a good place then. Even after Iranian war begin, many American companies here. Reagan send money, weapons, CIA helpers for Saddam— chemicals for battle. Saddam was America ally, you know this. Good days. I a teenager then, too, Suzuki 125, leather jacket, very cool. Talk in cafés with friends, all night. Girls, music, books, this stuff. We have future then. My wife's father have connections, so I don't join army. Thank the God. I got job in radio station, I work at Ministry of Information. War is over. At last, we think, Saddam spend money on country, on university, we become like Turkey. Then Kuwait happen. America says, 'Okay, invade, Kuwait is local border dispute.' But then—no. UN resolution. We all think, What the fuck? Saddam like cornered animal, cannot retreat with face. In Kuwait war my job was *verrry* creative—to paint defeat like victory for Saddam. But future was dark, then. At home, we listen to BBC Arab Service at home, in secret, my wife and me. So, so, so jealous of BBC journalists, who is free to report real news. That *I* wanted to do. But, no. We wrote lies about Kurds, lies about Saddam and sons, lies about Ba'ath Party, lies about how Iraq future is bright. If you try write truth, you die in Abu Ghraib. Then 9/11, then Bush say, 'We take down Saddam.' We happy. We scared, but we happy. Then, *then,* Saddam, that son of bitch, he gone. I thought, God is Great, Iraq begin again, Iraq rises like . . . that firebird, how you say, Ed?"

"Phoenix."

"So I think, Iraq rise like phoenix, I become *real* journalist. I think, I go where I want, I speak who I want, I write what I want. I think, My daughters will have careers, like my wife had career once, their future good now. Saddam statue pulled down by Iraqi and Americans—but by night looting begin from museum. U.S. soldiers, they just watch. General Garner said, 'Is natural, after Saddam.' I think, My God, America has no plan. I think, Here come Dark Ages. Is true. My daughters' school hit by missile, in war. Money for new school was stolen. So no school, for months and months now. My daughters not go out. Is too danger. All day they argue, read, draw, dream, wash if there is water, watch neighbor TV if there is power. They see teenage girls in America, in Beverly Hills, go to college, drive, date boys. TV girls, they have bedrooms bigger our apartment, *and rooms just for clothes and shoes.* My God! For my girls, dream is like torture. When America go, in Iraq, only two future. One future is place of guns, knives, Sunni fight Shi'a, it never end. Like Lebanon in 1980s. Other future is place of Islamists, Shariah, burkas. Like Afghanistan now. My cousin Omar, last year he escape to Beirut, then he go in Brussels to find girl to marry, any girl, old, young, any who have EU passport. I say, 'Omar, in name of God, you fucking crazy! You not marry a girl, you marry passport.' He say, 'For six years I treat girl nice, treat her parents nice, then plan careful, divorce, I EU citizen, I free, I stay.' He there now. He succeed. Today I think, No, Omar not crazy. We who stay, we crazy. Future is dead."

I didn't know what to say. The car edged past a crowded Internet café, full of slack-jawed boys holding game consoles and gazing at screens where American marines shot Arab-looking guerrillas in ruined streetscapes that could easily be Baghdad or Fallujah. The game menu had no option to be a guerrilla, I guess.

Nasser fed his cigarette butt out of the window. "Iraq. Broken."

I'M POSSIBLY A bit drunk. Holly's over by the silver punch bowls, among an asteroid belt of women talking nineteen to the dozen. Webbers, Sykeses, Corkonian Corcorans, A. N. Others . . . Who the hell *are* all these people? I pass a table where Dave's playing Connect 4 with Aoife and losing with theatrical dismay. I never play with Aoife like that; she giggles as her granddad clutches his head and groans, "Nooooo, you *can't* have won *again*! *I'm* the Connect 4 king!" Wishing I'd responded to Holly's frostiness earlier less frostily, I decide to offer Holly an olive branch. If she uses it to hit me across the face, then we'll clearly establish who's the moody cow and who occupies the moral high ground. I'm only three tight clusters of poshly attired people away from the woman officially known as my partner—when I'm intercepted and blocked by Pauline Webber, wielding a gangly young man. The lad's dressed for a teenage snooker tournament—purple silk shirt, matching waistcoat, pallid complexion. "Ed, Ed, Ed!" she crows. "Reunited at last. This is Seymour, who I told you *all* about. Seymour, Ed Brubeck, *real life* roving reporter." Seymour flashes a mouthful of dental braces. His handshake's a bony grab, like a UFO catcher's. Pauline smiles like a gratified matchmaker. "Do you know, I'd stab someone in the heart with a corkscrew for a camera right *now* just to capture the two of you?" Though she does nothing about commandeering one.

Seymour's handshake is exceeding the recommended limit. His brow is constellated with angry zits—see the squashed W of Cassiopeia—and the drunken feeling that I've already dreamt this very scene is superseded by the feeling that, no, I only dreamt the feeling that I've dreamt this very scene. "I'm a big fan of your work, Mr. Brubeck."

"Oh." A wannabe newshound, seduced by tales of derring-do and sex with Danish photojournalists in countries suffixed with -stan.

"You said you'd share a few secrets," says Pauline Webber.

Did I? "Which secrets did I say I'd share, Pauline?"

"You *devil,* Ed." She biffs my carnation. "Don't play hard to get with *me*—we're as good as family now."

I need to get to Holly. "Seymour, what do you need to know?"

Seymour fixes me with his ventriloquist's creepy eyes and wiry smile, while Pauline Webber's voice slashes through the din: "What makes a great journalist a great journalist?"

I need painkillers, natural light, and air. "To quote an early mentor," I tell the kid, " 'A journalist needs ratlike cunning, a plausible manner, and a little literary ability.' Will that do?"

"What about the *greats*?" fires Pauline Webber's voice.

"The greats? Well, they all share that quality Napoleon most admired in his generals: luck. Be in Kabul when it falls. Be in Manhattan on 9/11. Be in Paris the night Diana's driver makes his fatal misjudgement." I flinch as the windows blast in, but, no, that's not now, that's ten days ago. "A journalist *marries* the news, Seymour. She's capricious, cruel, and jealous. She demands you follow her to wherever on Earth life is cheapest, where she'll stay a day or two, then jet off. You, your safety, your family are *nothing*," I say it like I'm blowing a smoke ring, "*nothing,* to her. Fondly you tell yourself you'll evolve a modus operandi that lets you be a good journalist *and* a good man, but no. That's bollocks. She'll habituate you to sights only doctors and soldiers should ever be habituated to, but while doctors earn sainthoods and soldiers get memorials, *you,* Seymour, will earn lice, frostbite, diarrhea, malaria, nights in cells. You'll be spat on as a parasite and have your expenses questioned. If you want a happy life, Seymour, be something else. Anyway, we're all going extinct." Spent, I push past them and get to the punch bowls at bloody last . . .

. . . and find no sign of Holly. My phone vibrates. It's from Olive Sun. I scroll through the message:

> hi ed, hope wedding good, dufresne ok to interview thurs 22. can u fly cairns wed 21?
> dole fruits aunty take u direct from hotel. respond soonest, best, lr

My first thought is, *Result!* Having excellent grounds for assuming that *Spyglass*'s communications are being intercepted by several government agencies, Olive Sun texts in code: Dufresne is our *nom de texte* taken from *The Shawshank Redemption* for the Palestinian tunneler-in-chief under the Gaza-Egyptian border; "Cairns" is Cairo; "dole fruits" is Hezbollah; and an aunty is a handler. It's

exactly the sort of Bondesque stuff that kids like Seymour suppose
we do routinely, but there's nothing remotely glamorous about being
detained by the Egyptian security forces for seventy-two hours in a
downtown Cairo bunker, waiting for a bored interrogator to come
and ask you why you're there.

I pitched the story to Olive last autumn and she's pulled God
knows how many strings to set this up. Dufresne, if he's one man
and not ten, has a mythical status in Egypt, the Gaza Strip, and
Jordan. An interview would be a major coup and enhance our magazine's reputation in Arab-speaking countries by a factor of ten.
Blockades and sanctions have no news legs; there's little to say and
nothing to see. Who cares if Israelis ban imports of powdered milk
into Gaza? Stories about tunnels under walls, however, that's different. That's *Escape from Colditz* stuff, that's *The Count of Monte
Cristo,* and people eat that shit with a spoon. I'm about to reply
with a yes when I remember one catch: At seven P.M. next Wednesday, Miss Aoife Brubeck is appearing for one night only as the Cowardly Lion in St. Jude's C of E Primary School's performance of *The
Wizard of Oz,* and her daddy is expected.

What kind of self-centered bastard would miss his own daughter's star turn? Why care about other people's six-year-olds who'll
never perform anything because they died when Israeli bulldozers
or Hezbollah rockets destroyed their homes? They're not *our* kids.
We're clever enough to be born where such things don't happen.

See the problem, Seymour?

THE SECURITY GUYS on duty at the Safir Hotel checkpoint recognized Nasser's car, raised the barrier, and waved us through.
Crunching to a halt, Nasser told me, "Okay, Ed, so Aziz and me, we
come at ten tomorrow morning. You, me, we transcribe tapes. Aziz
bring photographs. Amazing story. Olive is very happy."

"See you at ten." Still in the car, I handed Nasser an envelope of
Spyglass dollars for the day's fee. We all shook hands, Aziz let me

out of his side, and the Corolla pulled away. It stopped after only a few yards. I thought it was mechanical trouble, but Nasser wound down his window and waved something at me. "Ed, take this."

I walked over and he put his little tape recorder into my hand. "Why? You're coming tomorrow."

Nasser made a face. "If here with you, is safer. Many good words on the tape." With that he drove around the roundabout and back to the checkpoint. I walked up the hotel steps. Every window was a dark rectangle. Even if the electricity is working, guests are warned to keep lamps off at night because of the risk of snipers. Meeting me in the metal-plated porch was Tariq, a security guard with a Dragunov. "How they hanging, Mr. Ed?" Tariq likes to practice his slang.

"Can't complain, Tariq. Quiet day?"

"Today quiet. Thanks to God."

"Is Big Mac back home already?"

"Yes, yes. The dude is in the bar."

I tip Tariq and his three colleagues generously to tell me if outsiders are asking questions about me, and to be vague with their replies. Not that I can ever be sure Tariq isn't pocketing fees from both sides, but the principle of the Golden Goose has held so far. From the porch I passed through the glass doors to the circular reception area, where a low-wattage lamp gleamed on the concierge's desk. A mighty chandelier hangs overhead, but I've never seen it illuminated, and now it's mightily cobwebbed. I never looked at it without imagining it crashing down. Mr. Khufaji, the manager, was helping a lad load used car batteries onto a luggage trolley. Dead batteries are exchanged for live ones every morning, like milk bottles when I was a kid. Guests use them to power laptops and sat-phones.

"Good evening, Mr. Brubeck," said the manager, dabbing his forehead with a handkerchief. "You'll be needing your key."

"Good evening, Mr. Khufaji." I waited while he fetched it from the drawer. "Could I have one of those batteries, please?"

"Certainly. I'll send the boy up when he returns."

"Most kind." We retain old-school manners, even if Baghdad has gone to hell and the Safir was less a five-star hotel and more of a serviced campsite inside a dead hotel.

"I thought I heard your dulcet tones." Honduran cigar in hand, Big Mac appeared from the dingy bar that served as common room, rumor mill, and favor exchange. "What time do you call this?"

"Later than you, which means you're buying the beers."

"No no no, the deal was the *last* one back buys the beers."

"That's a shameless lie, Mr. MacKenzie, and you know it."

"Hey. Shameless lies precipitate wars and make work for hungry hacks. Get any street action in Fallujah?"

"The cordon's too tight. What about you day-trippers?"

"Waste of time." Big Mac filled his lungs with cigar smoke. "Got to Camp Victory to be told the fighting had intensified, meaning the Marine Corps were too busy to keep our fat asses alive. We munched bullshit with press officers before being squeezed into a supply convoy heading back to Baghdad. Not the one that got IEDed into flying mince, obviously. You?"

"Better. We found a makeshift clinic for refugees from Fallujah, plus a shot-down Kiowa. Aziz took a few shots before a uniformed countryman of yours kindly suggested we leave."

"Not bad, but"—Big Mac crossed the floor and lowered his voice, even though Mr. Khufaji had exited—"one of Vincent Agrippa's 'well-placed sources' texted him twenty minutes ago about a 'unilateral cease-fire' coming into play tomorrow."

I doubted that. "Mac, the Fallujah militia won't roll over now. Perhaps as a regrouping exercise—"

"No, not the insurgents. The marines are standing down."

"Bloody hell. Where is this source? General Sanchez's office?"

"Nope. The army'll be spitting cold shit over this. They'll be, 'If you're going to take Vienna, take fucking Vienna.' "

"Do you think Bremer cooked this one up?"

"My friend: The Great Envoy couldn't cook his own testes in a Jacuzzi of lava."

"You'll have to give me a clue, then, won't you?"

"Since you're buying the beers, here's three." Big Mac took a five-second cigar break. "C, I, and A. It's a direct order from Dick Cheney's office."

"Vincent Agrippa has a source in the *CIA*? But he's French! He's a cheese-eating surrender monkey."

"Vincent Agrippa has a source in God's panic room, and it pans out. Cheney's afraid that Fallujah'll split the Coalition of the Willing—not that they're a coalition, or willing, but hey. Join us for dinner after you've freshened up—guess what's on the menu."

"Could it be chicken and rice?" There were fifty dishes on the Safir's official menu, but only chicken and rice was ever served.

"Holy shit, the man's telepathic."

"I'll be down after slipping into something more comfortable."

"Promises, promises, you tart." Big Mac returned to the bar while I climbed up to the first landing—the elevators haven't worked since 2001—the second, and the third. Through the window I looked across the oil-black Tigris at the Green Zone, lit up like Disneyland in Dystopia. I thought about J. G. Ballard's novel *High Rise,* where a state-of-the-art London tower block is the vertical stage for civilization to unpeel itself until nothing but primal violence remains. A helicopter landed behind the Republican Palace, where this morning Mark Klimt had told us about the positive progress in Fallujah and elsewhere. What do Iraqis think about when they see this shining Enclave of Plenty in the heart of their city? I know, because Nasser, Mr. Khufaji, and others have told me: They think a well-lit, well-powered, well-guarded Green Zone is proof that the Americans *do* own a magic wand capable of restoring order to Iraq's cities, but that anarchy makes a dense smokescreen behind which they can pipe away the nation's oil. They're wrong, but is their belief any more absurd than that of the 81 percent of Americans who believe in angels? I heard a *miaow* nearby and looked down to see a moon-gray cat melting out of the shadows. I bent down to say hello, which was the one and only reason why I wasn't scalped like a boiled egg when the explosion outside blew in the glass windows on the western face of the Safir Hotel, filling its unlit corridors with blast waves, filling our ear canals with solid roar, filling the spaces between atoms with the atonal chords of destruction.

I TAKE ANOTHER ibuprofen and sigh at my laptop screen. I wrote an account of the explosion on yesterday's flight from Istanbul with dodgy guts and not enough sleep, and I'm afraid it shows: Nonfiction that smells like fiction is neither. A statement from Rumsfeld about Iraq is due at eleven A.M. East Coast time, but that's fifty minutes away. I click on the telly to CNN World with the sound down, but it's only a White House reporter discussing what "a well-placed source close to the secretary of defense" thinks Rumsfeld might say when he comes on. On her bed, Aoife yawns and puts down her *Animal Rescue Ranger Annual 2004.* "Daddy, can you put *Dora the Explorer* on?"

"No, poppet. I was just checking something for work."

"Is that big white building in Bad Dad?"

"No, it's the White House. In Washington."

"Why's it white? Do only white people live in it?"

"Er . . . Yes." I switch the TV off. "Naptime, Aoife."

"Are we right under Granddad Dave and Grandma Kath's room?"

I should be reading to her, really—Holly does—but I have to get my article done. "They're on the floor above us, but not directly overhead."

We hear seagulls. The net curtain sways. Aoife's quiet.

"Daddy, can we visit Dwight Silverwind after my nap?"

"Let's not start that again. You need a bit of shut-eye."

"You told Mummy you were going to take a nap too."

"I will, but you go first. I have to finish this article and email it to New York by tonight." *And then tell Holly and Aoife that I won't be at* The Wizard of Oz *on Thursday,* I think.

"Why?"

"Where d'you think money comes from to buy food, clothes, and *Animal Rescue Ranger* books?"

"Your pocket. And Mummy's."

"And how does it get in there?"

"The Money Fairy." Aoife's just being cute.

"Yeah. Well, I'm the Money Fairy."

"But Mummy earns money at her job, too."

"True, but London's very expensive, so I need to earn as well."

I think of a pithy substitute for the florid "spaces between atoms" line, but my inbox pings. It's only from Air France, but when I get back to my article I've forgotten my pithy substitute.

"Why is London expensive, Daddy?"

"Aoife, *please*. I've got to work. Close your eyes."

"Okay." She lies down in a mock huff and pretends to snore like a Teletubby. It's *really* annoying, but I can't think of anything to say that's sharp enough to shut Aoife up but not so sharp that she won't burst into tears. Better wait this one out.

My first thought was, I type, *I'm alive. My second—*

"Daddy, why can't I go to see Dwight Silverwind on my own?"

Don't snap. "Because you're only six years old, Aoife."

"But I know the way to Dwight Silverwind's! Out of the hotel, over the zebra crossing, down the pier, and you're there."

Look at mini-Holly. "Your fortune's what you make it. Not what a stranger with a made-up name says. Now, *please*. Let me work."

She snuggles up with her Arctic fox. Back to my article: *My first thought was, I'm alive. My second thought was, Stay down; if it was a rocket-propelled grenade attack, there could be more. My—*

"Daddy, don't you want to know what'll happen in your future?"

I let a displeased few seconds pass. "No."

"Why not?"

"Because . . ." I think of Great-aunt Eilísh's mystic Script, and Nasser's family, and Major Hackensack, and cycling along the Thames estuary footpath on a hot day in 1984 and recognizing a girl lying on the shingly beach, in her *Quadrophenia* T-shirt, her jeans as black as her cropped hair, and asleep, with a duffel bag as a pillow, and thinking, *Cycle on, cycle on . . .* And turning around. I shut my laptop, walk over to her bed, kick off my shoes, and lie down next to her. "Because what if I found out something bad was going to happen to me—or, worse, Mum, or you—but couldn't change it? I'd be happier not knowing so I could just . . . enjoy the last sunny afternoon."

Aoife's eyes are big and serious. "What if you *could* change it?"

I squeeze her hair at her crown so it makes a sort of samurai top-knot. "What if I couldn't, Little Miss Pineapple Head?"

"*Hey,* I'm not"—she yawns—"Pineapple Head." I yawn too, and she says, "Ha! You caught my yawn."

"Okay, I'll take a snoozette with you." This isn't such a bad idea. Aoife'll be out for an hour, at least, while I'll wake up refreshed after a twenty-minute power nap, catch Rumsfeld's latest denial, finish my article, and figure out how to tell Holly and the Cowardly Lion that I have to be in Cairo on Wednesday. "Sleep tight," I tell Aoife, like Holly tells her. "Don't let the bedbugs bite."

"ED! ED!" I was dreaming Holly woke me up in a hotel room, her eyes panicky as a horse's when it knows it's going to die. It sounds like Holly's saying "Where's Aoife?" but she can't be because Aoife's asleep, next to me. Gravity's wrong, my limbs are hollow, and I try to say, "What's the matter?" Holly's like someone doing a bad impression of Holly. "Ed, where's Aoife?"

"Here." I lift the blanket.

There's only the Arctic fox.

Twenty thousand volts fry me into hyperalertness.

No need to panic. "In the bathroom."

"I just looked! Ed! Where *is* she?"

"Aoife? Come out, Aoife! This isn't funny!" I stand up and slip on *Animal Rescue Ranger Annual 2004,* fallen to the floor. I check the wardrobes; in the two-inch gap under the bed; and the bathroom, in the shower cubicle. My bones turn to warm Blu Tack. *She's missing.* "She was here. We were having a nap, just a minute ago." I look at the time on the TV frame: 16:20. Shit shit shit. I lurch over to the windows as if—as if I'll see her waving up at me from the teeming weekend crowds on the promenade below? My toe bangs something and the pain drills a hole: Aoife was asking where Dave and Kath's room is; and why she couldn't visit Dwight Silverwind. I look for Aoife's sandals. Gone. Holly's speaking but it's like I've forgotten my English, it's just vowels and consonants, and then she's stopped, and is waiting for me to respond.

"Either she went to find you, or to your mum and dad's room, or . . . or she's gone to the fortune-teller down the pier. You go to your parents' room. And tell Reception not to let a six-year-old girl in a—in a"—*fuck, what was she wearing?*—"a zebra T-shirt out of the building on her own. I'll check the pier." I ram my feet into my shoes, and as I leave the room Holly calls out, "Have you got your phone?" and I check and call back, "Yeah," then hurry into the corridor, down to the lifts where two old ladies from Agatha Christie in flowery frocks are waiting by an aspidistra of prehistoric size in a vast bronze pot and I punch the Down button, but no lift comes, and I punch it and realize I've been mumbling, "Shit shit shit shit shit," and the ladies are glaring, and finally it arrives, opens, and a Darth Vader points upwards with his light sabre and says, "Going up?" in a Belfast accent, and I'm walloped in the nuts by an image of Aoife up on the roof, so I get in. Miss Marple says, "We're going down, but I must say your costume's *splendid*." No, what am I thinking? Any door onto the roof'd be locked, that's stupid. Health and Safety. And, anyway, Aoife's on the pier. I get out, just as the doors close, and bark my shin, making the doors open again and Darth Vader says, "Make your mind up, pal." To the stairs. I follow the arrow marked STAIRS to another arrow marked STAIRS and follow that arrow to another and another and another. The carpet muffles my footfalls. Up ahead the two old ladies are getting into the lift so I shout, "HOLD THAT LIFT FOR ME!" and spring, like Michael Jordan, but trip over my undone laces and slide ten yards, friction-burning my Adam's apple and the doors rumble shut, and maybe the Agatha Christies could've held the lift for me and maybe they couldn't but they didn't, the bitches, and I hammer the button with my thumb but the bastard thing's gone and my trusting, innocent daughter's getting closer to that man on the pier, with his own lockable booth, who probably doesn't even bother with underpants underneath his Merlin robes. I do up my laces, and step back, and the lift stops at "7," and about a decade later it moves down to "6," and stays there another decade, and a scream's welling up, and then I notice stairs through a glass door, behind the aspidistra. For fuck's sake! Down the echoey stairwell I pound, like an action hero with dodgy knees, but what sort of action hero nods off while he's minding his only daughter, his only lovely, funny, perfect, fragile daughter? Down I run, floor after floor, on my Journey to the Center of the Earth, the smell of paint getting fumier, and past a decorator on stepladders: "Bloody hell take it easy mate or yer'll slip and dash yer brains out!" I reach a door marked EMERGENCY EXIT with a grimy little window and a view of an underground loading bay, so it's the back of the building when I need the front, and the door's locked anyway, and why didn't I just wait for the bloody lift? I hurtle along a service passage, skidding past a sign marked LEVEL ZERO ACCESS, and what's this prodding certainty that I'm in a labyrinth not only of turnings and doors but decisions and priorities, that I've been in it not just a minute or two but ages, years, and that I took some bad turns many years ago that I can't get back to, and I slam against a door marked ACCESS and turn the handle and pull but it doesn't open—that's because you're supposed to push so I push—

What? An exhibition space, opening up deeper and wider and higher even as I marvel that the Maritime Hotel could possibly contain this vastness extending—surely—under the foundations of the neighboring buildings, under the promenade, if not the English Channel. Thousands are perusing the rows and avenues of booths and stalls, and the noise is oceanic. Some are dressed in normal clothes but a majority are costumed: Supermen, Batmen, Watchmen; Doctor Spocks, Doctor Whos, Doctor Evils; a trio of C-3POs, a pair of Klingons, a lizardy Silurian; a file of female Chinese Harry Potters, a stubbly Catwoman adjusting his bra strap and a brace of apes from *The Planet of;* a posse of Agent Smiths from *The Matrix,* a walking Tardis, a blasted Schwarzenegger with bits of T-800 endoskeleton showing through; banter, laughter, earnest discussion. *What if Aoife fell into this reservoir of weirdos, geeks, and fantasists? How would she ever get out? How will I get out?* Through the big doors on the far side, of course, under a banner—BRIGHTON PLANET CON 2004. I hurry through the slow flow of browsers of manga, of Tribbles, of T-shirts bragging TREKKIES DO IT UP YOUR TURBO-SHAFT, self-assembly *USS Enterprise*s, metal die-cast *Battlestar Galactica*s; I pass a Dalek blasting out the lines "Golden lads and girls all must, As chimney-sweepers, come to dust"; I dodge an Invisible Man, swerve behind a Ming the Merciless, squeeze between some Uruk-hai, and now I've lost the way out, I've lost Aoife, I've lost my north, south, east, and west, so I ask Yoda which way's the way and he answers, "Next to the bogs, pal," and points, and at last I'm in the lobby, and I come between a cub reporter and Judge Dredd.

Out I plunge . . .

. . . into the Ready Salted afternoon, froggering between the traffic to the promenade. Horns beep but today I am exempt. The warm weather's brought out a hellish *Where's Wally?* of seaside humanity, of families who haven't lost their six-year-old girl through carelessness, through neglect, and I'd swap my soul for the chance to go back to our room an hour ago and I'd handle Aoife better, and I'd say, "Maybe I was a bit grumpy earlier, sorry, let's go and see Mr. Silverwind together," and if only I could have Aoife back I'd give the mystical old bastard my ATM card *and* wipe his arse for a year and a day. Or if I could jump forward an hour in time, after Aoife's turned up safe and sound, the first thing I'd do is to call Olive Sun and say, "Sorry, Olive, send Hari to interview Dufresne, send Jen." God, God, God: Let Aoife run through the crowd and jump into my arms. Let no stranger be bundling her into a van—*Don't go there, just don't go there.* A jostling river of people flows on and off the pier, I jog upstream, then slow down; mustn't miss her if she's walking back this way, looking for Daddy . . . Keep sweeping the faces, side to side, scan the faces for Aoife's; don't think about the headlines reading DAUGHTER OF WAR REPORTER

DISAPPEARS or the tearful TV appeals, or the solicitor's statements on behalf of the Sykeses, the Sykeses, who lived this nightmare once before, the very same one—TRAGEDY STRIKES TWICE FOR FAMILY OF JACKO SYKES; those weeks in 1984 when the Captain Marlow was shut "due to Family Circumstances," read the note on the locked door; the papers reported a few false sightings of a boy who could've been Jacko, but never was; and Kath'd say, "Sorry, Ed, she's not up to seeing anyone today"; in the end I didn't go Inter-Railing but worked at a garden center on the A2 roundabout all summer. I felt responsible, too: If I'd talked Holly into going home that Saturday evening, instead of picking the lock of that church, Jacko might not've gone walkabout; but I fancied her and hoped something might happen; and my phone trills—*Please, God, end this now;* it's Holly, tough-as-boots Holly, and I'm praying, *Please God Please God let it be good news,* and I say, "Any news?"

"Mum and Dad haven't seen her, no. You?"

"I'm still walking down the pier."

"I told the hotel manager. They've made an announcement on the PA, and Brendan's watching Reception. They say the police won't send anyone for a while, but Ruth's onto them."

"Call you as soon as I'm at the fortune-teller's."

"Okay." End call. I'm nearly at the Amusement Arcade—look look look look *look*! A little black-haired girl in a zebra T-shirt and green leggings slips inside the propped-open doors. Christ, that's her, it's got to be, and a hand grenade of hope goes off in my guts and I shout, "AOIFE!"

People turn around to spot the madman, but not Aoife.

I dodge between sunburned forearms, ice creams, and Slush Puppies.

The dark interior scrambles my senses. "Aoife!"

The chainsaw roars of Formula racing cars and *ackackackack-ack* of twenty-second-century laser blasters and the rubbled thunder of bombed-up buildings and—

There she is! Aoife! *Thank you, God, thank you, God, thank you.* She's gazing up at an older girl with a cutoff top and bangles on a Dance Dance Revolution gamefloor, and I lurch over, kneel at her side: "*Aoife, sweetheart, you mustn't wander off like this!* Me and Mum've had a heart attack! Come on." I put my hand on her arm. "Aoife, let's go back now."

But Aoife turns to me and she's got the wrong eyes, wrong nose, and a wrong face, and I'm pulled away by a powerful hand, by a well-built man in his fifties wearing a nasty acrylic shirt, and "What the *fuck* d'you think you're doing with my daughter?"

It just got worse, it really got worse. "I—I—I thought she was my daughter, I lost her, she was . . . But she—she . . ."

The guy's considering dismembering me. "Well, this isn't her—and you wanna watch it, mate. People get the wrong idea, or even the right idea—know what I'm sayin'?"

"I'm sorry, I—I—I . . ." I hurtle into the sunshine outside the arcade, like Jonah puked out of a smoky, chip-greasy whale.

This is your punishment for Aziz and Nasser.

Dwight Silverwind's my only hope. Sixty seconds away.

He wouldn't dare interfere with her here. Too public.

Maybe he'll tell her to wait till Daddy comes along.

Aoife'll be sitting there, like it's all a funny joke.

Does Aoife know Holly's mobile number? Don't know.

Past a burger stand; a netted basketball booth.

Past a giant teddy bear with a guy inside sweating buckets.

There's a little girl, gazing down at the lullabying sea.

Dwight Silverwind's jerks closer and closer, Brighton Pier sways, my ribs curl in, a woman's knitting outside the Sanctum, and a sign saying READING IN PROGRESS hangs on the door. I burst into the dark little cavern with one table, two upholstered chairs, three candles, incense, Tarot cards spread out, a surprised Dwight Silverwind and a black lady in a shell suit—and no Aoife. No Aoife. "*Er*—do you mind if we finish?" says the customer.

I ask Silverwind: "Has my daughter been here?"

The woman stands. "You can't barge in here like this!"

Silverwind's frowning. "I remember you. Aoife's dad."

"She's run off. From my hotel, the Maritime. I—I—I thought she . . ." They look at me like I'm a nutter. I need to vomit. ". . . might've come here."

"I'm so sorry, Mr. Brubeck," Dwight Silverwind's saying, as if she's passed away, "but we've seen neither hide nor hair of her."

I grip my skull to stop it exploding, the floor tilts through forty-five degrees, and if the woman hadn't caught me and sat me in the chair I'd've brained myself on the floor. "Let's get ahold of the situation," she says, in a Birmingham accent. "We've a missing child here, am I right?"

"Yes," I answer in a wafer-thin voice. *Missing.*

A no-nonsense manner: "Name and age?"

Missing. "Edmund Brubeck, I'm, uh, thirty-five."

"No, Edmund. The name and age *of the child.*"

"Oh. Aoife Brubeck. She's six. Only six!"

"Okay, okay. And what's Aoife wearing?"

"T-shirt with a zebra on it. Leggings. Sandals."

"Okay, rapid response is the name of the game, so I'll call pier security, and ask for the duty guys to watch out for your daughter. You write your number here." She hands me a pen and a name-card and I scribble my number down. "Dwight, you take Ed back down the pier, combing the crowds. I'll stay here. If you don't find her on the pier, go back to the Maritime Hotel and we'll have another confab. Ed, if Aoife shows up here, I'll call you. Now go. Go go go go!"

Back outside, my phone goes: Holly, asking, "Is she there?"

My unwillingness to answer gives it away: "No."

"All right. Sharon's texting all the wedding guests to search the hotel. Head back here. I'll be in the lobby with Brendan."

"Okay: I'll be right ba—" But she's ended the call.

Fairground music strobes from the funfair. Might Aoife be there? "They don't let kids under ten past the turnstyles without an adult's with them." Dwight Silverwind's still wearing his gem-encrusted waistcoat. "C'mon, let's sweep the pier. Miss Nichols in there"—he nods at his sanctum—"she'll hold the fort. She's a traffic warden."

"What about your"—I gesture at the booth—"you're working."

"Your daughter sought me out for a reason this morning, and I believe this is it." We walk back down the pier, checking every face, even in the arcade. No good. Where the pier ends, or begins, I manage to thank Dwight Silverwind for his help, but he says, "No, no; I sense I'm scripted to stay with you until the end."

I ask him, "What script?" but now we're crossing the road and entering the coolness of the Maritime Hotel, where all I have to show for my mad rush down the pier is this wizened druid in fancy dress, who doesn't even look that weird in this fantasy crowd. Behind the concierge's desk an operations center's been set up. A hassled manager, with a phone in the crook of his shoulder, is surrounded by Sykeses and Webbers who all look up at the shite father who caused this unraveling nightmare: Sharon and Peter, Ruth and Brendan, Dave and Kath, even Pauline and Austin. "She's not on the pier," I report, redundantly.

Ruth tells me, "Amanda's up in your room, in case she makes her way back there."

Pauline says, "Don't worry now, she'll show up any minute," and Austin nods at her side, telling me that Lee's taken his friends to the beach in case she took it into her head to go for a paddle. Dave and Kath look like they've gone through an age-accelerator and Holly scarcely notices I'm back.

The manager tells her, "Would you speak with the officer, Mrs. Brubeck?"

Holly takes the phone. "Hello . . . Yes. My daughter . . . Yes—yes, I *know* it's been less than an hour, but she's only six, and I want an all-service emergency call to go out now . . . Then *make* an exception, Officer! . . . No, *you* listen: My partner's a journalist at a national newspaper, and if Aoife's *not* found safe and sound, you are going to regret very, very, very badly if you don't put that 108 out now . . . *Thank* you. Six years old . . . Dark hair, shoulder length . . . A zebra T-shirt . . . No, not stripes, a T-shirt with a zebra on it . . . Pink trousers. Sandals . . . I don't know, wait a moment."

Holly looks at me, her face ashen. "Was her scrunchie gone from the room?"

I look dumbly. Her what?

"The silver spangly thing she ties her hair back with?"

I don't know. I don't know. I don't know. But before Holly can respond, her head lolls back at a weird angle and her face begins to shut down. What's happening now? Once I saw a diabetic colleague go into what he called a hypo and this looks a lot like that. Sharon says, "Grab her!" and I lurch forwards, but Brendan and Kath have Holly and stop her falling.

The manager's saying, "Through here, bring her through here," and Holly is half dragged, half supported into a back office.

Her breathing is now ferocious in-out-in-out and Kath, who took a nursing course in Cork years ago, tells everyone, "Space! Back back back!" as she and Brendan lower her onto a hastily cleared sofa. "Slow your breathing, darling," Kath tells her daughter. "Nice, slow breaths for me now . . ." I ought to be next to her but there are too many Sykeses in the way and the office is tiny, and, anyway, whose fault is all of this? I'm close enough to see Holly's eyes, though, and the pupils shrinking away to almost nothing. Pauline Webber says, "Why're her eyes doing that?"—and Peter's shoulder gets in the way—and Holly's face spasms—and Dave says, "Kath, shouldn't we call for a doctor?"—and Holly's face shuts down like she's lost consciousness altogether—and Brendan asks, "Is it some sort of attack, Mam?"—and Kath says, "Her pulse is going fierce fast now"—and the manager says, "I'm calling an ambulance"—but then Holly's lips and jaws begin to flex and she speaks the word *"Ten . . ."* blurrily, like a person profoundly deaf from birth, but huskier and tortuously slow, like a recording at the wrong speed, enunciating the syllable in drawn-out slow motion.

Kath looks at Dave and Dave shrugs: "Ten *what,* Holly?"

"She's saying something else, Kath," says Ruth.

Holly forms a second: *"Fifffff . . ."*

Peter Webber whispers, "Is that English?"

"Holly darling," says Dave, "what're you telling us?"

Holly's shaking slightly, so her voice does too: "Tee-ee-ee-een . . ."

I feel I ought to take charge, somehow. I mean, I am her partner, but I've never seen her—or anyone—like this.

Peter puts it together: "Ten-fifteen?"

Dave asks his daughter, "Love, what's happening at ten-fifteen?"

"It won't mean anything," says Brendan. "She's having an attack of some sort." The pendant with Jacko's last labyrinth on it slides off the edge of the sofa and swings there. Then Holly touches her head and winces with pain but her eyes are back to normal, and she blinks up at the array of faces frowning down. "Oh, f'Chrissakes. Don't tell me I fainted?"

Nobody's quite sure what to say at first.

"Sort of," says Sharon. "Don't sit up."

"Do you remember what you said?" asks Kath.

"No, and who cares, when Aoife—Yeah. Numbers."

"A time, Hol," says Sharon. "You said, 'Ten-fifteen.' "

"I'm feeling better. What happens at ten-fifteen?"

"If you don't know," says Brendan, "how can we?"

"None of this is helping Aoife. Did anyone finish my call with the police?"

"For all we knew," says Kath, "you were having a cardiac arrest."

"Well, I wasn't, Mam, thanks. Where's the manager?"

"Here," says the unfortunate guy.

"Get me the police station, please. They'll drag their heels on the 108 if I don't fire a rocket up them." Holly stands and steps towards the door and the rest of us shuffle back out. I reverse around behind the reception desk to make space—and a voice speaks: "Edmund."

I find Dwight Silverwind, whom I'd forgotten about. "It's Ed."

"That was a message. From the Script."

"A what?"

"A message."

"What was?"

"Ten-fifteen. It's a sign, a glimpse. It wasn't from Holly."

"Well, it certainly looked as if she said it."

"Ed, is Holly at all psychic?"

I can't hide my irritation. "No, she—" The Radio People. "Well, when she was younger, stuff happened, and she . . . A bit, yeah."

Even more lines appear on Dwight Silverwind's oak-grained, drooping face. "I won't deny that I'm as much a 'fortune discusser' as a 'fortune-teller.' People need to voice their fears and hopes in confidence, and I provide that service. But occasionally I *do* meet the real thing—and when I do, I know it. Holly's 'ten-fifteen.' It means something."

His Gandalfy face, my headache, the spinning pier, Eilísh . . . Any car could blow up at any time . . . The thought of Aoife being lost and scared and her mouth taped up—*stop it stop it stop it* . . .

"*Think,* Ed. Those numbers, they're not random."

"Maybe they're not. But I—I'm crap at codes."

"No, no—the Script's not some complex formula. As often as not it's just staring you in the face, so close you can't see it."

I need to look for Aoife, not have a discussion on metaphysics. "Look, I—I . . ." Dwight Silverwind is standing by the pigeonholes for the room keys. Room keys, these days, are a bit of an analog throwback, as most British or American hotels—not Iraqi—use re-writable plastic key cards with magnetic strips. Each pigeonhole is numbered with an engraved brass plaque that corresponds to the number on the ring of the key it houses. And six inches to the left of Dwight Silverwind's head is a pigeonhole labeled 1015. 1015. The key is there.

It's a coincidence—don't start "seeing signs" now.

Dwight Silverwind follows my faintly appalled gaze.

How improbable must a coincidence be before it's a sign?

"Cute," he mutters. "Sure as heck know what *I'd* do next."

The receptionist is turned away. Holly's waiting by the phone. The others are miserable, flapping, pale. One of Sharon's friends appears and says, "No sign of her yet, but everyone's looking," and Austin Webber's talking into his mobile, saying, "Lee? Any sign of her?"

I take the key to 1015; my feet get me to the lift.

It's waiting and vacant. I get in and press 10.

The doors close. Dwight Silverwind's still here.

The lift goes up to the tenth floor, no interruptions.

Silverwind and I step out into a tomblike silence I didn't expect in a busy hotel in April. Sunlight slants through dust. A sign says ROOMS 1000–1030 CLOSED FOR ELECTRICAL REWIRING UNTIL FURTHER NOTICE. STRICTLY NO ADMITTANCE. I walk to 1015, put the key into the lock, turn it, and go in. Silverwind stays outside and, ignoring the unlucky thought that says if Aoife isn't here I'll never see her again, I walk into the musty room and say, "Aoife?"

There's no reply. *Signs aren't real.* You've lost her.

Then the silence is ruffled. The coverlet moves. She's curled up on the bed, asleep in her clothes. "Aoife."

She wakes up, puzzled, sees me, and smiles.

These seconds burn themselves into my memory.

Relief this intense isn't relief anymore, it's joy.

"Aoife, poppet, you've given us all quite a fright."

We're hugging each other tight. "I'm sorry, Daddy, but after you fell asleep I still wasn't sleepy so I thought I'd go and find Granddad Dave for a game of Connect 4, so I went up some stairs, but then I—I got a bit lost. Then I heard someone coming, or I thought I did, and I was afraid I'd be in trouble so I hid in here but then the door wouldn't open. So I cried a bit, and I tried the phone but it didn't work, so then I slept. How much trouble am I in, Daddy? You can stop my pocket money."

"It's okay, poppet, but let's find Mum and the others."

There's no sign of Dwight Silverwind outside. Questions about how Holly could possibly, possibly have known will have to wait until later. They don't matter much. They don't matter at all.

. . .

THE NOISE OF the explosion died away, but half a dozen car alarms blasted out various pitches and patterns. I remembered being told that running outside wasn't clever in case gunmen were watching the site to pick off survivors and rescue workers. I just lay there shaking for a bit, I didn't know how long, until I got up and went back down to the lobby, my boots crunching on glass. Mr. Khufaji was crouched over the body of Tariq, the armed doorman, trying to curse him back to life. Probably I was the last person Tariq ever spoke to. Big Mac and some journalists were venturing out of the bar, nervous about a follow-up raid—often Bomber Number One clears the obstacles, while Bomber Number Two goes in and finishes off the tenderized targets.

The Safir was spared a double attack, however, and time lurched by until midnight. A paramilitary unit with an English-speaking "Detective Zerjawi" arrived sooner than usual because of the foreigners involved, and a torchlit survey of the hotel forecourt was carried out, with a shell-shocked Mr. Khufaji. I didn't go. Big Mac said several cars out front had been blown to smithereens and he'd seen a few body parts. Detective Zerjawi theorized that one of the security guys had killed the other—there was only one body—and let the car bomber through. The bomber had planned on driving through the glass porch and into the lobby to detonate the explosives there, hoping to bring down the building. This plan had been frustrated by an obstacle in the car park—"Who knows?"—causing the bomb to go off outside. God had been good to us, Detective Zerjawi explained in the bar, so now he, too, would be good to us: For only eight hundred dollars, he would spare three of his very best officers to stand guard in the shot-out lobby. Otherwise, it would be very difficult to guarantee our safety until the morning. Terrorists would know how vulnerable we were.

After organizing a whip-round, some of us headed to our laptops to write up the story, others helped Mr. Khufaji with the clean-up, and a few went to bed and slept the sleep of the lucky-to-be-alive. I was too wired for any of the above, and went up onto the roof, and put a call through to Olive in New York. Her PA took the message: The Safir in Baghdad had been hit by a car bomb, but no journalists had been killed. I also asked the PA to get the message to Holly in London. Then I just sat there, listening to the bursts of gunfire, the drone of engines and generators, shouts, barks, brakes, music, and more gunfire: a Baghdad symphony. The stars were feeble for a browned-out city and the moon looked like it had liver disease. Big Mac and Vincent Agrippa joined me to make their satphone calls. Vincent's wasn't working, so I lent him mine. Big Mac gave us a cigar to celebrate not being dead and Vincent produced a bottle of fine wine from God knew where. Under the influence of Cuban leaf and Loire Valley grapes, I confided how I'd have been dead if it hadn't been for a cat. Vincent, still a good Catholic, told me the cat was an agent of God. "Dunno what the cat was," Big Mac re-marked, "but *you,* Brubeck, are one lucky sonofa."

Then I texted Nasser to say I was okay.

The message failed to arrive.

I texted Aziz to tell Nasser I was okay.

That message failed to arrive, too.

I texted Big Mac to check the network was working.

It was. Then a terrible possibility hit me.

PROBABLY THE WORST hour of Holly's and my joint parenthood is already morphing into a multiuser anecdote, sprouting apocrypha and even one or two comic interludes. I told the jubilant crowd in the lobby I'd just had the thought that maybe Aoife had gone up *two* flights of stairs instead of one in search of her grandparents' room so I'd gone to check, and found a chambermaid who'd let me into all the rooms. The third one along, my shot in the dark had hit its mark. Luckily everyone was too relieved to examine my story closely, though Austin Webber huffed and puffed about Health and Safety and how doors that locked children in were a liability. Pau-line Webber declared, "Wasn't it *lucky* you thought of that? Poor

Aoife could've been trapped for *days*! You don't want to think about it!" and I agreed. Dead lucky. I didn't say what room number I'd found Aoife in: It all sounded too *X-Files,* and would've eclipsed Sharon and Peter's wedding. Until, that is, twenty minutes ago, when, on the balcony of the Maritime Hotel, looking down on the nighttime pier, I told Holly the full version. As usual, I couldn't tell what she was thinking.

"I'll take a quick shower," she said.

Aoife is tucked up in bed with Snowy, the Arctic fox.

A fleet of well-tuned motorbikes passes below.

WE'VE BEEN TALKING for ages. Which is a pleasant novelty. Holly's lying next to me now, with her head on my shoulder and her thigh over my torso. We haven't had sex, but still, there's an intimacy I'd almost forgotten. "It was different from the glimpses I used to get," Holly's explaining, "y'know, the glimpses of stuff that hadn't happened yet. The precognition."

"Was it more like the Radio People, when you were little?"

Long pause. "Today it was as if I *was* the radio."

"Like you were channeling someone else?"

"It's hard to describe. It's disturbing. Blanking out like that. Being in your body, but not being in your body. So em*barras*sing, too, coming back to myself with everyone standing round me like a—a Victorian deathbed scene. Christ only knows what the Webbers thought."

I've always put inverted commas around Holly's "psychic stuff" but today this same psychic stuff won us our daughter back. My agnosticism's badly shaken. I kiss her head. "Write about it, one day, darling. It's . . . fascinating."

"As if anyone'd be interested in my bonkers ramblings."

"You're wrong. People *ache* to believe there's more than . . ."

Screams from the funfair on the pier travel over the calm sea and through the slightly open window.

"Hol," I realize I'm going to say it all, "Nasser in Baghdad, my minder, and Aziz Al-Karbalai, my photographer. They were killed in the car bomb at the Safir last week. They're dead because of me."

Holly rolls off me and sits up. "What are you talking about?"

HOLLY CLASPS HER knees to her chest. "You should've told me."

I dab my eyes on the sheet. "Sharon's wedding bash wasn't the right time or place. Was it?"

"They were your colleagues. Your friends. S'pose Gwyn died, and I clammed up for days before telling you. Was there a funeral?"

"Yeah, for . . . the remains of them. But it was too dangerous for me to go." Drunken laughter lopes down the corridor outside our room. I wait for it to pass. "It was too dark to see much at night, but at dawn, when the sun came up, there were just . . . twisted pieces of the bomber's car, and of Nasser's Corolla . . . Mr. Khufaji keeps a—a—a few topiary shrubs in pots up front, y'know, bushes clipped into shapes. A token gesture of more civilized days. Between two of those pots, there was a—a—a shin, with a foot attached and a—a canvas shoe. God knows, I saw worse in Rwanda, and your average grunt in Iraq sees worse twenty times a day. But when I recognized the shoe—it was Aziz's—I puked myself inside out." *Get a grip.* "Earlier, Nasser'd recorded interviews with patients from a clinic outside Fallujah. The next day, this is just one week ago, he was going to come over and transcribe them. He gave me the Dictaphone for safekeeping. We said good night. I went into the hotel. Nasser's ignition was knackered, so Aziz probably got out to push-start it, or hook up a jump-lead, more likely. The bomber was aiming at the lobby, maybe hoping to bring down the building, I dunno, maybe it would've worked, it was a sizable blast, but anyway the car slammed into Nasser's and . . ." *Get a grip.* "God, I've got tears coming out of my nose now. Is that even anatomically possible? So, yeah—Nasser's daughters don't have a daddy now because Nasser dropped me off late, at car-bombing time, at a Westerners' hotel."

From next door's TV I hear a Hollywood space battle.

She touches my wrist. "You do know it's not that simple? As you always told me when I used to beat myself up over Jacko."

Aoife, in her dreams, makes a noise like a friendless harmonica.

"Yeah, yeah, it's 9/11, it's Bush and Blair, it's militant Islam, the occupation, Nasser's career choices, Olive Sun and *Spyglass,* a clapped-out Corolla that wouldn't start, tragic timing, oh, a million little switches—but also me. Ed Brubeck hired them. Nasser needed to feed his family. I *am* why he and Aziz were there . . ." I choke up and steady myself. "I'm an addict, Holly. Life *is* flat and stale when I'm not working. What Brendan denied implying yesterday, it's true. The whole truth, nothing but the truth. I . . . I'm a war-zone junkie. And I don't know what to do about it."

HOLLY'S CLEANING HER teeth, and a slab of vanilla light falls across Aoife. Look at her, this bright, bonkers, no-longer-so-little girl, who revealed herself from the mystery of ultrasound scans, nearly seven years ago. I remember us giving friends and family the big news; surprised joy from the Sykes clan and amused glances as Holly added, "No, Mum, Ed and I *won't* be getting married. It's 1997, not 1897"; and my own mum—whose leukemia was already getting to work on her bone marrow—saying, "Oh, Ed!" before bursting into tears and me asking, "Why're you crying, Mum?" and her laughing, "I don't know!"; and "Bump" swelling up until Holly's navel was inverted; and Bump's kicks; sitting in the Spence Café in Stoke Newington and compiling lists of girls' names—Holly *just knew,* of course; and my irrational anxiety during my trip to Jerusalem about London ice and London muggers; then on the night of November 30 Holly calling from the bathroom, "Brubeck, find your car keys"; and a dash to the maternity ward, where Holly got axed and shredded alive by a whole new pain called childbirth; and clocks that went at six times the speed of time, until Holly was holding a glistening mutant in her arms and telling her, "We've been expecting you"; and Dr. Shamsie the Pakistani doctor insisting,

"No, no, no, Mr. Brubeck, *you* will snip the cord, you absolutely *must*. Don't be squeamish—you've seen much worse on assignment"; and last, the mugs of milky tea and the plate of Digestive biscuits in a small room down a corridor. Aoife was discovering the joys of breast milk, and Holly and I found that we were both bloody ravenous.

Our very first breakfast as a family.

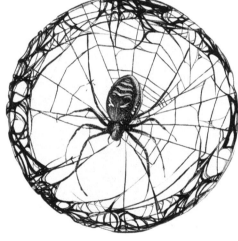

CRISPIN HERSHEY'S LONELY PLANET

2015

May 1, 2015

WELSH RAIN GODS PISS onto the roofs, festival tents, and umbrellas of Hay-on-Wye and also on Crispin Hershey, as he
strides along a gutter-noisy lane, into the Old Cinema Bookshop and makes his way down to its deepest bowel, where he rips
this week's *Piccadilly Review* to confetti. Who on God's festering
Earth does that six-foot-wide, corduroy-clad, pubic-bearded, rectal
probe Richard Cheeseman think he *is*? I shut my eyes but the words
of his review slide by like the breaking news: "I tried my utmost to
find something, *anything,* in Crispin Hershey's long-awaited novel
to dilute its trepanning godawfulness." How *dare* that inflatable
semen-stained Bagpuss write that after cosying up to me at the
Royal Society of Literature bashes? "In my salad days at Cambridge,
I got into a fistfight defending the honor of Hershey's early masterpiece *Desiccated Embryos* and to this day I wear the scar on my ear
as a badge of honor." Who sponsored Richard Cheeseman's application for Pen UK? *I* did. I did! And how does he thank me? "To
dub *Echo Must Die* 'infantile, flatulent, ghastly drivel' would be an
insult to infants, to flatulence, and to ghasts alike." I stamp on the
magazine's shredded remains, panting and gasping . . .

TRULY, DEAR READER, I could weep. Kingsley Amis boasted how a
bad review might spoil his breakfast, but it bloody wasn't going to
spoil his lunch. Kingsley Amis lived in the pre-Twitter age, when
reviewers actually read proofs and thought independently. Nowadays they just Google for a preexisting opinion and, thanks to Richard Cheeseman's chainsaw massacre, what they'll read about my

comeback novel is: "So why is *Echo Must Die* such a decomposing hog? One: Hershey is so bent on avoiding cliché that each sentence is as tortured as an American whistleblower. Two: The fantasy sub-plot clashes so violently with the book's State of the World pretensions, I cannot bear to look. Three: What surer sign is there that the creative aquifers are dry than a writer creating a writer-character?" Richard Cheeseman has hung a KICK ME sign around *Echo Must Die*'s neck, at the very time I need a commercial renaissance. It isn't the 1990s, when my agent, Hal "the Hyena" Grundy, could pluck a £500K book deal as easily as a plug of mucus from his giant honker. Now is the official Decade of the Death of the Book. I'm hemorrhaging £40K a year on school fees for the girls, and the little pied-à-terre in Montreal's well-heeled Outremont neighborhood may have put a smile back on Zoë's face but the expense has rendered me financially mortal for the first time since Hal the Hyena got me my book deal for *Desiccated Embryos*. My iPhone trills. Speak of the devil, it's a message from Hal.

gig kicks off 45mins o brother where art thou?

The Hyenas are howling. The show must go on.

MAEVE MUNRO, SALTY captain of BBC2's flagship arts show, gives a let's-roll nod to the stage manager. I'm waiting in the wings, miked up. Publicity Girl scrolls through her messages. Stage Manager asks me to check that my mobile is switched off. I check, and find two new messages: one from Qantas air miles and one about garbage collection. In our marital halcyon days, Mrs. Zoë Legrange-Hershey would send *Knock 'em dead, Genius*–type texts before my gigs, but these days she doesn't even ask what country I'm going to. Nothing from the girls, even. Juno will be playing remotely with her schoolfriends—or perverts pretending to be schoolfriends—on Tunnel Town or whatever the latest app is, while Anaïs will be reading a Michael Morpurgo book. Why don't *I* write kids' books about lonely children forging bonds with animals? Because I've spent two decades being the Wild Child of British literature, that's sodding why. In publishing it's easier to change your body than it is to switch genre.

House lights dim, stage lights brighten, and the audience falls silent. Maeve Munro's telegenic face shines and her trademark Orcadian lilt fills the tent. "Good evening, I'm Maeve Munro, broadcasting live from the Hay Festival, 2015. Ever since his debut novel *Wanda in Oils,* published while its author was still an undergraduate, Crispin Hershey has earned his stripes as a master stylist and a laser-sharp chronicler of our times. Our most lusted-after gong, the Brittan Prize, has—scandalously—eluded his grasp so far, but many believe that 2015 could finally be his year. With no further ado, reading from *Echo Must Die,* his first novel in five years, please join me and our very proud sponsors FutureNow Bank in welcoming—Crispin Hershey!"

Solid applause. I approach the lectern. A full house. Sodding well ought to be—they already moved me from the six-hundred seater PowerGen Venue to this "more intimate setting." Editor Oliver sits in the front row with Hyena Hal and his newest client and the Next Hot Young American Thing, Nick Greek. Let silence fall. Rain drums on the marquee roof. Most writers would now thank the audience for coming out on such a bad night, but Hershey treats 'em mean to keep 'em keen and opens *Echo Must Die* at page one.

I clear my throat. "I'll jump straight in . . ."

. . . my last line dispatched, I return to my chair. Swing high, sweet clap-o-meter; not bad for a contingent of securely pensioned metropolitans stuffed with artisanal fudge and organic cider. They guffawed as my protagonist Trevor Upward got duct-taped to the roof of the Eurostar; squirmed when Titus Hurt found a human finger in his Cornish pastie; and thrummed at my dénouement in the Cambridge pub, which flowers into Audenesque rhyme when spoken aloud at festivals. Maeve Munro gives me a cheerful that-went-well face; I give her a why-wouldn't-it? face back. Hershey spent his boyhood among thesps, and Dad's habit of ridiculing my brother and me for garbled diction has borne plump fruit. Dad's last words, as my memoir recounts, were "It's 'whom,' you baboon, not 'who' . . ."

"To kick off the Q and A," Maeve Munro addresses the tent, "I have some questions of my own. Then we'll turn it over to our roving mikes. So, Crispin, on last Friday's *Newsnight Review,* eminent critic Aphra Booth described *Echo Must Die* as 'a classic male midlife crisis novel.' Any response?"

"Oh, I'd say she's hit the nail on the head," I take a slow sip of water, "*if,* like Aphra Booth, your notion of 'reading' is to skim the back jacket in the green-room loo a minute before going on air."

My quip earns a fake smile from Maeve Munro, who is often seen wining and whining with Aphra Booth at the Mistletoe Club. "Right . . . And as for Richard Cheeseman's rather lackluster review—"

"What christening is complete without a jealous fairy's curse?"

Laughter; gasps; Twitterstorm ahoy. The *Telegraph* will report the line on page one of their arts section; Richard Cheeseman will get his gay-rights group to give me the Bigot of the Year Award; Hyena Hal will be thinking *Publi$ity,* while Nick Greek, bless, looks puzzled. American writers are so sodding *nice* to each other, hanging out in their Brooklyn lofts and writing each other's references for professorial chairs. "Let's move on," says Maeve Munro, her fluty trill flattening, "while we're ahead."

"What makes you think you're 'ahead,' Maeve?"

Little smile: "*Echo Must Die*'s protagonist is, like yourself, a novelist, yet in your memoir *To Be Continued* you dub novels about novelists 'incestuous.' Is Trevor Upward a U-turn, or is incest now a more attractive proposition?"

I lean back, smiling, while my interviewer's fan base expends its *gur-hurs.* "While I'd never lecture a native of the Orkney Islands, *Maeve,* on the subject of incest, I would maintain that *without* shifts in viewpoint, a writer could only write the same novel ad infinitum. Or end up teaching uncreative writing at a college for the privileged in upstate New York."

"Yet"—Maeve Munro is duly stung—"a politician who changes his or her mind is called a flip-flopper."

"F. W. de Klerk changed his mind about Nelson Mandela being a terrorist," I riff. "Gerry Adams and Ian Paisley changed their minds about violence in Ulster. *I* say, 'Let's hear it for the flip-floppers.'"

"Let me ask you this. To what degree is Trevor Upward, whose morality is decidedly elastic, modeled upon his maker?"

"Trevor Upward is a misogynist prick who gets ex*act*ly what he deserves on the final page. How, *dear* Maeve, could a royal arse like Trevor Upward"—I flash a smile of mock innocence—"*possibly* be modeled on a man like Crispin Hershey?"

SMUDGED WOODS AND Herefordshire hills rear up into a misty twilight. The moist air dabs my brow like a face flannel in business class. I, the Festival Elf, Publicity Girl, and Editor Oliver traverse the wooden walkways over the sodden sod past booths selling gluten-free cupcakes, solar panels, natural sponges, porcelain mermaids, wind chimes tuned to your own chi aura, biodegradable trays of GM-free green curry, eReaders, and hand-stitched Hawaiian quilts. Hershey dons his mask of contempt to ward off unwanted approaches, but a tiny voice is singing in his soul: *They know you, they recognize you, you're back, you never went away . . .* When we reach the signing tables at the bookshop tent, the four of us stop in astonishment. "Hell's bells, Crispin," says Editor Oliver, slapping my back.

Festival Elf declares, "Not even Tony Blair got a turnout like this."

Publicity Girl says, "Wayhay and hurrahs!"

The place is pullulant with punters, cordoned by festival heavies into a snaking queue of Crispin Hershey faithful. *Look on my works, Richard Cheeseman, and despair! They'll be reprinting*

Echo Must Die *by the weekend and a V2 of money is headed straight for the House of Hershey!* Victoriously, I gain my table, sit down, knock back the glass of white wine served by the Festival Elf, unsheathe the Sharpie . . .

. . . and realize that all these people are here not for me, God sod it, but for a woman sitting at a table ten feet away. My own queue numbers fifteen. Or ten. More frumpet than crumpet. Editor Oliver has turned the color of elderly chicken slices, so I scowl at Publicity Girl for an explanation. "That's, um, Holly Sykes."

Oliver's color returns. "*That's* Holly Sykes? Jesus."

I growl, "Who in the name of buggery is Holey Spikes?"

"Holly Sykes," says Publicity Girl, falling down the sar-chasm. "She's written a spiritual memoir called *The Radio People*. On *I'm a Celebrity Get Me Out of Here!* Prudence Hanson—the artist— was caught reading it, and sales spiraled into hyperspace. The Hay director arranged a last-minute gig and every seat in the Future-Bank Venue was sold out in forty minutes."

"Three cheers for the Woodstock of the Mind." I assess the Sykes woman: skinny, earnest, lined; midforties, black hair, with silvery outriders. She's kind to her punters: Each one gets a friendly word, which only proves how few books she's ever signed. Envious? No. If she believes her mystic-mumbo she's a deluded idiot. If she's cooked it all up, she's a snake-oil merchant. What's to envy?

Publicity Girl asks if I'm ready to start signing. I nod. Festival Elf asks if I want a drink. "No," I tell him. I won't be here long. My first punter approaches the table. His crumpled brown suit belonged to his dead father and his teeth are the color of caramel. "I'm your biggest, biggest, biggest fan, Mr. Hershey, and my late mother—"

Kill me now. "A G-and-T," I tell Festival Elf. "More G than T."

MY LAST PUNTER, a Volumnia from Coventry, treated me to her book group's thoughts on *Red Monkey,* which they "quite liked" but found the repetition of the adjectives "sodding" and "buggering" tiresome. Dear reader, Hershey missed not a beat: "So why choose the buggering book in the first sodding place?" A trio of dealers then descended, wanting a stack of first edition *Desiccated Embryos* signed, thereby increasing their value by five hundred pounds a pop. I asked, "Why should I?" One of the dealers gave me a sob story about driving up from Exeter "special, like, mate, and it's not like scribbling your name costs you anything," so I told him that if he paid me 50 percent of the markup on the nail, we'd have a deal. *Mate.* He vanished in a puff of poverty. Next stop is the first-night party at the BritFone Pavilion, where I am to endure a brief audience with Lord and Lady Roger and Suze Brittan. I stand up—and feel . . . a sniper's tracer on my forehead. Who's that? I look around and see Holly Sykes, watching me. She's probably curious about real writers. I click my fingers at Publicity Girl. "*I'm* a celebrity. Get *me* out of here."

On our way to the BritFone Pavilion, we pass the smoking tent, sponsored by Win²Win: Europe's premier facilitator of ethically sourced organs for medical transplant. I tell my minders I'll be along soon, and although Editor Oliver offers to join me I warn him there's a two-hundred-pound fine for nonsmokers who don't light up, and he takes the hint. Publicity Girl checks mumsily that I have my lanyard for getting past the bouncers.

I produce the plastic tag I refuse to wear around my neck. "If I get lost," I tell her, "I'll just follow the sound of knives sinking into vertebrae." Inside the Win²Win tent, fellow initiates of the Order of Nicotine sit on barstools chatting, reading, or gazing hollow-eyed at smartphones, fingers busy. We are relics from the days when smoking in cinemas, airplanes, and trains was the natural order; when the Hollywood hero was identified by his cigarette. Nowadays not even the villains smoke. Now smoking really *is* an expression of the rebel spirit—it's virtually sodding illegal! Yet what are we without our addictions? Insipid. Flavorless. Careerless! Dad was addicted to the hurly-burly of getting a film made. Zoë's addictions are fad diets, one-sided comparisons between London and Montreal, and obsessing over Juno and Anaïs's vitamin intake.

I light up, fumigate my alveolar sacs, and think dark thoughts about Richard Cheeseman. Someone needs to skewer *his* reputation; jeopardize *his* livelihood; see if *he* shrugs it off with an "I bloody well won't let it spoil my lunch." When I stub out my cigarette, I imagine it's into Cheeseman's fatuous eye.

"Mr. Hershey?" A short fat boy in glasses and a maroon Burberry jacket interrupts my revenge fantasy. His head is shaved and he's doughy and ill-looking, like Piggy in *Lord of the Flies.*

"My signing session's over. I'll be back in about five years."

"No, I wish to give you a book." The boy is a girl, with a soft American accent. She's Asian American, or semi–Asian American.

"And I wish to smoke. It's been a most exhausting few years."

Ignoring the hint, the girl proffers a thin volume. "My poetry." A self-funded volume, plainly. "*Soul Carnivores,* by Soleil Moore."

"I don't look at unsolicited manuscripts."

"Humanity asks you to make an exception."

"*Please* don't think me rude, Miss Moore, but I'd rather perform root-canal surgery on myself, or wake up next to Aphra Booth in the breeding pen of an alien menagerie, or take six shots in the heart at close range than *ever* read your poems. Do you understand?"

Soleil Moore flaunts her lunatic's credentials by staying calm. "Nobody wanted William Blake's work, either."

"William Blake had the merit of being William Blake."

"Mr. Hershey, if you don't read this and act, you'll be complicit in animacide." She places *Soul Carnivores* by the ashtray, wanting me to ask what that made-up word means. "You're in the Script," she says, as if that settles everything, before *finally* buggering off, as if she's just delivered a killer argument. I take a few more puffs, sifting a conversation nearby: "She said, 'Hershey': I *thought* it was him"; "Nah, can't be, Crispin Hershey's not *that* old"; "Ask him"; "No, you ask him." Cover blown, I crumple up my death-stick and flee my smoker's Eden.

THE BRITFONE PAVILION was designed by an eminent architect I've never heard of and "quotes" Hadrian's Wall, the Tower of London, a Tudor manor, postwar public housing, Wembley Stadium, and a Docklands skyscraper. What a sicked-up fry-up it is. A holographic flag of the BritNet logo flutters from its pinnacle and you ingress through a double-sized replica of 10 Downing Street's famous black door. The security men are dressed as Beefeaters, and one asks for my VIP lanyard. I check my jacket; my trousers; my jacket again. "Oh, sod a dog, I put it down somewhere—look, I'm Crispin Hershey."

"Sorry, sir," says the Beefeater. "No ID, no entry."

"Check your little list. Crispin Hershey. The writer."

The Beefeater shakes his head. "I got my orders."

"But I did a sodding event here only an hour ago."

A second Beefeater comes over, eyes ashine with fan-glow: "You're never—are you really . . . *him*? Oh, my God, you *are* . . ."

"Yes, I *am*." I glare at the first. "*Thank* you."

The Worthy Beefeater walks me through the small lobby where lesser mortals are patted down and have their bags checked. "Sorry about that, sir. The Afghan president's here tonight so we're on amber alert. My colleague back there's not au fait with contemporary fiction. And, to be fair, you do look older on your author photos."

I double-check this pleasing sentence. "Do I?"

"If I weren't such a fan, sir, I wouldn't have recognized you." We enter the pavilion proper, where hundreds are mingling, but the Worthy Beefeater has a favor to beg: "Look, sir, I shouldn't ask, but . . ." he produces a book from inside his ridiculous uniform, ". . . your new book's the best thing you've ever written. I went to bed with it and read *right through to dawn*. My fiancée's mother's a huge fan too, and, well, for premarital Brownie points, would you mind?"

I produce my fountain pen and the Beefeater hands me his book, already turned to the title page. Only when nib touches paper do I notice I am signing a novel called *Best Kept Secret* by Jeffrey Archer. I look up at the Beefeater to see if he's taking the piss, but no: "Would you write 'To Bridie on your Sixtieth Birthday from Lord Archer'?"

A famous columnist from *The Times* is standing three feet away. Dedication written, I tell the bouncer, "So glad you enjoyed it."

The pavilion contains enough celebrity wattage to power a small sun: I spy two Rolling Stones, a Monty Python; a teenage fifty-something presenter of *Top Gear* joshing with a disgraced American cyclist; an ex–U.S. secretary of state; an ex–football manager who writes an autobiography every five years; an ex-head of MI6 who cranks out a third-rate thriller annually; and a lush-lipped TV astronomer who writes, at least, about astronomy. We're all here for the same reason: We have books to flog. "I spy with my little eye the rarest of sights," an old codger purrs in my ear by the champagne bar, "a literary writer at a literary festival. How's life, Crispin?"

The stranger absorbs Hershey's withering stare like a man in his prime with nothing to fear, notwithstanding the damage that Time the Vandal has done to his face. The clawed lines, the whisky nose, the sagging pouches, the droopy eyelids. A silk handkerchief pokes up from his jacket pocket and he wears an elegant fedora, but Sodding Hell. How can the incurably elderly stand it? "And you are?"

"I'm your near future, my boy." He swivels his once-handsome face. "Take a good, long look. What do you think?"

What I think is that tonight is the Night of the Fruitcakes. "What I think is that I'm no fan of cryptic crosswords."

"No? I enjoy them. I am Levon Frankland."

I take the proffered champagne flute and make an underimpressed face. "No bells are going 'dong,' I must confess."

"I'm an old mucker of your father's from another time. We were both contemporaries at the Finisterre Club in Soho."

I maintain my underimpressed face. "I heard it finally closed down."

"The end of the end of an era. My era. We met," Levon Frankland tilts his glass my way, "at a party at your house in Pembridge Place in, ooh, sixty-eight, sixty-nine, around the time of the *Gethsemane* jazzamaroo. Amongst the various pies into which I had thrust my sticky fingers was artist management, and your father hoped that an avant-folk combo I represented would work on music for *The Nar-*

row Road to the Deep North. The plan came to nought, but I remember you, dressed up as a cowboy. You had not long mastered the art of bowel control and social intercourse was still years away, but I've followed your career with an avuncular interest, and read your memoir about your dad with relish. Do you know, every few months, I get it into my head to call him and arrange lunch? I clean forget he's gone! I do so miss the old contrarian. He was *sinfully* proud of you."

"Yeah? He did a sodding good job of hiding it."

"Anthony Hershey was an upper middle class Englishman born before the war. Fathers didn't do emotions. The sixties loosened things up, and Tony's films were a part of that loosening, but some of us were better than others at . . . deprogramming. Crispin, bury that hatchet. Hatchets don't work on ghosts. They cannot hear you. You only end up hatcheting yourself. Believe me. I know of what I speak."

A hand clasps my shoulder and I spin around to find Hyena Hal smiling like a giant mink. "Crispin! How was the signing?"

"I'll live. But let me introd—" When I turn back to Levon Frankland, he's been swept away by the party. "Yeah, the signing was fine. Despite half a million women wanting to touch the hem of some crank who writes about angels."

"I can spot twenty publishers from here who'll regret not snapping up Holly Sykes until their dying days. Anyway, Sir Roger and Lady Suze Brittan await the Wild Child of British Letters."

Suddenly I'm wilting. "Must I, Hal?"

Hyena Hal's smile dims. "The shortlist."

Lord Roger Brittan: onetime car dealer; budget hotelier in the 1970s; founder of Brittan Computers in 1983, briefly the U.K.'s leading maker of shitty word processors; acquirer of a mobile phone license after bankrolling New Labour's 1997 landslide, and setter-upper of the BritFone telecom network that still bears his name, after a fashion. Since 2004 he's been known to millions via *Out on Your Arse!*, the business reality show where a clutch of wazzocks humiliate themselves for the "prize" of a £100K job in Lord Brittan's business empire. Last year Sir Roger shocked the arts world by purchasing the U.K.'s foremost literary prize, renaming it after himself and trebling the pot to £150,000. Bloggers suggest that his acquisition was prompted by his latest wife, Suze Brittan, whose CV includes a stint as a soap star, face of TV's book show *The Unputdownables,* and now chairperson of the Brittan Prize's panel of uncorruptible judges. But we arrive at the canopied corner only to find Lord Roger and Lady Suze speaking with Nick Greek: "I hear what you're saying about *Slaughterhouse-Five,* Lord Brittan." Nick Greek possesses American self-assurance, Byronic good looks, and I already detest him. "But if I were forced at gunpoint to pick *the* twentieth-century war novel, I'd opt for Mailer's *The Naked and the Dead.* It's—"

"I *knew* you'd say that!" Suze Brittan performs a little victory jig. "I *adore* it. The only war novel to *really* 'get' trench warfare from the German point of view."

"I wonder, Lady Suze," Nick Greek treads delicately, "if you're thinking of *All Quiet on the Western—*"

"*What* German 'point of view'?" huffs Lord Roger Brittan. "Apart from 'Totally bloody wrong twice in thirty bloody years'?"

Suze crooks her little finger through her black pearls. "That's why *The Naked and the Dead* is so important, Rog—ordinary people on the wrong side suffer too. Right, Nick?"

"To put the shoe on the other foot is the novel's chief strength, Lady Suze," says the tactful American.

"Bloody shoddy product branding," says Lord Roger. "*The Naked and the Dead*? Sounds like a necrophilia manual."

Hyena Hal steps in: "Lord Roger, Lady Suze, Nick. Introductions are hardly necessary, but before Crispin leaves—"

"Crispin Hershey!" Lady Suze holds up both hands as if I'm the sun god Ra. "Your event was totes amazeballs! As they say."

I manage to lift the corners of my mouth. "Thank you."

"I'm honored," brownnoses Nick Greek. "In Brooklyn there's, like, a whole bunch of us, we literally worship *Desiccated Embryos.*"

"Literally"? "Worship"? I have to shake Nick Greek's hand,

wondering if his compliment is a camouflaged insult—"Everything you've done since *Embryos* is a crock of crap"—or a prelude to a blurb request—"Dear Crispin, totally awesome to hang out with you at Hay last year, would you dash off a few words of advance praise for my new effort?" "Don't let me interrupt," I tell the trio, "your erudite insights about Norman Mailer." I bowl a second googly at the young Turk: "Though for my money, the granddaddy of firsthand war accounts has to be Crane's *The Red Badge of Courage*."

"I didn't read that," Nick Greek admits, "because—"

"So many books, so little time, I know," I drain the fat glass of red that elves placed in my hand, "but Crane remains unsurpassed."

"—because Stephen Crane was born in 1871," counters Nick Greek, "*after* the Civil War ended. So can't really be firsthand. But if Crispin Hershey esteems it," he whips out an eReader, "I'll download it right now."

My gammon lunch repeats on me. "Nick's novel," Suze Brittan tells me, "is set in the Afghanistani war. Richard Cheeseman *raved* about it, and he's interviewing Nick on my program next week."

"Oh? I'll be glued to the set. I heard about it, actually. What's it called? *Highway 66*?"

"*Route 605*." Nick Greek's fingertips dance on the screen. "Named after the highway in Helmand Province."

"Were your sources any more firsthand than Stephen Crane's?" Obviously not: The closest this pallid boy ever came to armed combat was group feedback on his creative writing MA. "Unless, of course, you were a literate marine in an ex-life?"

"No, but that's a fair description of my brother. *Route 605* wouldn't exist without Kyle."

A small crowd, I notice, is now watching us, like tennis spectators. "I hope you don't feel overly indebted to your brother, or that he doesn't feel you've exploited his hard-won experiences."

"Kyle died two years ago." Nick Greek stays calm. "On Route 605, defusing a mine. My novel's his memorial, of sorts."

Oh, great. *Why* didn't Publicity Girl warn me that Nick Greek's a sodding saint? Lady Suze is looking like a Corgi just shat me out, while Lord Roger gives Nick Greek a fatherly squeeze on the biceps: "Nick, son, I don't know yer, and Afghanistan's a total bloody cock-up. But your brother'd be proud of yer—and I know what I'm on about, 'cause I lost my brother when I was ten. Drowned at sea. Suze was saying—weren't you Suze?—that *Route 605* is my sort of book. So yer know what? I'll read it over the weekend"—he clicks his fingers at an aide, who taps a smartphone—"and when Roger Brittan gives his word, he bloody well keeps it." Bodies come between me and the haloed ones—it's as if I'm being towed away on casters. The last familiar face is that of Editor Oliver, cheered by the future angle of *Route 605*'s sales graph. I need a drink.

HERSHEY IS *not* going to vomit. Did Hershey not pass this broken gate earlier? A hunchback tree, a brook that won't shut up, the puddle reflecting the BritFone holo-logo, the acid reek of cowshit. Hershey is *not* drunk. Just well oiled. Why am I here? "So far up his own arse he can see daylight." Gulp it down. The pavilion was a bottomless pit. The mascarpone trifle was ill-advised. "That wasn't Crispin Hershey, was it?" My shortcut across the car park back to my comfy room at the Coach and Horses has trapped me in a Möbius loop of Land Rovers, Touaregs, and slurping hoofed-up mud. I thought I saw Archbishop Desmond Tutu and I followed him to ask about something that seemed important at the time but it turned out not to be him anyway. So why am I here, dear reader? Because I need to keep my author profile high. Because the £500,000 advance that Hyena Hal extracted for *Echo Must Die* is gone—half to the Inland Revenue, a quarter to the mortgage, a quarter to negative equity. Because if I'm not a writer, what am I? "Anything new in the pipeline, Mr. Hershey? My wife and I adored *Desiccated Embryos*." Because of Nick sodding Greek and the Young Ones, eyeing my place in the throne room of English Literature. Oh, rum, sodomy, and the lash: Mount Vomit is ready to erupt; let us now kneel before the Lord of the Gastric Spasm and all pay homage . . .

P LAZA DE LA ADUANA IS THROBBING with Cartagenans
holding their iPhones aloft. Plaza de la Aduana is roofed by a
tropical twilight of Fanta Orange and oily amethyst. Plaza de
la Aduana is oscillating to the cod-ska chorus of "Exocets for
Breakfast" by Damon MacNish and the Sinking Ship. Up on his
balcony, Crispin Hershey taps ash into his champagne glass and
remembers a sexual encounter to the music of *She Blew Out the
Candle*—the Sinking Ship's debut album—around the time of his
twenty-first birthday, when the images of Morrissey, Che Guevara,
and Damon MacNish surveyed a million student bedrooms. The
second album was less well received—bagpipes and electric guitars
usually end in tears—and the follow-up's follow-up bombed.
MacNish would have returned to his career in pizza delivery had he
not resurrected himself as a celebrity campaigner for AIDS, for Sarajevo, for the Nepalese minority in the Kingdom of Bhutan, for any
cause at all, as far as I could see. World leaders eagerly submitted
themselves to two minutes of MacNish while the cameras rolled.
Winner of Sexiest Scot of the Year for three years running, tabloid
interest in his regularly rotating girlfriends, a steady trickle of okay
but mojoless albums, an ethical clothing brand, and two BBC seasons of *Damon MacNish's Five Continents* kept the Glaswegian's
star well lit until the last decade, and even today "Saint Nish" remains in demand at festivals, where he delivers a polished Q&A by
day and a tour through his old hits by night—for a mere $25,000
plus business-class travel and five-star accommodation, I understand.

I slap a mosquito against my cheek. The little bastards are the price for this delicious warmth. Zoë and the girls were due to join me here—I'd even bought the (nonrefundable) tickets—but then the shitstorm blew up about Zoë's earth-mother marriage counselor. £250+VAT for an hour of platitudes about mutual respect? "No," I told Zoë, "and, as we all know, no means no."

Zoë opened fire with every weapon known to woman.

Yes, the porcelain mermaid *was* launched from my hand. But had it been *aimed* at her, it would not have missed. Therefore I didn't mean to hurt her. Zoë, by now too hysterical to follow this simple logic, packed her Louis Vuitton bags and left with Lori the hairy au pair to pick up Anaïs and Juno from school, thence to her old friend's pad in Putney. Which was mysteriously available at zero notice. Crispin was supposed to proffer promises to mend his ways, but he preferred to watch *No Country for Old Men* with the volume up really loud. The following day, I wrote a story about a gang of feral youths who roam the near future, siphoning oil tanks of lardy earth mothers. It's one of my best. Zoë phoned that evening and told me she "needed space—perhaps a fortnight"; the subtext being, dear reader, *If you apologize grovelingly enough, I may come back.* I suggested that she take a month and hung up. Lori brought Juno and Anaïs to visit last Sunday. I was expecting tears and emotional blackmail, but Juno told me her mother had described me as impossible to live with, and Anaïs asked if she could have a pony if we got divorced, because when Germaine Bigham's parents got divorced she got a pony. It rained all day, so I ordered in pizza. We played Mario Carts. John Cheever has a short story called "The Season of Divorce." It's one of his best.

"STILL PUTS ON a decent show, don't he, f'ra fella his age?" Kenny Bloke offers me a smoke as Damon MacNish windmills through "Corduroy Skirts Are a Crime Against Humanity." "I saw the lads in Fremantle, back in . . . eighty-six? Fackin' A." Kenny Bloke's in his late fifties, sports ironmongery in his ear, and is a Noongar elder, according to the festival bumf. I observe how Damon MacNish and many of his contemporaries have turned into their own tribute bands, which must be a peculiar and postmodern fate. Kenny Bloke taps ash into the geraniums. "MacNish's sitting pretty compared to a lot of them, I reckon. Guess who was playing at Busselton Park not so long ago? Joan Jett and the Blackhearts. Remember them? Not a massive turnout, I'm afraid, but they've got pensions and kids to put through college, same as everyone. Us writers get spared that, at least, eh? Farewell tours on the nostalgia circuit."

I probe this not-necessarily-true remark. *Echo Must Die* cleared twenty thousand in the U.K. and the same in the States. Respectable . . .

. . . -ish, but for the new Crispin Hershey novel, disappointing. Time was I'd shift a hundred thousand units in both territories, no questions asked. Hyena Hal talks about eBook downloads reconfiguring the old paradigm, but I know exactly why my "return to form" novel failed to sell—Richard Cheeseman's Rottweilering. That one sodding review declared open season on the Wild Child of British Letters, and by the time the Brittan Prize longlist was announced, *Echo Must Die* was better known as *The One Richard Cheeseman Hilariously Shafted*. I scan the spacious ballroom behind us. Still no sign of him, but he won't resist the tug of coffee-skinned Latino butlers for long.

"Did you look around the old quarter today?" asks Kenny Bloke.

"Yes, it's pretty in a UNESCO way. If a touch unreal."

The Australian grunts. "My taxi driver told me how the FARC people and the intelligence services needed a place for a holiday, so Cartagena's their de facto demilitarized zone." He accepts one of my cigarettes. "Don't tell the missus—she thinks I've given up."

"Your secret's safe. I doubt I'll be coming to . . . ?"

"Katanning. Western Australia. Bottom-left corner. Compared to this"—Kenny Bloke gestures at the Latin Baroque glory—"it's a dingo's arse. But my people are buried there, from way, way back, and I wouldn't want to leave my roots."

"Rootlessness," I opine, "is the twenty-first-century norm."

"You're not wrong and that's why we're in the shit we're in, mate. If you belong nowhere, why give a tinker's toss about anywhere?"

Damon MacNish's drummer whacks out a solo and the sea of Latino youth below makes me feel WASPish and old. Friday, ten P.M. in London, no school tomorrow. Juno and Anaïs are handling my and Zoë's trial separation with suspicious maturity. Surely I deserve a few teary episodes. Has Zoë been readying them for a bust-up? My old mucker Ewan Rice told me *his* first wife had sought legal advice six months before the D-word, hence her cool million-quid settlement. When had the rot set in for me and Zoë? Was it there at the very beginning, hiding like a cancer cell, on Zoë's father's yacht, Aegean sea light playing on the cabin ceiling, an empty wine bottle rolling oh-ever-so-gently on the cabin floor, this way and that, this way and that? We'd been celebrating Hal the Hyena's text to say the auction for *Desiccated Embryos* had reached £750,000 and was *still* climbing. Zoë said, "Don't panic, Crisp, but I'd like to spend my life with you." This way and that . . . This way and that . . .

"Swim for it!" I want to shout at that moronic Romeo. Before you know it, she'll "study" for an online PhD in crystal healing and call you narrow-minded if you dare wonder aloud where the science is. She'll stop greeting you in the hallway when you get home. Her powers of accusation will *stupefy* you, young Romeo. If the au pair's lazy, it's your fault for vetoing the Polish troglodyte. If the piano teacher's too strict, you should have found a huggier one. If Zoë is unfulfilled, it's your fault for depriving her of the imperative to earn a living. Sex? Ha. "Stop pressuring me, Crispin." "I'm not pressuring you, Zoë, I'm just asking when?" "Sometime." "When *is* 'Sometime'?" "Stop *pressuring* me, Crispin!" Men marry women hoping they'll never change. Women marry men hoping they will. Both parties are disappointed, and meanwhile Romeo on the yacht kisses his soon-to-be-fiancée and murmurs, "Let's get hitched, Miss Legrange."

The drum solo ends and Damon MacNish bounds up to the

mike, does a "One-two-three-five" and the Sinking Ship strike up "Disco in a Minefield." I let my cigarette drop into an imaginary lake of gasoline and turn the plaza into a Doomsday *whooosh, k'bammm! Ommmmmm* . . .

I recognize a very familiar voice, mere feet away.

"So I told him," Richard Cheeseman is saying, " 'Uh, no, Hillary—I don't have a libretto of my own to show you, because I flush *my* shit down the toilet!' " Balding, midforties, round, and bearded. Hershey squeezes through the bodies and brings his hand down on the critic's shoulder, like a wheel clamp. "Richard Cheeseman, as I live and breathe, you hairy old sodomite! *How* are you?"

Cheeseman recognizes me and spills his cocktail.

"Oh dear," I emote, "all over your purple espadrilles, too."

Cheeseman smiles, like a man about to have his jaw ripped from his skull, which is what I've long dreamt of doing. "Crisp!"

Don't "Crisp" me, you wormfuck. "The stiletto I brought to skewer your cerebellum got seized at Heathrow, so you're in the clear." Those in the literary know are gravitating our way like sharks to a sinking cruise ship. "But my, oh, *my*," I dab Cheeseman's arm with a handy napkin, "you gave my last book a shitty review. *Didn't* you?"

Cheeseman hisses through his rictus grin. "Did I?" Up go his hands in a jokey surrender. "Candidly? *What* I wrote, or *how* some intern slapped it about, I no longer recall—but if it caused you any offense—any offense at all!—I apologize."

I could stop here, but Destiny demands a vengeance more epic, and who am I to deny Destiny? I address the onlookers. "Let's get this out in the open. When Richard's review of *Echo Must Die* appeared, many people asked, 'How did it feel, to read that?' For a while, my answer was 'How does it feel to have acid flung in your face?' Then, however, I began to think about Richard's motives. To a lesser writer, one could attribute the motive of envy, but Richard is himself a novelist of growing stature and a motive of petty malice didn't wash. No. *I* believe that Richard Cheeseman cares deeply about literature, and feels duty-bound to tell the truth as he sees it.

So you know what? Bravo for Richard. He misappraised my last novel, but this man"—again, I clasp his shoulder in its ruffled shirt—"is a bulwark against the rising tide of arselickery that passes for lit crit. Let the record show I harbor not a gram of animus towards him—provided he brings us both a *huge* mojito and *pronto,* you scurrilous, scabby hack."

Smiles! Applause! Cheeseman and I do a mongrel mix of a handshake and a high-five. "You got me back, though, Crisp," his sweaty forehead shines, "with your jealous-fairy line at Hay-on-Wye—look, I'll go and get those mojitos."

"I'll be on the balcony," I tell him, "where the air's a little cooler." Then I'm mobbed by a dollop of nobodies who seriously suppose I'd bother to remember their names and faces. They praise my noble fair-mindedness. I respond nobly and fair-mindedly. Crispin Hershey's magnanimity will be reported and retweeted and so it will become the truth. From across the plaza, through the balcony doors, we hear Damon MacNish bellowing: "Te amo, Cartagena!"

AFTER THE FINAL encore, the VIPs and writers are driven to the president's villa in a convoy of about twenty bombproof 4x4 limousines. Police sirens brush aside the riffraff and traffic lights are ignored as we levitate through nocturnal Cartagena. My traveling companions are a Bhutanese playwright, who speaks no English, and two Bulgarian filmmakers, who appear to be swapping a string of disgusting but funny limericks in their own language. Through the smoked-glass window of the limousine I watch a nighttime market, an anarchic bus station, sweat-stained apartment blocks, street cafés, hawkers selling cigarettes from trays strapped to their lean torsos. Global capitalism does not appear to have been kind to the owners of these impassive faces. I wonder what these working-class Colombians make of us? Where do they sleep, what do they eat, of what do they dream? Each of the American-built armored limousines surely costs more than a lifetime's earnings for these street vendors. I don't know. If a short, unfit British novelist in his late forties were ejected onto the roadside in one of these neighborhoods, I would not fancy his chances.

The presidential villa lies beyond a military training school, and security is rigorous. The party is al fresco in the villa's tasteful and floodlit gardens, where drinks are served and vol-au-vents circulated by crisply ironed staff, and a jazz combo is doing a Stan Getz thing. The swimming pool is lined with candles, and I cannot see it without imagining an assassinated politician floating facedown in it. Several ambassadors are holding court in huddles, reminding me of circles of boys in a playground. The British one's about somewhere. He's younger than me. Now the Foreign Office has gone all meritocratic our diplomats have lost their larger-than-life Graham Greeneness, and are of less novelistic use. The view across the bay is impressive, with its slapdash South American shorefronts erased by the night, and a baroque moon floats aloft a fecund, one might say spermy, Milky Way. The president himself is in Washington drawing down more U.S. tax dollars for the "War on Drugs"—one more push!—but his Harvard-educated wife and orthodontically majestic sons are busy winning hearts and minds for the family business. Piggishly, he admits, Crispin Hershey wonders whether there's an offshore prison where ugly Colombian women are incarcerated, because I don't recall seeing one since I arrived. Would I, dear reader, should I, were the opportunity to present itself? My wedding ring is six thousand miles away in the drawer where my rarely opened box of marital condoms is hurtling past its use-by date. If I am less married than at any point since my wedding day it is Zoë's doing, not mine—as is abundantly clear to any halfway-objective witness. In fact, if she were an employer and I her employee, I would have strong grounds for suing her for constructive dismissal. Look at how atrociously she and her family ostracized me during the Christmas holidays. Even three months later, on my third glass of champers, gazing at the Southern Cross and warmed by a balmy 20 degrees Celsius, I shudder . . .

. . .

. . . Zoë and the girls had flown out to Montreal as soon as school broke up, giving me a week to get stuck into my new book, a black comedy about a fake mystic who pretends to see the Virgin Mary during the Hay-on-Wye Literary Festival. It's one of my best three or four. Unfortunately that week without me also allowed Zoë's family to get to work on Juno and Anaïs, inculcating in my daughters the cultural superiority of the French-speaking world. By the time *I* arrived at our little pad in Outremont on December 23, the girls would only speak to me in English when I explicitly ordered them to. Zoë allowed them a treble budget of online games as long as they played *en français,* and Zoë's sister took them and their cousins out to a Christmas fashion show, in French, followed by some sort of teenybop boy-band concert, in French. Cultural bribery of the first degree—and when I objected, Zoë was all, "Well, Crispin, *I* believe in broadening the girls' horizons and giving them access to their family roots—and I'm astonished and depressed that *you* want them locked inside Anglo-American monoculture." Then, on Boxing Day, we all went bowling. The eugenically favored Legranges were astonished beyond words by my score: twenty. Not on one ball, but for the whole sodding game. I'm just not built for bowling; I'm built for writing. Juno flicked back her hair and said, "Papa, I don't know where to look."

"Creespin!" Here comes Miguel Alvarez, my Spanish-language editor, smiling as if he has a present for me. "Creespin, I have a small present for you. Follow me a little, to a place a little more discreet." Feeling like an Irvine Welsh character, I follow Miguel away from the hubbub of the main party to a bench in the shadow of a tall wall behind, indeed, a tangle of cacti. "So, I have items you ask for, Creespin."

"That's most obliging of you." I light a cigarette.

Miguel slips a small envelope the size of a credit card into my jacket pocket. "Enjoy, is shame to leave Colombia without tasting. Is very very pure. But a thing, Creespin. To use here, here in Cartagena, in private, is not big deal. But to transport, to carry to airport"—grimacing, Miguel slices his throat. "You understand?"

"Miguel, only a deadhead would consider taking drugs anywhere near an airport. Don't worry. What I don't use, I'll flush away."

"A good plan. Play safe. Enjoy. Is best in world."

"And were you able to find a Colombian phone?"

"Yes, yes." My editor hands me another envelope.

It, too, goes into my jacket pocket. "Thank you. Smartphones are great when they work, but if the coverage is dodgy you can't beat the little old phones for sending texts, I find."

Miguel tilts his head, not really agreeing, but thirty dollars, or however much the thing cost him, is a cheap price to keep the Wild Child of British Letters onside. "So, now you have all, and all is good?"

"Very good indeed, Miguel, thank you."

Like my best plots, this one is writing itself.

"Eh, Crispin," beckons Kenny Bloke, the Australian poet, as we pass a huddle of celebrants on the far gate of the cactus garden. "Some people here to meet." Miguel and I join the small group of writers, apparently, under a canopy of tree ferns. The foreign names don't really sink in—none has had a story in *The New Yorker,* so far as I'm aware, but when Kenny Bloke's introducing me to the pale, dark-haired, angular woman, I suffer a throb of recognition even before he names her: "Holly Sykes, a fellow Pom."

"Nice to meet you, Mr. Hershey," she says.

"You're vaguely familiar," I tell her, "if I'm not mistaken?"

"We were both at the Hay Festival on the same day, last year."

"Not that sodding awful party in that ghastly tent?"

"We were both in the signing tent, actually, Mr. Hershey."

"Hang on! Yes. You're that angel author. Holly Sykes."

"Not angels in the harps-'n'-haloes sense, though," interjects Kenny Bloke. "Holly writes about inner voices—and as I was just saying, there's a strong affinity with the spirit guides my people believe in."

"Miss Sykes," says Miguel, oleaginously. "I am Miguel Alvarez, editor of *Ottopusso,* editor of Creespin. Is great honor."

The Sykes woman shakes his hand. "Mr. Alvarez."

"Is true you sell over half-million books in Spain?"

"My book seemed to strike a chord there," she says.

"Uri Geller struck a chord everywhere." I'm drunker than I thought. "Remember him? Michael Jackson's best mate? Big in Japan? Huge." My cocktail tastes of mango and seawater.

Miguel smiles at me but swivels his eyes back to the Sykes woman like an Action Man figure I once owned. "You happy with your Spanish publishers, Miss Sykes?"

"As you pointed out, they sold half a million copies."

"Is fantastic. But in case of problem, here, my card . . ."

As Miguel hovers, another woman materializes by the tree fern's trunk like a *Star Trek* character. She's dark, golden, mid-to-late thirties, and impalingly attractive. Miguel says, "Carmen!" as if he's delighted to see her.

Carmen stares at Miguel's business card until it vanishes into his jacket pocket, then turns to Holly Sykes. I'm expecting a Latina accent full of thunder, but she speaks like a Home Counties domestic-science teacher. "I hope Miguel hasn't been making a nuisance of himself, Holly—the man is a shameless poacher. Yes, you *are,* Miguel—I *know* you haven't forgotten the Stephen Hawking episode." Miguel tries to look jokey-penitent, but misses and looks like a man in white jeans who underestimates a spot of flatulence. "Mr. Hershey," the woman turns my way, "we've never met. I'm Carmen Salvat, and I have the *singular* privilege"—a dart aimed at Miguel—"of being Holly's Spanish-language publisher. Welcome to Colombia."

Carmen Salvat's handshake is no-nonsense. She radiates. With her free hand she toys with her necklace of lapis lazuli.

Kenny Bloke pipes up: "Holly mentioned that you also publish Nick Greek in Spanish, Carmen?"

"Yes, I bought the rights to *Route 605* before Nick had finished the manuscript. I just had a good feeling about it."

"Bloody blew me away, that book did," says Kenny Bloke. "Totally deserved last year's Brittan Prize, I reckon."

"Nick has a lovely soul," says a Newfoundland poetess, whose name I've already forgotten but who has the eyes of a seal gazing out of a Greenpeace poster. "Truly lovely."

"Carmen knows how to pick a winner," says Miguel. "But I think, in sales, Holly is still streets ahead, no, Carmen?"

"Which reminds me," says Carmen Salvat. "Holly, the minister of culture's wife would love to meet you—could I be a pest?"

As the Sykes woman is led away, I watch Carmen Salvat's appetizing haunches and get to work on a fantasy in which my phone rings—right now: a doctor in London with the catastrophic news that Zoë's Saab was knocked off the Hammersmith flyover by a drunk driver. She and the girls were killed instantly. I fly home tomorrow for the funeral. My grief is ennobling, but crushing, and I withdraw from life. I'm glimpsed occasionally riding the obscurer London Tube lines, out in zones four and five. Spring adds, summer multiplies, autumn subtracts, winter divides. One day next year, Hershey finds himself at the end of the Piccadilly Line at Heathrow airport. He exits the Tube, wanders into Departures, and glances up at the board to see the name "Cartagena"—the last place on earth where he was still a husband and father. On an impulse he cannot explain, he buys himself a one-way ticket—for some reason he has his passport with him—and the evening of that very same day finds him wandering the streets of the old colonial quarter of the Colombian town. Girls in love with boys on scooters, screeching birds, tropical flowers on winding vines, *saudade,* and solitude, One Hundred Years of it; and then, as the tropical dusk darkens the corners of the Plaza de la Aduana, Hershey sees a woman, her fingers toying with a necklace of lapis lazuli, and they stand still as the world eddies about them. Surprisingly, neither is surprised.

MANY COCKTAILS LATER, I'm helping a royally bladdered Richard Cheeseman into the lift and back to his room. "I'm fine, Crisp, I look drunkier than I am, really." The lift doors open and we step inside. He staggers like a drugged camel in storm-force winds. "Jussamo, I f'got m'room number, I'll just"—Cheeseman takes out his wallet and drops it—"oh, bumplops'n'pissflaps."

"Allow me." I pick up Cheeseman's wallet and take out the swipe-card in its sleeve—405—before returning it. "There you go, squire."

Cheeseman nods his thanks and mumbles, "If th'numbers in y'room number add up to nine, Hersh, you'll never die in it."

I press 4. "First stop, your room."

"I'm fine. Icanfindmy—my—my way home."

"But I'm duty-bound to see you safe to your door, Richard. Don't worry, my intentions are entirely honorable."

Cheeseman snonks: "Y'not my type, y'too white'n'too saggy."

I see my reflection in the mirrored wall, and recall a wise man telling me that the secret of happiness is to ignore your reflection in mirrors once you're over forty. This year I'll be fifty. The door goes *ping* and we step out, passing a lean and tanned white-haired couple. "This place usedt'be a *nunnery*," Cheeseman tells them, "ful-lo'virgins," and croons an early hit by Madonna. We shuffle along a corridor half open to the Caribbean night. A crooked corner, then 405. I swipe Cheeseman's card through the lock and the handle yields. "'Snottalot," says Cheeseman, "burra callit home."

Cheeseman's room's lit by the bedside lamp, and the destroyer of my comeback novel staggers over to his bed, trips over his suitcase, and belly-flops onto the mattress. "Notteverynight," flobbers monsieur le critique, as he succumbs to an onslaught of giggles, "I get escorted home by the Wild Child of British Letters."

I tell him, Yes, that's hilarious, and sweet dreams, and if he's not up by eleven, I'll call up from Reception. "Ammabs'lutely fine," he drawls, "I truly, madly, deeply, truly, really am. Really."

Arms outspread, the critic Richard Cheeseman passes out.

I ORDER EGG-WHITE OMELETTE with spinach, sourdough toast, and organic turkey patties, freshly squeezed orange juice, chilled Evian water, and local coffee to wash down painkillers and entomb my hangover. Seven-thirty A.M., and the air in the roofed-over courtyard is still cool. The hotel's mynah bird sits on its perch, making improbable noises. Its beak is an enameled scythe and its eye is all-seeing and all-knowing. Were this a work of fiction, dear reader, my protagonist would wonder if the mynah bird intuits what he's planning. Damon MacNish, dressed in a striped linen suit like Our Man in Havana, sits in a corner half hidden by *The Wall Street Journal*. Funny how the trajectory of life can be altered by a few days in a Scottish recording studio at the end of one's teens. His girlfriend, who *is* still in her teens, is flipping through *The Face*. For her, their sex must be like shagging Sandpaperman. What's in it for her? Apart from first-class air travel, five-star accommodation, minglings with the rock aristocracy, movie directors, and charity tsars; exposure in every gossip magazine on Earth, and modeling contracts to match, obviously . . . I only hope that if Juno and Anaïs scale Mount Society they'll use their own talents and not just straddle the skinny thighs of a mediocre songwriter wrinklier than their dad. *For what we are about to receive may the Lord make us truly grateful.*

Can Literature Change the World? is the name of Cheeseman's event. This urgent and timely commingling of the cultural elite's finest minds is being held in a long, whitewashed hall on the top floor of the ducal palace, Ground Zero of Cartagena 2016. Things kick off when a trio of Colombian writers strolls onto the stage to a standing ovation. The three salute their audience like postwar resistance heroes. The moderator follows them—a twig-thin woman in a blood-red dress, whose fondness for chunky gold is visible even from my seat on the back row. Richard Cheeseman has opted for the English-consul look, with a three-piece cream suit and damson-purple tie, but just looks like a hairy twat off *Brideshead Revisited*. The Three Revolutionaries take their seats and we non-Hispanophones don our headphones for the English simultaneous translation. The female interpreter renders first the moderator's greeting, then the potted biographies of the four guests. Richard Cheeseman's biog is the scantiest: "A famous and respected English critic and novelist." In fairness to whoever wrote it, Richard Cheeseman's Wikipedia page is scanty too, though his "notorious demolition" of Crispin Hershey's *Echo Must Die* is there, and connected via hyperlink to the *Piccadilly Review* website. Hyena Hal tells me he's done his damnedest to get the link deleted, but Wikipedia doesn't take bribes.

South American readings are audience-participative affairs, like stand-up comedy at home. My in-ear Babelfish provides synopses of the passages rather than a running translation, but now and then the interpreter confesses, "I'm sorry, but I have no idea what he just said. I'm not sure the author knew, either." Richard Cheeseman reads a scene from his newest novel, *Man in a White Car,* about the final moments of a Sonny Penhallow, a Cambridge undergraduate who drives his vintage Aston Martin over a Cornish cliff. Cheeseman's prose lacks even the merit of being awful; it's merely mediocre, and one by one the earphones slip off and the smartphones come out. When Cheeseman's finished the applause is lackluster, though my own reading yesterday hardly brought the house down.

Then the "round table" starts and the bollocks gets going.

"Literature should assassinate," declares the first revolutionary. "*I* write with a pen in one hand and a knife in the other!" Grown men stand, cheer, and clap.

The second writer won't be outdone: "Woody Guthrie, one of the few great American poets, painted the words *This Guitar Kills Fascists* on his guitar; on *my* laptop, I have written *This Machine Kills Neocapitalism!*" Oh, the crowd goes wild!

A file of latecomers shuffles along the row in front of me. So perfect an opportunity, it might have been scripted. Behind this human shield, I slip out of the room and clip-clop down the whitewashed stairs. Across the open-air courtyard of the Claustro de Santo Domingo, Kenny Bloke is reading to a hemisphere of children. The kids are entranced. Dad had a story about a party where Roald Dahl arrived by helicopter and told everyone he met, "Write books for children, you know—the little shits'll believe anything." I exit the ducal gates onto the plaza where Damon MacNish performed last night. Five blocks along the not-quite-straight Calle 36, I light a cigarette, but drop it down a drain before taking a single puff. Cheeseman's given up smoking, and the tang of tobacco could be a lethal clue. This is serious shit. I've never done anything quite like it. On the other hand, no review ever killed a book as wantonly as Richard Cheeseman's killed *Echo Must Die*. Plantains sizzle at a stall. A toddler surveys the street from a second-floor veranda, clutching the ironwork, like a prisoner. Soldiers guard a bank with machine guns slung round their necks, but I'm glad my money isn't dependent on their vigilance; one's text-messaging while another flirts with a girl Juno's age. Is Carmen Salvat married? She made no mention.

Focus, Hershey. Serious shit. Focus.

STEP UP FROM the bright hot street into the cool marble-and-teak lobby of the Santa Clara Hotel. Pass the two doormen, who, one suspects, have been trained to kill. They assess clothes, gringocity quotient, credit rating. Remove sunglasses and blink a bit gormlessly—*See, boys, I'm a hotel guest*—but replace them as you skirt the courtyard, passing preprandial guests sipping cappuccinos and banging out emails where Benedictine nuns once imbibed deep drafts of Holy Spirit. Avoid the eye of the mynah bird and, beyond the sleepless fountain, take the stairs up to the fourth floor. Retrace last night's midnight steps to the inevitable forking path. A sunny corridor leads around the echoey well of the upper courtyard to my room, where Crispin Hershey bottles out, while the crookeder way twists off to Richard Cheeseman's Room 405, where Crispin Hershey extracts his due. A minnow of déjà vu darts by and its name is Geoffrey Chaucer:

> "Now, Sirs," quoth he, "if it be you so lief
> To finde Death, turn up this crooked way,
> For in that grove I left him, by my fay,
> Under a tree, and there he will abide . . ."

But it's justice, not death, that *I* be *so lief to finde*. Any eyewitnesses? None. The crooked way, then. A maid's trolley is parked outside Room 403, but there's no sign of the maid. Room 405 is around the corner, the last-but-one down a dead end. Leonard Cohen's "Dance Me to the End of Love" sashays through my head, and via an arch in the hotel's outer wall, four floors above street level, Hershey sees roofs, a blue stripe of Caribbean, and dirty cauliflower clouds . . . Far-off coastal skyscrapers, finished and unfinished. Room 405. Knock-knock. Who's there? Your come-sodding-uppance, Dickie Cheeseman. Down in the street, a motorbike revs up the octaves. Here's Cheeseman's spare swipe-card, retained after my act of Good Samaritanship last night, and here is Fate's chance to nix my best-laid plan: If Cheeseman noticed he was missing a swipe-card this morning and obtained a replacement with a new code, the little LED on the door will blink red, the door will stay shut, and Hershey must abort mission. But should Fate want me to press ahead, the LED will turn green. There's a lizard on the door frame. Its tongue flickers.

Swipe the card, then. Go on.

Green. Go go go go *go*!

The door closes. Good, the room's been tidied and the bed is made. If a maid arrives, just act like nothing's wrong. A shirt hangs from a cupboard door and *Independent People* by Halldór Laxness lies on the bedside table. In the same way that Muslim women are forbidden to touch the Koran during menstruation, a shit like Richard Cheeseman shouldn't be allowed to touch Laxness unless he's wearing a pair of CSI latex gloves. Excellent thought. Unfurl the Marigolds from your jacket pocket and don the same. Good. Find Richard Cheeseman's suitcase in the wardrobe. New, pricy, capacious: ideal. Open it up and unzip an inner pocket: The zip feels stiff and never-used. Take out the Swiss Army knife and carefully make a half-inch incision in the outer lining. Excellent. Remove the credit-card-sized envelope from your jacket pocket, *carefully,* and, just as carefully, snip off a corner, and scatter a tiny quantity of the white powder around the suitcase—undetectable to the human eye, but whiffy as skunk shit to a beagle's nose. Slip the envelope through the incision in the lining of the suitcase. Push it down deep. Rezip the inner pocket. Stow the suitcase back in the wardrobe and check Santa's left no trail of crumbs. Nothing. All good. Depart the crime scene. Rubber gloves off *first,* you idiot . . .

Outside, the maid unbends from behind her cart and gives me a tired smile, and my heart crunches its gears. Even as I say the short word "Hello," I know I've made a fatal slip. She mouths "Hello" back and her mestiza gaze glances off my sunglasses, but I've identified myself as an English speaker. Stupid, stupid, stupid. I hurry back down the crooked path. Slowly! Not like a scuttling adulterer. Did the maid see me remove my gloves?

Should I go back and retrieve the cocaine?

Calm down! To the illiterate maid, you're one more middle-aged white guy with sunglasses. To her, Room 405 was your room. She's already forgotten seeing you. I pass the heavies in the foyer, and take an alternative route back to Festival Ground Zero. This time I smoke. I deposit the rubber gloves in a bin behind a restaurant, and reenter the gates of the Claustro de Santo Domingo flashing my VIP lanyard. Kenny Bloke is telling a boy, "Now, that's a brilliant question . . ." Up via an alternative route, past a large hall of three hundred people listening to Holly Sykes on the far stage reading from her book. I stop. What the sodding hell do all these people see in her? Slack-jawed, focused, gazing devoutly at a translation of the Sykes woman's text on a big screen above the stage. Even the Festival Elves are neglecting their door duties to tune in to the Angel Authoress. "The boy looked like Jacko," the Sykes woman reads, "with Jacko's height, clothes, and appearance, but I knew my brother was in Gravesend, twenty miles away." Silence fills the hall like snow fills a wood. "The boy waved as if he'd been waiting for me to show up. So I waved back, and then he disappeared into the underpass." Audience members are actually crying as they listen to this tripe! "How had Jacko traveled that distance, so early on a Sunday morning? He was only seven years old. How had he found me? Why didn't he wait for me before dashing away into the underpass again? So I began running too . . ."

I hurry up another flight of steps and sidle back into my seat on the back row, unseen from the stage. People are talking, standing, texting. "But, no, I don't really agree poets are the unacknowledged legislators of the world," Richard Cheeseman is ruminating. "Only a third-rate poet like Shelley would believe such wishful thinking."

Soon the symposium ends and I make my way up to the stage. "Richard, you were the voice of reason, from beginning to end."

EVENING. ON NARROW streets laid out by Dutchmen and built by their slaves four centuries ago, grandmothers water geraniums. I climb steep stone steps onto the old city wall. Its stones radiate the day's heat through my thin soles and the rhubarb-pink sun's fattening nicely as it sinks into the Caribbean. Why *do* I live in my rainy bitchy anal country again? If Zoë and I go the whole divorce hog, why not up sticks and live somewhere warm? Here would do. Down below, between four lanes of traffic and the sea, boys are playing football on a dirt pitch: One team wears T-shirts, the other goes topless. Up ahead, I find a vacant bench. So. A last-minute stay of execution?

No sodding way. I spent four years on *Echo Must Die,* and that pube-bearded Cheeseman murdered it in eight hundred words. He elevated his own reputation at the expense of mine. This is called theft. Justice demands that thieves be punished.

I load up my mouth with five Mint Imperials, take out the pay-as-you-go phone Editor Miguel supplied, and, digit by digit, I enter the phone number I copied down from the poster at Heathrow airport. The noise of traffic and seabirds and the footballers fades away. I press Call.

A woman answers straight away: "Heathrow Customs Agency Confidential Line?" I speak in my crappest Sean Connery accent, the Mint Imperials jangling my voice further. "Listen to me. There's this character, Richard Cheeseman, flying into London from Colombia on BA713, tomorrow night. BA713, tomorrow. You getting all this?"

"BA713, sir. Yes, I'm recording it." That jolts me. Of course, they'd have to. "And the name was what again?"

"Richard Cheeseman. 'Cheese' and 'man.' He's got cocaine in his suitcase. Let a sniffer dog sniff. Watch what happens."

"I understand," says the woman. "Sir, may I ask if—"

CALL ENDED, say the chunky pixels on the tiny screen. The sounds of evening return. I spit out the Mint Imperials. They shatter on the stones and lie there, like bits of teeth after a fight. Richard Cheeseman committed the action: I am the *reaction.* Ethics are Newtonian. Maybe what I just said was sufficient to trigger a bag inspection. Maybe it wasn't. Maybe he'll be let off with a private caution, or maybe get his bum spanked in public. Maybe the embarrassment will cause Cheeseman to lose his column in the *Telegraph.* Maybe it won't. I've done my bit, now it's up to Fate. I go back down the stone steps, and pretend to tie my shoelace. Surreptitiously I slip the phone into a storm drain. Plop! By the time its remains are disinterred, if indeed they ever are, everybody alive on this glorious evening will have been dead for centuries.

You, dear reader, me, Richard Cheeseman, all of us.

APHRA BOOTH BEGINS the next page of her Position Paper, entitled *Pale, Male and Stale: The De(CON?)struction of Post-Post-Feminist Straw Dolls in the New Phallic Fiction.* I top up my sparkling water, *Glug*-splush-*glig*-splosh*glugsplshssssss* . . . To my right, Event Moderator sits with his professorial eyes half shut in a display of worshipful concentration, but I suspect he's napping. The glass wall behind the audience offers a view down to the Swan River, shimmering silver-blue through Perth, Western Australia. How long has Aphra been *droning*? This is worse than church. Either our moderator really is asleep, or he's too scared to interrupt Ms. Booth in mid-position. What am I missing? "When held up to the mirror of gender, masculine metaparadigms of the female psyche refract the whole subtext of an assymetric opacity; or to paraphrase myself, when Venus depicts Mars, she paints from below; from the laundry room and the baby-changing mat. Yet when Mars depicts Venus, he cannot but paint from above; from the imam's throne, the archbishop's pulpit or via the pornographer's lens . . ." I pandiculate, and Aphra Booth swivels around. "Can't keep up without a PowerPoint show, Crispin?"

"Just a touch of deep-vein thrombosis, Aphra." I win a few nervous giggles, and the prospect of a fight injects a little life into the sun-leathered citizens of Perth. "You've been going on for *hours.* And isn't this panel supposed to be about the soul?"

"This festival does not *yit* practice censorship." She glares at Event Moderator. "Am I correct?"

"Oh, totally," he blinks, "no censorship in Australia. Definitely."

"Then perhaps Crispin would pay me the courtesy," Aphra Booth sweeps her death ray back my way, "of letting me finish. As is *clear* to anyone out of his intellectual nappies, the soul *is* a pre-Cartesian avatar. If that's too taxing a concept, suck a gobstopper and wait quietly in the corner."

"I'd rather suck on a cyanide tooth," I mutter.

"Crispin wants a cyanide tooth! Can anyone oblige? *Please.*"

Oh, how the rehydrated mummies wheezed and tittered!

BY THE TIME Aphra Booth is finished, only fifteen of our ninety minutes remain. Event Moderator tries to lasso the runaway theme and asks me whether I believe in the soul, and if so, what the soul may be. I riff on notions of the soul as a karmic report card; as a spiritual memory stick in search of a corporeal hard drive; and as a placebo we generate to cure our dread of mortality. Aphra Booth suggests that I've fudged the question because I'm a classic commitmentphobe—"as we all know." Clearly this is a reference to my recent, well-publicized divorce from Zoë, so I suggest she stop making cowardly insinuations and say what she wants to say, straight up. She accuses me of Hersheycentricism and paranoia. I accuse her of making accusations she's too *gut*less to stand by, em- phasizing "gut" with everything I've got. Tempers fray. "The tragic paradox of Crispin Hershey," Aphra Booth tells the venue, "is that while he poses as the scourge of cliché, his whole Johnny Rotten of Literature schtick is the tiredest stereotype in the male zoo. But even *that* posturing is lethally undermined by his recent advocacy of a convicted drug smuggler."

I imagine a hair dryer falling into her bath: Her limbs twitch and her hair smokes as she dies. "Richard Cheeseman is victim of a gross miscarriage of justice, and using his misfortune as a stick to beat *me* with is vulgar beyond belief, even for Dr. Aphra Booth."

"Thirty grams of cocaine was found in the lining of his suitcase."

"I think," says Event Moderator, "we should get back to—"

I cut him off: "Thirty grams doesn't make you a drug lord!"

"No, Crispin; examine the record—I said drug *smuggler.*"

"There's no evidence Richard Cheeseman hid the cocaine."

"Who did, then?"

"*I* don't know, but—"

"Thank *you*."

"—but Richard would never take such a colossal, stupid risk."

"Unless he was a cokehead who thought his celebrity placed him above Colombian law, as both judge and jury concluded."

"If Richard Cheeseman were *Rebecca* Cheeseman, you'd be setting your pubic hair on fire outside the Colombian embassy, screaming for justice. The very least that Richard deserves is a transfer to a British jail. Smuggling is a crime against the country of destination, not the country of departure."

"Oh—so now you're saying Cheeseman *is* a drug smuggler?"

"He should be allowed to fight for his innocence from a U.K. prison, and not from a festering pit in Bogotá where there's no access to soap, let alone a decent defense lawyer."

"But as a columnist in the right-wing *Piccadilly Review,* Richard Cheeseman was very hot on prison as a deterrent. In fact, to quote—"

"Enough already, Aphra, you bigoted blob of trans fat."

Aphra springs to her feet and points her finger at me, like a loaded Magnum. "Apologize *now,* or you'll have a crash course in how Australian courts handle slander, defamation, and body fascism!"

"I'm sure all Crispin meant," says Event Moderator, "was—"

"I de*mand* an apology from that Weightist Male Pig!"

"Of course I'll apologize, Aphra. What I *meant* to call you was a preening, sexist, irrelevant, and bigoted blob of trans fat, who bullies her graduate class into posting five-star reviews of her books on Amazon and who was witnessed, on February the tenth at sixteen hundred hours local time, *purchasing a Dan Brown novel from the Relay Bookshop at Singapore Changi International Airport.* Some public-spirited witness has already downloaded the clip onto YouTube, you'll find."

The audience gasps as one, most gratifyingly.

"And don't say it was 'just for research,' Aphra, because *it won't wash.* There. I do hope this apology clarifies matters."

"*You,*" Aphra Booth tells Event Moderator, "shouldn't give a stage to rank, fetid misogynists, and *you,*" me, "will need a libel lawyer because I am going to *sue the living shit out of you!*"

Aphra Booth: Exit stage left to sound of thunder.

"Oh, don't be like that, Aphra," I call after her. "Your fans are here. Both of them. *Aphra* . . . Was it something I said?"

I CYCLE OUT of the strip of souvenir shops and cafés, but a minute later end up down a dead end at a dusty parade ground. There are Second World War–style huts, and I half recall being told that Italian prisoners of war were interned on Rottnest Island. This train of thought conveys me to Richard Cheeseman, as so many trains of thought do, these days. My fateful act of vengeance in Cartagena last year didn't so much backfire as explode with horrifying success: Cheeseman is now 342 days into a six-year sentence in the Penitenciaría Central, Bogotá, for drug trafficking. Trafficking! For one little sodding envelope! The Friends of Richard Cheeseman managed to wangle him a private cell and a bunk, but for this luxury we had to pay two thousand dollars to the gangsters who run his wing. Countless, countless times have I *ached* to undo my rash little misdeed but, as the Arabic proverb has it, not even God can change the past. We—the Friends—are using every channel we can to shorten the critic's sentence, or to have him repatriated to the U.K. at least, but it's an uphill struggle. Dominic Fitzsimmons, the suave and able undersecretary at the Ministry of Justice, knew Cheeseman at Cambridge and is on our side, but he has to act with discretion to avoid charges of cronyism. Elsewhere, sympathy for the lippy columnist is not widespread. People point to the life sentences doled out in Thailand and Indonesia and conclude Cheeseman got off lightly, but there's nothing "light" about life in the Penitenciaría. Two or three deaths occur in the prison every month.

I know, I know. One man alone could extract Cheeseman from his Bogotá hellhole and that is Crispin Hershey—but consider the cost. Please. By offering up a full confession, I'd be facing prison myself, quite possibly at Cheeseman's current address. The legal fees would be ruinous, and no friendsofcrispinhershey.org would procure *me* a private cell, either—it'd be straight to the piranha tank. Juno and Anaïs would cut me off forever. So a full confession would be tantamount to suicide, and better a guilty coward than a dead Judas.

I can't do it to myself. I just can't do it.

Beyond the parade ground the dusty track fizzles out.

We all take a few wrong turns. I turn my bike around.

THE AFTERNOON SUN is a microwave oven, door wide open, cooking all exposed flesh. Rottnest is small as islands go, only eight square miles of naked rock and baked gullies, twists, and bends, ups and downs, and the Indian Ocean is either always visible or always around the next bend. Halfway up a hill I dismount and push. My pulse bangs my eardrums and my shirt's sticking to my unflat torso. When did I get so sodding unfit? Back in my thirties I could've streaked up this slope, but now I'm so knackered I'm nearly puking. When did I last ride a bike? Eight years ago, give or take, with Juno and Anaïs in our back garden at Pembridge Place. One afternoon in the holidays I made an obstacle course for the girls with plank ramps, bamboo-stick slaloms, a tunnel out of a sheet and the washing line, and an evil scarecrow to decapitate with Excalibur as we cycled by. I called it "Scrambler Motocross" and the three of us held time trials. That French au pair, I forget her name, made ruby grapefruit lemonade and even Zoë joined the picnic in the fairy clearing behind the foaming hydrangeas. Juno and Anaïs often asked me to set the course up again, and I always meant to, but there was a review to write, or an email to send, or a scene to polish, and Scrambler Motocross ended up being a one-off. What happened to the kids' bicycles? Zoë must have disposed of them, I suppose. Disposing of unwanted items proved to be her forte.

Finally, gratefully, I reach the ridge, remount my bike, and coast down the other side. Iron trees untwist from the beige soil around gloopy pools. I imagine the first sailors from Europe landing here, searching for water in this infernal Eden, taking a quiet shit. Yobs from Liverpool, Rotterdam, Le Havre, and Cork; sun-blacked, tattooed, scurvied, calloused, and muscled as all buggery, and—

Suddenly I'm aware that I'm being watched.

It's strong. It's uncanny. It's disturbing.

I scan the hillside. Every rock, bush . . .

. . . no. Nobody. It's just . . . Just what?

I want to go back to the beginning.

AT THE NEXT turnoff, I follow the road to the lighthouse. No spray-cloaked monarch of the rocks, this; the Rottnest Light is a stumpy middle finger sticking up from a rocky rise, grunting, *"Sit on this, mate."* It keeps reappearing at odd angles and in wrong sizes, but refuses to let me arrive. There's a hill in *Through the Looking-Glass* that does the same until Alice stops trying to arrive there—maybe I'll try the same. What'll I think about, to distract myself?

Richard Cheeseman, who else? *All I wanted was to embarrass Richard Cheeseman.* I'd pictured him being held for a few hours at Heathrow airport while lawyers scrambled, and a much-humbled reviewer would be released on bail. That's all. How could I have predicted that British and Colombian police were enjoying a rare season of cooperation that might result in poor Richard being arrested at Bogotá International Airport, *pre*flight?

"Easily," my conscience replies. And yes, dear reader, I regret my actions very much, and I'm aiming to atone. With Richard's sister Maggie, I set up the Friends of Richard Cheeseman to keep his plight in the news—and, lamentable though my misdeed was, I'm hardly in the Premier Division of Infamy. I'm not a certain Catholic bishop who shuffled boy-raping priests from parish to parish to avoid embarrassment for the Holy Church. I'm not ex-president Bashar al-Assad of Syria, who gassed thousands of men, women, and children for the crime of living in a rebel-held suburb. All I did was punish a man who had smeared my reputation. The punishment was a little excessive. Yes, I'm guilty. I regret it. But my guilt is my burden. *Mine*. My punishment is to live with what I've done.

My iPhone trills in my shirt pocket. Needing a breather I pull over into the shade of a shed-sized boulder. I drop the phone and pick it up from the bleached grit by the Moshi Monsters strap that Anaïs attached to it. Appropriately, it's a text from Zoë or, rather, a photo of Juno's thirteenth birthday party at the house in Montreal. A house *I* paid for, owned by Zoë since the divorce. Behind a pony-shaped cake, Juno's holding the riding boots I paid for, and Anaïs's pulling a goofy face while holding a sign saying, BONJOUR, PAPA! Zoë's contrived to get herself into the background, obliging me to guess at the photographer's identity. It could be a member of La Famille Legrange, but Juno's mentioned some guy called Jerome, a divorced banker with one daughter. Not that I sodding care who Zoë puts it out to, but surely I've a right to know who's tucking my own daughters into bed at night, now their mother has decided it won't be me. Zoë's attached no message but the subtext is clear enough: *We're Doing Fine, Thank You Very Much.*

I notice a handsome bird on a branch, just a few meters away. It's white and black with red cap and breast. I'll photo it and send it to Juno with a funny birthday message. I get out of MESSAGES and press the camera icon, but when I look up I find the bird has flown.

TWO BIKES ARE leaning against the lighthouse when Crispin Hershey finally arrives, which displeases him. I dismount, sticky with sweat, my crotch saddle-sore. I walk out of the nuclear brightness to the shady side of the lighthouse—where, oh, great, two females of the species are finishing a picnic. The younger one's wearing a faux Hawaiian shirt, knee-length khaki shorts, and daubs of bluish sunblock over her cheekbones, cheeks, and forehead. The older one has earth-mother tie-dyed clothes, a floppy white sun hat, unruly black hair, and sunglasses chosen for maximum coverage. The younger one leaps up—she's still a teenager—and says, "Wow. Hi. You're Crispin Hershey." She speaks in estuary English.

"I am." It's been a while since I was recognized out of context.

"Hi. My name's Aoife, and, uh . . . Mum here's actually met you."

The older woman stands and removes her sunglasses. "Hello, Mr. Hershey. There's no reason in the world you'd remember, but—"

"Holly Sykes. Yes. We met at Cartagena, last year."

"*Wow,* Mum!" says Aoife. "*The* Crispin Hershey actually knows who you are. Aunt Sharon's going to be, like, '*Whaaa?*'"

She reminds me so much of Juno that I ache, a little.

"*Aoife.*" There's a note of maternal reprimand; the megaselling Angel Authoress is uneasy with her fame. "Mr. Hershey deserves some peace and quiet after the festival. Let's get back to town, hey?"

The young woman swats away a fly. "We only just *got* here, Mum. It'll look rude. You don't mind sharing a lighthouse, do you?"

"No need to rush off on my account," I hear myself saying.

"Cool," says Aoife. "Then have a seat. Or a step. We saw you on the ferry to Rottnest, actually, but Mum said not to disturb you 'cause you looked dead beat."

Angel Authoress seems keen to avoid me. How rude was I to her at the president's villa? "Jet lag won't take 'please' for an answer."

"You're not wrong." Aoife fans herself with her cap. "That's why Australia and New Zealand're, like, invasion-proof. Any foreign army'd only get halfway up the beach before the time difference'd kick in, and they'd just like *whoa,* and col*lapse* in the sand and that'd be it, invasion over. Sorry we missed your event earlier."

I think of Aphra Booth. "Don't be. So," this is to her mother, "you're appearing at the Writers Festival too?"

Holly Sykes nods, sipping from a bottle of water. "Aoife's doing a sort of gap year in Sydney, so this trip tied in nicely."

"My flatmate in Sydney's from Perth," adds Aoife, "and she's always saying, 'If you go to Perth, you got to go to Rotto.'"

Teenagers make me feel so sodding old. "'Rotto'?"

"Here. Rotto is Rottnest Island. Fremantle's 'Freo'; 'afternoon' is 'arvo.' Isn't it cool how Australians do that?"

No, I'd ordinarily reply, *it's baby talk for grown-ups.* But, then, whither humanity sans youth? Whither language sans neologisms? We'd all be Struldbrugs speaking Chaucerian.

"Fancy a fresh apricot?" Aoife offers me a brown paper bag.

MY TONGUE CRUSHES another perfumed fruit against the roof of my mouth. I throw away the apricot stones, thinking of Jack's mother throwing away the beans that'll turn into the beanstalk in the morning. "Ripe apricots taste exactly of their color."

"You talk like a *real* writer, Crispin," says Aoife. "My uncle Brendan's always teasing Mum, saying now she's this famous author she ought to talk posher, not all, 'Watch yer bleedin' marf or I'll clock yer one, innit.' "

Holly Sykes protests, "I do *not* talk like that!"

I miss Juno and Anaïs teasing me. "So what's this 'sort of' gap year of yours about then, Aoife?"

"I'll be studying archaeology at Manchester from September, but Mum's Australian editor knows a professor of archaeology at Sydney, so this semester I'm sitting in on the lectures in return for helping with a project at Parramatta. There was a factory there for convict women. It's been amazing, piecing their lives together."

"Sounds worthy," I tell Aoife. "Is your dad an archaeologist?"

"Dad was a journalist, actually. A foreign correspondent."

"What does he"—too late I spot the "was"—"do now?"

"Unfortunately a missile hit his hotel. In Homs, in Syria."

I nod. "Excuse my tactlessness. Both of you."

"It's eight years ago," Holly Sykes reassures me, "and . . ."

". . . and I'm lucky," now Aoife reassures me, " 'cause there's, like, a gazillion interviews with Dad on YouTube, so I can go online and there he is, chattering away, large as life. Next best thing to hanging out."

My dad's on YouTube too, but I find watching him makes him deader than ever. I ask Aoife, "What was his name, your dad?"

"Ed Brubeck. I've got his name, too. Aoife Brubeck."

"Not *the* Ed Brubeck? Wrote for *Spyglass* magazine?"

"That's him," says Holly Sykes. "Did you know Ed's writing?"

"We met! When was it? Washington, about 2002? My former wife's brother-in-law was on the panel for the Sheehan-Dower Prize. They awarded it to Ed that year, and I'd done a reading in town that day, so we shared a table at dinner that evening."

Aoife asks, "What did you and Dad talk about?"

"Oh, a hundred things. His job. 9/11. Fear. Politics. The pram in the writer's hallway. He had a four-year-old back in London, I recall." Aoife smiles with her whole wide face. "I was working on a journalist character, so Ed let me quiz him. Then we emailed from time to time, after that. When I heard the news, about Syria . . ." I exhale. "My very belated condolences, to both of you. For whatever they're worth. He was a bloody good journalist."

"Thank you," says one; and "Thanks," the other.

We gaze out across eleven miles of ferry-plowed sea.

Perth's dark skyscrapers stand against the light sky.

Twenty paces away, a medium-sized mammal I cannot identify lollops out of the scrub and down the slope. Chubby as a wallaby, reddish-brown, kangaroo forepaws, and a foxy wombat face. A tongue like a finger slurps the apricot stones. "Good God. *What* is *that*?"

"That charming devil is a quokka," says Aoife.

"What's a quokka? Besides a hell of a Scrabble score."

"An endangered marsupial. The first Dutch who landed here thought they were giant rats, so they called the place Rat's Nest Island: Rottnest, in Dutch. Most mainland quokkas got killed by dogs and rats, but they've managed to survive here."

"If the archaeology falls through, there's always natural history."

Aoife smiles. "I Wikipediaed them five minutes ago."

I ask, "Reckon they like apricots? There's a squishy one left."

Holly looks dubious. "What about 'Do Not Feed the Animals'?"

"It's not like we're chucking them Cherry Ripe bars, Mum."

"And surely," I add, "if they're endangered, they'll need all the Vitamin C they can get." I lob the apricot to within a few feet of the animal. It waddles over, sniffs, chomps, and looks up at us.

" 'Please, sir,' " Aoife does a trembly Oliver Twist voice, " 'can I have some more?' How *cute* is that? I've got to take a photo."

"Not too close, love," says her mother. "It's a wild animal."

"Gotcha." Aoife walks down the slope, holding out her phone.

"What a well-raised kid," I tell her mother, in a low voice.

She looks at me, and I see the signs of a full, fraught life around her eyes. If only she hadn't written a book full of angel bollocks for gullible women disappointed with their lives, we could be friends. It's a fair guess that Holly Sykes knows about my daughters and my divorce: the ex–Wild Child of British Letters may not be famous enough to sell books, but Zoë's huge "I Will Survive" splash for the *Sunday Telegraph* gave the world a very one-sided version of our troubles. We watch Aoife feed the quokka, while all around us Rottnest's bleached slopes buzz and whistle with insects, tinnitus-like. A lizard crosses the dust and . . .

The feeling of being watched comes back, stronger than ever. We aren't the only ones here. There are lots. Near. I could swear.

Acacia tree to wiry shrub to shed-sized rock . . . Nobody.

"Do you feel them too?" Holly Sykes is watching me. "It's an echo chamber, this place . . ."

If I say yes to this, I say yes to her whole flaky, nonempirical world. By saying yes to this, how do I refuse crystal healing, past-life therapy, Atlantis, Reiki, and homeopathy? The problem is, she's right. I do feel them. This place is . . . What's another word for "haunted," Mr. Novelist? My throat's dry. My water bottle's empty.

Down on the rocks blue breakers flume on rocks. I hear the boom, faint and soft, a second later. Further out, surfers at play.

"They were brought here in chains," says Holly Sykes.

"Who were?"

"The Noongar. Wadjemup, they called this island. Means the

Place Across the Water." She sniffs. "For the Noongar, the land couldn't be owned. No more than the seasons could be owned, or a year. What the land gave, you shared."

Holly Sykes's voice is flattening out and faltering, as if she's not speaking but translating a knotty text. Or picking one voice out from a roaring crowd. "The *djanga* came. We thought they were dead ones, come back. They forgot how to speak when they were dead, so now they spoke like birds. Only a few came, at first. Their canoes were big as hills, but hollow, like big floating rooms made of many many rooms. Then more ships, more and more, every ship it puked up more, more, more of them. They planted fences, waved maps, brought sheep, mined for metals. They shot our animals, but if we killed their animals, they hunted us like vermin, and took the women away . . ."

This performance ought to be ridiculous. But in the flesh, three feet away, a vein pulsing in her temple, I don't know what to make of it. "Is this a story you're working on, Holly?"

"Too late, we understood, the *djanga* wasn't dead Noongar jumped up, they was Whitefellas." Holly's voice is blurring now. Some words go missing. "Whitefella made Wadjemup a prison for Noongar. F'burning bush, like we always done, Whitefella ship us to Wadjemup. F'fighting at Whitefella, Whitefella ship us to Wadjemup. Chains. Cells. Coldbox. Hotbox. Years. Whips. Work. Worst thing is this: Our souls can't cross the sea. So when the prison boat takes us from Fremantle, our soul's torn from out body. Sick joke. So when come to Wadjemup, we Noongar we die like flies."

One in four words I'm guessing at now. Holly Sykes's pupils have shrunk to dots as tiny as full stops. This can't be right. "Holly?" What's the first-aid response for this? She must be blind. Holly starts speaking again but not a lot's in English: I catch "priest," "gun," "gallows," and "swim." I have zero knowledge of Aboriginal languages, but what's battling its way out of Holly Sykes's mouth now sure as hell isn't French, German, Spanish, or Latin. Then Holly Sykes's head jerks back and smacks the lighthouse and the word "epilepsy" flashes through my mind. I grip her head so that when she repeats the head-smash it only bashes my hand. I swivel upright and clasp her head firmly against my chest and yell, *"Aoife!"*

The girl reappears from behind a tree, the quokkas beat a retreat, and I call out, "Your mother's having an attack!"

A few pounding seconds later, Aoife Brubeck's here, holding her mother's face. She speaks sharply: "Mum! Stop it! Come back! Mum!"

A cracked buzzing hum starts deep in Holly's throat.

Aoife asks, "How long have her eyes been like that?"

"Sixty seconds? Less, maybe. Is she epileptic?"

"The worst's over. It's not epilepsy, no. She's stopped talking, so she's not hearing now, and—oh, *shit*—what's this blood?"

There's sticky red on my hand. "She hit the wall."

Aoife winces and inspects her mother's head. "She'll have a hell of a lump. But, look, her eyes are coming back." Sure enough, her pupils are swelling from dots to proper disks.

I note, "You're acting as if this has happened before."

"A few times," replies Aoife, with understatement. "You haven't read *The Radio People,* have you?"

Before I can answer Holly Sykes blinks, and finds us. "Oh, f'Chrissakes, it just happened, didn't it?"

Aoife's worried and motherly. "Welcome back."

She's still pasty as pasta. "What did I do to my head?"

"Tried to dent the lighthouse with it, Crispin says."

Holly Sykes flinches at me. "Did you listen to me?"

"It was hard not to. At first. Then it . . . wasn't exactly English. Look, I'm no first-aid expert, but I'm worried about concussion. Cycling down a hilly, bendy road would not be clever, not right now. I've got a number from the bike-hire place. I'll ask for a medic to drive out and pick you up. I strongly advise this."

Holly looks at Aoife, who says, "It's sensible, Mum," and gives her mother's arm a squeeze.

Holly props herself upright. "God alone knows what you must think of all this, Crispin."

It hardly matters. I tap in the number, distracted by a tiny bird calling *Crikey, crikey, crikey* . . .

FOR THE FIFTIETH time Holly groans. "I just feel so em*bar*rassed."

The ferry's pulling into Fremantle. "*Please* stop saying that."

"But I feel awful, Crispin, cutting short your trip to Rottnest."

"I'd have come back on this ferry, anyway. If ever a place had a karma of damnation, it's Rottnest. And all those slick galleries selling Aborigine art were eroding away my will to live. It's as if Germans built a Jewish food hall over Buchenwald."

"Spot the writer." Aoife finishes her ice pop. "Again."

"Writing's a pathology," I say. "I'd pack it in tomorrow, if I could."

The ferry's engines growl, and cut out. Passengers gather their belongings, unplug earphones, and look for children. Holly's phone goes and she checks it: "It's my friend, the one who's picking us up. Just a mo." While she takes the call, I check my own phone for messages. Nothing since the picture of Juno's birthday party earlier. Our international marriage was once a walk-in closet of discoveries and curiosities, but international divorce is not for the fainthearted. Through the spray-dashed window I watch lithe young Aussies leap from prow to quayside, tying ropes around painted steel cleats.

"Our friend's picking us up from the terminal building." Holly puts her phone away. "She's got space for you too, Crispin, if you'd like a lift back to the hotel."

I've got no energy to go exploring Perth. "Please."

We walk down the gangway onto the concrete pier, where my legs struggle to adjust to terra firma. Aoife waves to a woman waving back, but I don't zone in on Holly's friend until I'm a few feet away.

"Hello, Crispin," the woman says, as if she knows me.

"Of course," remembers Holly. "You two met in Colombia!"

"I may," the woman smiles, "have slipped Crispin's mind."

"Not at all, Carmen Salvat," I tell her. "How are you?"

L EAVING THE AIR-CONDITIONED FOYER of the Shanghai Mandarin we plunge into a wall of stewy heat and adoration from a flash mob—I've never seen anything like this level of fandom for a literary writer. More's the pity that writer isn't me—as they recognize him, the cry goes up, *"Neeeeeck!"* Nick Greek, at the vanguard of our two-writer convoy, has been living in Shanghai since March, learning Cantonese and researching a novel about the Opium Wars. Hal the Hyena has liaised closely with his local agent and now a quarter of a million Chinese readers follow Nick Greek on Weibo. Over lunch he mentioned he's been turning down modeling contracts, for sod's sake. "It's so embarrassing," he said modestly. "I mean, what would Steinbeck have made of this?" I managed to smile, thinking how Modesty is Vanity's craftier stepbrother. Some heavyweight minders from the book fair are having to widen a path through the throng of nubile, raven-haired, book-toting Chinese fans: "Neeck! Sign, please, please sign!" Some are even waving A4 color photos of the young American for him to deface, for buggery's sake. "He's a U.S. imperialist!" I want to shout. "What about the Dalai Lama on the White House lawn?" Miss Li, my British Council elf, and I follow in the wake of his entourage, blissfully unhassled. If I appear in any of the footage, they'll assume I'm his father. And guess what, dear reader? It doesn't matter. Let him enjoy the acclaim while it lasts. In six weeks Carmen and I will be living in our dream apartment overlooking the Plaza de la Villa in Madrid. When my old mucker Ewan Rice sees it he'll be *so* sodding jealous he'll explode in a green cloud of spores, even if he *has* won the Brittan Prize twice. Once we're in, I can divide my time more equally between London and Madrid. Spanish cuisine, cheap wine, reliable sunshine, and love. Love. During all those wasted years of my prime with Zoë, I'd forgotten how wonderful it is to love and to be loved. After all, what is the Bubble Reputation compared to the love of a good woman?

Well? I'm asking you a question.

MISS LI LEADS me into the heart of the Shanghai Book Fair complex, where a large auditorium awaits keynote speakers—the true Big Beasts of International Publishing. I can imagine Chairman Mao issuing his jolly-well-thought-out economic diktats in this very space in the 1950s; for all I know, he did. This afternoon the stage is dominated by a jungle of orchids and a ten-meter-high blowup of Nick Greek's blond American head and torso. Miss Li leads me out through the other side of the large auditorium and on to my own venue, although she has to ask several people for directions. Eventually she locates it on the basement level. It appears to be a row of knocked-through broom cupboards. There are thirty chairs in the venue, though only seven are occupied, not counting myself. To wit: my smiling interviewer, an unsmiling female translator, a nervous Miss Li, my friendly Editor Fang, in his Black Sabbath T-shirt, two youths with Shanghai Book Fair ID tags still round their necks, and a girl of what used to be known as Eurasian extraction. She's short, boyish, and sports a nerdy pair of glasses and a shaven head: electrotherapy chic. A droning fan stirs the heat above us, a striplight flickers a little, and the walls are blotched and streaked, like the inside of a never-cleaned oven. I am tempted to walk out—I really am—but handling the fallout would be worse than putting a brave face on the afternoon. I'm sure the British Council keeps a blacklist of badly behaved authors.

My interviewer thanks everyone for coming in Chinese, and gives what I gather is a short introduction. Then I do a reading from *Echo Must Die* while a Mandarin translation is projected onto a screen behind me. It's the same section I read at Hay-on-Wye, three years ago. Sodding hell, is it already three years since I last published? Trevor Upward's hilarious escapades on the roof of the Eurostar do not appear to amuse the select gathering. Was my satire translated as a straight tragedy? Or was the Hershey wit taken into custody at the language barrier? After my reading I endure the sound of fourteen hands clapping, take my seat, and help myself to a glass of sparkling water—I'm thirsty as hell. The water is flat and tastes of yeast. I hope it didn't come out of a Shanghai tap. My interviewer smiles, thanks me in English, and asks me the same questions I've been asked since I arrived in Beijing a few days ago: "How does your famous father's work influence your novels?"; "Why does *Desiccated Embryos* have a symmetrical structure?"; "What truths should the Chinese reader find in your novels?" I give the same answers I've been giving since I arrived in Beijing a few days ago, and my spidery, unsmiling translator, who also translated my answers several times yesterday, renders my sentences into Chinese without any difficulty. Electrotherapy Girl, I notice, is actually taking notes. Then the interviewer asks, "And do you read your reviews?" which redirects my train of thought towards Richard Cheeseman where it smashes into last week's miserable visit to Bogotá and comes off the tracks altogether . . .

HELL'S BELLS, THAT was one dispiriting visit, dear reader. Dominic Fitzsimmons had been pulling strings for months to get me and Richard's sister Maggie a meeting with his Colombian counterpart at the Ministry of Justice for us to discuss the terms of repatriation— only for said dignitary to become "unavailable" at the last minute. A youthful underling came in his place—the boy was virtually tripping over his umbilical cord. He kept taking calls during our twenty-seven-minute audience, and twice he called *me* Meester Cheeseman while referring to "the Prisoner 'Earshey." Waste of sodding time. The next day we visited poor Richard at the Penitenciaría Central. He's suffering from weight loss, shingles, piles, depression, and his hair's falling out too, but there's only one doctor for two thousand inmates, and in the case of middle-class European prisoners, the good medic requires a fee of five hundred dollars per consultation. Richard asked us to bring books, paper, and pencils, but he turned down my offer of a laptop or iPad because the guards would nick it. "It marks you as rich," he told us, in a broken voice, "and if they know you're rich they make you buy insurance." The place is run by gangs who control the in-house drug trade. "Don't worry, Maggie," Richard told his sister. "I don't touch the stuff. Needles are shared, they bulk out the stuff with powder, and once you owe them, they've got your soul. It'd kill off my chances of an early appeal." Maggie stayed brave for her brother, but as soon as we were out of the prison gates, she sobbed and sobbed and sobbed. My own conscience felt hooked and zapped by a Taser. It still does.

But I can't change places with him. It would kill me.

"Mr. Hershey?" Miss Li's looking worried. "You okay?"

I blink. Shanghai. The book fair. "Yes, I just . . . Sorry, um, yes . . . Do I read my reviews? No. Not anymore. They take me to places I don't wish to go." As my interpreter gets to work on this, I notice that my audience is down to six. Electrotherapy Girl has slipped away.

THE SHANGHAI BUND is several things: a waterfront sweep of 1930s architecture with some ornate Toytown set pieces along the way; a symbol of Western colonial arrogance; a symbol of the ascension of the modern Chinese state; four lanes of slow-moving, or no-moving, traffic; and a raised promenade along the Huangpu River where flows a Walt Whitman throng of tourists, families, couples, vendors, pickpockets, friendless novelists, muttering drug dealers, and pimps: "Hey, mister, want drug, want sex? Very near, beautiful girls." Crispin Hershey says, "No." Not only is our hero loyally hitched, but he fears that the paperwork arising from getting Shanghaied in a Shanghai brothel would be truly Homeric, and not in a good way.

The sun disintegrates into evening and the skyscrapers over the river begin to fluoresce: there's a titanic bottle opener; an outsize 1920s interstellar rocket; a supra-Ozymandian obelisk, plus a supporting cast of mere forty-, fifty-, sixty-floor buildings, clustering skywards like a doomed game of Tetris. In Mao's time Pudong was a salt marsh, Nick Greek was telling me, but now you look for levitating jet-cars. When I was a boy the U.S.A. was synonymous with modernity; now it's here. So I carry on walking, imagining the past: junks with lanterns swinging in the ebb and flow; the ghostly crisscross of masts and rigging, the groan of hulls laid down in Glasgow, Hamburg, and Marseille; hard, knotted stevedores unloading opium, loading tea; dotted lines of Japanese bombers, bombing the city to rubble; bullets, millions of bullets, bullets from Chicago, bullets from Fukuoka, bullets from Stalingrad, *ratatat-tat-tat-tat*. If cities have auras, like Zoë always insisted people do, if your "chakra is open," then Shanghai's aura is the color of money and power. Its emails can shut down factories in Detroit, denude Australia of its iron ore, strip Zimbabwe of its rhino horn, pump the Dow Jones full of either steroids or financial sewage . . .

My phone's ringing. Perfect. My favorite person.

"Hail, O Face That Launched a Thousand Ships."

"Hello, you idiot. How's the mysterious Orient?"

"Shanghai's impressive, but it lacks a Carmen Salvat."

"And how was the Shanghai International Book Fair?"

"Ah, same old, same old. A good crowd at my event."

"Great! You gave Nick a run for his money, then?"

" 'Nick *Greek*' to you," growls my green-eyed monster. "It's not a popularity contest, you know."

"Good to hear you say so. Any sign of Holly yet?"

"No, her flight's not due in until later—and, anyway, I've snuck off from the hotel to the Bund. I'm here now, skyscraper-watching."

"Amazing, aren't they? Are they all lit up yet?"

"Yep. Glowing like Lucy *and* the Sky *and* Diamonds. So much for my day, how was yours?"

"A sales meeting with an anxious sales team, an artwork meeting with a frantic printer, and now a lunch meeting with melancholic booksellers, followed by crisis meetings until five."

"Lovely. Any news from the letting agent?"

"Ye-es. The news is, the apartment's ours if we—"

"Oh that's fan*tast*ic, darling! I'll get on to the—"

"But listen, Crisp. I'm not quite as sure about it as I was."

I stand aside for a troop of cheerful Chinese punks in full regalia. "The Plaza de la Villa flat? It was far and a*way* the best place we saw. Plenty of light, space for my study, just about affordable, and *please*—when we lift the blinds every morning, it'll be like living over a Pérez-Reverte novel. I don't understand: What boxes isn't it ticking?"

My editor-girlfriend chooses her words with care. "I didn't realize how attached I am to having my own place, until now. My place here is my own little castle. I like the neighborhood, my neighbors . . ."

"But, Carmen, your own little castle is *little*. If I'm to divide my time between London and Madrid, we need somewhere bigger."

"I *know* . . . I just feel we're rushing things a bit."

That sinking feeling. "It's been a year since Perth."

"I'm not rejecting you, Crispin, honestly. I just . . ."

Evening in Shanghai is turning suddenly cooler.

"I just . . . want to carry on as we are for a while, that's all."

Everyone I see appears to be one half of a loving couple. I remember this *I'm not rejecting you, Crispin* from my pre-Zoë era, when it marked the beginning of breakups. Resentment snarls through the letterbox, feeding me lines to say: "Carmen, make your sodding mind up!"; "Do you *know* how much we're wasting on airfares?"; even, "Have you met someone else? Someone Spanish? Someone closer to your own age?"

I tell her, "That's fine."

She listens to the long pause. "It is?"

"I'm disappointed, but only because I don't have enough money to buy a place near yours, so we could establish some sort of Hanseatic League of Little Castles. Maybe if a film deal for *Echo Must Die* falls from the skies. Look, this call's costing you a fortune. Go and cheer up your booksellers."

"Am I still welcome in Hampstead next week?"

"You're always welcome in Hampstead. Any week."

She's smiling in her office in Madrid, and I'm glad I didn't listen to the snarls through the letterbox. "Thanks, Crispin. Give my love to Holly, if you meet up. She's hoping to. And if anyone offers you the deep-fried durian fruit, steer clear. Okay, bye then—love you."

"Love you too." And end call. Do we use the L-word because we mean it, or because we want to kid ourselves into thinking we're still in that blissful state?

BACK IN HIS hotel room on the twenty-ninth floor, Crispin Hershey showers away his sticky day and flumps back onto his snowy bed, clad in boxers and a T-shirt emblazoned with Beckett's "fail better" quote I was given in Santa Fe. Dinner was a gathering of writers, editors, foreign bookshop owners, and British Council folks at a restaurant with revolving tables. Nick Greek was on eloquent form, while I imagined him dying in spectacular fashion, facedown in a large dish of glazed duck, lotus root, and bamboo shoot. Hercule Poirot would emerge from the shadows to tell us who had poisoned the rising literary star, and why. The older writer would be an obvious choice, with professional jealousy as a motive, which is why it couldn't be him. I stare at the digital clock in the TV-screen frame: 22:17. Thinking about Carmen, I shouldn't be surprised at her reticence re: Our Flat. The "Honeymoon Over" signs were already there. She refused to be in London when Juno and Anaïs came over last month. The girls' visit was not a wholly unqualified success. On the way from the airport, Juno announced she was not into horses anymore so, of course, Anaïs decided that she was too old for pony camp as well, and as the deposit was nonrefundable, I expressed my displeasure perhaps a tad too much in the manner of my own father. Five minutes later Anaïs was bawling her eyes out and Juno was studying her nails, telling me, "It's no good, Dad, you can't use twentieth-century methods on twenty-first-century kids." It cost me five hundred pounds and three hours in Carnaby Street boutiques to stop them phoning their mother to get their flights back to Montreal rebooked for the next day. Zoë lets Juno get away with rejecting even the gentlest admonishment with a virulent "Oh, whatever!" while Anaïs is turning into a sea anemone whose mind sways whichever way the currents of the moment push her. The visit would have gone better if Carmen had pitched in, but she wasn't having any of it: "They don't need a stepmother laying down the law when holidaying in London with their dad." I said I felt a deep affection for my own stepmother. Carmen replied that after reading my memoir about Dad she could quite understand why. Subject deftly changed.

Classic Carmen Salvat strategy, that.

22:47. I PLAY chess on my iPhone, and indulge in a fond fantasy that my opponent isn't a mind of digital code but Dad: It's Dad's attacks I repel; Dad's defenses I dismantle; Dad's king scurrying around the board to prolong the inevitable. Stress will out, however; usually I win at this level, but today I keep making repeated slips. Worse, the old git starts taking the piss: "Superb strategy, Crisp; that's it, you move your rook there; so I'll move my knight here; pincer your dozy rook against your blundering queen and now there's Sweet Fanny Adams you can do about it!" When I use the undo function to take back my rook, Dad crows: "That's right—ask a sodding machine to bail you out. Why not download an app to write your next novel?" "Sod off," I tell him, and turn off my phone. I switch on the TV and sift through the channels until I recognize a scene from Mike Leigh's film *One Year*. It's appallingly good. My own dialogue is shite compared to this. Sleep would be a good idea, but I'm at the mercy of jet lag and I find I'm wired. My stomach isn't too sure about the deep-fried chunks of durian fruit, either; Nick Greek admitted to the British consul that he hadn't yet acquired the taste, so I ate three. I'd love a smoke but Carmen's bullied me into quitting so, yummy yummy, it's a zap of Nicorette. Richard Cheese-man's smoking again. How can he not, stuck where he is, poor bastard? His teeth are brown as tea. I flick through more channels and find a subtitled American import, *The Dog Whisperer,* about an animal trainer who sorts out psychotic Californians' psychotic pets. 23:10. I consider jerking off again, purely for medicinal purposes, and browse my mental Blu-ray collection, settling on the girl from that commune Rivendell somewhere in West London—but decide that I can't be bothered. So I open my new Moleskine, turn to the first page, and write "The Rottnest Novel" at the top . . .

. . . and find I've forgotten my main character's name again. Bugger it. For a while he was Duncan Frye, but Carmen said that sounded like a Scottish chip-shop owner. So I went with "Duncan McTeague" but the "Mc" is too obvious for a Scot. I'll settle with Duncan Drummond, for now. DD. Duncan Drummond, then, an 1840s stonemason who ends up in the Swan River Settlement, designs a lighthouse on Rottnest Island. Hyena Hal isn't sure about this book—"Certainly a fresh departure, Crisp"—but I woke up one morning and realized that all my novels deal with contemporary Londoners whose upper-middle-class lives have their organs ripped out by catastrophe or scandal. Diminishing returns were kicking in even before Richard Cheeseman's review, I fear. Already, however, a few problemettes with the Rottnest novel are mooning their brown starfishes my way: Viz., I've only got three thousand words; those three thousand are not the best of my career; my final new deadline is December 31 of this year; Editor Oliver has been sacked for "underperformance" and his aptly named successor Curt is making some unpleasant noises about paying back advances.

Would a quokka or two spice it up? I wonder.

Sod this. There must be a bar open somewhere.

HALLELUJAH! I WALK into the Sky High bar on the forty-third floor and it's still open. I sink my weary carcass into an armchair by the window and order a twenty-five-dollar shot of cognac. The view is to die for. Shanghai by night is a mind of a million lights: of orange dot-to-dots along expressways, of pixel-white headlights and red taillights; green lights on the cranes; blinking blues on airplanes; office blocks across the road, and smearages of specks, miles away, every microspeck a life, a family, a loner, a soap opera; floodlights up the skyscrapers over in Pudong; closer up, animated ad-screens for Omega, Burberry, *Iron Man 5*, gigawatt-brite, flyposted onto night's undarkness. Every conceivable light, in fact, except the moon and stars. "There's no distances in prisons," Richard Cheeseman wrote, in a letter to our Friends Committee. "No outside windows, so the furthest I ever see is the tops of the walls around the yard. I'd give a lot just for a view of a few miles. It wouldn't have to be pretty—urban grot would be fine—so long as there was several miles' worth."

And Crispin Hershey had put him there.

Crispin Hershey keeps him there.

"Hello, Mr. Hershey," says a woman. "Fancy finding you here."

I jump up with unexpected vigor. "Holly! Hi! I was just . . ." I'm not sure how to finish my sentence so we kiss, cheek to cheek, like fairly good friends. She looks tired, which is only to be expected for a time-zone hopper, but her velvet suit looks great on her—Carmen's taken her shopping a few times. I indicate an imaginary companion in the third chair: "Do you and Captain Jetlag know each other?"

She glances at the chair. "We go back a few years, yes."

"When did you get in from—was it Singapore?"

"Um . . . Got to think. No, Jakarta. It's Monday, right?"

"Welcome to the Literary Life. How's Aoife?"

"Officially in love." Holly's smile has several levels to it. "With a young man called Örvar."

"Örvar? From which galaxy do Örvars hail?"

"Iceland. Aoife went there a week ago, to meet the folks."

"Lucky Aoife. Lucky Örvar. Do you approve of the young man?"

"As it happens, yes. Aoife's brought him down to Rye a few times. He's doing genetics at Oxford, despite his dyslexia, don't ask me how that works. He fixes things. Shelves, shower doors, a stuck blind." Holly asks the waitress who brings my cognac for a glass of the house white. "What about Juno?"

"Juno? Never fixed a sodding thing in her life."

"No, you dope! Is Juno dating yet?"

"Oh. That. No, give her a chance, she's only fifteen. Mmm. Did you discuss boys with your father at that age?"

Holly's phone bleeps. She glances at it. "It's a message for you, from Carmen: 'Tell Crispin I told him not to eat the durian fruit.' Does that make any sense?"

"It does, alas."

"Will you be moving into that new place in Madrid?"

"No. It's a bit of a long story."

"ROTTNEST?" HOLLY FLICKS her wineglass with her fingernail, as if testing its note. "Well, as Carmen may have mentioned, at various points in my life, I've heard voices that other people didn't hear. Or I've been sure about things that I had no way of knowing. Or, occasionally, been the mouthpiece for . . . presences that weren't me. Sorry that last one sounds seancey, I can't help it. And unlike a seance, I don't summon anything up. Voices just . . . nab me. I wish they didn't. I wish very badly that they didn't. But they do."

I know all this. "You've got a degree in psychology, right?"

Holly sees the subtext, takes off her glasses, and pinches the indented mark on her nose. "Okay, Hershey, you win. Summer of 1985. I was sixteen. Jacko had been missing for twelve months. Me and Sharon were staying at Bantry in County Cork, with relatives. One wet day we were playing snakes and ladders with the smallies, when"—three decades later, Holly flinches—"I knew, or *heard*, or 'felt a certainty,' whatever you want to call it, what number the dice was next going to land on. My cousin'd rattle the eggcup and I'd think, *Five*. Lo and behold, the die landed on five. *One. Five. Three*. On and on. A lucky streak, right? Happens all the time. But on it went. For over fifty throws, f'Chrissakes. I wanted it to stop. Each time I thought, *This time it'll be wrong and I'll be able to dismiss it all as a coincidence* . . . but on and on it went, till Sharon needed a six to win, which I knew she'd roll. And she did. By now, I had a cracking headache, so I crawled off to bed. When I woke up, Sharon and our cousins were playing Cluedo, and everything was back to normal. And straightaway I started persuading myself that I'd only *imag*ined knowing the numbers. By the time I got back to boring old Gravesend, I'd half persuaded myself the whole thing'd just been just a . . . a one-off weirdness I was probably misremembering."

I think I'm drunker than I realized. "But it wasn't."

Holly picks at her ring. "That autumn, my mum got me enrolled on an office-skills course at Gravesend Tech, so at least I could do a bit of temping. I managed it okay, but one day in the canteen, I was on my own, as usual, when . . . Well, all of sudden, I *knew* that this girl, Rebecca Jones, who was sat chatting with friends on the table opposite, was going to knock her coffee onto the floor, in just a few seconds' time. I just *knew,* Crispin, like I know . . . your name, or that I'll go to sleep later. I've never believed in God, really, but I was praying, *Please don't, please don't, please don't.* Then Rebecca Jones flapped out her hand to illustrate her story, it hit her coffee cup and smashed it onto the floor. Little streams and puddles of coffee everywhere."

"What did you do?"

"Well, I bloody legged it, but . . . the certainties chased me. I knew that round the next corner I'd see a Dalmatian cocking its leg against a lamppost. As if I'd already seen it, only I hadn't. Round the corner, lo and behold, one Dalmatian, one lamppost, its hind leg up. A hundred yards from the railway bridge, I *knew* that when I crossed the bridge, the London train'd be passing under. Right again. On and on, all the way back to the pub. Then, as I passed through the bar, a regular, Frank Sharkey, was playing darts and . . ." she pauses to look at the goosebumps on her forearms, ". . . I knew I'd never see him again. I *knew,* Crispin. Sure," she winces, "I ignored it, it was nasty and morbid. Old Mr. Sharkey was as much a friend of the family as a regular. He'd watched us all grow up. I told Dad I'd come back from college 'cause of a migraine, which by now I had. Went to bed, woke up, felt tons better. It'd stopped. What'd happened was harder to dismiss as fantasy, of course; I couldn't. But I was just glad it'd stopped and tried not to think about Mr. Sharkey. But the next day, he didn't appear, and even then, I knew. I nagged Dad to call a neighbor who had a key. Frank Sharkey was found dead in his garden shed. He'd had a massive heart attack. The doctor said he'd have been dead before he hit the floor."

She's persuasive, and she's persuaded herself, I can see. But the paranormal *is* persuasive; why else does religion persist?

Holly stares sadly into her glass. "Many people need to believe in psychic powers. A lot of them latch onto my book so I get accused of milking the gullible. By people I respect, even. But s'pose it *was* real, Crispin, s'pose *you* had these certainties, which can't be altered or second-guessed—about, say, Juno or Anaïs. Would you think, *Happy Days, I'm psychic*?"

"Well, it depends . . ." I think about it. "No. At the risk of sounding like a GP, how long did all this last?"

She sucks in her lips and shakes her head. "Well . . . they've never stopped. Aged sixteen, seventeen, I'd be mugged by a bunch of facts that hadn't happened yet, every few weeks, rush home, and bury myself in my bed with my head in a duffel bag. Told no one, apart from my great-aunt Eilísh. What would I say? People'd just think I wanted attention. Aged eighteen, I went grape picking for the summer in Bordeaux, then worked winters in the Alps. At least if I was abroad, the certainties wouldn't be Brendan falling downstairs or Sharon getting hit by a bus."

"This precognition doesn't work long distance, then?"

"Not usually, no."

"And do you get inside info on your own future?"

"Thank Christ, no."

I hesitate to repeat my question, but I do. "Rottnest?"

Holly rubs an eye. "That was a strong one. Occasionally I hear a certainty about the past. I'm seized by it, I sort of . . . Oh, Christ, I can't avoid the terminology, however crappy it sounds: I was channeling some sentience that was lingering in the fabric of that place."

The barman's shaking a cocktail-maker. My friend watches with a discerning eye. "That guy knows what he's doing."

Again, I hesitate. "Do you know anything about Multiple Personality Disorder?"

"Yes. As a mature student, I wrote a thesis on it. It had a name-change in the 1990s to Disassociative Identity Disorder but, even by the standards of clinical psychiatry, its presentation is obscure." Holly fingers an earring. "It may explain things like Rottnest, but what about the precognition? Old Mr. Sharkey? Or how about when Aoife was little and we were at Sharon's wedding in Brighton and she took it into her head to run off, and a certainty *spoke through me* the very number of the room she'd got locked herself into? How could I have known that, Crispin? How? How could I've made that up?"

A group of East Asian businessmen explodes into laughter.

"What if your memory is inverting cause and effect?"

Holly looks blank, drinks her wine, and still looks blank.

"Take Rebecca Wotsit's coffee. Normally, your brain sees the cup knocked over first, and stores the memory of that event second. What if some neural glitch causes your brain to reverse the order—so the memory of the cup smashing on the floor was stored first, *before* your memory of the cup sitting on the edge of the table. That way, you believe in all sincerity that action B comes before A."

Holly looks at me like I just don't get it. "Lend us a coin."

I fish out a two-pound coin from the international collection that lives in my wallet. She holds it in her left palm, then, with the middle finger of her right hand, touches a spot on her forehead. I ask, "What's that in aid of?"

"Dunno, it just helps. Buddhism talks about a third eye in the forehead, but . . . Shush a mo." She shuts her eyes, and tilts her head. Like a dog listening to silence. The background bar noises—low-key chat, ice cubes in glasses, Keith Jarrett's "My Wild Irish Rose"— swell and recede. Holly hands me back the coin. "Flip it. Should be heads."

I flip the coin. "It's heads." Fifty-fifty.

"Heads again," says Holly, concentrating.

I flip the coin. "So it is." One in four against.

"Tails this time," says Holly. Her finger stays on her forehead.

I flip the coin: It's tails. "Three out of three. Not bad."

"Back to heads."

I flip the coin: It's heads.

"Tails," says Holly.

I flip the coin: It's tails. "How are you doing this?"

"Let's try a sequence," says Holly. "Heads, heads, heads, tails, and . . . tails again, but . . . *kneeling*? Crispin, why are you kneeling?"

"As you can see, I'm sitting here, *not* kneeling."

"Forget it. Three heads, two tails, in that order."

So I flip the coin: heads. And again: heads. How's she doing this? I rub the coin on my shirt, like a scratched disk, then flip it: heads, as predicted. "This is clever," I say, but I feel uneasy.

She's irritated by the adjective. "Two tails, now."

I flip the coin: tails. Nine out of nine. On the tenth flip, I fumble the catch and the coin goes freewheeling away. I give chase, and only when I draw it out from under a chair and see it's tails do I realize that I'm kneeling. Holly looks like someone being given the answer to a simple riddle. "Obviously. The coin runs away."

As I retake my seat, I don't quite trust myself to speak.

"Odds of 1,024 to 1 against a ten-digit sequence, if you're wondering. We can increase it to 4,096 to 1 with two more throws?"

"No need." My voice is tight. I look at Holly Sykes: Who *is* she? "That kneeling thing. How . . ."

"Maybe your brain is mistaking memories for predictions, too." Holly Sykes looks not at all like a magician whose ambitious trick just went perfectly, but like a tired woman who needs to gain a few pounds. "Oh, Christ, that was a mistake. You're looking at me in that way."

"In what way?"

"Look, Crispin, can we just forget all of this? I need my bed."

. . .

WE WALK TO the lift lobby without much to say. A pair of terra-cotta warriors don't think very much of me, judging from their expressions. "You've got a gazillion true believers who'd pay a year of their lives to see what you just showed me," I tell Holly. "I'm a cynical bastard, as you well know. Why honor me with that private demonstration?"

Now Holly looks pained. "I hoped you might believe me."

"About what? About your Radio People? Rottnest? About—"

"That evening in Hay-on-Wye, in the signing tent. We were sat a few yards away. I had a strange strong certainty. About you."

The lift doors close, and I remember from Zoë's flirtation with feng shui that lifts are jaws that eat good luck. "Me?"

"You. And it's an odd one. And it's never changed."

"Well, what's it saying about me, for heaven's sake?"

She swallows. " 'A spider, a spiral, a one-eyed man.' "

I wait for an explanation. None comes. "Meaning?"

Holly looks cornered. "I have absolutely no idea."

"But you usually find out what they mean after, right?"

"Usually. Eventually. But this is a . . . slow-cooking certainty."

" 'A spider, a spiral, a one-eyed man'? What *is* that? A shopping list? A dance track? A line from a sodding haiku?"

"Crispin, if I knew, I'd tell you, I swear."

"Then it may just be random gobbledegook."

Holly agrees too easily. "Probably, yes. Yep. Forget it."

An elderly Chinese guy in a pink Lacoste top, fudge-brown slacks, and golf shoes steps out of the lift. Hooked onto his arm is a blond model wearing a négligé sewn of cobwebs and gold coins, extraplanetary makeup, and not a lot else. They go around a corner.

"Maybe she's his daughter," says Holly.

"What did you mean just then, 'It's never changed'?"

Holly, I expect, regrets having started this. "In Cartagena, at the president's house, I heard the same certainty. Same words. At Rottnest, too, before I started channeling. And now, if I tune in. I did the coin thing so you might take the *spiral-spider-one-eyed-man* thing seriously, in case it's ever . . ." she shrugs, ". . . relevant."

The lifts hum in their turboshafts. "What's the use of certainties," I ask, "that are so sodding uncertain?"

"Oh, I don't *know,* Crispin. I'm not a bloody oracle. If I *could* stop them I would, like a bloody shot!"

These uncensored stupid words spill out: "You've profited from them well enough."

Holly looks shocked, hurt, then pissed off, all in under five seconds. "*Yes,* I wrote *The Radio People* because stupidly, *stupidly,* I thought if Jacko's alive and out there somewhere"—she sweeps an angry hand at the borderless city through the window—"he might read it, or someone who knows him might recognize him and get in touch. Fat bloody chance 'cause he's probably dead but I had to try. But I *endure* my certainties. I live *despite* them. Don't say I profit from them. Don't *dare* bloody say that, Crispin."

"Yeah." I close my eyes. "Look, it came out wrong. I . . ."

My crimes, my misdeeds. Where do I sodding begin?

Then I hear the lift doors close. Great. She's gone.

As I shamble back to my room, I send a text to Holly to apologize. I'll phone in the morning after we've both had a decent night's sleep, and we'll meet for breakfast. I arrive at Room 2929, where I find a black bag hung over my door handle. It's embroidered with runes in gold thread: a real labor of love. Inside is a book entitled *Your Last Chance* by Soleil Moore. Never heard of her. Or him. I already know it's dreck. No real poet would be rude enough to imagine that I'd read unsolicited sonnets, just because of a hand-embroidered bag. How did she find out my room number? We're in China. Bribes, of course. Not at the Shanghai Mandarin, surely. Ah, who cares? I'm so—soddingly—buggeringly—*tired.* I just go into my room, dump the book still in its lovely bag into the deep bin with the detritus of the day, empty my grateful bladder, crawl into bed, and sleep opens up like a sink-hole . . .

D ID YOU EVER ESPY a lonelier signpost, dear reader? North to Festap, east along the Kaldidadur Road, and west to Þingvellir, 23 kilometers. Örvar, I recall, taught me that "Þ" is a voiced "th" as in "lathe." Twenty-three kilometers on British back roads would be a mere twenty-minute drive, but I left the tourist center at Þingvellir an hour and a half ago. The tarmac road degenerated into a dirt track twisting its way up the escarpment and onto this rocky plateau under gunmetal mountains and churning clouds. On a whim, I pull over, kill the engine of my rented Mitsubishi, and climb up the stony hillock to sit on a boulder. Not a telephone pole, not a power line, not a tree, not a shrub, not a sheep, not a crow, not a fly, just a few tufts of coarse grass and a lone novelist. The valley in *The Fall of the House of Usher*. A terraforming experiment on a lesser moon of Saturn. A perfect opposite of end-of-summer Madrid, and I wonder how Carmen's doing, then remind myself that how she's doing is no longer my business. Driving around Iceland for a week before the Reykjavik Festival was her idea: "The Land of the Sagas! It'll be a blast, Crispin!" Dutifully I did the research, booked the rooms and the car, and was even reading *Njal's Saga* that London evening only eight weeks ago. When the phone went, I knew it was trouble: Holly would call it a "Certainty" with a capital C. My separation from Zoë was long forecast, but Carmen's declaration of independence came from a clear blue sky. Frantic, hurt, above all fearful, I began arguing that it's the challenges and routines that make a relationship real but I was soon incoherent as the house seemed to collapse and the sky fell in on top.

Enough. I had two years of love from a kind woman.

Cheeseman's on his third year in hell, and counting.

SOME TIME LATER, a convoy of 4x4s grinds past, coming back from the Kaldidur Road. I'm still here, sitting on my arse. A bit cold. The tourists watch me through grime-plastered windows, tires spitting stones and kicking up dust. The wind cuffs my ears, my stomach welcomes the tea and . . . Nothing else. Eerie. I treat the microflora to a bladderful of vintage novelist's urine. By the signpost a cairn of stones has accumulated over the centuries. Feel free to add a stone and make a wish, Örvar told me, but never remove one, or a spirit could slip out to curse you and your bloodline. The threat isn't as quaint up here as it sounded down in Reykjavik. The rim of Langjökull Glacier rises whalebone-white behind nearer mountains to the east. The few glaciers I've seen previously were grubby toes unworthy of the name—Langjökull is *vast* . . . The visible skull of an ice planet smooshed onto earth. Back in Hampstead I read about characters in the sagas getting condemned to outlawry, and imagined a jolly enough Robin-Hood-in-furs setup, but in situ I can see that outlawry Iceland-style was a de facto death sentence. Better push on. I put my stone on the cairn and notice, at close range, a few coins have been left here too. Down at sea level I wouldn't be so daft, but I find myself taking my wallet to retrieve a coin or two . . .

. . . and notice that the passport photo of me, Juno, and Anaïs is missing. Impossible. Yet the blank square of leather under the plastic sheath insists the photo is gone.

How? The photo's been in there years now, since Zoë gave me the wallet, since our last civilized Christmas as a family. We'd taken the photo a few days earlier, at the photo booth in Notting Hill Tube station. It was just to kill a little time while waiting for Zoë, before we went to the Italian place on Moscow Road. Juno said how she'd heard tribes in the rain forest or wherever believe photography can steal a piece from your soul, and Anaïs said, "Then this picture's got all three of our souls in it." I've had it ever since. It can't slip out. I used the wallet at the Þingvellir visitor center to buy postcards and water, and I'd have noticed if the photo was missing then. This isn't a disaster, but it's upsetting. That photo's irreplaceable. It's got our souls in it. Perhaps it's in the car, fallen down by the handbrake, or . . .

As I scramble down the slope, my phone rings. CALLER UNKNOWN. I take it. "Hello?"

"Afternoon—Mr. Hershey?"

"Who's speaking?"

"This is Nikki Barrow, Dominic Fitzsimmons's PA at the Ministry of Justice. The minister has some news regarding Richard Cheeseman, Mr. Hershey—if now's a convenient time?"

"Uh—yeah, yes, sure. Please."

I'm put on hold—sodding Vangelis's *Chariots of Fire*—while I sweat hot and cold. The Friends of Richard Cheeseman had thought our Whitehall ally had forgotten us. My heart's pounding; this will be either the best news—repatriation—or the worst—an "accident" in prison. Sod it, my phone's down to eight percent power. *Hurry.* It goes to seven percent. There's a burst of "Tell him I'll be there for the vote at five" in Fitzsimmons's plummy tones; then it's "Hi, Crispin, how *are* you?"

"Can't complain, Dominic. You have news, I gather?"

"I do indeed: Richard'll be on a flight back to the U.K. on Friday. I had a call from the Colombian ambassador an hour ago—he heard from Bogotá after lunch. And because Richard's eligible for parole under our system, he ought to be out by Christmas of next year, provided he keeps his nose clean, no tasteless pun intended."

I feel a lot of things, but I'll focus on the positives. "Thank Christ for that. And thank you. How definite is all of this?"

"Well, barring a major governmental tiff before Friday, it's very definite. I'll try to get Richard D-cat status—his mother and sister live in Bradford, so Hatfield may suit—it's an open prison in South Yorkshire. Paradise regained compared to his current digs. After three months he'll be eligible for weekend passes."

"I can't tell you how good it is to hear this."

"Yep, it's a decent result. The fact that I knew Richard in Cambridge meant that I kept a close eye on his case, but it also meant my hands were tied. By the same token, keep my name out of any social networking you may do, will you? Say an undersecretary got in touch. I spoke to Richard's sister five minutes ago and made the same request. Look, got to rush—I'm due at Number Ten. My best to your committee—and top job, Crispin. Richard's lucky to have had you fighting his corner when nobody else gave a monkey's toss."

WITH MY iPHONE's last two percent I text my congratulations to Richard's sister Maggie, who'll phone Benedict Finch at *The Piccadilly Review;* Ben's been handling the media campaign. This is what we've fought, connived, plotted, and prayed for, and yet, and yet, my joy's melting away even as I touch it. I committed an inexcusable wrong against Richard Cheeseman, and nobody knows. "A perjurer," I tell the Icelandic interior, "and a coward." A cold wind scuffs the black dust, same as it ever did, as it ever does, as it ever will do. I was going to beg for a wish from the cairn, but the moment passed. I'll take what luck I get. It's all I deserve.

What was I doing when Fitzsimmons called?

Yes, the photograph. That's a real pity. More than a pity. Losing the photo feels like losing the children again.

Down the slope I trudge to the Mitsubishi.

The photo won't be there, or anywhere.

FORTY OR FIFTY BIPEDS EXCLAIM, "Whale!" and "Look!" and "Where?" and "Over there!" in five, six, seven languages, hurry to the port bow and hold up devices at the knobbled oval rising from the cobalt sea. A locomotive huff of steam shoots from the blowhole, which the breeze combs over the shrieking, laughing passengers. An American boy about Anaïs's age grimaces: "Mommy, I'm *dripping* in whale boogers!" The parents look so glad. Decades from now they'll say, "Do you remember that time we went whale watching in Iceland?"

From my vantage point above the bridge I can see the whale's whole outline—not a lot shorter than our sixty-foot boat. "This is good, our patience is rewarded at the last minute," says the grizzled guide in his carefully trodden English. "The whale is a humpback—identifiable by the humps on its back. We saw a number of so-called friendlies in this location on this morning's tour, so I am happy that one is still hanging out here today . . ." My mind swims off to questions about how whales choose names for one another; whether flying feels like swimming; if they suffer from unrequited love too; and if they scream when explosive harpoons sink in and go off. Of course they must. The flippers are paler than the rest of its upper body, and as they flap I remember Juno and Anaïs floating on their backs in the swimming pool. "Don't let go, Daddy!" Standing waist-deep in the shallow end I'd assure them I'd never let them go, not until they asked me to, and their eyes were wide and true with trust.

Phone, I think at them, in Montreal. *Phone Dad. Now.*

I wait. I count from one to ten. Make it twenty. Make it fifty . . .

. . . it's sodding ringing! My daughters heard me.

No, actually. The screen reads Hyena Hal. *Don't answer.*

But I have to; it's about money. "Hal! Crispin here."

"Afternoon, Crispin. This signal's weird; are you on a train?"

"On a boat, actually. In the mouth of Húsavík Bay."

"Húsavík Bay . . . Which is—let me guess. Alaska?"

"North coast of Iceland. I'm doing the Reykjavik Festival."

"So you are, so you are. Top result regarding Richard Cheeseman, by the way. I heard on Monday morning."

"Really? But the government only found out on Tuesday."

His moniker notwithstanding, Hal's laugh isn't like a hyena's; it's a sequence of glottal stops, like the noise a body might make as it falls down wooden stairs into a basement. "Are Juno and Anaïs with you? Iceland's kid heaven, I'm told."

"No. Carmen was supposed to be joining me, but . . ."

"Ah, *yes,* yes. Well, fish in the sea, c'est la vie and pass the ammo—bringing us seamlessly to today's conference call with Erebus and Bleecker Yard. A frank discussion, resulting in an Action List."

Norman Mailer, J. D. Salinger, or even Dr. Aphra Booth would at this juncture toss the phone high into this clear air, and watch it *plop* into the depths. "Right . . . Are my advances on the Action List?"

"Moot Point Numero Uno. They *were* advances, when you signed the current deal, back in 2004. Fifteen years ago. Erebus and Bleecker Yard's view is that the new book's now *so* overdue, you're in breach of contract. What were advances are now debts repayable."

"Well, that's just sodding ridiculous. Isn't it. Isn't it, Hal?"

"Legally, I'm afraid, they're on tried and tested ground."

"But they own exclusive rights to the new Crispin Hershey."

"Moot Point Numero Dos—and there's no sugarcoating this one, I'm afraid. *Desiccated Embryos* sold a cool half-million, yes, but from *Red Monkey* onwards, your sales have resembled a one-winged Cessna. Your name is still known, but your sales are mid-list. Once upon a time, the Kingdom of Midlist wasn't a bad place to earn a living: middling sales, middling advances, puttering along. Alas, the kingdom is no more. Erebus and Bleecker Yard want their money back *more* than they want the new novel by Crispin Hershey."

"But I can't pay it back, Hal . . ." Here comes the harpoon, eviscerating my bankability, my self-esteem, my sodding pension. "I—I—I spent it. Years ago. Or Zoë spent it. Or Zoë's lawyers spent it."

"Yes, but they know you own property in Hampstead."

"No sodding way! They can't touch my house!" Disapproving faces look up from the deck—did I shout? "Can they? Hal?"

"Their lawyers are displaying worrying levels of confidence."

"What if I handed in a new novel in . . . say, ten weeks?"

"They're not bluffing, Crispin. They *truly* aren't interested."

"Then what the sodding hell do we do? Fake my suicide?"

I meant it as gallows humor, but Hal doesn't dismiss the option: "First they'd sue your estate, via us; then your insurers would track you down, so unless you sought political asylum in Pyongyang, you'd get three years for fraud. No, your best hope lies in selling the Australian lighthouse novel at Frankfurt for a fat enough sum to pacify Erebus and Bleecker Yard. Nobody'll pay you a bean up front now, alas. Can you send me the first three chapters?"

"Right. Well. The new novel has . . . evolved."

Hal, I imagine, mouths a silent profanity. He asks, "Evolved?"

"For one thing, the story's now set in Shanghai."

"Shanghai around the 1840s? Opium Wars?"

"More Shanghai in the present day, actually."

"Right . . . I didn't know you were a Sinologist as well."

"World's oldest culture. Workshop of the World. The Chinese Century. China's very . . . *now.*" Listen to me, Crispin Hershey pitching a book like a kid fresh off a creative-writing course.

"Where does the Australian lighthouse fit in?"

I take a deep breath. And another. "It doesn't."

Hal, I am fairly sure, is miming shooting himself.

"But this one's got legs, Hal. A jet-lagged businessman has the mother of all breakdowns in a labyrinthine hotel in Shanghai, encounters a minister, a CEO, a cleaner, a psychic woman who hears voices"—gabbling garbling—"think *Solaris* meets Noam Chomsky via *The Girl with the Dragon Tattoo*. Add a dash of *Twin Peaks . . .*"

Hal is pouring himself a whisky and soda: Hear it fizz? His voice is flat and accusative: "Crispin. Are you trying to tell me that you're writing a fantasy novel?"

"Me? Never! Or it's only one-third fantasy. Half, at most."

"A book can't be a half fantasy any more than a woman can be half pregnant. How many pages have you got?"

"Oh, it's humming along really well. About a hundred."

"Crispin. This is me. How many pages have you got?"

How does he *always* know? "Thirty—but the rest is all mapped out, I swear."

Hal the Hyena exhales a sawtoothed groan. "Shitting Nora."

THE WHALE'S TAIL lifts. Water streams off the striated flukes. "All tail flukes are unique," the guide is saying, "and researchers can recognize individuals from their patterns. Now we watch the whale dive . . ." The flukes slice into the water, and the visitor from another realm is gone. The passengers stare as if a friend's gone for good. I stare as if I squandered my one and only close encounter with a cetacean on a shitty business call. The American family pass round a box of cupcakes, and the caring way they make sure they've all had one injects me with fifty milliliters of distilled envy. Why *didn't* I invite Juno and Anaïs along on this trip, so *my* kids would have lifelong memories of being with their dad in Iceland, too? The boat's engines growl into life, and the vessel turns back towards Húsavík. The town's a mile away beneath a brooding fell. Harbor buildings, a fish-processing plant, a few restaurants and hotels, a wedding-cake church, one department store, steeply gabled houses painted all the shades of the color chart, WiFi masts, and whatever else 2,376 Icelanders need to get from one year to the next. One last time I look north between the muscled walls of the bay, towards the Arctic Ocean, where somewhere the whale is circling in its dark skies.

HALFWAY ALONG OUR JOURNEY *to life's end I found myself astray in a dark wood.* This fork in the path, these slender birches, that mossy boulder tilted upwards, like a troll's head. Finding oneself astray in any wood is a feat in Iceland, where even scraggy copses are rare. Zoë never let me navigate in our pre-satnav era; she said it was safer to drive with the road atlas on her lap. My tourist map of Ásbyrgi isn't any help; the mile-wide, horseshoe-shaped, forested ravine sinks beneath the surrounding land to a hundred-meter rock face, where a river dawdles in pools . . . But where am I in it? The river's vowels and the trees' consonants speak a not-quite-foreign language.

Minutes pass unnoticed as I gaze, transfixed, at the comings and goings of ants on a twig. Richard Cheeseman's sitting between a policeman and a consular official, somewhere over the Atlantic. I remember him griping at Cartagena that the festival hadn't flown him business class, but after three years in the Penitenciaría Central, even the Group 4 van from Heathrow up to Yorkshire is going to feel like a trip in a Rolls-Royce Silver Shadow.

A blundering wind scatters yellowed leaves . . .

. . . and I find one, dear reader, between my tongue and the roof of my mouth. Look. A little birch leaf. Sodding extraordinary. The wind's sharp fingers snatch away the evidence. Willows stand aside to reveal the towering rock slab in the center of Ásbyrgi . . . Perfect for snagging the anchor of a cloud-sailed longboat, or for a mothership from Epsilon Eridani to dock alongside. A torch-through-a-sheet sun. Hal sensed my China book would be a pile of crap, and he's right. One six-day trip to Shanghai and Beijing, and I think I can rival Nick Greek's knowledge of the place—what in buggery's name was I thinking? Let me write about an Icelandic road trip; a running man; backflashes galore; and slowly disclose what it is he's running from. Bring him to Ásbyrgi; mention how the ravine was formed by a slammed-down hoof of Odin's horse. Mention how it's the Parliament of the Hidden Folk. Have him stare at the rock faces until the rock's faces stare back. Breathe deep the resinous tang of the spruces. Let him meet a ghost from his past. Hear the bird, luring me in, ever deeper ever tighter circles. Where are you? There. On the toadstool-frilled tree stump.

"It's a wren," said Mum, turning to go.

AT MY TENTH birthday party, pass-the-parcel descended into a battle royale of half nelsons and Chinese burns. My father buggered off, leaving Mum and Nina the housekeeper to conduct riot control until Mr. Chimes the Magician showed up. Mr. Chimes was an alcoholic thesp-on-the-skids, whose real name was Arthur Hoare, upon whom Dad had taken pity. His halitosis could have melted plastic. From his magic hat, at the count of three, he produced Hermes the Magic Hamster, but Hermes had been flattened seriously enough to produce death, blood, feces, and innards. My classmates shrieked with disgust and joy. Mr. Chimes laid the rodent's mangled corpse in an ashtray and said: " 'For those whom thou think'st thou dost overthrow Die not, poor Death; nor yet canst thou kill me.' Boys." Mr. Chimes packed up his props. "John Donne lied, the bastard." Kells Tufton then announced he'd swallowed one of my miniature lead figurines, so Mum had to drive him to hospital. Nina was left in charge, a less-than-ideal arrangement, as she spoke little English and had suffered from bouts of depression ever since the Argentine junta's men had thrown her siblings from a helicopter over the South Atlantic. My classmates knew nothing and cared less about juntas and played the we'll-repeat-what-you-say game until

Nina locked herself in the third-floor flat where Dad normally wrote his screenplays. Now the blood-dimmed tide was truly loosed, and everywhere the ceremony of innocence was drowned—until a boy called Mervyn climbed a twelve-shelved bookcase and brought it down on himself. Nina dialed 999. The paramedic said Mervyn needed immediate attention, so Nina went off with the ambulance, leaving me to explain to our classmates' parents that our Pembridge Place house was as bereft of adults as all but the last two pages of *Lord of the Flies*. Mum and Nina got home after eight P.M. Dad got home much later. Voices were raised. Doors were slammed. The following morning I was awoken by the snarl of Dad's Jaguar XJS in the garage beneath my room. Off he went to Shepperton Studios—he was editing *Ganymede 5* at the time. I was eating Shredded Wheat over my comic *2000 AD* when I heard Mum lugging a suitcase down the stairs. She told me she still loved me and Phoebe, but that our father had broken too many promises, so she was taking a break. She said, "This one might be permanent." As my Shredded Wheat turned to mush, she spoke of how her swinging sixties had been a blur of morning sickness, washing nappies, wringing snot from Dad's handkerchiefs, and doing unpaid donkey work for Hershey Pictures; how she had turned a blind eye to Dad's "entanglements" with actresses, makeup girls, and secretaries; and how, when she was pregnant with Phoebe, Dad had promised to write and shoot a film just for her. Her role would be complex, subtle, and showcase her talent as an actress. Dad and his co-writer had completed the script, *Domenico and the Queen of Spain,* a few weeks before. Mum was to play Princess Maria Barbara, who became the titular queen. Now, this much we all knew. What I didn't know was that the day before, while anarchy reigned at Pembridge Place, the head of Transcontinental Pictures had phoned Dad and put Raquel Welch on the line. Miss Welch had read the script, she said, considered it a work of genius, and would play Maria Barbara. Had Dad explained that his wife, who had sacrificed her own acting career for the family, was to play the role? No. He had said, "Raquel, it's all yours." The doorbell rang and it was Mum's brother, my uncle Bob, come to pick her up. Mum said I'd learn betrayals came in various shapes and sizes, but to betray someone's dream is the unforgivable one. A bird hopped onto the foaming lilac outside. Its throat quivered; notes rose and fell out. As long as it kept singing and I kept staring, I told myself, I wouldn't start crying.

"It's a wren," said Mum, turning to go.

THE SUN'S SUNK behind the high lip of Ásbyrgi, so the greens are stewing to grays and browns. Leaves and twigs are losing three-dimensionality. When I remember my mother, am I remembering her, or just memories of her? The latter, I suspect. The glass of dusk is filling by the minute, and I don't really know where I left my Mitsubishi. I feel like Wells's time traveler separated from his time machine. Should I be getting alarmed? What's the worst that could happen to me? Well, I may *never* find my way out, and die of exposure. Ewan Rice will write my obituary for *The Guardian*. Or would he? At the housewarming/meet-Carmen party I threw last autumn Ewan almost went out of his way to emphasize his alpha literary male status: dinner with Stephen Spielberg on his last trip to L.A.; fifty thousand dollars for a lecture at Columbia; an invitation to judge the Pulitzer—"I'll see if I can fit it in, I'm so damn busy." So maybe not. My sister Phoebe'll miss me, even if the hatchets we've buried in the past are not buried very deep. Carmen would be distraught, I think. She might blame herself. Holly, bless her, would organize the logistics from this end. They'd both steal the show at my funeral. Hyena Hal will know about my death before I do, but will he miss me? As a client, I'm now a conspicuous underperformer. Zoë? Zoë won't notice until the alimony account runs dry, and the girls would sob their hearts out. Anaïs might, anyway.

This is ridiculous! It's a medium-sized wood, not a vast forest. There were some camper vans right by the car park. Why not just yell, "Help!" Because I'm a guy, I'm Crispin Hershey, the Wild Child of British Letters. I just can't. There's a mossy boulder that looks like the head of a troll, thrusting up through a thin ceiling of earth . . .

. . .

. . . by some trick of this northern light, a narrow segment of my 360-degree woodland view—it includes the mossy boulder and the X made by two leaning trunks behind—wavers and shimmers, like a sheet blown in a breeze, a breeze that isn't even there . . .

No: *Look*! A *hand* appears in the air, and pulls the sheet aside, a hand whose owner now steps out of the slitted air. Like a conjuring trick—a really, really astonishing one. A blond young man, dressed in jacket and jeans, has materialized here, in the middle of this wood. Midtwenties and with model-good looks. I watch, astonished: Am I . . . actually seeing a ghost? A twig cracks under his desert boot. No ghost and no materializing, you idiot; my "ghost" is just a tourist, like me. From the camper vans, like as not. Probably he just took a dump. Blame the twilight; blame another day spent in my own company. I tell him, "Good evening."

"Good evening, Mr. Hershey." His English sounds more expensively schooled British than sibilant Icelandic.

I'm gratified, I admit. "My. Odd place to be recognized."

He takes a few paces until we're at arm's length. He looks pleased. "I'm an admirer. My name's Hugo Lamb." Then he smiles with charisma and warmth, as if I'm a trusted friend he's known for years. For my part, I feel an unwanted craving for his approval.

"Nice, uh, to meet you then, Hugo. Look, this is all a bit embarrassing, but I've gone and mislaid the car park . . ."

He nods and his face turns thoughtful again. "Ásbyrgi plays these tricks on everybody, Mr. Hershey."

"Could you point me in the right direction, then?"

"I could. I will. But, first, I have a few questions."

I take a step back. "You mean . . . about my books?"

"No, about Holly Sykes. You've become close, we see."

With dismay I realize this Hugo's one of Holly's weirdos. Then with anger, as I realize, no, he's a tabloid "reporter"; she's had some bother with the telephoto lens gang at her new house in Rye. "I'd *love* to give you the lowdown on me 'n' Hol," I sneer at Handsome

Pants, "but here's the thing, sunshine: It's none of your *fucking* business."

Hugo Lamb is utterly unriled. "Ah, but you're wrong. Holly Sykes's business is very much our concern."

I start walking off, backwards, watchfully. "Whatever. Goodbye."

"You'll need my assistance to get out of Ásbyrgi," says the youth.

"Your assistance will fit neatly up your small intestine. Holly's a private person, and so am I, and I'll find my own way ba—"

Hugo Lamb has made a peculiar gesture with his hand, and my body is lifted ten feet into the air and squeezed in an invisible giant's fist: My ribs crunch; the nerves in my spine crackle and the agony is indescribable; begging for mercy or screaming is impossible, and so is enduring this torture for a second longer, but seconds pass, I think they're seconds, they could be days, until I'm thrown, not dropped, onto the forest floor.

My face is pressed into leaf mold. I'm grunting, quivering, and whimpering even as the agony fades. I look up. Hugo Lamb's face is that of a boy dismembering a daddy longlegs; mild interest and gleeful malevolence. A Taser might explain the incapacitating pain, but what about the ten-feet-off-the-ground bit? Something atavistic snuffs my curiosity now, however; I need to get away from him. I've pissed myself but I don't even care. My feet don't work, and a far-off voice might be roaring at me, "You'll never walk alone again," but I won't listen, I can't, I daren't. I crawl backwards, then pull myself upright, against a big tree stump. Hugo Lamb makes another gesture and my legs fold under me. There's no pain this time. Worse, almost, there's nothing. From my waist down, all sensation has gone. I touch my thigh. My fingers register my thigh but my thigh registers nothing. Hugo Lamb walks over—I cower—and perches on the tree stump. "Legs do come in handy," he says. "Do you want yours back?"

My voice is shaky as heck: "What *are* you?"

"Dangerous, as you see. You'll recognize these two cuties." He removes a little square from his pocket and shows me the passport photo of me, Anaïs, and Juno that I lost a few days ago. "Answer my questions honestly, and they'll have as decent a chance of a long and happy life as any child at Outremont Lycée."

This good-looking youth is the stuff of a bad acid trip. Obviously he stole the photo, but when and how, I cannot guess. I nod.

"Let's begin. Who is most precious to Holly Sykes?"

"Her daughter," I say hoarsely. "Aoife. That's no secret."

"Good. Are you and Holly lovers?"

"No. No. We're just friends. Really."

"With a woman? Is that typical for you, Mr. Hershey?"

"I guess not, but it's how it is with Holly."

"Has Holly ever mentioned Esther Little?"

I swallow and shake my head. "No."

"Think very carefully: Esther Little."

I think, or try to. "I don't know the name. I swear." I can hear how petrified I sound.

"What has Holly told you about her cognitive gifts?"

"Only what's in her book. In *The Radio People*."

"Yes, a real page-turner. Have you witnessed her channeling a voice?" Hugo Lamb notices my hesitation. "Don't make me count down from five, like some hokey interrogator in a third-rate movie, before I fry you. Your fans know how you detest cliché."

The hollow deepens as the trees lean over. "Two years ago, on Rottnest Island, near Perth, Holly fainted, and a weird voice came out of her mouth. I thought it was epilepsy, but she said how the prisoners had suffered, and then . . . she spoke in Aborigine . . . and—that's all. She hit her head. Then she was back."

Hugo Lamb tap-tap-taps the photo. Some part of me still able to analyze notices that although his face is young something about his eyes and intentness is much older. "What about the Dusk Chapel?"

"The what chapel?"

"Or the Anchorites? Or the Blind Cathar? Or Black Wine?"

"I never heard of any of those things. I swear."

Tap-tap-tap goes Hugo Lamb's finger on the photo of me and the girls. "What does Horology mean to you?"

This feels like some demonic pub quiz: "Horology? The study of the measurement of time. Or old clocks."

He leans over me; I feel like a microbe on a slide. "Tell me what you know about Marinus."

Wretched as a snitch and hopeful this will save my daughters, I tell my eerie interrogator that Marinus was a child psychiatrist at Gravesend Hospital. "He's mentioned in Holly's book as well."

"Has she met Marinus during the time you've known her?"

I shake my head. "He'll be ancient now. If he's still alive."

Is a woman laughing on the outer edge of my hearing?

"What is," Hugo Lamb watches me carefully, "the Star of Riga?"

"The capital of Estonia. No. Latvia. Or Lithuania. I'm not sure. One of the Baltic states, anyway. I'm sorry."

Hugo Lamb considers me. "We're finished."

"I—I told you the truth. Completely. Don't hurt my kids."

He swings off the mossy boulder and walks away, telling me, "If their daddy's an honest man, Juno and Anaïs have nothing to fear."

"You—you're—you're letting me go?" I touch my legs. They're still dead. "Hey! My legs! Please!"

"Knew I'd forgotten something." Hugo Lamb turns around. "By the by, Mr. Hershey, the critics' treatment of *Echo Must Die* was egregious. But, hey, you shafted Richard Cheeseman *royally* in return, didn't you?" Lamb's smile is puckered and conspiratorial. "He'll never guess, unless someone plants the idea in his head. Sorry about your trousers; the car park is left at the last fork. That much you'll remember. Everything else I'll redact. Ready?" His eyes fixing mine, Hugo Lamb twists the air into threads between his forefingers and thumbs, then pulls tight . . .

. . . a mossy boulder, big as a troll's head, on its side and brooding over an ancient wrong. I'm sitting on the ground with no memory of tripping, though I must have done; I'm aching all over. How the sodding hell did I get down here? A mini-stroke? Magicked by the elves of Ásbyrgi? I must have . . . what? Sat down for a breather, then nodded off. A breeze passes, the trees shiver, and a yellow leaf loop-the-loops, landing by a fluke of air currents on my palm. Look at that. For the second time today, I think of Mr. Chimes the conjuror. Not far away, a woman's laughing. The campsite's near. I get up—and notice a big cold stain down my thigh. Oh. Okay. The Wild Child of British Letters has suffered a somnambulant urethral mishap. Lucky there's no *Piccadilly Review* diarist around. I'm only fifty-three—surely still a bit young for incontinence pads? It's all chilly and clammy, like it happened a couple of minutes ago. Thank God I'm so close to the parking area, clean boxers, and trousers. Back to the fork, then turn left. Let us hurry, dear reader. It'll be night before you know it.

I T LOOKS LIKE HALLDÓR LAXNESS splurged most of the Nobel
dosh on Gljúfrasteinn, his white, blockist 1950s home halfway
up a mist-smudged vale outside Reykjavik. From the outside it
reminds me of a 1970s squash club in the Home Counties. A river
tumbles by and on through the mostly treeless autumn. Parked in
the drive is a cream Jag identical to the one Dad had. I buy my
ticket from a friendly knitter with a cushy job and walk over to the
house proper, where I put on my audio guide as directed. My digital spirit guide tells me about the paintings, the modernist lamps
and clocks, the low Swedish furniture, a German piano, parquet
floors, cherry-wood fittings, leather upholstery. Gljúfrasteinn is a
bubble in time, as is right and proper for a writer's museum. Climbing the stairs, I consider the prospect of a Crispin Hershey Museum. The obvious location is the old family home in Pembridge
Place, where I lived both as a boy and as a father. The snag is, the
dear old place was gutted by builders, the week after I handed over
the keys, subdivided into six flats and sold to Russian, Chinese,
and Saudi investors. Reacquisition, reunification, and restoration
would be a multilingual and ruinously expensive prospect, so my
current address on East Heath Lane, Hampstead, is the likeliest
candidate—assuming Hyena Hal can persuade Bleecker Yard's
and Erebus's lawyers not to whisk it away, of course. I imagine
reverent visitors stroking my varnished handrails and whispering
in awed tones, "My God, that's *the* laptop he wrote his trium-
phant Iceland novel on!" The gift shop could be squeezed into the
downstairs bog: Crispin Hershey key fobs, *Desiccated Embryo*
mouse mats, and glow-in-the-dark figurines. People buy such bol-

locks at museums. They don't know what else to do once they're
there.

Upstairs, the digital guide mentions in passing that Mr. and
Mrs. Laxness occupied different bedrooms. So I see. Strikes a sodding chord. Laxness's typewriter sits on his desk—or, more accurately, his wife's typewriter, as she typed up his handwritten
manuscripts. I wrote my debut novel on a typewriter, but *Wanda in
Oils* was composed on a secondhand Brittan PC handed down by
Dad as a birthday present, and it's been ever-lighter, ever-trustier
laptops ever since. For most digital-age writers, writing *is* rewriting.
We grope, cut, block, paste, and twitch, panning for gold onscreen
by deleting bucketloads of crap. Our analog ancestors had to polish
every line mentally before hammering it out mechanically. Rewrites
cost them months, meters of ink ribbon, and pints of Tippex. Poor
sods.

On the other hand, if digital technology is so superior a midwife
of the novel, where are this century's masterpieces? I enter a small
library where Laxness seems to have kept his overflow, and bend my
neck to graze upon the titles. Plenty of hardbacks in Icelandic, Danish, I guess, German, English . . . and sodding hell—*Desiccated
Embryos*!

Hang on, this is the 2001 edition . . .

. . . and Laxness died in 1998. Right.

Well, a kind gesture of the Hidden Folk.

GOING DOWNSTAIRS, I make way for a dozen teenagers trooping
up. Where do Juno and Anaïs go on their school trips in Montreal?
Not knowing saddens me. What a long-distance, part-time father I
am. These twenty-first-century children of Iceland are plugged into
headsets but still exude that Nordic confidence and sense of well-
being, even the two African Icelanders and a girl in a Muslim head-
dress. All have a 2 in front of their birth year and need barely scroll
down an inch when finding it on an online form. They carry a fra-
grance of hair conditioner and fabric conditioner. Their consciences

are as undented as cars in a dealership showroom, and all are bound for the world's center stage, where they'll challenge, outperform, and patronize us old farts at our retirement parties, as we did when we looked that beautiful. Their teacher brings up the rear and smiles his thanks at me, and as he passes, a rather fine mirror is revealed on the Laxness stairway. From its deep square well of grays peers out a haggard look-alike of Anthony Hershey. Look at that. My metamorphosis into Dad is complete. Did some evil spirit at Ásbyrgi suck out the last of my youth? My hair's thinner, my skin's tired, my eyes bloodshot; my neck's going all saggy and turkey-like . . . I summon a Tagore quote, for consolation: "Youth is a horse, and maturity a charioteer." Dad's aging lips twitch into a sneer and speak: "I see no charioteer. I see a sociology lecturer at a third-rate university who just learned that his department's being axed because nobody except future sociology lecturers studies sociology anymore. You're a joke, boy. Do you hear me? A joke."

My prime of life is going, going, gone . . .

Trudging down to the Mitsubishi waiting in Gljúfrasteinn's small car park, I check the time on my phone—and find a message from Carmen Salvat. It is not the message I might have wished to receive.

hello crispin pls can we talk? x yr friend C

I huff. My soul still aches from being dumped, but I'm handling it. I don't want to have to unhandle it, or un-unhandle it. We ingest our emotions, and grief for a lost relationship is not what I want to ingest. Carmen's "yr friend" is code for *"We won't be getting back together"* and "hello" instead of "hi" is the textual equivalent of a chilly air-kiss rather than a cheek-to-cheek contact kiss:

maybe not for a while, if that's ok. It still hurts and I'm bored of the pain. No offense meant and mind yourself. C.

After pressing send I wish I'd taken more care to sound less petulant and/or self-pitying. Suddenly the river's annoyingly clattery: How did Laxness get any work done, for buggery's sake? The gathering clouds are lead-lined gray, not Zen gray. The aging day's intersecting meanings form a crossword that defeats me, not inspires me, like it used to. I'm not as good a writer as Halldór Laxness. I'm not even as good a writer as the younger Crispin Hershey. I'm just as shit and uncommitted a dad as Dad, only his films will survive longer than my overregarded novels. My clothes are crumpled. My lecture's at seven-thirty. My heart is still crusty with emotional scabs, and I don't want them pulled off by a Spanish ex-partner.

No. We can't talk. I switch off my phone.

"THE NAME OF my lecture is *On Never Not Thinking About Iceland*." It's a decent turnout at the House of Literature, but half of the two hundred attendees are here because the Bonny Prince Billy concert was sold out, and a portion of the silver-haired contingent showed up because they love Dad's films. The only faces I know are Holly's, Aoife's, and Aoife's boyfriend Örvar's, sending me friendly vibes from the front row. "This car crash of a title," I continue, "is derived from an apocryphal remark of W. H. Auden's, spoken here in Reykjavik, for all I know on this very podium, to your parents or grandparents. Auden said that while he hadn't lived his life thinking about Iceland hourly or even daily, 'There was never a time when I *wasn't* thinking about Iceland.' What a delicious, cryptic statement. 'Never not thinking about Iceland'? Why not just say, 'Always thinking about Iceland'? Because, of course, double negatives are truth smugglers, are censor outwitters. This evening I'd like to hold Auden's double negative"—I raise my left hand, palm up—"alongside this double-headed fact about writing," right hand, palm up. "Namely, that in order to write, you need a pen and a place, or a study and a typewriter, or a laptop and a Starbucks—it doesn't matter, because the pen and the place are symbols. Symbols for means and tradition. A poet uses a pen to write but, of course, the poet doesn't *make* the pen. He or she buys, borrows, inherits, steals, or otherwise acquires the pen from elsewhere. Similarly, a poet inhabits a poetic tradition to write within, but no poet can single-handedly create that tradition. Even if a poet sets out to invent a new poetics, he or she can only react against what's already there. There's no Johnny Rotten without the Bee Gees." Not a flicker from my Icelandic audience; maybe the Sex Pistols never made it this far north. Holly smiles for me, and I worry at how thin and drawn she's looking. "Returning to Auden," I continue, "and his 'never not.' What I take from his remark is this: If you're writing fiction or poetry in a European language, that pen in your hand was, once upon a time, a goose quill held by an Icelander. Like it or not, know it or not, it doesn't matter. If you seek to represent the beauty, truth, and pain of the world in prose, if you seek to deepen character via dialogue and action, if you seek to unite the personal, the past, and the political in fiction, then you're in pursuit of the same aims sought by the authors of the Icelandic sagas, right here, seven, eight, nine hundred years ago. I assert that the author of *Njal's Saga* deploys the very same narrative tricks used later by Dante and Chaucer, Shakespeare and Molière, Victor Hugo and Dickens, Halldór Laxness and Virginia Woolf, Alice Munro and Ewan Rice. What tricks? Psychological complexity, character development, the killer line to end a scene, villains blotched with virtue, heroic characters speckled with villainy, foreshadow and backflash, artful misdirection. Now, I'm not saying that writers in antiquity were ignorant of all of these tricks but," here I put my balls and Auden's on the block, "in the sagas of Iceland, for the first time in Western culture, we find proto-novelists at work. Half a millennium avant le parole, the sagas are the world's first novels."

Either the audience is listening, or else they're merely snoozing with eyes open. I turn over my notes.

"So much for the pen. Now for the place. From the vantage point of continental Europeans, Iceland is, of course, a mostly treeless, mostly cold oval rock where a third of a million souls eke out a living. Within my own lifetime Iceland has made the front pages exactly four times: the Cod Wars of the 1970s; the setting for Reagan's and Gorbachev's arms-control talks; an early casualty of the 2008 crash; and as the source of a volcanic ash cloud that disabled European aviation in 2010. Blocs, however, whether geometric or political, are defined by their outer edges. Just as Orientalism seduces the imagination of a certain type of Westerner, to a certain type of southerner, Iceland exerts a gravitational force far in excess of its landmass and cultural import. Pytheas, the Greek cartographer who lived around 300 B.C. in a sunbaked land on the far side of the ancient world, he felt this gravity, and put you on his map: Ultima Thule. The Irish Christian hermits who cast themselves onto the sea in coracles, they felt this pull. Tenth-century refugees from the civil war in Norway, they felt it too. It was their grandsons who wrote the sagas. Sir Joseph Banks, enough Victorian scholars to sink a longship, Jules Verne, even Hermann Göring's brother, who was spotted by Auden and MacNeice here in 1937, they all felt the pull of the north, of your north, and all of them, *I* believe, like Auden—were never not thinking about Iceland."

The UFO-shaped lights of the House of Literature blink on.

"Writers don't write in a void. We work in a physical space, a room, ideally in a house like Laxness's Gljúfrasteinn, but we also write within an imaginative space. Amid boxes, crates, shelves, and cabinets full of . . . junk, treasure, both cultural—nursery rhymes, mythologies, histories, what Tolkien called 'the compost heap'; and also personal stuff—childhood TV, homegrown cosmologies, stories we hear first from our parents, or later from our children—and, crucially, maps. Mental maps. Maps with edges. And for Auden, for so many of us, it's the edges of the maps that fascinate . . ."

HOLLY'S BEEN RENTING her apartment since June, but she'll be moving back to Rye in a couple of weeks so it's minimally furnished, uncluttered, and neat, all walnut floors and cream walls, with a fine view of Reykjavik's jumbled roofs, sloping down to the inky bay.

Streetlights punctuate the northern twilight as color drains away, and a trio of cruise liners glitters in the harbor, like three floating Las Vegases. Over the bay, a long, whale-shaped mountain dominates the skyline, or would, if the clouds weren't so low. Örvar says it's called Mount Esja, but admits he's never climbed it because it's right there, on the doorstep. I biff away an intense wish to live here, intense, perhaps, because of its utter lack of realism: I don't think I'd survive a single winter of these three-hour days. Holly, Aoife, Örvar, and I eat a veggie moussaka and polish off a couple of bottles of wine. They ask me about my week on the road. Aoife talks about her summer's dig on a tenth-century settlement near Eglisstaðir, and nudges the amiable but quiet Örvar into discussing his work on the genetic database that has mapped the entire Icelandic population: "Eighty-plus women were found to have Native American DNA," he tells me. "This proves pretty conclusively that the Vinland Sagas are based on historical truth, not just wishful thinking. Lots of Irish DNA on the women's side, too." Aoife describes an app that can tell every living Icelander if and how closely related they are to every other living Icelander. "They've needed it for years," she pats Örvar's hand on the table, "to avoid those awkward, morning-after *in-Thor's-name-did-I-just-shag-my-cousin?* moments. Right, Örvar?" The poor lad half blushes and mumbles about a gig starting somewhere. Everyone in Reykjavik under thirty years old, Aoife says, is in at least one band. They get up to go, and as I'm leaving first thing in the morning they both wish me bon voyage. I get a niece's hug from Aoife and a firm handshake from Örvar, who only now remembers that he brought *Desiccated Embryos* for me to sign. While Örvar laces up his boots, I try to think of something witty to mark the occasion, but nothing witty arrives.

To Örvar, from Crispin, with best regards.

I've striven to be witty since *Wanda in Oils.*

Letting it go feels so sodding liberating.

. . .

I STIR, STIR, stir until the mint leaves are bright green minnows in a whirlpool. "The nail in the coffin of Carmen and me," I tell Holly, "was Venice. If I never see the place again, I'll die happy."

Holly looks puzzled. "I found it rather romantic."

"That's the trouble. All that beauty: in-*sodding*-sufferable. Ewan Rice calls Venice the Capital of Divorce—and set one of his best books there. About divorce. Venice is humanity at its ripped-off, ripping-off worst . . . I made this smart-arse remark about a rip-off umbrella Carmen bought—really, the sort of thing I say twenty times a day—but instead of batting it away, she had this look . . . like, '*Remind me,* why *am I spending the last of my youth on this whingeing old man?*' She walked off across Saint Mark's Square. Alone, of course."

"Well," Holly says neutrally, "we all have off days . . ."

"Bit of a Joycean epiphany, looking back. I don't blame her. Either for finding me irritating or for dumping me. When she's my age now, I'll be *sixty*-sodding-*eight,* Holly! Love may be blind, but cohabitation comes with all the latest X-ray gizmos. So we spent the next day moseying around museums on our own, and when we said goodbye at Venice airport, the last thing she said was 'Take care'; and when I got home, a Dear John was in my inbox. Couldn't call it unexpected. Both of us have been through a messy divorce already, and one's enough. We've agreed we're still friends. We'll exchange Christmas cards for a few years, refer to each other without rancor, and probably never meet again."

Holly nods and makes an "I see" noise in her throat.

A late bus stops outside, its air brakes hissing.

I fail to mention this afternoon's message to Holly.

My iPhone's still switched off. Not now. Later.

"LOVELY SHOT, THAT." There's a framed photograph on a shelf behind Holly showing her as a young mum, with a small toothy

Aoife dressed as the Cowardly Lion with freckles on her nose, and Ed Brubeck, younger than I remember, all smiling in a small back garden in the sun with pink and yellow tulips. "When was it taken?"

"2004. Aoife's theatrical debut in *The Wizard of Oz*." Holly sips her mint tea. "Ed and I mapped out *The Radio People* around then. The book was his idea, you know. We'd been in Brighton that weekend, for Sharon's wedding, and he'd always been Mr. There Has to Be a Logical Explanation."

"But after the room-number thing, he started believing?"

Holly makes an equivocal face. "He stopped disbelieving."

"Did Ed ever know what a monster *The Radio People* turned into?"

Holly shakes her head. "I wrote the Gravesend bits quite quickly, but then I got promoted at the center. What with that, and raising Aoife, and Ed being away, I never got it finished until . . ." she chooses words with practiced care, ". . . Ed's luck ran out in Syria."

Now I'm appalled by my own self-pity about Zoë and Carmen. "You're a bit of a hero, our Holly. Heroine, rather."

"You soldier on. Aoife was ten. Falling to pieces wasn't an option. My family'd lost Jacko so . . ." a sad little laugh, ". . . the Sykes clan does mourning and loss really bloody well. Taking up *The Radio People* and actually finishing it was therapy, sort of. I never imagined for a minute that anyone outside our family'd want to read it. Interviewers never believe me when I say that, but it's the truth. The TV Book Club, the Prudence Hanson endorsement, the whole 'The Psychic with the Childhood Scar' thing, I wasn't prepared for any of it, or the websites, the loonies, the begging letters, the people you lost touch with years ago for very good reasons. My first boyfriend—who really did *not* leave me with fond memories— got in touch to say he's now Porsche's main man in West London, and how about a test drive now my ship had come in? Uh, *no*. Then after the U.S. auction for *The Radio People* became a news item, all the fake Jackos crawled out from under the floorboards. My agent set the first one up via Skype. He was the right age, looked *sort of* like Jacko might look, and stared out of the screen, whispering, 'Oh, my God, oh, my God . . . It's you.' "

I feel like smoking, but I munch a carrot stick instead. "How did he account for the three missing decades?"

"He said he was kidnapped by Soviet sailors who needed a cabin boy, then taken to Irkutsk to avoid a Cold War incident. Yeah, I know. Brendan's bullshit detector was buzzing, so he shuftied me over and asked, 'Recognize me, Jacko?' The guy hesitated, then burst out, 'Daddy!' End of call. The last 'Jacko' we interviewed was Bangladeshi, but the imperialists at the British embassy in Dhaka refused to believe he was my brother. Would I send ten thousand pounds and sponsor his visa application? We called it a day after that. *If* Jacko's alive, *if* he reads the book, *if* he wants to locate us, he'll find a way."

"Were you still working at the homeless center all this time?"

"I quit before I went to Cartagena. A shame—I loved the job, and I think I was good at it—but if you're chairing a fund-raising meeting the same day a six-figure royalty payment slips into your bank account, you can't pretend nothing's changed. More 'Jackos' were trying their luck at the office, and my phone was hacked. I'm still involved with homeless charities at a patron level, but I had to get Aoife out of London to a nice sleepy backwater like Rye. So I thought. Did I ever tell you about the Great Illuminati Brawl?"

"You tell me less about your life than you think. The Illuminati: as in the lizard aliens who enslave humanity via beta-blocking mind waves beamed from their secret moonbase?"

"That's them. One fine April morning, two groups of conspiracy theorists hide in my shrubbery. Christ knows how it started—a stray remark on Twitter, probably. So, the two groups realize they're not alone, each group convinces itself that the other group are the Illuminati's agents. With me so far? Stop smirking; they kicked the crap out of each other. The police were up in a jiffy. After that I had to put up a security fence and CCTV. *Me*, f'Chrissakes, holed up like an investment banker! But what choice did I have? Next time the loonies might not be hell-bent on *defending* me but attacking me. So while the contractor was in, I went out to Australia, which was when Aoife and I met you on Rottnest." She pads over to draw the curtain on the night harbor. "Beware of asking people to question what's real and what isn't. They may reach conclusions you didn't see coming."

In the street two dogs bark furiously, then stop.

"If you don't publish again, the loonies'll move on."

"This is true," says Holly, looking evasive.

"*Are* you working on another book?"

Now she looks cornered. "Only a few stories."

I feel envious and pleased. "That's brilliant. Your publishers will be doing backflips down the corridors."

"There's no guarantee anyone'll read it. They're stories based on people I knew at the center. Not a psychic in sight."

"Right now, *The Collected Shopping Lists of Holly Sykes* would go straight to number one on preorders alone."

"Well, we'll see. But that's what I've been doing here all summer. Reykjavik's a good place to work. Iceland's like Ireland; being famous here's nothing special."

By chance our fingertips are almost touching. Holly notices at the same instant, and we pull our hands back onto our laps. I try to come up with a joke I can turn this micro-embarrassment into, but nothing springs to mind. "I'll call you a taxi, Crisp. It's gone midnight."

"No *way* is it that late." I check my phone: 00:10. "Sodding hell, it's tomorrow already."

"So it is! What time's your flight to London?"

"Nine-thirty, but can I ask you two last things?"

"Anything," she says. "Almost."

"Am I still 'the spiral, the spider, the one-eyed man'?"

"You want me to check?"

Like an atheist wanting to be prayed for, I nod.

As she did in Shanghai, Holly touches the spot on her forehead and lets her eyelids almost close. What a great face she has but . . . it shouldn't be that gray, or stretched. My eyes wander to her pendant. It's a labyrinth. Some symbolic mind-body-spirit thing, I guess. From Ed?

"Yes." Holly opens her eyes. "Same as ever."

A possible drunk laughs maniacally outside. "Will I ever know what that means? That's not my second question."

"Some day, yes. Let me know when you know."

"I promise." The second question's harder because one answer to it scares me very much: "Holly, you're not ill, are you?"

She reacts with surprise but not denial. She looks away.

"Oh, sod it." I want to unask my question. "Forgive me, it's not—"

"Cancer of the gall bladder." Holly attempts a smile. "Trust me to choose a nice rare one, eh?"

I can't even attempt a smile. "What's the prognosis?"

Holly wears the expression of someone discussing a tiresome inconvenience. "Too late for surgery—it's spread to my liver and . . . um, yeah, it's all over the shop. My oncologist in London gives me a—a—a five to ten percent chance of being here this time next year." Her voice croaks. "Not the odds I'd choose. With chemo and drugs the odds improve, up to twenty percent, maybe, but . . . do I want to spend a few extra months puking in bin-liners? That's the other reason I've been here in Iceland all summer, shadowing poor Aoife, like, y'know, whatsisface from *Macbeth*."

"Banquo. Aoife knows, then?"

Holly nods. "Brendan, Sharon, their kids, my mother, and Örvar too—I'm hoping he'll help Aoife when, y'know. When I can't. But nobody else knows. 'Cept you. People get so maudlin. I have to spend what energy I've got cheering them up. I wasn't going to tell you either but . . . you asked. Sorry to put a downer on a lovely evening."

I see her, and see Crispin Hershey through her eyes, and perhaps she sees Holly Sykes through mine. Suddenly it's later. Holly and I are standing by the table, hugging goodbye. It isn't an erotic hug. Truly it isn't, dear reader. I'd know.

It's this: As long I'm holding her, nothing bad can happen.

. . .

THE TAXI DRIVER has earlobes full of metalwork and just says, "Okay," when I tell him the name of my hotel. I wave goodbye until I can't see Holly anymore. I've arranged to go to Rye before Christmas, so I'll just ignore this unpleasant premonition that I'll never see her again. The radio's tuned to a classical-music station and I recognize Maria Callas singing "Casta Diva" from Bellini's *Norma*— Dad used it in the model-airplane scene in *Battleship Hill*. For a moment I forget where I am. I switch on my iPhone to text Holly, to thank her for the evening, and as I'm writing it, a message from Carmen gets relayed through. She sent it while I was delivering my lecture earlier. It has no text: it's just an image of . . . a blizzard?

A blizzard at night through a windscreen?

I tilt my head and rotate the phone.

Mashed-up asteroids? No.

It's an ultrasound scan.

Of Carmen's womb.

With a tenant in it.

THE *KEY* by Jun'ichirō Tanizaki: That's the one. But having found the title in my cupboard-under-the-stairs of once-read books, the mind of Crispin Hershey drifts away from Devon Kim-Ashkenazy's novel-in-progress (*Across the Wide Ocean*, three generations of abused women from Pusan to Brooklyn). I know it's happening, but I feel powerless to stop it. Up, up, and away my mind rises, through the ceiling tiles and roofing slates, over the bunker where the English Department has been temporarily housed since 1978. Espy the theater's curvaceous roof by Frank Gehry; skim over Lego-like accommodation blocks; circle the Gothic chapel from Lincoln's era; tumble amid the glass-and-steel science buildings; up to the president's house, red-bricked, gabled, ivy-veined; through the lych-gate to the cemetery, where Blithewood College lifers turn into trees at the speed of worms and roots, and up the highest tree of all, spirals Hershey's absent mind, known only unto squirrels and crows; the Hudson River stately winds between the Catskills' pigeon-toes; a train's revealed, a train's obscured, a quote around a broken cup, "I like to see it lap the miles and lick the valleys up." GoogleEarthlike soars his mind, through clouds where snowstorms brew; New York State has dropped away, and Massachusetts flew, and Newfoundland is ice-entombed and Rockall gull-beshatten, where no eye sees the lightning flash its momentary pattern . . .

"CRISPIN?" DEVON KIM-ASHKENAZY. "Are you okay?"

My postgrads' faces suggest it was a prolonged zone-out. "Yes. I was recalling a Tanizaki novel that does wonderful things with a similar diary-narrative to yours, Devon. *The Key.* It could save you from reinventing the wheel. But generally," I hand her back her manuscript, "good progress. My only cavil is the, uh, violation scene. Still a little adverb-rich, I felt."

"Fine." Devon uses a breezy tone to prove she's unoffended. "The violation in the flower shop or the violation in the motel?"

"The one in the carwash. Adverbs are cholesterol in the veins of prose. Halve your adverbs and your prose pumps twice as well." Pens scratch. "Oh, and beware of the verb 'seem'; it's a textual mumble. And grade every simile and metaphor from one star to five, and remove any threes or below. It hurts when you operate, but afterwards you feel much better. Japheth?"

Japheth Solomon (author of *In God's Country,* a Mormon bildungsroman-in-progress about a Utah boy escaping to a liberal East Coast college where sex, dope, and a creative writing program provoke existential angst) asks, "What if we can't decide if a metaphor's a three or a four?"

"If you can't decide, Japheth, it's only a three."

Maaza Kolofski (*Horsehead Nebula,* a Utopia about life after a plague destroys every male on earth) raises her hand: "Any holiday assignments, Crispin?"

"Yes. Compose five letters from five leading characters, to yourself. Does everyone know what a letter is?"

"A paper email," answers Louis Baranquilla (*The Creepy Guy in the Yoga Class* about a creepy guy in a yoga class). My pre-Internet credentials are an ongoing joke. "What do we put into these letters?"

"Your characters' potted life histories. Whom or what your characters love and despise. Details on education, employment, finances, political affiliations, social class. Fears. Skeletons in cupboards. Addictions. Biggest regret; believer, agnostic, or atheist. How afraid of dying are they?" I think of Holly, suppress a sigh and push on. "Have they ever seen a corpse? A ghost? Sexuality. Glass half empty, glass half full, glass too small? Snazzy or scruffy dressers? It's a letter, so consider their use of language. Would they say 'mellifluous' or 'a sharp talker'? Foul-mouthed or profanity-averse? Record the phrases they unknowingly overuse. When did they last cry? Can they see another person's point of view? Only one-tenth of what you write will make it into your manuscript, but when you knock on that tenth"—I rap my knuckles on the table—"you'll hear oaken solidity, not sawdust and glue. Ersilia?"

"Seems . . ." Ersilia Holt (a thriller named *The Icepick Man* about Triad gangs versus Taliban cells in Vancouver) scrunches her face, ". . . kinda deranged, to actually write *letters* to yourself?"

"Agreed, Ersilia. A writer flirts with schizophrenia, nurtures synesthesia, and embraces obsessive-compulsive disorder. Your art feeds on you, your soul, and, yes, to a degree, your sanity. Writing novels worth reading *will* bugger up your mind, jeopardize your relationships, and distend your life. You have been warned."

My ten postgrads look sober. So they should.

"Art feasts upon its maker," I tell them.

THE FACULTY STAFF room is empty but for Claude Mo (medievalist, not tenured) and Hilary Zakrewska (linguistics, not tenured either), who are engrossed in the fireside witticisms of Christina Pym-Lavit (head of political science, chair of the Tenure Committee). If their tenure track at Blithewood ends in failure, no other Ivy League college will be offering them a career. Christina Pym-Lavit waves me over. "Pull up a pew, Crispin, I was telling Hilary and Claude about the time I blew a tire while driving John Updike and Aphra Booth to the Iowa workshop, both of whom you knew, I believe?"

"Only ever so slightly," I say.

"Don't be coy," says the Tenured One, but I'm not. I interviewed Updike for *The New Yorker* back when I was the Wild Child and shifted units in the U.S.A. I haven't seen Aphra Booth since she threatened me with legal action in Perth, whenever that was. That pile of undergrad assignments back in my office suddenly doesn't strike me as such an awful prospect, so I make my excuses. "Grading, on the last day of the semester?" exclaims Christina Pym-Lavit. "Would that all the staff were as conscientious, Crispin." We agree to meet at the Christmas party later, and I head off down the corridor. As a guest lecturer I'm excused the cow's arse of campus politics, but if I'm offered a full-time position next year, I'll be burrowing so deep that only my shoes'll be showing. I'll need the salary, there's no doubt about it. Thanks to the "recoupment arrangement" ex-agent Hal negotiated, 75 percent of my ever-dwindling book royalties go to my ex-publishers to repay money I owe. I need a job with accommodation attached, too. I've kept the Hampstead house, just, but it's in the hands of a letting agent. I use the rent to pay alimony to Zoë. Alimony that Zoë refused point-blank to renegotiate: "Just because you got a Spanish girlfriend pregnant? Seriously, Crispin—why *would* I?" Carmen hasn't gone all legal on me, but child care costs an arm and a couple of legs even in Spain.

"Who da' man?" Inigo Wilderhoff clatters down the stairs with a mighty suitcase and his anchorman teeth flashing white. "I directed your friend to your office, just a minute ago."

I stop. "My friend?"

"Your friend from England."

"Did he give a name?"

Inigo strokes his professorial beard. "Do you know, I *don't* believe he did. Fiftyish. Tall. An eye patch. My taxi's waiting outside, I gotta fly. Enjoy tonight's party for me. Au revoir till January." I manage a "Take care," but Inigo Wilderhoff's suitcase is already *thwack-thwack-thwack*ing down the steps.

An eye patch? A one-eyed man.

Calm down. Calm down.

MY OFFICE DOOR is ajar. Our secretary is nowhere to be seen—security is lax at Blithewood College, two miles from the nearest town. In I peer . . . Nobody. Probably a mature student with corrective glasses who sounded a bit British to Wilderhoff, wanting a book signed for eBay. He'll have seen I'm out and gone for a tactful wander until my surgery hour at three P.M. Much relieved, I walk over to my desk.

"The door was open, Crispin."

I yelp, twist, knocking clutter from my desk onto the floor. A man is standing by my bookshelves. With an eye patch.

Richard Cheeseman stands still. "Quite an entrance."

"Richard! You scared the sodding *shit* out of me."

"Well, pardon me for scaring the sodding shit out of you."

We ought to be clapping each other's back, but I just gape. Richard Cheeseman's flab had melted away after a month of Latin American prison diet, but his civilian clothes accentuate how hard, gnarled, and leathered he's become. That eye patch—when did *that* happen?—gives him the air of an Israeli general. "I—I was all set to see you in Bradford after Christmas. I've arranged it with Maggie."

"Then it looks like I've saved you a trip."

"If I'd known you were coming here, I'd have . . ."

"Laid on champagne, a brass band? Not my style."

"So"—I try to smile—"to what *do* I owe this pleasure?"

Richard Cheeseman sighs and bites at a hangnail. "Back in the Penitenciaría, one method of slaying minutes was to plan my first trip to New York as a free man. The tinier the details, the more minutes my reverie would kill, you see. I used to refine my plans, night after night. *So,* when I found myself unable to face a family Christmas at Maggie's, full of jollity, pity, Christmas TV specials, then, naturally, New York was where I fled. And once there, what could be more appropriate than a ride up the Hudson Line to see the leading light, the chiefest friend of the Friends of Richard Cheeseman, Crispin Hershey?"

"The Friends of Richard Cheeseman was the least I could do."

His stare says, *The very fucking least you could do.*

I try to delay what I dread is coming. "Did you damage your eye in a fight, Richard?"

"No, no, not a knife fight, nothing so *Shawshank Redemption.* It was a spark from a welding torch on my very last day as a prisoner in Yorkshire. The doctor says the patch can come off in a week."

"Good." The framed photo of Gabriel is on the floor. I pick it up, and my visitor remarks, with sinister levity, "That's your son?"

"Yes. Gabriel Joseph. After Garcia Marquéz and Conrad."

"May your son be blessed with friends as true as mine."

He knows. He's worked it out. He's here for payback.

"Must be tough," remarks Cheeseman. "You here, him in Spain."

"It's less than ideal," I try to sound casual, "but Carmen has family in Madrid, so she's not alone. She'd been told she couldn't have children, you see, so for her, Gabriel was a minor miracle. Well, a major one. We were no longer an item by that point, but she was determined to go through with the pregnancy and"—I reposition Gabriel next to my sticky-tape dispenser—"he's the fruit of her labor. Won't you sit down? I could scare up a shot of brandy to celebrate . . ."

"What—to celebrate my four wasted years in prison?"

I can't look at him and I can't look away.

"You seem antsy, Crispin. I seem to be unnerving you."

"Seem" x 2 = textual mumble squared, I think, and notice that Richard Cheeseman's coat pocket is bulging and sagging. I can guess what heavy lethal object it may contain. He reads my thoughts. "Working out who put the cocaine in my suitcase, Crispin, and when, and even why—it didn't take me long."

Hot. Strange. My insides are being decanted out of me.

"I made up my mind not to confront my betrayer until I was out. After all, he was doing his damnedest to get me repatriated and released. Wasn't he?"

I can't trust my voice so I just nod, once.

"No, Crispin! He fucking well *wasn't* doing his best to get me out! If he'd confessed, I'd have been out in days. He let me *rot."*

Snow is falling again, I notice. The second hand on the clock lurches in tiny arcs. Nothing else moves. Nothing.

"As I lay in my cell in Bogotá, it wasn't only New York I dreamt of. I also dreamt of what I'd do to him. To the slug-fuck who came to see me, to gloat, who cared, but not enough to change places. Never that. I planned how I'd drug him, bind him, and kill him with a screwdriver over forty days. No script was ever polished as lovingly. Then I realized I was being silly. Teenage. Why take all that risk? Why not just meet him in America, buy a gun, and blow the fucker away in some out-of-the-way locale?"

I wish Betty the secretary or Inigo Wilderhoff was still pottering around. "Your tormentor," I try to keep my voice steady, "has been tortured by remorse."

Cheeseman's voice turns into barbed wire: "Tortured? Swanning around the globe? Fathering children? While I, *I,* was caged in Colombia with killers, drug addicts with HIV, and rusty razors. Which of these fates is torture?"

His hand goes to his coat pocket. A janitor walks down the corridor, whistling. I see him framed in the outer doorway of Betty's reception. *Yell for help!* urges Hershey the Sodding Terrified. Or run for it. Or beg for forgiveness: "Please don't orphan my children." Or negotiate. Or offer to write out a full confession. Or—or—or—

—or let him take his revenge. "Your tormentor," I begin, "wasn't gloating, when he came to visit you. He despised his own cowardice, and still does. But this changes nothing. He wants to pay, Richard. He's only a step away from personal bankruptcy, so if you want cash, he can't help you. But was it money that you wanted?"

"Weird thing is," he swivels his head, "now I'm here, I don't know what to take."

My shirt's glued to my body by hot and cold sweat. "Then I'll sit at my table," I tell him, "and wait for you to decide. Your tormentor didn't mean to get you banged up for years, he only meant a—a prank, a stupid prank, but it went nightmarishly wrong. What you decide he owes, he'll pay. All right?" No, dear reader, it's not all right. Here in my chair I'm disintegrating. Better to close your eyes. Shut out Richard Cheeseman, my books, the view of white woods. One blast to the head. There are worse ways to go. The kettle-drumming in my ears muffles whatever Richard Cheeseman is doing, and I barely hear the click of the safety catch, or the foot-steps. Curiously, I sense the muzzle of the handgun, an inch from my forehead. RUN! BEG! FIGHT! But like a suffering dog who knows what the vet's needle is for, I remain inert. Bowel and blad-der control stay operative. Small mercies. Final seconds. Final thoughts? Anaïs as a little girl, proudly presenting her handmade book, *The Rabbit Family Go on a Picnic.* Juno telling me how the coolest boy in her year told her that, to understand him, she had to read a book called *Desiccated Embryos.* Gabriel in Madrid, grow-ing so fast, so big, smelling of milk, marshy nappies, and talcum powder. A pity I won't know him, but maybe he'll find something of me in my best books. Holly, my only friend, really. I'm sorry about the upset my death will cause her. My favorite line from Roth's *The Human Stain:* "Nothing lasts, and yet nothing passes, either, and nothing passes just because nothing lasts." Of how, in a roundabout way, it's not Richard Cheeseman who's shooting me no in fact it's Crispin Hershey's finger on the trigger as he slips a tiny packet of cocaine into the lining of a suitcase in a hotel room long ago *now* I'm shuddering *now* I clench my body *now* and my eyes are stream-ing *now* I'm *sorry* I'm *sorry* and *now* he's *now* me *now* I'm *now* him *now now now* . . .

. . . and I'm alone. I'm alive, more to the sodding point.

Open your eyes. Go on, don't be afraid. Open up.

Same old room. The same, but not. Cheeseman's gone.

Down the faculty stairs he's walking, in the wake of Inigo Wil-derhoff. Across the lobby, through the big glass doors, along a track, out of my story . . . Hunkering into his coat as the snowy evening creeps through the trees, Vietcong-like. I scrutinize my hand for no reason I know of, marveling at its fleshy robotronics . . . Clasp the mug. Let the heat hurt. Raise the mug, bring it to your lips and sip. Tea from Darjeeling . . . Soily leaf and tannin sun bloom across my tongue. Marvel at my Rosetta Stone mouse mat; at the gray-pink beauty of a thumbnail; at how one's lungs drink in oxygen . . . Rattle a fruit Tic-Tac into your palm and pop it in: I know the flavors are synthetic chemicals, but to me it's a gustatory "Ode to Autumn" by Keats. Nothing attunes you to the beauty of the quotidian like a man who decides not to kill you after all. Scoop up the detritus I knocked to the floor: my pen holder, a plastic spoon, a memory stick, my Lego Man collection. Juno, Anaïs, and I send one another packets as jokey presents. I'm up to five: spaceman, surgeon, Santa, Minotaur—bugger. Who am I missing? I'm on my knees hunting for the fifth among the power cords when my laptop trills.

Sodding hell—I'm supposed to be Skyping Holly . . .

AOIFE'S STRONG, CLEAR voice comes through the speakers. "Crispin?"

"Hi, Aoife. I can hear you but I can't see you."

"You have to click the little green icon, cyberauthor."

I always get this bit wrong. Aoife appears on my screen in the kitchen at Rye. "Hi. Good to see you. How are things in Blithewood?"

"Great to see you too. Everything here's winding down for the holidays." I'm slightly afraid to ask: "So, how's the patient today?"

"Bit rough, to be honest. It's getting hard for her to keep food down, and she didn't sleep so well. Very migrainy. The doctor put her to sleep"—Aoife half grimaces—"could've phrased that better—an hour ago, so Mum said to say sorry she's stood you up today, but—" Someone offscreen speaks to Aoife; she frowns, nods, and mumbles a reply I don't catch. "Look, Crispin, Dr. Fenby wants a word, so I'll hand you over to my aunt Sharon, if that's okay?"

"Sure, Aoife, of course. Off you go, see you soon."

"Ciao then." Aoife stands up and leaves the screen, trailing pixels, and Holly's sister enters from the other side. Sharon's a stockier, worldlier Holly—the Jane Austen to Holly's Emily Brontë, though I've never told either of them that—but today she just looks knackered. "Hello, Globetrotter. How are things?"

Holly's the critically ill one but they keep asking me how I am.

"Uh, hi, Sharon, yeah, fine. It's snowing, and—" Richard Cheese-man just dropped by to kill me for letting him rot in a Colombian and British jail for four years, but luckily he changed his mind. "Who's this new Dr. Fenby Aoife just mentioned? Another consultant?"

"She's Canadian. She trained with Tom, our GP. A psychiatrist."

"Oh? Why does your sister need one of them?"

"Um . . . She's worked in palliative care with cancer patients for years, and Tom thought Hol might benefit from a new drug that Dr. Fenby—Iris—has been trialing in Toronto. I understood it when she explained it an hour ago, but if I try to repeat it I'll make it sound all flaky. Tom rates her very highly, though, so we thought—" Sharon yawns, massively. "Sorry, not very ladylike. What was I saying? Yeah, Iris Fenby. That's about it."

"Thanks for the update. You look exhausted."

Sharon smiles. "You look pale as a pot-holer's arse."

"Increase the color on your laptop, then. Give me a bronzed glow. Look, Sharon, Holly isn't—Monday won't be . . ."

The school principal gives me a meaningful look over her power-glasses. "Leave your black suit in New York State, mister."

"Anything I can bring with me?"

"Just yourself. Use your baggage allowance for Carmen and Gabriel. More clobber is not what Hol needs at this point."

"Does she know that *Wildflowers* is back at number one?"

"Yes, her agent emailed this morning. Holly said she ought to die more often, it's such a boost for sales."

"Tell her not to be so sodding ghoulish. See you Monday."

"Safe journey now, Crispin. God bless."

"When she wakes, tell her from me . . . just tell her she's the best."

Sharon looks at me at the wrong angle—Skype's little oddity—and says, "I promise." Like she's calming a scared little kid.

The Skype window goes blank. Hershey's ghost stares back.

. . .

MY OPEN OFFICE hours last until four-thirty P.M and usually I'm busy with a stream of students, but today a hushed apocalypse has depopulated the Hudson Valley and nobody bothered to let me know. I check my email, but there are only two new ones: spam from an antivirus company offering a better spam filter and a happier one from Carmen, saying Gabba's trying to crawl, and her sister's given her a pull-out sofabed so I won't have to knacker my back sleeping on cushions. I send a quick nothingy "Go for it, Gabba!" email back, zip off a second email to cancel my budget hotel in Bradford—I should get a full refund—and a third to tell Maggie that Richard dropped by to see me here at Blithewood, and he looked well. That tectonic plate-shifting encounter may have happened only thirty minutes ago, but already, *already,* it's turning itself into memory, and memory's a re-recordable CD-RW, not a once-and-forever CD-R. Lastly I email Zoë to say thanks but I'll give the ski day at Marc's parents' lodge a miss on New Year's Day. Zoë knows I don't ski—or renounce the gift of traction in any sphere—so why would I want to be humiliated by my ex-wife's gym-fit, Cayman Islands–tanned husband on the piste? I'll have an extra afternoon with the girls instead. Send. It's still only three forty-five, and the fact is I've nowhere to go but my empty room in a house I share with three other lecturers. Ewan Rice has three houses at his constant disposal. Crispin Hershey has one room and a shared kitchen. It's the English Department's party at a restaurant in Red Hook later, but squid-ink pasta and red snapper after my near-death experience just seems too . . . I don't know, I can't find the words for it.

Then I notice the kid in the doorway.

"Hello," I say. "Can I help you?"

"Hi. Yeah." She's a rather androgynous she, wrapped in a beetle-black knee-length thermal jacket with a few unmelted snowflakes on her shoulders; shaven-headed, Asian-eyelidded, and a puffy, marshmallow complexion. Can a gaze be both intense and vacant? A medieval icon's can be, and so is hers. She doesn't move.

"Come in," I prompt her. "Have a seat."

"I will." She walks as if distrustful of floors, and sits down as if she's had some bad experiences with chairs, too. "Soleil Moore."

She says her name as if I'll know it. Which, maybe, I do. "Have we met before, Miss Moore?"

"This would be our third encounter, Mr. Hershey."

"I see—remind me which department you're in."

"I dislike departments. I'm a poet and a seer."

"But . . . you *are* a student at Blithewood, right?"

"I applied for a scholarship when I learned you'd be teaching here, but Professor Wilderhoff described my work as 'delusional and not, alas, in a good way.' "

"That's certainly a frank assessment. Look, I'm afraid my surgery hours are only for students who are actually enrolled at Blithewood."

"We met at Hay-on-Wye, Mr. Hershey, back in 2015."

"I'm sorry, but I met a lot of people at Hay-on-Wye."

"I gifted you my first collection: *Soul Carnivores*."

Bells are ringing, albeit faint, underwater, and off-key.

". . . and attended your event at the Shanghai Book Fair."

I didn't believe this hour could possibly get trippier, but I could be wrong. "Miss Moore, I—"

"Miss S. Moore." She says it like it's a clever punch line. "I left my second book in an embroidered bag on the door handle of your hotel. Room 2929 of the Shanghai Mandarin. Its title is *Your Last Chance* and it's the big exposé."

"An exposé"—I sense a fragility here—"about what?"

"The secret war. The secret war waging around us, *inside* us, even. I saw you take *Your Last Chance* out of the bag. You'd spent an hour with Holly Sykes, up in the bar, flipping coins. You remember, Mr. Hershey. I know you do."

Twin facts: I have a stalker, and she is batshit crazy. "Proof of?"

"Proof that you're written into the Script."

"What script are you talking about?"

"*The* Script." She appears to be shocked. "The first poem in *Your Last Chance*. You *did* read it, Mr. Hershey. Didn't you?"

"No, I did not read your poetry, because it isn't my sodding—"

"*Stop!*" She lets out a corroded sob and sinks her fingers into the arm of the chair until they whiten. She tilts her head back and tells a face that isn't there on the ceiling: "He didn't even *read* it! Damn. Damn. *Damn.* Damn. *Damn!*"

"Young lady, you have to see things from—"

"*You* don't get to 'young lady' *me*. Not after," Soleil Moore's fingers writhe individually, "all that time! Money! Blood!"

"Why is it my job to get your poetry published?"

"Because *Soul Carnivores* explains about the apex predators; because *Your Final Chance* exposes the Anchorites' methods; because the Anchorites have a door to anywhere and can abduct *anyone;* and because you, Mr. Hershey, *you are of the Script.*"

"Look, Miss Moore—*what* sodding script?"

Her eyes flip open wider, like a mad toy's: "You're *in* it, Mr. Hershey. As am I. And Holly Sykes—the Anchorites took her brother. You do know that. You wrote yourself into the Script. You describe it in 'The Voorman Problem.' What you wrote, in that story, that's what the Carnivores do. You can't deny it. You can't."

" 'The Voorman Problem'? I wrote that years ago. Apart from the prison doctor and Belgium vanishing, I barely remember it."

"It no longer matters." Soleil Moore calms down, or appears to. "Plan A was to alert the world through poetry. That failed. So we'll have to resort to Plan B."

"Well," I want her gone, "the very best of luck with Plan B. Now I really must get back to work and—"

"You gave me Plan B yourself, at Hay-on-Wye."

"Miss Moore, please don't make me call security."

"Your role is to bring my work to the world's attention. I prayed and prayed that you'd do it by endorsement, but I didn't grasp the magnitude of the sacrifice necessary. I'm sorry, Mr. Hershey."

"That's quite all right, young lady. But please leave."

Soleil Moore stands up . . . in tears? "I'm sorry."

A SUPERNATURAL FORCE flung Hershey backward and off his swivel chair. Soleil Moore stood over him. Five more shots followed, so shocking, so close, they didn't even hurt. Hershey's cheek is against the rough carpet. His ribcage is punched open. Holy buggery. Shot. Really actually bloody shot, me, here, now. The carpet's drinking up blood. Mine. *Copious* quantities. COPIOUS. Seven-letter Scrabble score. Can Hershey move any part of his body, dear reader? No, he cannot. Snow boots. Inches away. Sno boots. No *w*. Listen. A voice. Loving, ebbing, flowing. Mum? Don't be so Disney. Soleil Moore. Miss S. Moore. Ah, of course! Esmiss Esmoore. E. M. Forster's best book. His best character. "You're famous, Mr. Hershey, so now they'll read my poems. The news, the Internet, the FBI, the CIA, the UN, the Vatican—not even the Anchorites can cover it up . . . We're martyrs, you and I, in the War. So was my sister. They lured her away, you see. She told me about them, but I thought it was just her illness talking. I'll never forgive myself. But I can wake up the world from its ignorance. Its deadly ignorance. Once humanity knows we are the Anchorites' food supply—its salmon farm—then we can resist. Rise up. Hunt them down." Soleil Moore's mouth continues to move, but the sound is gone. Reality's shrinking. It was up at the Canadian border; now it stops at Albany; now it's smaller than Blithewood Campus. The snowy woods, the library, the bunker, the bad cafeteria, all gone, all snuffed. Death by lunatic. Who would have thought it? Carpet of dots. Not dots. *Spirals.* All these weeks. Treading on spirals. Look. In the crack. Filing cabinet and skirting board. *Spider.* All dried out. Desiccated. Where the vacuum nozzle won't go. *A spider, a spiral, a* . . . what? The fifth Lego Man. Inches away. On his side. Like me. Look.

A pirate. Funny.

An eye patch.

One-eyed.

Lego *Man*
sodding
pirate.
Holly
tell
her
. . .
. .
.

AN HOROLOGIST'S
LABYRINTH

2025

M Y OLD HOUSE LOOKS haunted tonight, silhouetted against Toronto's smeary glow. Stars are caged like fireflies in the interlacing twigs. I tell the car, "Headlights off, radio off," and Toru Takemitsu's *From Me Flows What You Call Time* stops in midphrase. 23:11, says my car clock. I'm too weighed down to bestir myself. Are we mutants? Have we evolved this way? Or are we designed? Designed by whom? Why did the designer go to such elaborate lengths, only to vacate the stage and leave us wondering why we exist? For entertainment? For perversity? For a joke? To judge us? "To what end?" I ask my car, the night, Canada. My bones, body, and soul feel drained. I rose before five this morning to catch the six fifty-five flight to Vancouver, and when I arrived at Coupland Heights Psychiatric Hospital I found not a patient presenting Messiah Syndrome and acute precognition, but a press pack besieging the main entrance. Inside, my ex-student and friend Dr. Adnan Buyoya was enduring the worst day of his professional life. I sat in on a meeting with Oscar Gomez's wife, her brother, their lawyer, and a trio of senior managers. The representative from the hospital's private security company was "unavoidably absent," though their lawyer was taking notes. Mrs. Gomez's face was a mess of tear streaks. She swung from misery to fury: "There are TV cameras outside our house! The kids saw their dad on YouTube, but they don't know if he's a miracle worker or a criminal or a lunatic or . . . or . . . We daren't switch on the TV or go online, but we can't help it, either. Where *is* he? You're a secure unit—it says so on the signs! How can Oscar just vanish into thin air?"

Adnan Buyoya is a gifted young psychiatrist, but all he could say was he didn't yet know how Mr. Gomez had escaped from a locked room, unnoticed by hospital staff and unrecorded by the CCTV, which must have malfunctioned. The male nurse who was on duty last night had told Adnan that Mr. Gomez was claiming that Saint Mark had promised to bring Jacob's Ladder down during the night and take him up to heaven to discuss the building of the Kingdom of God on earth—but, of course, the nurse had hardly taken the warning seriously at the time. The hospital manager assured Mrs. Gomez that the first priority was to locate her husband, and promised a full inquiry into the security breach. Adnan observed that after 750,000 YouTube hits—probably millions by now—it could be only a matter of time before "The Seer of Washington Street" was identified. I said nothing until called upon to predict Mr. Gomez's next move. I noted that a majority of Messiah Syndromes are short-lived, but owing to Mr. Gomez's lack of a case history, I had no data upon which to base a guess. "Friggin' A," muttered Mrs. Gomez's brother, "yet another expert who can tell us doodly friggin' squat."

I could, in fact, have told Mrs. Gomez's brother doodly frigging everything, but some truths are inadmissible in the court of the sane. Anyway, Mrs. Gomez would not have believed that she is now a widow, and that her children will die wondering what happened to their father on April 1, 2025. After the meeting, all I could do was to stop Adnan apologizing for summoning me across three Canadian time zones to meet a patient who had escaped hours prior to my arrival. I bade my ex-student and colleague good luck and left Coupland Hospital via the kitchens. It took a while to locate my rented car in the vast, rainy parking lot. When I did, my day took an even stranger turn, and not in a good way.

A barn owl hoots. Move. I can't sit here all night.

A SHOEBOX-SIZED PARCEL forwarded by Sadaqat is waiting on the kitchen table, but I haven't eaten all day, so I put it aside and microwave a dish of stuffed aubergines prepared by my once-a-week housekeeper, Mrs. Tavistock. I crank up the heating. The snow's all melted but it doesn't yet feel like spring. I wash down my supper with a glass of rioja, and read an article in the *Korean Psychiatric Journal*. Only then do I remember the parcel. The sender is one Åge Næss-Ødegård from a school for the deaf in Trondheim, Norway, a country I haven't visited since I was Klara Koskov. I take the parcel into my study to check it with a handheld explosives detector. The LED stays green, so I remove the two outer skins of brown paper. Inside is a sturdy cardboard box, containing a cocoon of bubble wrap enclosing a second box crafted from mahogany. I lift its hinged lid to find a Ziplock plastic bag containing a Sony Walkman of a chunky 1980s design. Plugged into it is a set of earphones made of metal, plastic, and foam. The Walkman contains a C30 BASF cassette, a brand whose very existence I had forgotten. After deploying the explosives detector on the Walkman, I read the three-page letter that was also stowed in the mahogany box:

Øvre Fjellberg Skole for Døve
Gransveien 13,
7032 TRONDHEIM
Norge/Norway

15 March 2025

Dear "Marinus,"

First, I beg your pardon. I don't know if "Marinus" is Mr. or Mrs. or Doctor, your family name or your given name. Pardon also my poor English. My name is Åge Næss-Ødegård. Maybe Mrs. Esther Little told you my name, but in this letter, I will assume she did not. I am a seventy-four-year-old Norwegian man who lives in Trondheim, a town of my native Norway. In case you don't know why a stranger is sending you an old audio machine, here is the full story.

My father established the Øvre Fjellberg School in 1932, because his brother Martin was born with deafness and, in those days, attitudes were primitive. I was born in 1950 and I could sign fluently (in Norwegian, of course) before I was ten.

My mother managed the office of Øvre Fjellberg School and my uncle Martin became the groundsman, so, you can imagine, our school and its students were the life of our family. I graduated from Oslo University in 1975 with a degree in education, and I returned to Trondheim to teach at Øvre Fjellberg. I established a Music and Drama Department here, because also I love the violin. Many nondeaf people do not guess that deaf people can enjoy music in various ways, so it was our school's tradition to work with our local amateur orchestra to produce a spring concert for an audience of both deaf and nondeaf people. Signing, dance, amplification, images, and so on are used. In 1984, when this story happened, I chose Jean Sibelius's "The Swan of Tuenola" for our annual performance. It is very beautiful. Perhaps you know?

Anyway in 1984, we had one dark cloud above our landscape (do you say this in English?). Namely, the financial position of our school was critical. Øvre Fjellberg is a charitable foundation but we required a big subsidy from Oslo to pay for salaries, and so on. I will not bore you with old politics, but the national government at that time cut our subsidy, to oblige our students to attend another school, two hours away by car. We protested the decision, but without financial independence or political muscle, our precious school was to be shut, after half a century of excellent work. For our family, this was a tragedy.

However, one day in June of 1984, I received a visitor in my office. She was in her fifties, perhaps. She had short gray hair and masculine clothes and a face of many stories. She apologized for disturbing me in foreigner's Norwegian, then asked if we could speak English. I said yes. She said her name was Esther Little. Esther Little had attended our students' recent concert and enjoyed it greatly. She had also heard of the school's bad financial position, and she wished to assist, if possible. I said, "If you have a magic wand, please, I am listening." Esther Little put a wooden box on my desk. This

is the mahogany box I send to you. Inside was a portable
cassette player and one cassette tape. Then Esther Little
explained this deal. If I keep these items for some years, and
then post it to her friend "Marinus" at an address in New
York, she would tell her lawyers in Oslo to make a large
donation to our school.

Should I agree? Esther Little read my thoughts. She said,
"No, I am not a drug lord, or a terrorist, or a spy. I am an
eccentric philanthropist from Western Australia. The cassette
is a message to a friend, Marinus, who will need to hear it
when the time is right." As I write this letter today, I don't
know why I believed her, but sometimes you meet people
who you believe. It is an instinct. I believed Esther Little. Her
Oslo lawyers were a respectable conservative firm, so perhaps
this influenced my decision. I asked, why not did she simply
pay her Oslo lawyers to post her box to New York on a
certain date in the future? Esther Little said, "Lawyers come
and go. Even discreet ones are visible, and they all work for
money. But you are an honest man in a quiet corner of the
world, and you will live a long time." Finally, she wrote down
the donation she offered. I am sure my face became pale like
a ghost when I saw the number on the sheet of paper! Our
school would be safe for five years, at least. Esther Little said,
"Tell your board of governors that the money was donated
from a wealthy anonymous donor who believes in the work
of Øvre Fjellberg School. This is the truth." The box and our
deal should be our small secret, is what I understood.

We shook hands. Naturally, my last question was, "When
do I post the box to 'Marinus' in Manhattan?" Esther Little
took a small porcelain statue of Sibelius from a box, put it on
a high bookshelf, and said this: On the day Sibelius was
smashed into many pieces, that day I must post the box. I
thought I had not understood her English, so I examined her
request carefully. If the statue broke next week, I must post
the box next week. If it broke in year 2000, I must post the

box in year 2000. If I die before the statue breaks, then I never post the box. Yes, that was the deal, said Esther Little. "Like I said, I am eccentric," she said. We said goodbye and, to be honest, when she was gone I wondered if I dreamed her. But next day, the lawyer telephoned from Oslo for our bank account number, and every krone Esther Little promised was transferred. Øvre Fjellberg was safed. Three or four years later, the government ideas changed greatly and big investment was made for our school, but there is no doubt, Mrs. Esther Little rescued us at our worst time. In 2004, I became principal, and I retired a few years ago but I am still a governor, and even today, I use my former office as a study. All those years, Jean Sibelius watched my office, like a man who knows the secret.

You can guess the ending, I think. Yesterday was the first mild day of spring. Like most people in Norway, I opened the window for make air fresh in my office. Students was playing on tennis courts below my window. I left my study to make my morning coffee. I heard a noise. When I returned, Jean Sibelius was on the floor. His chest and head was in many little pieces. There was a tennis ball near. The chance was 10,000 of 1, but the time came. So I am sending the box, as I promised, with this strange story. I hope the message on the cassette is clear after forty years, but I never listened it. If Mrs. Little is still walking this world (if so, surely she is over 100 years old), give her thanks and regards from an honest man in a quiet corner of the world who has lived a long time indeed.

Sincerely,
Åge Næss-Ødegård

My heart is sprinting with no sign of a finishing line. A hoax? I get my slate and shirabu "Øvre Fjellberg Skole for Døve": There it is. A fake website? Possibly, but the Sibelius statue and the Norwegian backwater both smack strongly of Esther Little. If she was planting this marker in June of 1984, she was reacting to glimpses of the Script. If the First Mission was Scripted, then maybe, maybe, it was not the crippling defeat that we've believed it was for the last forty-one years. Yet how could the deaths of Xi Lo, Holokai, and Esther Little be part of a bigger scheme? Luckily I have some AA batteries in my desk drawer—they are also nearly extinct—and slot them into the Walkman. Will they still have any juice in them? I plug in the earphones, hesitate, and press play. The spindles rotate. There are a few seconds of silent "header," then magnetic hiss, then a clunk where the recording begins. I hear a distant motorbike, and a familiar voice whose timbre and croak make my breath catch and my heart ache for my long-lost friend.

"Marinus, it's Esther on . . . June 7, 1984. Before we all assemble in Gravesend, I've taken a little trip to Trondheim. Nice town. Not a lot going on. Very white—a taxi driver just asked what part of Africa I'm from." I hear her cackle slightly as she lights a cigarette. "But listen, I got glimpses of the Script, Marinus, about the First Mission. Sketchy and vague, to be sure, but I see fire . . . flight . . . and death. Death in the Dusk, and death in a sunny room. If the Script is accurate, I'll survive, in a manner of speaking, but I'll need a bolt-hole. I'll need asylum. It has to be hidden and locked, so when the Anchorites come looking for me, as Constantin will, they'll miss it. This means I'll need you to get me out again. I'll have to get the key to you." I hear a vitreous rumbling noise, and guess that Esther moved an ashtray across a table. "The Script showed me tombs among the trees, and this name: 'Blithewood.' Find it and go there, as soon as you can. You'll meet someone you know. That person gave me asylum. There are many locks, but already I sent you a sign to tell you which lock the key'll fit. Find that lock, Marinus. Open it. Bring me back from the dead." I hear the muffled chimes of an ice-cream van in that Norwegian summer. "Your hearing this cassette is a trigger. An enemy will make a proposal, very soon. Hide this sign. Hide this box. He's very close to you already. The Script doesn't say if you can trust him or not. His proposal'll be the seed of the Second Mission. Things'll move quickly now. In seven days the War will be over, one way or the other. If all goes well, we'll meet before then. Until then, then." Clunk.

The recording ends, the tape hisses, I press stop. I'm pummeled by guesses, half guesses, and questions. My friends and I have always believed that Esther's soul succumbed to its injuries after killing Joseph Rhîmes and redacting Holly Sykes's memory. How else to explain the absence of contact from Esther since 1984? This cassette flags up a dramatic alternative, however. That after the First Mission, Esther's soul unraveled to a critical, yet not *quite* fatal, degree. She then sought asylum deep inside an unknowing host, concealed so that no Shaded Way hunter guided by the Counterscript could find and kill her. And that by presending my keys and signs, I could locate and liberate her reraveled soul from its asylum, after forty-one years. This is so slim a hope as to be anorexic. Sentience dissipates after only a few hours in another's parallax of memories. After so many years of incorporeality, would Esther's soul even know its name?

I watch Iris Fenby's reflected face in the window-framed Kleinburg woods. The thickish lips, the flattish nose, the short curly black hair, silvered ever so slightly by middle age. These woods are remnants of the old forest that covered Ontario for most of the Holocene Era. The trees' war against subdivisions, agro-forestry, six-lane highways, and golf courses is more or less lost. Could Esther Little still be alive? I don't know. I just don't know. Esther had command of the Aperture, so why not seek asylum with an Horologist? Because that was too obvious, perhaps. What about the last part of Esther's message? "An enemy will make a proposal, very soon"? "He's very close to you already"? It's midnight in a shielded, bulletproofed house in a well-to-do rural retreat on the northwest fringes of Toronto, forty-one years in the future from the day that Esther spoke the words preserved on this magnetic tape. Even for a precognitive Horologist, it beggars belief that she could accurately have foreseen—

. . .

MY DEVICE TRILLS on my lamp stand. Before I answer an instinct makes me hide my parcel from Norway behind some books. My device can't identify the caller. It's late. Should I answer? "Yes?"

"Marinus," says a male voice. "It's Elijah D'Arnoq."

I'm shocked by the contact, though after Hugo Lamb's call in Vancouver, I shouldn't be. "This is . . . certainly a surprise."

A dead silence. "I imagine it must be. I'd feel the same."

" 'Imagine'? 'Feel'? You flatter yourself."

"Yeah." D'Arnoq's voice is pensive. "Maybe I do."

Keeping low, I unplug the lamp from the wall so I'm not visible from outside. "I don't want to seem rude, D'Arnoq, but would you skip to the bit where you gloat about Oscar Gomez, so I can just hang up? It's late and, as you know, I've had a long day."

A troubled, sloughing silence. "I want it to stop."

"Stop what? This call? Fine by me. Goodbye—"

"No, Marinus—I want to defect."

I check the last sentence for errors.

D'Arnoq repeats it like a sulky kid: "I want to defect."

"So I say, 'Really?' and you say, 'In your dreams.' When I last attended high school, it went something like that."

"I can't . . . can't endure another decanting. I want to defect."

Stranger than the Anchorite's words is his tone, denuded of the usual swagger. But I'm still a light-year from swallowing this. "Well, D'Arnoq," I say, "now you're au fait with the arts of feeling and imagining, try this: If you were on my end of the device, how would you respond to this show of remorse from a high-up Anchorite?"

"I'd be bloody skeptical. I'd ask, 'Why now?' "

"What an excellent place to begin. Why now?"

"It's not now. It's a . . . nausea that's grown over the last . . . twenty years. But I can't ignore it anymore. I . . . I . . . Look, last year, Rivas-Godoy, the Tenth Anchorite, sourced a five-year-old from Paraisópolis, a favela in São Paolo. Enzo was the kid's name. Enzo had no dad, he was bullied, friendless, his chakra-eye was vivid, and Rivas-Godoy became his big brother . . . A textbook sourcing. I did the ingress-check and Enzo was pure, no sign of Horology. So I approved him, and was in the Chapel for the Rebirthday when Rivas-Godoy walked Enzo up . . ."

I've bitten back five acidic interruptions already.

". . . to meet Santa Claus." There's a grimace in D'Arnoq's voice.

"Santa Claus. Caucasian male. About sixty. Nonexistent."

"Yeah. Enzo'd been picked on for saying Santa might be real. So Rivas-Godoy told Enzo he'd take him to Lapland. So the Way of Stones became the short cut to the North Pole, the Chapel was Santa's dining room, and the view over the Dusk, that was . . . Lapland. Enzo'd never left his favela, so"—D'Arnoq lets out a sigh through his teeth—"he didn't know any better. Rivas-Godoy said I was the vet in case the reindeer got sick. Enzo said, 'Wow.' Then Rivas-Godoy told Enzo, 'Go see Santa's papa, Enzo, in the painting. It's a magic talking picture, go say hello.' The last minute of Enzo's life was the happiest one, I suppose. But later, on the Solstice Rebirthday, as we drank the Black Wine, and Rivas-Godoy was laughing about this dumb-ass Brazilian kid . . . I could hardly empty my glass."

"But somehow you managed, of course."

"I'm a high-ranking Anchorite! What choice did I have?"

"Step out of the Aperture halfway down Mariana Trench? You'd cure your guilt, contribute to the local aquafauna, and spare me your oh-so-shiny crocodile tears."

D'Arnoq's whisper is broken. "The decanting has to stop."

"Enzo the São Paolo boy must've been *truly* cute. You ought to know, by the way, I'm not sure how secure this device—"

"I'm our hacker-in-chief, nobody can hear us. It wasn't just Enzo. Or Oscar Gomez, today. It's all of them. Since the day Pfenninger told me of the Blind Cathar, and what he built, and what it does, I've been party to . . . Look, if you need me to use the word 'evil,' I'll use it. I anesthetized myself against it, of course. I ate the lies. I digested the whole 'What's four a year out of eight billion?' schtick . . . But I'm sick of it. Of the sourcing, of the grooming, of the murder, of the animacide. Sick of the evil. Horology's right. You always were."

"And when your boyish good looks ebb away, D'Arnoq?"

"Then I'd be alive again, and not . . . what I am now."

Something creaks on the decking outside.

Am I being set up? I peer out: a raccoon.

"Did you share your new views with Mr. Pfenninger?"

"If you're going to sit there and take the piss, Marinus, *I'll* hang up on you. Apostasy is a capital crime in the Shaded Way Codex. A fact you ought to use, by the way—my only chance of survival is to help you annihilate your enemy before they kill me."

Damn Elijah D'Arnoq, but I have to ask: "How, exactly, do you suggest we annihilate our enemy?"

"By psycho-demolishing the Chapel of the Dusk."

"We tried that. You'll be aware of how it ended." Though I'm less sure I am, after tonight's box from Norway.

"Defeat for Horology, *but* on your First Trespass, you didn't know what you were dealing with. Did you?"

"Will you cure us of that ignorance?"

D'Arnoq's pause goes on a long, long time. "Yes, I will."

I'd give Elijah D'Arnoq's defection a five percent chance of being genuine, but Esther Little glimpsed it, and if I'm not mistaken, she wants me to treat D'Arnoq as an ally, or at least let him think I believe him. "I'm all ears."

"No. We need to meet face-to-face, Marinus."

Down to one percent. He'll propose a meeting in a man-trap, and its jaws will snap shut. "Where do you suggest?"

The raccoon turns its Zorro-masked face my way.

"Don't go all Deep Streamy on me, but I'm speaking from your car, on the drive. My balls are freezing. Get a fire going, will you?"

THE AIR IS SHARPER at the Poughkeepsie station than it was at Grand Central Station, but the sun is out and melting the last of the winter-long snow on the platform. With a cohort of students discussing skiing trips to Europe, internships at the Guggenheim, and viral zoonoses, I walk over the footbridge and through the turnstiles, the churchlike 1920s waiting room, and out to the curbside, where a woman a few years older than I is waiting in a black bodywarmer by a hybrid Chevrolet and holding a board for DR I. FENBY. Her foamy hair is dyed auburn but the gray is showing through, and her turquoise-framed glasses only heighten her sickly pallor. An unkind describer might refer to her face as like a party nobody's turned up to. "Good morning," I tell her. "I'm Dr. Fenby."

The driver tenses: "*You're* Dr. Fenby? *You?*"

Why the surprise? Because I'm black? In a campus town in the 2020s? "Ye-es . . . There's no problem, I trust?"

"*No.* No. No. Climb in. That's all the luggage you got?"

"I'm only a day-tripper." Still puzzled, I get into the Chevrolet. She climbs in behind the wheel and puts on her seatbelt. "So it's up to Blithewood campus today, Dr. Fenby?" Her voice is stippled with bronchial issues.

"That's right." Did I misgrade her reaction just now? "Drop me off by the president's house, if you know it."

"Not a problem. I must've driven Mr. Stein up and down a hundred times. Is it the president you're visiting today?"

"No. I'm meeting . . . someone else."

"Right." Her driver ID tag reads WENDY HANGER. "Off we go,

then. Chevrolet: ignition." The car turns itself on, the indicator blinks, and we pull away. Wendy Hanger looks jumpy on her ID photo, too. Maybe life's never allowed her to lower her guard. Maybe she's just clocked up a fourteen-hour shift. Maybe she just drank too much coffee.

We pass parking lots, a tire-and-exhaust fitters, a Walmart, a school, and a plastic moldings unit. My driver is the silent type, which suits me fine. My thoughts go back to last night's meeting held in the gallery at 119A. Unalaq, the local, arrived before me; Ōshima flew up from Argentina; Arkady, able to travel more freely now that he is eighteen, came over from Berlin, Roho from Athens, and L'Ohkna from Bermuda. It's been years since we were all gathered in the same place. Sadaqat submitted to an Act of Hiatus and we began. My five colleagues listened as I set out the facts of Elijah D'Arnoq's visit two nights ago to my Kleinburg house, his wish to defect, and the proposed Second Mission. Naturally, they were all skeptical.

"So soon?" asked Roho, peering over a canopy of interlaced fingers as slim, dark, and bony as the rest of him. Smooth-shaven, Egyptian-bodied Roho looks designed to slip through narrow spaces nobody else would even think of. He's young for an Horologist, on only his fifth resurrection, but under Ōshima's tutelage is becoming a formidable duelist. "The First Mission was five years in the planning, and it ended in disaster. To plan a Second Mission in a matter of days would be . . ." Roho wrinkles his nose and shakes his head.

"D'Arnoq makes it sound all too easy," remarked Unalaq. Her first life as an Inuit in northern Alaska dyed her soul indelibly with the far north, but her current midthirties body is pure Boston Irish redhead, though with skin swarming with so many freckles that her ethnicity is far from obvious. "Far too easy."

"We appear to agree," said Ōshima. Ōshima is one of the oldest Horologists in both his soul, dating back to thirteenth-century Japan, and body, dating back to 1940s Kenya. He dresses to accentuate what Roho calls his "unemployed jazz drummer" look, in an old trenchcoat and shabby beret. In a pyschoduel, however, Ōshima is more dangerous than any of us. "D'Arnoq's proposal has the word 'trap' written all over it. In flashing neon."

"But D'Arnoq *did* let Marinus scansion him," remarked Arkady. In stark contrast to his last, East Asian self, Arkady's soul now occupies a big-boned, gangly, blond, acne-prone, Hungarian male body whose teenage voice is not quite settled. "And the self-disgust, the grief about the Brazilian kid," Arkady double-checks with me, "you did locate them, in his present-perfect memory? And you're sure they were genuine?"

"Yes," I conceded, "although they could be implanted memories. The Anchorites would know that we wouldn't take a defector at face value without a frame-by-frame scansion. It's perfectly possible that D'Arnoq volunteered to be turned against the Shaded Way by Pfenninger himself, so that D'Arnoq is a true believer in his own false defection . . ."

"All the way to another firing squad in the Chapel," agreed Ōshima, "where Pfenninger would redact D'Arnoq's artificial remorse and psychoslay the Horologists it lured there. I have to admit, it's clever. It sounds like a Constantin ploy."

"My vote would be no." L'Ohkna is residing in a pale, balding, and puffy Ulsterman's body in its midthirties. L'Ohkna is the youngest Horologist, having been found by Xi Lo in a New Mexico commune in the 1960s during his first resurrection. While L'Ohkna's psychovoltage is still limited, he has become the principal architect of the Deep Internet, or "Nethernet," and his dozens of aliases are being fruitlessly hunted by every major security agency on earth. "One misstep and Horology dies. Simple as."

"But isn't the enemy taking a big risk, too?" asked Unalaq. "Turning one of their own strongest psychosoterics against the Anchorites and the Blind Cathar?"

"Yes," agreed Ōshima, "but they know what they're doing. They need to offer us a shiny prize and a juicy bait. But tell us, Marinus: What are your thoughts about this unexpected overture?"

"I think it's an ambush, but we should accept it anyway, then, between now and the Second Mission, engineer a means of ambusing the ambush. We'll never win the War by force. Every year, we save a few, but look at Oscar Gomez, snatched from a secure unit headed by one of my own students. Social media flag up active chakras before we can inoculate them. Horology's drifting towards irrelevance. There aren't enough of us. Our networks are fraying."

Arkady broke the gloomy silence: "If you think this, so must the enemy. Why would Pfenninger risk giving us access to the Blind Cathar when he can stalemate us to death?"

"Because of his cardinal vice: vanity. Pfenninger wants to annihilate Horology in one glorious act of slaughter, so he's offering us, his desperate enemy, this trap. But it'll also give us a narrow window of time inside the Chapel. It won't come again."

"And what do we do with that narrow window of time," countered L'Ohkna, "apart from being butchered, body and soul?"

"That," I confessed, "I cannot answer. But I heard from someone who may be able to. I didn't dare refer to this outside 119A, but now we're all here, lend an old friend your ears . . ." I produced an ancient Walkman and inserted a BASF cassette.

WENDY HANGER'S FINGERS drum on the wheel while four lanes of traffic cross the intersection. She has no ring on her finger. The light turns green, but she doesn't notice until the truck behind us blasts its horn. She pulls off, stalls, mutters, "Oh, for heaven's sake. Chevrolet, ignition!" We drive off, past a big Home Depot, and soon we've left Poughkeepsie behind. I ask, "How long to Blithewood?"

"Thirty, forty minutes." Wendy Hanger puts a nicotine gum stick into her mouth and her sternocleidomastoideus ripples with every chew. The road winds between and under trees. Their buds are on the cusp of opening. A sign says RED HOOK 7 MILES. We overtake a pair of cyclists, and Wendy Hanger musters the courage: "Dr. Fenby, could I . . . uh, ask you a question?"

"Ask away."

"This might sound like I'm outta my freaking tree."

"You're in luck, Ms. Hanger. I'm a psychiatrist."

"Does the name 'Marinus' ring any bells?"

I hadn't seen that coming. We don't hide our true names, but neither do we advertise them. "Why do you ask?"

Wendy Hanger's breathing is ragged. "Dunno how I knew it, but I knew it. Look, I—I—I'm sorry, I gotta pull over." Around the next bend there's a timely rest area with a bench and a view of woodland sloping down to the Hudson River. Wendy Hanger turns around. She's sweating and wide-eyed. Her dolphin air freshener swings in diminishing arcs. "Do you know a Marinus—or *are* you Marinus?"

The cyclists we passed not long ago speed by.

"I go by that name in certain circles," I say.

Her face trembles. It's scarred with childhood acne. "Ho-*ly* crap." She shakes her head. "*You* could hardly've been *born* yet. Jeez, I *really* need a smoke."

"Don't take your stress out on your bronchial tubes, Ms. Hanger. Stick to the gum. Now. I'm overdue an explanation."

"This isn't"—she frowns—"this isn't some kinda setup?"

"I wish it was, because then I'd know what was happening."

Suspicion, angst, and disbelief slug it out in Wendy Hanger's face, but no clear winner emerges. "Okay, Doctor. Here's the story. When I was younger, in Milwaukee, I went off the rails. Family issues, a divorce . . . substance abuse. My stepsister booted me out, and by the end, moms were, like, steering their kids across the road to avoid me. I was . . ." She flinches. Old memories still keep their sting.

"An addict," I state calmly, "which means you're now a survivor."

Wendy Hanger chews her gum a few times. "I guess I am. New Year's Eve 1983, though, the holiday lights all pretty—Jeez, I was no survivor then. I hit rock bottom, broke into my stepsister's house, found her sleeping pills, swallowed the entire freakin' bottle with a pint of Jim Beam. That movie *The Towering Inferno* was on, as I . . . sank away. You ever see it?" Before I can answer, a sports car storms by and Wendy Hanger shudders. "I woke up in the hospital with tubes in my stomach and throat. My stepsister's neighbor had seen the TV on, come over, and found me. Called an ambulance in the nick of time. People think sleeping pills are painless, but that's not true. I'd no idea a stomach could *hurt* that much. I slept, woke, slept some more. Then I woke in the geriatric ward, which *totally* freaked me out 'cause I thought I'd aged," Wendy Hanger does a bitter laugh, "and been in a coma for forty years, and was now, like, ancient. But there was this woman there, sitting by my bed. I didn't know if she was staff or a patient or a volunteer, but she held my hand and asked, 'Why are you here, Miss Hanger?' I hear her now. 'Why are you here, Wendy?' She spoke kinda funny, like with an accent, but . . . I don't know where from. She wasn't black, but wasn't quite white. She was . . . kind, like a . . . a gruff angel, who wouldn't blame you or judge you for what you'd done or for what life'd done to you. And I—I heard myself telling her things I . . ." Wendy Hanger gazes at the backs of her hands, ". . . I never told anyone. Suddenly it was midnight. This woman smiled at me and said, 'You're over the worst. Happy New Year.' And . . . I just freakin' burst into tears. I don't know why."

"Did she tell you her name?"

Wendy's eyes are a challenge.

"Was her name Esther Little, Wendy?"

Wendy Hanger breathes in deep: "She said you'd know that. She said you'd know. But you can't have been more than a girl in 1984. What's going on? How . . . *Jeez.*"

"Did Esther Little give you a message to give to me?"

"Yes. Yes, Doctor. She asked *me,* a homeless, suicidal addict whom she'd known for all of, like, two or three hours, to pass on a message to a colleague named Marinus. I—I—I—I asked, 'Is "Marinus" like a Christian name, a surname, an alias?' But Esther Little said, 'Marinus is Marinus,' and told me to tell you . . . to tell you . . ."

"I'm listening, Wendy. Go on."

"'Three on the Day of the Star of Riga.'"

The world's hushed. "Three on the Day of the Star of Riga?"

"Not a word more, not a word less." She studies me.

The Star of Riga. I know I've known that phrase, and I reach for the memory, but my fingers pass through it. No. I'll have to be patient.

"'Riga' meant nothing," Wendy Hanger chews what must now be a flavorless lump of gum, "back in my hospital bed in Milwaukee, so I asked her the spelling: R-I-G-A. Then I asked where I'd find this Marinus, so I could deliver the message. Esther said no, the time wasn't right yet. So I asked when the time would be right. And she said," Wendy Hanger swallows, her carotid artery pulsing fast, "'The day you become a grandmother.'"

Pure Esther Little. "Many congratulations," I tell Wendy Hanger. "Granddaughter or grandson?"

She looks more perturbed by this, not less. "A girl. My daughter-in-law gave birth in Santa Fe, early this morning. She wasn't due for another two weeks, but just after midnight, Rainbow Hanger was born. Her people are hippies. But, look, you gotta . . . I mean, I thought Esther maybe had on-and-off dementia, or . . . *Jeez*. What sane person'd beg such a wacko favor off of anyone, least of all an addict who'd just swallowed a hundred sleeping pills? I asked her. Esther said the addict in me *had* died, but that the real me, she'd survived. I'd be fine from now on, she said. She said the 'Riga' message and its due date were written in permanent marker, and on the right day, years from now, Marinus'd find me, but your name'd be different and—" Wendy Hanger's sniffling and her eyes are streaming. "*Why'm* I crying?"

I hand her a packet of tissues.

"Is she still alive? She'd be, like . . . ancient."

"The woman you met has passed on."

The newborn grandmother nods, unsurprised. "Pity. I'd've liked to thank her. I owe her so much."

"How so?"

Wendy Hanger looks surprised, but decides to tell me. "By and by, I fell asleep, and didn't wake until morning. Esther had gone. A nurse brought me breakfast, and said they'd be moving me to a private room later. I said there must a mistake, I didn't have insurance, but the nurse said, 'Your grandmother's settling your account, honey,' and I said, 'What grandmother?' The nurse smiled like I was concussed and said, 'Mrs. Little, isn't it?' Then, later, in my private room, a nurse brought a . . . like a black zip-up folder. In it was a Bank of America card with my name on it, a door key, and some documents. These," Wendy Hanger heaves an emotional sigh, "turned out to be the deeds to a house in Poughkeepsie. In my name. Two weeks later I was discharged from the hospital in Milwaukee. I went to my stepsister's, apologized for trying to kill myself on her sofa, and said I was heading east, to try to, y'know, make a fresh start, where no one knew me. I think my stepsister was relieved. Two Greyhound bus rides later, I walked into my house in Poughkeepsie . . . A house that a real live fairy godmother had apparently given me. Next thing I knew, forty years or more flew by. I still live there, and to this day my husband believes it was a gift from an eccentric aunt. I never told no one the truth. But every single time I turned my key in the lock, I thought of her, I thought, 'Three on the Day of the Star of Riga,' and pretty much every hour since I learned my daughter-in-law was pregnant, I'd wonder if I'd run into a Marinus . . . This morning, holy crap, was I a mess! The day I become a grandmother. My husband told me to stay at home, so I did. But Carlotta, who runs the cab company for us these days, deviced to say that Jodie'd twisted her ankle and Zeinab's baby was running a fever, so please, please, please, would I go to the station and pick up Dr. I. Fenby? And, y'know, there's no reason why *you'd* be Marinus, but when I saw you I . . ." she shakes her head, " . . . knew. That's why I was kinda spooked. Sorry."

Dappled sunshine shivers. "Forget it. Thank you."

"The Riga message. Does it make sense?"

I should be careful. "Partially. Potentially."

Wendy Hanger considers criminal networks, the FBI, *The Da Vinci Code*—but smiles, shyly. "Way, way over *my* head, hey? Y'know, I feel . . . lighter." She dabs her eyes with her wrists, notices the splodges of makeup, and checks in the mirror: "Holy crap, it's the Creature from the Black Lagoon. Can I just, like, fix myself?"

"I'll take the air, you take your time." I get out of the car and walk over to the bench. I sit down, gaze over the stately Hudson River at the Catskill Mountains, egress, transverse back to the car, and ingress into Wendy Hanger. First I redact everything that's happened since she pulled over. Then I trace the memory cord back forty-one years to a Milwaukee hospital. Redacting memories of Esther hurts, but it's for the best. The messenger will forget the message she's carried for so long, and everything else she just told me. At odd moments she may fret over a blank in her memory, but soon a Pied Piper thought will come dancing along and her untrained mind will follow . . .

WENDY HANGER SETS me down at the daffodil-clustered roundabout on Blithewood's campus, just below the president's ivy-veined house. "That *was* a pleasure, Iris."

"Thanks so much for the guided tour, Wendy."

"I like to show the place to folks who'd appreciate it, specially on the first real day of spring."

"Look, I know my assistant paid by charge card but"—I hand her a twenty-dollar bill—"buy a bottle of something silly to celebrate your life as a granny." She hesitates, but I press it into her hand.

"That's generous of you, Iris. I will, and my husband and I'll drink to your health. You're sure you're good for the trip back?"

"I'm good. My friend's driving us back to New York."

"Have a great meeting, then, and an excellent day, and enjoy the sunshine. The forecast's patchy for the next few days." She pulls away, waving, and is gone. I hear myself subaddressed in Ōshima's plangent tones: *Looking for your Sorority House?*

I try to spot him, but see only students crossing the well-tended lawns with armfuls of folders and bags. Four men are carrying a piano. *Ōshima, I just received a sign from Esther Little.*

The front door of the president's house opens and Ōshima, a slight figure with hands buried deep in his knee-length mugger's hoodie, emerges. *What sort of sign?*

A mnemocrypted key, I subreply, walking towards the house.

Wet catkins fur the twigs of a willow. *I haven't solved it yet, but I will. Is anyone at the cemetery?* I unbutton my coat.

Only squirrels, humping and jumping, Ōshima flips back his hood and angles his white-whiskered, septuagenarian Kenyan face to soak up the sun, *until a quarter-hour ago. Take the path leading up to your left from where I'm standing.*

I pass within a few yards. *Anyone we know?*

Go and see. She's wearing a Jamaican head-wrap.

I follow the path: *What's a Jamaican head-wrap?*

Ōshima shuts the door behind him and walks the other way. *Holler if you need me.*

UNDERFOOT, OLD LEAVES crackle and squelch, while overhead, brand-new leaves ooze unbundling from swollen buds and the wood is Bluetoothed with birdsong. At the base of a trunk the girth of a brontosaurus's leg, I find a gravestone. Here's another, and another smothered by ivy. Blithewood's campus cemetery, then, is not a regimented matrix of the dead but a wood whose graves are sunk between, and nourish the roots of, these pines, cedars, yews, and maples. Esther's glimpse was precise: *Tombs between the trees.* Rounding a dense holly tree I come across Holly Sykes, and think, *Who else?* I haven't seen her since my visit to Rye, four years ago. Her cancer is still in remission but she looks gaunter than ever, all bone and nerve. Her head-wrap is the red, green, and gold of the Jamaican flag. I scuff my feet to let her know someone's coming, and Holly slips on a pair of sunglasses that conceal much of her face. "Good morning," I venture.

"Good morning," she echoes neutrally.

"Sorry to bother you, but I was looking for Crispin Hershey."

"Right here." Holly gestures at the white marble stone.

CRISPIN HERSHEY

WRITER

1966–2020

"Short and sweet," I remark. "Clichéless."

"Yes, he wasn't a big fan of flowery prose."

"And a more peaceful, more Emersonian resting place," I say, "I can't imagine. His work is urban and his wit's urbane, but his soul is pastoral. One thinks of Trevor Upward in *Echo Must Die*, who finds peace only in the lesbian commune on the Isle of Muck."

Holly inspects me through her dark lenses; she last saw me through a fug of medication, so I doubt she'll recall me, but I'll stay prepared: "Were you a colleague of Crispin's here at the college?"

"No, no, I work in a different field. I'm a fan, though. I've read and reread *Desiccated Embryos*."

"He always suspected that book would outlive him."

"Attaining immortality is easier than controlling its terms and conditions." A blue jay swoops onto a fungus-ruffled tree stump by Hershey's grave, emits a volley of harsh jeers, then a breathy trill.

"They don't make those birds where I'm from," says Holly.

"A blue jay," I say, "or *Cyanocitta cristata*. The Algonquin name was *sideso* and the Yakama called it a *xwáshxway,* but their territory was over on the Pacific, so now I'm merely showing off."

Holly removes her sunglasses. "Are you a linguist?"

"By default. I'm a psychiatrist, here for a meeting. You?"

"Just here to pay my respects." Holly bends down, takes an oak leaf from the grave, and puts it into her purse. "Well, nice talking with you. Hope your meeting goes well."

The blue jay threads a flight path through stripes of brightness and stripes of mossy dark. Holly begins to walk off.

"So far so good, but it's about to get trickier, I fear."

Holly is struck by my strange answer and stops.

I clear my throat. "Ms. Sykes, we need to talk."

Down come the shutters, out comes her hardscrabble Gravesend accent. "I don't do media, I don't do festivals." She steps backwards. "I've retired from all that." A frond of pine tree brushes her head and she ducks nervily. "So, no, whoever you are, you can—"

"Iris Fenby this time around, but you know me as Marinus."

She freezes, thinks, frowns, and looks disgusted. "Oh, f'Chrissakes! Yu Leon Marinus died in 1984, he was Chinese, and if *you* have a Chinese parent, then I'm . . . Vladimir Putin. Don't force me to be rude. *That's* rude."

"Dr. Yu Leon Marinus was indeed childless, Holly, and that body died in 1984. But his soul, this 'I' addressing you now, is Marinus. Truly."

A dragonfly arrives and leaves like a change of mind. Holly's walking off. Who knows how many Marinuses she's met, from the mentally ill to fraudsters, after a slice of her royalties?

"You have two hours missing from July 1, 1984," I call after her, "between Rochester and the Isle of Sheppey. I know what happened."

She stops. "*I* know what happened!" Despite herself, she turns to face me again, properly angry now. "I hitched. A woman picked me up and dropped me off at the Sheppey bridge. *Please,* leave me alone."

"Ian Fairweather and Heidi Cross picked you up. I know you know those names, but you don't know you were at that bungalow that morning, that day, when they were killed."

"Whatever! Post the whole story at bullshitparanoia.com. The crazies'll give you all the attention you need." Somewhere a lawn-mover chugs into noisy life. "You digested *The Radio People,* sicked it up, mixed in your own psychoses, and made an occult reality show, starring yourself. Just like that wretched girl who shot Crispin. I'm going now. *Don't* follow, or I'll call the cops."

Birds crisscross and warble in the stripes of light.

That went well, subsays Ōshima the Unseen and Ironic.

I sit down on the blue jay's stump. *It's a beginning.*

"MY FAVORITE DISH on my menu, sweetheart, swear to God."
Nestor lays the plate in front of me. "People come in, they
sit down, they see 'vegetarian moussaka,' they think, *If
moussaka ain't meat it ain't moussaka,* so they order the steak, the
pork belly, the lamb chops. They dunno what they missing. Go on.
Taste. My own mother, God watch over her soul, that's her recipe.
Hell of a lady. Navy SEALs, ninjas, those Mafia guys, next to a
Greek momma, they a sack of quivering pussies. That's her, in the
frame, over the till." He points at the white-haired matriarch. "She
made this café. She invented no-meat moussaka too, when Mus-
solini invaded and shot every sheep, every rabbit, every dog. Mama
had to—wassaword?—improvise. Marinate the eggplant in red
wine. Simmer the lentils, *slow.* Mushrooms cooked in soy sauce—
she added soy sauce after she came to New York. Meatier than
meat. Butter in white sauce, cornflour, dash of cream. Heavy on the
paprika. That's the kick. *Bon appétit,* sweetheart, and"—he passes
me a clinking glass of iced tap water—"save space for dessert. You
too skinny."

"Skinny," I pat my midriff, "is *not* one of my worries."

Off he drifts, deftly avoided by higher-speed younger staff. I fork
an eggplant and squish up some white sauce, smoosh on a mush-
room and eat. Taste being the blood of memory, I remember 1969,
when Yu Leon Marinus was teaching only a few blocks away, Old
Nestor was Young Nestor, and the white-haired lady in the frame,
upon learning that the Greek-speaking Chinaman was a doctor,
held me up to her sons as the American Dream incarnate. She gave
me a square of baklava with my coffee every time I came here, which

was often. I'd like to ask when she passed away, but my curiosity might attract suspicion, so I downstream today's *New York Times* and flick to the crossword. But it's no good.

I can't stop thinking about Esther Little . . .

IN 1871 PABLO Antay Marinus turned forty. He had inherited enough Latino DNA from his Catalan father to pass as Spanish, so he signed as a ship's surgeon aboard an aging Yankee clipper, the *Prophetess,* at Rio de Janeiro, bound for Batavia in the Dutch East Indies, via Cape Town. Notwithstanding a typhoon of Old Testament fury, an outbreak of ship fever that killed a dozen sailors, and a skirmish with corsairs off Panaitan Island, we limped into Batavia on Christmas Day. Lucas Marinus had visited the place eighty years before, and the malarial garrison town I remembered was now a malarial city. One cannot cross the same river twice. I traveled inland to botanize around Buitenzorg, but the brutality meted out by Europeans to the Javanese natives robbed me of all pleasure in Javanese flora, and when the *Prophetess* slipped anchor in January for the youthful Swan River Colony in Western Australia, I wasn't sorry to leave. I'd never set foot on the southern continent in my entire metalife, so when our captain gave notice of a three-week layover in Fremantle for careening, I decided to spend two of them in the Becher Point wetlands. I engaged an eager-to-please local man named Caleb Warren and his long-suffering mule. Prior to the 1890s Gold Rush, Perth was a township of only a few hundred wooden dwellings, and within an hour Warren and I were making our way on a rough track through wilderness unchanged for millennia. As the rough track turned notional, Caleb Warren turned silent and moody. These days, I'd diagnose the man as bipolar. We walked through scrubby hills, swampy gullies, saltwater creeks, and copses of leaning paperbark trees. I was content. My sketchbook for February 7, 1872, contains drawings of six species of frog, a detailed description of a bandicoot, a botched sketch of a royal spoonbill, and a passable watercolor of Jervoise Bay. Night fell and we camped in a circle of rocks atop a low cliff. I asked my guide if Aborigines were likely to approach our fire. Caleb Warren slapped the butt of his rifle and announced, "Let the bastards try. We'll be ready." Pablo Antay recorded his impressions of the deep breakers and spatter of spray, the droning babel of insect scratches, mammalian barks, and the calls of birds. We ate "bush duff" with blood sausage and beans. My guide drank rum like water, and answered, "Who gives a damn?" to anything I said. Warren was a problem I'd have to fix the following day. I watched the stars and thought of other lives. I don't know how much time passed before I noticed a small mouse skip up Warren's forearm, onto his hand, and up the stick that served as a toasting fork to the greasy lump of sausage impaled there. *I* hadn't hiatused the man. Warren's eyes were open but he didn't reply or stir . . .

. . . as four tall natives with hunting spears slipped into the globe of firelight. A scrawny dog with a stumpy tail sniffed around. I stood up, uncertain whether to run, talk, brandish my knife, or egress. The visitors ignored Caleb Warren, who was still frozen out of time. They were barefoot and wore a mixture of settlers' breeches and shirts, Noongar skin cloaks, and loincloths. One wore a bone through his nose and all were ritually scarred. They were warriors. Whatever the costume, context, or century, one knows. I held up my hands to show I had no weapons, but the men's intentions were unreadable. I was afraid. Egression in those days took me ten or fifteen seconds, much longer than four spearmen needed to end Pablo Antay's peripatetic life, and death by skewering is quick but unpleasant. Then a pale, all skin-and-bone woman moved into the firelight. Her hair was tied back and she wore a shapeless cassock of the type handed out by missionaries faced with large quantities of native skin to cover up. Her age was hard to guess. She walked with a lopsided gait and she inspected me at close range with a critical eye, as if I were a horse she was having second thoughts about buying. "Don't fret. If we want kill, y'be dead hours ago."

"You speak English," I blurted.

"M'father taught me." She spoke to the warriors in what I would soon recognize as Noongar and sat on a rock by the fire. One of them prised the stick out of Caleb Warren's fingers and sniffed the sausage. He took a cautious bite, and another. "Y'guide's a bad-dun." The woman spoke to the fire while addressing me. "He's a plan to fill y'with grog, hit y'head, take y'money, throw y'off that cliff. Yer've more money'n he'll see in two year, see. Big . . ." she searched for the word, ". . . *tempting.* That the right word, issit?"

"Temptation, perhaps."

The woman clicked her tongue. "He's a plan t'tell Swan River whitefellas you go in bush'n never come back no more. Steal y'goods."

I asked her, "How can you know that?"

"Fly out." She touched her forehead and one-handedly mimed a fluttering. "Y'know how. Aye?" She watched my reaction.

I felt a rushing sensation in my chest. "You're . . . psychosoteric?"

She leaned closer to the fire. I saw European angles to her jaw and nose. "Big word, mister. Ain't speak English *boola* time. F'get *boola*. But my soul-spot bright." She tapped her forehead. "You, same. *Boylyada maaman.* Yurra spirit talker too."

I tried to etch every detail onto my memory. The four warriors were rifling through Warren's backpack. The stumpy dog sniffed about. Burning driftwood spat out sparks. Pablo Antay Marinus had happened upon a female Aborigine psychosoteric on the western edge of the Great Southern Continent. She was chewing a sausage now, and belched. "What y'name-it, this . . . pig-meat-stick?"

"A sausage."

"Sausage." She tasted the word. "Mick Little made sausages."

The statement begged the question: "Who's Mick Little?"

"This body's father. Esther Little's father. Mick Little kill pigs, make sausages, but he die." She mimed coughing and held out her hand. "Blood. Like this."

"Your body-father died of tuberculosis? Consumption?"

"That'sitsname it is, aye. Then men sell farm, Esther's mother, a Noongar woman, she go back in bush. She takes Esther. Esther die, and I go in her body." She frowned, rocking to and fro on her heels.

After a little time, I spoke up. "This body's name is Pablo Antay Marinus. But my true name is Marinus. Call me Marinus. Do you have a true name?"

She warmed her hands at the fire. "My Noongar name's Moombaki, but I've a longer name what I ain't tellin'."

Now I knew how Xi Lo and Holokai had felt upon entering the Koskov family's drawing room in Saint Petersburg, fifty years earlier. Quite possibly this Atemporal Sojourner would want nothing to do with Horology, nor care that there were others like her, scattered thinly throughout the world, but I felt heartened that we were a species one individual less endangered than fifteen minutes before. I asked my visitor my next question in subspeech: *So do I call you Esther or Moombaki?* Time passed and no answer came. The fire shifted its burning bones, and sparks spiraled up as the warriors spoke to one another in quiet voices. Just as I concluded that she wasn't telepathic, she subreplied: *You a wadjela, a whitefella, so t'you, I'm Esther. If yurra Noongar, then I'm Moombaki.*

"This is my thirty-sixth body," I told Esther. "You?"

Esther killed questions she found irrelevant by ignoring them, and she did it now. So I subasked, *When did you first come to this land? To Australia?*

She patted her dog: *I'm always here.*

A Sojourner has that luxury. *You never left Australia?*

She told me, "Aye. I stay on Noongar land."

I envied her. For a Returnee like myself, each resurrection is a lottery of longitudes, latitudes, and demography. We die, wake up as children forty-nine days later, often on another landmass. Pablo Antay tried to imagine an entire metalife in one place as a Sojourner, migrating out of one old or dying body into a young and healthy one, but never severing one's ties to a clan and its territory. "How did you find me?"

Esther gave the last lump of sausage to the dog. "The bush talks dunnit? We listen."

I noticed the four warriors taking the saddlebags from the mule. "Are you stealing my baggage?"

The half-Aborigine rose. *We carry y'bags. To our camp. You gunna come?*

I looked at Caleb Warren and subworried, *Something'll eat him, if we leave him here.* "Or he might just catch fire, or melt."

Esther inspected her hand. *Soon, he wake, his head like bees. He think he kill you already.*

WE WALKED MOST of the night to an outcrop whose Noongar name meant "Five Fingers" in English, not far from present-day Armadale. This was home for the warriors' clan, and the season's residence for Esther. When day broke, I tried to make myself as useful to my hosts as I could, but although I'd been resurrected as Itsekiri, Kawésqar, and Gurage tribespeople in earlier lives, I'd grown pampered as Lucas Marinus, Klara Koskov, and Pablo Antay, and two centuries had passed since I had hunted and foraged for dinner. I was of more use in helping the women to cure kangaroo hides, setting a broken arm, and gathering bush honey. I also busied myself gratifying my curiosity as a proto-anthropologist: My journals describe the burning of scrubland to smoke out game; totemic animals; a visit by five men from the south to trade red ocher for prized burdun wood; and a paternity suit, settled by Esther, who ingressed into a fetus to perform a psychosoteric DNA test. Esther's skingroup showed me the pity owed to a simpleminded uncle, a distrust of my Europeanness, and respect for a Boylyada maaman colleague of Moombaki's. The children were the least reserved. One boy named Kinta used to borrow my jacket and hat and strut about, and they all liked showing off their bushcraft skills to the clumsy pale visitor. My attempts to speak Noongar caused endless amusement, but with the tribe's help Pablo Antay compiled the best extant glossary of the Noongar language.

Moombaki, I learned, was not thought of as a god but a spirit guardian, a collective memory, a healer, a weapon of last resort, and a sort of assize judge. She moved from skin-group to skin-group at the start of each of the six Noongar seasons, helping each family and clan as best she could, and circulating the idea that violent resistance to the Europeans would result in more dead Noongar. Some called her a traitor, she told me, but by the 1870s her logic was demonstrable. The Europeans were too many, their appetites too voracious, their morality too fickle, and their rifles too accurate. The Noongar's slim hope of survival lay in adaptation, and if this altered what it meant to be Noongar, what choice was there? Without knowledge of the Ship People's minds, however, even this slim hope was doomed, and so Moombaki had chosen a ten-year-old half-caste girl for her present sojourn. Similarly, she had invited Pablo Antay to Five Fingers with a view to learning about the world and its peoples.

By night, then, Esther and I sat across the fire from each other at the mouth of her small cave and subspoke about empires, their ascents and falls; about cities, shipbuilding, industry; slavery, the dismemberment of Africa, the genocide of the natives of Van Diemen's Land; farming, husbandry, factories, telegraphs, newspapers, printing, mathematics, philosophy, law, and money and a hundred other topics. I felt like Lucas Marinus once did, lecturing in the houses of the Nagasaki scholars. I talked about who the settlers landing at Fremantle were, why they had voyaged here, and what they believed, desired, and feared. I tried to explain religion, too, but the Whadjuk Noongar had a distrust of priests after men had distributed blankets "from Jesus" to several clans up the Swan River, only for the recipients to die a few days later of what sounded like smallpox.

In most other subject areas, however, Esther was the teacher. Her metaage became apparent one night when she recited the names of all her previous hosts, and I lined up one pebble per name. There were 207 pebbles. Moombaki sojourned into new hosts when they were about ten and stayed until death, which implied a metalife stretching back approximately seven millennia. This was twice as old as Xi Lo, the oldest Atemporal known to Horology, who at twenty-five centuries was a stripling compared to Esther, whose soul predated Rome, Troy, Egypt, Peking, Nineveh, and Ur. She taught me some of her invocations, and I identified within them various tributaries to the Deep Stream from long before the Schism. On some nights we transversed together, and Esther enfolded my soul in hers so I could spirit-walk much further and faster than I was otherwise able. When she scansioned me I felt like a third-rate poet showing his doggerel to a Shakespeare. When I scansioned her, I felt like a minnow tipped from a jar into a deep inland sea.

TWENTY DAYS AFTER my arrival, I said my goodbyes and set out with Esther toward the Swan River valley accompanied by the four warriors who had escorted us from Jervoise Bay. We headed north from Five Fingers, climbing into the Perth Hills. My guides knew the wooded, trackless slopes as unerringly as Pablo Antay knew the thoroughfares and alleys of Buenos Aires. We camped in a dry creek near a water hole, and after a supper of yam, berries, and duck meat, Pablo Antay fell into steep-sided, slippery sleep. I slept until Esther subwoke me, which is a disorienting reveille. It was still dark, but a predawn wind was stirring the slanting trees into near speech. Esther was outlined against a banksia bush. Blearily, I subasked, *All well?*

Esther subreplied, *Follow.* We walked through a stretch of night-time forest of rustling she-oaks, up a sandstone ridge that cleared the treeline before trifurcating into three "prongs." Each of these ridges was only a few feet wide, but a hundred paces long, and with steep drops on either side I proceeded with great caution. Esther told me this place was called, descriptively, Emu's Claw, and led me along the central "toe." It ended at a lookout point over the Swan River. The looping watercourse was burnished pewter by starlight, and the land was a crumpled patchwork of light and dark blacks. A day's walk to the west, streaks of surf delineated the ocean, and I guessed that a rough clutter on the north bank of the river was Perth.

Esther sat, so I sat too. A currawong sang throaty gargle phrases in a peppermint tree. *I'm gunna teach y'm'true name.*

You told me, I subreplied, *it would take a day to learn.*

Aye, it's true, but I'm gunna speak it inside y'head, Marinus.

I hesitated. *This is a gift I'll struggle to repay. My true name is only one word long, and you already know that.*

"Ain't y'fault yurra savage," she said. "Shurrup now. Open up."

Esther's soul ingressed and inscribed her long, long, true name onto my memory. Moombaki's name had grown with the tens, hundreds, and thousands of years since Moombaki's mother-birth at the Five Fingers, back when it was known as Two Hands. While much of her true name lay beyond my knowledge of the Noongar language, as the minutes passed I understood that her name was also a history of her people, a sort of Bayeux Tapestry that bound myth with loves, births, deaths; hunts, battles, journeys; droughts, fires, storms; and the names of every host within whose body Moombaki had sojourned. With the word *Esther* her name ended. My visitor egressed and I opened my eyes to find slanted sunlight flaming the canopy below us sharp green, torching the scrub dark gold and reddening the whale-rib clouds, and countless thousands of birds, singing, shrieking, yammering. "Not a bad name," I said, already feeling the ache of loss.

A marri tree bled gum and starry blooms. *Corymbia calophylla.*

"Come back anytime," she said, "or y'kin y'spoke of."

"I will," I promised, "but my face will have changed."

"World's changin'," she said. "Even here. Can't stop it."

"How'll we find you, Esther? Me, or Xi Lo, or Holokai?"

Camp here. This place. Emu's Claw. I'll know. The Land'll tell.

I wasn't surprised to find that she'd gone back. So I set off for Perth, where a dishonorable man called Caleb Warren would soon suffer the fright of his life.

I FINISH FILLING in twenty-seven across—VERTIGO—before looking up to find Iris Marinus-Fenby mirrored in Holly Sykes's sunglasses. Today's head-wrap is lilac. I guess her hair only partly recovered from the chemo five years ago. Holly's indigo dress extends from the buttoned throat to her ankles. "I'm a world-class ignorer of attention-seekers," Holly slaps the envelope on the table, "but this is so crass, so intrusive, so bizarre, it's off the scale. So you win. I'm here. I walked down Broadway, and at every crossing I thought, *Why give even one minute to this head-meddling nutso?* I don't know how often I almost turned back."

I ask, "Why didn't you?"

"'Cause I need to know: If Hugo Lamb wishes to contact me, why not do it like everyone else and send an email via my agent? Why send *you* and this"—she knocks on the envelope—"this tampered-with photo? Does he think it'll impress me? Reignite old flames? 'Cause if he does he's in for a heck of a disappointment."

"Why not sit down and order lunch while I explain?"

"I don't think so. I only eat lunch with friends."

"Coffee, then? One drinks coffee with anyone."

With ill grace, Holly accedes. I mime a cup and mouth "Coffee" at Nestor, who makes a coming-right-up face. "First," I tell Holly, "Hugo Lamb knows nothing about this. We hope. He's gone by the name of Marcus Anyder for many years, incidentally."

"So if Hugo Lamb hasn't sent you, how can you possibly know that we met years ago in an obscure Swiss ski resort?"

"One of us resides in the Dark Internet. Overhearing things is what he does for a living, as it were."

"And you. Are you still a Chinese doctor who died in 1984? Or are you alive and female today?"

"I am all those four." I put a business card on the table. "Dr. Iris Marinus-Fenby. A clinical psychiatrist based in Toronto, though I consult further afield. And, yes, until 1984 I was Yu Leon Marinus."

Holly removes her sunglasses, scrutinizes the card, and me, with distaste. "I see I have to spell this out, so here goes: I haven't seen Hugo Lamb since New Year's Day 1992, when he was in his early twenties, yeah? He'll be in his midfifties by now. Like me. Now, the manipulator of this image shows Hugo Lamb *still* looking twenty-five years old, give or take, with the Helix Towers—built in 2018—and iShades hooked over his Qatar 2022 World Cup T-shirt. And the car. Cars didn't look like that in the nineties. I was there. This photo has been buggered about with. Two questions for you: 'Why bother?' and 'Who bothered?' "

A kid at the next table's playing a 3D app: A kangaroo's bouncing up a scrolling series of platforms. It's off-putting. "The photo was taken last July," I tell Holly. "It has not been altered."

"So . . . Hugo Lamb found the fountain of eternal youth?"

A young waiter with Nestor's heavyweight nose walks by with a T-bone steak sizzling on a hot plate. "Not a fountain, no. A place and a process. Hugo Lamb became an Anchorite of the Chapel of the Blind Cathar in 1992. Since his induction, he hasn't aged."

Holly takes this in and puffs out her cheeks. "Well, great. That's that cleared up. My one-night fling is now . . . let's say it, 'immortal.' "

"Immortal with terms and conditions," I equivocate. "Immortal only in the sense that he doesn't age."

Holly's exasperated. "And nobody's noticed, of course. Or does his family put it down to moisturizer and quinoa salad?"

"His family believe he drowned in a scuba-diving accident off Rabaul, near New Guinea, in 1996. Go ahead, call them." I give Holly a card with the Lambs' London number on it. "Or just shirabu one of his brothers, Alex or Nigel, and ask them."

Holly stares. "Hugo Lamb faked his own death?"

I sip my tap water. It's passed through many kidneys. "His new Anchorite friends arranged it. Obtaining a death certificate without a dead body is irksome, but they have years of experience."

"Stop talking as if I believe you. Anyway, 'Anchorites'? That's something . . . medieval, isn't it?"

I nod. "An Anchorite was a girl who lived like a hermit in a cell, but in the wall of a church. A living human sacrifice, in a way."

Nestor drifts up. "One coffee. Say, is your friend hungry?"

"No, thank you," says Holly. "I . . . I've got no appetite."

"Come on," I urge her, "you just walked from Columbus Circle."

"I'll bring a menu," says Nestor. "You a veggie, like your friend?"

"She's not my friend," Holly fires back. "I mean, we just met."

"Friend or not," says the restaurateur, "a body's got to eat."

"I'll be leaving soon," declares Holly. "I have to rush."

"Rush, rush, rush." Nestor's nasal hair streams in and out like seaweed. "Too busy to eat, too busy to breathe." He turns away and turns back. "What's next? Too busy to live?" Nestor's gone.

Holly hisses: "Now you made me piss off an elderly Greek."

"Order his moussaka, then. In my medical view, you don't eat—"

"Since you've raised the subject of medical matters, 'Dr. Fenby,' I knew the name was familiar. I checked with Tom Ballantyne, my old GP. You came to my house in Rye when I was very nearly dying of cancer. I could have your medical license revoked."

"If I was guilty of any malpractice, I would revoke it myself."

She looks both outraged and baffled. "Why were you in my home?"

"Advising Tom Ballantyne. I was involved in trials of ADC-based drugs in Toronto, and Tom and I both thought your gall-bladder cancer might respond positively. It did."

"You said you're a psychiatrist, not an oncologist."

"I'm a psychiatrist who owns a number of other hats."

"So you're claiming that I owe you my life now, are you?"

"Not at all. Or only partly. Cancer recovery is a holistic process, and while the ADCs contributed to your cancer's remission, they weren't the only curative agent, I suspect."

"So . . . you got to know Tom Ballantyne *before* my diagnosis? Or . . . or . . . just how long have you been watching my life?"

"On and off, since your mother brought you into the consulting room in Gravesend Hospital in 1976."

"Can you hear yourself? And it's your actual job to *cure* people of psychoses and delusions? Now for the last time, why did you send me a digitally jiggled image of a *very* brief, *very* ex-boyfriend?"

"I want you to consider that the clause of life which reads 'What lives must one day die' can, in rare instances, be renegotiated."

All the voices in the Santorini Café, all the gossiping, joking, cajoling, flirting, complaining, become, in my ears, a sonic waterfall.

Holly asks, "Dr. Fenby, are you a Scientologist?"

I try not to smile. "To believers in L. Ron Hubbard and the galactic Emperor Xenu, psychiatrists belong in septic tanks."

"Immortality"—she lowers her voice—"isn't—bloody—real."

"But Atemporality, with terms and conditions applied, is."

Holly looks around, and back. "This is deranged."

"People said that about you after *The Radio People*."

"If I could unwrite that wretched book, I would. Anyway, I don't hear those voices any longer. Not since Crispin died. Not that that's any of your goddamn business."

"Precognition comes and goes," I snowplow up some spilled sugar granules with my little finger, "mysteriously, like allergies or warts."

"The big mystery to me is why I'm still sitting here."

"Guess the name of Hugo Lamb's mentor in the dark arts."

"Sauron. Lord Voldemort. John Dee. Louis Cypher. Who?"

"An old friend of yours. Immaculée Constantin."

Holly rubs at a smear of lipstick on her coffee cup. "I never knew her first name. She's only referred to as 'Miss Constantin' in the book. And in my head. So why are you inventing her first name?"

"I didn't. It *is* her given name. Hugo Lamb's one of her ablest pupils. He's a superb groomer, and a formidable psychosoteric after only three decades following the Shaded Way."

"Dr. Iris Marinus-Fenby, what bloody planet are you *on*?"

"The same one as you. Hugo Lamb now sources prey, just as Miss Constantin sourced you. And if she hadn't scared you into reporting her so that Yu Leon Marinus was informed about and inoculated you, she would have abducted you and not Jacko."

Chatter and clinking cutlery is loud and all around us.

Behind us, a girl is dumping her boyfriend in Egyptian Arabic.

"Now, I"—Holly pinches the bridge of her nose—"want to hit you. *Really* hard. What *are* you? Some sort of head-screwing, life-trespassing, fantasy-peddling . . . I—I—I have no words for you."

"We're truly sorry for the intrusion, Ms. Sykes. If there was any alternative at all, we wouldn't be sitting here."

" 'We' being who, exactly?"

My back straightens a little. "We are Horology."

Holly heaves a long, long sigh, meaning, *Where do I start?*

"Please." I place a green key by her saucer. "Take this."

She stares at it, then me. "What is it? And why would I?"

A couple of zombie-eyed junior doctors troop by, talking medical prognoses. "This key opens the door to the answers and proof you deserve and need. Once inside, go up the stairs to the roof garden. You'll find me there with a friend or two."

She finishes her coffee. "My flight home leaves at three P.M. to-morrow. I'll be on it, heading home. Keep your key."

"Holly," I say gently, "I *know* you've met countless crazies thanks to *The Radio People*. I *know* the Jacko bait has been dangled at you before. But *please*. Take this key. Just in case I'm the real thing. It's a thousand to one, I know, but I might be. Throw it away at the airport, by all means, but for now, take it. Where's the harm?"

She holds my gaze for a few seconds, then pushes her empty cup and saucer away, stands, swipes up the key, and puts it into her handbag. She puts two dollars on the photo of Hugo Lamb. "That's so I owe you nothing," she mutters. "Don't call me 'Holly.' Good-bye."

I N THE SILT OF DREAMS, ill-wishers were cutting off my exits until the one way out was up. I can't remember which self I am until I find my nightlight's 05:09 imprinted on the overheated darkness. 119A. More than a mile away across Central Park on the ninth floor of the Empire Hotel, Arkady is preparing to dreamseed Holly Sykes with Ōshima standing guard. I pray he won't be needed. Staying here sticks in my craw, but if I went over to the Empire to help, I could end up triggering the very attack I so fear. Minutes limp by as I trawl New York's nighttime tinnitus for meaning . . .

Pointless. I switch on my reading lamp, and gaze around my room. The Vietnamese urn, the scroll of the monkey regarding its own reflection, Lucas Marinus's harpsichord from Nagasaki obtained by Xi Lo as a gift after a strenuous and improbable hunt . . . I turn to my place in Lucretius's *De Rerum Natura,* but my thoughts, if not my soul, are still a mile or two to the west. This never-ending, accursed War. On my weakest days, I wonder why we Atemporals of Horology, who inherit resurrection as birthright, who possess what the Anchorites kill to obtain a twisted variation of, why don't we just walk away from it? Why do we risk everything for strangers who'll never know what we've done, win or lose? I ask the monkey troubled by its mirrored self: "Why?"

THE HOLY SPIRIT entered Oscar Gomez during last Sunday's service at his Pentecostal church in Vancouver as the congregation recited Psalm 139. He described it to my friend Adnan Buyoya a few hours later as "knowing what lay in the hearts of his brothers and sisters in

Christ, what sins they had yet to repent or to atone for." Gomez's conviction that God had bestowed this gift upon him was unshakable, and he was setting about God's work without delay. He took the SkyTrain to Metropolis, a large suburban shopping mall in the city, and started preaching at the main entrance. Christian street preachers in secular cities are more ignored or mocked than they are listened to, but soon a crowd clotted around the short, earnest Mexican Canadian. Total strangers at Metropolis were baited, often to their astonishment, by Gomez's startling specificity. One man, for example, was exhorted by Gomez to confess to fathering his sister-in-law Bethany's baby. A hairdresser was begged to return the four thousand dollars she had stolen from her employer at the Curl Up and Dye hair salon. Gomez told a college dropout called Jed that the cannabis he was growing in his frail grandmother's garden shed was disfiguring his life and could only end in a custodial sentence. Some blanched, their jaws dropping, and fled. Some angrily accused Gomez of hacking into their slates or working for the NSA, to which he replied, "The Lord has all our lives under surveillance." Some began to weep, and ask for forgiveness. By the time the mall security guys arrived to escort Gomez from the premises, several dozen slates were filming the proceedings and a protective cordon of onlookers was surrounding the "Seer of Washington Street." The city cops were summoned. YouTube uploads caught Gomez asking one of his arresters to confess to stamping on the head of an Eritrean immigrant—named—three nights before, while beseeching the other officer to seek counseling for his child pornography addiction, naming both the officer's log-in and the Russian website. We can only guess at the conversation in the squad car, but en route to the precinct HQ, the destination was changed to Coupland Heights Psychiatric Hospital.

"Swear to God, Iris," Adnan emailed me that evening, "I walked into the interview room and my first thought was, *A seer? This guy looks straighter than my accountant.* Straightaway—as if I'd spoken out loud—Oscar Gomez told me, "My father was an accountant, Dr. Buyoya, so maybe I get my straightness from him." How do you conduct an assessment after that? I thought (or hoped?) I *had* spoken my initial thought aloud, but soon Gomez was referring to those events from my boyhood in Rwanda that I'd only ever told you and my own analyst about during training." In Adnan's second email, sent two hours later, patients at Coupland Heights were worshiping the new inmate as a god. "It's like 'The Voorman Problem,'" Adnan said, referring to a Crispin Hershey novella we both admired. "I know what my grandparents would call Gomez in Yoruba, but there's no way to talk about witchcraft in English and keep my job. Please, Iris. Can you help?"

VENI, VIDI, NON vici. By the time I'd located my car in the vast, rainy parking lot, I was drenched, and I got a run in my tights as I clambered in. I was also hammered by anger, despair, and a sense of impotence. I'd failed. My device warbled as a message arrived:

zlate marinus zlate. will mrs gomez believe the truth?

Answers and implications slid into place, like a self-solving Rubik's Cube. Topmost was the most obvious, that my device had been hacked by a Carnivore, a gloating Anchorite, who might be incautious and inexperienced enough to let his identity slip. I messaged a half-bluff:

hugo lamb buried his conscience but it never quite died

There was a chance that the "Saint Mark" who had promised to accompany Oscar Gomez up Jacob's Ladder was "Marcus Anyder," the Anchorite name of Hugo Lamb. My device sat in my clammy hand for one minute, two, three. Just as I gave up, a message arrived.

consciences r 4 bone clocks marinus, u r 1 beaten woman

My bluff had worked, unless I was being double-bluffed back. But, no, a carnivorous psychodecanter acting alone wouldn't pass up the chance to rub my nose in my wrong guess, and the "beaten woman" phrase matched L'Ohkna's profile of Hugo Lamb's misogyny. As I considered how best to make use of this contact, surely unsanctioned by Constantin or Pfenninger, a third message arrived:

c yr future marinus c yr rearview mirror

Instinctively, I ducked and tilted the rearview mirror until I could see through the rear window. The glass was beaded with rain. I switched on the car's battery, and clicked on the rear wiper, to remove the—

The passenger-side window exploded into a thousand tiny hailstones, and the mirror above my head was a brittle supernova of plastic and glass. One shard of plastic shrapnel, the size and shape of a fingernail clipping, lodged itself in my cheek.

I crouched, afraid. A logical portion of my mind was arguing that if the marksman had intended to kill me I would now be staring across the Dusk. But I stayed down for several minutes longer. Atemporality neutralizes death's poison, but it doesn't defang death, and old habits of survival linger on, even in us.

THAT IS WHY we prosecute the War, I remind myself in 119A, four days later. The window in my room turns under-ice gray. We bother because of Oscar Gomez, Oscar Gomez's wife, and his three children. Because nobody else would believe in the animacides committed by a syndicate of soul thieves like the Anchorites or by "freelancers" hunting alone. Because if we spent our metalives amassing the wealth of empires and getting stoned on the opiates of wealth and power, knowing what we know yet doing nothing about it, we would be complicit in the psychoslaughter of the innocents.

My device buzzes. It's Ōshima's tone. I fumble the thing like a panicky contestant, drop it, retrieve it, and read:

Done. No incidents.
Arkady returning now.
Will shadow Slim Hope.

I fill my lungs with oxygen and blessed relief. The Second Mission is one step closer. Daylight now leaks in around the window. 119A's ancient plumbing shudders and clanks. I hear feet, a toilet cistern, and cupboard doors. Two or three rooms away, Sadaqat is up.

"SAGE, ROSEMARY, THYME . . ." Sadaqat, our warden, minder, and would-be traitor, plucks a weed from the raised beds. "I planted parsley too, so we could dine on 'Scarborough Fair' but late frost killed it. Some herbs are feebler than others. I'll try again. Parsley's rich in iron. Here I planted the onions and leeks, tough customers, and I have high hopes for the rhubarb. Do you remember, Doctor, we grew rhubarb at Dawkins Hospital?"

"I remember the pies," I tell him.

We're speaking quietly. Despite the fine-sieved rain and his busy night, Arkady, my fellow Horologist, is practicing Tai Chi among the myrtle and witch hazel across the rooftop courtyard. "This will be a strawberry patch," Sadaqat points, "and the three fruiting cherry trees I'll fertilize with the tip of a paintbrush, due to a scarcity of bees here in the East Side. Look! A red cardinal, on the momiji maple. I bought a book about birds, so I know. Those birds on the cloister roof, those are mourning doves. We have starlings nesting under the eaves, up there. They keep me busy with the scrubbing brush, but their droppings make a nutritious fertilizer, so I don't complain. Here we have the fragrant quarter. Wintersweet, waxflower, and these thorny sticks will become scented roses. The trellis is for honeysuckle and jasmine."

I notice that Sadaqat's up-and-down British-Pakistani accent is flattening out. "You've worked magic up here, truly."

Our warden purrs. "Plants want to grow. Just let them."

"We should have thought of a garden up here decades ago."

"You are too busy saving souls to think of such things, Doctor. The roof had to be reinforced, which was a challenge . . ."

Watch out, subwarns Arkady, *or he'll tell you about load-bearing walls and girders until you lose the will to live.*

". . . but I hired a Polish engineer who proposed a load-bearing—"

"It's an oasis of calm," I interrupt, "that we'll cherish for years."

"For centuries," says Sadaqat, brushing droplets of mist off his vigorous but graying hair, "for you Horologists."

"Let's hope so." Through an ornate wrought-iron screen in the cloister wall, we look down on the street four floors below. Cars crawl along and honk in vain. Umbrellas overtake them, parting for joggers running contraflow. Level with us on the much taller building across the road, an old woman with a neck brace waters the marigolds in her window boxes. New York's skyscrapers vanish in cloud at about the thirtieth storey. If King Kong were up on the Empire State today, no one at our lowly altitude would believe the truth.

"Mr. Arkady's Tai Chi," Sadaqat murmurs, "reminds me of your magickings. How your hands draw on air, you know?" We watch him. Arkady may be gangly, Hungarian, and ponytailed, but the Vietnamese martial-arts master of his last self is still discernible, somehow.

I ask my former patient, "Are you still content with life here?"

Sadaqat is alarmed. "Yes! If I've done anything wrong . . ."

"No. Not at *all.* I just worry, sometimes, that we're depriving you of friends, a partner, family . . . The trappings of normal life."

Sadaqat removes his glasses and wipes them on his corduroy shirt. "Horology is my family. Partner? I am forty-five. I prefer to go to bed with *The Daily Show* on my slate, or a Lee Child novel and a cup of chamomile tea. Normal life?" He sniffs. "I have your cause, a library to explore, a garden to tend, and my poetry is becoming a little less awful. I swear, Doctor, every day when I shave I tell myself in the mirror, 'Sadaqat Dastaani, you are the luckiest schizophrenic, middle-aged, balding, British Pakistani in all Manhattan."

"If you ever," I strive to sound casual, "think differently . . ."

"No, Dr. Marinus. My wagon is hitched to Horology's."

Careful, Arkady subwarns me, *or he'll smell a guilty rat.*

I can't quite let it go. "The Second Mission, Sadaqat. We can't guarantee anyone's safety. Not yours, not ours."

"If you want me to go from 119A, Doctor, use your magickery-pokery because I won't jump ship of my own accord. The Anchorites prey on the psychiatrically vulnerable, yes? If I'd had the correct type of"—Sadaqat taps his head—"soul, they might have taken me, yes? So. Horology's War is my War. Yes, I am only a pawn, but a game of chess may hinge upon the conduct of a single pawn."

Marinus, our guest's arriving, Arkady subinforms me.

With a bruised conscience I tell Sadaqat, "You win."

Our warden smiles. "I am glad, Doctor."

"Our guest has arrived." We walk back to the ironwork to look down on Holly in her Jamaican head-wrap. Across the road, Ōshima shows his outline in the room we have above the violin maker's: *I'll watch the street,* he subsuggests, *in case any interested parties pass by.* Holly approaches the door with the green key I gave her yesterday at the Santorini Café. The Englishwoman's having a very strange morning. On a wand of willow very near my shoulder, a puffed-up red-winged blackbird performs a loop of arpeggios.

"Who's a handsome devil, then?" whispers Sadaqat.

I SPEAK FIRST. "We've been expecting you, Ms. Sykes. As they say."

"Welcome to 119A." Arkady's voice has a teenage croaky waver.

"You're safe, Ms. Sykes," says Sadaqat. "Don't be afraid."

Holly is flushed after her climb, but upon seeing Arkady her eyes widen: "It *is* you . . . you . . . *you* . . . *isn't* it?"

"Yes, I have some explaining to do," agrees Arkady.

Down in an alley, a dog is barking. Holly's trembling. "I *dreamt* you. This morning! You—you're the same. How did you *do* that?"

"The acne, right?" Arkady brushes his cheek. "Unforgettable."

"My dream! You were at my desk, in my room, in my hotel . . ."

"Writing this address on the jotter." Arkady picks up the sequence. "Then I asked you to bring Marinus's green key here and go in. I said, 'See you in two hours.' And here we are."

Holly looks at me, at Arkady, at Sadaqat, at me.

"Dreamseeding," I comment, "is one of Arkaday's métiers."

"My range is lousy," says my colleague, showing off his modesty. "My room was across the corridor from yours, Ms. Sykes, so I didn't have far to transverse. Then, when my soul was back in my body, I hurried back here. In a taxi. Dreamseeding of civilians runs counter to our Codex, but you needed some proof of the wild claims made by Marinus the other day, and we're at war, so I'm afraid we dreamseeded you anyway. Forgive us. Please."

Holly's at a nervous loss. "Who *are* you?"

"Me? Arkady Thaly, as of this self. Hi."

Up in the low cloud an airplane drags itself along.

"This is our warden," I turn to Sadaqat, "Mr. Dastaani."

"Oh, I'm just a glorified dogsbody, really," says Sadaqat, "and normal, like you—well, 'normal,' eh? Call me Sadaqat. It's said 'Sa-*dar*-cutt' with the stress on the 'dar.' Think of me as an Afpak Alfred." Holly looks none the wiser. "Alfred? Batman's butler. I take care of 119A when my employers are away. I cook. You're vegetarian, I am told? So are the Horologists. It's the"—he twirls his finger in the air—"body-and-soul thing. Who's hungry? I've mastered eggs Benedict with smoked tofu, a fine breakfast for a disorienting morning. Could I tempt you?"

119A'S FIRST-FLOOR GALLERY is dominated by an elliptical table of walnut wood that was here when Xi Lo bought the house in the 1890s. The chairs are mismatched, from various eras since. Pearly light enters through the three arched windows. The paintings on the long walls were gifts to Xi Lo or Holokai from the artists: a blushing desert dawn by Georgia O'Keeffe, A. Y. Jackson's view of Port Radium, Diego Quispe Tito's *Sunset over the Bridge of San Luis Rey,* and Faith Nulander's *Hooker and John in Marble Cemetery.*

At one end is Agnello Bronzino's *Venus, Cupid, Folly, and Time*. It is worth more than the building and its neighbors combined. "I know this one," says Holly, staring at the Bronzino. "The original's in the National Gallery, in London. I used to go and see it in my lunchbreak, when I worked at the homeless center at St. Martin in the Fields."

"Yes," I say. Holly doesn't need a story about how the National's copy and the original got switched in Vienna in 1860. Anyway, she's moved on to the Bronzino's unworthy companion, *Self Portrait of Yu Leon Marinus, 1969*. Holly recognizes the face and turns to me accusingly. I nod, sheepishly. "Absurd, of course, and sheer arrogance to hang it in this company, but Xi Lo, our founder, insisted. We keep it there for his sake."

Sadaqat enters from the door by the astrolabe, bringing our drinks on a tray. Nobody has the stomach for eggs Benedict. He asks, "Now, where is everyone sitting?" Holly chooses the gondola chair at the end, nearest the way out. Sadaqat asks our guest, "Irish Breakfast blend, Ms. Sykes? Your mother's Irish, I believe."

"She was, yes," says Holly. "That's grand, thanks."

Sadaqat places a matching willow-pattern teapot and teacup, a jug of milk, and a bowl of sugar on a mat. My green tea is brewing in a black iron teapot owned by Choudary Marinus, two selves ago. Arkady drinks coffee from a bowl. Sadaqat puts a lit candle in a stained-glass cup as a centerpiece. "To brighten the place up. It can get a little tomblike in here."

In a parallel universe the man's a design fascist, subsays Arkady.

"Just what we need, Sadaqat," I say. He leaves, pleased.

Holly folds her arms. "You'd better begin. I'm too . . ."

"We've invited you here this morning," I say, "to learn about us and our cosmology. About Atemporals and psychosoterics."

This sounds like a business seminar, Marinus, subsays Arkady.

"Hold on," says Holly. "You lost me at 'Atemporals.' "

"Prick us, we bleed," says Arkady, cupping his coffee bowl, "tickle us, we laugh, poison us, we die, but *after* we die, we come back. Marinus here has gone through this—thirty-nine lives, is it?"

"Forty, if we include poor Heidi Cross at her bungalow by the Isle of Sheppey." I notice Holly watching me for signs of a second head or a maniacal cackle.

"I'm still a newbie," says Arkady, "on my fifth self. Dying still *really* freaks me out, in the Dusk, looking over the Dunes . . ."

"What dusk?" asks Holly. "What dunes?"

"*The* Dusk," Arkady says, "between life and death. We see it from the High Ridge. It's a beautiful, fearsome sight. All the souls, the pale lights, crossing over, blown by the Seaward Wind to the Last Sea. Which, of course, isn't really a sea at all, but—"

"Wait wait wait." Holly leans forwards. "You're saying you've died? That you've seen all this yourselves?"

Arkady drinks from his coffee bowl, then wipes his lips. "Yes, Ms. Sykes, to both your questions. But the Landward Wind blows our souls back, like it or not. Back over the High Ridge, back into the Light of Day, and then we hear a noise like . . . a town being dropped, and everything in it smashing to bits." Arkady asks me, "Fair description?"

"It'll do. Then we wake up in a new body, a child's, usually in need of urgent repair, just vacated by its previous owner."

"At the café," Holly turns to me, "you said that Hugo Lamb's lot, the Anchorites, are immortal 'with terms and conditions.' Are you and they the same?"

"No. We live in this spiral of resurrections involuntarily. We don't know how, or why us. We never sought it. Our first selves died in one of the usual ways, we saw the Dusk as Arkady just described, then forty-nine days later we came back."

"From then on," Arkady unthreads and rethreads his ponytail, "we're stuck on repeat. Our second body grew, matured, died; *bam,* we're back in the Dusk; then, *whoosh,* forty-nine days later, we're waking up back on earth—in a body of the opposite gender, just to well and truly screw your head up."

Swearing won't make you more credible, I subreprimand him. "What matters," I tell Holly, "is that no one pays for our atemporality. Its cost we alone pay. Our phylum, if you will, is herbivorous."

From the street below we hear the screech of brakes.

"So," asks Holly, "the Anchorites are all carnivores?"

"Every last one." Arkady runs his finger round his bowl.

Holly rubs her temples. "Are we talking . . . vampires?"

Arkady groans. "Oh, the V-word! Here it comes again."

"Carnivores are only metaphorically vampiric," I tell Holly. "They look as normal, or as abnormal, as any other subset of the population—plumbers, bankers, diabetics. More's the pity they don't all look like David Lynch villains. Our work would be easier by far." I breathe in the bitter green-tea steam and anticipate Holly's next question. "They feed on souls, Ms. Sykes. Carnivores decant souls, which means abducting people, ideally children," I hold her freshly unsettled gaze as she thinks about Jacko, "which means killing them, I'm afraid."

"Which is not nice," says Arkady. "So Marinus, me, and a few other unthanked individuals—Atemporals for the most part, with some mortal collaborators—make it our business to . . . take them down. Individual Carnivores rarely give us that much bother—they tend to think they're the only ones, and operate as carelessly as shoplifters who refuse to believe in store detectives. The problems begin—our War started—when they hunt in a pack."

"Which is why we're here, Ms. Sykes," I sip my tea, "because of one particular pack. 'The Anchorites of the Chapel of the Dusk of the Blind Cathar of the Thomasite Order of Sidelhorn Pass."

"Too long for business cards." Arkady interlaces his fingers, inverts his hands, and lifts his arms. "Just 'Anchorites,' to friends."

"The Sidelhorn's a mountain," says Holly. "In Switzerland."

"Quite a climb it is, too," I remark. "Sidelhorn also lends its name to a pass in northern Italy, a road that was old even when Roman legions used it. A Thomasite monastery served as a hostelry on the pass, on the Swiss Valais side, from the ninth century to the last year of the eighteenth. There, in the 1210s, a figure known as the Blind Cathar ontologized into being a conduit into the Dusk."

Holly scans this blast of history. "The Dusk that lies between . . ."

"Life and death," says Arkady. "Good, you're listening."

Holly asks, "What's a Cathar?"

"The Cathars were twelfth- and thirteenth-century heretics," I say, "in Languedoc. They preached that the world was created not by God but the devil, that matter was evil, that Jesus, as a man, was therefore not the Son of God. The papacy did not approve. In 1198 Pope Innocent III proposed a landgrab that became known as the Albigensian Crusade. The King of France was otherwise engaged, but he gave barons from the north of France his blessing to ride south, kill Cathars, confiscate their lands, and subdue a disloyal region for the French Crown. Heresy is fissiparous, however. What was smashed, splintered. Our Blind Cathar had settled at a Thomasite monastery in distant Valais by, we guess, 1205, 1206. Why he chose the Sidelhorn, we do not know. His name, we do not know. His impetuses for delving into matter, noumena, logos, mind, the soul, the Dusk, we do not know. He appears in only one historical source. Mecthild of Magdeburg's history of the Episcopal Inquisition dates from the 1270s and describes how, in 1215, the Inquisition sentenced the 'Blind Cathar' of Sidelhorn monastery to death for witchcraft. The night before his execution, he was locked in a cell in the monastery. By dawn," I think of Oscar Gomez, "he had vanished. Mecthild arrived at the conclusion that the heretic's liege lord Satan had looked after his own."

"Don't worry," says Arkady. "We don't do Satan."

"The history lesson's almost over," I promise. "Earth spun on its axis, despite the Inquisition's insistence to the contrary, until the year 1799." I rest my fingertips on the iron teapot. "A stroke of Napoleon's pen merged the proud Swiss cantons into a single Helvetican Republic. Not all the Swiss approved of being a client state of France, however, and when promises of religious freedom were reneged upon, many began burning churches and turning on their Paris-appointed masters. Napoleon's enemies fanned the flames, and in early April a company of Austrian artillery came over the Sidelhorn Pass from Piedmont. Two hundred kegs of gunpowder were stored in the monastery's cowshed and, by carelessness or sabotage, exploded. Much of the monastery was destroyed, and a rockfall swept away a bridge crossing the chasm below. Which is only a footnote in the Revolutionary Wars, but that explosion, in *our* War, equates to the killing of Archduke Franz Ferdinand in Sarajevo. Shock waves from it ricocheted up to the Chapel of the Dusk, you see, and the Blind Cathar's long slumber ended."

The mantelpiece clock measures out eight delicate chimes.

"The Thomasite Order was by then a ghost of its pre-Reformation self, and lacked the money, means, and the will to rebuild its Alpine redoubt. The Helvetican government in Zürich, however, voted to repair the Sidelhorn bridge and position a barracks to guard the strategically vital pass. One Baptiste Pfenninger, an engineer from Martigny, was dispatched to the site to oversee the work, and on a night in late summer, as Pfenninger lay in his room at the barracks trying to sleep, he heard a voice calling his name. The voice sounded both miles away and inches away. His door was bolted on the inside, but Pfenninger saw a strip of air swaying at the foot of his bed. The engineer touched it. He found that the strip of air parted, like a curtain, and through it he saw a round floor and a person-high candle of the type one still finds before Catholic or Orthodox altars. Beyond were slabs of stone, climbing up into darkness. Baptiste Pfenninger was a pragmatic man, not drunk, and of sound mind. His room was on the second floor of a two-story building. Yet he passed through the impossible curtain in the air, known, by the way, as the Aperture, and climbed up the impossible steps. How are you holding up so far, Ms. Sykes?"

Holly's thumb sits in her clavicle. "I don't know."

Arkady is stroking his zits, content to let me talk.

"Baptiste Pfenninger became the first visitor to the Chapel of the Dusk. He found a portrait, or an icon of the Blind Cathar. It had no eyes, yet as Pfenninger stood there, and gazed at it, or was gazed at by it, he saw a dot appear in the icon's forehead and grow into the black pupil of a lidless eye and . . ."

"*I* saw that! Where's it from?"

I look at Arkady, who shrugs slightly in reply. "It's what the icon of the Blind Cathar does, shortly before it decants a soul."

Holly addresses me with a fresh urgency. "Listen. The weekend Jacko went missing. That dot-to-eye on a forehead thing. I—I—I had a—a daymare in an underpass, near Rochester. I left it out of *The Radio People*, it just read like a bad description of an acid trip. But it happened."

Arkady subasks me, *What if Xi Lo was cording images to her during the First Mission?*

Why keep that from us? I hunt for a better idea. *What if Jacko and Holly were already corded, as two psychosoteric siblings?*

Arkady's biting his thumb knuckle, a habit from his last life. *Possibly. The cord's remnants may have led Esther to Holly as you fled the Chapel. Like Hansel and Gretel's breadcrumbs.*

" 'Scuse me," Holly's saying, "but I *am* still here. What's Jacko got to do with this medieval monk and a Napoleonic engineer?"

The candle flame in its stained-glass jar is tall and still.

"The Blind Cathar and the engineer talked," I say, "and agreed upon a covenant, a pact of mutual assistance. We can't be sure—"

"Whoa, whoa, whoa. This monk had been in his Chapel of the Dusk for, what, six hundred years? Now he's inviting up visitors and making deals. What's he been eating since the Middle Ages?"

"Naturally, the Blind Cathar had transubstantiated," I explain.

Holly leans back. "Is transwhateveritis even a word?"

"The Blind Cathar's body had died," says Arkady, "but his mind and soul—which, for the purposes of our chat, are the same—had entered into the fabric of the Chapel. The Blind Cathar interfaced with Pfenninger via the icon."

Holly considers this. "So the builder became the building?"

"After a fashion," Arkady replies. "You could say so."

"The bridge and the garrison at the Sidelhorn Pass were finished ahead of winter," I pick up the thread, "and Baptiste Pfenninger returned to his family in Martigny. But the following spring he went on a fishing trip up to Lake d'Emosson, where, one evening, he took a boat onto the water. The boat was found, the body never was."

"I get it," Holly says. "The same as Hugo Lamb."

Rain is softly muttering at 119A's windows. "Jump forward six years to 1805. A new orphanage opened its doors in the Marais district of Paris. Its founder and director was a sturdy Frenchman called Martin Leclerc, whose father had amassed a colonial fortune in Africa, and who now wished to give sustenance, shelter, and scripture to the capital's war orphans. 1805 was a bad time to be a foreigner in Paris, and Leclerc's French had a Germanic slant, but his friends attributed his foreignness to a Prussian mother and a Hamburg education. These same friends, many of whom were the cream of imperial society, did not know that Martin Leclerc's real name was Baptiste Pfenninger. One imagines the accusations of insanity that would have greeted the idea that Leclerc had set up his orphanage to source and groom Engifted children. That is, children who showed evidence of psychosoteric voltage or an active chakra-eye."

Holly looks at Arkady, who narrows his eyes like a pondering interpreter. "Psychic gifts. Like you, aged seven."

"Why would a . . . a Swiss engineer, who faked his own death and is now a French orphanage owner—right?—want psychic children?"

Arkady says, "The Anchorites fuel their atemporality by feeding on souls, as Marinus said. But not just any old soul will do; only the souls of the Engifted can be decanted. Like organ donation, where only one in a thousand is a compatible match. Around every equinox and solstice, the soul's owner has to be lured up the Way of Stones into the Chapel. Once there, the hapless visitor stares at the icon of the Blind Cathar, who then decants the visitor's soul into Black Wine. The body is disposed of through a Chapel window, and the Twelve Anchorites assemble at a ritual known as a Rebirthday where they drink the Black Wine, and for a season—three months or so—no cellular subdivision occurs in their bodies. Which is why Hugo Lamb's body has remained in its midtwenties state, while his mind and soul are over fifty years old."

Holly suspends judgment, for now. "Why's Pfenninger now in Paris when you get to the 'Chapel' via a ruined Swiss monastery?"

"Any Anchorite can summon the Aperture anywhere." Arkady

lowers his palm over the candle flame. "And open it anywhere, too, from the inside. The Aperture's why this War's gone on for 160 years. For all intents and purposes the Anchorites are able to teleport themselves from place to place. It's both the ultimate getaway car and a method of surprise attack."

Holly's voice cracks as she realizes something: "Miss Constantin?"

"Immaculée Constantin is Pfenninger's deputy. We don't know why the First Anchorite recruited her as the Second, but she was the governess of the girls' wing of the Marais orphanage. No less a personage than Talleyrand referred to Madame Constantin as 'a Sword-wielding Seraphim in a Woman's Form.' Eighteen decades pass and we find her in Gravesend, grooming Holly Sykes. She made a rare error in your case, however, by spooking you, so that one of my ex-students brought you to my attention. I inoculated you by draining off your psychosoteric voltage and rendering you unfit for Black Wine. Miss Constantin was annoyed, of course, and although she never forgot Holly Sykes or her promising brother Jacko, she moved on."

"The arithmetic keeps them busy," says Arkady. "The Anchorites keep their numbers to twelve, so each individual member must source a decantible guest once every three years. Their prey can't be drugged, bagged, and dragged up to the Chapel. Anchorites must befriend their prey, like Constantin befriended you. If the prey isn't conscious and calm during decanting, the Black Wine's tainted. It's a delicate vintage."

The figures in the painting watch us. The stories they could tell.

"Am I to understand," Holly gathers her strength, "that Miss Constantin and the Anchorites abducted Jacko and . . . drank his soul? Is this what you're really saying?"

The clock's tick is either loud or quiet, depending.

"The thing about Jacko is . . ." I close my eyes and subsay *Wish me luck* to Arkady, ". . . he was one of us."

Maybe it's thunder somewhere, or maybe a garbage truck.

"Jacko was my brother." Holly speaks slowly. "He was seven."

"His body was seven," says Arkady. "But his body was the vehicle for the soul of Xi Lo, an Horologist. Xi Lo was much, *much* older."

Holly's shaking her head, wrestling with this outrage.

I ask, "Remember when Jacko had meningitis, when he was five?"

"Of course I do. He damn nearly died."

The only way is on. "Ms. Sykes, Jacko *did* die that day."

This is an affront, a trampling, and Holly's at breaking point. "*Er,* sorry—but he bloody didn't die! I was bloody there!"

There's no way to make this easier. "Jack Martin Sykes's soul left his body at two twenty-three A.M. on the sixteenth of October, 1981. By two twenty-four, the soul of Xi Lo, the oldest and best of Horologists, was in possession of your brother's body. Even as your father was yelling for a medic, Jacko's body was out of danger. But Jacko's soul was crossing the Dusk."

Ominous silence. "So . . ." Holly's nostrils dilate, ". . . my little brother's a zombie, you're saying?"

"Jacko *was* Jacko's body," says Arkady, "with Jacko's habits of mind, but with Xi Lo's soul and memories."

She shudders, lost. "Why *say* such a thing?"

"Good question," says Arkady. "Why would we, if it wasn't true?"

Holly stands up and her chair topples backwards. "It usually comes down to an attempt to get money."

"Horology was founded in 1598," Arkady says aloofly. "We've made a few investments down the years. Your nest eggs are safe."

Behave, I suborder Arkady. "Consider Jacko's oddities," I ask Holly. "Why would a British boy listen to Chinese radio?"

"Because . . . Jacko found it soothing."

"Mandarin was Xi Lo's mother tongue," I explain.

"*English* was Jacko's mother tongue! My mum was his mum! The Captain Marlow was his home. His family's us. We loved him. We still do." Holly's blinking back tears. "Even today."

"And Xi Lo–in–Jack loved you too," I say gently. "Very much. He even loved Newky, the smelliest dog in Kent. None of that love was a lie. But none of what we're telling is a lie, either. Xi Lo's soul was older than your pub. Older than England. Older than Christianity."

Holly's heard enough. She picks up the knocked-over chair. "My plane flies back to Dublin this afternoon, and I'll be on it. As you spoke, there were . . . bits I believed, bits I can't. A lot of it, I just don't know. The dreamseeding stuff was incredible. But . . . it's taken me so long to stop blaming myself for Jacko, and you're ripping that scar tissue off." She puts on her coat. "I lead a quiet life with books and cats in the west of Ireland. Little, local, normal stuff. The Holly Sykes who wrote *The Radio People,* she *might*'ve believed in your Atemporals, in your magic monks, but I'm not her anymore. If you are Marinus, good luck with . . . whatever." Holly retrieves her handbag, puts the green key on the table, and goes to the door. "Goodbye. I'm off."

Shall I suasion her to stay? subasks Arkady.

If her cooperation is coerced, it's not cooperation.

"We understand," I tell Holly. "Thanks for visiting."

Arkady subreminds me, *What about Esther?*

Too much, too fast, too soon. Say something nice.

"Sorry I was rude," says Arkady. "Growing pains."

Holly says, "Tell Batman's butler goodbye."

"I will," I answer, "and au revoir, Ms. Sykes."

Holly has closed the door. *By now the Anchorites'll know she's here,* substates Arkady. *Shall we have Ōshima shadow her?*

I'm unconvinced. *Pfenninger won't abort his meticulous plans on a premature strike.*

If they suspect that Esther Little is walled up inside Holly's head, Arkady's fingers make a gun, *they'll strike all right, and hard.*

I drink cooled tea, trying to see this morning from the Anchorites' view. *How could they know that Esther's in Holly?*

They can't know for sure. Arkady cleans his glasses on the sleeve of his Nehru shirt. *But they could guess, and off her to be safe.*

" 'Off her'? Too many gangster films, Arkady." My device trills. The screen reads PRIVATE CALLER and I intuit it's bad news even before I hear Elijah D'Arnoq: "Thank God, Marinus. It's me, D'Arnoq. Look, I just found out: Constantin dispatched a cell to abduct and scansion Holly Sykes. It won't be consensual. Stop them."

The words sink in. "When?"

"Right now," answers D'Arnoq.

"Where?" I ask.

"Probably at her hotel. Hurry."

ŌSHIMA'S WAITING ACROSS the road as I emerge, his collar up and his rain-spotted porkpie hat angled low. He points with a jerk of his head in the Park Avenue direction, subsaying, *I guess we failed the interview.*

I recognize Holly from behind by her long black coat and head-wrap. *My fault. I told her that Jacko was older than Jesus.* I step aside for a skateboarder. *More urgently, D'Arnoq was just in touch,* I subreply, *to say that a cell has been sent to pick her up for scansioning.* I put up my rainbow umbrella as a shield and we set off, Ōshima matching my pace and position on the south side of the street, me on the north.

Remind me, subsays Ōshima, *why we don't just suasion her into a nice deep sleep and then go in subhollering for Esther?*

One, it's against the Codex. Two, she is *chakra-latent, so she may react badly to scansion and redact her own memories, unraveling anyone who is in residence. Three . . . Well, that's enough for now. But we'll need her goodwill, and should only suasion her as a last resort.*

The green man flashes as Holly reaches Park Avenue, so Ōshima and I rush, dodge traffic, and get honked at to avoid being stranded on the island in the middle. We lengthen our strides and get to within twenty paces of Holly. Ōshima asks, *Do we have a strategy here, Marinus, or are we just following her like a pair of stalkers?*

Between here and her hotel, let's just secure her some head space to let her consider what she's just learned. New leaves and old trees drip, gutters slosh, drains gargle. *With luck, the park will work its magic on her. If not, we may have to use ours.* A doorman peers up at the rain from under an awning. We reach Madison, where Holly waits in the drizzle while I stand in the doorway of a boutique, watching that dog walker, those Hasidic Jews, the Arab-looking businessman over there. A couple of cabs slow down, hoping to lure a fare, but Holly is gazing into the small green rectangle of Central Park at the far end of the block. Her mind must be in turmoil. To write a memoir in which psychic events irrupt occasionally is one thing, but for psychic events to dreamseed you, serve you Irish tea, and spin you a whole cosmology, that's another. Maybe Ōshima's right; maybe I should suasion her back to 119A. A metalife of 1,400 years is no guarantee that you always know the right thing to do.

DON'T WALK turns to WALK and I miss my chance. Crossing Madison, I taste paranoia, and glance at people in the waiting vehicles, half expecting to see Pfenninger or Constantin staring back with hunters' eyes. The last block to the park is busier with foot traffic so I'm even jumpier. Is that iShaded jogger with the baby stroller really a jogger? Didn't that curtain twitch as Holly passed by? Why would a young surveyor with his tripod watch a gaunt woman in her fifties so closely? He eyes me up as well, so maybe he's just not fussy. Ōshima keeps pace on the pavement opposite, blending into the morning bustle far better than me. We pass Saint James's Church, whose red-brick steeple once towered above this rural neighborhood of Manhattan. Yu Leon Marinus attended a wedding here in 1968. The bride and groom will be in their eighties now, if they're still alive.

On Fifth Avenue traffic is lumbering and foul-tempered. Holly stands behind a cluster of Chinese tourists. They're agreeing in loud Cantonese how New York is smaller, tattier, and crappier than they'd expected. Across the road, Ōshima is leaning casually against the corner of the Frick Collection, his face hooded. A bus passes with a digital ad for the newly released movie of Crispin Hershey's *Echo Must Die,* but Holly is staring blankly at the park. I calm down. My instinct says we're safe from the enemy until we reach her hotel on Broadway. If she hasn't turned around by then, I'll have to ignore my scruples and perform an Act of Suasion on Holly for her own safety. The Anchorites won't try anything rash. The fallout from public assassinations is too messy. Reality on Fifth Avenue this drizzly morning is exactly as it appears.

A CHUNKY NYPD 4x4 pulls up onto the pavement, and a young black female officer swings out onto the sidewalk, holding her ID. "Ma'am? Are you Holly Sykes?"

Holly is yanked back to the here and now: "Yes, I—yes, is—"

"And you *are* the mother of Aoife Brubeck?"

I look for Ōshima, who's already crossing the street. A large male officer has joined his colleague. "Holly Sykes?"

"Yes." Holly's hand goes to her mouth. "Is Aoife okay?"

"Ms. Sykes," says the female officer in rapid-fire speech, "our precinct had a call earlier from the British consular office asking for us to put out an all-unit alert for you—we missed you by minutes at your hotel earlier. I'm afraid your daughter was involved in an auto collision in Athens last night. She's undergone surgery, she's stable for now, but you're being asked to fly home on the next plane. Ms. Sykes? You hearing me?"

"Athens?" Holly supports herself on the hood of the patrol car. "But Aoife's on an island . . . What . . . How badly—"

"Ma'am, we *really* don't have any details, but we'll drive you to the Empire Hotel so you can pack. Then we'll take you to the airport."

I step forward to do I don't know what, but Ōshima pulls me back: *I'm sensing intense psychovoltage in the car; if it's a high Anchorite and we engage in full combat on Fifth Avenue, every hippocampus within a fifty-meter radius'll get shredded, including Holly's. Feds, Homeland Security, who knows who'll be scouring footage of us, looking suspicious as all hell, tracking Holly from 119A?*

Ōshima's right, but: *We can't just let them take her.*

Meanwhile Holly's being half coaxed, half herded into the squad car. She's trying to ask more questions, but she's had a mind-bending morning and is scared into passivity. Perhaps she's being suasioned, too. In an agony of indecision, I watch the door slam shut and the vehicle pull off into the traffic, surging over the intersection just before the lights turn red. The windows are blacked out so I can't see who or what numbers we're dealing with. The sign says WALK and the pedestrians begin to cross. Sixty seconds was all it took to drop and smash our Second Mission.

ŌSHIMA LEADS ME over the crossing. "I'll do the transversing."

"No, Ōshima, it was my error of judgment so—"

"Strap on your horsehair shirt later. I'm the better transverser, and I'm just nastier. You know I am." There's no time to argue. We step over the low wall of the park by the Hunt Monument, where we sit on a damp bench. He grips one arm of the bench with one hand, and my hand with the other. *Cord yourself into my stream,* Ōshima subsuggests. *I'll need your advice, like as not.*

"Whatever that's worth. But I'll be with you."

He squeezes my hand, shuts his eyes, and his body slumps a little as his soul egresses through his chakra-eye. Even to psychosoterics, the soul is on the edge of what's visible, like a clear glass marble in a jar of water, and Ōshima's soul is lost in a second as it transverses upwards between the dripping twigs and the weather-stained old monument. I pull Ōshima's hat down to hide his face and shield both of us under my umbrella. A vacated body looks like a medical emergency, and at various points across my metalife I've ingressed myself only to find smelling salts up my nose, an artery being bled, or a stranger with halitosis administering inept CPR. Moreover, as I sync up our hand-chakras, Ōshima and I resemble a pair of lovers. Even by New York's laissez-faire standards, we would be worth a gawp.

I connect with Ōshima's cord . . .

. . . and images from Ōshima's soul stream directly into my

mind. He's gliding through a Cubist kaleidoscope of brake lights, roof racks, the tops of cars, branches, and budding leaves. Down we swoop, passing through the rear door of a van, between pig carcasses swinging on hooks, through the driver's tarry lung, then out through the windscreen, arcing over a United Parcels van, and still higher, scaring a collared pigeon off its streetlight perch. Ōshima hangs for a moment, searching for the squad car: *Are you with me, Marinus?*

I'm here, I subreply.

Can you see the squad car?

No. A garbage truck edges forward and I see the yellow of the school bus: *Try near that school bus.*

Ōshima flies down, through the back window of the bus, along the aisle, between forty children arguing, talking, clustered round a 3D slate, staring into space, and out past the driver and . . .

. . . the klaxon and lights of the police car, shunting along slowly. Ōshima enters through the rear windscreen and hovers for a moment, circling, to stream me a view of what we're dealing with. To Holly's left sits the female cop—or alleged cop. The driver is the burly male who helped hustle Holly into the car. Sitting on Holly's right is a man wearing a suit and a Samsung wraparound that half hides his face, but we know him. *Drummond Brzycki,* substates Ōshima.

An odd choice. Brzycki's the newest and weakest Anchorite.

Maybe they're not expecting trouble, guesses Ōshima.

Maybe he's a canary in a coal mine, I subreply.

I'll ingress the woman, subsays Ōshima, *and see if I can find out her orders.* He enters the female officer's chakra-eye and I now have access to her sensory input. "All we know, honey," she's telling Holly, "is what I already told ya. If I knew more I'd tell ya. I'm achin' for ya, honey, I am. I'm a mom too. Two little ones."

"But is Aoife's spine okay? How—how serious is the—"

"Don't distress yourself, Ms. Sykes." Drummond Brzycki flips up his wraparounds. Brzycki has Mediterranean-goalkeeper good looks, lush black hair, and a nasal voice, like a wasp trapped in a wineglass. "The consul's out of his meeting at ten. We'll device him direct, so whatever facts he has, you'll get from the horse's mouth. Okay?"

The squad car stops at a red light, and pedestrians stream across. "Maybe I can find the hospital's number," Holly says, getting her device from her handbag. "Athens isn't such a big—"

"If you speak Greek," says Brzycki, "go ahead, and good luck. Otherwise I'd keep your device free for incoming news. Don't jump to the bleakest conclusions. We'll use the emergency lane to get you on the eleven forty-five flight to Athens. You'll be with Aoife soon."

Holly puts her device back into her bag. "The police at home would never go to such trouble." A cycle courier zips by and the traffic lurches forward. "How on earth did you find me, Officer?"

"Detective Marr," says Brzycki. "Needles in haystacks really do get found. The precinct put out a Code Fifteen and although 'slim-built female Caucasian in her fifties in a knee-length black raincoat' hardly cuts the field down on a rainy day in Manhattan, your guardian angels were working overtime. Actually—it's maybe not appropriate to say this at this time—but Sergeant Lewis up front there, he's a *big* fan of yours. He was giving me a lift back from Ninety-eighth down to Columbus Circle, and Lewis said, 'My God, it's her!' Isn't that right, Tony?"

"Sure is. I saw you speak at Symphony Space, Ms. Sykes, when *The Radio People* was out," says the driver. "After my wife died, your book was a light in the darkness. It saved me."

"Oh, I'm . . ." Holly is in such a state that this rheumatic story passes muster, ". . . glad it helped." The meat truck draws up alongside. "And I'm very sorry for your loss."

"Thanks for saying so, Ms. Sykes. Truly."

After a few seconds, Holly menus her device. "I'll device Sharon, my sister. She's in England, but perhaps she can find out more about Aoife from there."

The stream flickers and dims. *The cord's thinning,* I subwarn Ōshima. *What have you found out about our host?*

Her name's Nancy, hates mice, she's killed eight times, comes the delayed answer. *A child soldier in South Sudan. This is her first job for Brzycki . . . Marinus, what's "curarequinoline"?*

Bad news. *A toxin. One milligram can trigger a pulmonary collapse in ten seconds. Coroners never test for it. Why?*

Nancy here and Brzycki have curarequinoline in their tranq guns. We can conclude it isn't for self-defense.

"I'll call my office again," says Brzycki, helpfully. "See if they can't get the name of your daughter's hospital in Athens. Then at least you'll have a direct line."

"I can't thank you enough." Holly's pale and sick-looking.

Brzycki flips down his wraparounds. "Anchor Two? Unit twenty-eight, you copying, Anchor Two?"

Unexpectedly, the earpiece in Nancy's helmet comes to life, and through it I hear Immaculée Constantin. "Clear as a bell. All things considered, let's play safe. Eliminate your guest."

Shock boils up but I rally myself: *Ōshima, get her out!* But my only reply is a blast of blizzard down the overstretched cord. Ōshima can't hear me, or he can't respond, or both.

Clarity returns. "Copy that, Anchor Two," Brzycki is saying, "but our present location is Fifth and East Sixty-eighth, where the traffic's still at a dead halt. Might I advise that we postpone the last order as per—"

"Give the Sykes woman a tranq in each arm," orders Constantin in her soft voice. "No postponement. Do it."

I subshout hard, *Ōshima, get her out get her out!*

But no answer comes either from his soul or his inert body, propped up by mine on the bench, a block from the police car. All I can do is watch via the cord as an innocent woman, whom I lassoed into our War, is killed. I can't transverse this distance, and even if I could I'd arrive too late.

"Understood, Anchor Two, will proceed as advised." Brzycki nods at Lewis in the mirror, and at Nancy.

Holly asks, "Any luck with the hospital number, Detective Marr?"

"Our secretary's on it." Brzycki unholsters his tranq gun and flicks off the safety catch, while left-handed Nancy, through whose viewpoint I must watch, does the same.

"Why," Holly's voice changes, "do you need your guns?"

On reflex, I try to suasion Nancy to stop, but one cannot suasion down a cord and I just watch in horror as Nancy fires the tranq—at Brzycki's throat, where a tiny red dot appears, on his Adam's apple. The Anchorite touches it, astonished, then looks at the red dab on his fingers, looks at Nancy, utters, "What the . . ."

Brzycki slumps, dead. Lewis is shouting, as if under water, "Nancy, you outta your fuckin' *MIND*?" or that's what Nancy thinks she hears, as she finds herself taking Brzycki's gun and firing it point-blank into Lewis's cheek. Lewis huffs out a falsetto vowel of disbelief. Nancy, whom Ōshima is suasioning ruthlessly, then finds herself clambering over Holly and onto the passenger seat as Lewis gibbers his last breath. She now cuffs herself to the steering wheel and unlocks the rear doors. As a parting gift, Ōshima redacts a broad swath of Nancy's present perfect and induces unconsciousness before egressing her and ingressing the traumatized Holly. Ōshima psychosedates his new host immediately, and I watch Holly in the first person as she puts on her sunglasses, checks her headwrap, climbs out of the squad car, and calmly walks back up Park Avenue toward the Frick. With a rip of corded feedback Ōshima's voice returns: *Marinus, can you hear me?*

I dare feel relief. *Breathtaking, Ōshima.*

War, subreplies the old warrior, *and now, logistics. We have a retired author in distinctive headgear leaving a patrol car containing two dead fake cops and one living fake cop. Ideas?*

Get Holly back here and rejoin your body, I subadvise Ōshima. *While you're doing that, I'll call L'Ohkna and ask for a catastrophic wipeout of all street cameras on the Upper East Side.*

Ōshima-in-Holly strides along. *Can that dope fiend do that?*

If a way exists, he'll find it. If no way exists, he'll make one.

Then what? 119A evidently isn't the fortress it once was.

Agreed. We'll go to earth at Unalaq's. I'll ask her to come and rescue us. I'm uncording now, see you soon. I open my eyes. My umbrella is still half hiding Ōshima's body and me, but a gray squirrel is sniffing my boot with curiosity. I swivel my foot. The squirrel is gone.

"HOME," ANNOUNCES UNALAQ. She stops the car level with her front door, next to the Three Lives Bookstore on the corner of Waverly Place and West Tenth Street. Unalaq leaves the hazard lights on and helps me as I guide Holly across the pavement while Ōshima stands guard like a monk-assassin. Holly's still doped from the psychosedation, and we've drawn the attention of a tall thin man with a beard and wire-framed glasses. "Hey, Unalaq, is everything okay?"

"All good, Toby," says Unalaq. "My friend just flew in from Dublin, but she's terrified of flying, so she took a sleeping pill to knock her out. It worked a bit too well."

"Sure did. She's still cruising at twenty thousand feet."

"Next time she'll stick with the glass of white, I think."

"Call down to the shop later. Your books on Sanskrit are in."

"Will do, Toby, thanks." Unalaq's found her keys but Inez has already opened the door. Her face is taut with worry, as if her partner, Unalaq, is the breakable mortal and not her. Inez nods at Ōshima and me and peers at Holly's face with concern.

"She'll be fine after a few hours' sleep," I say.

Inez's expression says, *I hope you're right,* and she goes to park the car in a nearby underground lot. Unalaq ushers us up the steps, inside, down the hallway, and into the tiny elevator. There's not enough space for Ōshima, who lopes up the stairs. I press up.

A dollar for your thoughts, subsays Unalaq.

One's thoughts cost only a penny when I was Yu Leon.

Inflation, shrugs Unalaq, and her hair goes boing. *Could Esther really be alive somewhere inside this head?*

I look at Holly's lined, taut, ergonomic face. She groans like a harried dreamer who can't wake. *I hope so, Unalaq. If Esther interpreted the Script correctly, then maybe. But I don't know if I be-*

lieve in the Script. Or the Counterscript. I don't know why Constantin wants Holly dead. Or if Elijah D'Arnoq's for real. Or if our handling of the Sadaqat issue is wrongheaded. "Truly, I don't know anything," I tell my five-hundred-year-old friend.

"At least," Unalaq blows the end of a strand of copper hair from her nostril, "the Anchorites can't exploit your overconfidence."

HOLLY'S ASLEEP, ŌSHIMA'S watching *The Godfather Part II,* Unalaq's preparing a salad, and Inez has invited me to play her Steinway upright, as the piano tuner came yesterday. There's a fine view of Waverly Place from the piano's attic, and the small room is scented with the oranges and limes that Inez's mother sends in crates from Florida. A photograph of Inez and Unalaq sits atop the Steinway. They're posing in skiwear on a snowy peak, like intrepid explorers. Unalaq won't have discussed the Second Mission with her partner, but Inez is no fool and must sense that something major is afoot. Being a Temporal who loves an Atemporal is surely as thorny a fate as being an Atemporal who loves a Temporal. It's not just Horology's future that my decisions this week will shape, but the lives of loved ones, colleagues, and patients who will get scarred if my companions and I never come back, just as Holly's life was scarred by Xi Lo–in–Jacko's death on the First Mission. If you love and are loved, whatever you do affects others.

So I leaf through Inez's sheet music and choose Shostakovich's puckish *Preludes and Fugues.* It's fiendish but rewarding. Then I perform William Byrd's *Hughe Ashton's Ground* as a palate cleanser, and a handful of Jan Johannson's Swedish folk songs, just because. From memory I play Scarlatti's K32, K212, and K9. The Italian's sonatas are an Ariadne's thread that connects Iris Marinus-Fenby, Yu Leon Marinus, Jamini Marinus Choudary, Pablo Antay Marinus, Klara Marinus Koskov, and Lucas Marinus, the first among my selves to discover Scarlatti, back in his Japanese days. I traded the sheet music off de Zoet, I recall, and was playing K9 just hours before my death in July 1811. I'd felt my death approaching for several weeks, and had put my affairs in order, as they used to say. My friend Eelattu cut me adrift with a phial of morphine I'd reserved for the occasion. I felt my soul sinking up from the Light of Day, up onto the High Ridge, and wondered where I'd be resurrected. In a wigwam or a palace or an igloo, in a jungle or tundra or a four-poster bed, in the body of a princess or a hangman's daughter or a scullery maid, forty-nine spins of the earth later . . .

. . . in a nest of rags and rotten straw, in the body of a girl burning with fever. Mosquitoes fed on her, she was crawling with lice, and weakened by an intestinal parasite. Measles had dispatched the soul of Klara, my new body's previous inhabitant, and it was three days before I could psychoheal myself sufficiently to take proper stock of my surroundings. Klara was the eight-year-old property of Kiril Andreyevich Berenovsky, an absentee landlord whose estate was bounded by a pendulous loop in the Kama River, Oborino County, Perm Province, the Russian Empire. Berenovsky returned to his ancestral lands only once a year to bully the local officials, hunt, bed virgins, and exhort his bailiff to bleed the estate even whiter than last year. Happiness did not enter feudal childhoods, and Klara's was miserable even by the standards of the day. Her father had been killed by a bull, and her mother was crushed by a life of childbearing, farmwork, and a peasant moonshine known as *rvota,* or "puke." Klara was the last and least of nine siblings. Three of her sisters had died in infancy, two others had gone to a factory in Ekaterinburg to settle a debt of Berenovsky's, and her three brothers had been sent to the Imperial Army just in time to be butchered at the Battle of Eylau. Klara's recovery from death was greeted with joyless fatalism. It was a long fall indeed from Lucas Marinus's life as a surgeon-scholar to Klara's dog-eat-dog squalor, and it was going to be a long, fitful, fretful climb back up the social ladder, especially in a female body in the early nineteenth century. I did not yet possess any psychosoteric methods to speed this ascent. All Klara had was the Russian Orthodox Church.

Father Dmitry Nikolayevich Koskov was a native of Saint Petersburg who baptized, preached to, wed, and buried the four hundred serfs on the Berenovksy estate, as well as the three dozen freeborn workers who lived and worked there. Dmitry and his wife, Vasilisa, lived in a rickety cottage overlooking the river. The Koskovs had arrived in Oborino County ten years before, full of youth and a philanthropic zeal to improve the lives of the rural peasantry. Long before I-in-Klara entered their lives, that zeal had been killed by the drudgery and bestiality of life in the Wild East. Vasilisa Koskov suffered from severe depression and a conviction that the world was laughing at her childlessness behind her back. Her only friends on the estate were books, and books can talk but do not listen. Dmitry Koskov's ennui matched his wife's and he cursed himself, daily if not hourly, for having forfeited the prospects of clerical life in Saint Petersburg, where his wife and his career could have blossomed. His yearly petitions to the church authorities for a pulpit closer to civilization proved fruitless. He was, as we'd say now, seriously Out of the Loop. Dmitry had God, but why God had condemned him and Vasilisa to sink in a bog of superstition and spite and sin like Oborino County for a landlord like Berenovsky, who showed more concern for his hounds than his serfs, the Almighty did not share.

To me-in-Klara, the Koskovs were perfect.

ONE OF KLARA'S chores, as soon as she was well again, was to deliver eggs to the bailiff, the blacksmith, and the priest. One morning in 1812, as I handed Vasilisa Koskov her basket of eggs at the kitchen door, I asked her shyly if it was really true I'd meet my dead sisters in heaven. The priest's wife was taken aback, both that the near-mute serf girl had spoken, and that I'd asked such a rudimentary question. Didn't I listen to Father Koskov in church every Sunday? I explained that the boys pinched my arm and tugged my hair to stop me listening to God's Word, so although I wanted to hear about Jesus, I couldn't. Yes, I was mawkishly, hawkishly manipulating a lonely woman for my own gain, but the alternative was a life of bovine labor, piggish servitude, and bile-freezing winters. Vasilisa brought me into her kitchen, sat me down, and taught me how Jesus Christ had come to earth in the body of a man to allow us sinners to go to heaven after we died, so long as we said our prayers and behaved as good Christians.

I nodded gravely, thanked her, then asked if it was true the Koskovs were from Petersburg. Soon Vasilisa was reminiscing about the operas, the Anichkov Theater, the balls at this archduke's name day, the fireworks at that countess's ball. I told her I had to go, because my mother would beat me for taking too long, but the next time I delivered the eggs, Vasilisa served me real tea from her samovar sweetened with a spoonful of apricot jam. Nectar! Soon the melancholic priest's melancholic wife found herself discussing her private disappointments. The little serf listened with wisdom far beyond her eight years. One fine day, I took a gamble and told Vasilisa about a dream I'd had. There was a lady with a blue veil, milky skin, and a kind smile. She had appeared in the hut I shared with my mother, and told me to learn to read and write, so that I could take her son's message to serfs. Stranger still, the kind lady had spoken strange words in a language I didn't understand, but they had stayed glowing in my memory, just the same.

What could it possibly mean, Mrs. Vasilisa Koskov?

PLEASED AS VASILISA's husband was by the improvement in his wife's nerves, Dmitry Nikolay was anxious about her being suckered yet again by yet another wily peasant. So the cleric interviewed me in the empty church. I wore a shy bewilderment at being noticed, let alone spoken to, by so august a figure, even as I nudged Dmitry towards a belief that here was a child destined for a higher purpose, a purpose that he, Father Dmitry Koskov, had been chosen to oversee. He asked me about my dream. Could I describe the lady I had seen? I could. She had dark brown hair, a lovely smile, a blue veil, no, not white, not red, but blue, blue like the sky in summer. Father Dmitry asked me to repeat the "strange words" the lady had told me. Little Klara frowned, and very shyly confessed that the words didn't sound like Russian words. Yes, yes, said Father Dmitry, his wife had said as much; but what were these words? Could I remember any? Klara shut her eyes and quoted, in Greek, Matthew 19:14: But Jesus said, Suffer little children, and forbid them not, to come unto me: for such is of the kingdom of heaven.

The priest's eyes and mouth opened and stayed open.

Trembling, I said I hoped the words meant nothing bad.

My conscience was clean. I was an epiphyte, not a parasite.

A few days later, Father Dmitry approached Sigorsky, the estate bailiff, to propose that Klara be allowed to live in their house, in order for his wife to train the girl as a servant for the Berenovksy house and give her a rudimentary schooling. Sigorsky granted this unusual request as pro bono payment for Father Dmitry averting his priestly gaze from the bailiff's assorted scams. I had no goods to bring with me to the Koskovs' cottage but a sackcloth dress, clogs, and a filthy sheepskin coat. That night Vasilisa gave me the first hot bath I'd enjoyed since my death in Japan, a clean frock, and a woolen blanket. Progress. While I was bathing, Klara's mother appeared, demanding a rouble "for compensation." Dmitry paid, on the understanding that she would never ask for another. I saw her around the estate, but she never acknowledged me, and the following winter, she fell drunk into a frozen ditch at night and never woke up.

Even a benign Atemporal cannot save everyone.

THE CLAIM IS immodest, but as a de facto if not a de jure daughter, I'd brought purpose and love back into the Koskovs' life. Vasilisa set up a class in the church to teach the peasant children their АБВs, basic numeracy, and scripture, and found time in the evening to teach me French. Lucas Marinus had spoken the language in my previous life, so I made a gratifyingly quick-learning student. Five years passed, I grew tall and strong, but every summer when Berenovksy visited, I dreaded his noticing me in church, and asking why his serf was being given airs above her natural station. In order to protect my gains and carry on climbing, my benefactors needed a benefactor.

Dmitry's uncle, Pyotr Ivanovich Chernenko, was the obvious, indeed the only, candidate. Nowadays he would be fêted as a self-made entrepreneur, with a gossip-magazine private life, but as a young man in nineteenth-century Saint Petersburg he had caused a scandal by eloping with and, even worse, marrying an actress five years his senior. Dissipation and disgrace had been gleefully predicted, but Pyotr Ivanovich instead had made first one fortune by trading with the British against the continental blockade, and was now making another by introducing Prussian smelters to foundries throughout the Urals. His love marriage had stayed strong, and the two Chernenko sons were students in Gothenburg. I persuaded Vasilisa that Uncle Pyotr must be invited to our cottage to inspect her estate school when he was next in Perm on business.

He arrived one morning in autumn. I ensured I shone. Uncle Pyotr and I spoke for an hour on metallurgy alone. Pyotr Ivanovich Chernenko was a shrewd man who had seen and learned a lot from his five decades of life, but he was beguiled by a serf girl who was so conversant on such manly concerns as commerce and smelting. Vasilisa said that the angels must whisper things in my ears as I slept. How else could I have acquired German *and* French so quickly, or known how to set a broken bone, or have grasped the principles of algebra? I blushed and mumbled about books and my elders and betters.

That night as I lay in bed I heard Uncle Pyotr Ivanovich tell Dmitry, "One bad-tempered whim of that ass Berenovksy, nephew, is all it needs to condemn the poor girl to a life of planting turnips in frozen mud and the spousal bed of a tusked hog. Something must be done! Something shall be done!" Uncle Pyotr left the next day in never-ending rain—spring and autumn alike are muddy hell in Russia—telling Dmitry that we had rotted away in this backwater for far too long already . . .

. . .

THE WINTER OF 1816 was pitiless. Dmitry buried about fifteen peasants in the iron-hard sod, the Kama River froze, the wolves grew bold, and even priests and their families went hungry. Spring refused to show until the middle of April, and the mail coach from Perm didn't resume its regular visits to Oborino County until May 3. Klara Marinus's journal marks this as the date when two official-looking letters were delivered to the Koskovs' cottage. They stayed on the mantelpiece until Dmitry returned in the late afternoon from administering last rites to a woodcutter's son, who had died of pleurisy several miles away. Dmitry opened the first letter with his paper knife and his face reflected the momentousness of its news. He puffed out his cheeks, said, "This affects you, Klara, my dear," and read it aloud: " 'Kiril Andreyvich Berenovsky, Master of the Berenovksy Estate in the Province of Perm, hereby grants to the female serf Klara, daughter of the deceased serf Gota, full and unconditional liberty as a subject of the Emperor, in perpetuity.' " In my memory, cuckoos are calling across the river and sunshine floods the Koskovs' little parlor. I asked Dmitry and Vasilisa if they would consider adopting me. Vasilisa smothered me in a tearful hug while Dmitry coughed, examined his fingers, and said, "I dare say we could manage that, Klara." We knew that only Pyotr Ivanovich could have brought about this administrative miracle, but some months would pass before we learned exactly how. My freedom had been granted in exchange for Uncle Pyotr settling my owner's account with his vintner.

In our excitement, we'd forgotten the second envelope. This contained a summons from the Episcopal Office of the Bishop of Saint Petersburg, requesting Father Dmitry Koskov to take up his new post as priest at the Church of the Annunciation of the Blessed Virgin on Primorsky Prospect, Saint Petersburg, on or before July 1 of that year. Vasilisa asked, quite seriously, if we were dreaming. Dmitry handed her the letter. As Vasilisa read it, she grew ten years younger before our eyes. Dmitry said he shuddered to think what

Uncle Pyotr had paid for such a plum post. The answer was a con-signment of Sienna marble to a pet monastery of the patriarch's but, again, we didn't hear this from Pyotr Ivanovich's lips. Human cru-elty can be infinite. Human generosity can be boundless.

NOT SINCE THE late 1780s had I lived in a sophisticated European capital, so once we were installed in our new house by Dmitry's church in Saint Petersburg, I engorged myself on music, theater, and conversation, as best a thirteen-year-old freed serf girl could. While I was expecting my lowly origins to be an obstacle in society, they ended up enhancing my status as an event of the season on the novelty-hungry Petersburg salon circuit. Before I knew it, "Miss Koskov the Polymath of Perm" was being examined in several lan-guages on many disciplines. I gave my foster mother due credit for my "corpus of knowledge," explaining that once she had taught me to read I could harvest at will the fruits of the Bible, dictionaries, almanacs, pamphlets, suitable poetry, and improving literature. Emancipationists cited Klara Koskov to argue that serfs and their owners differed only by accident of birth, while skeptics called me a goose bred for foie gras, stuffed with data I merely regurgitated without understanding.

One day in October a coach pulled by four white thoroughbreds pulled up on Primorsky Prospect, and the equerry of Tsarina Eliza-beth delivered to my family a summons to the Winter Palace for an audience with the Tsarina. Neither Dmitry nor Vasilisa slept a wink and were awed by the succession of sumptuous chambers we passed through on our journey to the Tsarina's apartment. My metalife had inoculated me against pomp centuries ago. Of Tsarina Elizabeth, I best recall her sad bass clarinet of a voice. My foster parents and I were seated on a long settle by a fire, while Elizabeth favored a high-backed chair. She asked questions in Russian about my life as a serf, then switched to French to probe my grasp of a variety of subjects. In her native German, she supposed that my round of engagements must be rather tiresome? I said that while an audience with a tsarina could never be tiresome, I would not be sorry when I was yesterday's news. Elizabeth replied that I now knew how an empress feels. She had the newest pianoforte from Hamburg and asked if I cared to try it out. So I played a Japanese lullaby I'd learned in Nagasaki, and it moved her. Apropos of I'm not sure what, Elizabeth asked me what sort of husband I dreamed of. "Our daughter is still a child, Your Highness," Dmitry found his tongue, "with a headful of girlish nonsense."

"I was wedded by my fifteenth birthday." The Tsarina turned to me and Dmitry lost his tongue again.

Matrimony, I remarked, was not a realm I yearned to enter.

"Cupid's aim is unerring," Elizabeth said. "You'll see. You'll see."

After a thousand years, dear Tsarina, I did not retort, *his arrows tend to bounce off me.* I agreed that no doubt Her Highness spoke the truth. She knew a fudged answer when she heard it, and suggested that I preferred books to husbands. I agreed that books tended not to switch their stories whenever it suited them. Dmitry and Vasilisa shifted in their borrowed finery. The jaded queen of a court in which adultery was a form of entertainment looked through me, the gold of the fire toying with the gold of her hair. "What an old sentence," she said, "from such youthful lips."

OUR VISIT TO the royal court triggered a new wave of gossip about Klara Koskov's true paternity that caused embarrassment for my foster father, so we brought my brief career as a salon curiosity to a timely close. Our decision coincided with Uncle Pyotr's return from a half year in Stockholm, and the Chernenko residence on Dzerzhinsky Street became a second home for us. Pyotr's ex-actress wife, Yuliya Grigorevna, became a loyal friend and held dinners where I met a broader cross section of Petersburgers than I had in the higher stratum of the salons. Bankers, chemists, and poets rubbed shoulders with theater managers, clerks, and sea captains. I continued to read voraciously, and wrote to many authors, signing myself "K. Koskov" to conceal my age and gender. Horology's archives still contain letters to K. Koskov from the physician René Laënnec, the inventor Humphrey Davy, and the astronomer Giuseppe Piazzi. University was not yet a possibility for women, but as the years passed, many of the liberal-leaning Petersburg intelligentsia visited the Chernenkos to discuss their papers with the cerebral bluestocking. In time, I even received a few marriage proposals, but neither Dmitry nor Vasilisa Koskov was eager to lose me, and I had no desire to become a man's legal property for a second time.

KLARA'S TWENTIETH CHRISTMAS came, and her twelfth with the Koskovs. She received fur-lined boots from Dmitry, piano music from Vasilisa, and a sable cloak from the Chernenkos. My journal records that on January 6, 1823, Dmitry gave a sermon on Job and the hidden designs of Providence. The choir of the Church of the Annunciation of the Blessed Virgin gave only a mediocre performance due to sore throats and colds. Snow lay deep in the gutters, fog and smoke filled the alleyways, the sun was a memory, icicles hung from the eaves, steam snorted white from the horses' frozen nostrils, and ice floes as big as boats floated on the thundercloud-gray Neva River.

After our midday meal, Vasilisa and I were in the parlor. I was writing a letter in Dutch about osmosis in giant trees to a scholar at Leiden University. My foster mother was marking the French compositions of some of her pupils. The fire gnawed logs. Galina, our housekeeper, was lighting the lamps and tutting about my eyesight when we heard a knock at our door. Jasper, our little dog of uncertain pedigree, went skating and yapping down the hall. Vasilisa and I looked at each other but neither of us was expecting a caller. Through the lace curtain we saw an unknown coach with a veiled window. Galina brought in a card, given to her by a footman at the door. Dubiously, my mother read it aloud: "Mr. Shiloh Davydov. 'Shiloh'? It sounds foreign to me. Does it sound foreign to you, Klara?" Davydov's address, however, was the respectable Mussorgky Prospect. "Might they be friends of Uncle Pyotr's?"

"*Mrs.* Davydov is in the coach, too, I'm told," added Galina.

With a sudden change of mind that I would later recognize as an Act of Suasion, Vasilisa's doubts evaporated. "Well, invite them in, Galina! What must they think of us? The poor lady'll be freezing!"

"PARDON OUR UNANNOUNCED intrusion," said a spry man with expansive whiskers, a plangent voice, and dark clothes of a foreign cut, "Mrs. and Miss Koskov. The fault is all mine. I had my letter of introduction written before church, but then our stable boy got kicked by a horse and we had to summon a doctor. With all this brouhaha afoot, I quite neglected to ensure that the letter I had written had in fact been brought to you. My name is Shiloh Davydov, and I am at your service." He handed his hat to Galina with a smile. "Of Russian extraction from my father, but resident in Marseille, in so far as I am 'resident' anywhere. And may I," even then, I noticed a Chinese cadence to his Russian, "may I present my wife, Mrs. Claudette Davydov, who, Miss Koskov, is better known to you"—he waggled his cane—"by her maiden and pen-name 'C. Holokai.'"

This was unexpected. I had corresponded with "C. Holokai," author of a philosophical text on the Transmigration of the Soul, several times, never dreaming that he might be a she. Mrs. Davydov's dark, inquisitive face hinted at Levantine or Persian extraction. She was dressed in dove-gray silk and wore a necklace of black and white pearls. "Mrs. Koskov," she addressed Vasilisa, "thank you for your hospitality to two strangers on a winter's afternoon." She spoke Russian more slowly than her husband, but enunciated with such great care that her listeners paid close attention. "We should have waited until tomorrow before inviting you to our house, but the name of 'K. Koskov' came up only an hour ago at the house of Professor Obel Andropov and I took it as a—as a sign."

"The professor is a friend," said my foster mother.

"And a classical linguist of the first rank," I added.

"Indeed. Well, Professor Andropov told me that the 'K' stood for 'Klara'; and then, on our way home, by chance I glanced out of our coach and saw your father's church. A hobgoblin told me to see if you were at home, and I'm afraid that I"—Claudette Davydov asked her husband in Arabic how to say the word "succumbed" in Russian, and Shiloh Davydov repeated it for her—"I succumbed."

"My, my," said Vasilisa, blinking at the exotic strangers whom she'd apparently invited into her house. "My. You're both welcome, I'm sure. My husband will be home presently. Make yourselves as comfortable as you can, I beg you. This is not a palace but . . ."

"No palace I ever saw was half so friendly." Shiloh Davydov looked around our parlor. "My wife's been excited about meeting 'K. Koskov' since the day I resolved to visit Petersburg."

"Indeed I have." Claudette Davydov handed Galina her muff of white fur with murmured thanks. "And to judge from Miss Koskov's surprise, we both wrote to the other in the mistaken belief that the other was a man—do I surmise correctly, Miss Koskov?"

"I cannot deny it, Mrs. Davydov," I said, as we all sat down.

"Is it not too much like an absurd farce for the stage?"

"A wrongheaded world," sighed Shiloh Davydov, "where women needs must deny their gender for fear that their ideas will be dismissed."

We considered the truth of this. "Klara dear," said Vasilisa, remembering her duty as hostess, "would you feed up the fire while Galina brings refreshments for our guests?"

"THE SEA IS my business, sir," replied Shiloh Davydov. Dmitry found the Davydovs' unexpected company to his liking, and for the men the tea and cakes were superseded by brandy and the box of cigars Shiloh had presented to my foster father. "Shipping, freight, shipyards, shipbuilding, maritime insurance . . ." He waved a hand vaguely. "I've journeyed to Petersburg at the behest of the Russian Admiralty, so naturally I must be discreet about details. We shall be employed here for a year at least, however, and I've been granted the use of a government house on Mussorgsky Prospect. Mrs. Koskov, how difficult will it be to engage domestic staff who are both capable and honest? In Marseille, I'm sorry to say, the combination is as rare as hen's teeth."

"The Chernenkos will help," said Vasilisa. "For Dmitry's uncle, Pyotr Ivanovich, and his wife, finding a few hen's teeth is a small matter. Is it not, Dmitry?"

"They'll come wrapped in a Golden Fleece, knowing Pyotr." Dmitry puffed appreciatively on his cigar. "How do you intend to wile away your months in our frozen northern wastes, Mrs. Davydov?"

"Like my husband, I have the soul of an explorer," said Claudette Davydov, as if that were a full answer. The fire spat sparks. "First, though, I intend to finish a commentary on Ovid's *Metamorphoses*. I had even entertained hopes that 'K. Koskov' would pay me the honor of casting her eye over my scribblings, if . . ."

I said that the honor would be mine, and that we clandestine female scholars were duty-bound to band together. Then I asked if "C. Holokai" had received my last letter, sent the previous August to the Russian legate in Marseille.

"Indeed I did," said Claudette Davydov. "My husband, whose love of philosophy is, as you see, as deep as my own, was as fascinated as I was to read about your notion of the Dusk."

Now Vasilisa was curious. "What dusk would that be, dear?"

I disliked lying even by omission to my foster parents, but Atemporality in a Godless, godless universe was not a profitable topic of discussion in our pious household. As I fabricated a prosaic explanation, my glance fell on Shiloh Davydov. His eyes had half closed and a spot glowed in what I knew from my Eastern resurrections was a chakra-eye. I looked at Claudette Davydov. The same spot glowed. Something was happening. I looked at my foster parents and saw that Vasilisa and Dmitry Koskov were as still as living waxworks. Vasilisa still wore her look of concentration, but her mind appeared to have shut down. Or have been shut down. Dmitry's cigar smoked in his fingers, but his body was motionless.

After twelve hundred years I had come to think of myself as immune to shock, but I was wrong. Time had not stopped. The fire still burned. I could still hear Galina chopping vegetables out in the kitchen. By instinct, I searched for a pulse in Vasilisa's wrist and found it, strong and steady. Her breathing was slow and shallow but steady. The same was true for Dmitry. I said their names. They didn't hear me. They weren't here. There could be only one cause or, more likely, a pair of causes.

The Davydovs, meanwhile, had returned to normal and were awaiting my response. Standing, feeling out of my depth but furious, I grabbed the poker and told the Davydovs, or whatever the Davydovs were, in a manner not at all like a twenty-year-old Russian priest's daughter, "If you've harmed my parents, I swear—"

"Why would we harm these sincere people?" Shiloh Davydov was surprised. "We've performed an Act of Hiatus on them. That's all."

Claudette Davydov spoke next: "We were hoping for a private audience with you, Klara. We can unhiatus your foster parents like that"—she clicked her fingers—"and they won't know they were gone."

Still viewing the Davydovs as threats, I asked whether a "hiatus" was a phenomenon akin to mesmerism.

"Franz Mesmer is a footling braggart," replied Claudette Davydov. "We are psychosoterics. Psychosoterics of the Deep Stream."

Seeing that these words only baffled me, Shiloh Davydov asked, "Have you not witnessed anything like this before, Miss Koskov?"

"No," I replied. The Davydovs looked at each other, surprised. Shiloh Davydov removed the cigar from Dmitry's fingers before it scorched them, and rested it in the ashtray. "Won't you put that poker down? It won't help your understanding."

Feeling foolish, I replaced the poker. I heard horses' hoofs, the jink of bridles, and the cries of a coalman on Primorsky Prospect. Inside our parlor my metalife was entering a new epoch. I asked my guests, "Who *are* you? Truly?"

Shiloh Davydov said, "My name is Xi Lo. 'Shiloh' is as close as I can get in Europe. My colleague here, who is obliged to be my wife in public, is Holokai. These are the true names we carry with us from our first lives. Our souls' names, if you will. My first question for *you*, Miss Klara Koskov, is this: What is your true name?"

In a most unladylike way, I drank a good half of Dmitry's brandy. So long ago had I buried the dream that I'd one day meet others like me, other Atemporals, that now it was happening, I was woefully, woefully unprepared. "Marinus," I said, though it came out as a husky squeak, thanks to the brandy. "I am Marinus."

"Well met, Marinus," said Claudette Holokai Davydov.

"I know that name," frowned Xi Lo–in–Shiloh. "How?"

"You would not have slipped my mind," I assured him.

"*Marinus.*" Xi Lo stroked his sideburns. "Marinus of Tyre, the cartographer? Any connection? No. Emperor Philip the Arab had a father, Julius Marinus. No. This *is* an itch I cannot scratch. We glean from your letter that you're a Returnee, not a Sojourner?"

I confessed that I didn't understand his question.

The pair looked unsettled by my ignorance. Claudette Holokai said, "Returnees die, go to the Dusk, are resurrected forty-nine days later. Sojourners, like Xi Lo here, just move on to a new body when the old one's worn out."

"Then, yes." I sat back down. "I suppose I am a Returnee."

"Marinus." Xi Lo–in–Shiloh watched me. "Are we the first Atemporals you ever met?"

The lump in my throat was a pebble. I nodded.

Claudette-Holokai stole a drag of her companion's cigar. "Then you're handling yourself admirably. When Xi Lo broke my isolation, the shock drove away my wits for hours. Some may say they never returned. Well. We bear glad tidings. Or not. There are more of us."

I poured myself more brandy from Dmitry's decanter. It helped to dissolve the pebble. "How many of you—of us—are there?"

"Not a large host," Xi Lo answered. "Seven of us are affiliated in a Horological Society housed in a property in Greenwich, near London. Nine others rejected our overtures, preferring isolation. The door to them stays open if they ever wish for company. We encountered eleven—or twelve, if we include the Swabian—'self-elected' Atemporals down the centuries. To cure these Carnivores of their predatory habits is a principal function of us Horologists, and this is exactly what we did."

Later I would learn what this puzzling terminology entailed.

"If you'll pardon the indelicate question, Marinus," Claudette-Holokai's fingers traced her string of pearls, "when were you born?"

"640 A.D.," I answered, a little drunk on the novelty of sharing the truth about myself. "I was Sammarinese in my first life. I was the son of a falconer."

Holokai gripped her armchair as if hurtling forward at an incredible speed. "You're more than twice my age, Marinus! I don't have an exact birth year, or place. Probably Tahiti, possibly the Marquesas, I'd know if I went back, but I don't care to. It was a horrible death. My second self was a Muhammadan slave boy in the house of a Jewish silversmith, in Portugal. King João died while I was there, tethering my stay to the fixed pole of 1433. Xi Lo, however . . ."

Clouds of aromatic cigar smoke hung at various levels.

"I was first born at the end of the Zhou Dynasty," said the man I'd been calling Mr. Davydov, "on a boat in the Yellow River delta. My father was a mercenary. The date would have been around 300 A.D. Fifty lifetimes ago, now, or more. I notice you appear to understand this language without difficulty, Miss Koskov, yes?"

Only as I nodded did I realize he was speaking in Chinese.

"I've had four Chinese lives." I pressed my rusted Mandarin back into service. "My last was in the middle years of the Ming, the 1500s. I was a woman in Kunming then. An herbalist."

"Your Chinese sounds more modern than that," said Xi Lo.

"In my last life I lived on the Dutch Factory in Nagasaki, and practiced with some Chinese merchants."

Xi Lo nodded at an accelerating pace, before declaring in Russian, "God's blood! Marinus—the doctor, on Dejima. Big man, red face, white hair, Dutch, an irascible know-it-all. You were there when HMS *Phoebus* blasted the place to matchwood."

I experienced a feeling akin to vertigo. "You were *there*?"

"I watched it happen. From the magistrate's pavilion."

"But—who *were* you? Or who were you 'in'?"

"I had several hosts, though no Dutchmen, or I might have known you for an Atemporal, and saved Klara Koskov a world of bother. You Dutch were marooned by the fall of Batavia, you'll recall, so my route in and out of Japan was via the Chinese trading junks. Magistrate Shiroyama was my host for some weeks."

"I visited the magistrate several times. There was a big, buried scandal around his death. But what took you to Nagasaki?"

"A winding tale," said Xi Lo, "involving a colleague, Ōshima, who was Japanese in his first life, and a nefarious abbot named Enomoto, who unearthed a pre-Shinto psychodecanter up in Kirishima."

"Enomoto visited Dejima. His presence made my skin creep."

"The wisdom of skin is underappreciated. I used an Act of Suasion to persuade Shiroyama to end Enomoto's reign. Poison. Regrettably, it cost the magistrate his life, but such was the arithmetic of sacrifice. My turn will come, one day."

Jasper the dog took advantage of Vasilisa's immobility to jump onto her lap, a liberty that my foster mother never granted.

I asked, "What's 'suasion'? Is it like a 'hiatus'?"

"Both are Acts of Psychosoterica," said Holokai-in-Claudette. "Where an Act of Hiatus freezes, an Act of Suasion forces. I presume your only present means of improving the lots of your lower-born lives," she indicated the Koskovs' warm but humble parlor, "is by acquiring patrons, patronesses, and such?"

"Yes. And the accrued knowledge of my lifetimes. I gravitate towards medicine. For my female selves, it's one of the few ways up."

Galina was still chopping vegetables in the kitchen.

"Let us teach you shortcuts, Marinus." Xi Lo leaned forward, his fingers drumming his cane. "Let us show you new worlds."

. . .

"SOMEONE'S MILES AWAY." Unalaq leans on the door frame, holding a mug emblazoned with the logo of Metallica, the death-defying heavy-metal group. "The mug? A gift from Inez's kid brother. Two updates: L'Ohkna's paid for seven days on Holly's hotel room; and Holly was beginning to stir, so I hiatused her until you're ready."

"Seven days." I put the felt cover over the piano keys. "I wonder where we'll be in seven days. To work, then, before Holly's snatched from under my nose again."

"Ōshima said you'd be flagellating yourself."

"He's not up and about already, is he? He didn't go to bed last night, and he spent the morning being an action hero."

"Sixty minutes' shut-eye and he's up and off like a cocaine bunny. He's eating Nutella with a spoon, straight from the jar. I can't watch."

"Where's Inez? She shouldn't leave the apartment."

"She's helping Toby, the bookshop owner. Our shield covers the shop, but I've warned her not to go further afield. She won't."

"What must she think of all this insanity and danger?"

"Inez grew up in Oakland, California. That gave her a grounding in the basics. C'mon. Let's go Esther-hunting." So I follow her downstairs to the spare room, where Holly is lying hiatused on a sofa bed. Waking her up seems cruel. Ōshima appears from the library. "Sweet tinkling, Marinus." He mimes piano fingers.

"I'll pass my hat around later." I sit down next to Holly and take her hand, pressing my middle finger against the chakra on her palm.

I ask my colleagues, "Is everyone ready?"

HOLLY JERKS UPRIGHT, as if her torso is spring-loaded, and struggles to make sense of a present perfect of homicidal policemen, of my Act of Hiatus, of Ōshima, Unalaq, and me, and of this strange room. She notices she's digging her nails into my wrist. "Sorry."

"It's perfectly all right, Ms. Sykes. How's your head?"

"Scrambled eggs. What part of it was real?"

"All of it, I'm afraid. Our enemy took you. I'm sorry."

Holly doesn't know what to make of this. "Where am I?"

"154 West Tenth Street," says Unalaq. "My apartment, mine and my partner's. I'm Unalaq Swinton. And it's two o'clock in the afternoon, on the same day. We figured you needed a little sleep."

"Oh." Holly looks at this new character. "Nice to meet you."

Unalaq sips her coffee. "The honor's all mine, Ms. Sykes. Would you like some caffeine? Any other mild stimulant?"

"Are you like . . . Marinus and the—the other one, that . . . ?"

"Arkady? Yes, though I'm younger. This is only my fifth life."

Unalaq's sentence reminds Holly of the world she's fallen into. "Marinus, those cops . . . they . . . I think they wanted to kill."

"Hired assassins," states Ōshima. "Real flesh-and-blood people whose job is not to fix teeth or sell real estate or teach math but to murder. I made them shoot each other before they shot you."

Holly swallows. "Who are you? If it's not rude . . ."

Ōshima's mildly amused. "I'm Ōshima. Yes, I'm another Horologist, too. Enjoying my eleventh life, since we're counting."

"But . . . *you* weren't in the police car . . . were you?"

"In spirit, if not in body. For you, I was Ōshima the Friendly Ghost. For your abductors, I was Ōshima the Badass Sonofabitch. Won't deny it, that felt good." The city's hiss and boom are smudged by steady drizzle. "Though our long cold War just got hotter."

"Thank you, then, Mr. Ōshima," says Holly, "if that's the appropri—" A barbed thought snags her: "*Aoife!* Marinus—those police officers, theytheythey said Aoife'd been in an accident!"

I shake my head. "They lied. To lure you into the car."

"But they know I've got a daughter! What if they hurt her?"

"Look, look, look. Look at this." Unalaq passes her a slate. "Aoife's blog. Today she found three shards of a Phoenician amphora and some cat bones. Posted forty-five minutes ago, at sixteen seventeen Greek time. She's fine. You can message her, but don't, *don't,* refer to any of today's events. That *would* risk embroiling her."

Holly reads her daughter's entry and her panic subsides a notch. "But just 'cause those people haven't hurt her yet, it doesn't—"

"This week the Anchorites' attention is focused on Manhattan," says Ōshima. "But to be safe, your daughter has a bodyguard. Roho's one of us, too." *And one that the Second Mission can ill spare,* Ōshima subreminds me.

Again, Holly is all at sea. She tucks some loose strands of hair under her head-wrap. "Aoife's on an archaeological dig, on a remote Greek island. How . . . I mean, why . . . No." Holly looks for her shoes. "Look, I just want to go home."

I break the brutal truth gently: "You'd get as far as the Empire Hotel, but you wouldn't leave the building alive. I'm sorry."

"Even if you slip through that net," Ōshima extends the brutal truth more bluntly, "the next time you used an ATM card, your device, your slate, an Anchorite would find you within a few minutes. Even without using those methods, unless you're hidden by a Deep Stream cloak, they could get to you with a quantum totem."

"But I live in the west of Ireland! That's not gangster country."

"You'd not be safe on the goddamn International Space Station, Ms. Sykes," says Ōshima. "And the Anchorites of the Chapel of the Dusk belong to a higher order of threat than gangsters."

She looks at me. "So what must I do to be safe? Stay here forever?"

"I think," I tell her, "you'll only be safe if we win our War."

"If we don't win," says Unalaq, "it's over for all of us."

Holly Sykes shuts her eyes, giving us one last chance to vanish and to return to her life as it was at Blithewood Cemetery before a slightly chubby African Canadian psychiatrist strolled into view.

Ten seconds later, we're still here.

She sighs and tells Unalaq, "Tea, please. Splash of milk, no sugar."

" 'HOROLOGY'?" REPEATS Holly in Unalaq's kitchen. "Isn't that clocks?"

"When Xi Lo founded our Horological Society," I say, "the word meant 'the study of the measurement of time.' It was a sort of self-help group, you could say. Our founder was a London surgeon in the 1660s—he appears in Pepys's diary, by the by—and acquired a house in Greenwich as a headquarters, a storage facility, and a noticeboard to help us stay connected down through time, from one self to the next."

"In 1939," says Unalaq, "we shifted to 119A—where you visited this morning—because of the German threat."

"So Horology is a social club for you . . . Atemporals?"

"It is," says Unalaq, "but Horology has a curative function, too."

"We assassinate," states Ōshima, "carnivorous Atemporals—like the Anchorites—who consume the psychovoltaic souls of innocent people in order to fuel their own immortality. I thought Marinus told you this earlier."

"We do give them a chance to mend their ways," says Unalaq.

"But they never do," says Ōshima, "so we have to mend their ways for them, permanently."

"They are serial killers," I tell Holly. "They murder kids like Jacko, and teenagers like you were. Again and again and again. They don't stop. Carnivores are addicts and their drug is artificial longevity."

Holly asks, "And Hugo Lamb is one of these serial killers?"

"Yes. He's sourced prey eleven times since . . . Switzerland."

Holly swivels her eternity ring. "And Jacko was one of you?"

"Xi Lo founded Horology," says Ōshima. "Xi Lo led me to the Deep Stream. To psychosoterica. He was irreplaceable."

Holly thinks of a small boy with whom she shared only eight Christmases. "How many of there are you?"

"Seven, definitely. Eight, possibly. Nine, hopefully."

Holly frowns. "Quite a small-scale war, then, isn't it?"

I think of Oscar Gomez's wife. "Was there anything 'small-scale' about Jacko's disappearance for the Sykes family? Eight is very few, but we were only ten when we inoculated you. We build networks. We have allies and friends."

"And how many Carnivores are there?"

"We don't know," says Unalaq. "Hundreds, worldwide."

"But whenever we find one," Ōshima inserts a meaningful pause, "there soon becomes one less."

"The Anchorites endure, however," I say. "The Anchorites are our enemy through time. Can we prevent all the Carnivores in the world from committing animacide? No. But whom we save, we save, and every one is a victory."

Pigeons croon and huddle on Unalaq's window boxes.

"Let's say I believe you," says Holly. "Why me? Why do these Anchorites want to—Christ, I can't believe I'm saying this—want to kill me? And what am I to you?" She looks around the table. "Why do I matter in your War?"

Ōshima and Unalaq look at me. "Because you said 'Yes,' forty years ago, to a woman named Esther Little, who was fishing off a rickety wooden pier jutting out over the Thames."

Holly stares at me. "How can you possibly *know* that?"

"Esther told me about the encounter. That day, in 1984."

"*You* were in Gravesend? That Saturday Jacko went?"

"My body was. My soul was in Jacko's skull, as Jacko lay in his bed in the Captain Marlow. Esther Little's soul was there too, as was the soul of Holokai, another colleague. With Xi Lo's soul, that made four Greeks hiding in the belly of the Trojan Horse. Miss Constantin appeared in the room, through the Aperture, and ushered Jacko up the Way of Stones into the Chapel of the Dusk."

"The place the Blind Cathar built?" Holly's voice is dry.

"The place the Blind Cathar built." Good, she'd taken it in. "Jacko was Constantin's bait. We'd poked her eye by inoculating you, and we gambled on her not being able to resist poking ours in return by grooming and abducting the saved sister's brother. That part worked, and for the first time Horologists gained access to the oldest, hungriest, and best-guarded psychodecanter in existence. Before we could figure out a means of destroying the place, however, the Blind Cathar awoke. He summoned all the Anchorites and, well, it's hard to describe a psychosoteric battle at close quarters . . ."

"Think of those tennis-ball firing machines, but loaded with hand grenades," offers Ōshima, "trapped in a shipping container, on a ship caught in a force-ten gale."

"It was the worst day in Horology's history," I say.

"We killed five Anchorites," says Ōshima, "but they killed Xi Lo and Holokai. Killed-killed."

"Didn't they just get . . . resurrected?" asked Holly.

"If we die in the Dusk," I explain, "we die. Terms and conditions. Somehow the Dusk prevents resurrection. I survived because Esther Little fought her way to and fled down the Way of Stones with my soul enwrapped in hers. Alone, I would have perished, but even in Esther's safekeeping I suffered grievous damage, as did Esther. She opened the Aperture very near where you were, Holly, in the garden of a certain bungalow near the Isle of Sheppey."

"I'm guessing the location was no accident?" asks Holly.

"It was not. While Esther's soul and mine were reraveling, however, the Third Anchorite, one Joseph Rhîmes, arrived on the scene. He had followed our tracks. He slew Heidi Cross and Ian Fairweather for the hell of it, and was about to kill you, too, when I reraveled myself enough to animate Fairweather. Rhîmes kineticked a weapon into my head, and I died. Forty-nine days later I was resurrected in this body, in a broken-down ambulance in one of Detroit's more feral zip codes. For a long time I assumed Rhîmes had killed you in the bungalow, and that Esther's soul had been too badly damaged to reravel. But when I next made contact with 119A, Arkady—in his last self, not the self you met earlier—told me that you hadn't died. Instead, Joseph Rhîmes's body had been found at the crime scene."

"Only a psychosoteric could have killed Joseph Rhîmes," says Ōshima. "Rhîmes followed the Shaded Way for seventeen decades."

Holly understands. "So you think it was Esther Little?"

Unalaq says, "It's the least implausible explanation."

"But Esther Little was a . . . sweet old bat who gave me tea."

"Yes," snorts Ōshima, "and I'm a sweet old boy who rides around all day on my senior citizen's bus pass."

"Why don't I remember any of this?" says Holly. "And where did Esther Little go *after* killing this Rhîmes man?"

"The first question's simpler," says Unalaq. "Any psychosoteric can redact memories. It takes skill to do it with precision, but Esther had that skill. She could have done it on her way in."

Unconsciously, Holly grips the table. "On her way in—to where?"

"Into your parallax of memories," I say. "To the asylum you offered her. Esther's soul was battered in the Chapel of the Dusk, flamed as she fought our way out down the Way of Stones, and drained to the last psychovolt by killing Joseph Rhîmes."

"Her soul would have needed years to reravel," says Unalaq. "Years when Esther was as vulnerable to attack as someone in a coma."

"I . . . sort of get it." Holly's chair creaks. "Esther Little 'ingressed' me, got me away from the crime scene, wiped my memories of what happened . . . Okay. But where did she go *after* she . . . recovered?"

Ōshima, Unalaq, and I all look at Holly's head.

Holly frowns, then understands. "You're bloody joking."

BY SEVEN O'CLOCK, twilight is draping the attic in blues, grays, and blacks. The little lamp on the piano glows daffodil yellow. Four storys below us, I see the manager of the bookshop bidding a staff member good night. He then walks off arm in arm with a petite lady. The couple make an old-fashioned sight under the mist-haloed solars of West Tenth Street. I draw the curtains on the drizzle-streaked bulletproof glass. Ōshima, Unalaq, and I spent the afternoon debriefing Holly further on Horology and our War with the Anchorites, and eating Inez's pancakes. Going outside would have been a needless risk after this morning's near disaster, and we'll avoid 119A until our rendezvous with D'Arnoq on Friday. Arkady and the Deep Stream cloak will keep the place safe. On the evening news the "Police Impostor Fifth Avenue Shootout" was a lead story, with reporters speculating that the dead men were bank robbers who'd had a fatal argument prior to their heist. The national networks haven't run with the story, due to yesterday's gun massacre at Beck Creek, Texas, the reignited Senkaku/Diaoyu standoff between China and Japan, and Justin Bieber's fifth divorce. The Anchorites will know Brzycki was killed by psychosoteric intervention, but how it affects any plans they have for our Second Mission, I cannot guess. I've heard nothing from our defector, Elijah D'Arnoq. I hear Unalaq and Holly's feet on the creaky stairs, and they appear in the doorway.

"You have a psychiatrist's couch," says Holly.

"Dr. Marinus will see you now," I say. "Again. Ready?"

Holly unslippers her feet, and lies back. "I've got over half a century of memories stored away, right?"

I roll up the sleeves of my blouse. "A finite infinity, yes."

"How do you know where to look for Esther Little?"

"I was sent a clue via a cabdriver in Poughkeepsie," I say.

Unalaq puts a cushion under Holly's head. "Relax."

"Marinus?" Holly flinches. "Will you see *everything* I ever did?"

"That's how scansion works. But I'm a psychiatrist from the seventh century, remember. There's not much left that I haven't seen."

Holly's unsure what to do with her hands. "Do I stay conscious?"

"I can hiatus you while I scansion you, if you wish."

"Uh . . . No need. Yes. I dunno. You decide."

"Very well. Tell me about your house, near Bantry."

"O-*kay*. Dooneen Cottage was originally my great-aunt Eilísh's cottage. It's on the Sheep's Head Peninsula, this rocky finger sticking out into the Atlantic. There's a drop to a cove at the end of the garden, and a path going down to the pier and . . ."

As I ingress, I hiatus her. It's kinder, somehow. Holly's present-perfect memory, I notice, is dominated by today's bizarre events, but older memories soon billow around my passing soul like windblown sheets on a washing line. Here's Holly catching a taxi from the Empire Hotel early this morning. Meeting me at the Santorini

Café, and at Blithewood. Landing in Boston last week. I go further back, back to Holly's pluperfect memory. Holly painting in her studio, spreading seaweed on her potato patch, watching TV with Aoife and Aoife's boyfriend. Cats. Storm petrels. Jump leads. Mixing mincemeat at Christmas. Kath Sykes's funeral in Broadstairs. Deeper, faster, like rewind on an old-style DVD, showing one frame every eight, sixteen, thirty-two, sixty-four . . . Too fast. Slow down. Too slow, this is like searching for an earring dropped somewhere in Wyoming, I must take care. Here's a vivid memory of Dr. Tom Ballantyne: "I sent off three samples to three different labs. Remissions are fickle, yes, but for now, you're clear. I won't pretend to understand it—but congratulations." Deeper, further. Memories of Holly meeting Crispin Hershey in Reykjavik, in Shanghai, on Rottnest Island. They loved each other, I see, but both only half guessed it. Holly's first U.S. book tour for *The Radio People*. Holly's office at the homeless center. Her Welsh friend and colleague Gwyn. Aoife's face when Holly tells her that Ed died in a missile strike. Olive Sun's voice on the phone, an hour earlier. Happier days. Watching Aoife perform in *The Wizard of Oz* while holding Ed's hand in the darkness. Psychology lectures with the Open University. Look, a glimpse of Hugo Lamb . . . *Stop*. Their night in a room in a Swiss ski town, which is none of my business, but what muffled, baffled joy shines in the young man's eyes. He loved her, too. But the Anchorites came knocking. Fateful or fated? Scripted, Counterscripted? No time. Hurry. Deeper. A vineyard in France. A slate-gray sea—is the asylum here? There's no sign of the freighter. Too far or not far enough? Look closely. The wind must be squally and the engines churning. Stop. No time, no noise. Passengers become photographs of themselves. Gulls, balancing gravity and the battering wind. A squaddie's tossed away his cigarette, it hangs there, threads of smoke, vapor trailing . . . This is Holly's first Channel crossing, back before the tunnel was built. Back further, a year or two or three . . . An iced "17" on a birthday cake . . . Further. An abortionist's clinic in the shadow of Wembley Stadium, a young man on a Norton motorbike outside. Slowly now . . . A slope of gray months, after Jacko's disappearance. Picking strawberries . . .

And look—look! Blank, redacted scenes. Two hours' worth. Neatly done. That must be the bungalow murders. Before the blanks I find scenes of a petrol station, and a bridge. Rochester? There are ships below, but we're still the day *after* the Star of Riga, not the day *of* it. Church bells. Back through the night, spent in a church, with a teenage Ed Brubeck. The Script loves foreshadow. Back to the day before the First Mission. Holly on the back of Ed's bike, fish and chips by the sea, more cycling, Ed's T-shirt glued to his back with sweat. We pass a couple of anglers, but both look male and neither sports Esther's famous hat. Esther fished alone. "Angling's like prayer," she said. "Even together, you're alone." Slow right down. Holly looks at her watch at 4:20, at 3:49, and again at 3:17 before Ed came along. Her backpack's rubbing her skin, though backpacks were called "rucksacks" in 1984. Holly's thirsty, angry, and upset. She glances at her watch at 2:58. I've gone back too far. "Three on the Day," begins my marker. I reverse and inch forward, *slowly,* to the Thames on my left, and . . . Oh.

I've found you.

FAR OUT IN the Thames sits a cargo ship, halfway between Kent and Essex, and the name of this quarter-mile-long signpost is the *Star of Riga.* Esther Little saw the ship "now," at three P.M. exactly, on June 30, 1984. I had seen the ship earlier in Tilbury Docks, as I waited in a rented flat in Yu Leon Marinus's body before transversing over the Thames to the Captain Marlow to ingress Jacko's head. Esther submentioned the freighter as we all waited for Constantin. Holokai submentioned he'd lived in Riga for a few months as Claudette Davydov.

There Esther sits, at the end of the jetty, as Holly saw her on that hot, thirsty day. I transverse down the embankment and along the planks. Like an Oriental ghost I lack feet, but my progress is soundtracked by Holly's memories of her own footsteps. Look. Esther's cropped gray hair, grubby safari shirt, and floppy leather hat.

I subspeak: *Esther? It's Marinus.*

But Esther doesn't react in any way.

I transverse around her, to study her face.

My old friend flickers like a dying hologram.

Am I wrong? Is this just Holly's memory of Esther?

Then her chakra-eye glows dimly. Holly couldn't have seen it. I subaddress her: *Moombaki of the Noongar People.*

Nothing. Esther fades like a shadow as the sun goes in.

Her chakra-eye flickers open, shuts, open, shuts. I try to ingress, but instead of strong, coherent memories, like in Holly's parallax, I find only a nebula of moments. Dewdrops, clinging to a spider's web on a golden wattle flower; a dead infant, flies drinking from his eyes; eucalyptus trees crackling into flame and parrots shrieking through smoke; a riverbed alive with naked-backed men panning for gold; the warbling throat of a butcher bird; a line of Noongar men in chains, lugging blocks of stone; and then I'm out the other side of Esther's head. Her mind's gone. It's smashed. Just those shards remain.

The hologram solidifies and speaks: "Cold tea do you?"

False hope hurts like a broken rib: *Esther, it's Marinus.*

"Five perch. One trout. A slow afternoon."

This is recorded ghost speech, uttered by the Esther Little whom Holly remembers, not spoken by Esther's soul here and now.

Esther, you're trapped in a memory in the mind of Holly Sykes.

A bee lands on the brim of her hat. "Lucky you're not fussy."

Esther, you sought asylum here, but you forgot who you are.

"I may need asylum." She watches me, sniperlike. "A bolt-hole."

Horology needs you for a Second Mission to the Chapel of the Dusk, Esther. You left me signs.

"You won't find a shop until you and the boy arrive at Allhallows-on-Sea . . ."

Esther, what do I do? How can I bring you back?

She fades to a shimmer. I'm too late, years too late. Esther's soul has cooled to an ember that only Esther herself, or maybe Xi Lo, could have breathed back to life. I cannot. The misery I feel at finding her but losing her this way is insupportable. I look out across the memory-generated Thames. What now? Abort the Second Mission? Resign myself to managing Horology's slow decline? Circles radiate out from Esther's float. And Holly's memory-Esther takes a stick of chalk from her pocket and writes on a slat of wood: MY—

Another word on the next slat: LONG—

Then one more word: NAME—

AS ESTHER WRITES the final E the loop ends, the time resets to three P.M. Once more Esther sits gazing at the *Star of Riga,* going nowhere, the weather-bleached planks by her foot not yet written on.

Yet those three words mattered. They matter now.

Holly must have thought that Esther Little was a crazy old witch but what if Esther was transmitting an instruction to me? I begin to subrecite Esther Little's name, her true name, her living name that she taught me three selves ago, to Pablo Antay Marinus in the half hour between night and the pink-and-blue Australian dawn on the Emu's Claw rock over the Swan River valley. Esther fixed it indelibly, she said. Could she truly have seen so far ahead, so long ago? One by one I subintone the syllables. Hesitantly at first, afraid to make an error and invalidate the sequence, but the pace picks up until the name is the player and I the instrument. Is it wishful thinking, or do I sense a coalescence in the head of the memory-Esther? Word by phrase by line, archaic Wadjuk Noongar gives way to nineteenth-century Wadjuk Noongar. The space around us brightens as particles and threads of Esther's soul reassemble, reintegrate, reravel . . .

. . . and without noticing I've finished, I've finished.

Esther Little gazes out at the *Star of Riga.* The ship blasts its horn. Across the water, in Essex, a vehicle reflects a tiny pinprick of June sunshine. Esther picks up her flask and peers down it. It looks as if the loop is restarting.

Why hasn't it worked?

A subvoice tells me, *You speak Noongar like a chain saw.*

My soul pulses. *My teacher disappeared for forty-one years.*

The oldest Horologist looks into her bucket. *Not many fish, for forty-one years. I guess my signs found you?*

One from Trondheim and one from Poughkeepsie.

Esther allows herself an amused growl. *The Script contained an invitation to the Chapel. Is a Second Mission in the offing?*

Two days away, or possibly only one by now.

Time we were back, then. Esther's soul egresses the chakra of her long-ago remembered forehead and hovers, rotating through 360 degrees. *Goodbye,* she tells the vanished day.

Esther's soul egresses from Holly's forehead first and I follow, into a new morning. Holly is still lying on the couch, motionless, with my body next to her, motionless. They haven't seen us. Unalaq is reading a book and Arkady, over from 119A, is writing on his slate. I ingress Iris Marinus-Fenby and rethread my soul to my brain. My nose smells burned toast, my ears hear traffic, my calves and toes are cramped, my stomach's empty, and my mouth feels like a rodent died in it. Finding my optic nerves always takes longer. Suddenly Unalaq is laughing with astonishment and delight and says, "Be my guest!" so I know where Esther's soul went. My eyes, when I manage to lift the lids, see Arkady peering up close. "Marinus? Are you back?"

"You're supposed to be minding Sadaqat."

"L'Ohkna flew back in last night. Did you find Esther?"

"Why don't you ask Unalaq if she's seen her?"

Arkady turns around in time to see Esther-in-Unalaq drop her book, lift her hand, and stare at it, as if freshly fitted. "Fingers," she says, sounding a little drunk. "You forget. Hell, listen to me." She flexes the muscles around her mouth. "Arkady. Apparently."

Arkady leaps to his feet like a guilty character in a melodrama.

"I turn my back for a few paltry decades," growls Esther-in-Unalaq, "and you go from being a Vietnamese neurologist to a . . . a power forward with the New York Knicks?"

Arkady looks at me. I nod. "My God. My *God*. My God."

"You'll have to lose that ponytail. And what's that you're holding? Don't tell me that's what televisions have evolved into?"

"It's a tab, for the Internet. Like a laptop, minus keyboard."

Esther-in-Unalaq looks at me. "Was that English? What else has changed since 1984?"

"Oil's running out," I say, checking Holly's pulse and the second hand of the clock. "Earth's population is eight billion, mass extinctions of flora and fauna are commonplace, climate change is foreclosing the Holocene Era. Apartheid's dead, as are the Castros in Cuba, as is privacy. The USSR went bankrupt; the Eastern Bloc collapsed; Germany reunified; the EU has gone federal; China's a powerhouse—though their air is industrial effluence in a gaseous state—and North Korea is still a gulag run by a coiffured cannibal. The Kurds have a de facto state; it's Sunni versus Shi'a throughout the Middle East; the Sri Lankan Tamils got butchered; the Palestinians still have to eke out a living off Israel's garbage dumps. People outsourced their memories to data centers and basic skills to tabs. On the eleventh of September 2001, Saudi Arabian hijackers flew two airliners into the Twin Towers. As a result Afghanistan and Iraq got invaded and occupied for years by lots of American and a few British troops. Inequality is truly Pharaonic. The world's twenty-seven richest people own more wealth than the poorest five billion, and people accept that as normal. On the bright side, there's more computing power in Arkady's slate than existed in the world when you last walked it; an African American president occupied the White House for two terms; and you can now buy strawberries at Christmas." I check the clock again. "Holly's pulse is okay, but we should unhiatus her. She'll be dehydrated. Where's Ōshima?"

"I heard," Ōshima appears in the doorway, "that Rip van Winkle was honoring us with an appearance."

Esther-in-Unalaq looks at her on-and-off partner. "I'd say, 'You haven't aged a day,' Ōshima, but it wouldn't be true."

"If you'd let us know that you'd be dropping by, I'd have gone out and found me a prettier body. But we all thought you were dead."

"I damn near was dead, after finishing with Joseph Rhîmes."

"A teacher in *Norway* got the truth! A Milwaukee junkie got the truth! Or was not telling me 'obeying the Script'?"

"No, it was common bloody sense, Ōshima."

Arkady subasks me, *Can you believe these two?*

"If the Anchorites even suspected I'd survived the First Mission," says Esther-in-Unalaq, "they would have gone after any possible asylum-giver. Back in 1984, Xi Lo agreed that if our foray to the Chapel ended badly, Pfenninger and Constantin might wipe out all remaining Horologists to give themselves an open field for a decade. That meant you were a target, Ōshima. You would've only died, you Returnee, but as an unraveled Sojourner I would've *died*-died. The safest play was to seek asylum in a tough Temporal kid who'd survive a few decades, and let nobody know until it was time to wake me up."

"Holly's been tough," I say. "We should let her go now."

Esther runs Unalaq's ruby thumbnail up the stem of a purple tulip. "You miss purple, after a few years . . ."

When Esther dodges a question, I worry. "Holly's paid enough, Esther. Please. She deserves to be left in peace."

"She does," says Esther. "But it's not that simple."

"According to the Script?" asks Ōshima.

Esther fills Unalaq's lungs and slowly exhales. "There's a crack."

None of us understands. Arkady asks, "A crack in what?"

"A crack in the fabric of the Chapel of the Dusk."

THE LIBRARY IN Unalaq and Inez's apartment is a deep square well, walled with bookshelves. Its parquet floor has just enough room for the round table, but a corkscrew staircase winds up not to one but two narrow balconies that give access to the upper bookshelves, and the Monday-morning sunshine enters through a skylight twenty feet above us. It illuminates an oblong of book spines. Ōshima, Arkady, Esther-in-Unalaq, and I sit around the table and talk about Horology business until there's a knock at the door and Holly enters, fed, freshly showered, and dressed in baggy clothes borrowed from Inez. Her new head-wrap is deep blue, scattered with white stars. "Hi," says the tired, lined woman. "I hope I haven't kept you all waiting."

"You hosted me for forty-one years, Ms. Sykes," says Esther-in-Unalaq. "A few minutes is the least I owe you."

"Make it Holly. Everyone. Wow. Look at all these books. It's rare to see so many, these days."

"Books'll be back," Esther-in-Unalaq predicts. "Wait till the power grids start failing in the late 2030s and the datavats get erased. It's not far away. The future looks a lot like the past."

Holly asks, "Is that, like . . . an official prophecy?"

"It's the inevitable result," I say, "of population growth and lies about oil reserves. But please. This chair's for you."

"What a beautiful table," remarks Holly, sitting down.

"It's older than the nation we're in," says Arkady.

Holly runs her fingers for a moment over the grain and knots of the yew wood. "But younger than you lot, right?"

"Age is a relative concept," I say, rapping my knuckles on the old, old wood.

Esther-in-Unalaq pushes back Unalaq's bronze hair from her face. "Holly. Years ago you made a rash promise to a fisherwoman on a jetty. You couldn't know the true consequences of that promise, but you kept it anyway. Doing so pulled you into Horology's War with the Anchorites. When Marinus and me egressed from you earlier, your first role in our War ended. Thank you. From me, from Horology. I owe you my life." The rest of us signed our agreement. "The good news is this. By six o'clock tomorrow evening, according to the world's clocks, the War will be over."

"A peace treaty?" asks Holly. "Or a fight to the death?"

"A fight to the death," answers Arkady, raking his fingers through his lush hair. "Poachers and gamekeepers don't do peace treaties."

"If we win," says Esther-in-Unalaq, "you're home free, Holly. If not, we won't be able to stage any more dramatic rescues. We'll be dead-dead. And we won't lie. We can't know how our enemy'd respond to victory. Constantin, specially, has a long memory."

Holly's troubled, naturally. "Aren't you precognitive?"

"*You* know precognition, Holly," says Esther. "It's a flicker of glimpses. It's points on a map, but it's never the whole map."

Holly considers this. "My first role in your War, you just said. Implying there's a second."

"Tomorrow," I take over, "a high-ranking Anchorite named Elijah D'Arnoq is due to appear in the gallery at 119A. D'Arnoq proposes to escort us to the Chapel of the Dusk and to help us destroy it. He claims to be a defector who can no longer stomach the moral evil of decanting innocent 'donors.' "

"You don't sound as if you believe him."

Ōshima drums his fingers on the table. "*I* don't."

Holly asks, "Can't you enter the defector's mind to check?"

"I did," I explain, "and what I found backed his story up. But evidence can be tampered with. All defectors have a complex relationship with truth."

Holly asks the obvious: "Then why take the risk?"

"Because now we have a secret weapon," I answer, "and fresh intelligence."

We all look at Esther-in-Unalaq. "Back in 1984," she tells Holly, "on what we call our First Mission to our enemy's fastness, I detected a hairline crack running from the apex to the icon. I believe that I . . . may be able to split this crack open."

"Dusk," I explain further, "would then flood the Chapel, and destroy it. The Blind Cathar, whose half-sentient vestiges reside *within* the Chapel, would perish. Any Anchorites touched by the Dusk would die. Any Anchorites elsewhere would have lost their psychodecanter, and be as susceptible to the aging process as the rest of humanity."

Holly asks the less-than-obvious: "You said the Blind Cathar was a genius, a mystic Einstein who could 'think' matter into being. Why didn't he notice his masterpiece has a chink in its armor?"

"The Chapel was built by faith," replies Esther. "But faith requires doubt, like matter requires antimatter. That crack, that's the Blind Cathar's doubt. It dates from before he became what he later became. Doubt that he was doing God's work. Doubt that he had the right to take the souls of others so that he could cheat death."

"So you plan to . . . stick dynamite into the crack?"

"Nitroglycerin won't scratch the paintwork," says Ōshima. "The place has withstood the Dusk for centuries. A nuclear explosion might do the job, but warheads aren't very portable. What's needed is psychosoteric dynamite."

Esther clears Unalaq's throat. "That would be me."

Holly checks with me: "A suicide mission?"

"If our defector is fake, and his promise to show us how to safely demolish the Chapel is a lie and a trap, then that contingency is real."

"Marinus means yes," says Ōshima. "A suicide mission."

"Christ," says Holly. "So are you going up alone, Esther?"

Esther shakes Unalaq's head. "If D'Arnoq is luring the last Horologists up the Way of Stones, he'll want *all* of the last Horologists, not just one. If the Second Mission *is* an ambush, I'll need the others to buy me time. Detonating your soul isn't a beginner's party trick."

I hear the piano, faintly. Inez is playing "My Wild Irish Rose."

Holly asks, "So *if* Esther has to blow up this—enemy HQ, say, and assuming she succeeds . . ." She looks at the rest of us.

"Dusk dissolves living tissue," says Ōshima. "The End."

"Unless," I venture, "there was a way back to the Light of Day that we don't yet know about. One built by an ally. On the inside."

Half a mile above us, a cloud passes between our skylight and our nearest star and the oblong of sunshine fades away.

Holly reads me. "What is it you still haven't told me?"

I look at Esther, who shrugs Unalaq's shoulders: *You've known her the longest.* So I say what I won't be able to unsay later: "On the First Mission, neither I nor Esther actually saw Xi Lo die."

At certain rare moments, a library is a kind of mind. Holly shifts in her seat. "What did you see?"

"Not a lot in my case," I say. "I was pouring all my psychovoltage into our shield. But Esther was next to Jacko when Xi Lo's soul egressed and . . ." I look at my colleague.

"And ingressed the chakra-eye on the icon of the Blind Cathar. He wasn't being dragged like a victim. Xi Lo transversed in, like a bullet. And . . . the instant before he vanished, I heard Xi Lo subtell me three words: *I'll be here.*"

"We don't know," I admit, "if this was a spur-of-the-moment act, or a plan that Xi Lo hadn't shared, for reasons of his own. If Xi Lo hoped to sabotage the Chapel, he failed. One hundred and sixty-four people have lost their lives and souls in the Chapel of the Dusk since 1984. One poor man was abducted from a secure psychiatric ward in Vancouver only last week. But . . . Esther thinks that Xi Lo has been preparing the way for the Second Mission. Holly? Are you okay?"

Holly dabs the sleeves of Inez's shirt against her eyes. "Sorry, I . . . That 'I'll be here,'" she says. "I heard it too. In my daymare, in the underpass, outside Rochester."

Esther is fascinated. "Your voices, your certainties, are silent for you now, but do you remember when it used to insist on something? Maybe the sense was obscure, but the Script refused to change. Do you remember how that felt?"

Holly swallows and composes herself. "I do."

"The Script insists that Xi Lo is, somehow, alive. To this day."

"I don't know," I say, "if you view Xi Lo as a body snatcher or"—a fierceness is growing in Holly's whole demeanor—"as a bookshelf, say, of many books, the newest of which is called *Jacko Sykes*. None of us is saying, 'If you join the Second Mission, you'll get your brother back,' because we're so much in the dark ourselves, but—"

"Your Xi Lo," Holly interrupts, "is my Jacko. You loved your founder, your friend, as I loved—*love*—my brother. Dunno, maybe that makes me an idiot. I mean, you're a club of immortal professors who've probably *read* these books"—she indicates the four walls of bookshelves, rising to the skylight—"while I left school without one A-level, even. Or maybe I'm even sadder than that, maybe I'm just clutching at straws, magic straws, hoping, *hoping,* pathetically, like a mother paying her life savings to a psychic shyster to 'channel' her dead son . . . But y'know what? Jacko's still my brother, even if he *is* better known as Xi Lo and older than Jesus, and if the shoe was on the other foot, he'd come and find me. So, Marinus, if there's one chance in a thousand that Xi Lo or Jacko is in this Chapel of the

Dusk or Dunes or wherever and this Second Mission of yours'll get me to him, I'm in. You're not stopping me. Just you bloody try."

The oblong of light is back and motes of dust swirl in the sunshine slanting down the wall of books. Golden pollen.

"Our War must strike you as otherworldly, but dying in the Chapel is just as final as dying in a car crash here. Consider Aoife—"

"Earlier, you said you can't guarantee Aoife's safety, or mine, unless these Anchorites are taken down. That *is* right, yeah?"

My conscience wants a recess, but I must agree. "Yes, I stand by that statement. But our enemy is dangerous."

"Look, I'm a cancer survivor, I'm in my fifties, and I've never shot an air pistol even, and I've got no"—her hand dances—"psychopowers. Not like you, anyway. But I'm Aoife's mother and Jacko's sister and these—these individuals have harmed, or threatened, people *I* love. So here's the thing: *I'm* dangerous."

For what it's worth, subremarks Ōshima, *I believe her.*

"Sleep on it," I tell Holly. "Decide in the morning."

INEZ DRIVES. She's wearing dark glasses to hide the effects of a sleepless abysmal night. The wipers squelch every few seconds. We don't say much and there's not a lot to say. Unalaq sits up front, and Ōshima, Holly, Arkady, and I are squashed into the back. Ōshima's hosting Esther today. New York is damp, in a hurry, and indifferent to the fact that we Horologists plus Holly are risking our metalives and life for total strangers, their psychovoltaic children, and for the unborn whose parents have not yet met. I notice details I ordinarily overlook. Faces, textures, materials, signs, flows. There are days when New York strikes me as a conjuring trick. All great cities do and must revert to jungle, tundra, or tidal flats, if you wait long enough, and I should know. I've seen it with my eyes. Today, however, New York's *here*-ness is incontestable, as if time is subject to it, not it subject to time. What immortal hand or eye could frame these charted miles, welded girders, inhabited sidewalks, and more bricks than there are stars? Who could ever have predicted these vertical upthrusts and squally canyons in Klara Koskov's lifetime, when I first traveled here with Xi Lo and Holokai—my friends the Davydovs? Yet all this was already there, packed into that magpie entrepôt like an oak tree packed into an acorn or the Chrysler Building folded up small enough to fit inside the brain of William Van Alen. If consciousness exists beyond the Last Sea and I go there today, I'll miss New York as much as anywhere.

Inez turns off Third Avenue into our street. For the last time? These thoughts don't help. Will I die without ever reading *Ulysses* to the end? Think of the case files I'm leaving back in Toronto, the paperwork, the emails, the emotions that my colleagues, friends, neighbors, and patients will pass through as I change from being "the AWOL Dr. Fenby" to "the Missing Dr. Fenby" to "Dr. Fenby, presumed dead." No, don't think. We pull up to 119A. If Horology has a home, it's this place, with its oxtail-soup red bricks and dark-framed windows of differing shapes. Inez tells the car, "Park," and the hazards lights flick on.

"Be careful," Inez says to Unalaq. Unalaq nods.

"Bring her back," Inez says to me.

"I'll do my best," I say. My voice sounds thin.

119A RECOGNIZES HOROLOGISTS and lets us in. Sadaqat greets us behind the inner shield on the first floor. Our faithful warden is dressed like a parody survivalist, with army fatigues and a dozen pockets, a compass around his neck. "Welcome home, Doctor." He takes my coat. "Mr. L'Ohkna's in the office. Mr. Arkady, Miss Unalaq, Mr. Ōshima. And Ms. Sykes." Sadaqat's face drops. "I only hope you have recovered from the vicious and cowardly attack by the enemy. Mr. Arkady told me what happened."

Holly: "I've been well taken care of. Thank you."

"The Anchorites are abominable. They are vermin."

"Their attack persuaded me to help Horology," says Holly.

"Good," says Sadaqat. "Absolutely. It is black and white."

"Holly is joining our Second Mission," I tell our warden.

Sadaqat shows surprise, and a gram of confusion. "Oh? I was not aware that Ms. Sykes had studied Deep Stream methodology."

"She hasn't," says Arkady, hanging up his coat. "But we all have a role to play in the hours ahead, don't we, Sadaqat?"

"True, my friend." Sadaqat insists on collecting everyone else's coat for the closet. "So true. And are there any other last minute . . . modifications to the Mission?"

Sadaqat's been well prepared, but he can't quite keep the hunger out of his voice.

"None," I say. "None. We will act with acute caution, but we will take Elijah D'Arnoq at face value—unless he betrays us."

"And Horology has its secret weapon." Sadaqat glows. "Myself. But it is not yet ten o'clock, and Mr. D'Arnoq is not due to appear until eleven, so I made some muffins. You can smell them, I think?" Sadaqat smiles like a buxom chocolatier tempting a group of dieters who know they want to. "Banana and morello cherries. An army cannot march on an empty stomach, my friends."

"I'm sorry, Sadaqat," I step in, "but we shouldn't eat. The Way of Stones can induce nausea. An empty stomach is in fact best."

"But surely, Doctor, just a *tiny* mouthful can't hurt? They are fresher than fresh. I put white chocolate chips in the mix, too."

"They'll be just as awesome on our return," says Arkady.

Sadaqat doesn't push it. "Later, then. To celebrate."

He smiles, showing twenty thousand dollars' worth of American dental care, paid for by Horology, of course. Sadaqat owns very little not earned from or given by Horology. How could he? He spent most of his life in a psychiatric hospital outside Reading, England. A freelance Carnivore had got herself employed as a secretary in the hospital, and had groomed a psychovoltaic patient who had shared confidences with Sadaqat before the poor woman's soul was decanted. I disposed of the Carnivore after quite a strenuous duel in her sunken garden, but rather than redact what Sadaqat had learned about the Atemporal world, I set about isolating the section of his brain harboring his schizophrenia and severing its neural pathways to the unimpaired regions. This cured him, after a fashion, and when he declared his undying gratitude I brought him over to New York to be the warden of 119A. That was five years ago. One year ago our faithful retainer was turned during a series of incorporeal encounters and rendezvous in Central Park, where Sadaqat exercises daily, whatever the weather. Ōshima, who first noticed the Anchorites' fingerprints on our warden, was all for redacting the last six years from Sadaqat's memory and suasioning him aboard a container ship to the Russian Far East. A mixture of sentimentality and a reluctant intuition that we could deploy the Anchorites' mole against his new masters persuaded me to stay Ōshima's hand. It has been a perilous twelve months of second- and third-guessing our enemy's intentions, and L'Ohkna had to recalibrate 119A's sensors to detect toxins in case Sadaqat was ordered to poison us, but it all comes to an end this very morning, for good or for ill.

How I loathe this war.

"Come," Ōshima tells Sadaqat. "Let's check the circuitry in our box of tricks one last time . . ."

They go upstairs to ensure the hardware needs no last-minute adjustments. Arkady goes up to the garden to do Tai Chi in the half-hearted drizzle. Unalaq retreats to the common room to send instructions to her Kenyan network. I go to the office to transfer the Horology protocols to L'Ohkna. The task is soon done. The young Horologist shakes my hand and tells me he hopes we'll meet again, and I tell him, "Not as much I do." Then he departs 119A through the secret exit. Thirty minutes remain before D'Arnoq's appearance. Poetry? Music? A game of pool.

I go down to the basement, where I find Holly setting up. "I hope it was okay to help myself. Everyone sort of vanished, so I just . . ."

"Of course. May I join you?"

She's surprised. "You play?"

"When not battling with the devil over a chessboard, nothing calms the nerves like the click of cue tip on phenolic resin."

Holly lines up the pack of balls and removes the triangle. "Can I ask another question about Atemporals?" I give her a *fire-away* face. "Do you have families?"

"We're often resurrected into families. A Sojourner's host usually has blood relatives around like Jacko did. We form attachments, like Unalaq and Inez. Until the twentieth century, traveling alone as an unmarried woman was problematic."

"So you've been married yourself?"

"Fifteen times, though not since the 1870s. More than Liz Taylor and Henry the Eighth combined. You're curious to know if we can conceive children, however." I make a gesture to brush her awkwardness away. "No. We cannot. Terms and conditions."

"Right." Holly chalks her cue. "It'd be tough, I s'pose, to . . ."

"To live, knowing your kids died of old age decades ago. Or that they *didn't* die, but won't see this loon on the doorstep who insists he's Mom or Dad, reincarnated. Or discover you've impregnated your great-great-grandchild. Sometimes we adopt, and often it works well. There's never a shortage of children needing homes. So I've never borne or fathered a child, but what you feel for Aoife, that unhesitating willingness to rush into a burning building, I've felt that too. I've gone into burning buildings, as well. And one sizable advantage of infertility was to spare my female selves getting banged up as breeding stock all their lives, as was the fate of most women between the Stone Age and the Suffragettes." I gesture at the table. "Shall we?"

"Sure. Ed always said I've got this nosy streak. Which was brass-necked of Mr. Journalist, mind you." She takes a coin from her purse. "Heads or tails?"

"Throw me a heads."

She flips the coin. "Tails. Once I'd've known that." Holly lines up her shot and breaks. The cue grazes the pack, bounces off the bottom cushion, and floats back up to the top.

"I'm guessing that wasn't beginner's luck."

"Brendan, Jacko, and me played at the Captain Marlow, on Sundays when the pub was shut. Guess who usually won?"

I copy Holly's shot, but play it less well. "He'd been playing since the 1750s, remember. More recently, too. Xi Lo and I played daily on this very table, for most of 1969."

"Seriously? On this very table?"

"It's been reupholstered twice since, but yes."

Holly runs her thumb along the cushion. "What did Xi Lo look like?"

"Shortish, early fifties in 1969, bearded, Jewish, as it happened. He set up comparative anthropology at NYU. There are photos in the archives, if you'd like to see him."

She considers the offer. "Another time, when we're not off on a suicide mission. Xi Lo was male back then, too?"

"Yes. Sojourners often have a gender they're most at home in. Esther prefers being female. We Returnees alternate gender from one resurrection to the next, whether we like it or not."

"That doesn't screw your head up?"

"It's odd for the first few lives, but you get used it."

Holly hits the cue ball off the side and bottom cushions, and into the loosened pack. "You say things like that as if it's so . . . normal."

"Normal is whatever you have come to take for granted. To your ancestor in 1024, your life in 2024 would seem equally improbable, mystifying, full of marvels."

"Yeah, but . . . it's not quite the same. For that ancestor and me, when we die, we die. For you . . . What's it *like,* Marinus?"

"Atemporality?" I rub blue chalk dust onto the fleshy pad at the base of my thumb. "We're old, even when young. We're usually leaving, or being left behind. We're wary of ties. Until 1821, when Xi Lo and Holokai found me, my loneliness was indescribable yet had to be endured. Even now, what I'd call the 'ennui of eternity,' if you will, can be debilitating. But being a doctor, and an horologist, gives my metalife a purpose."

Holly readjusts her moss-green head-wrap, half removing it, to reveal a scalp of trimmed tufty down. She hasn't done this in my presence before, and I'm touched. "Last question: Why do Atemporals exist? I mean, did Returnees and Sojourners evolve this way, like the great apes or whales? Or were you . . . 'made'? Was it something that happened to you, in your first life?"

"Not even Xi Lo has an answer to that. Not even Esther knows." I hit the orange 5 ball into the bottom left. "I'm spots, you're stripes."

AT TEN-FIFTY, HOLLY pots the black to beat me by a single ball. "I'll give you a rematch later," she says, picking up her daypack. We walk upstairs to the gallery, where the others are assembled. Ōshima lowers the blinds. Holly goes into the kitchen for a glass of tap water—*Only tap water,* I subcall after her. *Don't touch the bottled water. It could have been tampered with,* I subwarn her—and she returns a minute later, strapping on a small daypack, as if we're going for a short hike in the woods. I lack the heart to ask her what she's packed—a flask of tea, a cardigan, a bar of Kendal mint cake for energy? This just isn't that sort of expedition. We look at the paintings. What's left to say? We discussed strategy to the saturation point in Unalaq's library; sharing our fears at this point is unhelpful, and we don't want to fill the last moments with small talk. Bronzino's *Venus, Cupid, Folly, and Time* calls me over. Xi Lo told me he regretted never switching it for the copy in London, but he couldn't face all the Acts of Suasion, skulduggery, and subterfuge needed to right the wrong. Fifty years later I stand there with the same regret. For Atemporals, our tomorrows feel like a limitless resource. Now I've none left.

"The Aperture," Unalaq says. "I feel it."

Six of us look around for the unzipping line . . .

"There," says Arkady, "by the Georgia O'Keeffe."

A vertical black slit draws itself in front of the horizontal yellows and pinks of the New Mexico dawn. A hand appears, the line widens to a slash, and Elijah D'Arnoq emerges. Softly, Holly mangles a swear word and says, *"Where did he come from?"* and Arkady mutters, "Where we're going."

Elijah D'Arnoq needs a shave and his wiry hair looks unkempt. Yes, the strain of being a traitor ought to show. "You're punctual."

"Horologists have no excuse for being late," replies Arkady.

D'Arnoq recognizes Holly. "Ms. Sykes. I'm glad you were rescued the other day. Constantin regards you as unfinished business."

Holly can't yet speak to the man who steps out of thin air.

"Ms. Sykes will join our demolition party," I tell D'Arnoq. "Unalaq will channel her psychosoteric voltage into the cloaking operation."

Elijah D'Arnoq looks dubious, and I wonder if this might jeopardize the Second Mission. "I can't guarantee her safety."

"I thought you'd covered all angles?" says Arkady.

"War has no guarantees. You all know that."

"And Mr. Dastaani here," I indicate Sadaqat, "will also be joining us. I presume you are familiar with our warden at 119A?"

"Everybody spies," says D'Arnoq. "What's Mr. Dastaani's role?"

"To park his ass," says Ōshima, "halfway up the Way of Stones and unleash a force-ten psychoferno if anyone wanders up after us. Temporal, Atemporal—anyone in the conduit will be ash."

D'Arnoq frowns. "Is a psychoferno a Deep Stream invocation?"

"No," says Ōshima. "It's my word for what happens if the bomb made of N9D—the famous Israeli-made nano-explosive—currently in Mr. Dastaani's backpack goes off inside the Way of Stones."

"It's insurance against an attack from the rear," I say, "while we're taking apart the Chapel."

"A smart precaution," says Elijah D'Arnoq, looking impressed. "Though I pray to God you don't have to use it."

"How do you feel?" Ōshima asks D'Arnoq. "Defection's a big step."

The 128-year-old Carnivore regards the eight-centuries-old Ōshima with defiance. "I've been party to decades of indiscriminate evil, Mr. Ōshima. But today I'll also be party to stopping it."

"But without your Black Wine," Ōshima reminds him, "you'll age, you'll fade away, you'll die in a care home."

"Not if Pfenninger or Constantin stop us before we've smashed the Chapel of the Dusk, I won't. And so. With no further ado?"

ONE BY ONE, we slip through the dark Aperture onto the round floor of rock ten paces across. The unflickering, paper-white Candle of the Dial stands as tall as a child. I'd forgotten the dual claustrophobia and agoraphobia, the smell of locked spaces, and the thin air. Residual color and light from the gallery filters in through the Aperture, held open like a drape by D'Arnoq now for Holly, now for Sadaqat, with his explosive backpack. Sadaqat's face is a study of nervous awe, while Ōshima, the last to enter, is a study of sulky nonchalance. "This isn't the Chapel, is it?" Holly mutters. "And why's my voice so quiet?"

"This is the Dial of the Way of Stones," I reply. "The first of the many steps that climb up to the Chapel. The edges of the Dial absorb light and sound, so raise your voice a little to compensate."

"There's no color," observes Holly. "Or is it me?"

"The Candle's monochrome," I answer. "It's been burning for eight centuries." Behind us, Elijah D'Arnoq is sealing the Aperture. I catch a brief glimpse of Bronzino's Venus, lightly holding her golden apple, before our way back is gone. No dungeon was ever so secure. Only Esther or a follower of the Shaded Way can unseal the Aperture and get us home. I suffer a jabbing flashback to my last time on the Dial, incorporeally, my and Esther's souls unraveling, Joseph Rhîmes hard on her heels and gaining. Esther, nestled and hidden in Ōshima's head, is no doubt remembering too.

"There are letters cut into the stone," Holly remarks.

"The Cathar alphabet," I tell her. "No one can read it now, not even heresiologists. The alphabet is descended from Oc, a language older even than Basque."

"Pfenninger told me," says D'Arnoq, "the letters are a prayer to God, requesting His help to rebuild Jacob's Ladder. That's what the Blind Cathar believed he was building, apparently. Don't touch the walls. Whatever it's made of, it and atomic matter"—he produces a coin from his pocket—"do not get on." He tosses the coin out of the Dial's perimeter. It vanishes in a blink of phosphorescence. "Don't lose your footing on the Way of Stones."

"Which is where?" asks Ōshima.

"It's cloaked," D'Arnoq shuts his eyes and opens his chakra-eye, "and moving, to keep out the riffraff. One moment." He takes short, slow steps to the edge of the Dial, symboling in the staccato manner of the Shaded Way and mumbling an Act of Reveal. Keeping his back to the Candle, he shuffles sideways around the perimeter. "Got it." Off the edge of the Dial and about one foot higher, a stone slab appears, as long and wide as a table. A second slab leads up from the first, and a third, and a fourth, higher into the blackness.

"Marinus," Holly asks in my ear, "is this technology? Or . . ."

I know the missing word. "If you'd cured Henry the Seventh's TB with a course of ethambutol, or given Isaac Newton an hour's access to the Hubble telescope, or shown an off-the-shelf 3-D printer to the regulars at the Captain Marlow in the 1980s, you would have had the M-word thrown your way, too. Some magic is merely normality that you're not yet used to."

"*If* the professor of semantics wouldn't object," says Ōshima, "perhaps she'd finish her seminar later?"

ELIJAH D'ARNOQ GOES first, I follow, then Holly, Arkady, Unalaq, and Sadaqat, with ten kilos of N9D in his bag, and last Ōshima as our rear guard. On the fifth or sixth stone I look back over my companions' heads, but the Dial is already out of view. Even the Way of Stones' irregularity is irregular. There are stretches where the steps twist upward, sharp and steep, a stairway in a spire. There are stretches where long slabs of stone form a gently climbing road. There are even places where the climber must jump across from slab to slab, like stepping stones in a river. Better to ignore thoughts of slipping. Soon I work up a sweat. Visibility is poor, akin to climbing a narrow mountain track at night, in grainy fog. The stones glow with a pale light, like that of the Candle of the Dial, but only as we approach, creating an illusion that the Way is building itself as we make our ascent. The darkness all around is oppressive, and seems to conjure up voices from my metalife. I hear my birth father, explaining in vernacular late Latin how to feed a dormouse to a kestrel. Now it's Sholeetsa, an herbalist of the Duwamish tribe, scolding me for overboiling a root. Now the corvine cackle of Arie Grote, a warehouseman on Dejima. Their bodies were compost long ago, their souls passed to the Last Sea. We Horologists agreed not to subspeak, for fear of being overheard, but I wonder if the others also hear voices from their past lives. I don't ask in case I distract them from where they're putting their feet. Who falls off the Way of Stones falls into nothing.

. . .

WE ARRIVE AT the only triangular slab on the whole climb. It is concave in its center and large enough for all six of us to stand on. "Welcome to the Halfway Station," says D'Arnoq, and I recall Immaculée Constantin naming it in the same way to Jacko on the First Mission. "I think we've found our lookout point for you, Sadaqat," says Ōshima. "The line of sight looking down is as good it gets. Lie in this hollow, here in the middle, and you'll see any visitors before they see you." Sadaqat nods, looks at me and I nod back. "Very good, Mr. Ōshima." With due diligence, Sadaqat sits down and takes from his backpack a heavily adapted iCube and a thin metallic cylinder. He places the iCube towards the "downhill" corner of the slab.

"Is that the firebomb?" D'Arnoq asks with professional curiosity.

"It's a Deep Stream cloak generator," Sadaqat flips open the cuboid's air-screen and scrolls through options, "and a soul alarm. This noise sounds"—a wild-goose signal honks repeatedly—"when it detects an unidentified soul, such as yours, Mr. D'Arnoq . . ." Sadaqat's fingers sidescroll and the air-screen throbs as D'Arnoq's brain signature is stored. "Now it will know friend from foe."

"A wise gadget," says D'Arnoq, "and a clever one."

"The generator prevents a psychosoteric from using an Act of Suasion to make me deactivate the N9D." Sadaqat unscrews the top of the metallic cylinder. "And the detector alerts me to the fact that someone has tried—and that it is time to detonate the firebomb, which, of course, is this." Tripod legs shoot out from the lower end of the cylinder and Sadaqat stands it up. "Ten kilos of N9D have been compressed into this tube—sufficient to turn the Way of Stones into a conduit of flame at five hundred degrees Celsius. If the goose goes 'honk,'" Sadaqat looks at D'Arnoq, "psychoferno."

"Stay alert," says Ōshima. "We're depending on you."

"I have made my oaths, Mr. Ōshima. This is what I am for."

"You have a loyal lieutenant," D'Arnoq tells me. "Ready to make a . . . the ultimate sacrifice."

"I know how lucky we are," I say to Sadaqat.

"Don't look so grim, Doctor!" Sadaqat stands and shakes hands with us all. "We'll see each other soon, my friends. I am sure it is Scripted." When he reaches me he slaps his heart. "Here!"

WE KEEP CLIMBING, stone after stone after stone, but it's difficult to track how high or how far we've come since the Dial of the Way, or how many minutes have gone by since we left Sadaqat on sentry duty at the Halfway Station. We left our devices and watches at 119A. Time exists here but it isn't easily measured, even in an Horologist's mind. My resolve to count the steps has been sidelined by the voices of the long-dead. So I just follow Elijah D'Arnoq's back, staying as alert as I can until at last we come to a second circular slab of stone, identical in most features to the Dial at the base of the climb. "The Summit, we call this one," says D'Arnoq, visibly nervous. "We're here."

"Isn't this where we came in?" asks Holly. "The candle, the circle, the stone circle, the engravings . . ."

"The stone inscription differs," I say. "Mr. D'Arnoq?"

"Never studied it," admits the defector. "Pfenninger is big into philology, and Joseph Rhîmes used to be as well, but for most of us, the Chapel's a . . . sentient machine that we have a deal with."

" 'Don't blame me, I'm only the little guy'?" says Arkady.

D'Arnoq looks worn thin. "Yeah. Maybe so. Maybe that *is* what we tell ourselves." He rubs imaginary dust from his eye. "Okay, now I'll unseal the Umber Arch—the way in—but first a warning: The Blind Cathar should be safely in stasis, in his icon, in the north corner. You'll sense him. He shouldn't sense us. So—"

" 'Shouldn't'?" queries Ōshima. "What's this 'shouldn't'?"

"Deicide has its risks," D'Arnoq scowls, "or it wouldn't be deicide. If you're afraid, Ōshima, go and join Sadaqat down below. But here are three don'ts to reduce the risk: Be wary of looking into the Blind Cathar's face on the icon; don't make any loud noises or sudden movements; don't perform any acts of Deep Stream psychosoterica, not even subspeech. I can invoke Shaded Way acts without disturbing the Chapel, but the Cathar'll detect psychosoterica from the far side of the Schism. Your 119A is fitted with alarms, shields, and cloaks; so is our sanctum, and if the Blind Cathar is aware of Horologists in the house before the walls come tumbling down, the day will end badly for all of us. Understood?"

"Understood," says Arkady. "Dracula can be safely awoken only when the stake's already in his heart."

D'Arnoq barely hears as he evokes an Act of Reveal. A modest, trefoiled, man-high portal shimmers into being at the edge of the Summit Stone. The Umber Arch. Through it we see the Chapel, and inwardly I recoil, even as I follow Elijah D'Arnoq forwards. "In we go," somebody says.

THE CHAPEL OF the Dusk of the Blind Cathar is the body of a living being. One senses it, immediately. Taking the Umber Arch as south, the rhombus-shaped nave of the Chapel is maybe sixty paces along its north-south axis, thirty paces from east to west, and loftier than it is long. Every plane points to, refers to, or mirrors the icon of the Blind Cathar, hanging in the narrow "northern" corner, so one must concentrate hard on not gazing at the icon. Walls, floor, and pyramidal ceiling are all crafted from same milky, flint-gray stone. The Chapel's sole furnishings are a long oaken table placed along the north-south axis, two benches on either side, and one large picture on each wall. Immaculée Constantin explained the gnostic paintings to Jacko last time: the Blue Apples of Eden at Noon on the Eighth Day of Creation; the Demon Asmodeus, tricked by Solomon into building the King's Temple; the true Virgin, suckling a pair of infant Christs; and Saint Thomas standing in a rhombus-shaped chamber identical to the Chapel of the Dusk. Floating below the roof's apex is a writhing snake wrought in chatoyant stone, in the circular act of consuming its own tail. The Chapel's blockwork is flawless and fused and creates the illusion that the chamber was hewn from inside a mountain, or that it was crystalized into being. The air here is not fresh or stale or warm or cool, though it carries the tang of bad memories. Holokai died here, and despite what we've allowed Holly to hope, I have no proof that Xi Lo didn't.

"Give me a minute," murmurs D'Arnoq. "I need to revoke my Act of Immunity, so we can merge our psychovoltage." He closes his eyes. I walk over to the oblique-angled west corner, where a window offers a view over one mile or a hundred miles of Dunes, up to the High Ridge and the Light of Day. Holly follows me. "See up there?" I tell her. "That's where we're from."

"Then all those little pale lights," whispers Holly, "crossing the sand, they're souls?"

"Yes. Thousands and thousands, at any given time." We walk over to the eastern window, where an inexact distance of Dunes rolls down through darkening twilight to the Last Sea. "And that's where they're bound." We watch the little lights enter the starless extremity and go out, one by one by one.

Holly asks, "Is the Last Sea really a sea?"

"I doubt it. It's just the name we use."

"What happens to the souls when they get there?"

"You'll find out, Holly. Maybe I will, one day." *Today?*

We return to the center, where D'Arnoq is still inside himself. Ōshima points up to the apex of the Chapel, and traces an invisible line down to the north corner where the icon appears to be watching us. I shut my eyes, open my chakra-eye, and scan the ceiling for the crack mentioned by Esther . . .

It takes a moment, but I find it. There, starting at the apex and curving down to the shadows in the north corner.

Yes, it's there, but it's a terribly thin crack on which to gamble five Atemporal metalives and one Temporal life.

"Is it me," Holly is asking, and I close my chakra-eye and open up my physical eyes, "or does that picture . . . sort of . . . reel you in?"

"It's not you," replies Elijah D'Arnoq, who is now back with us. We look at the icon. The hermit wears a white cloak, his hood draped about his shoulders to expose his head and a face with blanks instead of eyes. "But don't stare at him," D'Arnoq reminds us. On the Way of Stones, sound was muffled so you had to speak twice as loudly. Here in the Chapel, whispers, footsteps, and even the swish of our clothing sound amplified, as if collected by hidden microphones. "Look *away*, Ms. Sykes. He may be dreaming at present, but he's a light sleeper."

Holly forces herself to look to one side. "It's those empty eye sockets. They drag your eyeballs into them."

"This place has a sick mind," remarks Arkady.

"Then let us put it out of our misery," says D'Arnoq. "The Act of Anesthesia is done. As per the plan, then: Marinus and Unalaq, you hiatus the icon to ensure he won't wake while Arkady, Ōshima, and I psychoflame the icon with every volt we've got."

We approach the northern corner, where the eyeless figure gleams pale as a shark's underbelly. "So all you have to do to bring down this place," Holly asks me, "is trash that painting?"

"Only now, at this point in the cycle," D'Arnoq answers on my behalf, "while the Blind Cathar's soul is housed inside the icon. At other times he resides in the fabric of the chapel, and then he would have sensed our intent and melted us like plastic figurines in the flame of a blowtorch. Marinus: Begin."

If Elijah D'Arnoq is betraying us, he's keeping up a convincing act until the last minute. "You take the left," I tell Unalaq, "I'll take the right." We stand in front of the Blind Cathar and shut our eyes. Our hands intone in synchronicity. Xi Lo taught Klara Marinus Koskov the Act of Hiatus in Saint Petersburg, and as my Indian self, I taught Unalaq. To strengthen and deepen the act, our lips recite it, silently, from memory, like a pianist's eye navigating a complex but familiar musical score. I sense the Blind Cathar's consciousness rise to the icon's surface, like a swarm of bees. We push it back. We succeed. Partly. I think. "Quickly," I tell Elijah D'Arnoq. "It's more a local anesthetic than a deep coma."

Unalaq and I step aside. D'Arnoq stands before his ex-master, or his current master, I do not know, and holds out his hands at his sides, palms up. To his left and his right, Arkady and Ōshima press their palm-chakras against D'Arnoq's. "Don't even *think* about getting off on this," mumbles Ōshima.

Pallid and sweaty, D'Arnoq shuts his eyes, opens his chakra-eye, and channels the ember-red light of the Shaded Way at the throat of the Holy of Holies.

The Blind Cathar is no longer dreaming. He knows he's being attacked. Like a drugged giant, like my house in Kleinburg in the grip of an Arctic gale, the Chapel strains and struggles. I stagger, I think I blink, and the Blind Cathar's mouth is twisted into aggression. His chakra begins to dilate, a black spot appearing on his forehead, growing like an ink stain. If it opens fully, we're in severe trouble. An earthquake is trapped in the Chapel walls, and Elijah D'Arnoq is making a high, inhuman sound. Channeling so much psychovoltage is killing him. His defection must be genuine; this will kill him. I think I blink again and the icon is firelit and smoking and the depicted monk is roaring with agony, as two-dimensional flames burn him alive, his chakra-eye flickering here and not-here, here and not-here, here and . . .

GONE. SILENCE. THE Blind Cathar's icon is a charcoal square and Elijah D'Arnoq is heaving, bent over double. "We've done it," he gasps. "We've bloody well done it."

Wordlessly, we Horologists consult with one another . . .

. . . and Unalaq confirms it. "He's still there." Her words are our death sentence. The Blind Cathar has merely left the icon and fled to the floors, walls, and ceiling. We have been participants in a charade to allow the Anchorites time to stream up the Way of Stones. Their arrival is imminent. D'Arnoq's defection was indeed a trap, and the Second Mission has become a kamikaze attack. I'd subsend an apology to Inez and Aoife if I could, but their world is out of range. "Holly? Stand behind us, please."

"Did it work? Is—is—is Jacko going to . . . appear?"

I'd like to hiatus her now so she won't die hating me. The Script has failed us. At Blithewood Cemetery I should have turned around, called Wendy Hanger, explained there'd been a mix-up, and gone back to Poughkeepsie station. "I don't know," I tell Holly the mother, sister, daughter, widow, writer, friend. "But stand behind us."

Message from Esther, subreports Ōshima. *She's started the Last Act. She'll need up to a quarter hour.*

"We had to try," Unalaq says. "While there was hope."

Elijah D'Arnoq is still pretending: "What are you talking about?" He even smiles. "We've won! The Blind Cathar's dead. Without him to maintain the Chapel fabric, where we're standing will all be Dunes and Dusk within six hours."

I look at what, in spy-novel terms, is an old-fashioned double agent. I don't even need scansion to be sure. Elijah D'Arnoq isn't as skillful a liar as he believes. For part one of the deception, at my house outside Toronto, he had indeed been "turned" into a genuine *penitento,* but at some point in the last few days, Pfenninger or Constantin turned him back to the Shaded Way.

"May I, Marinus?" asks Ōshima. "Please?"

"As if *my* permission ever mattered to you. But yes. Hard."

Ōshima fakes a sneeze and suckerkinetics D'Arnoq along the table, clean off the end. He comes to a halt only at the Umber Arch.

Xi Lo did the same to Constantin, I subremark, *though he only managed to bowl her about halfway down the table.*

"D'Arnoq's more of a lightweight," says Ōshima. "It's an obvious play: long, smooth, table; annoying person. Who could resist?"

"I . . . guess this means he's not one of us," says Holly.

"You," Elijah D'Arnoq picks himself up and is shouting from the far end of the Chapel, "you," he points, "will *smoulder* and *shrivel* in the *heat*!" Nine men and a woman melt from the air around him.

"GUESTS, GUESTS, GUESTS!" Baptiste Pfenninger claps his hands and smiles. The First Anchorite is a tall man, utterly at ease in his well-toned, well-dressed body. He sports a fastidiously trimmed, silver-tinged beard. "How the old place loves guests, and so many!" I'd forgotten his bass, actorly voice. "One per quarter is the usual quota, so today's a very special occasion. Our second very special occasion." All the men are wearing dinner jackets of various cuts and fashions. Pfenninger's looks Edwardian. "Marinus, Marinus, welcome. Our only repeat visitor in the Chapel of the Dusk's history, though, of course, last time you'd left your body back on earth. Ōshima, you're looking old, burned, tired, and in need of a resurrection. It won't occur. Thank you for killing Brzycki, by the by; he was showing signs of vegetarianism. Who else? 'Unalaq'—do I pronounce it correctly? It sounds awfully like a brand of superglue, however one says it. Arkady, Arkady, you've got taller since I last sawed your feet off. Remember the rats? Dictators really were dictators in the days of Salazar's Lisbon. Seventy-two hours you took to die. I'll see if I can't beat it with Inez, eh?" Pfenninger clicks his tongue. "A pity L'Ohkna and Roho can't be here, but Mr. D'Arnoq," the First Anchorite turns to his double agent, "netted the fattest fish. Good boy. Oh! Last and least, Holly Sykes, mystic lady author turned Irish egg farmer. We've never met. I'm Baptiste Pfenninger, interlocutor of this miraculous"—he gestures at the walls and dome—"engine, and, oh, titles, titles, they drag behind one like Marley's chains, Jacob's not Bob's. Two of our number are even more thrilled than I to see you here at last, Holly . . ."

Dressed in a black velvet gown and gratuitous webs of diamonds, Immaculée Constantin steps forwards. "My singular young lady is all grown-up . . . menopausal, cancerous, and fallen in with quite the wrong sort. So. Do I match my voice?"

Holly looks at this faceless girlhood figure, speechless.

Constantin's smile fades, though it was never sincere. "Jacko could carry a dialogue. Only he wasn't really Jacko by then, was he? Tell me, Holly, did you believe Marinus when she claimed your brother just happened to die of natural causes while Xi Lo was hovering nearby, mmm?"

Seconds pass. Holly's voice is dry. "What are you saying?"

"Oh, my." Constantin's smile fades into pity. "You *did* believe them? Forget everything I said, I beg you. Gossip is the devil's radio, and I shan't be a broadcaster, but . . . try to put two and two together before you die. I'll take care of Aoife, too. Just so, you know, she won't miss you. In *fact,* why not go the whole hog and kill Sharon and Brendan and collect the full Sykes family set? As it were."

Esther's had about three minutes. The Sadaqat denouement should take five, if Pfenninger's feeling voluble. I calculate our chances for when the psychoduel begins. The newest three Anchorites shouldn't cause us too much trouble, but the Chapel is devoid of projectiles to kinetic and eleven against four is still eleven against four. We'll need to buy Esther about seven minutes. Can we hold them off that long?

"You *will* regret threatening my family," Holly's saying. "I swear. I swear to God."

"Oh, you *swear,* do you? To God, no less?" Immaculée Constantin looks concerned. "But God's dead. Why don't we check if I'll regret my promises with our friends the Radio People, shall we?" She cups her diamonded ear and pretends to listen. "No, Holly, no. You're misinformed. I'll regret nothing; *you,* however, are going to *writhe* with remorse that you deserted your secret friend Miss Constantin when you were sweet, seven, and psychic. Think about it. Only one Sykes would have died, instead of five Sykeses plus a Brubeck. You'll positively *scream* with regret! Well, Mr. Anyder? Was this brittle-boned widow a screamer in her pliable, pheromonal days?"

Hugo Lamb steps into view. Cleft-chinned, his body preserved at twenty-five years of age, and scornful-eyed. "She was the silent type. Hello, Holly. Funny how things turn out, isn't it?"

Holly steps back. Being warned about a ghost and seeing him are not the same. "What did they *do* to you?"

Some of the Anchorites laugh. Hugo looks back at his long-ago lover. "They"—he looks about the Chapel—"cured me. They cured me of a terrible wasting disease called mortality. There's a lot of it about. The young hold out for a time, but eventually even the hardiest patient gets reduced to a desiccated embryo, a Strudlebug . . . a veined, scrawny, dribbling . . . bone clock, whose face betrays how very, very little time they have left."

" 'Betrays'?" Pfenninger steps up. "A segue, Marinus. Did you know we have a supergrass among your Inner Circle?"

I resist the temptation to say, "Yes, we've known for a year now."

"Not Mr. D'Arnoq," Pfenninger continues. "He only duped you for seven days. Someone who's been making a monstrous bloody tit of you for a whole year."

I've been dreading this scene. "*Don't*, Pfenninger."

"Yes, it hurts, but *veritas vos liberabit*—and remember, amusing me is your only means of squeezing out a few extra minutes . . ."

True. I think of incorporeal Esther, invoking a real psychoferno inside Ōshima's head. Every second matters. "Amaze and dismay me."

Pfenninger clicks his fingers at the Umber Arch, and in strolls Sadaqat. His demeanor has changed from humble warden to captain of firing squad. "Hello again, dear friends. Here was my choice: twenty more years of housework, laundry, weeding, growing old, catheters, prostate trouble, *or* eternal life, free training in the Shaded Way, and the deeds to 119A. Mm. Let me think. For about twenty seconds. Well, well, well, the Way of the Butler just wasn't for me."

Holly is shocked: "They trusted you! They were your friends!"

"If you'd known Horology for longer than five days, Ms. Sykes," Sadaqat walks up to the far end of the long table and leans on it as if he owns it, "you would *even*tually wake up to the fact that Horology is a club for immortals, who prevent others from attaining their own privileges. They are aristocrats. They are *very* like a white country—so sorry to bring race into this, but the analogy is spot on—a rich, white, imperial, exploitative bastion, which torpedoes the refugee boats coming from the Land of the Huddled Brown Masses. What I have done is to choose survival. Any living being would do the same."

"Congratulations on the new job, Sadaqat." Arkady's sincerity is flawless. " 'Soul-harvester.' Couldn't happen to a nicer guy."

Sadaqat sneers: "Fancy your servile little Pakistani butler spotting your subtle Arkadian irony."

Ōshima asks, "What's your hipster new name going to be, Sadaqat? Major Integrity? Mr. Snitchfink? Judas McJanus?"

"Here's what my name is *not*—Mr. Don't-Worry-About-Sadaqat-He's-Happy-to-Have-the-Privilege-of-Blowing-Himself-Up-on-the-Stairs-to-Save-Our-Pious-Atemporal-Asses."

"Sadaqat's played his part," I tell Pfenninger. "Let him go."

Pfenninger flicks his bow tie. "Don't pretend to know my mind, Marinus. You'd not *know*ingly nurture a spy."

"Fine, I had no idea. He followed your orders. Spied on us. Threw away his ten kilos of Blu Tack. Let him go."

Sadaqat snarls in a way he hasn't done since I first treated him at Dawkins Hospital in Berkshire, England: "It wasn't Blu Tack! It was N9D. Hyperexplosives, which *you* as good as strapped to my chest!"

"Actually, Marinus, he's half right," Arkady tells me. "The Blu Tack people make it, but technically its brand-name is White Tack."

Sadaqat stands on the bench. "Liar! You dragged me along as your human land mine!"

"Three times I tried to persuade you not to join the Second Mission, Sadaqat," I remind him.

"You could've suasioned me, if you cared so much. And Mr. Pfenninger isn't going to 'let me go'! I'm the Twelfth Anchorite."

"Forgive me for raising the specter of race," Arkady says, "but look at Anchorites One through Eleven. Any ethnic commonalities jump out at you?"

Sadaqat is immune to doubt. "I've been recruited to improve the—the—the balance of the Anchorites."

Arkady's snorting laugh turns into a cough. "Sorry, a bit of saliva went down the wrong way. And *why* did the All Whites choose *you*?"

"My psychovoltage is *off the scale,* is why!"

"You poor sap." Ōshima yawns. "I've eaten trays of dim sum with more psychosoteric potential than you."

"I'm curious, Marinus," says Immaculée Constantin. "Your pet schizophrenic just sold you down the river. Will nothing make you despise a person?"

"Homicide and animacide work just fine. But I blame you for bending Sadaqat's fear of dying into treachery. I'm sorry, Sadaqat. It's the War. I had to let them believe you were their ace in the hole. Thank you for the garden, at least. This won't change that."

"I *am* the Twelfth Anchorite. Tell them, Miss Constantin, what you told me. About my potential as a follower of the Shaded Way."

"You have the potential to whinge people to death, Sadaqat." When Constantin's tone turns maternal I know time's running out. "No. Psychosoterically speaking, you fire blanks. Worse, you're a traitor. A talentless, chakraless, *brown* traitor."

Sadaqat looks round at the tall white Anchorites disbelievingly. I can barely look at his changed expression, but I owe him this. Then, mercifully, he turns his back to us to take a few shaky steps towards the Umber Arch. Two of the rearguard block his way. Sadaqat flees for the exit but Pfenninger psycholassos him, reeling him in with mighty pulls, then kinetics him twenty feet high. I can't intervene. The Second Mission depends on us preserving every volt for the coming duel. Constantin hand-symbols an Act of Violence, and Sadaqat's head is twisted through 360 degrees. "There," purrs Constantin. "We're not such sadists, are we? Nice and quick. Chickens suffer more when you wring their necks, don't they, Holly?"

Sadaqat's broken body drops onto the ground, and a lesser Anchorite kinetics it through the east window, like a trash bag of household waste. His soul, at least, will find its way to the Last Sea, unlike those of other "guests," who are brought here to be psychodecanted.

They're about to attack, Unalaq subwarns me.

Feeling like a conductor raising his baton for the Orchestra of All Hell Breaks Loose, I say, *"Now."*

UNALAQ INVOKES A shield from wall to wall, closing off the northern quarter of the Chapel. Even at thirty paces, its force shoves

Pfenninger, Constantin, Hugo Lamb, and D'Arnoq back a few feet. The shield is rooted in Unalaq's raised palms, and shimmers, a blue lens of Deep Stream force. Pfenninger and Constantin look on from the outer edge of the shield with condescension. Why? Elijah D'Arnoq makes a megaphone of his hands and shouts at us. His words take a few seconds to penetrate Unalaq's shield, and arrive fragmented but discernible: "It's behind you!"

I look behind us. Sickeningly, the charred icon of the Blind Cathar is restoring itself. The monk's skin is emerging, and the gold halo is starting to shine. Worse, the black dot of the chakra-eye's returning. Once it's fully dilated, the Cathar will be able to decant us one by one.

Pfenninger taunts us: "See who you've locked yourself in with!"

"This one's mine," Ōshima calls out. "Marinus, Arkady, keep the shield up. Goodbye Esther." Esther's soul egresses from Ōshima, transversing to one side, pulsing with her evocation of the Last Act. Then the grizzled warrior turns, grips the edges of the icon, and holds his head one foot away from the Blind Cathar's. He shuts his physical eyes and pours Deep Stream voltage from his own glowing chakra straight at the black pupil on the icon's forehead. Ōshima cannot win against this incorporeal generator of the Shaded Way, but he might win us a precious extra minute.

Pfenninger sees the stowaway soul, however, and barks an order. The Anchorites advance towards our shield, two rows of five on either side of the table, hands symboling furiously. Constantin's voice reaches me: "Smash that shield and kill the stowaway first!" Arkady, Unalaq, Holly, and I are knocked back by a barrage of jagged emberfire, laser-whiplash, and sonic bullets. I feel Unalaq's nervous system scream with every impact. Arkady and I fire back, our Deep Stream projectiles passing from our palm-chakras through Unalaq's shield. Those that hit their targets will hiatus, sedate, or redact an Anchorite out of the battle, but Shaded Way psychoincendiaries will fry our flesh. The Anchorites have flamethrowers, while we have tranq darts and a riot shield, a riot shield beginning to crack. Through the oscillating blaze I see that Arkady and I have scored a couple of lucky strikes. Cammerer, the Eighth Anchorite, crumples and Osterby, the Sixth, is hiatused off-balance and topples over like a side of pork, but now Du Nord enacts a Shaded Way shield to prevent further losses.

We're still outnumbered nine to three, penned in with a malign demigod whom Ōshima surely cannot occupy for much longer. Holly crouches by the wall. I don't have time to guess what she's thinking. Unalaq shudders as the enemy's red shield slams into hers with the force of a freight train and the shriek of an angle-grinder. The Deep Stream blue turns a leprous purple at the point of contact, and Unalaq is shoved back a pace, and another, another, another, reducing our little triangle of territory to a few square meters. I don't have time to check that Holly has shuffled back with us to stay on Horology's side of the shield, because two more Anchorites now raise their palm-chakras and, through a rattle of psychobullets, I hear Constantin's cry: "Crush them like ants!"

Arkady now pours his voltage into Unalaq's shield, which bolsters it temporarily, but the Anchorites' cascade of fire doubles, trebles, quadruples in intensity. The psychoduel becomes too magnesium-bright to look at, so it is through my chakra-eye that I see the long table rise ten feet into the air, hang there for a second like a bird of prey, then hurtle straight at Arkady and Unalaq. On reflex, I hand-sign the fastest countermand of my life, and stop it a fist's width from Arkady's clenched face, the two ends of the table on either side of the jammed-together shields. Now begins not a tug-of-war but a push-of-war, in which Pfenninger tries to bludgeon Unalaq or Arkady and so knock out the shield, while I try to stop him. We wrestle for control of the table for a long, slippery moment, but fresh Anchorites join Pfenninger, and suddenly I'm overpowered and the table smashes into the head of Dr. Iris Marinus-Fenby. Luckily, the table has fallen on our side of the shield so it can no longer be used as a weapon, but my body's skull is half staved in so I egress before my brain shuts down. Cause of death: flying table. That's a first and, after I die-die in the Dusk, a last.

Through an ever-redder shade of purple I see Pfenninger, Constantin, and other outlines just a few paces away directing their fire at Unalaq until a puncture rips our shield wide open. Baptiste Pfenninger smiles like a proud father, raises his palm at Unalaq, and a pinprick of brilliant light scorches a line in the air between his hand and Unalaq's heart. The psychodumdum semi-inverts my colleague's body, my dead colleague's ex-body, until it deflates in a withered mess of bones and viscera. Pfenninger and Constantin's eyes shine with delight. Arkady is trying desperately to repair our pale blue barrier and all the while Ōshima is locked into a losing one-to-one duel with the Blind Cathar's shining icon.

Seeing my dead body against the wall, the Anchorites reason that no psychosoteric can now attack them, and their red shield flickers out. They'll pay for this mistake. Incorporeally, I pour psychovoltage into a neurobolas and kinetic it at our assailants. It smacks into Imhoff and Westhuizen, the Fifth and Seventh Anchorites, respectively, and down they go. Three against seven. I ingress into Arkady to help him repair the shield, which turns a stronger blue and pushes back the remaining Anchorites. When Arkady glances back at Ōshima, however, I see his fight is lost. His body is evaporating as we look. *Go to Holly,* suborders Arkady. I obey without even thinking to bid him goodbye, an omission I regret even as I transverse to Holly, ingress, evoke an Act of Total Suasion, and . . . Now what?

Infuriated by the loss of Imhoff and Westhuizen, the seven remaining Anchorites cannon Arkady with everything they have, and the blue shield dies. Arkady's spent. He straightens up and gives Baptiste Pfenninger the finger. The Blind Cathar evaporates him from behind with a short, sharp psychobolt. The battle's over. They'll kill Holly or try to decant her, perhaps. I can neither see nor communicate with Esther, but in seconds the Blind Cathar will psycholocate her soul, annihilate it, and Horology will have lost its hundred-year War with the Anchorites who—

THE LIGHT FILLS the Chapel, passing through hands pressed over eyes, through the eyelids behind those eyes, through corneas and vitreous humors, through bodies, through souls . . . The white is so white it's black. Esther did it. Esther won. I wait for the bone-snapping crack as the Chapel splits down the middle. I wait for the screams of the Anchorites as their immortality machine disintegrates about them.

Seconds unspool . . . Many seconds.

The black beyond white fades back to white.

The white slips off its layers, back to milky flint-gray.

Vision returns. I open Holly's eyelids and look up from where her body lies, up at the Chapel roof. It hasn't fallen in.

I think, *Esther's Last Act wasn't powerful enough.*

I think, *The Blind Cathar took countermeasures.*

It hardly matters why Esther failed. The Second Mission was the last chance. Horology is now just L'Ohkna, a hacker, and Roho, a bodyguard. Horology lost and the Anchorites won.

Holly's body wants to groan and retch, but I keep it in a state of deathlike stillness while I work out . . . What? I don't have enough voltage left for a single psychoprojectile. Try to save my soul? Egress Holly, try to cloak myself, and hover nearby as she is slain or decanted, until the Blind Cathar notices the frightened little piggy, hiding in the corner? I almost envy Esther. At least she died in the false belief she had won Horology its ultimate victory.

The surviving Anchorites take stock. Pfenninger's still standing at the center of the rhombus nave. Constantin, D'Arnoq, Hugo Lamb, Rivas-Godoy, Du Nord, and O'Dowd remain. One or two of the other fallen may wake in a while, or may not. The Anchorites will be knocked back, but they'll have lists of possible Carnivores, and in a decade or two they'll be operating, and abducting, at full strength. The Chapel of the Dusk is unscratched. Beyond the up-ended table and benches, and a lesser icon hanging at the wrong angle, there is no sign of the battle that raged here only a minute ago. I don't know what to do, so I just stay inside Holly's head, paralyzed by indecision.

Elijah D'Arnoq asks, "What was that light?"

"A Last Act," says Pfenninger. "A powerful one. The question is, who invoked it?"

"Esther Little," says Constantin, "in incorporeal form. The Counterscript never acknowledged her death, as you know. I sensed her. She attacked the Chapel's doubt-line, in hopes of splitting it open and making the sky fall in. Who else but her could have engineered this attack? We're lucky her last big bang wasn't quite as explosive as she hoped."

"So we've won the War?" asks Rivas-Godoy.

Pfenninger looks at Constantin. As one, they announce, "Yes."

"Oh," admits Pfenninger, "there'll be a few mopping-up operations. We have a few wounds to lick, but Horology is dead. My one regret? That Marinus didn't live long enough to learn how utterly, how miserably, she had failed. The Blind Cathar must have slain her at some point between killing Ōshima and Arkady."

"Let's tip the Sykes woman after Sadaqat," says Constantin, stepping over towards us. She asks D'Arnoq, "Why *did* Marinus bring her along? I don't . . . Wait a minute." She peers at me with not-quite-human eyes. "Mr. Pfenninger. I do believe we have an after-dinner mint." Constantin takes a few cautious steps closer. She smiles. "My my my, Holly Sykes is—what's the term?—playing possum. How—"

A ROARING, PERCUSSIVE KA–*BOOOOOOOOOMMM* . . . fills the Chapel. Constantin falls to the floor, as do the others. I-in-Holly stare up at the crack, terror transmuting into hope, then a savage joy as an uprooting, tearing, steel-hull-on-a-reef noise howls louder, and the hairline crack becomes a black line zigzagging down the north roof to the back of the icon. Slowly, the sickening sound dies away, but it leaves behind a heavily pregnant threat of more . . . From where I-in-Holly am crouching I see the halo-shaped gnostic serpent swing, then drop. It smashes like a thousand dinner plates, fragments dashing and smattering across the stone floor, like ten thousand little living fleeing beings. A chunk as big as a cricket ball just misses Holly's head. I hear Baptiste Pfenninger declaim a histrionic "Shit! Did you see that, Ms. Constantin?" It occurs to me to test Holly's own psychovoltage, and I find a deeper reserve than I expected.

"That's the least of our problems," snaps Constantin. "Can't you see the crack?" Silently, I invoke an Act of Cloaking. If a psychosoteric looks at me directly they'll see a faded outline, but it's better than nothing, and the seven Anchorites are now worried about the Chapel's fabric. As well they should be. Moving along the wall towards the west window, we hear the creak of stressed stone.

Elijah D'Arnoq notices first. "The Sykes woman!"

O'Dowd, the Eleventh Anchorite, asks, "Where did she go?"

"The bitch is hosting," booms Du Nord. "Someone's cloaked her!"

"Shield the Umber Arch!" Constantin orders Rivas-Godoy. "It's Marinus! Don't let her out! I'll evoke an Act of Exposure and—"

An ogre groans overhead and stones rain from the crack, which now widens into a jagged gash. I understand. Esther's Last Act worked, and only the Blind Cathar has kept the Chapel intact. But now even his ancient strength is failing.

"Pfenninger, MOVE!" shouts Constantin.

But the First Anchorite, whose survival instinct has perhaps been dulled by two centuries' Black Wine, health, and wealth, looks up to where Constantin is staring before, not after, he dives to safety. A slab of Chapel roof the size of a family car is the final thing that Baptiste Pfenninger sees before it smashes him, like a sledgehammer striking an egg. More masonry explodes off the floor. I revoke my cloak and invoke a body-shield. Du Nord, a French captain who followed the Shaded Way from 1830 to the present day, is too slow to protect himself from a volley of shrapnel, and although it doesn't kill Du Nord, yet, his current wife wouldn't recognize him. Three or four body-shielded figures are running for the Umber Arch but, like an ice sheet calving icebergs, the south roof slides down and blocks the exit. Our tomb, then, is sealed.

Through the crumbling gaps in the roof, a roiling, grainy, smoky tentacle of Dusk spills, gropes, and uncoils into the Chapel. It hums, not quite like bees, and mutters, not quite like a crowd, and susurrates, not quite like sand. A tendril of the stuff uncurls behind Elijah D'Arnoq as he shifts backwards to avoid a falling slab of rock. Unimpeded by his body-shield, the Dusk brushes D'Arnoq's neck, and he is turned into a man-shaped cloud of Dusk, whose form lasts only a moment.

"Marinus, is this you in here?" asks Holly.

Sorry, I suasioned you without permission.

"We beat them, didn't we? Aoife's safe."

Everyone's family is safe from the Anchorites, now.

We look across the rubble and body-strewn Chapel. Only three of the ember-red shielded figures are visible. I recognize those of Constantin, Rivas-Godoy, and Hugo Lamb. In its corner, the icon of the Blind Cathar is peeling and decaying, as if spattered by acid. The place is growing darker by the second. The arms of the Dusk fill a quarter of the Chapel now, at least.

"That Dusk stuff," says Holly. "It doesn't look so painful."

Sorry I let you get tangled up in this.

"It's all right. It wasn't you, it was the War."

It'll only be a few moments now.

A SPLITTING NOISE from the northern corner turns into the discordant jangle of a bell. Where the icon hung, an ellipse has opened up, emitting a pale moonlight. "That noise," says Holly, "sounded like the time-bell at the Captain Marlow. What is it, Marinus?"

A few feet away, the psychosedated body of Imhoff is licked into nonexistence by a tongue of Dusk.

I have no idea, I subadmit. *Hope?*

Certainly the three surviving Anchorites reach a similar conclusion and make for the north corner. I-in-Holly follow, or try to, but a long plume of Dusk sweeps in through the now-unshielded east window. I slip in a puddle of what used to be Baptiste Pfenninger, and dodge into a safe pocket of clear air that drifts up the nave, before a column of the swarming gray forces me over to the west wall. The Chapel is now more than half Dusk, and the thirty paces to the ellipse are a shifting airborne minefield. I stumble over my old body, lying at an undignified angle, but in mere seconds Dr. Fenby will cease to be. Miraculously, our luck holds, and we arrive at the ellipse. Constantin and her two companions are nowhere in sight. Some sort of emergency chute? It doesn't feel like a design feature of the Blind Cathar. The oval glow brightens as the Chapel darkens. It's a membrane across which clouds appear to stream, like speeded-up sky. I take one last look at the Chapel, now Dusk-filled. The eastern roof slides in. "What do we have to lose?" asks Holly.

I fill my host's lungs with a deep breath, and step in . . .

. . . and out into a passageway, little wider than a person, little taller, lit by the Chapel's dying light and the surface through which we just passed, apparently harmlessly. The bellow of the disintegrating Chapel is still audible, but it sounds a good mile behind us, not a few meters. The passageway slopes down ten paces before reaching a wall, then branches off to the left and right. It's warmer here. I touch the wall. It's skin temperature, and has the Mars-red hue and texture of adobe. If sound, light, and flesh can travel through the membrane, however, then I'm afraid the Dusk will soon be following us. A body-shield would be wise, especially with three Anchorites up ahead, but Holly's psychovoltage is low and mine is virtually spent, so I walk down the passage to the end. Both the left-hand and right-hand corridors curve away into darkness. *It feels like necropolis,* I subsay to Holly, but . . .

"The Blind Cathar doesn't bother with bodies, right?"

No. Like Sadaqat's corpse, the psychodecanted are just ejected.

I look up the corridor behind us. The ellipse is fading as the Chapel dies. I subask Holly, *What do you think? Left or right?*

"Marinus, I think I just saw letters, on the wall, at waist height."

I peer down and find, inscribed like a sculptor's mark:

JS

"JS?" says Holly. "Jacko? Marinus, that's how he used to sign his—" A noise like a bell struck under water interrupts her, and we can tell by a change of the air that the Dusk is following us in. *"Left,* Marinus," Holly orders. "Go left."

There's no time to ask if, or why, she's so sure. I obey, hurrying us along the narrow, curving, claustrophobic, and graphite-black passageway. Holly's fifty-six-year-old heart is pounding hard and I think I sprained her ankle in our last dash across the Chapel. She's a decade older than Iris, I need to remember. "Trail my fingers along the wall," she tells me, in little more than a whisper.

If you're up to driving, I'll hand you back the controls.

"Yes. Do it." She steadies herself against the wall for a moment until her vestibular sense rights itself. "Christ, that was weird."

I could light a psycholamp, but it might attract company.

"If my wild guess is right, I won't need light. If I'm wrong, a light won't help. I'll know one way or the other fairly soon. This passage is still following a curve, wouldn't you say?"

Yes. It's an arc, for sure. About a hundred paces so far.

Holly stops. We hear her ragged breath, her thumping heart, and the murmuring of the Dusk. She looks behind us, and a monochromatic gleam blooms in the darkness. Holly holds up her hand and we see its black outline, and even the faint sheen of her wedding ring. *The Dusk has its own phosphorescence,* I report. *It's flooding the passage behind us, at walking pace. Keep moving.*

"Diabolical," says Holly. She sets off again, and although I'm tempted to scansion her present tense to see what she's thinking, I decide to trust in her. Fifty more paces and Holly stops, out of breath. Her fear is charged with hope, now. "Am I imagining that, Marinus? What are my right fingertips touching?"

I check, and double-check. *Nothing.*

She turns to her right, putting out her palms against a void. She touches the sides, and we feel a narrow entrance in the wall. "A little light now, please—just a match-flame?"

I half egress from Holly's chakra-eye, and invoke a faint glow. My host has seen too much today to be taken aback by light shining from the center of her forehead. In front of us, a short connecting tunnel ends five paces away at another left-right junction. To our left, the original passage curves away. To our right, the Dusk is not far around the bend. "We're *in* it," Holly whispers. "Light off, please. I'd rather trust my memory than my eyes."

If you can talk and *walk*, I subsay, *I'm very, very curious.*

Holly walks forwards through the connecting tunnel until her palms meet the wall of a new left-right passage. Holly turns right. "The last time I saw Jacko," she keeps her voice very low, "I was packing a bag to leave home. Did Xi Lo ever tell you any of this?"

Maybe—I don't know. It was so long ago.

We've gone about ten paces through the darkness when Holly's left hand registers empty air. Another "connecting" archway. She enters it, walks five paces to another left-right passage, and turns left. These corridors appear to be concentric to one another. "Well, as I was packing, Jacko appeared, with a—a—a labyrinth. He used to draw these big, intricate mazes, just for fun, like. There should be another one opening soon . . ." After another ten paces of curving darkness, Holly finds a gap on the right and goes through it. For fear of putting her off, I say nothing about the maze Xi Lo once designed for King William of Orange. Through the arch is another left-right branch. Holly goes right. "The labyrinth Jacko gave me that day, though, it was plainer. Just a nest of nine circles, with a few connecting gaps between them. He made me promise to learn it. To learn it so well that, if I ever needed to, I could find my way through it in the darkness, without one mistake . . ."

And now we're in it, I finish the sentence.

"Now we're in it. I s'pose how hardly matters?"

Transubstantiation. The Blind Cathar's soul became the Chapel of the Dusk. Xi Lo's soul, I believe, entered the fabric of the Chapel during the First Mission. Once it was inside, Xi Lo became this labyrinth. Like a benign cancer, perhaps?

Holly hurries on. "But why would he do that?"

So that there would be a way back to the world after the Second Mission, but one that only you could navigate. Anyone else . . .

Both Holly and I think of the three Anchorites who arrived here before us, trapped in a dead end, with a wall of Dusk closing in.

"Does Jacko know we're here, do you think?"

Transubstantiation is an arcane, powerful act. I can't invoke it and I don't know its modii. Xi Lo never even told me he was studying it. The Blind Cathar knew we were in the Chapel, however, so it stands to reason that, yes, Xi Lo—Jacko—knows you're here.

Holly finds an archway in the right-hand wall, and enters.

If the labyrinth's round, I subpoint-out, *we're now moving away from the center.*

"You have to go out to go in again. This next junction should be a crossroads. A little light, please?" I egress and glow for a moment. A crossroads. Holly takes the left branch. I ingress and fade.

You kept your promise, then, I subsay, *to memorize the path.*

"Yeah. Those were Jacko's last words to me. I stormed off to my boyfriend's house, and never saw my little brother again. Ruth, my sister-in-law, she was into jewelry making, and turned his sketch into a sort of pendant, made of silver. When I left home I took it away with me. Probably every week of my life I've studied it. Left turn coming up."

We take the left, and pain explodes in our head. Holly spins as she falls and tumbles. Fresh pain shoots through her ankles and knees, and our scorched retinas are dazzled by petals of temporary colors. Through these, as my host lifts her head, I glimpse Constantin, her chakra-eye glowing rose-red, standing over us. "Show me the exit," the Second Anchorite says maternally, "or I'll turn you into a screaming human torch to light my path." Her palm-chakras are glowing red too, a psychobolt in each ready to make good her threat. Holly's shaking and muttering, "Please don't please don't please don't." I don't know what Constantin just heard, how much she knows, how much psychovoltage she's retained after the battle. Enough to kill us both several times over, I think. I decide to draw her away from Holly, back to the Dusk, so Holly at least has a chance of getting out alive.

I egress, glowing.

Icy and scalding, Constantin demands, "Which one are you?"

Marinus, I subannounce.

"Marinus. It would be. Time's short. Lead."

If you kill us both, you die too.

"Then I'll die happier, knowing who I killed in the last scene."

Before I can think of a strategic reply, Constantin's chakra-eye goes out, her head tilts back, and she slumps to the floor. "I *TOLD YOU!*" Holly makes a throat-scraping, berserking yell, and brings down an indistinct clublike object on our attacker's head a second time. "NOBODY THREATENS MY FAMILY!" And a third time. I glow brightly to find Holly panting over the slumped form of Immaculée Constantin. The Second Anchorite's head is a mess of blood, white-gold hair, and diamonds. I ingress back into Holly, finding a supernova of fury melting into many other emotions. A few seconds later, Holly empties her stomach in three powerful bursts.

It's okay, Holly, I say. *I'm here, it's fine.*

Holly vomits a fourth time.

I synthesize a drop of psychosedative in her pituitary gland. *Okay, I think you're finished now.*

"I killed someone." Holly's shaking. "I killed. It just . . . sort of . . . It's like I wasn't me. But I know it was."

I tweak out a little dopamine. *She may be alive . . . sort of. Shall I check?*

"No. No. I'd rather not know."

As you wish, but what's the murder weapon?

Holly drops the thing. "Rolling pin."

Where did you find a rolling pin in here?

"I nicked it from your kitchen at 119A. Put it in my bag."

Holly stands up. I sedate her ankle and knees. *Why?*

"You were all talking about the War, but I didn't even have a Swiss Army knife. So—yeah, I *know,* hysterical woman, rolling pin, big fat cliché, Crispin would've rolled his eyes and said, 'Oh, come *on!*' but I wanted . . . y'know . . . *something.* I hate the sight of blood so I left the knives in the drawer and . . . so. *Shit,* Marinus. What have I done?"

Killed a 250-year-old Atemporal Carnivore with a fifty-dollar kitchen implement, after putting on a fine impersonation of a sniveling, scared middle-aged woman.

"The sniveling part was easy."

The Dusk's coming, Holly. Which way now?

She pulls herself together. "A bit of light, please." I half egress and glow, illuminating the narrow crossroads where the woman lying dead or dying ambushed us. "Which way were we going?"

We spun as we fell, I remember. And Constantin moved around us before she threatened us. I glow brighter, but this just enhances our view of a dead ambusher and a puddle of vomit. *I can't be sure.*

Panic surges through Holly. I psychosedate it back down.

Then we hear the hum of the approaching Dusk. *Shall I drive?*

"Yeah," Holly croaks. "Please."

I look at the four passageways. They're identical.

They're not. One looks a little lighter. *Holly, there's only one way through the labyrinth, right?*

"Yeah."

I take the passage that leads to the light, turn right, and ten paces in front of us is the Dusk, filling the tunnel like starry, slow-motion water. There are voices in its smothered ululation. *It doesn't hurt,* they say in unlabeled languages, *it doesn't hurt . . .*

"What are we doing?" Holly's voice rings out.

I turn back. *This is the way we came in. The Dusk's following us. We came to the crossroads—here.* I step us over Constantin's body. *Picture Jacko's maze in your head again. The pendant.*

"I've got it. Straight on." I obey. "Left. There'll be a turning to the right, but ignore it, it's a dead end . . . Keep going. Through the next right." I pass through the tunnel, thinking of the Dusk spilling over Constantin's body. "Left. On a few paces . . . On a few more, we're near the middle, but we have to go out in a circle to avoid a trap ahead. That's this next left. Go on, through the arch . . . Now turn right." I walk a few paces, still hearing the slosh of the Dusk catching up as the ever-shortening side tunnels and dead ends drain off less and less of its mass and energy. "Ignore that gap to your left . . . Now turn right. Over the crossroads. Hurry! Turn right, turn left, and we should be—" The archway before us is black, not black with shadow, but solid black, black like the Last Sea is black, a blackness that absorbs the chakra-light I shine from Holly's palms and bounces nothing back.

I step into—

—A DOMED ROOM of the same dead Mars-red walls as the labyrinth, but alive with the sharp shadows of many birds. The room is lit by the evening light of a golden apple. "My . . ." Despite all we've seen today, Holly's breath catches in her throat. "Look at it, Marinus." The apple hangs in the middle of the chamber, at head-height, with no means of support. "Is it alive?" asks Holly.

I would say, I subspeculate, *it's a soul.*

Golden apples I've heard of in poems and tales throughout my metalife. Golden apples I've seen in paintings, and not just the one Venus holds in the Bronzino original that Xi Lo knew so well, though that golden apple strengthens my suspicions about this one. I've even held an apple wrought from Kazakh gold in the eleventh century by a craftsman at the court of Suleiman VI, with a leaf of emerald-studded Persian jade and dewdrops of pearl from the Mauritius Islands. But the difference between those golden apples and this one is the difference between reading a love poem and being in love.

Holly's eyes are welling. "Marinus . . ."

It's our way back, Holly. Touch it.

"*Touch* it? I can't touch it. It's so . . ."

Xi Lo created it for you, for this moment.

She takes a step closer. We hear air in feathers.

One touch, Holly. Please. The Dusk's coming.

Holly reaches out her well-worn, grazed hand.

As I egress from my host, I hear a dove trill.

Holly is gone.

THE SHADOW-BIRDS VANISHED with the apple, and the domed chamber feels like a rather dingy mausoleum. Now I die. I die-die. But I die knowing that Holly Sykes is safe, knowing that a debt Horology owed her has been paid. This is a good way to finish. Aoife still has a mum. I invoke a pale gleam and subask Hugo Lamb, *Why die alone?*

He uncloaks and melts out of the air. "Why indeed?" He touches his badly gashed cheek. "Oh, *shit,* look at the state of me! Bloody dinner jackets. My tailor's this Bangladeshi chap in Savile Row, and he's a genius, but he only makes twenty suits a year. Why did Xi Lo only leave the one magic ticket back to the world?"

I transverse to where the golden apple hung. Every subatomic particle of it is gone. *Transubstantiation's draining. The Blind Cathar kept getting fed fresh meat, remember. Xi Lo sustained all this on batteries. Why didn't you take the one magic ticket back?*

He dodges the question. "Got any cigarettes on you, Marinus?"

I'm incorporeal. I don't even have a body on me.

A trickle of Dusk appears from the black doorway, like sand.

You've sourced, lied, I subsay, *groomed, lured, murdered . . .*

"They were clinical murders. They died happy. Ish."

. . . as Marcus Anyder, you even killed your old self.

"Do you really want to spend your final moments interviewing me? What do you want? Some big dramatic mea culpa?"

I'm just curious as to why a predator, I subspell out the obvious, *who has thought about* nothing *but himself for so many years, and who only last week gloated about killing Oscar Gomez, should now —*

"You're not still angry about that, are you?"

—should now nobly lay down his artificially suspended life for a common bone clock. Go on. I promise I won't tell a soul.

The muttering of the Dusk is growing. I push the voices away.

Hugo Lamb dusts his sleeves. "You scansioned Holly, I presume?"

Extensively. I had to, to locate Esther Little.

"Did you find us in La Fontaine Saint-Agnès? Holly and I?"

I hesitate too long.

"So you had a good gawp. Well. Now you have your answer." More Dusk spills in, promising us it won't hurt, it won't hurt, it won't hurt. A third of the floor is covered now. "Did you see her lay into Constantin? Irish blood, Gravesend muscle. Talk about breeding."

You stood by and watched that?

"Never been the have-a-go-hero type, me."

Constantin recruited you. She was the Second Anchorite.

"I've always had a problem with authority figures. Rivas-Godoy turned right when we entered the labyrinth, so that was him finished from the outset, but I followed Constantin. Yes, she recruited me, but she bought into the women-and-children-first doctrine bigtime. So I cloaked myself, got lost, heard Holly, followed you . . . And here we are. Death-buddies. Who would have thought it?" We watch the sandy Dusk fill the domed chamber, getting deeper. I'm nagged by a thought that I've missed something obvious. Hugo Lamb coughs. "Did she love me too, Marinus? I don't mean after she found out about my little . . . dalliance with a paranormal cult that scarred her family and attempted to animacide her brother. I mean, that night. In Switzerland. When we were young. Properly young. When Holly and I were snowed in."

Two-thirds of the floor is covered. Lamb the corporeal has sixty seconds of life before the Dusk reaches him. I can hover a little longer, until the dome is full to the roof, if I really want to.

Then it hits me, what I've missed. Hugo Lamb missed it too. Even Constantin missed it. Dodging falling masonry, trying to avoid the Dusk, we all forgot an alternative exit. I could sublaugh. Will it work? If the Dusk got into the Way of Stones and erased the conduit, no . . . But it was a long way down.

I subask Lamb, *How much voltage do you have left?*
"Not a lot. Why? Fancy a psychoduel?"
If I ingress you, we might have enough together.
He's confused. "To do what?"
To summon the Aperture.

SHEEP'S HEAD

2043

AT THE FOOT OF THE STAIRS I hear this thought, *He is on his way*, and goosebumps shimmy up my arms. Who? Up ahead, Zimbra turns to see what's keeping me. I sift the sounds of the late evening. The stove, clanking as it cools. Waves, shoulder-barging the rocks below the garden. The creaking bones of the old house. The creaking bones of Holly Sykes, come to that. I lean over the banister to peer through the kitchen-sink window up the slope to Mo's bungalow. Her bedroom light's on. All well there. No feet on the gravel garden path. Zimbra doesn't sense a visitor. The hens are quiet, which at this hour is the way we want it. Lorelei and Rafiq are giggling in Lorelei's room, playing shadow puppets: "That looks nothing *like* a kangaroo, Lol!"; "How would *you* know?"; "Well, how would *you* know?" Not so very long ago, I thought I'd never hear my two orphans laugh like that again.

So far so normal. No more audible thoughts. Someone's always on their way. But, no, it was "*He* is on his way," I'm sure. Or as sure as I can be. The problem is, if you've heard voices in your head once, you're never sure again if a random thought *is* just a random thought, or something more. And remember the date: the five-year anniversary of the '38 Gigastorm, when Aoife's and Örvar's 797 got snapped at twenty thousand feet, theirs and two hundred other airliners crossing the Pacific, snapped like a boy in a tantrum snapping the Airfix models Brendan used to hang from his bedroom ceiling.

"Oh, ignore me," I mutter to Zimbra, and carry on up the stairs, the same stairs I once flew up and flew down. "Come on," I tell Zimbra, "shift your bum." I stroke the whorl of fur between his ears, one sticky-uppy and one floppy. Zimbra looks up, like he's reading my mind with those big black eyes. "You'd tell me if there was anything to worry about, wouldn't you, eh?"

Anything *else* to worry about, that is, besides the fear that the dragging feeling in my right side is my cancer waking up again; and about what'll happen to Lorelei and Rafiq when I die; and about the Taoiseach's statement about Hinkley Point and the British government's insistence that "a full meltdown of the reactor at Hinkley E is not going to happen"; and about Brendan, who lives only a few miles from the new exclusion zone; and about the Boat People landings near Wexford, and where and how these thousands of hungry, rootless men, women, and children will get through the winter; and about the rumors of Ratflu in Belfast; and our dwindling store of insulin; and Mo's ankle; and . . .

Worrying times, Holly Sykes.

"I KNEW THAT was going to happen!" says Rafiq, swamped in Aoife's old red coat that now serves as his dressing gown, hugging his knees at the foot of Lorelei's bed. "When Marcus found the brooch was missing from his cloak, that was a—a *dead* giveaway, like. You can't nick a golden eagle from a tribe like the Painted People and expect to get away with it. For them, it's like Marcus and Esca have stolen God. Of *course* they'll come and hunt them down." Then, 'cause he knows how much I love *The Eagle of the Ninth,* he tries his luck: "Holly, can't we have just a bit of the next chapter?"

"It's almost ten," says Lorelei, "and school tomorrow," and if I close my eyes I can almost imagine it's Aoife at fifteen years old.

"All right. And is the slate recharged?"

"Yes, but there's still no thread and no Net."

"Is it *really* true," Rafiq shows no sign of shifting from Lorelei's bed, "that when you were my age you used to get as much electricity as you wanted *all* the time, like?"

"Do I detect a bedtime postponement tactic, young man?"

He grins. "Must've been *magno* to have all that electricity."

"It must've been what?"

"Magno. Everyone says it. Y'know: boss, class, epic, good."

"Oh. Looking back, yes, it was 'magno,' but we all took it for granted back then." I remember Ed's pleasure at unlimited electricity each time he got back to our little house in Stoke Newington from Baghdad, where he and his colleagues had to power their laptops and satellite phones with car batteries brought by the battery guy. Sheep's Head could do with a battery guy now, but his truck'd need diesel, and there isn't any spare, which is why we need him.

"And airplanes used to fly *all* the time, right?" sighs Rafiq. "Not just people from Oil States or Stability?"

"Yes, but . . ." I flounder for a way to change the subject. Lorelei, too, must be thinking dark thoughts about airplanes tonight.

"So where did you go, Holly?" Rafiq never tires of this conversation, no matter how often we do it.

"Everywhere," says Lorelei, being brave and selfless. "Colombia, Australia, China, Iceland, Old New York. Didn't you, Gran?"

"I did, yes." I wonder what life in Cartagena, in Perth, in Shanghai is like now. Ten years ago I could have streetviewed the cities, but the Net's so torn and ragged now that even when we have reception it runs at prebroadband speed. My tab's getting old, too, and I only have one more in storage. If any arrive via Ringaskiddy Concession, they never make it out of Cork City. I remember the pictures of seawater flooding Fremantle during the deluge of '33. Or was it the deluge of '37? Or am I confusing it with pictures of the sea sluicing into the New York subway, when five thousand people drowned underground? Or was that Athens? Or Mumbai? Footage of catastrophes flowed so thick and fast through the thirties that it was hard to keep track of which coastal region had been devastated this week, or which city had been decimated by Ebola or Ratflu. The news turned into a plotless never-ending disaster movie I could hardly bring myself to watch. But since Netcrash One we've had hardly any news at all and, if anything, this is worse.

The wind shakes the windowpane. "Lights out now. Let's save the bulb." I have only six bulbs left, too, stowed under the floorboards in my bedroom with the final slate since the spate of break-ins up Durrus way. I kiss Rafiq's wiry-haired head as he traipses out to his tiny room, and tell him, "Sweet dreams, love." I mean it, too: Rafiq's nightmares are down to one night in ten, but when they come his screams could wake the dead.

Rafiq yawns. "You too, Holly."

Lorelei snuggles down under her blankets and sheepskin as I close her door. "Sleep tight, Gran, don't let the bedbugs bite." Dad used to say that me, I used to say it to Aoife, Aoife passed it on to Lorelei, and now Lorelei says it back to me.

We live on, as long as there are people to live on in.

IT'S PROPERLY DARK, but now I'm in my seventies, I need only a few hours—one of the rare compensations of old age. So I feed the stove another log, turn up the globe, and get out my sewing box to patch an old pair of Lol's jeans so Rafiq can inherit them, and then I need to repair some socks. Wish I could stop longing for a hot shower before bed. Occasionally Mo and I torment each other with memories of the Body Shop, and its various scents: musk and green tea, bergamot, lily-of-the-valley; mango, brazil nut, banana; coconut, jojoba oil, cinnamon . . . Rafiq and Lorelei'll never know these flavors. For them, "soap" is now an unscented block from "the Pale," as the Dublin manufacturing zone is known. Until last year you could still buy Chinese soap at the Friday market, but whatever black-market tentacle got it as far as Kilcrannog has now been lopped off.

When I'm sure the kids are asleep, I turn on the radio. I'm always nervous that there'll just be silence, but it's okay: All three stations are on air. The RTÉ station is the mouthpiece of Stability and broadcasts officially approved news on the hour with factual how-to programs in between about growing food, repairing objects, and getting by in our ever-more-makeshift country. Tonight's program is a first-aid repeat about fitting a splint to a broken arm, so I switch to JKFM, the last private station in Ireland, for a little music. You never know what you'll get, though obviously it's all at least five years old. I recognize the chorus of Damon MacNish and the Sinking Ship's "Exocets for Breakfast," and remember a party in Colombia, or was it Mexico City?, where I met the singer. Crispin was there as well, if I'm not wrong. I know the next song, too: "Memories Can't Wait" by Talking Heads, but it reminds me of Vinny Costello so I try our third station, Pearl Island Radio. Pearl Island Radio is broadcast from the Chinese Concession at Ringaskiddy, outside Cork. It's mostly in Mandarin, but sometimes there's an international news bulletin in English, and if the Net's unthreaded this is the only way to get news unfiltered by Stability. Of course, the news has a pro-Chinese slant—Ed would call it "naked propaganda"—and there'll be not a whisper about Hinkley E, which was built and operated by a Chinese-French firm until the accident five years ago when the foreign operators pulled out, leaving the British with a half-melted core to ineffectively contain. There's no English news tonight, but the sound of the Chinese speakers soothes my nerves and, inevitably, I think of Jacko; and then of those days and nights with the Horologists in New York, and out of New York, nearly twenty years ago . . .

THE CHAPEL, THE battle, the labyrinth: Yes, I believe it all took place, even though I know that if I ever described what I saw, it'd sound like attention-seeking, insanity, or bad drugs. If it'd just been the trippier parts that I remembered, if I'd woken up in my room at the Empire Hotel, I might be able to put it down to delusion, or food poisoning, or an "episode" with memory loss, or false memories. There's too much other stuff that won't be explained away, though: Stuff like how, after touching the golden apple in the domed room of the bird shadows I vanished in a head-rush of vertigo and found myself not waking up in my hotel room but in the gallery at 119A, with my middle finger touching the golden apple on the Bronzino picture, a dove trilling on the windowsill outside, and all the Horologists gone. The marble rolling pin was missing from the kitchen drawer. My knees were scabbed and sore from when Constantin ambushed me in the labyrinth. I never knew why Marinus didn't travel back in my head—maybe the golden apple only worked for one passenger. Last of all, when evening came and I gave up waiting for a friendly Atemporal to appear, I got a cab across Central Park back to my room, where I found all charges for the week had been paid by a credit card that wasn't mine. If a New York hotel receptionist tells you your room's been paid for, you can bet your life you weren't dreaming it.

So, yes, it happened, but ordinary life carried on at the speed of time, and the following day doesn't care about all your paranormal adventures in the days before. To the cabdriver, I was just another fare to LaGuardia Airport who'll leave her glasses on the backseat if he doesn't check. To the Aer Lingus air steward, I was just another middle-aged lady in economy whose earphones weren't working. To my hens, I'm a two-legged giant who throws them corn and keeps stealing their eggs. During my "lost weekend" in Manhattan I may have seen a facet of existence that only a few hundred in history have glimpsed, but so what? I could hardly tell anyone. Even Aoife or Sharon would've gone, "I believe you believe it, but I think you may need professional help . . ."

There has been no sequel. Marinus, if she got out of that domed room, has never reappeared and it isn't going to happen now. I streetviewed 119A a few times and found the tall brownstone townhouse with its varied windows, so someone's still looking after it—New York real estate is still New York real estate, even as America disintegrates—but I've never been back, or tried to find out who's living there. Once I deviced the Three Lives Bookstore, but when a bookseller answered, I chickened out and hung up before asking if Inez still lived upstairs. One of the last books Sharon sent me before post from Australia stopped getting through was about the twelve Apollo astronauts who walked on the moon, and I sort of felt my time in the Dusk was a bit like that. And now that I was back on earth, I could either go slowly crazy by trying to get back to that other realm, to psychosoterica and 119A and Horology, or not, and just say, "It happened, but it's over," and get on with the ordinary stuff of family and life. At first, I wasn't sure if I could, I dunno, write up the minutes for the Kilcrannog Tidy Towns Committee, knowing that, as we sat there discussing grants for the new playground, souls were migrating across an expanse of Dusk into a blankness called the Last Sea—but I found I could. A few weeks before my sixteenth birthday, I met a woman twice my age in an abortion clinic in the shadow of Wembley Stadium. She was posh and composed. I was a scared, weepy mess. As she lit a new cigarette from the dying ember of the last one, she told me this: "Sweetheart, you'll be astounded by what you can live with."

Life has taught me that she was right.

. . . Zimbra's barking in my dreams. I wake up in my chair next to the stove, and Zimbra's still barking, on the side porch. Fuddled, I get up, dropping the half-darned sock, and walk over to the porch: "Zimbra!" But Zimbra can't hear me; Zimbra's not even Zimbra, he's a primeval canine scenting an ancient enemy. Is anyone out there? God, I wish the old security floodlight was still working. Zimbra's barking stops for one second—long enough for me to hear the terror of hens. Oh, no, not a fox. I grab the torch, open the door only a crack but our dog barges through and scrabbles at what's probably the fox's hole under the wire. Dirt flies over me and the chickens are going berserk around the wire walls of their coop. I shine the torch in and can't see the fox but Zimbra's in no doubt. One dead hen; two; three; one feebly flapping; and there, two disks on the head of a reddish blur on top of the hen coop. Zimbra—fifteen kilos' worth of German shepherd crossed with black Labrador with bits of the devil knows what else—squeezes into the cage and launches himself at the henhouse, which topples over while the hens squawk and flap around the wire-mesh enclosure. Quick as a whip, the fox leaps back to the hole and its head's actually through before Zimbra's sunk his fangs into its neck. The fox looks at me for a split second before it's yanked back, shaken, flung, and pounced on. Then its throat's ripped out and it's all over. The hens keep panicking until one notices the battle's over, then they all fall quiet. Zimbra stands over his prey, his maw bloodred. Slowly he returns to himself and I return to myself. The porch door opens and Rafiq's standing there in his dressing gown. "What happened, Holly? I heard Zim going mental."

"A fox got into the chickens, love."

"Oh, bloody hell, no!"

"Language, Rafiq."

"Sorry. But how many did it get?"

"Only two or three. Zim killed it."

"Can I see it?"

"No. It's a dead fox."

"Can we eat the dead chickens, at least?"

"Too risky. Specially now rabies is back."

Rafiq's eyes go even wider: "*You* weren't bitten, or . . ."

Bless him. "Back to bed, mister. Really, I'm fine."

SORT OF. RAFIQ has plodded upstairs and Zimbra is locked on the porch. It's four dead hens, not three, which is a medium-sized loss, with eggs being my main bartering token at the Friday market, as well as Lorelei and Rafiq's main source of protein. Zimbra looks okay, but I can only hope he doesn't need veterinary attention. Synthetic meds for humans have all but dried up; if you're a dog, forget it. I turn down the solar, dig out a bottle of Declan O'Daly's potato hooch, and pour myself what Dad would've called a goodly slug. I let the alcohol cauterize my nerves and look at the backs of my old, old hands. Ridged tendons, snaky veins, vacuum-packed. My left hand trembles a little these days. Not much. Mo's noticed, but pretends not to. If you're Lol and Raf's age, all old people're trembly, so they're not worried. I pull my blanket over me, like Little Red Riding Hood's grandmother, who I feel like, in fact, in a world of too many wolves and not enough woodcutters. It's chilly out. Tomorrow I'll ask Martin the Mayor if we're likely to see a delivery of coal this winter, though I know he'll just say, "If we see any, Holly, the answer's yes." Fatalism's a weak antidepressant, but there's nothing stronger at Dr. Kumar's. Through the side window I see my garden chalkdusted by the nearly full moon, rising over the Mizen Peninsula. I should harvest the onions soon and plant some kale.

In the window I see a reflection of an old woman sitting in her great-aunt's chair and I tell her, "Go to bed." I haul myself to my feet, ignoring the twinge in my hip, but pausing for a moment at the little driftwood box shrine we keep on the dresser. I made it five years ago during the worst grief-numbed weeks after the Gigastorm, and Lorelei decorated it with shells. Aoife and Örvar's photo is inside, but tonight I just stroke my thumb across the top edge, trying to remember how Aoife's hair felt.

"Sleep tight, sweetheart, don't let the bedbugs bite."

U P BEFORE DAWN to pluck the feathers from four dead hens. Only twelve hens left, now. When I first moved to Dooneen Cottage—a quarter of a century ago—I couldn't have plucked a hen if my life depended on it. Now I can stun, decapitate, and gut one as casually as Mam used to make a beef and Guinness stew. Necessity's even taught me how to skin and dress rabbits without puking. One old fertilizer bag of feathers later I put the dead hens into the wheelbarrow and walk down the end of the garden via the hen coop, where I add the fox's body to my one-wheeled hearse. He's male, I see. Don't touch fox's tails, Declan says. A fox's brush is a bacteriological weapon, barbed with disease. Probably got fleas, too, and we've had enough trouble with fleas, ticks, and lice as it is. The fox looks like he's having an afternoon nap, if you ignore the ripped-out throat. One of his fangs protrudes slightly, pressing in his lower lip. Ed's tooth did that. I wonder if the fox has cubs and a mate. I wonder if the cubs'll understand that he's never coming back, if the heart'll be ripped out of their lives, or if they'll just carry on foraging without a second thought. If they do, I envy them.

The sea's ruffled this morning. I think I see a couple of dolphins a few hundred yards out, but when I look again, they've gone, so I'm not sure. The wind's still from the west and not the east. It's an awful thing to think, but if Hinkley is spewing radioactive material, which way the wind happens to be blowing could be a matter of life or death.

I tip the wheelbarrow's grisly cargo off the stone pier. I never name our hens, 'cause it's harder to wring the neck of something you've named, but I'm sad they had such frightened deaths. Now they're drifting away with their killer into the open bay.

I want to hate the fox, but I can't.

It was only trying to survive.

BACK AT THE house, Lorelei's in the kitchen spreading a bit of butter on yesterday's rolls for her and Rafiq's lunch. "Morning, Gran."

"Morning. There's dried seaweed, too. And pickled turnip."

"Thanks. Raf told me about the fox. You should've woken me."

"No point, love. You can't raise chickens from the dead, and Zim dealt with the fox." I wonder if she's remembered the date. "There's a few strips of corrugated iron from the old shed—I'll try sinking some underground walls around the coop."

"Good idea. It should 'outfox' the next visitor."

"That's one gene you inherited from Granddad Ed."

She likes it when I say that sort of thing. "It's, uh," she makes an effort to sound breezy, "Mum and Dad's Day, today. The twenty-seventh of October."

"It is, love. Want to light the incense?"

"Yes, please." Lorelei goes to the little box shrine and opens up its front. The photo shows Aoife and Örvar and a ten-year-old Lorelei, against the background of a dig at L'Anse aux Meadows. It was taken in spring of 2038, the year they died, but its greens and yellows are already fading and the blues and magentas blotting. I'd pay a lot for a reprint but there's no power or ink cartridges to print one, and no original to make a reprint from; my feckless generation trusted our memories to the Net, so the '39 Crash was like a collective stroke.

"Gran?" She's looking at me like my mind's gone walkabout.

"Sorry, love, I was, um . . ." Often, there are just blanks.

"Where's the tin with the incense sticks?"

"Oh. I tidied it up. Put it somewhere safe. Um . . ." Is this happening more these days? "The tin, above the stove."

Lorelei lights the new incense stick at the stove, then blows out the tiny flame. She crosses the kitchen, placing the stick in the holder in the little shrine. On the ledge are a Roman coin, which Aoife gave to Lorelei, and an old windup watch Örvar inherited from his grandfather. We watch the sandalwood smoke unthread itself from the glowing tip. Sandalwood, yet another old-world scent. The first year we did this, I'd prepared a prayer and a poem, but I started weeping so uncontrollably that I appalled Lorelei; since then we've tacitly agreed that we just stand here for a little while and sort of be alone together with our memories. I remember waving them off at Cork airport five years ago—the last year that ordinary people could buy diesel, drive cars, and fly, though ticket prices were spiraling through the roof, and they couldn't have gone if the Australian government hadn't paid Örvar's way. Aoife went to see her aunt Sharon and uncle Peter, who'd moved out there in the late twenties and who I hope are still alive and well in Byron Bay, but there've been no news-threads to—and precious little information from—Australia for eighteen months. How easily, how instantly we used to message anyone, anywhere on earth. Lorelei holds my hand. She would've gone with her parents if she hadn't been getting over chicken pox, so Aoife and Örvar drove her here from Dublin, where they were living that year. A fortnight with Grandma Holly was the consolation prize.

Five years later, I take a deep, shuddery breath to stop myself crying. It's not just that I can't hold Aoife again, it's everything: It's grief for the regions we deadlanded, the ice caps we melted, the Gulf Stream we redirected, the rivers we drained, the coasts we flooded, the lakes we choked with crap, the seas we killed, the species we drove to extinction, the pollinators we wiped out, the oil we squandered, the drugs we rendered impotent, the comforting liars we voted into office—all so we didn't have to change our cozy lifestyles. People talk about the Endarkenment like our ancestors talked about the Black Death, as if it's an act of God. But we summoned it, with every tank of oil we burned our way through. My generation were diners stuffing ourselves senseless at the Restaurant of the Earth's

Riches knowing—while denying—that we'd be doing a runner and leaving our grandchildren a tab that can never be paid.

"I'm so sorry, Lol." I sigh, looking around for a box of tissues before remembering our world no longer has tissues.

"It's all right, Gran. It's good to remember Mum and Dad."

Upstairs, Rafiq is hopping along the landing—probably pulling on a sock—as he sings in hybrid Mandlish. Chinese bands are as cool to kids in the Cordon as American New Wave bands were to me.

"We're luckier, in a way," Lorelei says quietly. "Mum and Dad didn't . . . Y'know, it was all over so quickly, and they had each other, and at least we know what happened. But for Raf . . ."

I look at Aoife and Örvar. "They'd be so proud of you, Lol."

Then Rafiq appears at the top of the stairs. "Is there any honey for the porridge, Lol? Morning, Holly, by the way."

SCHOOL BAGS PACKED, lunches stowed, Lorelei's hair braided, Rafiq's insulin pump checked and his blue tie—the last vestige of a uniform the school at Kilcrannog can reasonably insist on—done again and redone, we set off up the track. Caher Mountain, whose southern face I've looked at in all seasons, all weathers, and all moods nearly every day over the last twenty-five years, rises ahead. Cloud shadows slide over its heathered, rocky, gorse-patched higher slopes. Lower down is a five-acre plantation of Monterey pines. I push the big pram that was already a museum piece when me and Sharon used to play with it during summer holidays here in the late seventies.

Mo's up and out. She's hanging clothes on her line as we get to her gateway, wearing a fisherman's *geansaí* so stretched it's almost a robe. "Morning, neighbors. Friday again. Who knows where the weeks go?" The white-haired ex-physicist grabs her stick and hobbles across the rough-cropped lawn, handing me her empty ration box to take to town. "Thanks in advance," she says, and I tell her, "No bother," and add it to Lorelei's, Rafiq's, and mine in the pram.

"Let me help with that washing, Mo," says Lorelei.

"The washing I can handle, Lol, but yomping off to town," as we call the village of Kilcrannog, "I can't. What I'd do without your gran to fill up my ration box, I cannot imagine." Mo whirls her cane like a rueful Chaplin. "Well, actually I can: starve by degrees."

"Nonsense," I tell her. "The O'Dalys'd take care of you."

"A fox killed four of our chickens last night," says Rafiq.

"That's regrettable." Mo glances at me, and I shrug. Zimbra sniffs a trail all the way up to Mo, wagging his tail.

"We're lucky Zimmy got him before he killed the lot," says Rafiq.

"My, my." Mo scratches behind Zimbra's ear and finds the magic spot that makes him go limp. "Quite a night at the opera."

I ask, "Did you have any luck on the Net last night?" Meaning, *Any news about the Hinkley Point reactor?*

"Only a few minutes, on official threads. Usual statements." We leave it there, in front of the kids. "But drop by later."

"I was half hoping you'd mind Zimbra for us, Mo," I say. "I don't want him going all *Call of the Wild* on us after killing the fox."

"Course I will. And, Lorelei, would you tell Mr. Murnane I'll be in the village on Monday to teach the science class? Cahill O'Sullivan's taking his horse and trap in that day and he's offered me a lift. I'll be borne aloft like the Queen of Sheba. Off you go now, I mustn't make you late. C'mon, Zimbra, see if we can't find that revolting sheep's shin you buried last time . . ."

AUTUMN'S AT ITS tipping point. Ripe and gold is turning manky and cold, and the first frost isn't far off. In the early 2030s the seasons went badly haywire, with summer frosts and droughts in winter, but for the last five years we've had long, thirsty summers, long, squally winters, with springs and autumns hurrying by in between. Outside the Cordon the tractor's going steadily extinct and harvests have been derisory, and on RTÉ two nights ago there was a report on farms in County Meath that are going back to using horse-drawn plows. Rafiq trots ahead, picking a few late blackberries, and I encourage Lorelei to do the same. Vitamin supplements in the ration boxes have grown fewer and further between. Brambles grow as vigorously as ever, at least, but if we don't shear them back soon, our track up to the main road'll turn into the hedge of thorns round Sleeping Beauty's castle. Must speak to Declan or Cahill about it. The puddles are getting deeper and the boggy bits boggier, too, and here and there Lorelei has to help me with the pram; more's the pity I didn't have the whole track resurfaced when money still got things done. More's the pity I didn't lay in better, deeper, bigger stores, too, but we never knew that every temporary shortage would turn out to be a permanent one until it was too late.

We pass the spring that feeds my cottage's and Mo's bungalow's water tanks. It's gurgling away nicely now after the recent rains, but last summer it dried up for a whole week. I never pass the spring without remembering Great-aunt Eilísh telling me about Hairy Mary the Contrary Fairy, who lived there, when I was little. Being so hairy the other fairies laughed at her, which made her so cranky she'd reverse people's wishes out of spite, so you had to outwit her by asking for what you *didn't* want. "I *never* want a skateboard" would get you a skateboard, for example. That worked for a bit till Hairy Mary cottoned on to what people were doing, so half the time she gave people what they wished for, and half the time she gave them the opposite. "So the moral is, my girl," Great-aunt Éilish says to me across the six decades, "if you want a thing, get it the old-fashioned way, by elbow grease and brain power. Don't mess with the fairies."

But today, I don't know why, maybe it's the fox, maybe it's Hinkley, I take my chances. *Hairy Mary, Contrary Fairy: Please, let my darlings survive.* "Please."

Lorelei turns and asks, "You okay, Gran?"

WHERE DOONEEN TRACK reaches the main road we turn right and soon pass the turnoff leading down to Knockroe Farm. We meet the farm's owner, Declan O'Daly, hauling a handcart of hay. Declan's around fifty, is married to Branna, has two older boys plus a daughter in Lorelei's class, owns two dozen Jerseys and about two hundred sheep, which graze on the rockier, tuftier end of the peninsula. His Roman brow, curly beard, and lived-in face give him the air of a Zeus gone to seed a bit, but he's helped Mo and us out more than a few times and I'm glad he's there. "I'd give you a big hug," he says, walking across the farmyard to the road in stained overalls, "but one of the cows just knocked me over into a huge pile of cow shite. What's so funny," he mock-fumes, "young Rafiq Bayati? By God, I'll use you as a rag . . ."

Rafiq's shaking with silent giggling and hides behind me as Declan lumbers over like a manure-spattered Frankenstein.

"Lol," Declan says, "Izzy told me to say sorry but she's gone on into the village early to help her aunt get her veg boxed up for the Convoy. You're coming for a sleepover later, I am informed?"

"Yes, if that's still okay," says my granddaughter.

"Ach, you're hardly a rugby squad now, are ye?"

"It's still good of you to feed an extra mouth," I say.

"Guests who help with the milking are more than—" Declan stops and looks up at the sky.

"What's *that*?" Rafiq squints up towards Killeen Peak.

I can't see it at first but I hear a metallic buzzing, and Declan says, "Would you look at that now . . ."

Lorelei asks, disbelievingly, "A plane?"

There. A sort of gangly powered glider. At first I think it's big and far, but then I see it's small and near. It's following Seefin and Peakeen Ridges, aiming towards the Atlantic.

"A drone," says Declan, his voice strained.

"*Magno,*" says Rafiq, enraptured: "A real live UAV."

"I'm seventy-four," I remind him, sounding grumpy.

"Unmanned aerial vehicle," the boy answers. "Like a big remote-control plane, with cameras attached. Sometimes they have missiles, but that one's too dinky, like. Stability has a few."

I ask, "What's it doing here?"

"If I'm not wrong," says Declan, "it's spying."

Lorelei asks, "Why'd anyone bother spying on us?"

Declan sounds worried: "Aye, that's the question."

"'I AM the daughter of Earth and Water,'" recites Lorelei, as we pass the old rusting electrical substation,

> "And the nursling of the Sky;
> I pass through the pores of the oceans and shores;
> I change, but I cannot die."

I wonder about Mr. Murnane's choice of "The Cloud." Lorelei and Rafiq aren't unique: Many kids at Kilcrannog have had at least one parent die as the Endarkenment has set in. "Oh, I can't be*lieve* I've forgotten this bit again, Gran."

"For after the rain . . ."

"Got it, got it.

> "For *after the rain when with never a stain,*
> *The pavilion of Heaven is bare,*
> *And the winds and sunbeams with their convex gleams—*"

"Um . . .

> "Build up the blue dome of air . . ."

Unthinkingly, I've looked up at the sky. My imagination can still project a tiny glinting plane onto the blue. Not an overgrown toy like the drone—though that was remarkable enough—but a jet airliner, its vapor trail going from sharp white line to straggly cotton wool. When did I last see one? Two years ago, I'd say. I remember Rafiq running in with this wild look on his face and I thought something was wrong, but he dragged me outside, pointing up: "Look, look!"

Up ahead, a rat runs into the road, stops, and watches us.

"What's a 'convex'?" asks Rafiq, picking up a stone.

"Bulging out," says Lorelei. " 'Concave' is bulging in, like a cave."

"So has Declan got a convex tummy?"

"Not as convex as it was, but let Lol get back to Mr. Shelley."

" 'Mr.'?" Rafiq looks dubious. "Shelley's a girl's name."

"That's his surname," says Lorelei. "He's Percy Bysshe Shelley."

"Percy? Bysshe? His mum and dad must've *hated* him. Bet he got crucified at school." He throws his stone at the rat. It just misses and the rat runs into the hedgerow. Once I would've told Rafiq not to use living things for target practice but since the Ratflu scare, different rules have applied. "Go on, Lol," I say. "The poem."

"I think I've got the rest.

> *"I silently laugh at my own cenotaph,*
> *And out of the caverns of rain,*
> *Like a child from the womb, like a ghost from the tomb,*
> *I arise and unbuild it again."*

"Perfect. Your dad had an amazing memory, too."

Rafiq plucks a fuchsia flower and sucks its droplet of nectar. Sometimes I think I shouldn't refer to Örvar in front of Rafiq, 'cause I never met his father. Rafiq doesn't sound upset, though: "The womb's where the baby is inside the mum, right, Holly?"

"Yes," I tell the boy.

"And what's a senno-thingy?"

"A cenotaph. A monument to a person who died, often in a war."

"I didn't get the poem either," says Lorelei, "till Mo explained it. It's about birth and rebirth *and* the water cycle. When it rains, the cloud's used up, so it's sort of died; and the winds and sunbeams build the dome of blue sky, which is the cloud's cenotaph, right? But then the rain that *was* the old cloud runs to the sea where it evaporates and turns into a new cloud, which laughs at the blue dome—its own gravestone—'cause now it's resurrected. Then it 'unbuilds' its gravestone by rising up into it. See?"

A gorse thicket scents the air vanilla and glints with birdsong. "I'm glad we're doing 'Puff the Magic Dragon,'" says Rafiq.

AT THE SCHOOL gate Rafiq tells me, "Bye!" and scuttles off to join a bunch of boys pretending to be drones. I'm about to call out, "Mind your insulin pump!" but he knows we've only one more in store, and why embarass him in front of his friends?

Lorelei says, "See you later, then, Gran, take care at the market," as if she's the adult and I'm the breakable one, and goes over to join a cluster of half-girls, half-women by the school entrance.

Tom Murnane, the deputy principal, notices me and strides over. "Holly, I was after a word with you. Would you still be wanting Lorelei and Rafiq to sit out of the religion class? Father Brady, the new priest, is starting Bible study classes over in the church from this morning."

"Not for my two, Tom, if it's no bother."

"That's grand. There's eight or nine in the same boat, so they'll be doing a project on the solar system instead."

"And will the earth be going round the sun or vice versa?"

Tom gets the joke. "No comment. How's Mo feeling today?"

"Better, thank you, and I'm glad you mentioned it, my mem—" I stop myself saying, "My memory's like a sieve," because it's not funny anymore. "Cahill O'Sullivan's bringing her in on his horse-trap next Monday, so she can teach the science class, if it still suits."

"If she's up to it she's welcome, but be sure and tell her not to bust a gut if her ankle needs more time to recuperate." The school bell goes. "Must dash now." He's gone.

I turn around and find Martin Walsh, the mayor of Kilcrannog, waving goodbye to his daughter, Roisín. Martin's a large pink man with close-cropped white hair, like Father Christmas gone into nightclub security. He always used to be clean-shaven, but disposable razors stopped appearing in the ration boxes eighteen months ago and now most men on the peninsula are sporting beards of one sort or another. "Holly, how are ye this morning?"

"Can't complain, Martin, but Hinkley Point's a worry."

"Ach, stop—have ye heard from your brother in the week?"

"I keep trying to thread a call, but either I get a no-Net message, or the thread frays after a few seconds. So, no: I haven't spoken with Brendan since a week ago, when the hazard alert went up to Low Red. He's living in a gated enclave outside Bristol, but it's not far from the latest exclusion zone and hired security's no use against radiation. Still," I resort to a mantra of the age, "what can't be helped can't be helped." Pretty much everyone I know has a relative in danger, or at least semi-incommunicado, and fretting aloud has become bad etiquette. "Roisín was looking right as rain just now, I saw. It wasn't mumps, after all?"

"No, no, just swollen glands, thanks be to God. Dr. Kumar even had some medicine. How's our local cyberneurologist's ankle?"

"On the mend. I caught her hanging out washing earlier."

"Excellent. Be sure to tell her I was asking after her."

"I will—and actually, Martin, I was hoping for a word."

"Of course." Martin leans in close, holding my elbow as if he, not I, is the slightly deaf one—as public officials do to frail old dears the week before election in a community of a mere three hundred voters.

"Do you know if Stability'll be distributing any coal before the winter sets in?"

Martin's face says, *Wish I knew.* "If it gets here, the answer's yes. Same old problem: There's a tendency for our lords and masters in Dublin to look at the Cordon Zone, think, Well, that bunch are living off the fat of the land, and wash their hands of us. My cousin at Ringaskiddy was telling me the collier docked last week with a cargo of coal from Poland, but when there'll be fuel enough to fill the trucks to distribute it is another matter."

"And a shower o' feckin' thieves 'tween Ringaskiddy and Sheep's Head there are so," says Fern O'Brien, appearing from nowhere, "and coal falls off lorries at a fierce old rate. I'll not be holding my breath."

"We raised the subject," says Martin, "at the last committee meeting. A few o' the lads and me're planning a little excursion up Caher Saddle for a spot o' turf cutting. Ozzy at the forge has made a—what's the word?—a compressor for molding turf logs, so big." Martin's hands are a foot apart. "Now sure it's not coal, but it's a sight better than nothing, and if we don't leave Five Acre Wood alone, it'll be No Acre Wood in no time, like. Once we've the logs dried, I'll have Fíonn drop down a load each to you and Mo on his next diesel run to Knockroe Farm—whoever you cast your ballot for. Frost doesn't care about politics, and we need to look after our own."

"I'm voting for the incumbent," I assure him.

"Thank you, Holly. Every last vote will count."

"There's no serious opposition, is there?"

Fern O'Brien points behind me to the church noticeboard. Over I go to read the new, large hand-drawn poster:

> ENDARKENMENT IS GOD'S JUDGMENT
> GOD'S FAITHFULL SAY "ENOUGH!"
> VOTE FOR THE LORD'S PARTY
> MURIEL BOYCE FOR MAYOR

"Muriel Boyce? *Mayor?* But Muriel Boyce is, I mean . . ."

"Muriel Boyce is not to be underestimated," says Aileen Jones, the ex–documentary maker turned lobster fisherwoman, "and thick as thieves with our parish priest, even if they can't spell 'faithful.' There's a link between bigotry and bad spelling. I've met it before."

I ask, "Father McGahern never did politics in church, did he?"

"Never," Martin replies. "But Father Brady's cut from a different cloth. Come Sunday I'll be sat there in our pew while our priest tells us that God'll only protect your family if you vote for the Lord's Party."

"People aren't stupid," I say. "They won't swallow that."

Martin looks at me as if I don't see the whole picture. I get this look a lot these days. "People want a lifeboat and miracles. The Lord's Party's offering both. I'm offering peat logs."

"But the lifeboat isn't real, and the peat logs are. Don't give up. You've a reputation for sound decisions. People listen to reason."

"Reason?" Aileen Jones is grimly cheerful. "Like my old doctor friend Greg used to say, if you could reason with religious people, there wouldn't be any religious people. No offense, Martin."

"I'm beyond offense at this point, Fern," says our mayor.

UP CHURCH LANE we come to Kilcrannog square. Ahead is Fitzgerald's bar, a low, rambling building as old as the village. It's been added to over the centuries and painted white, though not recently. Crows roost on its ridge tiles and gables as if up to no good. On our right's the diesel depot, which was a Maxol garage when I first moved here, and where we used to fill up our Toyotas, our Kias, our VWs like there was no tomorrow. Now it's just for the Co-op tanker that goes around from farm to farm. On the left's the Co-op store, where the ration boxes'll be distributed later by the committee, and on the south side of the square's the Big Hall. The Big Hall also serves as a marketplace on Convoy Day, and we go in, Martin holding the door open so I can wheel in my pram. The hall's noisy but there's not a lot of laughter today—Hinkley Point casts a long shadow. Martin says he'll see me later and goes off electioneering, Aileen looks for Ozzy to speak about metal parts for her sailboat, and I start foraging through the stalls. I browse among the trestle tables of apples and pears and vegetables too misshapen for Pearl Corp, home-cured bacon, honey, eggs, marijuana, cheese, home-brewed beer and poitín, plastic bottles and containers, knitted clothes, old clothes, tatty books, and a thousand things we used to give to charity shops or send to the landfill. When I first moved to the Sheep's Head Peninsula thirty years ago, a West Cork market was where local women sold cakes and jam for the *craic,* West Cork hippies tried to sell sculptures of the Green Man to Dutch tourists, and people on middle-class incomes bought organic pesto, Medjool dates, and buffalo mozzarella. Now the market's what the supermarket used to be: where you get everything, bar the basics found in the ration boxes. With our modified prams, pushchairs, and old supermarket trolleys, we're a hungry-looking, unshaven, cosmetic-less, jumble-sale parody of a Lidl or Tesco or Greenland only five or six years ago. We barter, buy, and sell with a combination of guile, yuan, and Sheep's Head dollars—numbered metal disks engraved by the three mayors of Durrus, Ahakista, and Kilcrannog. I turn forty-eight eggs into cheap Chinese shampoo you can also use to wash clothes; some bags of seaweed salt and bundles of kale into undyed wool from Killarney to finish a blanket; redcurrant jelly—the jars are worth more than the jelly—into pencils and a pad of A4 paper to stitch some more exercise books, as the kids' copy books have been rubbed out so often that the pages are almost see-through; and, reluctantly, a last pair of good Wellington boots I've had in their box for fifteen years into sheets of clear plastic, which I'll use to make rain capes for the three of us, and to fix the polytunnel after the winter gales. Plastic sheeting's hard to find, and Kip Sheehy makes a predictable face, but waterproof boots are even rarer, so by saying, "Maybe another time, then," and walking off I get him to throw in a twenty-meter length of acrylic cord and a bundle of toothbrushes as well. I worry about Rafiq's teeth. There's very little sugar in our—or anyone's—diet, but there are no dentists west of Cork anymore.

I chat with Niamh Murnane, Tom Murnane's wife, who's sitting at a table with hemp sacks of oats and sultanas; Stability no longer has any yuan to pay teachers, so it's sending out salaries of trade-able foodstuffs instead. I was hoping to find sanitary towels for Lorelei, too, as Stability no longer includes them on the list of neces-sities, but I'm told there weren't any on the last Company container ship. Branna O'Daly uses strips of old bedsheets, which we'll need to wash, 'cause even old bedsheets are getting rarer. If only I'd had the foresight to lay in a store of tampons a few years back. Still. Complaining is rude to the three-million-odd souls who have to somehow survive outside the Cordon.

. . .

IN THE ANNEX, Sinéad from Fitzgerald's bar serves hot drinks and soup made on the kitchen range that keeps the Big Hall warm in winter. As I trundle up with my pram, Pat Joe, the Co-op mechanic, pulls up a chair for me with his giant oily hands, and by now I need the sit-down. The road from Dooneen gets longer every Friday, I swear, and the pain in my side's more acidy than before. I should've spoken with Dr. Kumar, but what could she do if it's my cancer waking up? There's no CAT scans anymore, no drug regime. Molly Coogan, who used to design websites but who now grows apples in polytunnels up below Ardahill, and her husband, Seamus, are also at the table. As the Englishwoman there, I'm asked if I know anything about Hinkley Point, but I have to disappoint them.

Nobody else has had any luck with threading out of the island of Ireland for two or three days now. Pat Joe spoke with his cousin in Ardmore in East Cork last night, however, and holds court for a few minutes. Apparently two hundred Asylumites from Portugal landed on the beach in five or six vessels, and are now living in an old zombie estate built back in the Tiger Days. "As bold as you please," says Pat Joe, nursing his soup, "as if they own the place, like. So the Ardmore town mayor, he leads a—a deputation up to the zombie estate, my cousin was one of them, to tell the Asylumites that, very sorry and all, but they can't winter there, there's not enough food in the Co-op or wood in the plantation for the villagers as it is, let alone two hundred extra mouths, like. This big feller walks out, takes out a gun, cool as you please, and *shoots Kenny's hat off his head,* like in an old cowboy western!"

"Shocking! Shocking!" Betty Power is a theatrical matriarch who runs Kilcrannog's smokehouse. "What did the mayor do?"

"Sent a messenger to the Stability garrison in Dungarvan, asking for assistance, like—only to be told their jeeps had no feckin' diesel."

"The *Stability* jeeps had no diesel?" asks Molly Coogan, alarmed.

Pat Joe purses his lips and shakes his head. "Not one drop. The mayor was told to 'pacify the situation' as best he could. Only how's yer man s'posed to manage that when his deadliest weapon's a feckin' staple gun?"

"*I* heard," says Molly Coogan, "that the *Sun Yat-sen*"—one of the Chinese superfrigates that accompanies the Chinese container ships on the polar route—"sailed into Cork Harbor last week with five hundred marines on deck. A bit of a show of force, like."

"Sure you're missing a zero, there, Moll," says Fern O'Brien, who leans over from the next table. "My Jude's Bill was on loading duty at Ringaskiddy that day so he was, and he swears there wasn't a man under five *t'ousand* trooping the color under the Chinese flag."

I can imagine Ed, my long-dead partner, making hang-dog eyes at the authenticity of this so-called news but there's more to come as talk switches to a sister-in-law of Pat Joe's cousin in County Offaly, who knows a "Man in the Know" at Stability Research in the Dublin Pale who reckons the Swedes have genomed a rustproof, self-fertile strain of wheat. "I'm only passing on what I've been told," says Pat Joe, "but there's talk of Stability planting it all over Ireland next spring. If people have full bellies, the Jackdawing and rioting'll stop."

"White bread," sighs Sínead Fitzgerald. "Imagine that."

"I'd not want to go pissing on your snowman now, Pat Joe," says Seamus Coogan, "but was that the same Man in the Know who said the Germans had a pill that cured Ratflu, or that the States was reunited again, and the president was sending airdrops of blankets, medicine, and peanut butter to all the NATO countries? Or was it that friend of a friend who met an Asylumite outside Youghal who swore on his mother's life that he'd found a Technotopia where they still have twenty-four-hour electricity, hot showers, pineapples, and dark chocolate mousse, in Bermuda or Iceland or the Azores?"

I think about Martin's remarks on imaginary lifeboats.

"I'm only passing on what I've been told," sniffs Pat Joe.

"Whatever the future has in store," says Betty Power, "we're all in the hollow of God's hand, so we are."

"That's certainly how Muriel Boyce sees it," says Seamus Coogan.

"Martin's doing his best," says Betty Power, crisply, "but it's clear that only the Church can take care of the devilry falling over the world."

"Why will a loving God only help us if we vote for him?" asks Molly.

"You have to ask," blinks Betty Power. "That's how prayer works."

"But Molly's saying," says Pat Joe, "why can't He just answer our prayers directly? Why does he need us to vote for him?"

"To put the Church back where it belongs," says Betty Power. "Guiding our country."

The conversation heats up but I may as well be listening to children arguing about the acts and motives of Santa Claus. I've seen what happens after death, the Dusk and the Dunes, and it was as real to me as the chipped mug of tea in my hand. Perhaps the souls I saw were bound for an afterlife beyond the Last Sea, but if so, it's not the afterlife described by any priest or imam. There is no God but the one we dream up, I could assure my fellow parishioners: Humanity is on its own and always was . . .

. . . but my truth sounds no crazier than their faith, no saner either; and who has the right to kill Santa? Specially a Santa who promises to reunite the Coogans with their dead son, Pat Joe with his dead brother, me with Aoife, Jacko, Mum, and Dad; and even put the Endarkenment into reverse, and bring back central heating, online ordering, Ryanair, and chocolate. Our hunger for our loved ones and our lost world is as sharp as grief; it howls to be fed. If only that same hunger didn't make us so meekly vulnerable to men like Father Brady.

"Fallen pregnant?" Betty Power covers her mouth. "Never!" We're back to Sheep's Head gossip. I'd like to ask who's pregnant, but if I do so at this point they'll all wonder if I'm going deaf or turning senile.

"That's the problem." Sinéad Fitzgerald leans in. "Three lads went off with young Miss Hegarty after the harvest festival, they were all off their faces"—she mimes smoking a joint—"so until the baby's features are clear enough to play Spot the Daddy, Damien Hegarty doesn't know who to point the shotgun at. A proper mess it is."

The Hegartys keep goats lower down the peninsula, between Ahakista and Durrus. "Shocking," says Betty Power, "and Niamh Hegarty not a day over sixteen, too, am I right? No mother in the house to lay down the rules, that's what this is about. They just think anything goes. Which is exactly why Father Brady's—"

"Hear that," says Pat Joe, holding up a finger and listening . . .

. . . cups are poised in midlift; sentences dangle; babies are shushed; nearly two hundred West Corkonians fall silent, all at once; and then let out a collective sigh of relief. It's the Convoy: two armored jeeps, ahead of and behind the diesel tanker and the box truck. Inside the Cordon we still have tractors and harvesters, and Stability vehicles still drive on the old N71 to Bantry to service the garrisons and the depots, but these four shiny state-of-the-art vehicles rumbling up Church Lane are the only regular visitors to Kilcrannog. For anyone over Rafiq's age, say, the sound evokes the world we knew. Back then, traffic was a "noise," not a "sound," but it's different now. If you close your eyes as the Convoy arrives you can imagine it's 2030, say, back when you had your own car and Cork was a ninety-minute drive away, and my body didn't ache all the time, and climate change was only a problem for people who lived in flood-prone areas. Only I don't close my eyes these days, because it hurts too much when I open them. We all go outside to watch the show. I take my pram. It's not that I don't trust the villagers not to steal from an old lady with two kids to raise, but you shouldn't tempt hungry people.

THE HEAD JEEP pulls up past the diesel store. Four young Irish Stability troops jump out, enjoying the impact their uniforms, guns, and swagger makes on the yokels; it's not by chance that Kilcrannog's single girls wear their dwindling supplies of makeup and best clothes on Convoy Days. Corinna Kennedy from Rossmore Farm married a Convoyman and now she's living in the Bandon garrison with five hours of electricity a day. The head Irish guard speaks rapid-fire "Mandlish" into his transband to confirm their current position to the Main Convoy. "Each of them helmets'd cost more than my house," Pat Joe tells me, not for the first time, "if you had the contacts to turn it into hard yuan."

Three Chinese troops jump down from the rear jeep, in the uniforms of the Pearl Occident Company, or POC. They are taller than their Irish counterparts, their teeth are better, and their guns are more, as teenage Aoife would've said, badass. The Irish troops will chat a little, but the Chinese troops are under orders not to fraternize with the locals. Bantry is the western, wilder end of the Lease Lands, and the diesel they're delivering is more precious than gold. One of the Irishmen spots Kevin Murray's lit pipe too close to the tanker and barks, "Sir, we need you to put that pipe out right now!" Mortified, Kevin shuffles back into the Big Hall. Convoymen never need to threaten. The Convoys are our umbilical cord to the Ringaskiddy depot and its special items, no longer manufactured in Ireland, or anywhere in Europe, for all we know.

The two week in, week out Convoymen are Noel Moriarty, the tankerman, and Seamus Li, the chief merchant. Noel Moriarty, a busy-eyed, quick-witted, pale, and balding man in his midthirties, shakes hands and chats with Martin while the driver fits nozzle to intake. Martin asks Noel if he has any information about Hinkley Point. Noel says his POC boss told him the Chinese are monitoring the site from low-altitude satellites, but the whole complex appears to have been deserted. This news flies round the onlooking crowd in less than a minute, but as ever it's difficult to draw reliable conclusions from such scant facts. Noel Moriarty and Martin sign each other's clipboards, then the tankerman pulls the red handle that starts the flow of diesel into the Co-op tank. We try to catch a whiff of the stuff, and suffer a fresh round of pangs for the Petrol Age.

The box truck, meanwhile, has backed into the Co-op warehouse across the square, where Seamus Li speaks with Olive O'Dwyer,

Kilcrannog's deputy mayor. Items loaded onto the truck are mostly farm produce; from the deep freeze come recently slaughtered beef, bacon, turkey, rabbit, mutton, and lamb, and from the fresh store come boxes of cured tobacco, leeks, kale, onions, potatoes, pumpkins, and late fruit. Most of the fruit and vegetables will feed the Ringaskiddy Concession, where the POC officials live with their families, or the crews of the People's Liberation Navy's Atlantic Fleet. The meat, uncloned and cesium-free—so far—will be sold for jaw-dropping prices in Beijing, Chongqing, and Shanghai. Milk is powdered at Ringaskiddy, and is a major export.

In return, the three Sheep's Head Co-ops of Durrus, Ahakista, and Kilcrannog receive diesel, fertilizer, insecticide, machine parts, lightbulbs, tools, hardware, as well as the special requests— including vital medicines like Rafiq's insulin—agreed upon every month by the town committee. The POC also has a deal with Cork Stability to deliver the basic commodities for our weekly ration boxes, though the quality of these has been going downhill in recent months. The most important item delivered by the Company, however, is security. The POC protects its Lease Lands by paying for the Stability Militia to man the sixty-mile Cordon, which is why the ten-mile coastal strip from Bantry to Cork has been spared the worst of the lawlessness that plagues much of Europe as the Endarkenment switches off power networks and emaciates civic society. The men in Fitzgerald's bar mutter that the Chinese aren't here out of love, and that the POC is no doubt turning a tidy profit from its operation, but even the drunkest lout can imagine how savage life on Sheep's Head would soon become without the three Cs: Company, Convoy, and Cordon.

It's our Great Wall of China, so to speak.

MY PRAM AND me are at the school gate at three o'clock sharp. I remember the various kindergartens and schools in north London and Rye where I used to collect Aoife. The main topic of conversation is the half-empty ration box, returned to us irrespective of age from the Co-op with a 400-gram bag of oatmeal bulked out with husk and straw, 200 grams of brown rice, 200 grams of lentils, 50 grams of sugar and 50 grams of salt, a packet of ten Dragon Brand teabags, half a small bar of DMZ soap, a tub of Korean detergent two years past its use-by date, a small bottle of iodine labeled in Cyrillic, and, bafflingly, a Hello Kitty cola-flavoured eraser. What isn't used will become currency in future Friday markets, but to-day's ration box is the worst in the six years since the system was introduced in the wake of the '39 crop failure. "I know it's a disgrace," Martin's saying to a group of the disgruntled, "but I'm your mayor, not a magician. I've threaded messages to Stability in Cork till I'm blue in the face, but how can I make them answer if they won't? Stability is not a democracy; they'll look after their own first and answer only to Dublin."

Martin's saved, sort of, by the bell. The kids troop out, and my two and I set off along the main road out of Kilcrannog, Lorelei and Rafiq taking it in turns to sniff the cola eraser. The scent awakens very early memories for Lorelei, but Rafiq's too young to have tasted the real thing, and he keeps asking, "But what *is* cola? A fruit or a herb or what?"

The last house out of the town happens to be Muriel Boyce's, standing alone after a row of terraced houses. It's big and blockish, every window has net curtains, and its conservatory is now a greenhouse, like most other conservatories round here. The three houses before Muriel Boyce's are occupied by three of her four big thumping sons and their wives, who seem to give birth only to boys, so the houses are referred to collectively as "Boyce Row." I remember Ed saying how in tribal areas of Afghanistan sons mean power; the Endarkenment's taking us the same way. Crosses are painted over Boyce Row's windows and doors. Muriel Boyce has always been devout, organizing trips to Lourdes in the old days, but since her husband "was called to the Lord" two years ago—appendicitis—her piety has grown fangs and she's let the hedge grow tall, though that doesn't stop her seeing out, somehow. We've already passed her house when I hear her call my name. We turn, and she appears at her garden gate. She's dressed nunnishly and has her lumpish twenty-year-old son, Dónal, with her. Dónal wears cutoff shorts and a wife-beater's vest. "Beautiful evening it's turned into, Holly. Lorelei, aren't ye after shooting up tall into a pretty young thing? And hello, Rafiq. What class are ye in at our school up above?"

"Fourth," says Rafiq, cautiously. "Hello."

"Lovely day, Lolly," says Dónal Boyce, and Lorelei nods and looks away.

Muriel Boyce says, "Ye're after having fox trouble, I hear?"

"You heard correctly, yes," I reply.

"Now isn't that fierce unlucky?" She tuts. "How many birds are you after losing altogether?"

"Four."

"Four, is it?" She shakes her head. "Any of your best layers?"

"One or two." I shrug, wanting to move on. "Eggs are eggs."

"That hound o' yours got the fox, I gather?"

"He did." Hoping she'll ask me to vote for her so I can give a vague reply and go, I say, "I see you're running for mayor."

"Well, I didn't want to, but the Lord insisted so I'm obeying. People're free to vote as they choose, of course—you won't catch *me* giving my friends and neighbors the 'hard sell.'" *Father Brady's doing that for you,* I think, and Muriel brushes away a fly. "No, no. It's about the youngsters," she smiles at Lorelei and Rafiq, "that I was wanting a word with ye, Holly."

The kids look puzzled. "I haven't done anything," protests Rafiq.

"Nobody's saying you have," Muriel Boyce looks at me, "but is it true you're refusing to let Father Brady speak to them about the Lord's Good News?"

"Are you talking about the religion class?"

"About Father Brady's Bible study, yes."

"We've opted out. Which is a private matter."

Muriel Boyce looks away, sighing over Dunmanus Bay. "The whole parish admired how you've rolled up your sleeves, so to speak, when the Lord gave these two to your care—at your point in life. And when one isn't even your blood! Nobody could fault you."

"Blood doesn't come into it." Now I'm riled. "I didn't give Rafiq a home because the parish admires me, or because 'the Lord' wanted me to—I did it because it was the right thing to do."

Muriel Boyce's smile is pained. "Which is ex*act*ly why the parish is so dismayed, now ye're hell-bent on neglecting their spiritual needs. The Lord's *so* disappointed. Your own angel's crying, right next to you, right now. Youngsters in these godless times *need* the power of prayer more than ever. It's as if ye're not feeding them."

Lorelei and Rafiq look around and see, of course, nothing.

"Oh, I can see all your angels, children." Muriel Boyce gives a glazed look above our heads, just as prophetesses are supposed to. "Yours is like a bigger sister, Lorelei, but with long golden hair, and Rafiq's is a man, a darkie but sure so was one o' the Wise Men, but all three are sad, so sad. Your grandmother's angel is weeping her blue eyes red, so she is. It breaks my heart. She's begging ye to—"

"Enough of this, Muriel, f'Chrissakes."

"Yes, it *is* for the sake of Our Lord Jesus Christ that I'm—"

"No no no no no. First off, *you* are not the parish. Second, I'm afraid the angels you 'see' happen to agree with Muriel Boyce too often to be plausible. Third, Lorelei's parents weren't churchgoers and Rafiq's mum was from a Muslim background, so as the children's guardian I'm respecting their parents' wishes. We're done here. Good day to you, Muriel."

Muriel Boyce's fingers clutching the top of her gate remind me of talons. "There's many who were 'atheists' when Satan was dazzling them with money, abortions, science, and Sky TV but who're sorry now they've seen what it's all led to." With one hand she holds her crucifix towards me as if it'll awe me into submission. "But the Lord forgives sinners who seek forgiveness. Father Brady's willing to come and speak with ye—at home. And it's churches not mosques we have in *this* part of the world, thanks be to God."

Dónal, I notice, is nakedly eyeing up Lorelei.

I push the pram away and tell the kids, "C'mon."

"We'll see if ye change your tune," Muriel Boyce calls after me, "when the Lord's Party's controlling the Co-op, deciding what's going into whose ration boxes, so we will."

Shocked, I turn around. "Is that a threat?"

"It's a fact, Holly Sykes. Here's another: The food in your bellies is Irish food. Christian food. If it's not to your liking, there's lots of houses going begging in England, I hear, near Hinkley."

I hear wood being chopped. "Sheep's Head is my home."

"There's plenty hereabouts who won't be seeing things that way, not when belts are tighter. Ye'd do well to remember."

My legs feel weak and stiff, like stilts, as I walk off.

Dónal Boyce calls after us, "I'll be seeing you, Lol."

He's a leery, muscly, horny threat. We leave the village passing the SLÁN ABHAILE sign and the old 80 KPH. speed limit sign. "I don't like the way Dónal Boyce was looking at me, Gran," says Lorelei.

"Good," I tell her. "I didn't, either."

"Me neither," says Rafiq. "Dónal Boyce is a jizbag."

I open my mouth to say, "Language," but don't.

FORTY MINUTES LATER we arrive home, at the end of the bumpy Dooneen track. "Dooneen" means "little fortress" and that's how our cottage feels to me, even as I stow the food, items from the market and our ration boxes. While the kids get changed I try my tab to see if I can get through to Brendan, or even one of my closer relatives in Cork, but no luck; all I get is a SERVER NOT DETECTED message, and IF PROBLEMS PERSIST, CONTACT YOUR LOCAL DEALER. Useless. I check the hens and retrieve three fresh eggs from the coop. When Rafiq and Lorelei are ready, we go through the thicket between our garden and Mo's, and over to her back door. It's open, and Zimbra comes padding into the kitchen wagging his tail. He used to jump up more when he was a puppy, but now he's calmer. Mo's ration box and the eggs go in her cupboard. I click it shut to keep out the mice. We find Mo in her sunroom playing two-handed Scrabble with herself. "Welcome back, scholars. How were school and the market?"

"Okay," says Rafiq, "but we saw a *drone* this morning."

"Yes, I saw it too. Stability must have fuel to burn. Odd."

Lorelei studies the Scrabble board. "Who's winning, Mo?"

"I'm demolishing myself: 384 versus 119. Any homework?"

"I've got quadratic equations," says Lorelei. "Yummy."

"Ah, sure you can do those in your sleep now, so you can."

"I've got geography," says Rafiq. "Ever see an elephant, Mo?"

"Yes. At zoos, and at a reservation in South Africa."

Rafiq's impressed. "Were they really as big as houses? That's what Mr. Murnane said."

"As big as small cottages, maybe. African elephants were bigger than Indian ones. Magnificent beasts."

"Then why did people let them go extinct?"

"There's plenty of blame for everyone, but the last herds were slaughtered so that people in China could show how rich they were by giving each other knickknacks made of ivory."

Mo isn't one to sugar pills. I watch Rafiq's face go almost sulky as he digests this. "I wish I'd been born sixty years ago," he says. "Elephants, tigers, gorillas, polar bears . . . All the best animals've gone. All we've got left is rats and crows and earwigs."

"And some first-class dogs," I say, patting Zimbra's head.

We all fall quiet at once, for no obvious reason. Mo's husband, John, fifteen years dead, smiles out of his frame above the hearth. It's a beautiful likeness in oils painted on a summer's day in the garden of Mo and John's old cottage on Cape Clear. John Cullin was blind and his life wasn't always an easy one, but he lived at a civilized time in a civilized place where people had full bellies. John wrote fine poetry. Admirers wrote to him from America.

That world wasn't made of stone, but sand.

I'm afraid. One bad storm is all it will take.

LATER, LORELEI GOES off to Knockroe Farm for her sleepover. Mo comes down to the cottage for dinner, where Rafiq and us two old ladies eat broad beans and potatoes fried in butter. At Rafiq's age

Aoife would have turned her nose up at such plain fare, but before he reached Ireland Rafiq knew real stomach-gnawing hunger and he never turns anything down. Dessert is blackberries we picked on the way home and a little stewed rhubarb. Dinner is quieter without our resident teenager, and I'm reminded of when Aoife first left home to go to college. Once the dishes are done, we all play crib-bage listening to an RTÉ program about how to dig a well. Rafiq then escorts Mo home before it gets dark, while I empty the latrine bucket into the sea below and check the wind direction; still east-erly. I round the hens up into their house and bolt its door shut, wishing I'd done so last night as well. Rafiq comes back, yawns, strip-washes in a bucket of cold water, cleans his teeth, and takes himself up to bed. I read an old copy of *The New Yorker* from De-cember 2031, savoring a story by Ersilia Holt and marveling at the adverts and the wealth that existed so recently.

At eleven-fifteen P.M. I switch on my tab to patch Brendan, but when the thing asks for my password, I blank. My password. F'Chrissakes. I never change it. It was something to do with dogs . . . Years ago I'd laugh about these flashes of forgetfulness, but at my age, it's like the beginning of a slow-motion death sentence. If you can't trust your mind anymore, you're mentally homeless. I get up to retrieve my little book where I write things down, but Zimbra's on my foot, and I remember: NEWKY, the name of the dog we had when I was a girl. I enter the password and try to thread Brendan. After five days of letdowns I'm ready for the error message, but on the first go I get a hi-res image of my brother frowning into his tab, 250 miles away in his study in his house on Exmoor. Something's wrong: His strands of white hair are a mess, his haggard, puffy face is a mess, his voice is a nervous mess. "*Holly?* I can see you! Can you see me?"

"And hear you, Brendan, clear as a bell. What's happened?"

"Well, apart from"—he reaches offscreen to get a drink, and I'm left looking at a photo on his shelf of a twenty-years-ago Brendan Sykes shaking hands with King Charles on Tintagel Gated Village's opening day—"apart from the west of England looking more like the Book of Revelation and a nuclear reactor down the road about to blow? Jackdaws. We had a visit two nights ago."

I feel sick. "In the village, or in your actual house?"

"The village, but that was bad enough. Four nights ago our dedicated guards all buggered off, taking half the food in the store *and* the backup generator." Brendan's half drunk, I realize. "Most of us stayed—where'd we go to?—and we drew up a security rota."

"You could come here."

"If I don't get sliced and diced by highwaymen at Swansea. If the trafficker doesn't cut my throat a mile off the Welsh coast. If Immigration at Ringaskiddy takes my bribe."

I know now, if I didn't before, that I'll never see Brendan in the flesh again. "Maybe Oisín Corcoran could help?"

"They're all too busy trying to survive to help an eighty-year-old English Asylumite. No, you reach an age when . . . journeys, voyages, are for other people, not you." He drinks his whisky. "I was telling you about the Jackdaws. At one o'clock or so this morning the alarms all went off, so I got dressed, got my .38 and went to the storehouse, where about a dozen of the bastards with guns, knives, and face-masks were loading up a van. Jem Linklater walked up and told the organizer, 'That's our food you're thieving, sunshine, and we've the right to defend it.' He shone a solar right in Jem's face and said, 'It's ours now, Granddad, so back off, and that's your last warning.' Jem didn't back off, and Jem"—Brendan shuts his eyes—"Jem got his head blown in."

My hand's over my mouth. "Jesus. You *saw* this?"

"From ten feet away. The murderer said, 'Any more heroes?' Then a gun went off and the guard went down, and total bloody anarchy broke out, and the Jackdaws realized we weren't quite the doddery old farts they'd expected. Someone shot out the headlamps on the van. It was too dark to know who was where, what was what, and"—Brendan's chest's heaving—"I ran into the tomato polytunnel, where a Jackdaw came pounding at me, waving a machete, I thought . . . And my .38 was suddenly in my hand with the safety off, a bang sounded, and something skidded into me . . . His mask'd come away, somehow, and I saw—I saw he was a boy, younger than Lorelei. The machete was a garden trowel. And"— Brendan controls his voice—"I shot him, Hol. Straight through the heart."

My brother's trembling and his face is shining, and a memory comes to me of a woman lying at a crossroads in an impossible lab- yrinth with her head staved in and a marble rolling pin dropping from my hand. I manage to say, "Under the circumstances . . ."

"I know. I thought it was him or me and some reflex kicked in. I dug his grave myself, at least. That's a lot of earth to shift, at my age. We got four of them, they got six of us, plus Harry McKay's boy, who's in a bad way with a punctured lung. There's a clinic in Exmouth, but care standards are pretty Middle Ages, by all ac- counts."

"Bren, if you can't come here, perhaps I could try to—"

"*No!*" For the first time Brendan looks afraid. "For your sake, for Lol's sake, for Rafiq's sake, for God's sake stay put. Traveling's too dangerous now, unless you've ten armed men willing to kill, and Sheep's Head Peninsula's probably the safest place in western Eu- rope. When Pearl Occident first leased the West Cork coastal strip I thought, *What a humiliation for the Paddies,* but at least you've still got law and order there, of sorts. At least—"

Brendan's features freeze in midsyllable, as if the wind changed direction just as he pulled a weird face. "Brendan? Can you hear me?" Nothing. I groan with frustration and Zimbra looks up, wor- ried. I try rethreading, I try resetting my tab, I try waiting. I didn't even ask if he'd heard from Sharon in Australia, but now the cover- age has gone and something tells me it won't be coming back.

UP IN MY room, I can't get to sleep. Shadows bloom in the corners, swaying a little against darker darkness. The wind's risen, the roof creaks, the sea booms. What Brendan said is on imperfectly remem- bered, nonstop shuffle repeat: I think of better things to say, calm- ing things, but as usual it's too late. My big brother, the onetime multimillionaire property developer, looked so hollowed out and so fragile. I envy the God-intoxicated Boyces of the world. Prayer may be a placebo for the disease of helplessness, but placebos can make you feel better. At the end of my garden the sound of waves dies and gives birth to the sound of waves, forever and ever, Amen. Across the corridor, Rafiq says something in his sleep, quite loud and afraid and in Arabic. I get up, go to his room, and say, "You okay, Raf?" but he's asleep and mumbling, so I go back to my warm bed. My stomach makes a buried squeal. Once upon a time "my body" meant "me," pretty much, but now "me" is my mind and my body is a selection box of ailments and aches. My molar throbs, the pain in my right side is jaggedy, rheumatism rusts my knuckles and knees, and if my body was a car I'd have traded it in, years ago. But my small, late, unexpected family—me, Lorelei, Rafiq, Zimbra, and Mo—will last only as long as my body functions. The O'Dalys would look after the kids as best they could, I know, but the world is getting worse, not better. I've seen the future and it's hungry.

My fingers find Jacko's silver labyrinth, looped on its cord over my bedpost, and I press it against my forehead. The pattern of its walls, passageways, and junctions cools my hot brain down a bit. "I doubt you survived," I murmur to any real angel, to any surviving Horologist, "so I doubt you'll hear me. But let me be wrong. Give me one final abracadabra. Two golden apples, if you can spare them. Get the kids out of here, somewhere safe, if anywhere is safe. Please."

M Y OLD CURTAIN FILTERS the early rose-orange sun, but it's cold rose-orange, not warm rose-orange. The wind and waves sound busy this morning, rather than relentless, like last night. I hear Zimbra coming up the stairs, and here he is, nosing his way into my room and wagging his tail to say good morning. Strange how he always knows when I'm awake. I'm aware I've forgotten something, something deeply unpleasant. What was it? Brendan. I wonder how he is this morning. I hope he's being looked after. Only five years ago I could have booked myself a seat on an airplane, driven to the airport, flown over to Bristol, and within the hour been at Tintagel Gated Village. Now it's like a trip to the moon . . .

What can't be helped can't be helped. I've jobs to be doing. I get out of bed like an old lady, carefully, open the curtains and open my window. Dunmanus Bay's still a bit choppy, but I see a sailboat— probably Aileen Jones, out checking her lobster pots. The sea holly and myrtle at the end of the garden are being buffeted; back they bend towards the cottage, then spring up, then bend back towards the cottage. This means something. Something I'm missing, even though it's there in front of me, as plain as day.

It's an east wind, blowing from England; from Hinkley Point.

RADIO POC ISN'T broadcasting this morning; there's just a looped message saying the station is off the air today for operational reasons. So I switch to JKFM and leave it playing the Modern Jazz Quartet as I quarter an apple for my breakfast and heat up a couple of potato cakes for Rafiq. Soon he smells the garlic and clops down the stairs in his makeshift dressing gown and he tells me about a zipwire some of the older village boys are planning up in Five Acre Wood. After we've eaten I feed the chickens, water the pumpkins in the polytunnel, make a few days' worth of dog biscuits from oats, husk, and mutton fat, and sharpen the hair scissors while Rafiq cleans our drinking-water tub, refills it by taking the long hosepipe up to the spring, then goes down to the pier with his fishing rod. Zimbra joins him. Later he comes back with a pollack and a mackerel. Rafiq has bits of memories of fishing in sunny blue water before he came to Ireland, he says, and Declan O'Daly says the boy's a natural angler—luckily for his and Lorelei's diet, as they only eat meat once a month, at most. I'll bake the fish for dinner tonight, and serve them up with mashed swede. I make a pot of mint tea and start cutting Rafiq's hair. He's long overdue a trim and it'll be head-lice season at school soon. "I saw Aileen Jones through my telescope earlier," he says. "Out on the bay in the *Lookfar,* checking her lobster pot."

"That's great," I say, "but I hope you were careful—"

"—not to point it at the sun," he says. " 'Course I didn't, Holly. I'm not a total doofus, y'know?"

"Nobody's saying you're even a partial doofus," I tell him mildly. "It's just once you're a parent, a sort of . . . accident detector switches on, and never switches off. You'll see, one day, if you're ever a father."

"*Euuuyyyuckh*" is what Rafiq thinks of that prospect.

"Hold still. Lol should be doing this. She's the better stylist."

"No way! Lol'd make me look like a boy in Five-star Chongqing."

"Like a boy in what?"

"Five-star Chongqing. They're Chinese. All the girls fancy them."

And dream dreams of lives of plenty in Shanghai, I don't doubt. They say there are only two women to every three men in China 'cause of selective feticide, and when the Lease Lands were new and buses still ran to Cork, my relatives there told me about local girls being recruited as "China brides" and sailing away to full stomachs, 24/7 electricity, and Happy Ever After. I was old enough to have my doubts about the recruiting agencies' testimonials. I switch the radio from JKFM to RTÉ in case there's a report about Hinkley, which went unmentioned on the eight A.M. news. Zimbra comes and puts his head on Rafiq's lap and looks up at the boy. Rafiq musses his head. The RTÉ announcer reads the birth notices, where people thread the program the names of new babies, birthweights, the parents' names, parishes, and counties. I like hearing them. Christ knows these kids' lives won't be easy, especially for the majority who are born beyond the Pale or the Cork Cordon, but each name feels like a tiny light held up against the Endarkenment.

I snip a bit more around Rafiq's right ear to match his left.

I snip off too much, so now have to snip around his left.

"I wish all this never had to change," says Rafiq, unexpectedly.

I'm pleased he's content and sad that a kid so young knows that nothing lasts. "Change is sort of hardwired into the world."

The boy asks, "What does 'hardwired' mean?"

"A computer phrase from the old days. I just mean . . . what's real changes. If life didn't change, it wouldn't be life, it'd be a photograph." I snip the hairs up his neck. "Even photos change, mind. They fade."

We say nothing for a bit. I accidentally spike the bit between the tendons on Rafiq's neck and he goes, "Ouch," and I say, "Sorry," and he says, "No bother," like an Irishman. Crunchie, a semiwild tomcat I named after a long-ago chocolate bar, strolls across the kitchen windowsill. Zimbra notices, but can't be bothered to make a fuss. Rafiq asks, "Holly, d'you think Cork University'll be open again by the time I'm eighteen?"

I love him too much to puncture his dreams. "Possibly. Why?"

" 'Cause I want to be an engineer when I grow up."

"Good. Civilization needs more engineers."

"Mr. Murnane said we need to fix stuff, build stuff, move stuff, like oil states do, but do it all without oil."

And start forty years ago, I think. "He's right." I pull up a chair in front of Rafiq. "Lower your head, I'll do your fringe."

I lift up his fringe with a comb and snip off the hair that shows through its teeth, leaving a centimeter. I'm getting better at this. Then I see Rafiq's got this strange intense look on his face; it makes me stop. I turn the radio down to a mumble. "What is it, Raf love?"

He looks like he's trying to catch a far-off sound. Then he looks at the window. Crunchie's gone. "I remember someone cutting my hair. A woman. I can't see her face, but she's talking Arabic."

I lean back and lower the scissors. "One of your sisters, perhaps? Someone must've cut your hair before you were five."

"Was my hair short when I got here?"

"I don't remember it being long. You were half starved, half drowned, then you nearly died of hypothermia. The state of your hair didn't register. But this woman, Raf—can you see her face?"

Rafiq scrunches up his face. "It's like, if I don't look, I see her, but if I look at her, her face melts away. When I dream, I sometimes see her, but when I wake up, the faces've gone again, leaving just the name, like. One was Assia, I *think* she's my aunt . . . or maybe a sister. Maybe it's her with the scissors. Hamza and Ismail, they were my brothers, on the boat." I've heard this a few times, but I don't interrupt Rafiq when he's in the mood to study the surviving fragments of his life before Ireland. "Hamza was funny, and Ismail wasn't. There were so many men on the boat—we were all jammed up with each other. There were no women, and only one other boy, but he was a Berber and I didn't understand his Arabic very well. Most of the passengers were seasick, but I was okay. We all went to the toilet over the side. Ismail said we were going to Norway. I said, 'What's Norway?' and Ismail said it's a safe place where we could earn money, where they didn't have Ebola and nobody tried to shoot you . . . That sounded good, but the days and nights on the boat were bad." Rafiq's frown deepens. "Then we saw lights across the water, down a long bay, it was night, and there was a big fight. Hamza was saying to the captain in Arabic, 'It can't be Norway,' and the captain was saying, 'Why would I lie to you?' and Hamza had a sort of compass in his hand, saying, 'Look, we're not north enough,' and the captain threw it over the side of the boat and Hamza told the others, 'He's lying to us to save fuel. Those lights aren't Norway, it's somewhere else!' Then all the shouting began, and then the guns were going off, and . . ." Rafiq's eyes and voice are hollow. "That's where I am for most of my nightmares. We're all jammed in too tight . . ."

I remember how the Horologists could redact bad memories, and wish I could grant Rafiq the same mercy. Or not, I dunno.

". . . and most times it's like it was, with Hamza throwing a ring into the water, telling me, 'We'll swim together,' and he throws me into the water first, but then he never follows. And that's all I have." Rafiq dabs his eyes on the back of his hand. "I've forgotten everything else. My own family. Their faces."

"Owain and Yvette Richie of Lifford, up in County Donegal," says the radio guy, "announce the birth of their daughter Keziah—a dainty but perfect six pounds . . . Welcome aboard, Keziah."

"You were five or six, Raf. When you washed up on the rocks below you were in shock, you had hypothermia, you'd seen slaughter at close quarters, you'd drifted for heaven only knows how long in the cold Atlantic, you were alone. You're not a forgetter, you're a survivor. I think it's a miracle you remember anything at all."

Rafiq takes a clipping of his own hair, fallen onto his thigh, and rubs it moodily between his finger and thumb. I think back to that spring night. It was calm and warm for April, which probably saved Rafiq's life. Aoife and Örvar had only died the autumn before, and Lorelei was a mess. So was I, but I had to pretend not to be, for Lorelei's sake. I was speaking with my friend Gwyn on my tab in my chair when this face appeared at the door, staring in like a drowned ghost. I didn't have Zimbra yet, so no dog scared him off. Once I'd recovered, I opened the door and got him inside. Where he puked up a liter of seawater. The boy was soaked and shivering and didn't understand English, or seemed not to. We still had fuel for our boiler at that time, just about, but I understood enough about hypothermia to know a hot bath can trigger arrhythmia and possibly a cardiac arrest, so I got him out of his wet clothes and sat him by the fire wrapped in blankets. He was still shivering, which was another hopeful sign.

Lorelei had woken up by this point, and was making a cup of warm ginger drink for the boy from the sea. I threaded Dr. Kumar but she was busy at Bantry helping with an outbreak of Ratflu, so we were on our own for a couple more days. Our young visitor was feverish, malnourished, and suffered from terrible dreams, but after about a week we, with Mo's and Branna O'Daly's help, had nursed him back to relative health. We'd worked out his name was Rafiq by that stage, but where had he come from? Maps didn't work so Mo Netsourced "Hello" in all the dialects a dark-skinned Asylumite might speak: Moroccan Arabic rang the bell. With Mo's help, Lorelei studied the language from Net tutorials and became Rafiq's first English teacher, pulling herself out of mourning for the first time. When an unsmiling Stability officer arrived with Martin, our mayor, to inspect the illegal immigrant about a month later, Rafiq was capable of stringing together basic English sentences.

"The law says he has to be deported," stated the Stability officer.

Feeling sick, I asked where he'd be deported to, and how.

"Not your problem, Miss Sykes," stated the Stability officer.

So I asked if Rafiq'd be driven outside the Cordon and dumped like an unwanted dog, 'cause that's the impression I was getting.

"Not your problem, Miss Sykes," said the Stability officer.

I asked how Rafiq could legally stay on Sheep's Head.

"Formal adoption by an Irish citizen," stated the Stability officer.

Thanking my younger self for acquiring Irish citizenship, I heard myself say that I hereby wished to adopt Rafiq.

"It's another ration box for your village to fill," stated the Stability officer. "You'll need permission from your local mayor."

Martin read my face and said, "Aye, she has it."

"*And* you'd need authorization from a Stability officer of level-five status or above. Like me, for example." He ran his tongue along between his front teeth and his closed lips. We all looked at Rafiq, who somehow sensed that his future—his life—was hanging in the balance. All I could think of to say to the Stability officer was "Please."

The Stability officer unzipped a folder he'd had tucked inside his jacket all along. "I have children too," he stated.

"AND LAST BUT by no measure least," mumbles the radio, "to Jer and Maggs Tubridy of Ballintober, Roscommon, a boy, Hector Ryan, weighing in at a whopping eight pounds and ten ounces! Top job, Maggs, and congratulations to all three of you." Rafiq gives me a look to say he's sorry he went a bit morbid on me, and I give my adopted grandson a look to say there's nothing to be sorry about, and get back to cutting the wild whorl of hair about his crown. What little evidence we have suggests Rafiq's parents are dead, and if they're not, I don't know how they'll ever discover their son's fate—both the African Net and the Moroccan state had pretty much ceased to exist by the time Rafiq arrived at Dooneen Cottage. But now he's here, Rafiq's a part of my family. While I'm alive I'll look after him the best I can.

The RTÉ news theme comes on, and I turn it up a little.

"Good morning, this is Ruth O'Mally with the RTÉ News at ten o'clock, Saturday, the twenty-eighth of October, 2043." The familiar news fanfare jingle fades. "At a news conference at Leinster House this morning, the Stability Taoiseach Éamon Kingston confirmed that the Pearl Occident Company has unilaterally withdrawn from the Lease Lands Agreement of 2028, which granted the Chinese consortium trading rights with Cork City and West Cork Enterprise Zone, known as the Lease Lands."

I've dropped the scissors, but all I can do is stare at the radio.

"A Stability spokesman in Cork confirms that control of the Ringaskiddy Concession was returned to Irish authorities at oh four hundred hours this morning, when a POC container vessel embarked with a People's Liberation Navy frigate escort. The Taoiseach told the assembled journalists that the POC's withdrawal had been kept secret to ensure a smooth handover of authority, and stated that the POC's decision has been brought about by questions of profitability. Taoiseach Éamon Kingston added that in no way can the POC's withdrawal be linked to the security situation, which remains stable in all thirty-four counties. Nor is the decision of the Chinese linked to radiation leaks from the Hinkley Point site in north Devon."

There's more news, but I'm no longer listening.

Hens cluck, croon, and crongle in their enclosure.

"Holly?" Rafiq's scared. "What's 'unilaterally withdrawn'?"

Consequences spin off, but one thumps me: *Rafiq's insulin.*

"DA'S SAYING IT'LL be okay," Izzy O'Daly tells us, "and that Stability'll just keep the Cordon intact, where it is now." Izzy and Lorelei came running back across the fields from Knockroe Farm and found Rafiq, Zimbra, and me up in Mo's tidy kitchen. Mo'd heard the same RTÉ report as us, and we've been telling Rafiq that not much'll change, only Chinese imported goods'll be a little trickier to get hold of than before. The ration boxes will still be delivered by Stability every week, and provision will still be made for special medicines. Rafiq's reassured, or pretends to be. Declan O'Daly gave Izzy and Lorelei an equally upbeat assessment. "Da says," Izzy goes on, "that the Cordon was a fifteen-foot razor-wire fence before ten o'clock and it still is after ten o'clock, and there's no reason for the Stability troops to abandon their posts."

"Your dad's a very wise man," I tell Izzy.

Izzy nods. "Da 'n' Max've gone into town to check on my aunt."

"Fair play to Declan now," says Mo. "Kids, if you'd give Zimbra a run in the garden, I'll make pancakes. Maybe I've a dusting of cocoa powder left somewhere. Go on, give Holly and me a little space, hey?"

Once they're out, a grim and anxious Mo tries to thread friends in Bantry, where the Cordon's westernmost garrison is stationed. Calls to Bantry normally get threaded without trouble, but today there isn't even an error message. "I've got this nasty feeling," Mo stares at the blank screen, "that we've kept our Net access as long as we have because our threads were routed via the server at Ringaskiddy, and now the Chinese have gone . . . it's over."

I feel as if someone's died. "No more Net? *Ever?*"

Mo says, "I might be wrong," but her face says, *No, never.*

For most of my life, the world shrank and technology progressed; this was the natural order of things. Few of us clocked on that "the natural order of things" is entirely man-made, and that a world that kept expanding as technology regressed was not only possible but waiting in the wings. Outside, the kids're playing with a frisbee older than any of them—look closely, you'll see the phantom outline of the London 2012 Olympics logo. Aoife spent her pocket money on it. It was a hot day on the beach at Broadstairs. Izzy's showing Rafiq how you step forward and release the frisbee in one fluid motion. I wonder if they're all putting on a brave face about the end of the Lease Lands, and that really they're as scared as we are by the threat of gangs, militiamen, land pirates, Jackdaws and God knows what streaming through the Cordon. Zimbra retrieves the frisbee and Rafiq does a better throw, lifted by the wind. Lorelei has to spring up high to catch it, revealing a glimpse of shapely midriff. "Medicine for the chronically ill is one worry," I speak my thoughts aloud, "but what kind of life will women have, if things carry on the way they are? What if Dónal Boyce *is* the best future the girls in Lol's class can hope for? Men are always men, I know, but at least during our lives, women have gathered a sort of arsenal of legal rights. But only because, law by law, shifting attitude by shifting attitude, our society became more civilized. Now I'm scared the Endarkenment'll sweep all that away. I'm scared that Lol'll just be some bonehead's slave, stuck in some wintry, hungry, bleak, lawless, Gaelic-flavored Saudi Arabia."

Lorelei throws the frisbee, but the east wind biffs it off course into Mo's wall of camellias.

"Pancakes," says Mo. "I'll measure the flour and you crack a few eggs. Six should be enough for the five of us?"

. . .

"WHAT'S THAT SOUND?" asks Izzy O'Daly, half an hour later. Mo's kitchen table is strewn with the wreckage of lunch. Mo, of course, did unearth a small tub of cocoa powder from one of her bottomless hidden nooks. It must be a year since the last square of waxy Russian chocolate appeared in the ration boxes. Neither me nor Mo had any ourselves, but watching the kids as they ate their chocolate-laced lunch was a sight more delicious than the taste. "There," says Izzy, "that . . . crackly noise. Didn't you hear it?" She looks anxious.

"Raf's stomach, probably," says Lorelei.

"Sure I only had one more than you," objects Rafiq. "And—"

"Yeah, yeah, you're a growing boy, we know," says his sister. "Growing into a total pancake monster."

"There," says Izzy, making a *shush* gesture. "Hear it?"

We listen. Like the old woman I am, I say, "I can't hear—"

Zimbra leaps up, whining, at the door. Rafiq tells him, "Shush, Zimbra!"

The dog shushes, and—there. A spiky, sickening sequence of bangs. I look at Mo and Mo nods back: "Gunfire."

We rush out onto Mo's scrubby, dandelion-dotted lawn. The wind's still from the east and it buffets our ears but now another burst of automatic fire is quite distinct and not far away. Its echo reaches us a couple of seconds later from Mizen Head across the water.

"Isn't it coming from Kilcrannog?" asks Lorelei.

Izzy's voice is shaky. "Dad went into the village."

"The Cordon can't have fallen al*ready*," I blurt, wishing I could stuff the words back in, 'cause by saying it, I feel I've helped to make it real. Zimbra is snarling towards the town.

"I'd better get back to the farm," says Izzy.

Mo and I exchange a look. "Maybe, Izzy," Mo says, "until we know what we're dealing with, your parents'd prefer you to lie low."

Then we hear the noise of jeeps, this side of town, driving along the main lane. More than one or two, by the sound of it.

"Must be Stability," says Rafiq. "Only they have diesel. Right?"

"Speaking as a mum," I say to Izzy, "I *really* think you ought—"

"I—I—I'll stay hidden, I'll be careful, I promise." Izzy swallows, and then she's gone, vanished through a gap in the tall wall of fuchsia.

I hardly have time to dismiss the unpleasant feeling that I've just seen Izzy O'Daly for the final time before we notice the timbre of the jeeps has changed, from fast and furious to cautious and growly.

"I think one of the jeeps is coming down our track," says Lorelei.

Vaguely, I wonder if this blustery autumn day is going to be my last. But not the kids. Not the kids. Mo's had the same thought: "Lorelei, Rafiq, listen. Just on the off chance this is a militia unit and not Stability, we need you to get Zimbra to safety."

Rafiq, who still has some cocoa powder in the corner of his lips, is appalled. "But Zim and me are the bodyguards!"

I see Mo's logic: "If it's militiamen, they'll shoot Zim on sight before they even start talking to us. It's how they work."

Lorelei's scared, which she should be. "But what'll you do, Gran?"

"Mo and I'll talk to them. We're tough old birds. But please"—we hear a jeep engine roar in a low gear, sickeningly near—"both of you, go. It's what your parents would be saying. Go!"

Rafiq's eyes are still wide, but he nods. We hear brambles scraping against metal sides and small branches being snapped off. Lorelei feels disloyal going, but I mouth *"Please"* and she nods. "C'mon, Raf, Gran's counting on us. We can hide him at the sheep bothy above the White Strand. C'mon, Zim. Zimbra. Come *on*!"

Our spooked, wise dog looks at me, puzzled.

"Go!" I shoo him. "Look after Lol and Raf! *Go*!"

Reluctantly, Zimbra allows himself to be pulled off and the three are clear of Mo's garden and over the garden wall behind the polytunnel. We have a wait of about ten seconds before a Stability jeep barges its way through the overgrown track and up onto Mo's drive, spitting stones. A second jeep appears a few seconds later. The word Stability is stenciled along the side. The forces of law and order. So why do I feel like an injured bird found by a cat?

. . .

YOUNG MEN CLIMB out, four from each vehicle. Even I can tell they're not Stability; their uniforms are improvised, they carry mismatched handguns, automatic weapons, crossbows, grenades, and knives, and they move like raiders, not trained soldiers. Mo and I stand side by side, but they walk past us as if we're invisible. One, perhaps the leader, holds back and watches the bungalow as the others approach it, guns out and ready. He's scrawny, tattooed, maybe thirty, wears a green beret of military origin, a flak jacket, like Ed used to wear in Iraq, and the winged figure off a Rolls-Royce around his neck. "Anyone else at home, old lady?"

Mo asks him, "What's the story here, young man?"

"If anyone's hiding in there, they'll not be coming out alive. That's the story here."

"There's nobody else here," I tell him. "Put those guns away before somebody gets hurt, f'Chrissakes."

He reads me. "Old lady says it's all clear," he calls to the others. "If she's lying, shoot to kill. Any blood's on her hands now."

Five militiamen go inside, while two others walk around the outside of the bungalow. Lorelei, Rafiq, and Zimbra should be across the neighboring field by now. The strip of hawthorn should hide them from then on. The leader takes a few steps back and examines Mo's roof. He jumps onto the patio wall to get a better view.

"Will you *please* tell us," says Mo, "what you want?"

Inside Mo's bungalow, a door slams. Below, in their coop, my surviving chickens cluck. Over in O'Daly's pasture, a cow lows. From the road to the end of Sheep's Head, more jeeps roar. A militiaman emerges from Mo's shed, calling out, "Found a ladder in here, Hood. Shall I bring it out?"

"Yep," says the apparent leader. "It'll save unloading ours."

The five men now reemerge from Mo's bungalow. "All clear inside, Hood," says a bearded giant. "Blankets and food, but there's better in the village store."

I look at Mo: Does this mean they killed people in Kilcrannog?

Militiamen kill. It's how they carry on being militiamen.

"We'll just take the panels, then," says Hood, telling us, "Your lucky day, old ladies. Wyatt, Moog, the honor is yours."

Panels? Two of the men, one badly scarred by Ratflu, prop the ladder against the end gable of the bungalow. Up they climb, and we see what they want. "No," says Mo. "You can't take my solar panels!"

"Easier'n you'd think, old lady," says the bearded giant, holding the ladder steady. "One pair o' bolt cutters, lower her down gently, job's done. We've done it a hundred times, like."

"I need my panels for light," protests Mo, "and for my tab!"

"Seven days from now," Hood predicts, "you'll be praying for darkness. It'll be your only protection 'gainst the Jackdaws. Look on it as a favor we're doing you. And you won't be needing your tabs anymore, neither. No more Net for the Lease Lands. The good old days are good and gone, old lady. Winter's coming."

"You call yourself 'Hood,'" Mo tells him, "but it's 'Robbing Hood,' not Robin Hood, from where I'm standing. Would you treat *your* elderly relatives like this?"

"Number one is to survive," answers Hood, watching the men on the roof. "They're all dead, like my parents. They had a better life than I did, mind. So did you. Your power stations, your cars, your creature comforts. Well, you lived too long. The bill's due. Today," up on the roof the bolt is cut on the first panel, "you start to pay. Think of us as the bailiffs."

"But it wasn't us, personally, who trashed the world," says Mo. "It was the system. We couldn't change it."

"Then it's not us, personally, taking your panels," says Hood. "It's the system. We can't change it."

I hear the O'Dalys' dog barking, three fields away. I pray Izzy's okay, and that these men with guns don't molest the girls. "What'll you do with the panels?" I ask.

"The mayor of Kenmare," says Hood, as a couple of his men carry the first of Mo's panels over to the jeep, "he's building himself quite a fastness. Big walls. A little Cordon of his own, with surveil-

lance cameras, lights. Pays food and diesel for solar panels." A bolt
affixing Mo's second solar panel is cut. "These and the ones from
the house below"—he nods at my cottage—"are going to him."

Mo's quicker than me: "My neighbor has no solar panels."

"Someone's telling porkies," singsongs the bearded giant.
"Mr. Drone says they do, and Mr. Drone never lies."

"That drone yesterday was yours?" I ask, as if it'll help.

"Stability finds the booty," says the giant, "we go 'n' get it. Don't
look so gobboed, old lady. Stability's just another clan o' militia,
nowadays. Specially now the Chinks've gone."

I imagine my mother saying, It's "Chinese," not "Chinks."

Mo asks, "What gives you the right to take our property?"

"Guns gives us the right," says Hood. "Plain 'n' simple."

"So you're reinstating the law of the jungle?" asks Mo.

"You were bringing it back, every time you filled your tank."

Mo stabs the ground with her stick. "A thief, a thug, and a killer!"

He considers this, stroking his eyebrow ring. "Killer: When it's
kill or be killed, yeah, I am. Thug: We all have our moments, old
lady. Thief: Actually, I'm a trader, too, like. You give me your solar
panels—I'll give you glad tidings." He reaches into his pocket and
brings out two short white tubes. I'm so relieved it's not a gun I
extend my hand when he holds them out. I stare at the pill canisters,
at their skull and crossbones, their Russian writing. Hood's voice is
less mocking now. "They're a way out. If the Jackdaws come, or
Ratflu breaks out, or whatever, and there's no doctor. Instant anti-
emetic," he says, "and enough pentobarbital for a dignified ending
in thirty minutes. We call 'em huckleberries. You drift away painless, like. Childproof container, too."

"Mine's going into the cesshole," says Mo.

"Give it back, then," Hood says. "There's plenty who'll want
one." Mo's second solar panel's off the roof and is being carried past
us to the jeep. I slip both canisters into my pocket: Hood notices and
gives me a conspiratorial look I ignore. "Anyone in the house down
below," he nods at the cottage, "the lads need to know about?"

With acute retrospective envy, I remember how Marinus could

"suasion" people into doing his bidding. All I have is language. "Mr. Hood. My grandson's got diabetes. He controls it with an insulin pump that needs recharging every few days. If you take the solar panels, you'll be killing him. Please."

Up the hill, sheep bleat, oblivious to human empires rising and falling. "That's bad luck, old lady, but your grandson's born into the Age of Bad Luck. He was killed by a bossman in Shanghai who figured, 'The West Cork Lease Lands ain't paying their way.' Even if we left your panels on your roof, they'd be Jackdawed off in seven days."

Civilization's like the economy, or Tinkerbell: If people stop believing it's real, it dies. Mo asks, "How do you sleep at night?"

"Number one is to survive," Hood repeats.

"That's no answer," snorts my neighbor. "That's a huckleberry you force-feed to what's left of your conscience."

Hood ignores Mo and, with a gentleness I'd not have guessed at, he cups my hand under his larger one and presses a third canister into the hollow of my palm. Hope seeps through holes in the soles of my feet. "There's no one in the house below. Don't hurt my hens. Please."

"We'll not touch a feather, old lady," promises Hood.

The bearded giant's already carrying the ladder down the track to Dooneen Cottage when an explosion punches a hole through the tight quiet of the afternoon. Everyone crouches, tense—even Mo and me.

From Kilcrannog? There's an echo, and an echo's echo.

Someone calls out, "What the *holy feck* was that?"

The Ratflu-scarred kid points and says, "Over there . . ."

Rising into view above the fuchsia thicket we see a fat genie of orange-tinged oil-black smoke fly upwards, before the wind sucks it away over Caher Mountain. A raspy voice says, "The feckin' oil depot!"

Hood slaps his earset and flips up a mike piece. "Mothership, this is Rolls-Royce, our location's Dooneen, one mile west of Kilcrannog. What's with that big bang? Over."

Across the fields we hear the sickening percussion of gunfire.

"Mothership, this is Rolls-Royce—d'you need help? Over."

Through Hood's helmet we hear a smear of frantic speech, panicky static, and nothing more.

"Mothership? This is Rolls-Royce. Respond, please. Over." Hood waits, staring at the smoke still streaming up from the town. He slaps his headset again: "Audi? This is Rolls-Royce. Are you in contact with Mothership? And what's happening in town? Over." He waits. We all do, watching him. More silence. "Lads, either the peasants are revolting or we've got company from across the Cordon sooner than we thought. Either way, we're needed back at the town. Fall back."

The eight militiamen return to the jeeps without a glance at Mo or me. The jeeps reverse down Mo's short drive, and thump their way back up the track towards the main road.

Towards Kilcrannog, the gunfire grows more intense.

We can still recharge Rafiq's insulin pump, I realize.

For now, at least: Hood said the Jackdaws are coming.

"Didn't even put my bloody ladder back," mutters Mo.

FIRST I GO and get the kids from White Strand. The waves in Dunmanus Bay never look sure which way to run when the wind's from the east. Zimbra runs out of the old corrugated-iron shelter, followed by a nervy, relieved Lorelei and Rafiq. I tell them about the militiamen and the solar panels, and we walk back to Dooneen Cottage. Gunshots still dot-and-dash the afternoon, and as we turn back we see a drone circle over the village at one point. After a sustained burst of gunfire, Rafiq's keen eyes see it shot down. A jeep roars along the road up above. We find a giant puffball at the edge of the meadow, and although food's the last thing on my mind we pick it and Lorelei carries it home like a football. Fried in butter, its sliced white flesh will make the bones of a meal for the four of us—Christ knows when, or if, we'll be seeing a ration box again. Probably I have about five weeks' food in my parlor and the polytunnel, if we're careful. Assuming no gang of armed men steals it.

Back at the cottage I find Mo feeding the hens. She tried to patch friends in the village, in Ahakista, Durrus, and Bantry, but the Net's well and truly dead. As is the radio, even the RTÉ station. "All across the bandwidths," she says, "it's the silence of the tomb."

What now? I have no idea what to do: Barricade us in, send the kids to some remoter spot, like the lighthouse, go to the O'Dalys at Knockroe Farm to see what happened to Izzy and her family, or what? We've got no weapons, though given the number of rounds being fired on the Sheep's Head this afternoon, a gun's likelier to get you killed than save your life. All I know is that unless danger is careering down the Dooneen track in a jeep, I'm less fretful if Lorelei and Rafiq are right by me. Of course, if we're all absorbing high levels of radioactive isotopes it's all pretty academic, but let's take it one apocalypse at a time.

The commodity we're most in need of is news. The gunfire's stopped in the village, but until we know the lie of the land, we should steer clear. The O'Dalys'll probably know more, if Declan's got back okay. Their farm feels a long way off on such a violent afternoon, but Lorelei and I set out. I ask Rafiq to stay at the cottage with Zimbra to guard Mo, but tell him that, whatever happens, his first duty is to stay alive. That's what his family in Morocco would want; that's why they tried to get him to Norway. Which maybe wasn't the best thing to say, but if there was a book called *The Right Things to Do and Say as Civilization Dies,* I've never read it.

WE FOLLOW THE shore to Knockroe Farm, past the rocks where I harvest carrageen sea moss and kelp, and across the O'Dalys' lower grazing pasture. Their small herd of Jerseys approaches us, wanting to be milked; not a good sign. The farmyard's ominously quiet too, and Lorelei points out that the solar panels on the old stables are gone. Izzy said earlier that Declan and the eldest son, Max, went into the village this morning, but Tom or Izzy or their mum, Branna, should be around. No sign of the farm sheepdog, Schull, either, or English Phil the shepherd. The kitchen door's banging in the wind and I find Lorelei's hand in mine. The door was kicked in. We pass the manure pile, cross the yard, and my voice is trembling as I call into the kitchen, "Hello? Anyone home?"

No reply. The wind trundles a can along.

Branna's wind chime's chiming by the half-open window.

Lorelei shouts as loud as she dares: "IZZY! IT'S US!"

I'm afraid to go farther into the house.

The breakfast plates are still in the sink.

"Gran?" Lorelei's as scared as me. "Do you think . . ."

"I don't know, love," I tell her. "You wait outside, I'll—"

"Lol? Lol!" It's Izzy, with Branna and Tom following, crossing the yard behind us. Tom and Izzy look unhurt but shaken, but Branna O'Daly, a black-haired no-nonsense woman of fifty, has blood all over her overalls. I almost shriek, "Branna! Are you hurt?"

Branna's as puzzled as I am horrified, then realizes: "Oh, Mother of Jesus, Holly, no no no, it's not a gunshot wound, it's one of our cows, calving. The Connollys' bull got into the paddock last spring, and she went into labor earlier. Timing, eh? She didn't know that the Cordon'd fallen and gangs of outlaws were roaming the countryside taking solar panels at gunpoint. A messy breech birth, too. Still, she gave birth to a female, so one more milker."

"They took your panels, Branna," says Lorelei.

"I know, pet. Nothing I could do to stop them. Did they pay a courtesy call down Dooneen track, I wonder?"

"They stole Mo's panels off her roof too," I say, "but when they heard the explosion they left, before they took mine."

"Yes, our crew cleared off at the same time."

I ask Branna, "What about Declan and Max?" and she shrugs and shakes her head.

"They're not back from the village," says Tom, adding disgustedly, "Mam won't let me go and find them."

"Two out of three O'Daly males in a war zone is enough." Branna's worried sick. "Da told you to defend the home front."

"You made me hide," Tom's sixteen-year-old voice cracks, "in the fecking hay loft with Izzy! That's not defending."

"I made you hide in the *what*?" says Branna, icily.

Tom scowls, just as icily. "In the loft with Izzy. But why—"

"Eight bandits with the latest Chinese automatics," Izzy tells him, "versus one teenager with a thirty-year-old rifle. Guess the score, Tom. Anyway: I believe I hear a bicycle. Speak of the devil?"

Tom has only just time to say, "What?" before Schull starts barking at the farm gate, wagging his tail, and round the corner—on a mountain bike—comes Tom's brother Max.

He skids to a halt a few yards away. He's got a nasty gash across one cheekbone and wild eyes. Something terrible's happened.

"Max!" Branna looks appalled. "Where's Da? What's happened?"

"Dad's—Dad's," Max's voice wobbles, "alive. Are you all all right?"

"Yes, thanks be to God—but your eye, boy!"

"It's fine, Ma, just a bit of stone from a . . . The fuel depot got blown to feckereens and—"

His mum's hugging Max too tight for him to speak. "What's with all the cussing in this house?" says Branna, over his shoulder. "Your father and I didn't raise you to speak like a gang o' feckin' gurriers, did we? Now tell us what happened."

WHILE I CLEAN Max's gashed cheek in the O'Dalys' kitchen, he drinks a glass of his father's muddy home brew to steady himself and a mug of mint tea to muffle the taste of the home brew. He finds it hard to begin until he begins. Then he hardly pauses for breath. "Da and me'd just got to Auntie Suke's when Mary de Búrka's eldest, Sam, calls round, saying there's an emergency village meeting at the Big Hall. That was noon, I think. Pretty much the whole village was there. Martin stood up first, saying he'd called the meeting because of the Cordon falling and that. He said we should put together Sheep's Head Irregular Regiment—armed with whatever shotguns we had at home—to man roadblocks on the Durrus road and the Raferigeen road, so if or when Jackdaws break through the Cordon, we'd not just be sat around like turkeys waiting for Christmas, like. Most of the boys thought it was a sound enough idea, like. Father Brady spoke next, saying that God would let the Cordon fall because we'd put our faith in false idols, a barbed-wire fence, and the Chinese, and the first thing to do was choose a new mayor who'd have God's support. Pat Joe and a few o' the lads were like, 'F'feck's sake, this is no time for electioneering!' so Muriel Boyce was shrieking at them that they'd burn, burn, burn because whoever thought a pack o' sheep farmers with rusty rifles could stop the Book of Revelation coming true was a damned eejit who'd soon be a dead damned eejit. Then Mary de Búrka *nnhgg-gffftchtchtch* . . ." Max grimaces as I extract a small flake of stone from his cut with a pair of tweezers.

"Sorry," I say. "That was the last bit of grit."

"Thanks, Holly. Mary de Búrka was saying it'd do us no harm to follow the principle that the Lord helps those who help themselves, when we heard engines, lots of them, roaring our way. Like the Friday Convoy but much, much louder. The hall emptied, and into the square drove twenty Stability jeeps, plus a tanker, too. Four, five, six men got out of each. Big bastards, Ma. Big mean bastards. Stability guys *and* militiamen obviously from outside the Cordon. We were about matched man to man, but there'd not be much of a fight. They were armed to the teeth and trained to kill, like. This big Dub, he climbed on a jeep roof and spoke through a megaphone. Said his name was General Drogheda, and the former West Cork Lease Lands were now under martial law following the collapse o' the Cordon. He'd been sent by Cork Stability to requisition all the solar panels on Sheep's Head for government use, and to commandeer in Stability's name the diesel that'd been delivered yesterday. Well, we looked at each other, like, 'Not feckin' likely.' But then yer man Drogheda said that any opposition would be treated as treason. And treason, under Clause Whatever of the Stability Law Act of Whenever, would be dealt with by a bullet through the head. Mar-

tin Walsh walked up to this General Drogheda's jeep and introduced himself as mayor of Kilcrannog and asked for a closer look at
the requisition orders from Cork HQ, like. Your man got out his
revolver and shot the road between Martin's shoes. Martin jumped
six foot in the air and six foot back. Drogheda, if that's his real
name, said, 'Is that a close enough look, Mr. Mayor?' Then he said
if any hero tried to stop them they'd empty the food depot, too, and
we'd be eating stones all winter."

"Stability'd not behave like that," says Branna. "Would they?"

Max drinks the brew, winces, and shudders. "Nobody's sure
about anything now. After Drogheda'd said his piece, about ten of
the jeeps left the village along the main road heading Dooneen way,
another ten drove to the edges of the town to get to work, while the
rest stayed put. Then out came ladders from the back o' the jeeps,
and up went men from each crew onto every roof with a panel. A
pair stayed below fingering their weapons, like, to discourage any
argument. Meanwhile the tanker was emptying the fuel depot. We
were all muttering and furious, like—these robbers're robbing our
feckin' diesel!—but if we'd tried to stop them they'd have mown us
down, cold, like, and taken the panels anyway. We knew that and
there was feck all we could do. By and by the tanker was full, the
roofs stripped of panels, and jeeps were coming back into the square,
waiting for the ones that'd gone down the Knockroe road to come
back, I guess. Then . . . it happened. I didn't see it kick off, but I was
with Da and Sean O'Dwyer when I heard a godalmighty ruckus
from by General Drogheda's jeep . . ."

Sparingly, I dab Max's cut with antiseptic cream and he winces.

"Drogheda was yelling at a militiaman. He had an Audi symbol
round his head, saying *he* was head of operations, and if yer man
din't like it, then he could . . . Well, it was to do with his mother's . . . Doesn't matter. The wind had dropped, the shouting echoed
round the square, and I watched another o' the scruffier militiamen
stroll up behind Drogheda and, uh . . ." Max frowns, swallows,
tries to stop himself crying, can't, and the wheels come off his voice.
"Shot his brains out. Point blank. Right feckin' . . . there."

"Oh, God, no," whispers Izzy.

"Oh, my poor boy," says Branna. "You *saw* that?"

Max hides his face in his hands and steadies himself for a few seconds, breathing deeply. "Oh, that was just for starters, Mam. The Stability men and the militias went at each other like dogs, dogs with guns. It was a hailstorm but with bullets, like, not hail." He's angry with himself for blubbing. "Like an old war film, with stuntmen falling off roofs, men crawling on the pavement . . ." Max looks away and shuts his eyes hard to keep out the picture but he can't. "Us villagers scrambled clear, as best we could, but . . . Mam . . . Seamus Coogan got a bullet."

I can't help it: "Seamus Coogan's hurt?"

Max starts shaking and he shakes his head.

Tom asks, wide-eyed, "Seamus Coogan's *dead*?"

Max just nods. Izzy, Branna, Lorelei, Tom, and me look at one another and feel the cold wind of the near future. I was talking to Seamus Coogan only yesterday. Max drinks up the rest of the homebrew and carries on as if his sanity depends on telling us what saw, and maybe it does. "I—I tried to . . . but . . . it was all instant, like." Max shuts his eyes, shakes his head, and sort of wipes the air with his hand. "Da pulled me off, shouting there was nothing we could do for him. We legged it round the back o' the Fitzgeralds' and hid in their garage. Just in time. The tanker in the square got hit and—you heard that, right?"

"They must've heard it up in Tipperary," says Branna.

"Time went by," says Max, "I dunno how long. We heard guns, saw a guy get shot on the Fitzgeralds' drive . . . An hour? Dunno. Can't've been, but suddenly the jeeps were driving off, up the mountain road to Finn MacCool's seat, and . . . And then it was all quiet again. Birds singing, like. We all appeared from our hiding places . . . stunned, like, like . . . had that *really* happened? Here? In Kilcrannog?" Max's eyes well up again. "Yes. There were the bodies and the wounded to prove it. Bernie Aitken tried to defend his panels with his rifle, and he got shot. He's in a bad way. I think he's going to die, Mam. The village square's a—a—it's—it's . . . *Don't* go and see it," he tells Tom, Izzy, and Lorelei, "just don't. Not till it's been cleaned up and rained on. I—I—I wish to feck I'd not seen it. There's twenty, thirty graves to dig, like. Several injured militiamen, too, who can't walk, like. Some o' the lads said we should just dump them in the sea, that's what they'd do to us"—anger ignites in Max's face, driving away his shock for a few seconds—"but Dr. Kumar's doing what she can for them. They'll probably die anyway. There's a crater where the depot was and all the windows blasted out around the square. Josey Malone's house has had the front ripped off it. Oh, and the pub's a right feckin' mess now."

Dimly, I worry about Brendan; these pitched battles for dwindling reserves must be happening all over Europe, with only small variations in uniforms and scenery. I wonder where Hood and the bearded giant are now: dead, running, dying in Dr. Kumar's clinic. Swallowing a huckleberry.

Branna asks softly, "What's Da doing now, Max?"

"Helping Mary de Búrka direct the cleanup. Martin Walsh and a couple of others have cycled up to Ahakista to discuss roadblocks. It's more urgent now, not less. Make a short Cordon of our own, maybe; from Durrus cross-country to Coomkeen, then down the road to Boolteenagh on the Bantry side. Sure until we can get it fenced and dug it'd just be a few of the lads with guns in tents, but there's automatic weapons going begging, and Martin's cousin's at the Derrycahoon garrison. Was, anyway. Stability men'll need a safe place for their families, too. Anyway, I ought to get back, with a couple o' shovels."

"No, Max," says Branna. "You're in shock. Lie down. There'll be plenty of work tomorrow."

"Mam," says Max, "if we don't get some sort of roadblocks in place there mightn't *be* a tomorrow. There's work to do."

"Then I'm coming with you," states Tom.

"*No,*" say Branna and Max together.

"I am so. I'm sixteen. Ma, you can handle the milking?"

Branna rubs her face. All the rules are changing.

. . .

LORELEI HELPS WITH the milking while I feed the Knockroe chickens. Then we walk home along the shore, gathering a bag of sea spinach. Sandhoppers ping off my exposed shin, and oystercatchers pick their way between stones and bladderwrack, stabbing the mud for lugworms. A gray heron fishes off a rock twenty feet out and the sun emerges. The wind's swinging around to the south, brushing up stragglier clouds, like sheep's wool caught on barbed wire. We find a big bough of bleached driftwood that should keep the stove fed for a couple of days in winter. Below the cottage we find Rafiq fishing off the pier, a favorite sedative of his. We give him the edited gist of Max O'Daly's story—he'll hear it sooner or later anyway—as he helps us lug the driftwood up to the cottage. Mo is snoozing in Eilísh's old chair, with Zimbra lying on her feet and a biography of Wittgenstein on her lap. Perhaps she'll move into our granny flat now her own bungalow has no electricity at all. I had it built when I learned Aoife was pregnant so that she, Örvar, and the baby could have a bit of privacy when they visited, but over the years it's become a storeroom.

Zimbra gets up when we walk in, Mo wakes, and Lorelei makes us a pot of green tea with leaves she fetches from Mo's polytunnel. I begin by telling her about Seamus Coogan's death, then the rest of Max's report on the massacre. Mo listens without interruption. Then she sighs and rubs her eyes. "Martin Walsh is right, unfortunately. If we want a quality of life higher than that of the Middle Ages ten years from now, we need to act like soldiers. The barbarians won't turn on each other twice."

My clock says five. Rafiq stands up. "I'd like to catch another couple of fish before it gets dark. Is Mo staying for tea, Holly?"

"I hope so. We ate her out of house and home at lunch."

Mo thinks of her unlit stove and the useless lightbulbs in her bungalow. "I'd be honored. Thank you. All three of you."

When Rafiq's left, I say, "I'll go into town tomorrow."

"I'm not sure how wise that'd be now," says Mo.

"I need to speak with Dr. Kumar about insulin."

Mo sips her tea. "How much do you have?"

"Six weeks' worth." Lorelei keeps her voice down. "One more insulin pump, and three packets of catheter nozzles."

Mo asks, "How much does Dr. Kumar have?"

"That's what I want to ask." I scratch an insect bite on my hand. "Yesterday's convoy brought nothing, and after today . . . I don't think there'll be anymore. We have water, maybe we'll be okay for food and security if we can act like a socialist Utopia, but you can't synthesize insulin without a well-equipped laboratory."

Mo asks, "Has Rafiq raised the subject?"

"No, but he's a bright kid. He knows."

Through the side window, a screen of late afternoon sunlight is projected onto the wall. Shadows of birds flit across it.

Some shadows are sharp, some shadows are blurry.

I've seen them before in another time and place.

"Gran?" Lorelei's waiting for my answer to a question.

"Sorry, love. I was just . . . What were you saying?"

THE RADIO'S STILL dead. Mo asks Lorelei if she's up to playing a tune on the fiddle after a day like that. My granddaughter chooses "She Moved Through the Fair." I wash the sea spinach while Mo guts the fish. We'll fry the puffball in butter at the last minute. If I was younger I'd be in town helping with the grisly business, but I wouldn't be much use there at my age, digging graves for makeshift coffins. Father Brady'll be busy. Probably he's claiming the salvation of Kilcrannog was a case of divine intervention. Lorelei plays the ghostly refrain beautifully. She inherited her dad's musical flair as well as his fiddle, and if she'd belonged to my or Aoife's generation she might've thought about a musical career, but I'm afraid music will be one more nonsurvival pursuit that the Endarkenment snuffs out.

Rafiq makes us all jump as he barges open the door; something's wrong. "Rafiq," says Mo, "what on earth's the matter?"

He's panting for breath. My first thought is diabetes, but he's pointing back down to the bay. "There!"

Lorelei stops playing. "Deep breaths, Raf—what is it?"

"A ship," Rafiq gasps, "a boat, and men, and they've got guns, and were coming closer, and they spoke to me through a big cone thing. But I didn't know what to say. 'Cause of—of what happened today."

Mo, Lorelei, and me look at each other, confused.

"You're not making a whole lot of sense," I say. "Ship?"

"*That!*" He points out at the bay. I can't see, but Lorelei goes over, looks out, and says, "*Jesus.*" At her astonishment I hurry over, and Mo hobbles behind. At first I see only the bluish, grayish waters of the bay, but then see dots of yellow light, maybe three hundred meters out. "A patrol boat," says Mo, at my side. "Can anyone see a flag on it?"

"No," says Rafiq, "but they launched a littler boat and it moved dead fast, straight towards the pier. There's men in it. When it was near one of the men spoke through this cone thing that made his voice louder, like this." Rafiq mimes a megaphone.

"In English?" asks Mo, just as Lorelei asks, "What did he say?"

"Yeah," replies Rafiq. "He asked, 'Does Holly Sykes live here?'"

Mo and Lorelei look at me; I look at Rafiq. "Are you *sure*?"

Rafiq nods. "I thought I'd heard it wrong, but he said it again. I just sort of froze, and then," Rafiq looks at Lorelei, "he asked if you live here. He knew your full name. Lorelei Örvarsdottir."

Lorelei sort of clutches at herself and looks at me.

Mo asks, "Could you see if they were foreign?"

"No, they had combat goggles. But he didn't sound very Irish."

The patrol boat sits there. It's big, with a tower and globes and big twin guns at each end. Can't remember when I last saw a steel hull in the bay. "Might it be British?" suggests Mo.

I don't know. "I heard the last six Royal Navy vessels were rusting in the Medway, waiting for fuel that never arrived. Anyway, don't British ships always fly the Union Jack?"

"The Chinese or Russians would have the fuel," says Lorelei.

"But what would the Chinese or Russians want with us?"

"More raiders," Lorelei wonders, "after our solar panels?"

"Look at the size of the ship," says Mo. "She must be displacing three, four thousand tons? Think of the diesel it cost to get here. This isn't about swiping a few secondhand solar panels."

"Can you see the launch?" I ask the kids. "The motorboat?"

After a moment, Lorelei says, "No sign of it."

"It could be behind the pier," says Rafiq, edgily. At this point Zimbra pushes through between my calf and the door frame and growls at the lumpy denseness in the hawthorn by our gate. The wind brushes the long grass, gulls cry, and the shadows are sharp and long.

They're here. I know. "Raf, Lol," I murmur, "up to the attic."

Both of them start to object, but I cut them off: *"Please."*

"Don't be alarmed," says a soldier at the gate, and all four of us jump. His camo armor, an ergohelmet, and an augvisor conceal his face and age and give him an insectoid look. My heartbeat's gone walloping off. "We're friendlier than your earlier visitors today."

It's Mo who collects her wits first. "Who are you?"

"Commander Aronsson of the Icelandic Marines, that ship is the ICGV *Sjálfstæði.*" The officer's voice has a military crispness, and when he turns to his left, the bulletproof visor reflects the low sun. "This is Lieutenant Eriksdottir." He indicates a slighter figure, a woman, also watching us through an augvisor. She nods by way of hello. "Last, we have 'Mr.' Harry Veracruz, a presidential adviser who is joining us on our mission."

A third man steps into view, dressed like a pre-Endarkenment birdwatcher in a fisherman's sweater and an all-weather jacket, un-zipped. He's young, hardly into his twenties, and has somewhat African lips, sort of East Asian eyes, Caucasianish skin, and sleek black hair, like a Native American in an old film. "Afternoon," he tells me, in a soft anywhere-voice. "Or have we crossed the boundary to evening?"

I'm flustered. "I . . . uh, don't know. It's, um . . ."

"I'm Professor Mo Muntervary, formerly of MIT," says my neighbor, crisply. "How can we help you, Commander Aronsson?"

The commander flips up his augvisor so we can see his classically Nordic, square-jawed chin. He's thirtyish, squinting now in the direct light. Zimbra gives a couple of gruff barks. "First, please calm down your dog. I do not want him to hurt his teeth on our body armor."

"Zimbra," I tell him. "Inside. Zimbra!" Like a sulky teenager, he obeys, though once inside he peers out between my shins.

Lieutenant Eriksdottir pushes back her augvisor too. She's midtwenties and intensely freckled; her Scandinavian accent is stronger and *ess*-ier. "You are Holly Sykes, I think?"

I'd rather find out what they want before telling them that, but Mr. Harry Veracruz says, with an odd smile, "She certainly is."

"Then you are the legal guardian," continues Lieutenant Eriksdottir, "of Lorelei Örvarsdottir, an Icelandic citizen."

"That's me," says Lorelei. "My dad was from Akureyri."

"Akureyri is my hometown also," says Commander Aronsson. "It's a small place, so I know Örvar Benediktsson's people. Your father was also"—he glances Mo's way—"a famous scientist in his field."

I feel defensive. "What do you want with Lorelei?"

"Our president," says the commander, "has ordered us to locate and offer to repatriate Miss Örvarsdottir. So, we are here."

A bat tumbles through the dark and bright bands of the garden. My first thought is, *Thank Christ, she's saved.*

My second thought is, *I can't lose my granddaughter.*

My third thought is, *Thank Christ, she's saved.*

The hens peck, cluck, and goggle around their coop, and the brittle, muddy garden swishes in the evening wind. "*Magno,*" declares Rafiq. "Lol, that massive ship sailed here from Iceland just for you!"

"But what about my family?" I hear Lorelei saying.

"Permission to immigrate is for Miss Örvarsdottir," Aronsson addresses me, "*only*. That is not negotiable. Quotas are strict."

"How can I leave my family behind?" Lorelei's saying.

"It is difficult," Lieutenant Eriksdottir tells her. "But please consider it, Lorelei. The Lease Lands have been safe, but those days are over, as you learned today. There is a broken nuclear reactor not far enough away, if the wind blows wrongly. Iceland is safe. This is why the immigration quota is so strict. We have geothermal electricity and your uncle Halgrid's family will care for you."

I remember Örvar's older brother from my summer in Reykjavik. "Halgrid's still alive?"

"Of course. Our isolation saves us from the worst"—Commander Aronsson searches for the word—"hardships of the Endarkenment."

"There must be a lot of Icelandic nationals around the globe," says Mo, "praying for a deus ex machina to sail up to the bottom of the garden. Why Lorelei? And why such a timely arrival?"

"Ten days ago we learned that the Pearl Occident Company was planning to withdraw from Ireland," says the commander. "At that point, one of the president's advisers," Aronsson looks sideways at Harry Veracruz with something like a scowl, "persuaded our president that your granddaughter's repatriation is a matter of national importance."

So we look at Harry Veracruz, who must be more influential than he appears. He's leaning on the gate like a neighbor who's dropped by for a chat, making a what-can-I-say face. He tells me in his young voice: "Normally I'd try to prepare the ground better, Holly, but this time I lacked the opportunity. To cut a long story short, I'm Marinus."

I'm sort of floating up, as if lifted by waves; my hands grasp the nearest things, which are the door frame and Lorelei's elbow. I hear a sound, like the pages of a very thick book being flicked, but it's only the wind in the shrubberies. The doctor in Gravesend; the psychiatrist in Manhattan; the voice in my head in the labyrinth that couldn't exist, but did; and this young man watching me, from ten paces away.

Wait. How do I know? Sure Harry Veracruz looks honest, but so do all successful liars. Then I hear his voice in my head: *Jacko's labyrinth, the domed chamber, the bird shadows, the golden apple.* His gaze is level and knowing. I look at the others. Nobody else heard. *It's me, Holly. Truly. Sorry for this extra shock. I know you're having a hell of day here.*

"Gran?" Lorelei sounds panicky. "You want to sit down?"

A mistlethrush is singing on my spade in the kale patch.

With effort, I shake my head. "No, I . . ." Then I ask him, in a croak, "Where have you *been*? I thought you were dead."

Marinus—I remember the verb—"subspeaks." *Long story. The golden apple was a one-soul escape pod, so I had to find another route and another host. It proved to be circuitous. Eight years passed here before I was resurrected in an eight-year-old in an or-phanage in Cuba, neatly coinciding with the 2031 quarantine. It was 2035 before I could get off the island, when this self was ten. When finally I reached Manhattan the place was half feralized, 119A was deserted, and it took three more years to connect with the remnants of Horology. Then the Net crashes happened and tracing you became nigh-on impossible.*

"What about the War?" I ask. "Did you—did we—win?"

The young man's smile is ambivalent. *Yes. One could say we won. The Anchorites no longer exist. Hugo Lamb helped me es-cape the Dusk, in fact, though what fate befell him I do not know. His psychodecanting days are over and his body will be middle-aged, if indeed he has survived this long.*

"Holly?" Mo's got an is-she-losing-her-marbles face. "What war?"

"This is an old friend," I reply, "from . . . my, uh, author days."

For some reason, Mo looks more worried, not less.

"The *son* of an old friend, Holly means, of course," says Marinus. "My mother was a psychiatrist colleague of Holly's, back in the day."

Commander Aronsson receives a luckily timed message and turns away, speaking Icelandic into his headset. He checks his watch, signs off, then turns back to us: "The captain of the *Sjálfstæði* wants to depart in forty-five minutes. Not long for a big decision, Lorelei, but we do not wish to attract attention. Please. Discuss matters with your family. We"—he glances at Lieutenant Eriksdottir—"will check you are not disturbed."

Voles, hens, sparrows, a dog. A garden's full of eyes.

"You'd better come in," I tell Harry Marinus Veracruz.

The gate squeaks as he opens it. He crosses the yard. How do you greet a resurrected Atemporal you've not seen for twenty years? Hug? A double-sided cheek kiss? Harry Veracruz smiles and the Marinus within subsays, *Weird, I know. Welcome to my world. Or welcome back to it, albeit briefly.* I stand aside to let him into the cottage, and something occurs to me. "Commander Aronsson? I have one question for you."

"Ask it," says Commander Aronsson.

"D'you still have insulin in Iceland?"

The man frowns, but Marinus calls over his shoulder: "It's the same in Icelandic, Commander. *Insúlín.* The drug for diabetes."

"Ah." The officer nods. "Yes, we manufacture this drug at a new unit, near the airbase at Keflavík. Two or three thousand of our citizens require it, including our minister of defense. Why do you ask? Does your granddaughter have diabetes?"

"No," I reply. "I was just curious."

BACK IN OUR kitchen, I put on the solar lamp. It flickers like a candle. Dinner is almost ready, but suddenly none of us is hungry. "Gran," says Lorelei. "I can't go to Iceland."

This'll be one of the hardest sells of my life.

"You've *got* to, Lol!" says Rafiq, and I bless him. "You'll have a good life there. Won't she, Mr. Vera—Verac—"

Marinus is already peering at the books on the shelves. "Those whom I respect I ask to call me 'Marinus,' Rafiq, and, yes, your sister will enjoy an incomparably better-nourished, better-educated, and safer life than on Sheep's Head. As today has proven, I believe."

"Then, Lol," Rafiq says for me, "that ship's your lifeboat."

"A one-way lifeboat," Lorelei asks Marinus. "Right?"

The young man frowns. "Lifeboats don't do return tickets."

"Then I'm not going to sail off and leave you all here." Lorelei sounds so like Aoife when she's making a stand, it wakes up my old grief. "If you were in my shoes, Raf, you wouldn't go."

Rafiq takes a deep breath. "If you were in *my* shoes, you'd be diabetic in a country without insulin. Think about it."

Lorelei looks away miserably and says nothing.

"I have a question," Mo says, lowering herself onto a chair at the kitchen table and hooking her stick over its edge. "Three, in fact. Holly knew your mother, Mr. Marinus, which is all well and good, but why should she trust you to do the right thing by Lorelei?"

Marinus puts his hands into his pockets and rocks on his heels, like a young man with supple joints. "Professor, I can't prove to you that I'm the trustworthy, honorable human being that I claim to be, not in forty minutes. I can only refer you to Holly Sykes."

"It's a long, long story," I tell Mo, "but Marinus—or his mother, I mean, it's complicated, she saved my life."

"There's a Marinus in *The Radio People*," says Mo, the careful and retentive reader, "who plays quite a major role. The doctor in Gravesend." Mo looks at me. "Any relative?"

"Yes," I admit, badly not wanting to get into Atemporals now.

"That Dr. Marinus was my grandfather," Marinus only sort of lies, "on my Chinese side. But Holly did a great service to my mother, Iris, and her friends back in the twenties. Which may pre-empt another of your questions, Professor. I owe Holly Sykes a debt of honor, and giving her granddaughter the chance of a pre-Endarkenment life is one way to repay it."

Mo nods at Marinus's correct guess. "And you're so up to speed with current events on Sheep's Head because?"

"We hack into spy satellites."

Mo nods coolly, but the scientist within inquires: "Whose?"

"The Chinese array is the best, and the Russian satellites work well in clear conditions, but we stream our images from the last functioning American Eyesat. The Pentagon's given up on security."

Rafiq's incredulous. "You can see what's going on on Sheep's Head, from space? That's like . . . being God. That's like magic."

"It's neither." Marinus smiles at the boy. "It's technology. I saw the fox attack on your chickens, the other night, and *you*," he fondles the ears of Zimbra, who clearly trusts this stranger, "you killer." He looks at me. "Some months ago L'Ohkna, our IT specialist, detected a tab signal from this area that corresponded to recordings of your voice, Holly, and of course I remembered that you'd retired here, but a chain of crises in Newfoundland distracted us. After the Hinkley Point reactor went critical, though, and we learned about the POC's withdrawal, I acted with greater urgency, and here we are." Lorelei's fiddle catches Marinus's eye. "Who is the musician?"

"I play a bit," says Lorelei. "It was Dad's."

Marinus picks it up and examines it, like an instrument maker, which for all I know he once was. "Beautiful lines."

I ask, "What are you doing in Iceland, Marinus?" My feet are hurting too, so I join Mo at the table.

"We operate a think tank. L'Ohkna named it—modestly— 'Prescience' before I arrived. Roho, who kept an eye on Aoife during your Manhattan week twenty years ago, is with us, plus a handful of others. We have to be more interventionist politically than—than my mother used to be. By and large, the president values our advice, even if we occasionally put the military's nose a little out of joint." Marinus plucks the strings on Lorelei's fiddle, one by one, testing its tone. "Only thirty minutes to settle Lorelei's future, Holly."

"It's already settled," my granddaughter declares. "I can't leave Gran and Raf. Or Mo."

"A noble and worthy response, Lorelei. May I play a few bars?"

Taken a bit aback, Lorelei says, "Sure."

Marinus takes up the bow, puts the fiddle under his chin, and skims through a few bars of "Don't Cry for Me Argentina." "Warm tone. Is the E-string a little . . . flat? Holly, a possibility is occurring to you."

I'd forgotten how Marinus knows, or half knows, what you're thinking. "If Lorelei left with you—*if*, Lol—she really would be safer?"

"Indubitably, yes."

"So that ship in the bay *is* a lifeboat to civilization?"

"Metaphorically, yes."

"Commander Aronsson said only Lorelei can go?"

"Technically, yes."

"Could you turn that one space to two spaces? Using your . . . y'know . . ." I do a spell-casting gesture with my hands.

Marinus resembles a lawyer whose line of questioning is proceeding as planned. "Well, now. I'd need to enforce a powerful Act of Suasion on the commander and the lieutenant outside, as they wait; then, as the launch approached the *Sjálfstæði,* I'd need to transverse to the captain and the first mate and enforce the same act upon them, to ensure poor Rafiq wasn't returned to shore immediately. *Then,* during the voyage north, I'd have to renew the Act of Suasion continuously until we were past the point of no return, when all the protagonists would be wondering what had got into them. I won't lie: It would be a tall, tall order. Only a truly adept follower of the Deep Stream could pull off a trick like that . . ."

I feel mild annoyance, gratitude, and hope. "You can do it, then?"

Marinus puts down the fiddle. "Yes, but only for Lorelei and Rafiq. Many of the *Sjálfstæði's* crew members have children of their own, so they'll be unconsciously sympathetic, and much easier to keep suasioned. Perhaps Xi Lo or Esther Little could have squeezed you and the professor aboard, but I know my limits, Holly. If I tried it would all come tumbling down. I'm sorry."

"Doesn't matter. In Reykjavik, can Lol and Raf stay together?"

"We'll find a way." Marinus's young eyes are big, gray, and as truthful as Iris Fenby's. "They can stay with me. We're housed in the old French consulate. It's roomy." He tells Lorelei and Rafiq, "Don't panic. I'm a more experienced guardian than I look."

The clock ticks. We have only twenty-five minutes now.

"I don't quite understand, Holly," says Raf.

"One moment, love. Lol, if you go, Raf can go with you, up to the land of insulin. If you don't go, sooner or later there'll be a medical emergency and . . . nothing to treat him with. Please. Go."

Upstairs a door bangs shut. The evening sunlight's a mandarin color. Lorelei's on the edge of tears, and if she starts, there'll be no stopping me. "Who'd look after *you*?"

"*I'll* look after her!" Mo acts grumpy to stop Lorelei crumpling.

"And the O'Dalys," I tell her, "the Walshes and the all-new, fortified Sheep's Head Republic. I'll get myself elected Minister for Seaweed, so they'll give me a guard of honor." Lorelei's face is unbearable so I look away at the smiling, fading dead, watching me from the mantelpiece from safer worlds, from beyond wooden, plastic, and mother-of-pearl frames. I stand, and press both kids' heads against my old, aching sides and kiss the tops of their heads. "I promised your mum and dad, Lol, that I'd look after you, and I promised you the same, Raf. Getting you two on that boat, that's keeping my promise. *Nothing* will give me more peace or—or," I swallow, "joy, than knowing you two are safe from all of—all of," I sweep my hand in the direction of the town, "oh, what happened today. What's to come. *Please.* My two treasures. Give me this. If you—" No. *If you love me* sounds like blackmail. "Be*cause* you love me," my throat's so tight I can hardly say the word, "go."

OUR LAST MINUTES together were rushed and blurred. Lorelei and Rafiq hurried upstairs to pack for the two-day voyage. Marinus said they'd go shopping in Reykjavik for warmer clothes, as if shops are the most natural thing in the world. I still dream of shops: Harrods in London, Brown Thomas in Cork, even the big Supervalu in Clonakilty. While the kids were still upstairs, Marinus sat in Eilísh's chair, shut his eyes, and Harry Veracruz's body and face went still and vacant, while my psychosoteric friend's soul went outside to implant a strong, false, urgent memory in the minds of the two officers. Mo watched, fascinated, muttering only that I'd have a lot of explaining to do later. Moments later, Marinus's soul was back in Harry Veracruz's skull and the two Icelandic officers appeared, saying that the captain had just that minute told them the president was extending his offer of asylum to Lorelei Örvarsdottir's foster brother, Rafiq Bayati. Both appeared just a trifle dazed as they spoke, like drunk people trying their best to act sober. Harry Veracruz thanked Commander Aronsson and confirmed that both youngsters would be taking up the president's offer—and would he kindly have the sea chest sent up from the launch at the pier? The officers went and Mo said that she could think of three laws of physics that Marinus had apparently broken but, given time, she was confident of coming up with a few more.

Soon after, two marines arrived with a carbon-fiber trunk. Marinus unpacked it in my kitchen, taking out ten large sealed containers, each with eighty vacuum-packed tubes of powder inside. "Concentrated field rations," Marinus said. "Each tube has fifteen hundred calories, plus nutrients and vitamins. Mix with water for supergoo. I'm afraid the only flavor the depot had in stock was Hawaiian pizza, but if you can ignore the pineapple and cheese, they'll last the two of you nearly three years. Better yet . . ." He took out a pack of four sheathed tabs and handed me one, explaining they were ethered to one another, so they wouldn't need the Net to thread a connection. "One for you, me, Lorelei, and Rafiq. Not the same as having them in your kitchen, of course, but this way they're not gone from your life once we round the headland. They're powered bioelectrically just by holding them, too, so they'll function without solar panels."

Rafiq's head appeared between the banisters. " 'Scuse me, Mr. Marinus? Do you have toothbrushes in Iceland?"

"A lifetime's supply. Dentists, too. And it's just 'Marinus.' "

"Cool. Okay. Holly, what's a dentist again?"

THE BLUR'S OVER. We're on the pier as dusk dims the Dunmanus Bay, Lorelei, Rafiq, Marinus, six Icelanders, Zimbra, and me, and it's actually happening. We had to leave Mo up at my gate 'cause the path down's too crumbled away for her ankle. Her brave face and the kids' gasps and tears have given me a taster of my own very near future. "Wrap up well," Mo had told them. "And wave at Dooneen Cottage as the ship leaves the bay. I'll be waving back."

The patrol vessel's half hidden against the darkening mass of Mizen Head. Only a few spots of light mark its position. On any other evening there'd be skiffs and dinghies taking a closer look at the incredible steel visitor, but today people're still too occupied with, and too traumatized by, the aftermath of the violence in Kil-crannog, so the Icelandic vessel sits there undisturbed.

Marinus's sea chest is being loaded back onto the launch moored to the concrete pier. It now contains the kids' clothes as well as the *Eagle of the Ninth* books, Lorelei's box shrine, her fiddle, and Rafiq's box of fishing floats and hooks—Marinus assured him the salmon fishing in Iceland is world-class. Rafiq's key to Dooneen Cottage is still around his neck, by accident or design I don't know, but it's his. He picked up two white pebbles from the strip of beach by the pier, I noticed, and put them in his saggy coat pocket. Then the three of us hug, and if I could choose one moment of my life to sit inside of for the rest of eternity, like Esther Little did for all those decades, it'd be now, no question. Aoife's in here too, inside Lorelei, as is Ed, as is Zimbra, with his cold nose and excited whine. He knows something's up. "Thanks for everything, Gran," says Lorelei.

"Yeah," says Rafiq. "Thanks."

"It was my honor," I tell them.

We separate, at last. "Take care of them," I tell Marinus.

That's why I came, he subreplies, and says, "Of course."

"Say bye from me to Izzy and the O'Dalys and . . . everyone," says Lorelei, her eyes streaming, not with the cold.

"And from me too," says Rafiq, "and tell Mr. Murnane sorry I didn't get my fractions homework done."

"Tell them yourselves," says Marinus. "Via the tab."

I can't say "Goodbye" because that word's too painfully final, but I can't just say "See you then" because when will I ever see these precious people, really, in the flesh? Never again: That's when. So I just do my best to smile as if my heart isn't being wrung out like an old dishcloth and watch as Lorelei and Rafiq are helped aboard the launch by Lieutenant Eriksdottir, followed by the youthful ancient Marinus. "We'll thread you once we're safe ashore at Reykjavik," he calls up to me from the boat. "It should be the day after tomor-row." I call back, "That's great, do that." My voice is thin and stretched, like a violin string wound too tight. Rafiq and Lorelei look up from the deck, not sure what to say. Marinus subwishes me, *Good luck, Holly Sykes,* and I sense that somehow he knows about my resurgent cancer, and my huckleberries in their childproof canisters, stowed safely for if and when. So I just nod back at Harry Marinus Veracruz, no longer trusting my voice. A tall marine unmoors the boat and hunkers down in the prow. Owls in the Knockroe pines hoot. The outboard motor is ripped into life. The noise jolts Lorelei rigid and alert and she's scared now, and I am too. This is the moment of no turning back. The launch pulls away from the pier in a tight curve. Lorelei's hair streams across her face. Did she remember her woolly hat? Too late now. Above Knocknamadree Mountain on Mizen Head swim a pair of blurry overlapping moons. I wipe my eyes on the cuff of my ratty old fleece and the two captive planets become one again. Pale gold and badly scratched. I shiver. We're in for a cold night. Now the launch is skimming off at full speed over the dark and choppy water, and Rafiq's waving and Lorelei's waving and I'm waving back until I can't make out the figures in the noisy blue murk anymore, and the white wake from the outboard engine is widening behind the launch . . . But not for long. Incoming waves erase all traces of the vanishing boat, and I'm feeling erased myself, fading away into an invisible woman. For one voyage to begin, another voyage must come to an end, sort of.

Acknowledgments

Michel van der Aa, Lisa Babalis, Tom Barbash, Nikki Barrow, Avideh Bashirrad, Manuel Berri, Dominika Bojanowska, John Boyne, Adam Brophy, Ken Buhler, Amber Burlinson, Evan Camfield, Gina Centrello, Rajiv Chandrasekaran's *Imperial Life in the Emerald City,* Noah Chasin, Kate Childs, Rachel Clements, Patrick Cockburn and his book *The Occupation,* Toby Cox, Louise Dennys, Walter Donohue, Margaret Drabble, Susan Fletcher, Dominique Fortier, Kirsten Foster, Daniel Galera, Tally Garner, Claire Gatzen, Sam Greenwood, Dominic Gribben, Sophie Harris, Aleksandar Hemon, Kazuo Ishiguro, Susan Kamil, Trish Kerr of Kerr's Bookshop Clonakilty, Jessica Killingley, Martin Kingston (founder of Kilcrannog), Katie Kitamura (sorry I woke Ryu), Hari Kunzru, Seth Marko, Nick Marston, Sally Marvin, Meriç Mekik the Treasure Hunter, Mrs. MacIntosh, Katie McGowan, Caitlin McKenna, Jan Montefiore, Ray Murnane, Neal Murren, Lawrence Norfolk and family, Alasdair Oliver, Hazel Orme, David Peace, Thomas E. Ricks's *Fiasco,* Wendell Steavenson's *The Weight of a Mustard Seed,* Juan Gabriel Vásquez, Lana Wachowski, Bing West's *No True Glory,* Camilla Young. Apologies to anyone I've overlooked—it's my memory, not ingratitude.

Thanks to Kathleen Holland Designs for crafting Jacko's labyrinth.

Singled-out thanks to David Ebershoff, Jonny Geller, Doug Stewart, and Carole Welch.

Final thanks to my family.

About the Author

DAVID MITCHELL is the award-winning and bestselling author of *The Thousand Autumns of Jacob de Zoet, Black Swan Green, Cloud Atlas, Number9Dream,* and *Ghostwritten.* Twice shortlisted for the Man Booker Prize, Mitchell was named one of the 100 most influential people in the world by *Time* magazine in 2007. With KA Yoshida, Mitchell translated from the Japanese the internationally bestselling memoir *The Reason I Jump.* He lives in Ireland with his wife and two children.

davidmitchellbooks.com
Facebook.com/DavidMitchellBooks